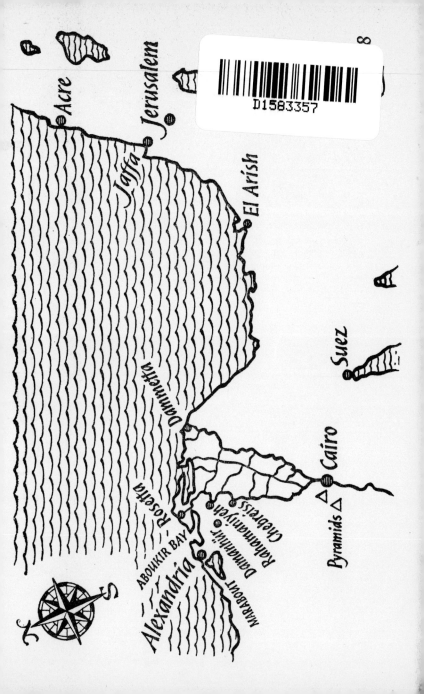

THE SULTAN'S DAUGHTER

THAT famous critic, Howard Spring, wrote of *The Launching of Roger Brook*, 'I look forward with pleasure to the spectacle of Roger Brook turning the Scarlet Pimpernel pale pink.'

Since then Roger's exploits as Prime Minister Pitt's most resourceful secret agent, and his hectic love-affairs, have gained him a permanent place among the leading characters in period fiction.

That, in part, is due to his adventures always being presented against a background of the facts of history. Dennis Wheatley never takes liberties with dates or events. These, and the portrayal of such famous people as General Bonaparte, Josephine, Nelson, Emma Hamilton, Sir Sidney Smith, Djezzar Pasha, Talleyrand and Fouché—all of whom play large parts in the present story—are in accordance with the most reliable sources. Even the accounts of the capture of the heroine's mother by Barbary pirates and of Napoleon's shocking mental collapse on the fateful 18th Brumaire are strictly authentic.

From the England of 1798 the reader accompanies Napoleon on his conquest of Egypt; then witnesses Nelson's brilliant victory at the Battle of the Nile, Sir Sidney Smith's heroic defence of Acre, the escape of King Ferdinand and Queen Caroline from Naples and, finally, is taken behind the scenes during Napoleon's desperate gamble for supreme power. Meanwhile, Roger himself is in almost constant peril and, driven crazy by his passion for the beautiful half-French, half-Turkish Zanthé, risks ruin and death in order to sleep with her.

Dennis Wheatley's books sell over a million copies a year; so it is safe to say that many more than a million people are eagerly awaiting this *tour de force* by 'The Prince of Thriller Writers'. They will not be disappointed.

DENNIS WHEATLEY

THE
SULTAN'S
DAUGHTER

THE BOOK CLUB
121 CHARING CROSS ROAD
LONDON W.C.2

HUTCHINSON & CO. (*Publishers*) LTD
178-202 Great Portland Street, London, W.1

First published 1963
Reprinted 1964

PRINTED IN GREAT BRITAIN BY
NORTHUMBERLAND PRESS LIMITED
GATESHEAD ON TYNE

For

DERRICK MORLEY

Ambassador Extraordinary and 'Most Secret'
during the years we spent together in the
Offices of the War Cabinet
and for
MARIE JOSÉ,

this tale of great days in France.
With my love to you both

DENNIS

Contents

7

CONTENTS

1

The Great Risk

IT was late on a dismal February afternoon in the year 1798. For the past ten days the weather had been so bad in the Channel that no ship had dared to put out from the little harbour of Lymington with a reasonable hope of running the blockade and safely landing a passenger, or a cargo of smuggled goods, on the coast of France.

But in the lofty rooms of Grove Place, the home of Admiral Sir Christopher Brook, a small, square mansion looking out across the Solent to the Isle of Wight, it was warm and quiet. The heavy curtains were already drawn, shutting out the winter cold and the steady pattering of the rain. In the dining room the soft light of the candles glinted on the silver and crystal with which the mahogany table was laid. Opposite each other sat two people— the Admiral's son Roger and his guest Georgina, the widowed Countess of St. Ermins. They had just finished dinner.

Suddenly Roger pushed back his chair, looked directly into the lovely face of his companion and declared, 'Georgina, I must be the stupidest fellow alive in that despite all the opportunities I've had, I've lacked the sense to force you into marrying me.'

Georgina's dark curls danced as she threw back her head and gave her rich low laugh. 'What nonsense, Roger. We have oft discussed the matter and——'

'Aye,' he interrupted, 'and reached the wrong conclusion. God never put breath into a couple more suited to share the trials and joys of life; and you know it.'

He was just over six feet tall, with broad shoulders and slim hips. His brown hair swept back in a high wave from a fine forehead. Below it a straight, aggressive nose stood out between a

9

pair of bright blue eyes. From years of living dangerously as Prime Minister 'Billy' Pitt's most resourceful secret agent, his mouth had become thin and a little hard, but the slight furrows on either side of it were evidence of his tendency to frequent laughter. His strong chin and jaw showed great determination, his long-fingered hands were beautifully modelled, and his calves, when displayed in silk stockings, gave his tall figure the last touch of elegance.

She was a head shorter, and the full curves of her voluptuous figure were regarded in that Georgian age as the height of feminine beauty. Her face was heart-shaped, her eyes near-black, enormous and sparkling with vitality. Her eyebrows were arched and her full, bright-red lips disclosed at a glance her tempestuous and passionate nature.

But, apart from the physical attractions with which both of them had been blessed, Roger was right in his contention that neither had ever met another human being in whose company each had known so much happiness.

After a moment Georgina shrugged her fine shoulders, smiled and said, 'Dear Roger, that no two lovers could have had more joy of one another I'd ne'er deny; but marriage is another thing. We agreed long since that did we enter on wedlock the permanent tie would bring ruin to our love. 'Tis because I have been your mistress for only brief periods between long intervals that the flame of our desire for one another has never died.'

'Of that you cannot be certain, for we have never put it to the test. Besides, physical desire is but one ingredient of a successful marriage. Another factor is that we both have young children. That you care for my little Susan like a daughter and let her share your Charles's nursery is a debt I'll find it hard ever to repay; but it would be far better for them if we were legally united, so that we became "mother" and "father" to both.'

'In that you have an argument I find it difficult to refute, for I know none I'd as lief have to bring up my little Earl to be a proper man. Yet it does not shake my opinion that other considerations outweigh it.'

'I'll revert, then, to the point I made a moment since. It was that we have never made trial of our passion for long enough to form an idea of how durable it might prove. Look back, I pray you, on our past. There was that one unforgettable afternoon when I was but a boy and you seduced me——'

' Fie, sir! Seduced you, indeed! 'Tis always the man who——'

' Fiddlesticks, m'dear. You had already allowed another to rob you of your maidenhead, whereas I——'

' Pax! Pax! ' Georgina laughed. 'Let's say that both of us had just reached an age when there was naught for it but to succumb to the hot blood of our natures.'

' So be it,' he smiled back. ' But that was in the summer of '83 and it was well on in the autumn of '87 before I held you in my arms again. After a few months of bliss we had to separate once more, and then——'

Georgina gave a sudden giggle. 'I'll ne'er forget that night in '90 when we made our pact that if I accepted my Earl you would marry Amanda. Then we slept together.'

' And, shame upon us,' Roger smiled, ' became lovers again for the six weeks before our respective marriages. But after that we played fair by our spouses. At least you did, although I deceived Amanda four years later with Athenaïs de Rochambeau and she me with the Baron de Batz. It was not until I got back from the West Indies in the spring of '96 that, after near six years and Amanda's death, I once more shared your bed.'

' We had that glorious spring together, though. Three whole months of bliss.'

' Could I have foreseen that our idyll was to be so abruptly terminated through that fiend Malderini, I'd not have been content to spend those months lotus-eating, but would have persuaded you then to marry me.'

' No, Roger! No! Years before that we had decided that to marry would be to court disaster.'

He shrugged. ' Anyway, I missed my chance and was forced to flee the country. While I was travelling in India and with General Bonaparte in Italy, another eighteen months sped by. This Christmas brought me the sweetest present I could ever wish for— your lips on mine the night after my return. Yet here we are a bare six weeks later and I must once more tear myself away from you.'

Roger leaned forward and went on earnestly, ' Think on it, my love. It is now fourteen years since the sweet culmination of our boy-and-girl romance. We vowed then that, although we'd con- sider ourselves free to make love where we listed, each of us would ever hold first place in the other's heart. We have kept that vow, yet in all these years we have lived scarce ten months together.'

Georgina slowly shook her head. 'Dear Roger, I am most sensible of it and have oft felt a great yearning for you when you have been in distant lands. Yet your own statement is the answer to your argument. Had we married, with yourself abroad for years at a stretch it could have been no more than a mockery of the state. Made as I am, unless I'd taken lovers during your long absences I'd have burst a blood vessel, and had you not done likewise you would have returned to me as dried up as a sack of flour. It would have meant either that or spending our brief reunions reproaching one another for discovered infidelities.'

'Nay. Matters need never have come to such a sorry pass as you envisage. Had we faced up to our situation after Humphrey's death and married then, I would have changed my whole life so as to remain with you.'

'You changed it when you married Amanda, but for how long did you remain content with domestic felicity? In less than two years you succumbed to the urge to go adventuring again. How can it possibly profit us to con over all these " might-have beens "? Above all at such a time as this, when within a few hours you will again be on your way to France? '

''Tis just that which causes me to do so,' he replied promptly. 'Your having volunteered to brave the winter journey and accompany me here for the sake of spending a last night or two with me, then tempests having delayed my departure for ten days, have given us a new experience of one another.'

'You refer to our having for the first time in our lives been for so long completely alone? '

'I do. With my father absent in his Command at Harwich, and the cousin who keeps house for him staying with friends in London, we might have been marooned on a desert island except for the servants providing us with every comfort. We have eaten, slept and loved, or sat engrossed in conversation by a roaring fire, just as we listed, without a single duty to perform or any social obligation. And for my part I have never been nearer to dwelling in heaven.'

'In that you speak for me, too,' she smiled. 'Time has ceased to be our master, and each night when I have fallen asleep in your arms I have known the sweetest contentment. I would that living with you in this world apart could have gone on for ever.'

'Then, sweet, have I not made my case : that as soon as it is possible we should marry? '

Georgina sadly shook her head. 'Nay, my beloved. We must not allow ourselves to be led astray by these halcyon days that we have snatched from life's normal round. As I've already said, to be faced during long separations with the alternative of maintaining a dreary chastity or deceiving one another would be fatal to our love.'

'There is yet another alternative. I am too far committed to my present mission to ask to be excused of it; but when I return to England I could resign from Mr. Pitt's service.'

'Can you say, within a month or two, when you expect your return to be?' Georgina asked.

He shook his head. 'Alas, no. Unfortunately there is nothing definite about my mission. It is simply that having established myself as *persona grata* with the men who now rule France, and particularly with Barras and General Bonaparte, I should return there, keep Mr. Pitt informed, as far as possible, of their intentions and do what I can to influence their policies in favour of British interests.'

'Then you may have to remain abroad for a year, or perhaps two, as you did during the Revolution.'

'I trust not, yet I cannot altogether rule out such a possibility. You will recall that when recounting my more recent activities I told you that in Italy General Bonaparte made me one of his A.D.C.s with the rank of Colonel. While I have been in England he has believed me to be on sick leave at my little château in the South of France. My orders were to report back to him at the end of January, and I would have done so had not storms delayed my passage. When I do rejoin his staff I must go where he goes; but the odds are that even he does not yet know how the Directory will employ him, now that Austria has signed a peace with France.'

'Since our nation alone now remains in arms against the French, surely they must strike at us. You have said yourself on more than one occasion that they might attempt an invasion in the spring, and that if so this little Corsican fire-eater will be the man to lead it.'

'You may take it as certain that the Directory favours such a move; and Bonaparte himself becomes like a man crazed with excitement whenever anyone raises in his mind the vision of the glory that would be his if he succeeded in marching an Army into London. At least, that was his dearest ambition until I secretly stacked the cards that led to his being given the command of the Army of Italy; and it may well be that now he is once more dreaming of himself as the conqueror of England.' Giving a twisted smile, Roger added, ' If so I'll be back quite soon, but in a foreign uniform and making it my first business to ensure your not being raped by the brutal and licentious invaders.'

Georgina snorted, ' 'Tis more likely that you'll find yourself back in the sea with a British pitchfork stuck in your bottom.'

' I've good hopes of escaping such a fate,' he laughed, ' for it's my opinion that the French will never get ashore at all. The attempt would be at best a desperate gamble, and Bonaparte has an uncanny way of assessing odds correctly. I think it more than probable that he will decide against staking his whole future on such a hazardous undertaking.'

' What, then, are the alternatives? '

' He has several times mentioned to me a grandiose project for leading an expedition to conquer the glamorous East and make himself another Alexander.'

' Should he do so I assume, from what you have said, that you would perforce accompany him? '

' No, no! ' Roger laughed. ' That I will not do. I've no mind to spend the rest of my life fighting Saracens and savages. Were I faced with such a grim and profitless prospect I'd think up some way to relieve myself smoothly of my aide-de-campship. Personally, though, I think it unlikely that the Directory would agree to Bonaparte taking a large army overseas for his own aggrandizement. Since France is still bankrupt, despite the immense treasure Bonaparte looted out of Italy for her, I count it probable that the minds of the Directors run on renewing the war across the Rhine, or sending him to invade smaller States that have remained neutral, to act again as a robber for France. But all this is speculation. It would, therefore, be unfair in me to disguise from you the possibility that new developments in France might prevent my return this year, or even next.'

For a long moment Georgina was silent, then she said, ' I am very conscious that I owe it to my little Charles to marry again, so that he should have a father to bring him up. At any time I might meet a suitable *parti*. Not one who could ever take your place in my heart, but a home-loving man of probity and charm for whom I could feel a genuine affection. Since you may be away for so long, I must hold myself free against such an eventuality. You too might meet some charming woman with whom you may feel tempted to share your future. If so, as in the past, you must also consider yourself free to marry again; for I can hold out little hope that I will ever alter my opinion that this unique love of ours can be preserved only by our never remaining together long enough to weary of one another. All I can promise is that should we both be still unwed when you do return to England I'll give your proposal serious consideration.'

Roger refilled their glasses with port and said, 'In fairness I can ask no more, and I pray that my return may be neither in a French uniform nor delayed beyond the summer. Let's drink to that.'

She raised her glass and they both drank. As she set it down, she sighed, 'I would to God I could be certain that you will return at all. Each time you leave me to set out upon these desperate ventures my stomach contracts with the horrid fear that I'll never see you more. You've been monstrous lucky, Roger; but every day you spend among your enemies is tempting Fate anew. Hardly a week passes but I think of you and am harrowed by the thought that you may make some slip, be caught out and denounced as an English spy.'

He shrugged. 'My sweet Georgina, you need have little fear of that. I have spent so long in France that my identity as a Frenchman is established there beyond all question. Anyone who challenged it would be laughed at for a fool.'

'How you have managed that I have never fully understood.'

'The fact that I lived there for four years in my youth formed a sound basis for the deception. To account for my foreign accent, before I rid myself of it, I gave out that my father was of German stock and my mother English, but that I was born in the French city of Strasbourg. I further muddied the waters of my origin by giving out that both my parents died when I was at a tender age; so I was sent to my English aunt, here in Lymington, and brought up by her. My story continues that I hated England, so as soon as I was old enough ran away back to my native France. In that way I became known there as the Chevalier de Breuc.'

'But later, Roger, you became the trusted henchman of Danton, Robespierre and other sanguinary terrorists. Such men have since been guillotined, or at least proscribed. How did you succeed in escaping a similar fate?'

'In that, I am one of many. Tallien, who directed the Red Terror in Bordeaux; Fréron, who was responsible for the massacres in Marseilles; and numerous others whose crimes cry to heaven have proved such subtle politicians that they rode out the storm, succeeded in whitewashing themselves and still lord it in Paris. There are, too, scores of *ci-devant* nobles who, until the Terror made things too hot for them, had, for one reason or another, found it expedient to collaborate with the Revolutionaries. Some were thrown into prison, others went into hiding. After the fall of Robespierre they all emerged with specious stories of how from the beginning they had worked in secret against the Revolution; so it has become the height of bad form to enquire closely of anyone about their doings previous to '94.'

'Thus on my return from Martinique, in the spring of '96, I needed only to imply that I, too, had been playing a double game, to be welcomed into the most fashionable salons which have sprung up in the new Paris. Such terrorists as survived know that I had a hand in bringing about Robespierre's fall, so they naturally now accept it that I fooled them when they knew me as a *sans-culotte*, and was all the time a young nobleman disguised. The aristocrats whose acquaintance I made earlier in the galleries of Versailles look on my as one of themselves—a clever enough schemer and liar to have saved my neck throughout the Revolution.'

'I should find it most repellent to have to move in such a dubious society.'

'But for a few exceptions they are indeed a despicable crew. At times it makes my gorge rise to learn that some woman of noble birth has become the mistress of a man well known to be a thief and a murderer, or that a Marquis is giving his daughter in marriage to some gutter-bred ex-terrorist who has climbed to influence and wealth over the bodies of that nobleman's relatives. Yet it is in the fact that the Revolution has brought to the surface a scum composed of the worst of both worlds that my security lies. To them, there is nothing the least surprising that a youth educated abroad by rich relatives should have returned to become a fervent patriot, having risen to the rank of Citizen Representative, have conspired against Robespierre and now be an aide-de-camp to General Bonaparte.'

'There are gaps in your career in Franch, of which you have made no mention: one of two years while you were first married to Amanda, another while you were Governor of Martinique and yet another while you were in India. If seriously questioned, surely you would have difficulty in accounting for them; and there must be at least a few Frenchmen who have seen you when you have been wearing your true colours, in England or elsewhere, as Admiral Brook's son, and would recognize you again.'

'No.' Roger shook his head. 'My absences from Paris are all accounted for. And to guard against such chance recognition as you suggest I long ago invented two mythical cousins, both of whom strongly resemble me. One is myself, the English Admiral's son, Roger Brook; the other, on my mother's side, as a bearded fellow named Robert MacElfic. Should any Frenchman think that he has seen me where I should not have been I'd vow it was one or other of these cousins they saw and mistook him for myself.'

'Lud! One must admire you for a cunning devil,' Georgina laughed. 'Can there then be no single man in all France who knows you for an Englishman and can give chapter and verse to prove it?'

Roger's face became a little grave. 'There are two. Joseph Fouché, the terrorist who was responsible for mowing down with cannon the Liberal bourgeoisie of Lyons, is one. But when we last came into conflict he was without money or influence and on the point of quitting Paris as a result of an Order of Banishment forbidding him to reside within twenty leagues of the capital. Fortunately he is not among those terrorists who succeeded in whitewashing themselves; so from fear of the reactionaries seeking to be avenged on him he is most probably still living quietly in some remote country village.'

'Then your chances of coming face to face with him are, thank God, slender. Who is the other?'

'Monsieur de Talleyrand-Périgord. His name was struck from the list of *émigrés* in '95, but he did not return from America until the autumn of '96; so he had not yet arrived in Paris when I was last there. He has since been made Foreign Minister, as I learned in Italy while assisting Fauvelet de Bourrienne with General Bonaparte's correspondence.'

'It is a certainty, then, that before you have been for long back in Paris you will run into him at some reception.'

'True, but I have little apprehension on that score.' Roger shrugged. 'He and I have long been firm friends. Moreover, he is greatly in my debt. It was I who saved him from the guillotine

B

by providing him with forged papers that got him safely out of
Paris. He is not the man to forget that; and, although he knows
me to have been born an Englishman, it should not be difficult
to persuade him that I have served France well and have for long
been French at heart.'

Georgina slowly shook her head. 'You are the best judge of
that. Yet I shall still fear that, through some accident, the fact
that you are a secret agent sent from England will come to light.'

He frowned. 'Knowing so well your psychic gifts, it troubles
me somewhat to hear you say so. I only pray that your foreboding
may not be due to the capacity that you have oft displayed for
seeing into the future. Yet I do assure you that such a risk gives
me small concern compared with a far greater one that always
plagues me when I set out upon my missions.'

'What greater risk could there be than of a discovery which
would be almost certain to lead to your death?'

'It is that, having acquired considerable influence with Barras,
the most powerful man in the Directory, I may use it wrongly.
On more than one occasion I have formed my own judgment
and have acted in direct opposition to what I knew to be the
official British policy.

'In three separate matters upon which great issues hung I have
done this, and all three times fortune has favoured me. But it is
in the taking of such decisions that lies the real anxiety of my
work. Each time I am faced with some crisis, in which a word
from me may serve to sway the balance, I am beset with a desperate fear that I will adopt the wrong course. So far my judgment has proved right, but there can be no guarantee that it
will continue so; and sooner or later, should I again take it upon
myself to act contrary to Mr. Pitt's instructions, I may find that I
have committed an error that will cost our country dear.'

'I understand and sympathize, dear Roger.' Georgina stretched
out a hand across the table and took his. 'But in this new mission
you have no cause for such a fear. You told me a while back that
it was entirely nebulous. As no specific task has been enjoined
upon you, you'll have no nerve-racking decision to take concerning the best way to accomplish it.'

He nodded. 'You are right in that my terms of reference are,
in general, vague. But Mr. Pitt has many minor agents in France
whose regular reports have enabled him to follow the development of events in Paris. Upon them, he and his cousin Grenville

at the Foreign Office have formed more or less correct assessments of the most important men there. They regard General Bonaparte as the best soldier who has emerged from the Revolution. In that I concur, and I would go further. Having worked under him in Italy, I know him also to be a great administrator, and I naturally informed them of my opinion. During the Revolution he was an extremist, and in recent months there have been strong rumours that he contemplates overthrowing the Directory by a *coup d'état*. You will readily appreciate that the very last thing Mr. Pitt and his colleagues would wish is to see France under a dictator who is not only a great General but has proclaimed it as a sacred cause to carry the doctrines of the Revolution by fire and sword through every country in Europe. In consequence, while I have been offered only opinions on how it might prove most profitable to develop my relations with other leading men, I have been definitely instructed to do my utmost to ruin General Bonaparte.'

'Surely that makes sound sense and, apart from any qualms you may feel about harming a man who has given you his friendship, should cause you no uneasiness.'

'Unfortunately it does, for I am by no means convinced that Mr. Pitt is right in his assumption that, given supreme power, the brilliant young Corsican would become the ogre that he supposes. Admittedly Bonaparte owed his first chance to show his abilities as a soldier to the patronage of Robespierre, and he has since deposed the sovereigns of the Italian States he overran in order to convert them into so-called " People's Republics ". Yet he went out of his way to treat the Pope with civility and formed a Court about himself at Montebello at which even his brother Generals kow-towed to him as though he were a reigning Monarch.'

'You think, then, that he is already by way of abandoning his Republican principles? '

'I think that any man so intelligent must realize the hopelessness of endeavouring to impose them upon Austria, Russia, Prussia and England; and, rather than challenge these mighty monarchical Powers, he would prefer to initiate an era of peace in which to build a new and prosperous France out of that country's present ruin.'

'Does this mean that you have in mind to ignore again your master's orders and assist in furthering the ambitions of General Bonaparte? '

'No, I would not say that. To start with it is most unlikely that it will ever lie in my power to make or mar the career of such an exceptional man. But there is just a chance that some card might fall into my hand by playing which at the right time I could put a serious check to his designs, or even, perhaps, bring to naught a *coup d'état* launched by his followers with the object of making him the uncrowned King of France. Should such a chance occur, I would have to decide whether to play that card or withhold it. What greater risk could there be than that of making a wrong judgment which might perhaps bring death and disaster to Europe for a generation?'

2

A Most Unwelcome
Encounter

As Roger finished speaking, Jim Button, the elderly houseman who had been with the family since his boyhood, came in and said, 'The carriage is at the door, Master Roger, and Dan was set on driving you down; so I've given him your valise.'

'Thanks, Jim.' Roger stood up and Georgina with him. She had insisted on accompanying him down to the harbour; so her maid, Jenny, was waiting in the hall with the great hooded cloak of Russian sables in which Georgina always travelled in the winter.

Roger, who loved colourful clothes, was, for him, dressed very quietly in a grey cloth suit, black boots and a plain white cravat. Over them he put on a heavy, tight-waisted, multi-collared travelling coat. In one of the pockets of its wide skirt reposed a big flask of French cognac, in the other a small double-barrelled pistol. Having bidden Jim and Jenny a cheerful farewell, he donned a beaver hat with a flower-pot-shaped crown and led Georgina out to the carriage.

The port was little more than a quarter of a mile away and during the short drive they sat in silence, Roger with his arm round Georgina, her head upon his shoulder.

Down at the quay a boat was waiting. As they got out, a Petty Officer came forward and touched his forelock. Dan Izzard, Roger's devoted servant, climbed down from the box and put a small valise in the stern of the boat. Then, with a grumble that he was not going too, he wrung his master's hand and wished

21

him a safe return. Turning, Roger took Georgina in his arms. For a long moment they embraced. All they had to say had already been said and their hearts were too full for further words, but as they kissed he felt the tears wet on her cheeks. Releasing her, he stepped into the stern of the boat, the Petty Officer gave the order to cast off and a moment later the oars were dipping rhythmically as they drew away in the early winter twilight.

Aboard the sloop her Captain, Lieutenant Formby, was waiting to greet his passenger. Roger had already made the young man's acquaintance on the ship's arrival at Lymington ten days earlier, and had not been very favourably impressed. It was not that Formby lacked a pleasant personality, but Roger would have much preferred to be taken across by an older and more experienced man; for it had emerged during their conversation that Formby had been transferred recently from service in the Bristol Channel. However, Roger knew the French coast so well that he felt confident that he could identify headlands and bays along it of which Formby might be in doubt; so he had no serious misgivings on the score of possibly failing to locate the cove, a few miles south of Dieppe, at which he wished to land.

The rain had ceased and the wind had died down. While the little ship tacked out through the Channel to the Solent, then west along it, Roger remained on deck making desultory conversation with her Captain. But when she rounded the Needles she came head-on to a sullen swell that was the aftermath of the recent tempest. Roger had always been a bad sailor; so he decided to turn in and try to get some sleep while he could, in case it should become rougher when they were well away from land.

He slept soundly and did not wake until the Lieutenant's servant roused him at six o'clock with a mug of ale and a plate of meat sandwiches. Sitting up in his narrow cot he slowly drank the ale, but eyed askance the doorstep slices of bread with their filling of red, underdone beef. Knowing the sort of fare which would be set before him during such a crossing, he had come provided with food more to his taste. Opening his little valise, he took from it two hard-boiled eggs and a partridge—one of the last of the season—which he gnawed to the bone.

Seeing no reason to get up, he lay in his bunk all the morning reading a book. At midday he dressed and went on deck. It was Formby's watch below and his Second-in-Command, a stodgy, moon-faced fellow named Trumper, stood near the binnacle, keeping an eye on the sails. Having acknowledged Trumper's greeting, Roger quickly turned away and began to pace the narrow quarter-deck.

As he reached its limit amidships, he noticed one of the hands coiling down a rope at the foot of the mast. The man's face seemed vaguely familiar, so he stopped and asked, 'Have I not seen you somewhere before?'

The sailor straightened himself and replied with a surly frown. 'Aye. My name be Giffens and you knows me well enough though it be a few years since we met. I were groom up at Walhampton to Miss Amanda afore you married she.'

Roger nodded. 'I recall you now. But I find it surprising that you should have chosen to go to sea rather than continue to care for horses.'

'Chosen!' Giffens echoed with a snort. 'There were no choice about it. I were catched by the Press Gang in Christchurch three months back.'

'Indeed. But the servants of the quality are immune from pressing. You had only to show that you were in Sir William Burrard's service to secure your release.'

'I were so no longer. Sir William got to know that I were a member of the Corresponding Society. 'E were that angry that 'e took 'is cane to me and drove me from Walhampton 'Ouse. Aye, and with 'alf a week's wages owing me ter boot.'

'So,' remarked Roger coldly, 'you are a member of the Corresponding Society. As such, you would no doubt like to see the King dethroned and a bloody revolution here, similar to that there has been in France?'

Giffens eyed him angrily. 'I've naught against King George, but I 'ave against gentry the like o' you. To further your own fortune in some way you've a mind to go to France, an' a word with others of your kidney is enough to 'ave a sloop-of-war bidden to land ye there. Yet what of us afore the mast who 'as the doin' of it? Should we be taken by the Frenchies us will find ourselves slaves chained to an oar in them's galleys.'

It was a point of view that Roger had never before had put to him. Had he heard it voiced in other circumstances he would have agreed that it was hard upon the common seaman that his lot, perhaps for years, should he be made a prisoner-of-war, would be the appalling one of a felon. On the other hand, the officers who ordered him into danger could count upon being treated fairly decently and were often, after only a few months of captivity, exchanged for enemy officers of equivalent rank.

But for some years past there had been serious unrest in England. Among the lower orders the doctrines of atheism and communism rampant in France had spread alarmingly. In Bristol, Norwich and numerous other cities troops had had to be used to suppress riots and defend property. In London mobs many thousands strong had publicly demanded the abolition of the Monarchy and the setting up of a People's Republic. Mr. Pitt had found it necessary to suspend Habeas Corpus and had passed a law sentencing to transportation for life street agitators caught addressing more than four people. Such measures might appear harsh but, having witnessed the horrors of the French Terror, Roger felt that no severity against individual trouble-makers was too great, when only by such means could they be prevented from bringing about the destruction in a welter of blood and death of all that was best in Britain. By admitting to being a member of the revolutionary Corresponding Society, Giffens had virtually revealed himself as a potential *sans-culotte*; so Roger said to him sternly:

'I go to France not for my own pleasure or profit, but upon the King's business. And since you are now one of His Majesty's seamen, however unwillingly, it is your duty to accept any risk there may be in doing your part to land me there.'

Giffens spat upon the deck. 'Aye! Duty and weevilly biscuits, that's our lot. But you're not one of my officers; so it's not for you to preach duty to me.'

'Speak to me again like that,' Roger snapped, 'and I'll have the Captain order you strapped to a grating for six lashes of the " cat ".' Then he swung on his heel and recommenced pacing the quarter-deck.

Within a few minutes he had dismissed Giffens from his mind and was thinking of his last conversation with Mr. Pitt. Together they had surveyed the international situation and, for Britain, it could hardly have been worse.

Between March '96 and April '97 Bonaparte's victorious army had overrun Piedmont, the Duchies of Milan, Parma and Modena, the Republic of Genoa and an area as big as Switzerland in north-east Italy that had for centuries been subject to Venice. He had dethroned their rulers, set up People's Governments and merged a great part of these territories into a new Cisalpine

Republic. He had also invaded the Papal States and had black-mailed both the Pope and the Duke of Tuscany into making huge contributions to the cost of his campaign. As a result, the whole of northern Italy now lay under the heel of France.

Yet he had fallen short of achieving his great plan, as he had described it to Roger before setting out for Italy. It had been that he should fight his way up to the Tyrol while the French Army of the Rhine marched south to make junction with him there; then with this overwhelming force, he would thrust east and compel the Austrians to sign a peace treaty in Vienna. He had reached the Tyrol, but the Army of the Rhine had failed him; so, to give it further time, he had agreed to an armistice with the Austrians. For six months the plenipotentiaries had wrangled over peace terms at Leoben. By then autumn had come again, and the Army of the Rhine had made little progress. Although the great prize, Vienna, lay less than a hundred miles away, Bonaparte did not dare, with snow already falling in the mountains, resume his advance alone and risk a defeat so far from his base. Reluctantly he had come to terms and signed a peace treaty with the Austrians at Campo Formio on October 17th.

When making peace Austria had not consulted Britain, thus betraying the ally who had sent her many millions in subsidies to help her defend herself. Still worse, by the terms of the Treaty, she surrendered all claim to her Belgian territories. Her flat refusal to do so previously had been the stumbling block which Mr. Pitt had felt he could not honourably ignore when he had had the opportunity to agree a general pacification with France some two years earlier.

Still earlier Prussia, too, had betrayed Britain by making a separate peace; and although Frederick William II had died in the previous November his succssor, Frederick William III, as yet showed no inclination to re-enter the conflict against the Power that threatened every Monarchy in Europe.

Catherine of Russia had realized belatedly the danger, and had promised to send an Army against France. But she had died just a year before the King of Prussia, and her death had proved another blow to Britain. Her son, who succeeded her as Paul I, had detested his mother so intensely that he senselessly sought to be avenged upon her in her grave by reversing every policy she had favoured and, overnight, he tore up the agreement by which Russia was to join the Anglo-Austrian alliance.

Holland lay at the mercy of France, Portugal had signed a separate peace and Spain had gone over to the enemy. The Kingdom of the Two Sicilies alone, owing to the influence of Queen Caroline, the sister of the martyred Marie Antoinette, pursued a neutrality strongly favourable to Britain, and would have entered the war again if she could have been supported. But she could not. The combination of the French and Spanish Fleets, after Spain had become the ally of France in '96, gave them such superiority that Britain had been forced to withdraw her Fleet from the Mediterranean; so for the past two years Naples had remained cut off.

At sea in all other areas Britain had more than held her own. She had driven her enemies from every island in the West Indies, with the one exception of Guadeloupe, and in the previous October Admiral Duncan had inflicted a shattering defeat on the Dutch Fleet at Camperdown. This had proved more than a great naval victory, for the French had been using the Dutch Fleet to convoy a large body of troops to the Clyde, on the somewhat dubious assumption that an enemy landing there would force the British Government to withdraw troops from Ireland and thus enable the Irish malcontents to launch a successful rebellion.

For several years past the French had been sending agents to stir up trouble in Ireland. They had met with such a fervent response from the discontented elements there that the Directory had promised to send ten thousand troops to act as a spearhead of rebellion against the hated British. Had this force succeeded in landing, it might well have proved impossible for Britain, with her other commitments, to hold the sister island, in which case it would have become the base for a great French Army able to invade at will England, Scotland or Wales.

Even as things stood, the League of United Irishmen was thirty thousand strong and pledged, with or without French help, to rise and fight to the death for Irish independence at the signal of its leader, Wolfe Tone. So at any time unhappy Britain might find a bloody civil war forced upon her as a further drain on her desperately stretched resources.

Outside the Mediterranean the British Navy had proved more than a match for the combined Fleets of France and Spain. Just on a year before, Admiral Sir John Jervis, now Earl St. Vincent, had so thoroughly defeated the Spanish Fleet, off the Cape from which he had taken his title, that only a small remnant of it now remained. Great seaman as he was, he had also had the greatness of mind to give a large part of the credit for his victory to Commodore Nelson who, on his own initiative, had broken station to cut through the Spanish line of battle, thus throwing the enemy Fleet into confusion.

Later that year this dashing junior officer had shown exceptional skill and gallantry in a series of attacks on the harbour of Cadiz. Then in July St. Vincent had given him command of a Squadron detached for the purpose of capturing the island of Tenerife. In that Nelson's luck had failed him. The Military Commanders in Gibraltar and the Channel Isles both had considerable bodies of idle troops under their orders, but both refused to lend any part of them to St. Vincent for this expedition. On account of lack of troops Nelson had not sufficient men to land forces which could have surrounded the town and had to rely on his limited number of marines and his ' tars ' to take it by direct assault.

On the night of July 22nd, when he launched his attack, many of the boats, owing to dense fog, failed to reach their landing points and others were driven off. Refusing to acknowledge defeat, Nelson decided to lead a second assault in person two nights later. The first attack had alerted the Spanish garrison and they were ready for him. It soon transpired, too, that the troops who garrisoned the Spanish colonies were of far finer mettle than those of their home Army.

Before Nelson even got ashore his right arm was shot away above the elbow by a cannon ball. But his men, most gallantly led by officers some of whom were later to become that famous ' Band of Brothers ', his Captains, fought their way into the city and held a part of it for several hours. Their position was, however, so evidently untenable that the seriously wounded Commodore agreed with the chivalrous Spanish Governor to a cease-fire and an exchange of prisoners.

In spite of this defeat, there was something about Nelson that had already caused the British people to take him, although still a comparatively junior Commander, to their hearts; and on his return to England in September they had hailed him as a hero. Throughout the autumn his wound had caused him great pain, but by early in December the stump had healed; so he was now recovered and, report had it, pestering the life out of the Admiralty to be sent to sea again.

In France the 'Five Kings'—as the members of the Directory which had taken over the Government after the fall of Robespierre were called—were still all-powerful. Under the new Constitution which had elevated them to office there were two Chambers: the *Corps Législatif*, popularly known as the Five Hundred, and the *Anciens*, which consisted of two hundred and fifty older statesmen elected from the former body. But the two Houses were no more than forums for debating proposed changes in the law. They had no executive power and Ministers were neither allowed to be members of either House nor were in any way responsible to them.

The Ministers were appointed by the Directory and were little more than chief clerks of departments under them. The Directory also appointed all military officers of senior rank, all diplomatic representatives and all the principal civilian officials of the State. As the majority of the Directors were unscrupulous men, the patronage in their gift had led to a degree of bribery and corruption never known in any country before or since.

All five of the Directors had voted for the King's death, so it was essential to their own safety that they should check the tide of reaction against the Terror that was sweeping France. To achieve this they secured agreement that one-third of the members of the new legislative body should consist of men who had sat in the old extremist Convention. Thus, against the will of the people, they ensured a majority which would refuse to pass any law which might bring retribution on themselves.

Paul de Barras, a man of noble birth and a soldier of some ability, was the acknowledged figurehead of the Directory. He was handsome, brave, gay, utterly corrupt and shamelessly licentious. Jean-François Rewbell was its strength and brain. A dyed-in-the-wool terrorist, he was foul-mouthed, brutal and dictatorial, but possessed a will of iron and in indefatigable appetite for work. Larevellière-Lépeaux was a lawyer, deformed, ill-tempered and vain, with one all-absorbing passion—a positively demoniacal hatred of Christianity. These three had united to form a permanent majority unshakably determined to oppose the popular movement for a greater degree of liberty and tolerance under a truly representative Liberal government.

Nevertheless, the new Constitutional Movement, as it was called, had by the preceding year gained such momentum that it caused Barras and his cronies considerable alarm. They feared that General Pichegru was about to stage a *coup d'état*, and it was even rumoured that in the Club de Clichy, where the leaders of the Constitutional Party had their headquarters, a plot was being hatched to restore the Monarchy.

When news of the landslide in public opinion percolated to the Armies in the field they too became disturbed, for a high proportion of the soldiers were former *sans-culottes*. The Divisions of the Army of Italy drew up fiery proclamations which they sent to Paris, declaring that if the *Corps Législatif* ' betrayed the Revolution ' they would return and slaughter its members.

Bonaparte had also shown his old colours. As the war was at a stalemate owing to the armistice with Austria, he could have gone to Paris and organized a *coup d'état*, but he was too shrewd a politician to lead personally a movement in support of the unpopular Directors. Instead he sent General Augereau, a huge, swashbuckling bully of a man imbued with violently revolutionary opinions.

Augereau was not a man to take half-measures and on his arrival in Paris he immediately announced that he had come to kill the Royalists. Having concerted measures with Barras, he dealt with the *Corps Législatif* on 4th September—18th Fructidor, Year V, in the revolutionary calendar—much as Cromwell had dealt with the Long Parliament. Arriving at their Chamber with two thousand troops he overawed their guard, arrested the Constitutional leaders and dispersed the remainder of the members.

Generals Pichegru and Miranda and thirty-eight other prominent Constitutionalists were sentenced to the ' dry guillotine ', as it was called, and transported to the fever-ridden swamps of Cayenne. The *Corps Législatif* was then purged of more than two hundred members, leaving a rump that was entirely subservient to the Directors.

The *coup d'état* of 18th Fructidor had also made infinitely more remote any possibility of Roger influencing some of the French leaders in favour of negotiating a peace. After five years of executions, street fighting, massacres, civil war in La Vendée and wars against half a dozen foreign nations, the French people were utterly sickened by blood-letting in all its forms. They longed for peace every bit as much as did the British. Had the Constitutionalists triumphed they would have given the people peace but, once again, as always happens at times of crisis, the Liberals, lacking the determination and ruthlessness of their extremist opponents, had been swept away. The Directory, on the other hand, was as determined as ever to carry the doctrines of the Revolution into every country in Europe, both by the thousands of agitators it sent abroad as secret agents and by force of arms. In consequence, Roger saw little hope of peace as long as the present rulers remained in power, and felt that he would be extremely lucky if he could succeed even in diverting some part of the French war effort from England.

Soon after four o'clock he was abruptly roused from his gloomy musings by a series of orders shouted from the after deck. Men tumbled up from below, others ran to the ropes and hauled on them. The vessel heeled over, the sails sagged and flapped noisily for a moment, then billowed out again as they refilled with wind. For most of the day the ship had been proceeding under a fair wind, east-south-east; now she had swung round to east by north.

At eight bells Lieutenant Formby had come up on deck to take his watch. With his telescope to his eye he had his back turned and was looking aft from the break of the low poop. Roger ran up the short ladder to it and asked him why he had changed course.

Formby frowned and pointed to the south-west. Hull-up on the horizon, but only just perceptible to the naked eye, lay a three-masted ship. 'From this distance I can't be certain,' he said, ' but she looks to me like a Frenchie. If so, she's a frigate out of Cherbourg.'

Taking the glass the young Lieutenant offered, Roger focussed it until he could see the ship quite clearly. 'She is certainly a warship,' he remarked, ' but I am not sufficiently acquainted with such matters to give an opinion on her nationality.'

As Roger handed back the telescope, Formby went on, 'Had we continued on course we'd have had to pass within a mile of her, and that's a risk I dare not take.'

' Stap me, no! ' Roger agreed emphatically. ' We'd be completely at the mercy of a ship that size did she prove an enemy. Do you think she will have sighted us? '

' I doubt it. This vessel being so much smaller, it would be harder to pick up. If she has, we can only pray that she did not observe our change of course.'

' You mean that seeing us turn away would arouse her

Captain's suspicions that we are either up to no good or are British?'

'Hell's bells!' Formby exclaimed, quickly putting up his telescope again. 'She *has* sighted us. Even with the naked eye you can now discern that her three masts are merging into one. She is coming round, so intends to pursue us.'

Roger shrugged. 'She is still miles away. Surely you can out-distance her with this sloop?'

Formby's forehead was creased with a frown. 'Should she crowd on all sail, I'd not wager on it.'

For the first time Roger felt a slight apprehension as he said, 'At least, your ship is much more easily manœuvrable. Unless she gets near enough to menace us with a broadside you have naught to fear except some balls from her bow-chaser. Visibility, thank God, is bad. By taking avoiding action, you should escape being hit until darkness closes down and we can get away under cover of it.'

'I could, with luck, had I a first-rate crew,' the Lieutenant replied bitterly. 'But more than half my men were pressed and were landlubbers until a few months back. With such ham-handed swabs, and slow at that to obey orders, I'll not be able to get the best out of her.'

Roger refrained from comment. From his father he knew only too well how, during the years of peace, half the ships of the Navy had been allowed to rot, while the men who had manned them either starved or settled into jobs ashore. During the past few years many new ships had been built and somehow crews had been got together for them, but nearly every ship in the Navy was undermanned and there was still a great shortage of trained seamen with long service.

Anxiously now he continued to stand beside Formby, peering at the outline of the frigate in the grey light of the February afternoon. After twenty minutes she appeared appreciably larger, so it was clear that she was gaining on them.

From time to time Formby used his glass to scan the horizon to the north. He said now, 'I turned up-Channel in the hope that we might meet with a ship of the Dover Squadron. That would scare the Frenchman off; but, unfortunately, we're a long way from the Narrows yet.'

Another half-hour went by, while officers and crew stood about, or leaned on the rail, watching with growing apprehension as the frigate gradually crept up on them. When two bells were struck, announcing five o'clock, individual sails on the jib boom and fore-mast of the frigate could be distinguished. From the waterline she presented a diamond shape with a fraction of the downward point cut off, nine-tenths of the remainder being made up of bulging white canvas.

At ten minutes past five a puff of smoke billowed out from her bows and some seconds later they heard the report of the gun. But the shot fell far astern of the sloop and was obviously intended only as a summons to her to heave to.

By twenty past they could clearly see the crest of foam on either side of the frigate's cut-water. Five minutes later she opened fire in earnest with her bow-chaser. The first shot was short by a good two hundred yards, and half a dozen others, fired at the rate of one a minute, failed to reach their target. Yet the spouts of water sent up from the sea by the fall of each shot gradually came nearer.

Roger, endeavouring to assess their chances of getting away, thanked all his gods that the sky was overcast. Sunset could not be far off and darkness should hide them from the enemy well before six o'clock. Yet within the next quarter of an hour they might easily be dismasted, and so compelled to surrender. With one half of his mind he was trying to think up a plausible story to tell about himself in the event of capture.

Suddenly a cannon ball clanged on the iron post of the stern lantern, bounced on the deck and whistled harmlessly off at a tangent. Formby turned to Roger. His eyes were wide and his young face white as he said, 'I've never fought a ship before, sir, and our twelve-pounder in the stern is useless at this range. What do you advise? Should we continue to hold our course or risk a tack?'

Angry that his safety should have been entrusted to such an inexperienced man, yet sorry for him, Roger replied, 'You are the Captain of this ship, so it is for you to decide. Were I in your place I would hold my course but run up the white flag. That would fox them into ceasing fire temporarily. The French are not such fools as to sink a ship if they think there is a good chance of capturing her. While their Captain is nurturing a false belief that we have surrendered, with luck we'd get away in the darkness.'

'No, no!' Formby protested. 'I could not do that. It would be dishonourable so to deceive our enemies.'

Roger gave a cynical laugh. 'When you have played tag with the French as long as I have you will realize that since the Revolution the majority of them who now wear officer's uniform are unscrupulous scoundrels and would think no trick too low to get the better of you. But, I repeat, the responsibility of saving this ship from capture is yours, so you must take such action as you think best.'

For some time past he had been increasingly perturbed by recalling his conversation with Georgina, and her fear that through some ill-chance he might be caught out as a spy. Once safely landed in France, he had little fear of that, but there was now no escaping the fact that a few more direct hits by the frigate's cannon balls might force the sloop to surrender.

At best that would mean imprisonment and an indefinite post-ponement of his mission, but it might have far more serious developments. Should someone aboard the frigate, or in France when he was landed there as a prisoner, chance to have known him during the years he had spent in that country under the name of Breuc, it was going to be no easy matter to explain his presence aboard a British ship-of-war. A little grimly, he realized that he was now in grave danger from exactly that 'lesser risk' of which he had made so light.

3

The Lesser Risk

BARELY concealing his disgust at Roger's 'dishonourable' attitude
to waging war, Formby ordered the Jack to be run up. The
frigate's captain was already doing his utmost to sink the sloop
or compel her to surrender, so openly proclaiming her to be
British added nothing to their danger. But as the little stern gun
could not have sent a shot within hundreds of yards of the enemy,
or have done her serious damage even had the shot landed,
the Lieutenant's gesture was no more than one of futile
defiance.

Roger was not at all surprised that his advice had been rejected;
but since it had, and there was no other means of gaining a
temporary respite from the frigate's fire, he felt that he should
no longer delay taking such steps as he could for his own protection. Within the next quarter of an hour he might be killed or
drowned, and that was a risk there was no escaping; but, if he
did survive this one-sided action, he meant to do everything he
could to preserve his identity of Colonel Breuc and, with his
usual resourcefulness, he had thought of a plan which, as far as
the French were concerned, should give him a fair chance of
doing so.

Turning again to Formby he said, 'The Government having
placed this sloop at my disposal to take me to France is sufficient
indication of the weight they attach to my mission. If we are
captured it is of the utmost importance that the French should
not realize that I am an Englishman. Therefore, should you
shortly decide that you have no option but to surrender, I desire
that you first have me put in irons and locked in the lazaret,
then tell our captors that I am a Frenchman and that you picked

34

me up this mid-day endeavouring to get to France in a small sailing boat which was near sinking.'

'If that is your wish, I'll see it carried out,' Formby replied. Then he added with a sudden show of spirit, 'But, dam' me, I'll not surrender my ship; not till she's either dismasted or holed below the waterline.'

Clapping him on the shoulder, Roger smiled. 'To hear you express such a sentiment warms my heart, Lieutenant. Since your crew leaves much to be desired in handling ship, let us then continue to take our punishment while forging dead ahead, and pray that fortune may aid us to escape.'

As he spoke, the frigate's bow-chaser boomed again. Next moment the Quartermaster at the wheel gave a single scream and collapsed upon the deck. The cannon ball had taken him squarely in the small of the back, cutting him nearly in half and spattering his blood in all directions.

Luckily the spent shot had not seriously damaged the wheel, only shearing off one of the spokes, and it was quickly secured by the bo'sun. But the ball had cleft the air barely a yard from Roger, so that he had felt the wind of it brush his cheek. More than once he had owed his life to having no false shame about taking cover when under fire and, while others about him were still gaping at the gory remains of the unfortunate Quartermaster, he left the poop in two swift bounds for the greater safety of the well-deck below it.

He had scarcely picked himself up and stationed himself under the ladder, where he would be protected not only from a direct hit but also from flying splinters should a shot smash into the deck forward of him, than the frigate's gun boomed again. This time she missed, but her next shot smacked through the sail above him, leaving a large rent in it.

Crouching there, he thanked his stars that he was only a passenger and had no duty to perform or obligation to set an example by remaining exposed upon the poop, as was the case with Formby.

The young Lieutenant, meanwhile, white-faced but determined, remained at his post, cursing his inability to return the frigate's fire. But he ordered the after gun to be run out and loaded in readiness, for it looked as if their pursuer would soon be in range of his smaller armament.

Dusk had now fallen and the enemy's next two shots went wide.

After the second, knowing there would be a minute's interval before another could be fired, Roger swung himself round the ladder and ran a few steps up to it to get a quick look astern over the taffrail. The semi-darkness obscured the outline of the frigate but her position could still be clearly seen because she had lit her lanterns.

At that moment there came a sharp crack and flash. Formby had just given the gunner the order to fire the little twelve-pounder. Instead of ducking back, as he had been about to do, Roger leapt up the remaining steps of the ladder on to the poop. His action nearly cost him his life. Another ball smacked into the deck only a few feet in front of him. It would have carried off his head had it not landed on a ring-bolt which caused it to ricochet and whine away over his shoulder. Dashing forward he grabbed Formby by the arm, and shouted:

'Are you mad to fire upon the frigate?'

Angered by such arbitrary treatment, Formby jerked his arm away. 'How dare you address me in such terms?' he cried hotly. 'Get back to your funk hole and leave me to fight my ship.'

'Funk hole be damned,' Roger retorted. 'I've killed more men than you've been months at sea. Unless you want your ship shot to pieces order your gunner to blow out his match.'

Drawing himself up, Formby snapped, 'For this impertinence, sir, I could have you put in irons. I am the Captain of this ship and——'

'I care not if you are the King of Spain,' roared Roger. 'Have you not the sense to realize that though we can see the frigate on account of her lights, she can scarce see us as ours are still unlit? To her we can now be no more than a dark shadow. Another few minutes and we'll be hidden by the blessed dark. But do you continue to fire your popgun you'll be giving her a mark by which she may yet sink us.'

The frigate's gun boomed again. Seconds later the shot crashed through the stern rail, sending deadly splinters flying in all directions. One caught the Yeoman of Signals in the fleshy part of the thigh, and he gave vent to a spate of curses. But this fourth hit gave point to Roger's argument and Formby had the grace to admit that he was right. Fighting down his humiliation, he gulped:

'I stand corrected, Mr. Brook. The temptation at least to show fight got the better of my judgment. We'll not fire on her again and in a few minutes we'll chance a tack with the hope of getting clear of her altogether.'

Several more shots came over but no further hits were scored. As eight bells sounded, signifying the end of the first dog-watch, they turned on to a new course and, shortly afterwards, the firing ceased. They had been saved by the early coming of the winter night.

Now that the action was over, Roger began to consider how it might have affected his plans. When they had sighted the frigate they had been about five hours' sailing from Dieppe, given a continuance of the wind in roughly the same force and direction. Although by nine o'clock it would have been fully dark, only the fisher folk would have turned in for the night at that hour, so he had intended to have the sloop hold off a couple of miles or so from the shore until midnight. But for the past two hours they had been sailing away from Dieppe, and the wind would be less favourable heading back in that direction. Therefore it would now be midnight, or perhaps one in the morning, before they reached the normally deserted cove in which he intended to land. The loss of an hour was of no importance, or two for that matter. His only definite requirement was that he should be put ashore in ample time to get well away from the coast before morning.

To Formby he said, 'Now that we are out of trouble, Lieutenant, I pray your leave to retire to my cabin. I've a hard day ahead of me tomorrow, and it's unlikely that I'll get any sleep for the best part of twenty-four hours; so I've a mind to put in a few hours before I land.'

'That would certainly be wise,' the Lieutenant agreed, 'and you should have a good meal too. Shortly now the galley will produce something for us, and Trumper will relieve me while I have the pleasure of entertaining you.'

Roger shook his head. 'I thank you, but beg to be excused. I am a poor sailor and hot meals at sea are apt to play the devil with my stomach. I've some hard tack in my cabin which will suit me better, should I feel hungry.' Then, not wishing to seem churlish to the young officer after having been so brusque with him, he added with a smile, 'But if you chance to have a decanter of wine handy I'd be delighted to take a glass with you before I turn in.'

'Indeed I have.' Formby's face brightened. 'Let's go below.'

In his cabin he produced some very passable Madeira, of which they drank two glasses apiece, while wishing one another good fortune. Then, having asked to be called at midnight, Roger went to his own cabin.

There he made a scratch meal from his small but carefully chosen stock of provisions, then undressed and, still ruminating on his good luck at having escaped capture, fell asleep.

At midnight the Lieutenant's servant woke him. A quarter of an hour later he had dressed and, carrying his small valise, went up on deck. There was no moon and as cloud obscured the greater part of the heavens it was almost totally dark; so it was a perfect night for a secret landing. Groping his way up to the poop, Roger saw Formby's face lit by the glow from the binnacle. Stepping up to him, he asked:

'How long should we be now? Whereabouts on the French coast do you estimate us to be at the moment?'

Looking up, Formby replied, 'As far as I can judge by dead reckoning, the coast on our beam should be a few miles south of Le Touquet.'

'Le Touquet!' Roger echoed, aghast. 'But that is not far from Boulogne, and sixty miles or more north of Dieppe. What in hell's name led you to bring your ship up-Channel?'

The Lieutenant bridled. 'After our experience this afternoon surely you would not have had me go about and again risk capture? We might well have run into that frigate.'

'In darkness and with our lights out there would not have been one chance in five hundred of our doing so,' Roger snapped. 'And here am I, a half-hour after midnight, still several hours' distant from the place at which I wished to land.'

'I'm sorry, Mr. Brook.' Formby's voice held evident contrition. 'I was under the impression that you'd mentioned that cove south of Dieppe only as a preference, and that it would have served your purpose to be landed at any quiet spot on the French coast. But I'll put her about and beat down to Dieppe if you wish.'

Roger considered for a minute. With the wind in its present quarter it was unlikely that they could reach Dieppe before six o'clock in the morning, and that was much too late to risk a landing. He could require Formby to turn back towards England, cruise off the Sussex coast for twelve hours, then run in again to put him ashore near Dieppe the following night. But that would mean the loss of yet another day in reporting to General Bonaparte; worse, the wind might change, rendering it impossible for him to land in France for another forty-eight hours or more.

Although he hated being at sea in uncertain weather, he had deliberately chosen the much longer crossing to Dieppe, rather than the short one across the Straits of Dover. It had been only a minor consideration that Lymington was one of the most convenient ports from which to cross to Dieppe and that, if he were held up by the weather, he could wait there in the comfort of his old home instead of a draughty inn in Margate or Sandwich. His choice had been governed by the fact that, whereas Calais was over a hundred and fifty miles from Paris, Dieppe was less than a hundred.

In the days of the *ancien régime* the difference would have mattered little. The *corvée*—the system of conscripting the peasants once a year for forced labour on the roads—had been one of the most bitterly resented impositions of the Monarchy, but it had kept the roads in excellent condition. Moreover, every few miles there had been Royal Post Houses—well-run hostelries at which travellers could secure good meals and relays of horses without delay or difficulty.

All that had been entirely changed by the Revolution. The roads had become nobody's responsibility. After six years of neglect they had fallen into an appalling state of disrepair, pock-marked with pot-holes sometimes as much as two feet deep and, in wet weather, having in places stretches of almost impassable mud. So many horses had been commandeered for the Army that relays often took hours to obtain, and the inns in which travellers were compelled to wait had become bug-ridden dens staffed by surly servants. To frequent breakdowns and other discomforts had to be added the lawless state of the countryside with the risk of being held up and robbed by bands of deserters.

In consequence, where in the old days it had been possible to travel from Calais to Paris overnight, it could now take up to four days in winter, with the certainty of passengers having time and again to get out, unload their vehicle and, knee-deep in mud, manhandle it out of the deep ruts in which it had become bogged down.

With fury in his heart, Roger thought of the additional fifty miles of such nightmare travel he would now have to face if he were landed in the neighbourhood of Boulogne. But he decided that he could not afford to risk another night at sea, with the possibility that the weather might turn foul and delay his landing by several days.

Turning to Formby, he said coldly, ' Very well, then. Run in, and we will reconnoitre the coast for a place suitable for me to be put ashore.'

At the Lieutenant's command the sloop altered course to north-east. Twenty minutes later they picked up a winking light on their starboard quarter which they decided must be the harbour beacon of the little fishing village of Le Touquet. Although the sky was mainly overcast. a faint starlight percolated through a few rents in the scudding clouds and, as they drew closer inshore, it was just sufficient for them to make out patches of white cliff against the dead blackness of the night sky above them.

While the sloop ploughed on until the Le Touquet beacon had become only a speck astern, Roger and Formby alternately studied the coast through the latter's night glass, until Roger said, ' Somewhere here should serve.'

Formby gave orders to stand in, start sounding and prepare to lower a boat. For some minutes a monotonous chant broke the silence as a seaman swung the lead. When he called four fathoms the command was given to heave to, and the sails came rustling down. A kedge-anchor was thrown out and the boat lowered and manned. Formby wished Roger luck, they shook hands, then Roger climbed down into the stern of the boat.

It had a crew of six: the coxswain, four oarsmen and a man in the bow to jump out with the painter. No sooner had it started to pull away than Roger's attention was caught by the loud splashing of the oars. For a secret landing such as this the oars should have been muffled and it was another indication of Formby's lack of experience that this precaution had been neglected. It was now too late to do anything about it, but Roger said to the coxswain in a low voice:

' Go easy. Tell the men to dip their oars gently; and there's to be no talking.'

As the coxswain passed on his order, Roger reflected that it was hardly necessary to observe caution to the point where it would double the time it would take for the boat to reach the shore, and he realized that he had given it only as a result of habit. Even so, perhaps it had been wise, since the coast here was so much nearer to England than at Dieppe that it was much more fre-quently patrolled, and one could not be too careful.

Slowly the boat nosed its way in, was lifted slightly by the surf and grounded on the beach. The bowman jumped out and threw his weight on the painter to keep the boat from being sucked back by the undertow. But the man was still standing calf-deep in water and as the wavelets broke they were wetting him up to the thighs. Seing this by the faint starlight, Roger said to the coxswain:

' Be good enough to have the boat hauled up for me. It will be many hours before I can secure a change of clothes and I have no mind to spend the night in those I am wearing half soaked with seawater.'

' Aye, aye, sir! ' The coxswain spoke sharply to his crew. The four oarsmen shipped their oars, scrambled over the side into the surf and set about dragging the boat up out of the sea. When the bow was clear of the water Roger stood up, with a word of thanks slipped a guinea into the coxswain's hand, scrambled over the thwarts and jumped ashore.

When he sprang out the men were still heaving and cursing, and as they dragged at the boat the keel was making a loud, grating sound on a patch of shingle. It was these noises which had prevented any of them hearing other sounds up by the cliff face. Before Roger caught them he had taken a dozen paces along the shore in the direction of Le Touquet. His heart began to hammer. They were, unmistakably, the footfalls of men running towards the sea. At this hour, in such a deserted spot, it could only be a French patrol that had seen the faint outline of the sloop or heard the boat approaching from her.

He gave a swift glance round. The seamen were now endeavouring to re-launch the boat. He could dash back to it. But would they get it off in time? Even if they did it was certain that the French patrol would be armed with muskets and the boat still within point-blank range.

The alternative was to chance taking to his heels. The men in the patrol would, without doubt, head straight for the boat, in the hope of capturing it as well as its crew. If they reached it before it was afloat a fight would ensue. They would then be too fully occupied to come after him before the darkness had rendered it impossible for them to tell the direction he had taken. He was already some way from the boat and as soon as the patrol came within sight of it the eyes of all of them would be riveted on it; so he might even escape their notice and get clear away without fear of pursuit.

While these thoughts were racing through his mind, the seamen were shouting in alarm and urging one another to greater efforts to get the boat off. Through their shouting cut cries of challenge from the French and demands by them to stand or be fired upon. Without waiting another second, Roger plunged forward and pelted along the shore as fast as his legs would carry him.

Before he had covered fifty yards a shot rang out. Fearing that it might have been aimed at him, he did a quick swerve, then looked back over his shoulder. A second was fired at that moment and for an instant its flash lit the scene behind him as brightly as daylight. Two groups of black silhouettes stood out sharply. The boat had been got off, and the coxswain stood in the stern, his arm extended, pointing a pistol; but three of the seamen, clustered round the bow, had not yet managed to clamber aboard. No more than fifteen feet away the French patrol was charging down the slope. It was led by a figure waving a sword and some of the men had their muskets raised, with the evident intent of firing as they ran. Roger judged there to be at least a dozen of them, but it was obvious that their whole attention was concentrated on the boat's crew and he doubted if any of them had given even a glance in his direction.

To put as great a distance as he could between them and himself while he had the chance, he clutched his valise to his chest, threw back his head, tucked his elbows into his sides and sprinted a good hundred yards. Panting for breath, he then eased his pace, stumbled a few more paces, halted and again looked back. Shouts and curses still echoed back from the chalk cliffs, but darkness now completely hid the scene. Suddenly another firearm flashed.

The boat was well away; a good twenty feet out from the water's edge. Two of the men in her had got out oars and were pulling for the ship. Some of the French had followed the boat out into the sea and were brandishing their weapons but they were already waist-deep and had halted, so it was clear that she would get away. None the less, their skirmish with the crew had not proved altogether a failure. They had captured one of the seamen. Before darkness again blanketed the scene Roger glimpsed a group of them dragging him away, still struggling, up the slope of the beach.

After gulping in a few breaths, he ran on again, but at a

steadier pace until he had covered about a quarter of a mile. The shooting and yelling in his rear had ceased. Suddenly, in the renewed silence, he heard the steps of someone running towards him.

Next moment the faint starlight revealed two figures emerging from the gloom ahead. Swerving, Roger spurted towards the greater darkness beneath the cliff. But it was too late. They had seen him. One of them shouted, '*Qui vive?*', then they, too, both swerved inland to intercept him.

With bitter fury he realized that, already winded as he was, there could be no hope of evading them. The only course appeared to be to fight it out. Dropping his valise he thrust his hand into the pocket of his coat, pulled out the little double-barrelled pistol and cocked it as he ran. A dozen yards from the water's edge his path and theirs intersected. The bigger of the two was leading. He had drawn a sabre and swung it high to cleave Roger's head. While the sabre was still pointing skyward Roger fired. The bullet struck the man in the right shoulder. With a howl of pain he dropped his arm and the sabre slipped from his grasp. As he staggered away, the second man came at Roger with a short sword. Roger fired his second barrel, but missed. Dodging the man's thrust, he ran in and smashed the fist that held the pistol with all his force into his antagonist's face. He, too, dropped his weapon, clapped his hands to his broken nose and bleeding mouth, then lurched away moaning.

For a moment it seemed that Roger would yet escape capture but, even as he stood there, his chest heaving painfully from his efforts, he caught the sound of more thudding footfalls fast approaching. It flashed upon him then that the two men he had rendered *hors de combat* must be only the first to appear of a second patrol stationed further along the coast. It must have been alerted by the sound of firing as the first patrol attacked the boat.

Desperately, he looked about him. To run back the way he had come meant certain capture. The cliff was much too high to scale and it shut him off from attempting to escape inland. But there was still the sea. Sobbing for breath he swung about, pounded down the slope, splashed through the shallows, then flung himself headlong into the water.

It was icy. As his head came up above the surf his heart contracted in a spasm and a shudder ran through him. But, still almost entirely submerged, he stumbled and thrust his way out until, with only his head above water, his feet could just touch the sea-bed.

He had decided to take the plunge on a sudden inspiration that he might get away by swimming out to the sloop. But he had temporarily overlooked the fact that it was early February. As he stood there, up to his neck in the sea, he knew that had he attempted to swim the Channel his chances of success would have been no more hopeless. Strong swimmer though he was even if he could have wriggled out of his heavy travelling coat and rid himself of his boots the cold would have numbed him into insensibility before he had swum a hundred yards.

Yet he still had one faint hope. Racked with pain as they were, the two men he had wounded might not have seen which way he had gone. If so, the patrol would divide to search the shore for him in both directions. Then, if he could stand the cold long enough, he might crawl out and find a hiding place under the cliff until the coast was clear of his enemies. To fortify himself against the ordeal he foresaw he got out his flask of brandy and took a long pull from it. The spirit coursed through his veins like a fire, yet gave him only temporary relief from the deadly chill.

And his hope proved vain. The man he had shot in the shoulder had seen him run off and splash into the sea. As the main body of the patrol came up he began shouting to them, and Roger could plainly hear him giving an account of what had happened. In the faint starlight he could just make out the group of figures as it split up, and the men spread themselves along the shore, evidently peering seaward in an endeavour to spot him.

With only his head above water, and against the black background of the sea, he knew that it would prove impossible for them to do so. But his lips were blue with cold and shudders ran through him every moment. He felt certain now that if his body remained for another five minutes in the grip of those icy waters he would die there. Miserably he admitted to himself that there was nothing for it but to surrender, so he began to wade ashore.

As soon as his chest was above the level of the sea, he feebly waved an arm and cried in French, 'Don't shoot! I give myself up to you.'

No sooner had he spoken the words than he realized that, taken by surprise, he had committed an appalling blunder. Instead of firing his pistol when attacked, those were the very words he should have used, adding, 'I am a Frenchman, and have just escaped from the English.'

To account for himself he could have told the story he had given to Formby—that he had been picked up by the sloop while attempting to get to France in a small sailing boat, or that he was a French prisoner-of-war who had escaped from the Isle of Wight and had bribed the Captain of the sloop to bring him over. By wounding two men of the patrol he had quite unnecessarily declared himself to be an enemy. Now it was going to be the very devil of a job to make his captors believe otherwise.

With his mind almost atrophied by cold, he vaguely berated himself for his folly, while lurching and stumbling his way ashore. When he reached the strand he collapsed upon it.

Laughing at the obvious madness of this Englishman who had endeavoured to escape by taking refuge in the sea when it was near freezing, but by no means lacking in humanity, the men of the patrol stripped off his heavy coat and pummelled a little warmth back into his shuddering limbs. Then one of them produced a flask of cognac and at short intervals tipped the greater part of it down Roger's throat.

After this treatment he was sufficiently recovered to gulp out that he was a Frenchman, and would later give them the story of how he had escaped from England. At that, they exclaimed in great surprise and at once asked why, if that were so, he had attacked their two comrades. Roger stammered out that by coming upon him suddenly in the dark they had caught him unawares, and that he had been forced to it in self-defence, otherwise they would have cut him down before he had had a chance to explain himself.

His French accent was so impeccable that, to his great relief, they no longer appeared to have doubts about his nationality; but they obviously remained extremely puzzled about his behaviour.

As soon as he could stand, the officer said, 'We will get to the bottom of this later. Let's take him along to the other patrol and find out what has happened there.'

Two of the men then took Roger by the arms and helped him walk the quarter of a mile back to the place on the beach where he had landed. The rents between the clouds were larger now, so the brighter light from the stars enabled him to see that opposite this place there was a dark gap in the cliff leading up to higher

ground. In the entrance to it the other patrol was gathered and
several of the men had lit lanterns. Their officer came forward
and exchanged reports with the one who led Roger's party. Then
they all moved up to the entrance to the gap.

Just inside it there was a rough lean-to, which was evidently
used by the patrol as a shelter in bad weather. Stretched out on
the ground under it, half propped up against a wooden bench, lay
an unconscious figure. Roger guessed that it must be the seaman
who had been captured, and that to put an end to his struggles he
had been given a knock on the head. A moment later, by the
light of one of the lanterns, he recognized the man as Giffens.

The two officers conferred again, and from what they said
Roger gathered that he and Giffens were to be taken to a nearby
house and locked up there till morning. A few minutes later, led
by the officer of the first patrol, and with two men carrying the
unconscious Giffens, a party with Roger in its midst set off up
the steep slope through the gap between the cliffs. Roger, still
swaying with exhaustion, had to be helped, but on reaching the
top of the cliffs they had not far to go. In a hollow a quarter of
a mile beyond the cliffs lay a small farmhouse, which had been
taken over by the Military. The shutters were closed so no lights
showed from the windows, but inside the kitchen a bright fire was
burning and two lanterns hung from the central beam of the
room.

For the first time Roger had the chance to get a good look at
his captors. The officer was a medium-sized man with a long,
droopy nose, prawn-like eyebrows and a greying moustache. He
was dressed in a threadbare uniform, and one of his men had
just addressed him as Citizen Lieutenant Tardieu.

Roger was shaking as though he had the ague, and a pot of
soup was bubbling on the stove; so one of the men gave him a
bowl of it. He swallowed about half the soup in a succession of
gulps, then the Lieutenant said, ' Now you must give me an
account of yourself.'

Pulling himself together, although his teeth were still inclined
to chatter, Roger replied, ' I can go into no details in my present
condition. I can only ask you to accept my statement that my
name is Breuc, and that the sufferings I endured during my
escape from England were such that I was half out of my wits
when those two men attacked me, so I automatically defended
myself. In due course I shall have no difficulty in proving my

identity. I hold the rank of Colonel and while in Italy had the honour to be one of General Bonaparte's aides-de-camp.'

Citizen Tardieu's eyes widened. 'What's this you say? Aide-de-camp to General Bonaparte! I can scarce credit that.' Then after a moment he added, 'Still, since you aver it, I'll give you the benefit of the doubt and treat you with the respect due to the rank you claim.'

He then gave orders to two of his men who were standing by to fetch blankets and heat them by the fire. Ten minutes later the men helped Roger upstairs to a bedroom, assisted him to get out of his waterlogged clothes, then wrapped him in the blankets and put him to bed.

When they left the room he heard one of them lock the door, but if it had been left wide open he would not have had the strength to stagger down the stairs in a bid to escape. As things were, he would not have made the attempt, even had he been able to do so, for he felt confident that he now had little to fear. Before he was questioned again he could trust to his fertile mind to have ready a convincing story of an escape from England and, even if he were kept prisoner for a week or so, it should not be difficult to produce evidence that he was, in fact, one of General Bonaparte's aides. Greatly relieved in mind, he dropped off to sleep.

When he awoke it was broad daylight and the Lieutenant was standing beside his bed. With a pleasant smile his visitor asked, 'Well, and how is General Bonaparte's aide-de-camp feeling this morning?'

Rousing himself, Roger returned the smile and replied, 'Very different from last night, and almost myself again, I thank you.'

The smile suddenly left Citizen Tardieu's face, and he snapped, 'A taller, more impudent story I have never heard. General Bonaparte's aide-de-camp, indeed! Through an interpreter I have questioned the seaman we captured. He says he knows you well. You are the son of no less a person than Admiral Sir Brook, and an accursed Englishman sent here as a spy.'

4

A Desperate Situation

FOR a moment Roger was utterly taken aback. He had been roused from a sound sleep barely two minutes earlier, and the events of the previous night were only just assuming their proper sequence in his mind. Yet almost his first memory was of his last conscious thought before he slept—that the officer beside him had agreed temporarily to give his claim to be one of General Bonaparte's aides-de-camp the benefit of the doubt, and his own confidence that he would find means in the morning to substantiate that claim.

Now he recalled having seen Giffens lying unconscious in the patrol's lean-to but, at that time, owing to his own recent ordeal, he had been hardly conscious himself. It had not even entered his mind that the disgruntled ex-groom might betray him. Taken entirely by surprise, he propped himself up in bed on one elbow and stammered :

'I . . . I don't know what you're talking about. Admiral Brook? I . . . I've never heard of him. Giffens . . . the man is lying.'

'I do not think so,' replied Tardieu coldly. 'He says that he has known you for several years, and has given us chapter and verse about you. From him we also know that the ship from which you landed was a British sloop-of-war. What purpose could a naval vessel have for standing in here secretly at night other than to put ashore a spy? I mean to see that you get your deserts before you are much older. Get up now and dress yourself.'

Roger made no further attempt to protest his innocence. Experience had taught him that when in a dangerous situation the less said the better. He feared that he had already said too much. To have protested that he had never heard of his own father had been unnecessary; worse, by mentioning Giffens by name he had admitted that he knew the seaman, which might later be difficult to explain if he was to get his story accepted that he had been picked up in the Channel.

As he thrust back the blankets he saw that his clothes were in a bundle on a nearby chair. Evidently they had been dried during the night and put there while he was still asleep. Tardieu walked towards the door. When opening it, he glanced back and, seeing that Roger was looking in the direction of the window, snapped:

'Don't imagine you can give us the slip that way. I've a sentry posted outside with orders to shoot you should you so much as show your head.'

'My compliments, Citizen, upon your forethought,' Roger replied tartly.

Left to himself, he took his time in dressing and used it to take stock of his alarming situation. It was, he decided, about as tough a corner as any in which he had ever found himself. Any immediate attempt to escape was obviously out of the question, and his only course was to await developments while saying as little as possible. His one consolation was that he had taken no harm from his immersion in the freezing sea. The brandy and hot soup he had been given, and his sound sleep between the warm blankets, had saved him from pneumonia or even from catching a severe chill.

When he felt that he could delay no longer he went down the narrow stairs to the kitchen. Tardieu was standing there with three of his men. Giffens was sitting on a stool in a corner mopping up with a hunk of bread what remained of a bowl of soup. As Roger appeared he gave him one swift, hostile glance, then kept his eyes averted.

Roger looked towards the kitchen range, upon which a pot was bubbling, hoping that he was about to be given some breakfast. Guessing his thought, Tardieu pulled at his grey moustache, then said with a sneer, 'It would be a waste of a meal to give you one. You won't need it where you're going.' Then, turning to one of his men, he added, 'Tie his hands, Corporal, then bring him outside.'

At that Roger's scalp began to prickle and the palms of his hands suddenly became damp. He could only conclude that there

C

and then they meant to take him out and shoot him. Instantly he broke into violent protests, demanding a trial, a lawyer, a priest.

Ignoring his outburst, Tardieu drew a pistol, cocked it and pointed it at him. Faced with the probability of immediate death if he resisted, he had no alternative but to allow the Corporal to tie his hands behind his back. When the man had knotted the cord securely he said:

'No need to keep him covered any longer, Citizen Lieutenant. Should he try any tricks now we've only to give him a good kick.'

Tardieu put up his pistol and led the way out. Roger was pushed after him by the three soldiers and Giffens brought up the rear. Drawn up in front of the farmhouse there was a small, covered cart with a single horse harnessed to it and two other horses tethered nearby. At the sight of them Roger, now wide-eyed and sweating at the thought that they had intended to put him up against the rear wall of the farmhouse and shoot him, felt a surge of temporary relief. Evidently he was to be taken some-where in the cart, and even a brief postponement of his execution might yet give him a chance to save his life.

Two of the men bundled Roger into the cart. At a sign from the Corporal, Giffens clambered in after him and the two soldiers climbed on to the driver's seat. Mounting one of the horses, Tar-dieu took the lead; then, with the Corporal bringing up the rear on the other horse, they set off.

The road was no more than a rutted track, and the rumble of the cartwheels on the hard ground drowned all other sounds; so, as soon as Roger had recovered a little from the ghastly five minutes he had just been through, he wriggled into a more comfortable position and said to Giffens:

'Are you not utterly ashamed of yourself?'

'Why should I be?' muttered the man surlily.

'For having betrayed a fellow-countryman, of course.'

Giffens shrugged. 'I don't hold with nationalities. There's rich and poor in the world, that's all. And you be on the other side to I. Besides, it were either me or you.'

'What makes you suppose that?'

'Why, they'd 'ave sent I to the galleys. But by givin' you away I've saved me bacon, ain't I?'

Roger managed an unpleasant little laugh. 'I wouldn't count on that. These Frenchmen of the Revolution have a nasty habit of using one enemy to bring about the death of another, then ridding themselves of his betrayer. I ought to know, seeing that I am a Frenchman myself.'

'You a Frenchie!' Giffens snorted. 'Don't give me such gab. I know different. You're Admiral Brook's son, just as I tells the officer when 'e questions me an 'our back.'

'I've no doubt you believe so,' Roger said quietly. 'But in that you are wrong. How long is it since you think you last saw me?'

Giffens scratched his head. 'Let's see now. Miss Amanda were married in the summer o' ninety, weren't she? Then you come down to Walhampton with she the following spring; so 'twould be getting on seven year agone. But I seed you many a time afore that.'

'No, it was my English cousin, Roger Brook, you saw. We are near the same age and have a striking resemblance. But I am of the French branch of the family and was born in Strasbourg. That is why my name is spelt B-r-e-u-c.'

'Them's a pack o' lies fit only for the marines. Seems to 'ave slipped your memory that only yesterday you played the fine English gentleman an' threatened me with a floggin'. You was Mr. Roger Brook then, right enough, an' made no pretence otherwise.'

'Indeed, no; and I'd have been out of my mind to do so, seeing that I was passing myself off as him in order to get back to France.'

'That's another tall one. 'Ow come it that you recognized me, then? It was you as said to me, "'Aven't I seen your face some place afore?" Remember?'

'Certainly. And I had. On several occasions while our two countries were still at peace I stayed at Lymington with my relatives, and more than once I visited Walhampton with the Admiral—or Captain Brook, as he then was.'

Giffens was evidently shaken, but he stubbornly shook his head and declared, 'I'll not believe it. I'll be danged if I do.'

Sensing the doubt he had sown in the man's mind, Roger pressed his advantage, and retorted, 'You will continue to disbelieve me at your peril. Listen, Giffens. Believe it or not, I am a Frenchman and a Colonel on the Staff of the most important General in France. There are hundreds of officers in the French Army to whom my face is well known. When we reach the place to which we are being taken I shall demand to see the local Military Commander. I'll then have no difficulty in establishing my true identity. I shall, of course, at once be freed. But what of you? If you persist in this idea of yours and make it more difficult for me to get a fair hearing I vow I'll see to it that you are sent to the galleys. If, on the other hand, you are prepared to admit that you may have been mistaken I'll see that you are treated decently and perhaps even arrange an exchange for you.'

For the better part of a minute Giffens remained silent, then he muttered, ' I'll 'ave to think about it. I told the bloke what did the interpreting that my politics was red-'ot Republican, an' arter that they treated me very friendly-like. So as things be I ain't afraid they'll send me to the galleys. But say I goes back on what I said about ye, all the odds is they'll act very different. I've still 'alf a mind that you'se lying; but even given I'm wrong about that, maybe none'll be found as knows you for a French Colonel, so they'll shoot you just the same. That 'ud be 'ard luck on you, but on me too. No sayin' I were a Republican would do me no good then. They'd clamp the fetters on me an' afore you was cold in your grave I'd find meself a slave in a dockyard.'

There was sound reasoning behind Giffen's argument. As Roger knew only too well, the chances of coming across an officer with whom he could claim acquaintance were all too slender and, although he continued to argue with the man for some while longer, he could not persuade him to commit himself.

Nevertheless, being by nature an optimist, Roger derived some little comfort from their conversation. It was Giffens who had denounced him and if, as he now thought probable, he was to be given some form of trial, Giffens would be the principal witness against him. It was no small achievement to have both sown doubt in his mind and scared him. Whereas before he would undoubtedly have given his evidence with malicious gusto, it now seemed fairly certain that even if he did not hedge he would exercise some degree of caution in what he said.

As the cart jogged on across the windswept downs both its occupants began to suffer from the cold. Giffens could slap his arms across his chest now and then to keep his circulation going. He had also had a hot breakfast, whereas Roger had an empty stomach and, with his hands tied behind him, could do no more than drum with his feet on the floorboards of the cart. Except that it had a hood the cart might easily have been taken for a tumbril and after an hour in it Roger's spirits had again fallen so low that he began to think of it as one in which he was being driven to the guillotine.

At length, between the undrawn curtains above the backboard, glimpses of occasional houses could be seen. Then the cart clattered down a succession of mean streets, to pull up outside a big building in a square, after a journey that had lasted about two hours. As Roger was helped out, he recognized the place as Boulogne and the building as its Hôtel de Ville.

His guards hustled him inside, took him down a flight of stone stairs to a basement and handed him over to a turnkey, who locked him, cold, hungry and miserable, into a cell. But he was not left to shiver there for long. After a quarter of an hour the turnkey returned with a companion, and they marched him up to the ground floor again, then into a spacious courtroom.

Earlier that morning the uniforms of Roger's captors had confirmed his belief that they were not Regular troops but Coastguards, with similar functions to the English Preventives, whose principal task was to stop smuggling. In consequence, as he had feared might be the case, he now saw that he was about to be tried not by a military but by a civil court. That meant that he would stand less chance of convincing its members that he was a Colonel in the French Army.

At one time the courtroom had been a handsome apartment, but the walls were now stained with damp, the windows long uncleaned, with numerous cracked panes, and the straw on the floor badly in need of changing. Yet the state of it was far from being as bad as that of many so-called Courts of Justice that Roger had seen during the worst days of the Revolution. The walls of the room were not lined with pipe-smoking, spitting, out-at-elbows National Guards, or the public benches packed with an evil mob of both sexes which, at the first sign of the judges inclining to show mercy, would intimidate them by howling for the blood of the accused.

Here there were no more than half a dozen casual spectators: Tardieu with his men, Giffens, a handful of depressed-looking advocates in the well of the Court and three magistrates, who were sitting at a table on a dais. On the wall behind it the *Axes and Fasces* surmounted by the Cap of Liberty had long since replaced the Royal Arms of France.

As Roger was put in the dock he swiftly scrutinized the three magistrates seated on the dais. The only thing they had in common was that they all wore tricolour sashes. The Chairman was a tall, lean individual. He had a bulging forehead, was wearing steel-rimmed spectacles, a shiny suit of dark-green cloth and looked as if he might be a lawyer. On his right sat a heavy-jowled, fattish man with black, curly hair. He wore a bright-blue coat, a big horseshoe pin was stuck in his cravat and he was sucking a straw, so Roger put him down as probably a farmer or a horse-dealer. The third man was small, with apple-red cheeks, a snub nose, and was dressed very neatly in a snuff-coloured suit with silver buttons. His appearance suggested the well-to-do bourgeois merchant who had succeeded in living through the Terror.

One of the advocates, who was evidently the Public Prosecutor, got to his feet. He was elderly, thin-faced and had a rat-trap mouth. After taking a pinch of snuff, most of which fell upon his already snuff-stained gown, he opened the trial. In a tired, indifferent voice, he stated that he did not think the present matter would occupy the Court for long, as there was ample evidence to show that the prisoner was an English spy. He then called Tardieu.

Speaking quickly and using many gestures, the Coastguard Lieutenant gave an account of the happenings of the previous night. From time to time he ran a finger down his long nose and shot a malicious sideways glance at Roger, who rightly assumed that Tardieu, having been fooled into giving his prisoner the benefit of the doubt to start with, and a night in a comfortable bed, was now working off his spite. But he said nothing that Roger had not expected him to say.

The next witness was one of the men who had acted as escort from the farm. It transpired that he belonged to the second patrol and had been among the first to reach the two men whom Roger had wounded. In a gruff voice he described the injuries they had sustained and how Roger had taken refuge in the sea, but had been compelled, on account of the cold, to come up out of it and surrender.

Roger had been offered no legal aid; so he asked permission of the Court to cross-examine the witness, and it was granted. In reply to his questions, the man at once agreed that there had been no moon and that none of his party was carrying lanterns. Then, after some pressing, he admitted that it had been very dark and the starlight so feeble that an approaching figure could not be seen at more than a few paces.

The Prosecutor then informed the Court that the next witness would be a seaman of the British Navy. He was a member of the crew of the sloop-of-war that had brought Roger to France and had been captured when landing him from a boat. He would swear to having known the prisoner for a number of years and that he was an Englishman, the son of Admiral Sir Brook.

Giffens was put in the box and, by a series of little more than nods and grunts, confirmed, through an interpreter, the Prosecutor's statement. But Tardieu was not satisfied by this and took it on himself to prime the Prosecutor with further questions. This resulted in Giffens repeating, in dribs and drabs but fully, the statement he had volunteered so readily to the Coastguards early that morning. Roger could see that he had succeeded in scaring the man to a point at which he gave these details only with reluctance, but he could not prevent particulars of himself, his home at Lymington, his visits to Walhampton and his marriage to Amanda from coming out.

When they had finished with Giffens, Roger cross-examined him and, greatly to his relief, found that the seaman had made up his mind to hedge. He agreed almost eagerly that before Roger boarded the sloop at Lymington he had not seen him for nearly seven years, so might perhaps have mistaken him for the Admiral's son.

Roger then made a bold attempt to trade on Giffen's fears by saying, ' As you were at Walhampton before the war with France began, you surely must remember a French gentleman who came there several times with the Admiral: a cousin of young Mr. Brook, who strongly resembled him? '

Giffens gave him a startled look, shook his head, then, thinking better of it, mumbled something that the interpreter translated as, 'Well, perhaps. There were a lot of Frenchmen who were refugees from the Revolution living in Lymington in those days, and some of them visited at Walhampton. But I couldn't be certain.'

Although that left the matter in doubt, Roger felt, as Giffens stood down, that he had scored a valuable point and when the Prosecutor began to question him he gave his story with quiet confidence.

It was that General Bonaparte, knowing that he had spent

several years of his boyhood in England and was bilingual, so
could pass as an Englishman, had sent him there to report on
the measures being taken by the English to resist invasion.

He had been landed on the Kentish coast by smugglers, and
had spent the past six weeks staying in small towns on the Kent,
Sussex and Hampshire coasts, working his way westward until
he reached Lymington.

There, four nights ago, at an inn, he had got into conversation
with a naval Lieutenant. This young man had been drinking
heavily and, after they had talked for some while, confided that
owing to gambling he had got himself into serious money troubles.
The Lieutenant had also mentioned earlier that he was under
orders to sail his sloop up to Dover as soon as the weather
permitted.

Having covered the territory assigned him by his General,
Roger was anxious to get back to France. Normally he would
have had to wait until he could get in touch with another gang of
smugglers working from the Hampshire coast; but the sloop had
seemed too good an opportunity to miss if he could persuade the
Lieutenant to put him over. He had, therefore, told the Lieutenant
that he was a Government agent seeking a passage and asked his
help. The officer had, at first, demurred, on the grounds that he
would be acting without orders and might risk his ship if he
stood in too near the French coast; but Roger had played on his
anxiety about money and had overcome his scruples by offering
him the considerable sum he would have had to pay a smuggler
to run him across.

The Prosecutor then asked him a number of questions about
his parentage, upbringing in England, later career in France,
recent stay in England and whether, during it, he had been to
Grove Place to see any of his English relatives.

Assuming the last question to be a trap, Roger replied
promptly, 'Certainly not. With a war in progress how could I
possibly have explained my presence in England to them? They
would have felt compelled to hand me over to the authorities.
On the contrary, while I was in Lymington I was in constant fear
of being recognized; so I spent nearly all the two days I was
there in my room at the inn. I would never have gone to Lymington at all had it not been a part of my instructions to report on
the shipping in the harbour.'

To all the other questions he gave the stock answers which were now second nature to him, adding for full measure references to many of his well-known acquaintances in Paris and descriptions of some of the outstanding scenes he had witnessed there during the Revolution. Since he spoke without the slightest hesitation and in French that was beyond reproach, he felt confident by the time he had finished that he had convinced the Court that he was a Frenchman. Yet one matter arose out of his examination that caused him a few nasty moments.

From beneath the table at which he was sitting, the Prosecutor produced the little valise that Roger had brought ashore, and to which he had clung during his flight along the beach until he was compelled to drop it on meeting the two men who had attacked him. Opening the valise, the Prosecutor took from it a small squat bottle and handed it up to the magistrates for them to look at.

As Roger recognized it his heart gave a thump. The bottle bore a handwritten label, 'Grove Place; Cherry Brandy.' Old Jim Button made a couple of gallons or so of the cordial every year with the morello cherries that grew in the garden. Knowing Roger's fondness for this home-made tipple he had slipped a bottle of it into the valise just before Roger's departure.

'You have told the Court,' said the Prosecutor, 'that while in Lymington you deliberately kept away from Grove Place. How comes it, then, that you had in your valise a bottle of this liqueur which has the name of the Admiral's residence upon it?'

'I bought it,' Roger declared, after only a second's hesitation. 'I saw it with other bottles in the coffee room of the inn, and chose it as most suitable to keep me warm during my crossing.'

The fat magistrate in the bright-blue coat was examining the bottle and he said, 'The handwritten label shows this to be a private brew. Inns buy their liquor from merchants, not from amateur cordial makers.'

'It may have been stolen,' Roger countered. 'Perhaps one of the servants at the house sold it for half its value to the innkeeper.'

The magistrate shook his head. 'Such things happen, but not in this case. You say you saw it in the coffee room of the inn. No landlord who had bought stolen goods would be such a fool as to display them publicly in his coffee room. I'm an innkeeper myself and can vouch for that.'

' Then you had best drink it, Citizen,' Roger quipped. ' You will find it very good.'

His sally raised a titter, but next moment he could have bitten off his tongue. The Chairman of the Bench was on him in a flash. ' This bottle is unopened, yet you admit to knowledge of its contents. Therefore, you must be well acquainted with the cordial and must have drunk it recently. I regard this as evidence that you did visit Grove Place and were given the bottle there.'

A slight shiver ran through Roger. The courtroom was warmed only by a charcoal brazier; so it was distinctly chilly, and by this time his having had nothing to eat since the previous night was beginning to tell upon him. With an effort, he shrugged his shoulders and said:

' Citizen Chairman, you err in counting that against me. I recommended the cordial on the grounds that I recall enjoying it when as a youth I lived at Grove Place and I saw no reason to suppose that its quality had deteriorated.'

A frown momentarily wrinkled the bulging forehead of the Chairman, then he said, ' We will leave that question for the moment and enquire further into an outstanding feature of the case. You have stated that your recent visit to England was as an agent for General Bonaparte, and that having completed your mission you fooled the Captain of a British sloop into bringing you back to France. Evidence has been given that you were landed safely and covered near half a kilometre along the shore away from the boat before you were challenged by two members of the second patrol. At that distance, had you declared yourself in what you assert to be your true colours, the members of the boat's crew could not have shot you down or even heard you. Yet, instead of hailing your compatriots with joy, you shot one of them with a pistol and smashed the butt of it into the face of the other. If you are, as you claim, a Colonel in the Army of France, what possible explanation have you to offer for attacking two members of our Coastguard Service? '

This was the big fence and, pulling himself together, Roger took it to the best of his ability. Pointing to the Coastguard who had been among the first to arrive on the scene of the affray, he said, ' That man has told the Court that at the time of the occurrence the beach was lit only by starlight so faint that it was impossible to see an approaching figure at more than a few yards' distance. The men who attacked me were running full tilt towards me and I towards them. In such circumstances a yard can be covered in less than a second. They were upon me before I had even the time to shout. One of them had a sabre raised above his head with intent to cleave my head from scalp to chin. Instinctively, as the only chance of saving my life, I fired upon him. As he fell his companion charged at me. I barely escaped his thrust, and in swerving struck wildly at him with the hand that held my pistol. It caught him in the face and he went down.'

'And then,' the Chairman remarked acidly, 'instead of remaining to give such aid as you could to these compatriots you had injured, you ran off into the sea, leaving them, perhaps, to bleed to death.'

'There was no question of their bleeding to death,' Roger cried indignantly. 'The one was shot only in the shoulder and the other had but a bloody nose. Besides, their comrades came up with them no more than two minutes later. It was the thudding of the patrol's footsteps on the sand as they came charging towards me that caused me to act as I did. Had I remained beside the men I had wounded, their comrades would not have waited to listen to any explanations but would have struck me down where I stood and made an end of me. My only hope of preserving my life lay in an immediate flight and the hope that their resentment against me would have cooled a little by the time I gave myself up.'

The Prosecutor made no attempt to sum up, neither did the magistrates leave the Court to debate the evidence in private. No further evidence being offered, they began openly to discuss the case among themselves. The Chairman asked his two colleagues for their opinions and the little man with the ruddy cheeks, who had not so far spoken, said:

'He is a Frenchman. There can be no doubt about that. And he has an answer for everything. One must admit that his account of himself is entirely plausible.'

'Except about the Cherry Brandy,' put in the innkeeper. 'I am convinced that he was lying about that.'

'If so,' commented the Chairman, 'he was then lying to us on other matters. If he obtained the bottle from Grove Place that means he did contact his relatives at the house. His doing so would greatly increase the probability that he is Sir Brook's son rather than a French cousin who could not readily have accounted for his presence in England and who, on disclosing himself, would almost certainly have been detained.'

At that, Tardieu jumped to his feet and cried, 'He is lying, Citizen Chairman; and I can prove it. When I woke him this morning and charged him with being Admiral Sir Brook's son, his first words were, "Admiral Brook? I've never heard of him." Yet now he declares himself to be a French relative of the Admiral and tells us that he spent several years of his youth in the Admiral's house. He cannot have it both ways.'

Shaken as Roger was by this bolt from the blue, he rallied all his resources to meet it. Leaning out of the dock, he pointed at Tardieu and shouted indignantly, 'It is the Lieutenant who is lying! I said no such thing! What I said was that I had not seen Admiral Brook since the war started. He has twisted my words because he is disgruntled. Having convinced himself this morning that I am a spy, he feels that I made a fool of him last night and that his men must be laughing at him for having accepted my statement that I am Colonel Breuc and an aide-de-camp to General Bonaparte.'

'Lies! More lies!' shouted Tardieu. 'I swear to what I have said.'

'Then you should be charged with perjury,' Roger shouted back.

'Silence!' cried the Chairman. 'Silence!' and banged hard on the table with his gavel. When quiet was restored he went on:

'The Court has taken notice of the Lieutenant's statement, also of the prisoner's denial, although I can hardly credit that the reason he suggests constitutes sufficient grounds to have caused the Lieutenant to commit perjury. If we accept his statement it shows how anxious the prisoner was to conceal the truth about his activities while in Lymington and throws the gravest doubt on a great part of what he has said about himself.'

'I told you he was lying about that Cherry Brandy,' the inn-keeper declared in a self-satisfied voice. 'Displaying stolen liquor in a coffee room, indeed! Is it likely?'

Roger needed no telling that since Tardieu's intervention things were beginning to look black for him; but the little man with the ruddy face created a diversion by remarking, 'Whatever the truth may be about what he was up to in Lymington, I'll not believe that he's an Englishman. As my Citizen colleagues know, up till the Revolution I'd lived all my life in Paris, and it would be hard to find a man with a more definite Parisian accent.'

The Chairman nodded. 'On consideration, I think you are right, Citizen colleague, and the seaman's evidence, which is all we have to go on about that, was inconclusive. He must be a Frenchman or, at least, have French blood in his veins. From his statement, too, it can hardly be doubted that he has lived for a great part of his life in France. But even if, as he says, he was born here, that is no guarantee that he is a loyal Frenchman. Every country has its quota of traitors, and in recent years France has suffered far more in that respect than others, owing to the thousands of *émigrés* who now live abroad and intrigue against her.'

The innkeeper gave a snort. 'Ah, now you've hit on it, Citizen. Look at those fine hands of his. He's an aristo, I'll be bound, and has never done an honest day's work in his life. An *émigré*, that's what he is, and come here to sell us to our enemies.'

After pursing his thin lips for a moment, the Chairman nodded again. 'Yes, that would explain everything: his impeccable French, the English landing him here and his dread of capture. Well, the law is clear on the subject of *émigrés*. If caught re-entering France such traitors are liable to the death penalty. If my Citizen colleagues agree, I am in favour of passing it.'

'I am not an *émigré*!' Roger broke in hotly. 'I am one of General Bonaparte's aides-de-camp and were we in Paris I'd have no difficulty in proving that. The Director Barras, Citizens Tallien, Fréron and many other important men would all vouch for me. I met General Bonaparte as far back as the siege of Toulon. I was with him in Paris on 13th *Vendémiaire*. I——'

'Enough!' snapped the Chairman, rapping on the desk with his gavel. 'We have given you a fair hearing and have already listened overlong to your lies.'

But Roger was determined to defend himself to the last ditch. Ignoring the interruption, he cried, 'You dare not have me executed! You dare not! My friends, the men I served with in Italy—Junot, Murat, Duroc, Lannes, Berthier and half a dozen other Generals—will exact vengeance on you if you do. Aye, and my great master Bonaparte himself will call you to reckoning. I demand——'

'Silence! Silence! Silence!' the Chairman shouted, redoubling his banging on the table, and Roger, now white-faced and exhausted, realized the futility of continuing, so ceased his angry threats.

There followed a moment's hush, then the Chairman turned to the innkeeper and asked, 'Do you agree?'

His colleague nodded. 'Yes, he's a spy, right enough. I made up my mind on that as soon as the fool tried to gull us about where he got the Cherry Brandy. Have him taken outside and finished with.'

A sad little smile twitched at Roger's lips. Although there was not an atom of humour in his terrible situation, it had suddenly struck him how incongruous it was that after all the dangers from which he had escaped during his life he was about to be sent to his death because dear old Jim Button had popped a bottle of Cherry Brandy into his valise.

Turning to his other colleague, the Chairman asked, 'And you, Citizen?'

The little man tilted back his head so that the nostrils of the snub nose between the apple cheeks looked like two round holes in his chubby face. Then, in a quiet voice, he appeared to address the ceiling.

'Yes, Citizen Chairman, I agree. Whether or not the man be an *émigré*, he landed clandestinely on French soil from a British war vessel. He resisted arrest and seriously wounded two of our people. The account he has given of himself lacks the ring of truth, and on several matters there can be no reasonable doubt that he has lied to us. All the evidence points to his having come to France as a secret agent, and in times such as these we cannot afford to take chances. That being so it is our duty to send him to his death.'

For a moment he was silent, then he went on, 'But there is an aspect of this case which I would like my Citizen colleagues to consider. Let us suppose, just suppose, for one moment, that he has told us the truth in one important particular: namely, that he is an aide-de-camp of our national hero, the brilliant young General who has restored the glory of France by his conquest of Italy. Should we decree this man's execution—what then, Citizen colleagues? General Bonaparte is back in France. In a matter of a few months he has become, after the Directors, the most powerful man in the country. He has only to express a wish and others spring to gratify it. To incur his displeasure might bring about our ruin.'

Roger's eyes had remained riveted on the cherubic, upturned face. His throat seemed to contract and he held his breath in an agony of suspense as he waited to learn if this new development would prove the thread by which hung his life.

For a full minute, with a frown of uncertainty on his thin, bony face, the Chairman stared at his small, plump colleague, then he said, 'You are right, Citizen, in that it might go hard with us did we make an enemy of General Bonaparte; but I count the risk of our doing so exceedingly small. We are all convinced that the prisoner is unquestionably a liar, so it is improbable that he has ever even set eyes on the General.'

'Maybe, maybe,' replied the other. 'But why should we take any risk at all?'

'*Ventre du Pape!*' exclaimed the innkeeper. 'Surely you do not suggest that we should let the rogue go free to spy on us and sell our secrets to the accursed English; or that we should even send him to a prison from which he might in time escape and still do the Republic some serious injury?'

'Besides,' the Chairman argued, 'you say yourself that it is our duty to pass sentence of death upon him, and that being so——'

'I did not say that,' retorted the little man, suddenly sitting up. 'I said that it was our duty to send him to his death. It does not follow that we should make ourselves responsible for his execution; and I, for one, will have no hand in it.'

The innkeeper banged his great fist on the table and cried angrily, 'What in hell's name do you mean by that?'

Simultaneously, the Chairman shook his head and said in a testy voice, 'You talk in riddles, Citizen colleague. Put a plain meaning on what you have in mind.'

'It is quite simple,' came the smooth reply. 'In calling for water and washing his hands before sending the Nazarene to be executed, Pontius Pilate set us an admirable example. The prisoner declares himself to be a Colonel in the Army of France. Moreover, spies are normally court-martialled, as this one would have been had he been caught by a patrol of soldiers instead of by Coastguards. Therefore, in a double sense, this is a military matter. Let us send him to the senior officer in the district, with a message to the effect that after giving him a fair trial we came to the unanimous conclusion that he is a spy and probably an *émigré*, and so deserving of death; but that on consideration we decided that he should never have been brought before this Court, so we are handing him over for them to deal with as they see fit.'

The innkeeper gave a great bellow of laughter. The Chairman smiled, patted the little man on the shoulder and said, 'Most ingenious, my dear Citizen colleague. We will most certainly adopt your admirable suggestion.'

He then said to Tardieu, 'Citizen Lieutenant, the Court is returning the prisoner to you. I charge you to deliver him safely into the hands of General Desmarets at his headquarters outside the town.' Turning to the Prosecutor, he added, 'You, Citizen Corbiel, will accompany the Lieutenant, inform the General of the Court's reasons for sending the prisoner to him and give him a full account of all that has taken place here.'

Having so delivered himself, he gave the table one sharp rap with his gavel and declared the Court adjourned.

As Roger stepped from the dock a sigh of relief escaped him. He was not, after all, fated to be led out right away to be hanged, or to face a firing party. Yet he could not disguise from himself that his reprieve was only a temporary postponement of the issue. It was, too, an unnerving thought that he was to be brought before General Desmarets, of whom he had never heard, as a spy who had already been tried and convicted. Even so, he felt that his chances of living out the day were considerably better now that he was to be handed over to the Military. They would surely give a more considerate hearing to a man who claimed to be General Bonaparte's aide-de-camp and, vast as the French Army was, these must be officers or soldiers in the camp to which he was being taken who could, if only they could be found, vouch for it that he was Colonel Breuc.

The strain of the trial upon him had been appalling, as he had not dared to relax for an instant in case he missed an opportunity to make some point that would have counted in his favour. Now he was so terribly exhausted that he stumbled several times when being escorted out to the small covered cart in which he had been brought to the Court.

His hands were again tied behind him and he was bundled into the cart. There was a slight delay while Citizen Prosecutor Corbiel was provided with a horse, then the little cavalcade set off.

Just before Roger had been bundled into the cart he had caught a glimpse of the Town Hall clock and had been amazed to see that it was still a few minutes before eleven. It seemed to him as though many hours had passed since Tardieu had roused him in the farmhouse bedroom that morning. While the trial had been in progress his mind had been so desperately concentrated on its twists and turns, for and against himself, that he had been only vaguely conscious of cold and hunger; but now, as the cart trundled out of the town, he began to shiver and could hear his stomach rumbling. Miserably, while the jolting of the cart again bruised his limbs against the hard floorboards, he longed for food, warmth and comfort, at the same time endeavouring to convince himself that the most dangerous stage in his ordeal was over.

Three-quarters of an hour later he heard a command ring out to halt. The cart pulled up and a soldier poked his head in over the backboard. Withdrawing it, he shouted, 'You may proceed,' and the cart moved on through the gates of a big cantonment, which had been set up on the downs when the numbers of troops garrisoning the coast had become too large to be accommodated in the town barracks.

Five minutes later the cart pulled up again in front of a long, low building facing a parade ground, but only Tardieu and Citizen Prosecutor Corbiel entered it. Another quarter of an hour elapsed before the Lieutenant came out and had his men escort Roger into the building, then along to an office at the back that had a view across distant sand-dunes to the sea.

It then transpired that General Desmarets was absent from the camp and would not be free to attend to any business until he had returned and had his dinner. For the moment, Roger's affair was being dealt with by the General's adjutant, a pleasant-faced young Major, who was lolling behind a desk. When Roger was brought before him he looked at him with lazy interest and said:

'So you are the Englishman and spy?'

'I am neither,' declared Roger firmly. 'This whole business is a ghastly mistake. I am Colonel Breuc and an aide-de-camp to General Bonaparte.'

The young Major sat back and roared with laughter.

'How dare you laugh!' Roger cried indignantly. 'This is a

very serious matter.' Yet, could he have seen himself, he would have realized that his statement, coupled with his appearance, gave ample grounds for mirth. His unshaven chin was covered with unsightly stubble, his undressed brown hair looked like a bird's nest and his clothes, which had not been pressed since their immersion in the sea, hung as they had rough-dried, in ugly folds and ridges about him. At that moment he could hardly have looked less like the Staff officer to a General-in-Chief that he claimed to be.

Recovering himself, the Major made him a mocking little bow. 'I'm sorry—yes, let us call you " Colonel "; although I gather you would find it mighty difficult to substantiate your claim to that rank.'

'By no means,' Roger replied firmly. 'And I am relying on you, Major, to enable me to do so. In this cantonment there must be many men who served with General Bonaparte in the Army of Italy. I most earnestly request that you will have them sought out and confront me with them. I count it certain that a number of them will readily vouch for my identity. I pray you, too, to give heed to the fact that my life hangs upon your doing as I have asked.'

The young man's face had suddenly become grave. 'Your request would be pointless did you not expect to vindicate yourself through it. The great majority of the men who fought in General Bonaparte's victorious campaign are still with the Army of Italy. Few of them have been transferred to us here in the north. But I will at once have enquiries set on foot for such as have come to us from Italy.'

After pausing a moment, he went on, 'However, it will take some time to collect them. By then General Desmarets should be available and, no doubt, he will wish to adjudicate in this matter in person. Meanwhile, although it seems possible that I may have the pleasure of welcoming you to our Mess later in the day, for the present I am sure you will appreciate that I have no alternative but to have you confined in the guard-room.'

Roger bowed. 'Major, I am deeply grateful to you for acceding so promptly to my request, and for your courtesy. I have only one more boon to ask. This morning I was given no breakfast; so I am terribly hungry. Could I perhaps be brought something to eat while I am in the guardroom, and a pallet on which to lie, with several blankets, for I am both cold and desperately tired.'

'Certainly you shall be provided with these things,' the Major agreed. Turning to an Orderly Sergeant who was standing by the door, he gave him the necessary instructions.

Under a guard of soldiers, Roger was marched away to the guardroom. Ten minutes later, his hands untied, he was making a hearty meal of stew, followed by bread-and-cheese. He then lay down on a straw-filled mattress and drew a single blanket over himself. There was no need for more, since the room was heated by a roaring brazier.

At last the awful fears which had harrowed him since morning were lifted from his mind. Although a civilian himself, he had spent so much of his time with military men that he always felt at home with them. Once the young Major had grasped the facts of the case he had treated him with consideration and kindness. Even if there were no great number of men in the cantonment who had served with the Army of Italy there must be a dozen or more. A single one who could identify him would be enough to get him out of all his troubles. Confident that by evening he would be a free man again, he dropped asleep.

It was soon after three o'clock when the Sergeant of the Guard roused him and escorted him between two privates back to the headquarters building. They marched him through the room in which he had been interviewed and into a larger one next door. Standing there were Tardieu, Citizen Prosecutor Corbiel and the young Major. Behind a large desk sat an elderly man with a slightly pockmarked chin and grey hair that fell in lank strands on either side of his face. Obviously he was General Desmarets, and Roger put him down as an N.C.O. of the old Royal Army who had risen, owing to the Revolution, by years of conscientious but unspectacular service, to this minor Command.

Giving a nod in the direction of Tardieu and Corbiel, the General said in a gruff voice to Roger, 'These Citizens have told me about you. Three worthy Citizen magistrates have heard all you have to say and have decided that you are guilty of charges that merit death. You have advanced a preposterous claim to be one of General Bonaparte's aides-de-camp, and say that you served with him in the Army of Italy. We shall soon learn how much truth there is in that.'

His tone and attitude were ominous, but Roger remained

optimistic. A door to a passage was opened by the Major and nine
men filed into the room. Six of them were officers and the other
three senior N.C.O.s. Eagerly Roger's glance ran from face to
face. Then his heart sank a little; not one of them was familiar to
him. But he could still hope that some of them might have
noticed him while he was in attendance on their hero, the General-
in-Chief.

Briefly Desmarets questioned each of them about his service in
Italy. All of them had fought there and had later been granted
leave, on one ground or another, to transfer to the Army of the
North. Roger had not joined Bonaparte in Italy until three
months after the Armistice of Leoben was signed, and all but
two of the men had left Italy before he arrived there. Of the
remaining two, only one had visited the General-in-Chief's headquarters at Montebello. He firmly declared that he had never
heard of a Colonel Breuc. All of them agreed that Bonaparte's
aides-de-camp during the Italian campaign had been Marmont,
Junot, Duroc, Lavalette and Sulkowsky.

General Desmarets shrugged his powerful shoulders. 'There we
are, then. I thought from the beginning this would prove a farce.'
He glanced at the nine veterans of the Italian campaign and said,
'I am sorry, Citizens, that you should have been brought here
for no useful purpose. You may go.' As they filed out, he
pointed to Roger and gave an order to the Sergeant of the Guard.

'Take this man away and have him shot.'

Seized once again with terror at the thought of the fate now
rushing upon him, Roger broke into violent speech. He pleaded
that other men who had served in Italy should be sought,
explained that he had not joined General Bonaparte's staff until
a few months before the General's return to Paris, and begged
for a postponement of sentence until he could communicate with
the General. But in vain. Desmarets ignored his outburst, the
guards on either side of him seized his arms and hustled him
away.

Back at the guardroom, the Sergeant told his Corporal to turn
out the reserve guard and take over. Then he selected six of his
men to act as a firing party. Just before they left the guardroom
he took a spade from a corner, handed it to Roger and
said:

'Here, take a grip o' that. An' don't you dare drop it in a fit
of the funks or you'll get a kick up the backside.'

Roger stared aghast at the spade and stammered, 'What . . . what is this for?'

The Sergeant replied with a sneer, 'Where yer bin all yer life? Don't expect us ter get ourselves sweaty making an 'ole for an English spy to lie comfortable in, do yer? Before sentence is carried out the likes of you 'as ter dig 'is own grave.'

5

Roger Digs his Grave

ALMOST overcome with horror at the idea of digging his own grave, Roger gave a gulp; but he took the spade. The six soldiers closed round him, the Sergeant gave an order and the firing party set off.

As they marched through the cantonment, men lounging in the doorways of the huts and others cleaning arms or harness stared at Roger with curiosity. Apparently the fact that he was a civilian carrying a spade and obviously under arrest was enough to tell them that he was going to his death. Evidently, too, a rumour had already run round the camp that he was an English spy, for several of them shook their fists at him, with shouts of '*A la mort, cochon!*' and '*Sale Anglais*'. He was well aware of the hatred with which the French regarded Britain; so their abuse meant nothing to him, and his whole mind was occupied in an attempt to think of an eleventh-hour ruse by which he might save himself, or at least postpone his execution.

His hot meal and three hours' sleep had restored him physically, but the shock of finding that none of the men from the Army of Italy had even heard of him, and the abrupt way in which General Desmarets had dealt with his case, had robbed him temporarily of his wits. It was half past three on a chilly but sunny afternoon, and all he could think of was how pleasant it would be to have a good horse between his knees and be cantering across the downs. At the same time he was terribly conscious, as they marched towards the sea, that with every step he took the moments of his life were running out. Yet, try as he would, he could not bring himself to concentrate.

After twenty minutes they came to within half a mile of the

shore at a place where, between a break in the cliffs, there was a wide area of sand-dunes in which steep mounds alternated with depressions and shallow valleys. Some of the mounds had coarse grass growing in patches on them; but there was no other vegetation, except at some distance inland, for as far as the eye could see.

When they had laboriously made their way for some two hundred yards across this desolate waste they slithered down into a broader dip than any they had so far crossed. The Sergeant called a halt and grunted, ' This'll do.'

The men surrounding Roger fell out and moved a little way away from him. For a moment he was tempted to make a dash for it. But with slopes of loose sand rising twelve feet or more on every side he realized that it would be hopeless to do so. He would have been riddled with bullets before he could have reached even the top of the nearest crest. Such is the instinct in a healthy man to cling to life until the very last moment that, although he felt certain that within another quarter of an hour his body would in any case have six lumps of lead in it, he could not bring himself to make the bid against the virtual certainty that he would be killed before he took another dozen breaths.

The Sergeant picked one man to stand by Roger with his musket at the ready; the other five piled theirs in a pyramid, with the long thin bayonets pointing to the sky. They then sat down in a group on a nearby slope to take their ease and began a game of cards. Pointing to the flattish bottom of the hollow, the Sergeant said to Roger:

' Get to it. And don't waste time diggin' a trench more'n what's big enough to take yer body. Should be a metre deep, though; else the sand'll blow off and leave bits of yer stickin' out. We don't want ter tumble over any nasty stinkin' English corpses when we're next out 'ere doin' our trainin'.'

The mental picture that the old ghoul's words conjured up in Roger's mind, of his own body rotting and creeping with maggots, filled him with nausea. Yet there was nothing for it but to begin digging. Although he had found it impossible to concentrate while being marched to the dunes, he had kept looking about him in the wild hope that an officer carrying a reprieve would come galloping up from the cantonment, or that some unforeseen diversion would occur that might give him a chance to escape. But on all sides the landscape had remained empty. By the time

they arrived at this hollow where he was about to dig his grave
he knew that there could be no living creature within miles,
except for the seagulls that wheeled overhead and the men who
had been ordered to execute him.

The sand was soft and as soon as he began to dig the trench he
found that a good part of each spadeful trickled back into it.
That brought him the sudden thought that if he could prolong his
gruesome task until darkness fell he would stand a worthwhile
chance of attempting a breakaway. But it was not yet four o'clock,
so there was a long time to go before it became even twilight.
Moreover, in this wildly optimistic idea for delaying matters till
sundown, he had counted without the Sergeant.

Seeing that he was allowing most of the sand he dug up to slide
from his spade before he threw the remainder aside, the N.C.O.
said with an oath, 'Think we want ter stay 'ere all night? Put
some guts into it, you English bastard. Shovel quick and toss
it as far as you can. That's the way to make a trench in this soft
stuff.'

Roger responded by digging faster, but still at no great speed;
so the Sergeant suddenly struck him smartly across the shoulders
with a swagger cane he was carrying and cried, 'Lively, I said!
Lively! If yer not sweating within two minutes I'll cut yer face
ter ribbons wiv this cane o' mine.'

Again Roger had no option but to obey, and within a few
minutes he was sweating profusely. But some of the sand continued to trickle back into the trench and before he had dug out
more than a third of the amount that had to be shifted he was
puffing like a grampus. Thrusting his spade upright in the sand
for a moment, he took off his heavy coat and threw it down
behind him.

As he resumed his digging, the Sergeant remarked, 'That's a
real aristo's coat yer got there. Should sell for a tidy sum, so I'll
take it as my share of yer kit. Be a sin ter bury good clothes like
yours. The others can cast lots for the rest of yer duds.'

After a minute he added, 'I bet yer got a bit o' money on yer
too. I'll give you a spell from diggin' if yer'll hand it over.'

Roger's heart bounded. A 'spell' might mean anything from a
few minutes to an indefinite period. The Sergeant's offer sounded
like an overture to him to buy his life. On reaching Paris he had
meant to draw his back pay and, should he need more, there
were means by which he could draw on British Secret Service

funds; so he had not brought a large sum with him. He had only fifty *louis d'or* to cover immediate expenses and they were in a money-belt round his waist. Yet those fifty louis, which would have done no more than see him to Paris and buy him a new uniform when he got there, would be regarded by the Sergeant as a magnificent windfall. Even if he had to give five louis apiece to his men to keep their mouths shut that would still leave twenty for him, and that was more than the pay he would receive in a whole year.

The Sergeant spoke again. 'Come on. Yer can't take it wiv yer. If yer 'and it over I can split it wiv the boys now. That'll save us a lot o' time arguing about shares when ye're a gonner, an' we'll get back to camp the sooner.'

His words instantly dashed Roger's hopes. He felt that he must be out of his mind not to have realized that they would search his body for cash and valuables before they filled in his grave. As they would come by the money anyhow, why should they risk condign punishment by letting him buy his life with it.

Yet even in his extremity it went against the grain to make the Sergeant a gratuitous present; and he thought it possible that it might not occur to them that he was wearing a money-belt. If so, they might strip him only to his underclothes and so fail to find his gold. In the hope of depriving them of it, he said tersely to the N.C.O.:

'If you've been counting on lining your pockets, Sergeant, you are unlucky. The Coastguards searched me last night and took from me every sou I had.'

'Then that's bad luck for yer, too,' the Sergeant snarled. 'I'll give yer no spell, an' if yer drop while yer work I'll have the boys jab their bayonets in yer an' finish yer off that way.'

Once more, under the N.C.O.'s threats and his baleful glare, Roger set about digging. After another ten minutes the sweat was pouring off him and he had managed to scoop out a trench, the middle of which was over two feet deep. But the sides sloped and it still required a lot more work before his body could have been laid in it and well covered.

It was now nearly half an hour since he had started on the job and the hard work had made him uncomfortably hot; but that was far from being the case with the firing party. The sun had gone in and the chill of a February afternoon had descended on the dunes. Of the group of five sitting on the slope nearby playing cards, one or more was now standing up every few minutes to stamp his feet and flail his arms to keep his circulation going.

To ease his aching arms, Roger risked a blow from the cane to pause for a breather. As he did so, the Sergeant snapped, 'Keep at it, damn yer, or we'll all freeze to death afore yer done.' Then he added as an afterthought, 'What wouldn't I give for a good tot of schnapps to warm me up! '

Instead of going on with his digging, Roger stared at him for a moment. He had just remembered that after taking a few gulps from his brandy flask while in the sea he had managed to get it back into his pocket. To the N.C.O. he said, 'The Coastguards didn't rob me of my flask and it's still three-quarters full of cognac. You'll find it in the left-hand skirt pocket of my travelling coat.'

The Sergeant's eyes widened eagerly and he exclaimed, '*Mort de Dieu!* Yer may be a pig of an Englishman, but I'll see to it yer gets a quick, clean death for that.' Then he turned about and began swiftly to rummage in the coat that Roger had thrown behind him.

The guard holding his musket at the ready was standing a yard away on Roger's other side. He, too, was feeling the cold and as time had gone on he had ceased to give his whole attention to the prisoner.

Suddenly Roger lifted the spade and slashed sideways at him with it. The edge of the spade caught the man on his right hand, severing two of his fingers. With a scream of agony he dropped his musket. The Sergeant had just found the pocket in Roger's coat and, bent right over, was pulling the flask out of it. The guard's scream had hardly rent the air before Roger had turned on his heel, swung the spade high and brought its blade down with all his force on the back of the Sergeant's neck. The blow almost severed it. From the terrible wound his blood spurted out in a jet over the sand, and he collapsed without uttering a sound.

Without losing an instant, Roger threw aside the spade that had served him so well as a weapon and made a dash for the slope furthest from the other five men. With the sand slithering beneath his boots he scrambled up it. Jumping to their feet, the men ran to their stacked muskets, shouting imprecations and calling on him to halt. In their haste two of them collided, fell and rolled into the trench. The other three grabbed up their firearms and levelled them.

From the moment Roger had thought of his brandy flask and realized that it could be used as a snare by which he might possibly save his life, his wits had come back to him. It had been the apparent hopelessness of his situation that had so clouded his mind from the moment General Desmarets had ordered his execution. The germ of a plan had scarcely formed before he had a clear-cut picture of exactly how he must act. His perfect sense of timing had done the rest and it did not now desert him.

At a glance he had measured the slope and judged that by the time he reached the crest the men would have their weapons in their hands and be ready to fire at him. Up there, against the skyline, and only some twelve yards distant, he would provide a perfect target that they could not fail to hit. Without pausing to look behind him to see if he had judged aright, he flung himself flat.

Three muskets banged in quick succession. Bullets whistled through the air a good three feet above him. He knew that there should be two more, but dared not wait where he lay for more than another few seconds. Picking himself up, he ran on, the hair now prickling on his scalp from the horrid expectation that at any moment one of those other two bullets would smack into his back.

He plunged into a dip, then breasted another slope. A furious shouting broke out behind him, but no bullets either hit him or whined past. From that he could only conclude that the muskets of the two men who had not yet fired could not have been loaded. On reaching the second crest he risked a glance over his shoulder. Three of the soldiers were leaping down the slope, twenty yards behind him, the other two were ten yards in the rear, had reached the top of the first mound and were taking aim at him.

Again he flung himself flat. Again the bullets hummed through the air above him. Again he scrambled to his feet and dashed headlong down the slope ahead. But throwing himself down, although only for thirty seconds, had cost him a good part of his lead. The three nearest men had come up to within fifteen feet of him.

Yet as he pounded on he was far from giving up hope. None of the five could reload his musket as he ran. If they halted to do so, by the time they had rammed home the charges and the bullets and primed their weapons they would have to be good marksmen to hit him. As they must know that themselves, he thought it certain that they would put their trust in running him down. But unless there were trained runners among them he felt confident that he could out-distance them; because he had shed his topcoat, whereas they were wearing theirs, and, in addition, they were weighed down by their heavy equipment.

In that he proved right. By the time he had covered a quarter of a mile he had gained a fifty-yard lead on his pursuers. But he had had no choice in the direction he should take and saw that he was heading almost directly for the sea. To continue on his course was to risk that when he reached the beach they would spread out and hem him in against the water. With his previous night's experience still fresh in mind, he would have thought twice before seeking refuge in the sea even had it been fully dark. As it was still daylight, it would have been completely futile to do so.

His only alternative was to alter direction slightly until, by making a wide curve, he would be running parallel with the shore. That, he feared might cost him much of his lead, but after covering another two hundred yards another swift look over his shoulder filled him with elation. His pursuers were obviously tiring. Two of them had dropped out and the others, staggering now as they ran, were still a good hundred yards behind him.

By then he had come to the end of the dunes, where they sloped down to a wide stretch of foreshore. The sand was firmer there so he took to it and, although he was tiring, it enabled him to increase his pace slightly. Some distance ahead of him, a little way inland, he could now see a farmhouse among a group of stunted trees. The sight of them lent him new strength and determination. If only he could reach them well ahead of his pursuers he might find a place to hide there until darkness had fallen.

For some time past the soldiers had ceased their shouting, but now it suddenly broke out again. Looking back to see the reason, Roger gave a gasp of dismay. A quarter of a mile off, trotting along the shore behind him, were three horsemen, and they were in uniform. The men in pursuit of him were pointing at him and yelling to them:

' A spy! An English spy. He has escaped from us! He killed our Sergeant and got away! After him! After him! Ride him down! '

Even as Roger grasped this new peril that had come upon him like a bolt from the blue, the three riders put spurs to their horses and urged them into a gallop. The only thing he could do was to turn away from the shore and head up into the sand-dunes, in the wild hope that the loose sand and sudden dips there would make it more difficult for the horsemen to come up with him.

By this time he had run over a mile and most of it had been across soft sand that made the going very heavy. His face was dripping with sweat, his leg muscles were aching abominably and he was catching his breath in sobbing gasps.

To be captured and dragged back to death when he had escaped it four times within the past twenty-four hours, and only a moment since had been in a fair way to regain his freedom, seemed so utterly unjust a fate that he rebelled against it. There was nowhere he could hide, he knew that he had no possible hope of out-distancing the horsemen; yet he staggered on, bent almost double as he charged the upward slopes and slithering wildly as he careered down into the valleys beyond them.

The chase lasted barely four minutes. The murmur of the horses' hooves behind him increased to a loud thudding. His foot caught in a tuft of coarse sand-grass. He stumbled and fell. As he rolled over and picked himself up he found himself facing the three horsemen. Their leader was an infantry officer wearing a shako, the two others were Hussars, with straps wound round their tall busbies. All three had drawn their swords and were waving them on high. It was evident that they meant to give no quarter to an English spy who had just killed a Sergeant and escaped.

In spite of the inescapable destruction with which Roger was now confronted, the instinct to cheat death until the very last moment was still strong in him. To turn and run further was utterly useless. Before he had taken another dozen paces they would cut him down from behind. But he could fling himself flat between two of the onrushing horses in the slender chance that he would escape both their hooves and the swords of their riders. At the pace they were going, if they overshot him that would give him a few more minutes before they could wheel and come at him again. What would he do then, or what could possibly occur to save him during those few fleeting minutes, he had not, as yet, the faintest idea.

Then, as the living torrent of snorting horses and yelling men came rushing upon him, he realized that his idea of possibly escaping them by throwing himself to the ground had been no better than a pipe-dream. Into his mind there flashed a memory of a military gymkhana which he had once attended. It had been on a sunny afternoon with officers in colourful uniforms and pretty women in sprigged muslin crowding the enclosure. On the programme one contest had been for mounted men to ride full tilt at a row of turnips stuck on low pegs. Leaning low from their saddles, they had picked the turnips up, one after another, on the points of their swords. If he did throw himself flat it would only be to have a sword thrust through his back.

Three horsemen were now within ten feet of him, the officer in the centre and leading by half a length. With distended eyes, Roger stared at him. He was a small man, neat and elegant, but with a fierce expression compressing his lips and thrusting out his determined jaw. Suddenly, Roger's mouth opened and he yelled:

'Lannes! Lannes! Do you not know me? I am Rojé Breuc!'

From frowning slits, due to concentration, the officer's eyes sprang wide open. His sword was already descending to cleave Roger's skull. With a flick of the wrist, of which only an expert swordsman could have been capable, he diverted the stroke, so that the blade curved away into a horizontal position and became extended at a right-angle to his body. Thus it not only passed a good six inches above Roger's head but prevented the Hussar on his other side from getting a clear cut at him.

The three horses thundered by. Roger, almost hysterical with relief, remained where he stood, still choking for breath. In the next valley the horsemen checked their foam-flecked mounts, brought them round in a wide semi-circle and came cantering back to him.

'Lannes!' Roger croaked, lurching forward and grasping the bridle of the officer's horse to support himself. 'Lannes, by all that's holy! Never . . . never was the arrival of any friend more opportune.'

'Ten thousand devils!' exclaimed the officer. 'When you shouted I could scarce believe it. But you are . . . you are Colonel Breuc.'

Roger gave an unsteady laugh. 'Indeed I am; but I've been within an ace of losing my life because till now I could not prove it.'

'*Sang Dieu!* What luck then that I chanced to be riding by. Those infantrymen who were giving chase to you yelled to me

that you were an English spy and had just got away after killing
their Sergeant. It sounds like Beelzebub's own mess that you've
been in.'

'It was; and I did kill the brute. Had I not I'd be dead myself
by now. As for my being an Englishman, a pack of fools jumped
to the conclusion that I was one simply because I was caught
last night landing clandestinely on the coast below Boulogne. But
I'll give you full details later of the ghastly time I have been
through.'

At that moment, still puffing from their exertions, three soldiers
of the firing squad appeared over a nearby ridge. With bayonets
levelled and shouts of triumph at the sight of Roger, they ran
down the slope to surround him.

'Halt!' snapped out Lannes. 'Put up your weapons. Ground
arms!'

As Lannes was a Brigadier-General, they pulled up and stood
to attention after only a moment of surprised hesitation. Then
one of them panted out:

'Thanks, Citizen Brigadier, for . . . for 'elping us recapture
our prisoner. Us is a firing party an' we was on the point of
shootin' 'im, but 'e got away.'

'I know it, and it is as well for your Commander that he did.'

'But . . . but . . .' stammered the man, ''e's an English spy,
an' 'e's just killed our Sergeant.'

'He is nothing of the kind. He is a Colonel in the French Army
and well known to me. You will return to camp and tell the
officer who gave you your orders of the absurd mistake that has
been made. Meanwhile, I will be responsible for Colonel
Breuc.'

An older, truculent-looking man put in, 'We can't do that. 'E's
our prisoner, an' 'oever you says 'e is, 'e killed our Sergeant.
Near sliced 'is 'ead off wiv the bloody spade.'

'Silence!' roared Lannes, who was an impatient man. 'Another
word from you and I'll have you given a month's pack-drill for
having allowed your prisoner to escape.'

Roger was standing within two feet of his rescuer. Looking up
at him, he said in a low voice, 'These men were acting under
orders. Would it not be best if we all went to the camp and got
the business straightened out properly?'

The Brigadier-General pulled a big turnip watch from his fob
pocket, glanced at it and said, 'I must not be late in getting

back to Calais to make my report, but I can spare about twenty minutes. Very well, then. We'll do as you suggest.'

Turning to one of the Hussars, he ordered the man to dismount so that Roger could have his horse, then told him to march back with the others. Roger was hardly in the saddle before Lannes set off at a canter, and ten minutes later they entered the cantonment.

As the sentry on the gate presented arms, he stared with astonishment at Roger, now riding at ease beside a Brigadier-General, and when they trotted on towards the headquarters building several other men who had seen him marched off to execution imagined for a moment that they were seeing a ghost. When they pulled up, the young Major was just coming out of the main door with some papers in his hand. His mouth fell open, then he exclaimed:

'Shades of Robespierre! If it's not the English spy!'

Springing from his horse, Lannes said, 'I am told by Colonel Breuc that General Desmarets commands here.'

'Then this man is . . . is who he said he——' stammered the Major.

'He is,' Lannes cut him short. 'But I have no time to waste. Take me at once to your General.'

Pulling himself together, the Major gave a stiff salute, turned on his heel and led them through to the General's office. Desmarets was sitting at his desk, smoking a clay pipe. At the sight of Roger he gave an angry frown and cried, 'What the hell are you doing here? I gave orders——'

Without waiting for him to finish, Lannes, having snapped to attention and saluted him as his superior, said, 'General, I had the good fortune to prevent a most culpable miscarriage of justice. This gentleman is Colonel Breuc and a personal friend of mine. I understand that you ordered his execution. Being an officer of courage and resource he killed the Sergeant in charge of the firing party and got away. He was being pursued by the remainder of the squad when I chanced to be riding by and was able to identify him. I have come here only to report what has taken place, and to inform you that Colonel Breuc will be accompanying me to Calais.'

The General came slowly to his feet. 'He . . . he killed the Sergeant, do you say?'

'It was his life or mine,' Roger put in.

'So you confess to it? Then, whoever you may be, it was murder; and you will have to answer for it.'

'No man who has not deserved death could be expected to allow himself to be shot without putting up a fight,' said Lannes quickly. 'That the Sergeant should have lost his life in this affair is most regrettable; but if anyone will be called on to answer for that it will be yourself.'

'What the devil do you mean?' demanded Desmarets angrily.

'Why, for having ordered Colonel Breuc's execution without first satisfying yourself that he was guilty of the crime imputed to him.'

'He was tried by the magistrates in Boulogne, and their opinion was unanimous. He was sent to me only because it is usual for spies to be executed by the Military.'

'And you, a General, accepted the verdict of a bunch of civilians when the prisoner sent to you claimed to be an officer of the French Army!' Lannes cried indignantly. 'I consider your conduct to have been disgraceful.'

Desmarets's dark brows drew together. With an oath he roared, 'How dare you use such language to your superior! I intend to hold the man for further inquiry. Even if you are right about his identity it is a moot point whether any man is justified in killing a member of his escort in order to escape. Now you may go.'

'Start any judicial proceedings you like,' Lannes retorted. 'I will make myself responsible for Colonel Breuc's appearance at them when required. But I'll not leave without him.'

'Then you have asked for trouble and you shall have it. I'll arrest you for insubordination and you shall kick your heels in confinement with him until I see fit to consider further measures.'

As the interview had proceeded, Roger had grown more and more apprehensive. He knew at least that his life was now safe, but what view would a court martial take of his having killed the Sergeant? With luck, they would take Lannes's view that his act had been justifiable homicide. But if there were a straw-splitter among his judges it might be held that to injure an escort during an attempt to escape was one thing, and to kill him another. That could mean a verdict of manslaughter and a severe prison sentence. It was, too, unpleasantly clear that, in order to distract attention from the negligent way in which he had handled matters to start with, Desmarets would do all he could to make the case

D

against his prisoner as black as possible. Roger's one hope lay in Lannes, and glancing anxiously at his friend he sought to comfort himself by recalling what he knew of him.

Jean Lannes was a Gascon, and a year or so younger than Roger. He had had little education and as a boy had been apprenticed to a dyer. Espousing with fervour the cause of the Revolution, he had joined the Army and during the war with Spain reached the rank of *Chef de Brigade*, although he was then only twenty-five. The Thermidorian reaction had led to him being dismissed from the Service, owing to his political views, but he had re-enlisted as a volunteer in the Army of Italy and had again fought his way up to Brigadier.

In Italy his name had become legendary for valour. He made his mark within ninety-six hours of the opening of the campaign by carrying the village of Dego at the point of the bayonet. He led the final assault on the bridge at Lodi in the face of a hail of grapeshot and captured the enemy guns. At Arcola, when victory wavered in the balance, although already suffering from three wounds, he thrust his way out of the field hospital, took command of a column, led the assault that saved the day and was the first man to cross the Adda. Many times wounded and covered with glory, dauntless and indefatigable, he was the best leader of infantry that Bonaparte had, and the General-in-Chief had publicly acknowledged it by presenting him with captured enemy standards.

On the field of battle Lannes did not know what fear was, but this was a different matter. He had already committed himself much deeper than most men would have cared to do by defying an officer of higher rank than himself. But now that he was threatened with arrest, would he back down, apologize and, in order to make his peace, agree to leave Roger there at the mercy of Desmarets? Next moment Roger knew that his fears had been groundless.

Drawing himself up, the little Gascon cried furiously, 'Do you know who I am? I am Lannes! I fought with General Bonaparte at Montebello. I captured the guns at Lodi. I was the first Frenchman across the Adda. Arrest me at your peril. General Bonaparte lies this night in Calais. I'll send one of my orderlies to him with a report of your disgraceful mishandling of this affair. Before morning all hell will break about your ears. Unless you allow Colonel Breuc and myself to depart this instant you might as well tear your rank badges off here and now, for you'll not need them tomorrow.'

Although a rough, uncultured man, Desmarets was no fool. He realized that he had unwittingly put his head into a hornets' nest. To arrest a national hero and court the anger of the terrible little Corsican who was his master spelled certain ruin. Yet he lacked the tact to give way graciously. With a sullen scowl he muttered :

'I'm not afraid of Bonaparte, and I've done my duty as I saw it. Still, I've never been one to make trouble. Have your way, then, and we'll say no more of this.'

'I'll make no promise about that,' snapped Lannes. Then jerking his head towards the door he added to Roger, 'Come, Breuc. We must ride hard. The General-in-Chief is expecting me and he does not like to be kept waiting.'

Five minutes later the young Major had produced a mount for Roger. With the two Hussars behind them, he and Lannes clattered out of the camp and took the road to Calais. Alternately they cantered, trotted and walked their horses to give them a breather. During the latter spells Roger gave his friend an account of his misadventure and, in turn, Lannes brought him up-to-date with what had been taking place since Roger had left Bonaparte to go on sick leave.

He said that on leaving Italy Bonaparte had gone to Rastatt where, it had been agreed, the details of the Peace Treaty should be settled. Francis II was in a somewhat difficult position, for he was Emperor of Austria and also the titular head of the Holy Roman Empire. This latter consisted of numerous Germanic States that, centuries earlier, had formed a Federation giving allegiance to a Monarch elected by their Princes as the representative of the hereditary power derived from ancient Rome. In more recent times the Emperor of Austria, being by far the most powerful among them, had, almost automatically, been elected as their Suzerain. But Francis had signed a peace with Bonaparte only in his capacity as Emperor of Austria; so he now had to arrange matters with the numerous satellite, semi-independent rulers who had given him their support as the head of the Holy Roman Empire.

Under a secret agreement entered into with Bonaparte by the Emperor's Foreign Ministers, Baron Thugut and Count Cobenzl, certain Princes whose realms had been overrun by the French, or were to be ceded to them, were to be compensated by being given other territories, and some of the German Prince-Bishops were to be deprived of their ancient fiefs altogether.

It was to initiate these delicate negotiations that Bonaparte had gone to Rastatt. However, soon foreseeing the endless wrangles that must ensue at such a conference, and detesting long hours of inaction spent listening to argument, he had, after a few days, left the plenipotentiaries appointed by the Directory to handle matters.

During his progress through the Swiss cantons the republicans in the cities had hailed him with enthusiasm as the 'Liberator of the Italian People'. A few minorities had even gone to the length of handing him petitions asking that he should free them from their feudal overlords.

His journey thence through France had been a triumph. His name, almost unknown eighteen months earlier, had since become synonymous with victory and the renewal of French glory. In every town and village the people had fought to touch his hand and had showered gifts upon him. When he reached Paris on December 15th the enthusiasm of the crowds had been indescribable. He was the man of the hour, and rich and poor alike went wild about him.

It was no secret that the Directors were very perturbed by his popularity, jealous of it and a little frightened of him. However, they donned the absurd, pseudo-classical robes which the Assembly had decreed as their costume for official occasions and gave the young conqueror a State welcome, during which they, in turn, embraced him, acclaimed him as a hero and urged him to undertake further conquests for the glory of France.

He had accepted all this as his due, but with commendable modesty, and had afterwards withdrawn himself on all occasions when it seemed likely that he would receive a public ovation.

He had been living quietly with his wife Josephine in their house in the Rue Chautereine, refusing to receive any visitors except his personal friends. To honour him, the Municipality had changed the name of the street to Rue de la Victoire, but the only honour which appeared to give him real pleasure had been his election to the Institute. His name had been put forward to fill the vacancy created by Carnot's flight on 18th *Fructidor*, and he had been unanimously elected. At his inauguration as a member of this learned body he had addressed the assembled savants with humility and declared, to thunderous applause, that the only conquests of real value to mankind were those wrested by science from the universe for the benefit of humanity as a whole.

When Roger asked how it came about that Lannes had been riding along the beach between Calais and Boulogne, the Brigadier replied, ' The Directory have appointed our little man General-in-Chief for the invasion of England; so at the moment he is carrying out a reconnaissance of the coast to assess the shipping available for such a project. He has brought with him only de Bourrienne, myself and, as his aide-de-camp, Sulkowsky.

' While he carried out an inspection of Calais harbour this afternoon, he sent me to report on the beaches south of Calais, to see if there were any coves or small river mouths in which shallow-draught vessels might be assembled. But I found none, and I cannot think that he will chance the destruction of an Army in such an operation. The British Navy commands the Channel. Until we have built up a Fleet to equal it, and have made preparations on a scale which would take many months to complete, I doubt if more than a handful of us would ever get ashore in England, and those of us who did would be massacred by that ferocious people.'

This was excellent news to Roger, as Lannes was one of Bonaparte's most trusted officers, and so exceptionally well placed to judge the way his mind was working. Moreover, the fact that the only senior officer Bonaparte had brought with him on this important reconnaissance was Lannes showed the value he set on the fiery Gascon's judgment. Being also a very outspoken man, Lannes would not hesitate to oppose the project should ambition tempt the Corsican to face the risks involved.

It was close on two years since Roger had first mentioned to Mr. Pitt the name of Bonaparte and had informed him that, although the newly promoted General had not then commanded even a Brigade in the field, he was a man to watch. He had said that conversations with that gaunt young Artillery officer had convinced him that Bonaparte had an extraordinary grasp of military matters, a mind capable of conceiving strategic plans on the grand scale and was fired by a boundless ambition; so that with Barras behind him it was certain that he would soon be given an important Command. Roger had then warned the Prime Minister that should that Command be the Army of the North he must expect an invasion that summer, as Bonaparte had maintained that the only means of ensuring permanent peace and prosperity to France lay in the destruction of her great commercial rival, Britain, and that the dearest of all his dreams was to march into London at the head of a French Army.

The Prime Minister had taken the warning seriously and had put certain measures in train to strengthen the defences on the south coast, but not long afterwards Bonaparte had been given the Command of the Army of Italy. As a result, with the *laissez-faire* habitual to the British, preparations to resist invasion had been allowed to slacken off. Roger was well aware that little of value had been done, and the danger of the French making a successful landing was as great as ever. It comforted him, therefore, to learn that Lannes thought it unlikely that Bonaparte would attempt it.

By taking the inland road they covered the twelve miles to Calais in good time and entered the town a little before seven o'clock. Lannes said that their General had taken up his quarters for the night at the house of the Military Commandant, General Réveillon. It was a spacious mansion which, before the Revolution, had been the property of a wealthy noble. In the courtyard Lannes and Roger handed their mounts over to the two Hussars and the Brigadier led the way inside.

In the hall they ran into another old friend of Roger's, Fauvelet de Bourrienne. He was a *ci-devant* noble and as a youth had been a cadet at the Military Academy at Brienne with Bonaparte, although he had later gone into the Diplomatic Service instead of entering the Army. During the Revolution he had been recalled from his post in Germany but, fearing that as an aristocrat he would be sent to the guillotine, he had refused to return to France; so he had been listed as an *émigré*.

When peace negotiations were about to be entered into, following the signing of the armistice at Leoben, Bonaparte had felt the need of a really capable man, on whose devotion he could rely, to act as his *Chef de Cabinet*. At Brienne, Bonaparte, as the poor son of a landless Corsican gentleman, had been almost ostracized by his rich and noble schoolfellows. Bourrienne had been one of the few who, as well as being a star pupil, had befriended him; so he had written and offered him the post. Bourrienne had accepted, joined him in Italy and soon showed such ability that Bonaparte had every reason to be pleased with his choice.

On seeing Roger, Bourrienne opened wide his arms, embraced him and cried, '*Mon ami*, what a joy to have you back with us!

But what a state you are in! You look as though you have been dragged through a hedge backwards. What the deuce have you been up to?'

Between them Roger and Lannes gave him a rough outline of what had occurred, the latter promising a more detailed account later. Then Bourrienne took him into a room at the front of the house which their host used as an office.

General Réveillon was sitting there: a big, red-faced, jolly-looking man in his late forties. Having welcomed Roger, he took him up to a bedroom on the third floor and ordered a soldier servant to bring up cans of hot water so that Roger could wash and tidy himself up. As he was about to leave, he said:

'When you are ready, come down to the big salon on the first floor. Supper will be ready in about three-quarters of an hour, and I have asked some of my officers to meet the General-in-Chief; so we'll be quite a big party.'

Half an hour later, having made himself as presentable as he could and with a light heart now that all his troubles were over, Roger went downstairs and entered the salon. There were nearly twenty officers there, and Bonaparte was standing near one of the tall windows, talking to Réveillon. The young conqueror was then twenty-eight and a half, so was some eighteen months younger than Roger.

The eagle eyes in the pale face of the weedy-looking little Corsican lit on Roger immediately. With an abrupt gesture he beckoned him over. Roger drew himself up, walked forward and stood stiffly to attention.

Bonaparte, whose memory was prodigious, said sharply, 'Breuc, you were due to report back from leave not later than January 31st. You are twelve days late. Explain yourself.'

Roger replied with quiet confidence, '*Mon Général*, it was in your service. I recovered from the wound I received in Venice more speedily than I had expected; so I decided to put the remainder of my sick leave to good purpose. Since you have often spoken to me of your intention, sooner or later, to invade and conquer England, and since I can so easily pass for an Englishman, I had myself smuggled across the Channel. My return was delayed by appalling weather, but in the six weeks I spent there I carried out a reconnaissance of the present state of defence on the south coast, from Ramsgate to Lymington.'

A sudden smile twitched Bonaparte's thin lips and his large

dark eyes lit up as he murmured, 'That was well done, Breuc. Well done indeed. I have always counted on your value when we make our descent on England, and now you will be worth an extra Division to me.'

When he had first addressed Roger so sharply a sudden hush had descended on the room. Now, raising his voice so that all could hear, he laid his hand on Roger's arm and said, 'I appoint you my Aide-de-Camp-in-Chief for the invasion of England, and I have today decided to lead the Army of the North against that accursed island before the spring is out.'

6

The New Babylon in 1798

BONAPARTE'S pronouncement was received with great enthusiasm. Lannes alone among the assembled officers refrained from joining in the cheers and for a moment it looked as if he were about to voice a protest. But evidently considering the time and place inappropriate, he refrained and confined himself to exchanging an uneasy glance with Bourrienne.

Having dealt with Roger, the General-in-Chief resumed his conversation with Réveillon; so Roger tactfully withdrew and mingled with the others. When supper was announced they filed into a large dining room where, although Réveillon was the host, he insisted on Bonaparte taking the head of the long table. The gesture showed Roger that his chief had by his return to France lost nothing of the status he had achieved for himself in Italy.

There, at Montebello, during the peace parleys with Austria, he had in a few months transformed his position from that of a fighting soldier, who shared all hardships with his strongly Republican officers and men, to that of an almost royal personage. He had formed a Court at which his wife, mother and sisters set the tone for the many other ladies who had been invited from France to join his senior officers. Even his oldest friends no longer dared to 'thee and thou' him. Like royalty, he dined every night in state, with his family and only a few others whom, from time to time, he chose to honour. The drawing rooms and antechambers of the Palace were always crowded, not only with his Generals but with a score of German and Italian nobles sent by their Princes to fawn upon him and win his goodwill.

He talked almost incessantly and now, as then, everyone hung upon his words while his agile mind flashed from subject to subject, hardly waiting for answers to the questions he shot at those nearest him. Réveillon had taken the place on his right and Bourrienne was on his other side. Lannes and Roger were on the opposite side of the table, a few places down. The meal was nearly over when, during a brief pause in the conversation, Lannes said to his master:

'But for my arrival on the scene this afternoon you would have been short of an aide-de-camp. At four o'clock Breuc was on the point of being shot as a spy.'

Bonaparte gave Roger an amused glance. 'That would have been carrying your pretence of being an Englishman a little too far. Tell us how you got yourself into such a predicament.'

One of Roger's most valuable gifts was his ability as a *raconteur*. He plunged into his story with gusto, deliberately raised several laughs against himself, gave a graphic description of the terror he had felt and belittled his achievement of having got away from seven armed men.

He could afford to adopt such an attitude because Bonaparte believed him to be fearless. At the siege of Toulon, soon after they first met, Roger had got himself into a position where he had no alternative but to lead an assault on an enemy battery over open ground in full daylight, and the out-at-elbows little Commander of the Artillery was under the impression that he had deliberately volunteered to undertake this suicidal act. More recently, too, on an island near Mestre, he had defended himself against a dozen Venetians under the eyes of the General-in-Chief, and in so doing had saved him from their most unwelcome attentions. He had received a sword of honour as a reward and a mention in Army Orders that had established his reputation for valour.

As Bonaparte loved stories he listened attentively, interrupting only to tell Roger what he ought to have done on several occasions when he might have taken some different line in his defence. By the time the tale was completed everyone had finished eating, the wine was circulating freely and several officers had lit cheroots. Bonaparte's comment on Roger's account of himself was:

'Like myself, Breuc, you were born under a lucky star. Desmarets I know only by name. He is one of those Old Guard Generals who owes his rise to the Revolution. Most of them should never have been promoted above Sergeant-Major. His attitude shows laziness as well as irresponsibility. On that account

I shall take steps to have him removed from his Command. Now tell me the impression you formed of the defences of England.'

In replying, Roger had to be extremely careful. It was in the interests of his country to report that the south coast now bristled with formidable obstacles designed to prevent an enemy landing. However, he knew that the French must have numerous spies in England who would be sending back more or less accurate assessments; so he dared not depart very far from the truth. With a thoughtful look, he said:

'The English have certainly not made the best of the time they have been given since you last contemplated a descent on their shores, but they are now definitely in a position to give us a hotter reception. In '96, apart from such great castles as Dover, Walmer and so on they had virtually no fixed coast defences, whereas they have since built a chain of forts along the Kent and Sussex beaches. There is one every few miles and they call them Martello Towers.'

'That I had heard. What are they like? Are they armed with cannon? Do you consider them formidable?'

'They are round, with inward-sloping walls and thirty or forty feet in height. Some have cannon on their roofs, the others are expected to receive their armament shortly.' In the latter statement Roger lied, as he knew the deliveries from the arsenal to be hopelessly behindhand. He continued, 'To storm them will not be easy, as they will be defended by resolute men.'

Bonaparte smiled. 'To have built them with inward-sloping walls was folly. That makes it less easy for a garrison to thrust the top of a scaling ladder back and cast it down with the men upon it.' Looking across at Bourrienne, he added, 'But we shall need many scaling ladders. Make a note to treble the quantity normally allotted to each Division.' To Roger he said:

'You consider the morale of the British to be good?'

'About that I have no doubts. In every past campaign they have displayed their doggedness in defence. And you may be certain that in defending their own soil they will fight like tigers. You may recall, *mon Général*, that when you asked my view on this two years ago I told you that not only will the troops show great bravery but people of all ages for miles round will come to their aid with shotguns and pitchforks, and I have seen no reason to change my opinion.'

'Unorthodox resistance of that kind will be only temporary,'

Bonaparte shrugged. 'After I have had a few hundred of them shot as *francs tireurs* the others will be glad enough to run back and tend their pigs. But what of Regular forces? Have these been materially increased?'

'Not greatly,' Roger admitted, 'but to some extent. However, they will now have the support of a considerable Militia. Virtually every able-bodied gentleman and yeoman within twenty miles of the coast has been embodied in these volunteer units, given a uniform and equipped with weapons.'

'Pah!' exclaimed the General. 'My veterans will make mincemeat of such amateurs. And you say that the Regular forces have not been much increased? Well, God is always on the side of the big battalions. Once ashore we shall drive all before us.'

Lannes suddenly put in, 'But we have first to get ashore. And in its present state our Navy is no match for that of the English.'

'What of that?' Bonaparte replied promptly. 'Looked at on a map, the Channel appears to be no more than a gulf between the two countries; but in fact it consists of hundreds of square miles of water. The English Fleet cannot be everywhere at once and it should take us only about seven or eight hours to get across. If we make our crossing on a foggy night the chances of running into their Fleet will be negligible.'

'We might run into one of its frigates,' argued Lannes. 'If so, the frigate would bring the Fleet speedily down on us, to our destruction.'

Bonaparte gave him an impatient glance. 'Should that happen our own escorting ships-of-war would swiftly overwhelm the frigate. Even if she did escape, the odds are that it would be many hours before, in fog, she could locate the Fleet and bring it down upon us. By then we should be safely ashore and with our artillery landed.'

'Would not fog prove as great a handicap to us as to the enemy?' Roger asked. 'Surely our flotillas would be liable to become dispersed. Many units would then find themselves lost and fail to reach their objectives.'

'I should take precautions against that. Each ship or barge would carry a fog-horn and keep in touch with her companions by sounding recognition signals at short intervals.'

Bonaparte's only experiences of sea travel were his brief crossings between Corsica and France, whereas Roger had voyaged many thousand miles. Moreover, he had learned much during his boyhood of the storms and currents of the Channel, so he did not think it all likely that this idea could be made to work in practice. But he refrained from voicing his opinion.

After a moment Bonaparte asked, ' Do you know who has been nominated to oppose me when I land in England with an Army? '

Roger smiled. ' Alas, no! I was neither in the confidence of Downing Street nor the Horse Guards. I think it almost certain, though, that the Duke of York would assume command in person.'

' What! That barber's block whom Pichegru chased out of Holland in '95? '

' Since he is the King's son and Commander-in-Chief of the Army, it is hardly likely that he will allow himself to be passed over.'

' Then I will eat him for breakfast.'

After the laughter had died down Roger remarked, ' He could, of course, have a Second-in-Command well qualified to advise him. Faced with such a desperate situation, they would probably recall Sir Ralph Abercrombie from Ireland.'

' He did well in the West Indies,' Bonaparte admitted. ' But he is an old man now. He must be well over sixty and, I am told, near blind; so he will give me little trouble.'

The conqueror of Italy would have spoken less disparagingly of Sir Ralph could he have foreseen that three years later the Army he had left to garrison Egypt was to be totally destroyed by this veteran.

' It is possible,' Roger suggested, ' that Lord Cornwallis might be given the post, or even the Command. He has a great reputation——'

' Reputation! ' Bonaparte snorted. ' That fellow! Why, he lost the war in America for the British! He allowed himself to be boxed up in York Town by a mob of colonial farmers and was compelled to surrender. He is, too, nearly as old as Sir Abercrombie.'

' I think you underrate him. In America it was not his strategy that was at fault but the Navy's failure to break the blockade and bring him reinforcements and supplies. Later, in India, he did extremely well in the wars against the native Princes.'

' Oh, India! What chance could any horde of natives, armed with spears and javelins, stand against well-trained European troops equipped with modern artillery?' Bonaparte's eyes suddenly lit up. 'One day I will go to India and throw the English out. That done, within half a year I could make myself master of the whole sub-continent, from the Himalayas to Ceylon.'

Roger smiled. 'I have no doubt of that, *mon Général.* I agree too that, as was proved in Italy, Commanders of over sixty could have little hope when confronted with your new, swift and audacious methods of waging war. But, from what I have heard, the English now have a number of younger officers who show considerable promise. I became quite intimate with one such when I was in India. His name was Arthur Wellesley. Although only a Colonel, they thought so highly of him that he was given the Command last spring of an expedition to Manila and charged with ousting the Dutch from their East Indian possessions.'

'I had intelligence of that. But you raise a matter that will prove of immense advantage to us in our invasion. The commitments of the British in India and the West Indies compel them to keep all their best regiments and officers abroad, and in the latter theatre thousands of them are carried off each year by yellow fever. That leaves the island but poorly defended and by an Army of the old type similar to that of France before the Revolution. Young men of noble families buy their commissions in it, but are soldiers only in so far as the fine uniforms they wear. Often, for years at a stretch, I am told, they are allowed to be absent from their regiments; so they know nothing of the art of war.'

'Besides,' put in Bourrienne, 'this officer of whom Breuc speaks is only a Colonel; so even if recalled he could not hope for the Command of more than a Brigade.'

'True; true. But Breuc is right in his contention that they have certain officers on the way up who show promise. There was one who greatly distinguished himself at the taking of Calvi, when the English invaded Corsica. He was a Colonel John Moore, and he showed not only great dash and courage but also intelligence. Later, when the island was subdued, he was made Adjutant-General to the forces there. He then took considerable pains to become acquainted with the leading Corsican families and showed them much kindness, thereby lessening the hostility to the English garrison stationed in the island.'

Roger nodded. 'I recall hearing of that, because on learning that Colonel Moore had been fraternizing with the patriots the Viceroy, Sir Gilbert Elliot, became furious, and ordered him to

leave the island within forty-eight hours. The Viceroy's action
was much criticized; so it had no harmful effect on Moore's career.
Shortly afterwards he was promoted to Brigadier and sent out
to the West Indies, where he became Sir Ralph Abercrombie's
right-hand man and again distinguished himself in numerous hot
actions.'

'Where is he now?' asked Bonaparte.

'I have no idea. I heard no mention of him during my recent
stay in England.'

'No matter.' The General-in-Chief abruptly stood up. 'Write
a full report of all you saw and heard while there and give it
to Bourrienne. You will, of course, accompany me when I leave
in the morning.' Turning to Réveillon, he added, 'I shall now get
some sleep.' Then, without excusing himself further, he nodded
absently in reply to a chorus of 'Good nights' and walked
quickly from the room.

Réveillon led the others back into the Salon and a number of
them crowded round Roger, pressing him for further particulars
of the desperate time he had been through. But it was now getting
on for seventeen hours since Tardieu had roused him to face one
of the most gruelling days he had ever spent. Reaction had set in
and only Bonaparte's electric presence at the supper had enabled
Roger to keep going through the meal; so he begged to be released
and went up to bed.

Next morning he was roused at four o'clock and by five they
were on their way. It was typical of Bonaparte's furious urge to
get anything he undertook completed swiftly that he would not
allow his progress to be slowed down by the bad state of the
roads. He travelled in a big carriage that had reinforced springs
and was drawn by six strong horses. Two pairs of extra horses
accompanied it, so that the team could be increased to ten when
going up steep hills, and it was escorted by a Squadron of Hussars
who were always on hand to hoist it out of ruts should it get
stuck. As the weather continued fine, their progress was not
impeded by deep mud or landslides.

Lannes, Bourrienne and the Polish aide-de-camp Sulkowsky
travelled in the carriage with the General. Roger rode alongside
it on a horse that had been provided for him and was thankful
to escape the constant jolting of the vehicle, which must have
been very wearing to its occupants. At first he wondered why
they, too, did not ride; until he realized that Bonaparte, who

never wasted a moment, was employing his time by dictating notes to Bourrienne about the state of the coast and that, despite the bumping, that hard-worked official was somehow managing to take them down.

Their first stop was Dunkirk, and there Roger asked Bourrienne for some of the back pay due to him. The *Chef de Cabinet* unlocked a brass-bound chest in the boot and gave him a small bag of gold coin together with a great bundle of *assignats*. The latter were paper money issued by the Government some years previously on the security of the lands confiscated from the Church and nobility. In exchange for gold they had since dropped to a fraction of their face value, but shopkeepers were still compelled by law to accept them. Dividing the bundle into three, Roger arranged for them to be sent to the young Major at General Desmarets's headquarters with the request that they be passed on to the soldier whose fingers he had cut off with the spade and the two Coastguards whom he had injured, as some compensation for the wounds they had sustained while only doing their duty.

Bonaparte had sent Sulkowsky to the harbour-master with an order that he should collect any Captains of ships, fishermen and smugglers whom he could readily find and bring them to the local military headquarters. As soon as these worthies arrived the General fired a series of questions at them about the capacity of the wharves, the amount of shipping of all kinds based on Dunkirk, the effect of off-shore currents and so on. He then carried out a personal inspection of the port. Roger, meanwhile, took the opportunity to buy himself a hat and topcoat, also a razor, change of linen and a few other things.

Lannes had already been sent ahead to ride along the beach to Furnes, where they picked him up in mid-morning. They then drove on to Nieuport and, after Bonaparte had carried out a brief inspection, snatched a hurried meal there. By four o'clock they reached Ostend and in this larger port the procedure at Dunkirk in the morning was repeated.

For some years past the Belgian Netherlands had been absorbed into the French Republic; so they spent that night at the residence of the Military Commandant. But during the evening Roger managed to get a little time in which to carry out a highly private matter of his own.

Having secured pen, ink and paper, he took them with him

when he went up to the bedroom he had been given to wash in before supper. On two of the sheets of paper he scrawled a semi-literate letter in French. Anyone reading it would have accepted it as a communication from some small distributor of smuggled goods to his opposite number in England. The greater part of it concerned current prices for French cognac and scent and for Brussels lace, and asked for large consignments of English cloth. But near the end he inserted a paragraph that read as follows:

I hear that great quantities of jelly-fish are breeding on the French coast. The spring tides will, people say, carry them to England. You owning fishing smacks should warn your fellows of this, else they'll do great damage to the nets. Big shoals of them can likely be spotted in daylight, but not so at night, and especially in foggy weather.

He addressed an envelope for the letter to Mr. George Peabody at the Crown Inn, Dover. Then he put it in another envelope addressed to Citizen Cammaerts, *Patron de l'Auberge du Bon Voyage.* He had to wait until after supper before he could slip away, but down by the docks he soon found a man who could direct him to the inn. It was one of the secret post-offices that had been established in all the principal ports along the French coast to enable English agents to have their reports smuggled over. Roger had never previously made use of this one but it was a part of his business to memorize them all.

As he was not yet in uniform he could go into the inn without fear of arousing unwelcome comment in connection with his clandestine business. Even so, he took advantage of the prevailing fashion to arrange his voluminous cravat so that it should hide the lower part of his face.

He would, if necessary, have left his letter with a potman but, having called for a drink, he felt very much happier on learning that the little, wizened-faced man behind the bar, with gold rings in his ears, was Citizen Cammaerts. After knocking back the tot of brandy he had ordered, he slipped the letter and a louis across to the landlord, who took them both, ripped open the outer envelope, glanced at the inner one and slipped it into his pocket with a nod but no word.

Roger had put a special mark on the envelope, so that when Mr. Peabody received it he would pay the bearer five guineas then without delay forward the letter to an address in Queen Anne's Gate. Mr. Pitt and Lord Grenville at the Foreign Office would receive copies of it very shortly afterwards and, from the paragraph about the jelly-fish, they would have no difficulty in deducing that a French invasion could be expected on a foggy night before the spring was out.

When Roger got back to the Commandant's house Bourrienne asked him where he had been, but he shrugged the question off by replying that he had drunk so much wine at supper that he had felt he must get a breath of fresh air. Then, very pleased at having got this urgent information safely away, he went up to bed.

Next day they drove further up the coast and crossed to the island of Walcheren. After Bonaparte had assessed its possibilities as an invasion base, they went on to Antwerp. There they had another quick midday meal, after which Bonaparte questioned a number of people and inspected the port. By nightfall they arrived in Brussels and early on the 16th set out on the long drive to Paris.

It had been a whirlwind tour. Bonaparte had left Paris on the 10th, so in seven days he had covered well over five hundred miles. He alone among the party appeared unaffected by the strain. Even the tough little Lannes was showing it, but when they drew up in the newly named Rue de la Victoire the pale-faced, frail-looking Corsican told the unfortunate Bourrienne to come into the house with him so that they could look through such correspondence as had arrived in his absence.

Roger took his leave and jogged on wearily to La Belle Étoile, almost falling from his saddle outside the inn. By then it was past midnight so the place was in darkness, but persistent knocking brought the landlord, Maître Blanchard, down to the door. He was swathed in a woollen robe and still wearing his cotton nightcap.

The worthy Norman believed Roger to be a Frenchman, but had known him to be an aristocrat and secretly a Royalist during those desperate times when he had passed himself off as a fervid revolutionary. But he had always kept Roger's secret, proved the staunchest of friends and still had up in his attic a big trunk of clothes, varying from the tattered garments of a *sans-culotte* to the elegant attire of a young exquisite, that Roger had used as occasion required during the long periods in which he had made La Belle Étoile his home.

On recognizing Roger, Maître Blanchard welcomed him with delight, roused a serving boy from a cubby-hole under the stairs to take his horse, and led him in. Seeing his exhausted state, he tactfully refrained from asking what had become of him during the past two years, and took him up to a comfortable bedroom. There he pressed Roger to let him bring him up a grog or hot posset, but Roger declared that he would sleep like a log without any aid to somnolence.

Flopping into bed he was almost instantly asleep, and he slept on well into the following morning. When he did become fully awake he rang for the chambermaid and told her to bring him a substantial breakfast. Hungry as a hunter, he ate it in bed, then proceeded slowly to wash and dress himself in becoming clothes from the chest that had been brought down from the attic. While doing so he groaned more than once, for he was terribly stiff from his long ride on the previous day and the insides of his thighs were almost raw.

It was midday before he made his way downstairs and encountered the landlord coming out of the coffee room. With a smiling bow to him, Maître Blanchard addressed him in a low voice as 'Monsieur le Chevalier' then said, 'Knowing one of your favourite dishes to be duck, my wife is about to braise one in the Normandy fashion for dinner. We should be greatly honoured if you would join us.'

Roger had enjoyed many a good meal in the Blanchards' private parlour, and he assented with the utmost readiness. He whiled away an hour scanning the latest issues of the *Moniteur*, then was summoned and went through to greet his motherly hostess.

Over the meal, which they washed down with two bottles of excellent Chambolle Musigny, Roger told them of the voyage he had made to India, of his return via Egypt and Venice and of his having been given a post on General Bonaparte's staff. To this simple couple India seemed as distant as another planet and they listened with rapt attention while he was describing its strangeness, colour and marvels. Then, when Maître Blanchard produced a dust-encrusted bottle of his native Calvados, Roger—knowing that his host followed all political developments with shrewd interest and that his clients kept him well informed about what was going on—said:

'But enough of myself. Tell me now how you have fared, and the latest gossip in this great city of Paris.'

'Monsieur, we cannot complain,' replied Blanchard. 'In fact by last September things had become quite like old times and——'

'Old times!' interrupted his wife. 'How can you say that when those who rule us flaunt their godlessness and lechery so shamelessly?' Turning to Roger, she went on indignantly, 'Paris has become another Babylon, monsieur. The Christian faith is mocked at, the men have made money their god, and the women of all classes sell themselves; the richer ones for jewels, and the poorer ones for a good dinner or a few ribbons.'

'That was already the case when I was last here,' Roger commented. 'While one does not approve such a state of things, it is, to some extent, understandable. Having lived in fear for so long, when any display of rich living could lead to the guillotine and all forms of enjoyment were frowned on by the Committee of Public Safety, it is hardly surprising that when the Terror ended a wave of hysterical relief should sweep people into giving free rein to their baser passions.'

'You misunderstood me, my love,' added her husband. 'By "old times" I meant that there was much more money about, men were beginning to address one another as *"Monsieur"* again, instead of *"Citoyen"*, and many people who had been in prison or had fled from the Terror were once more freely walking the streets of Paris.'

'The 18th *Fructidor* altered all that,' Madame Blanchard put in quickly.

Her husband nodded. 'As I was about to say, we have since suffered another revolution and, but for the threat of the guillotine, we again suffer under a tyranny almost as bad as that of Robespierre.'

'That was General Augereau's doing, was it not?' Roger remarked.

'Yes. He arrived here from Italy in the late summer. Covered with jewels and prancing about on his great charger, he rode round the city stirring up trouble wherever he went. By early September he had hatched a plot with Barras. On the 4th he led two thousand soldiers to the Legislative Assembly, arrested the officers of its guard and suborned their men. When the Deputies asked him by what right he dare break into their Chamber he waved his sabre in their faces and bellowed, "By the law of the sword." He arrested some of them and dispersed the rest. By nightfall it was all over. Barras placarded the city with announcements that a Royalist plot had been discovered and that the revolution had been saved only by immediate action. Over two hundred Constitutionalist Deputies were permanently deprived of their seats. Carnot got away, but Barthélemy refused to flee. He, General Pichegru and some dozen other leaders of the Moderates were condemned to transportation and shipped off to Cayenne.'

Madame Blanchard raised her eyes and hands in horror. 'Monsieur, you cannot conceive that even the worst of men could treat others of their kind with such brutality. They were trundled across France all the way to Rochefort in open iron cages on wheels, half-starved, and at every stop that was made their guards allowed mobs of ruffians to pelt them with refuse. Even worse followed, for it has since been learned that their voyage to America lasted seven whole weeks. For all that time they lay battened down in the hold with only weevilly biscuits and brackish water to sustain them.'

'Indeed, madame,' Roger agreed, with a sad shake of his head, 'the "dry" guillotine is far more to be feared than the "wet" one Many of them, too, were men advanced in years who, as in the case of poor Barthélemy, had rendered valuable service to their country. It is disgraceful that they should have received such treatment.'

After a moment he turned to Blanchard and asked, 'Is it believed that there was a Royalist plot?'

'No; not the ghost of one,' the landlord declared firmly. 'I doubt if there was a single Deputy who wanted a King back, and most of the Constitutionalists differed so widely from one another in their views of what ought to be done that no group would have been large enough to overthrow the Directory.'

'Since they had in common the aims of securing a greater degree of tolerance and bringing about a peace, I find it surprising that sufficient of them did not combine to form a powerful party.'

'That can be partly explained by the seating arrangements in the Chamber, initiated by the Thermidorians. With the object of preventing the formation of such formidable blocs as the " Mountain ", which might have opposed them, the Directors got a law passed that a separate chair and desk should be provided for each Deputy, and once a month they had to draw lots for where they were to sit. The result was that no two of them sat side by side for more than four weeks. Men of similar opinions could not get together and consult with one another during a session, so their opposition was unco-ordinated and haphazard.'

' From what I am told, I gather the Jacobins again have complete control of the situation.'

' Yes; and they've brought back all the old repressive measures. They have removed every magistrate and official in the Departments where the expelled Deputies were elected, and reinstated their own cronies. Between 10th *Thermidor* and 18th *Fructidor* over fifteen thousand names were struck from the lists of *émigrés,* but there have since been very few. Hearing of the turn things had taken, thousands of other exiles returned, without waiting to be struck off the lists. They were publicly welcomed by their friends and no action was taken against them. Now they are in hiding and again in fear of their lives. Should they be denounced to one of these Jacobin courts I was speaking of they are certain to be shot, as the penalty for returning without a permit is death.'

' And the poor Fathers,' lamented Madame Blanchard. ' All over France they had come out of hiding and, although the churches remained closed to them, no objection was raised to their celebrating Mass. Everywhere people were crowding into rooms to hear them, and had begun publicly to observe Sundays again. But now, wherever they can be found, they are seized and killed. On Sundays, too, these abominable atheists compel everyone to work and the children to attend school, while on every tenth day shops must close and anyone who lifts a finger is liable to a heavy fine.'

Her husband nodded. ' Yes, the persecution of the religious is as fierce as ever it was. And, of course, that has set La Vendée aflame once more. General Hoche had done a fine thing there. They sent him to exterminate the Breton priests and their followers. But he was a clever man as well as a brave one. After defeating the Chouans he met their leaders and agreed to grant them a degree of religious tolerance. The country was pacified in no time so, instead of a great Army being tied up there burning villages and massacring indiscriminately men, women and children, he was able to send the greater part of his troops to reinforce our Armies abroad under General Bonaparte and General Moreau.'

'I heard tell of Hoche's wise conduct while I was in Italy,' Roger said. 'It was a tragedy that he should have been carried off by consumption last September. And doubly so for a man like him, for one may be certain he would have been far happier had he died in action with his troops, even if it had been when their transports were caught and sunk by Admiral Duncan at the battle of Camperdown.'

'His death is a great loss; but I know one man who has no cause to regret it,' remarked the landlord shrewdly, 'and that's General Bonaparte.'

Roger smiled. 'You are right. Hoche was the only General with the ability, charm and strength of character to have become his rival. Now the "Little Corporal's" place as first soldier in the Armies of France cannot be disputed.'

For an hour or so longer they continued to talk, then Roger thanked his good friends for the excellent meal and went out to pay his respects to his master.

The house occupied by Bonaparte in the Rue de la Victoire had been given by Barras to Josephine—whom most people believed to have been his mistress—before her marriage. A soldier now stood on guard between two stone lions flanking a long passage that led from the street. He accompanied Roger along to the small, two-storeyed villa at its end where, having sent in his name, Roger was allowed to enter. A servant took him through to the back of the house and into a drawing room with french windows looking on to a little garden.

Bonaparte was standing in a corner, talking animatedly in his harsh voice with its strong Italian accent to Pléville Le Pelay, the Minister of Marine. He acknowledged Roger's entrance with only a nod. But Josephine was seated by the fireplace, with the son and daughter she had had by her 'first' husband, the Vicomte de Beauharnais, and all three of them greeted Roger with obvious pleasure.

Josephine was then in her thirty-fifth year and was a dark, well-preserved beauty. Her well-rounded form was supple, her manner languorous and she gave the impression that if a man took her in his arms she would give a sigh and melt in his embrace. Her reputation was far from spotless, but no worse than the majority of the women who made up the high society of the post-revolutionary era, and she was the soul of kindness. Her only physical shortcoming was that she had bad teeth.

Roger was one of the very few people who knew that her marriage to Beauharnais had been bigamous, as when a very young girl in Martinique passion had led her into a secret marriage with a youth named William de Kay. Just before she married Bonaparte, Roger had succeeded in saving her from the public exposure of her youthful folly and she had more than repaid the debt sixteen months later by saving his life; so they were firm friends.

The boy, Eugène, was now close on seventeen: a high-spirited and charming lad. In response to his desperate pleading, Bonaparte had taken him to Italy as his junior aide-de-camp; so, in his fine uniform, he now considered himself very much a war-hardened soldier. But he had not forgotten that it was Roger who had given him his first brace of pistols, or the friendship they had developed when they had met again in Italy. The girl, Hortense, was younger by a year or so. She was no great beauty, but had a pair of fine blue eyes and a mass of fuzzy, fair hair.

Someone must have told Josephine that Roger had narrowly escaped being shot as a spy, as she at once made him sit down and tell them about his terrible adventure. When he had finished he asked her about herself, upon which she began loudly to lament her husband's conduct.

'His behaviour is absurd,' she declared. 'When he first returned to Paris he was given a tremendous reception and quite graciously accepted the homage of the crowds; but since then he has gone like a snail into its shell. He refuses all invitations and declines to entertain here. I can get him to the Opera, because he enjoys that, but when the audience learn that he is in the house and call for him for minutes on end he flatly refuses to give them the pleasure of even seeing him. He sits through the whole performance in the back of the box, while Bourrienne, Junot or some other friend he takes with him is made to sit in front with me, so that he can pretend not to be there.'

Knowing Josephine's love of excitement and parties, Roger could well understand how disappointed she must feel at being deprived of a wife's right to share the glory of the national hero, particularly as before her husband's return she had had a wonderful time, being hailed everywhere she went as 'Our Lady of

Victories'. But Bonaparte had caught what she said and, striding over, reproved her:

'Madame, you are talking foolishly. There is nothing so fickle as the applause of the mob. Did I go here, there and everywhere I would be fawned on for a fortnight and then become just one more General. If I stood up at the front of the box each time we go to the Opera I would be wildly cheered once or twice, but on the fourth or fifth occasion the audience would not even turn their heads to look at me. No, I mean to keep the place that I have won in the imagination of the people by my victories. That is why I am anxious to get away from Paris as soon as possible.'

Turning to Roger he added, 'For the moment, Breuc, I have no matters on which I can employ you. Leave your address in the hall so that you can be sent for if required. Should you not hear from me, report here again a week from today. By then I expect to have settled plans for the future. You may go now when you wish.'

As Roger's call had already lasted about half an hour he stayed only for a few minutes longer, talking to Josephine and her children, then he took his leave.

That evening he went to the Palais du Luxembourg, in which each of the Directors occupied a handsome suite of apartments. Mounting the marble staircase to the long, lofty gallery that had been allotted to Barras as his ante-room, he found it packed with people. They were assembled there to ask favours or simply, by showing themselves as his courtiers, to retain the great man's goodwill. Among them he found a score of acquaintances and soon learned that the story of his misadventures were already the talk of Paris.

Nothing could have pleased him better, for the more widely it was believed that he had an English cousin who resembled him, and for whom a British seaman had mistaken him, the stronger his position became.

In due course the great double doors at the end of the gallery were thrown open and handsome, flamboyant 'King Paul' emerged through them. The crowd divided, making a lane down which he slowly progressed, receiving petitions which he passed to a secretary who followed him and bestowing smiles of greeting on his friends.

On coming opposite Roger he paused and said with a smile,

'I hear that you have been in even greater danger than when you charged that battery of cannon at Toulon. You must join us for supper and tell us about it.'

When he had made his way back up the lane two score or more of people, with Roger among them, whom he had invited followed him into the spacious supper room. Long tables were set along three of the walls, weighed down with every expensive food and extravagant confection that a great chef could devise. There was a row of silver wine-coolers, each holding half a dozen quarts of Champagne, and, for those who preferred them, there were Burgundy, Claret, Anjou, Tourraine, Sauternes, Florence wine, Alicanti, Rhenish and Moselle.

For the better part of three hours the company ate, drank and made merry, until the tables were a shambles, their clothes were slopped with spilt wine and the women, whose fashion in dress had progressed from *décolletée* to little more than a gold-trimmed tunic slit up one side to the hip, were openly allowing the men to take the freest liberties with them.

Roger enjoyed it up to the point when many of the women became maudlin. Nearly all were attractive and some were really beautiful. During the course of the evening two out of three who had aroused his interest made it clear that they were quite prepared to leave the party for anywhere he chose to take them. But the memory of the nights he had spent with the incomparable Georgina were still too fresh in his mind for him to spoil them wilfully by a casual night of lechery with one of these young women, who were highly desirable but anybody's property; so in the early hours of the morning he took a coach back to La Belle Étoile on his own.

Next day he went to the best tailor in Paris and ordered new uniforms, as he had had to leave his others at his little château in the south of France. The tailor was used to obliging officers who had received orders to leave at short notice for one of the battle-fronts, and promised to have Roger's uniforms finished in three days.

During the week before he was to report to Bonaparte again he visited all his old haunts, and in the evenings attended the salons of Mesdames Tallien, de Château-Renaul, de Staël and de Récamier. They were crowded with *émigrés* who had received permission to return from exile, ex-terrorists who had survived the Thermidorian purge, foreign diplomats, Army contractors who had made fortunes and lovely women who had made a name for themselves by their looks and immorality.

By this time they had recovered from the shock of *Fructidor* and spoke with cynical amusement of those who had been destroyed by it through not having been clever enough to ensure themselves of the protection of Barras and his cronies. No secret was made of the fact that such protection could be bought for a round sum down, and the bribes that had been paid to Ministers and officials for various services were talked of openly. In this connection the name of Talleyrand was mentioned as frequently as that of Barras. It was said that the Foreign Minister had black-mailed the ambassadors of several countries to the tune of over a million francs and demanded huge sums from them before he would consent to clauses which would benefit their countries being embodied in trade agreements.

On February 23rd Roger, now resplendent in one of his new uniforms, again repaired to the house in the Rue de la Victoire. After sending in his name he was kept waiting for some time, then ushered into a small room which his master used as an office. Bonaparte was seated at a table strewn with papers, with Bour-rienne beside him. Looking up he said:

'I am glad you have come, Breuc, because we shall all be active again shortly. I have today sent in my report to the Direc-tors. In it I have said that a descent on England is not practical for the present. Before that can be accomplished safely our Navy must be built up to a strength which would ensure its protecting my flotillas from the British Fleet, and hundreds of barges will have to be assembled in the estuaries along our north coast to carry our men across.

'Such preparations would require many months. With the end-ing of spring there will be little fog in the Channel and a foggy night would best favour our chances of landing without inter-ference on the English coast. All this I knew when I set out on my recent tour of inspection, and I undertook it only as a blind. It is of the first importance that the English should continue to believe that within a few months an invasion will be launched against them. They will then retain such troops as they have on their south coast and, perhaps, even augment them. In any case, they will not send them elsewhere to some place where they might be used against us.

'It is important, too, that our own people continue to believe this. Your own arrival at Calais was most opportune, since it enabled me to launch my deception plan among General Réveillon's officers in a most natural manner. And it is certain that they will talk. All that I am telling you now is, therefore, of the highest secrecy.

'With regard to the future, I am determined to leave Paris shortly in order to win fresh glory for France. I have told the Directors that they must either give me the Army of the Rhine and consent to my invading the Germanic States with it, or allow me to take an Army to Egypt and so put an end to England's invaluable trade with the Levant. The choice, theoretically, is theirs. But you are aware of my inclinations and you may count on my making these fellows let me have my way.

'Such an expedition will need detailed planning and preparations of the greatest magnitude. For this I must rely exclusively on my Staff, since the strictest secrecy must be maintained. So get what sleep you may, while you can. From now on you will report to me each morning at eight o'clock. You may go.'

Roger clicked to attention, wheeled about and left the room. His head was in a whirl. Bonaparte had fooled him as well as Réveillon's officers, and he had sent false information to his real master, Mr. Pitt. That must be rectified as soon as possible and news of the Corsican's true intentions sent across. He was now also threatened with being carted off to Egypt and, perhaps, becoming involved in some wild adventure to conquer half Asia, which might prevent his returning to England for years. But, somehow, he would find a means of wriggling out of such a crazy business, even if it meant quarrelling with Bonaparte.

As he walked down the passage to the street, his mind still working overtime on this new situation, he suddenly noticed a black-clad figure advancing towards him. It was that of a man in the prime of life, who adhered to the pre-Revolution fashion of wearing his hair powdered. He was carrying a malacca cane and walked with a slight limp. Next moment, Roger recognized his old friend the ex-Bishop M. de Talleyrand-Périgord.

Halting, the Foreign Minister smiled at him and said, 'Breuc, my dear fellow. How delightful to see you. I heard that you were back. Why have you not called upon me?'

Roger had thought several times of doing so, but a subconscious nervousness about his ability to establish a satisfactory new relationship with de Talleyrand had caused him to postpone this delicate interview. With a smile, he said:

'I had meant to call and offer my congratulations on your return to France, and your appointment as Foreign Minister. But, for the few days I have been in Paris, I have been prodigious busy, getting myself fitted with new clothes and a score of other tiresome matters.'

'New clothes,' de Talleyrand murmured, putting his quizzing glass to his eye and lazily surveying Roger from head to toe. 'Your omission to look in on an old friend was not, perchance, on account of this gorgeous new plumage, I suppose. But I must say I find it passing strange to come upon an Englishman attired in the uniform of a French Colonel.'

7

When Greek Meets Greek

CHARLES-MAURICE DE TALLEYRAND-PÉRIGORD had just passed his
forty-eighth birthday. His face was chubby and inclined to be
rosy; his mouth was beautifully modelled but had a slightly
ironic twist; his nose was *retroussé,* and his eyes, under heavy
lids fringed with thick lashes, were large and piercing. He was of
medium height, had a slim figure and, despite his limp, moved
with grace. His dress was always faultless, no man had more
charming manners and he was an aristocrat to his fingertips.

His limp was due to his nurse having dropped him at the age of
four and the subsequent neglect of the injury to his foot, which
could have been corrected with proper care. The resulting
deformity had repercussions which altered his whole life. As he
could not go into the Army his parents dispossessed him of his
rights, although he was their eldest son, and, early in his 'teens,
put him into the Church.

He bitterly resented this and soon became the most irreligious
priest in an age celebrated for its cynicism and immorality. He
rarely wore clerical garments, even when created Bishop of
Autun, but dressed in silks and satins with exquisite taste, and
exercised his extraordinary charm in seducing a long series of
beautiful young women at the Court of Versailles. At sixteen he
had as his first mistress a charming little actress named Dorothy
Dorinville. At seventy he was still to have a mistress and another
Dorothy, who was his own niece—the Duchess de Dino.

From the first calling together of the Three Estates in 1789, he
had, as a representative of the Clergy, at once made his mark—
but in another role. By his able brain and gifts as a speaker, he
had emerged as one of the leaders of the Liberal nobility. He

110

was not an anti-Monarchist, but he saw the urgent necessity for sweeping reforms which had been long overdue.

As the Revolution progressed he had held many important offices; and when the breakaway from Rome was formally executed he became the first Bishop in the new, reformed National Church of France. In January 1792 he had been sent on a diplomatic mission to London. Having always held the opinion that an alliance between France and Britain was essential to the lasting prosperity of both countries he had, while there, strongly pressed for it, but without success. Later in that year, after his return to Paris, the Commissioners of the Convention had gone through the King's papers that had been seized during the sack of the Tuileries and had found two letters written by him, privately advising the King to adopt a policy contrary to the interests of the revolutionaries.

In consequence he had been denounced as an 'Enemy of the People', and had escaped from Paris only just in time to save his life. In London, where he returned, he was ostracized by the majority of the French *émigrés,* and by a large section of the British aristocracy, because of the part he had played in the Liberal Revolution. So he had moved on to the more sympathetic atmosphere of the newly-created United States.

However, he still had many powerful friends and acquaintances in France who respected his abilities and, after the fall of Robespierre, they began to work for his return. Among these friends was one of his many mistresses, the clever intriguer Madame de Staël. She had persuaded Barras to allow him to return, and in the previous July she had secured for him the post of Foreign Minister.

Confronted by this shrewd and again-powerful man, who knew the truth about him, Roger did not lose his nerve. To have shown the least trace of apprehension would have given away the fact that he had something to hide. With a laugh, he gaily paraphrased Shakespeare:

'The world is but a stage and men play many parts upon it. I am glad you find my uniform becoming. And, if I may say so, it suits me better than yours did when you were a Bishop.'

Talleyrand raised an eyebrow. 'Indeed! I had no idea you were a church-goer, and so ever saw me in it. May I suggest, though, that your presence here dressed as a French officer requires some explanation?'

'It is quite simple,' Roger shrugged. 'As you must be aware, I have spent a great part of my manhood in France, and have become so enamoured of this country that I now regard myself as a Frenchman. I have been wounded more than once in the service of France and my title to this uniform is beyond dispute. When I was in Italy no less a person than the General Bonaparte did me the honour to make me one of his aides-de-camp.'

'How prodigious interesting.' Talleyrand gave a slight bow. 'Allow me to congratulate you, my dear fellow, on this signal distinction. I cannot, alas, linger to converse longer with you now, as the General is expecting me. But we must foregather to discuss old times: over breakfast, perhaps, when our enjoyment of one another's company will not be diverted by the presence of others. Let me see. Friday, I think, is the first day I have free. May I have the pleasure of receiving you at nine o'clock?'

'You are most kind,' Roger smiled. 'There is nothing I should enjoy more.'

Exchanging another bow, they parted and Roger went on his way. The brief conversation had gone as well as he could have expected. To all appearances Talleyrand had accepted his explanation, but all the same it was a most delicate situation and he knew that, on the coming Friday, he would have all his work cut out to convince the astute statesman that he had really abandoned for good all his ties with England.

Yet it was the line he had already decided to take when they did meet, as it was inevitable that they would, and the only line possible.

It was nearly twelve years since, when he had been assistant secretary to the Marquis de Rochambeau, he had first met Talleyrand. An occasion had arisen when the Marquis had an urgent need to have a long, confidential document copied overnight, and the work was to be done at Talleyrand's house out at Passy. Talleyrand, Roger and the Marquis's senior secretary, the Abbé d'Heury, had set off together in a coach for Passy, but when nearing their destination the coach had been held up by footpads. Talleyrand had defied the brigands and an affray had ensued. D'Heury had been shot dead—which had led to Roger's promotion—and a second ball had wounded Roger in the head, rendering him unconscious. When he came to, in bed in Talleyrand's house, he learned that during his delirium he had been raving in English. Since at that time he had been passing himself off as a

Frenchman only as a matter of convenience, he had freely admitted his real nationality and had given Talleyrand full particulars of himself. Roger felt certain that he would not have forgotten them, so it would have been futile for him to deny now that he was the son of Admiral Sir Christopher Brook.

However, a strong bond of friendship had long since developed between them. It was Roger who had tricked Danton into giving him the passport which had enabled Talleyrand to escape from Paris when to remain would have cost him his life; so Roger had no fear whatever that his old friend would regard him as an enemy, let alone have him arrested.

After a few minutes his mind turned to the *volte-face* in plans that Bonaparte had sprung upon him that morning. The news that there was to be no invasion of England that year, but that instead the conqueror of Italy was pressing the Directory to let him follow in the path of Alexander the Great, must be sent without delay to Mr. Pitt.

Returning to La Belle Étoile, he wrote a long despatch and put it into a double envelope. He then had his midday meal and afterwards went out to send off his letter. He was always reluctant to use secret post-offices because, although they were usually in back streets unlikely to be frequented by the sort of people he knew, some risk that he might be recognized or followed from the post-office by the man who ran it, should he have turned double traitor, was unavoidable. In the past he had had to use them rarely, as during the Revolution he had been able to send his despatches by members of Sir Percy Blakeney's League of the Scarlet Pimpernel, and on the last two occasions he had been in Paris he had been employed on special missions which did not call for him to send back regular reports. But in the present circumstances he had no option.

In a mental index he carried three addresses. One was an old one that he had used before, and two were new ones that he had been given when last in London. But it proved his unlucky day, for the afternoon brought him only frustration. Calling first at the old address, he learned that the forwarding agent there had died shortly before Christmas. At the next address he was told that the man he wanted had left that morning to visit relatives in the country and was not expected back until the end of the week. At the third address a slatternly woman told him that her husband had been carried off by the police a fortnight before.

E

Had his news been of great urgency and importance, he would seriously have considered sending a message to Bonaparte by Maître Blanchard saying that he had met with an accident which would keep him in bed for a few days. He would then have used the time to ride all-out to Dieppe and back, with the certainty that he would be able to get his despatch off by a smuggler there. But a few days' delay could make no material difference to the value of his news; so he resigned himself to awaiting the return of the man who had gone to the country.

Friday was three days away and, although he reported to Bonaparte each morning, the General-in-Chief still had no use for him. He filled in the time much as he had done during the previous week: riding in the mornings, putting in an hour or two in a fencing school or a pistol gallery in the afternoons and attending the salons in the evenings.

The denizens of the latter were now largely young '*Incroyables*', with sickle-moon hats, enormous cravats on either side of which their hair dangled in 'dog-ears' and trousers so tight that they could not sit down without risk of splitting them. Their female opposite numbers had their hair piled high and banded, *à la Grecque,* or cut short *à la Romaine* and, having given up both corsets and underclothes, wore skin-tight dresses so revealing as to be near indecent.

Among these bizarre creatures, with their affected voices and languid manner, Roger sought out the older, more serious people. From them he built up the store of knowledge he was acquiring about trends in Government policy and learned the latest rumours. Among those current was one to the effect that the Swiss had risen *en masse* against a body of French troops under General Ménard, whom Republicans in Lausanne had asked should be sent to protect them from oppression. Another rumour was that a French Army had entered Rome.

This last news filled everyone with delight, as the French had a score to settle with the Papacy. Bonaparte had overrun a great part of the Papal States and incorporated them in his Cisalpine Republic, but he had refrained from sending his troops into the Eternal City. His orders from the atheist Directory had been to dethrone the Pope and abolish the Papacy. However, he was well aware that the greater part of the French people were still Christian at heart and had been far too shrewd to make himself responsible for a sacrilege which they would have held against him for as long as he lived. Instead he had menaced the Pope into paying a huge indemnity, blackmailed him into handing over the finest art treasures in the Vatican and had his own eldest brother, Joseph, appointed Ambassador to the Holy See.

Joseph Bonaparte was a mild man, an able administrator, and one who believed in conciliation. As the representative of the new France that had arisen from the ashes of an ancient absolute Monarchy, it was natural that the Republican Party in Rome should urge him to approve of and support them in violent measures against what they termed ' their tyrants '. But he stead-fastly refused to do so.

The malcontents had, therefore, decided to provoke a collision with the object of its resulting in French intervention. On December 27th they staged a great demonstration in the Via Medici and were dispersed by the cavalry of the Papal Guard. Next day a similar scene took place outside the French Embassy. General Duphot, a young officer who had served with great distinction under Bonaparte in the north, ran out into the courtyard of the Embassy waving a drawn sword. It was said that he ran out to make peace; but more probably it was to lead the insurgents, and he was shot dead by the *Papalini*. Joseph Bonaparte had seen no alternative but to demand his passports, after what was regarded as the assassination of his military adviser, and the arrogance of the French had by then reached such a pitch that nothing short of the occupation of Rome would satisfy them for Duphot's untimely death.

On leaving Italy, Bonaparte had nominated his Chief-of-Staff, General Berthier, as Commander of the French Army occupying the Cisalpine Republic, and Berthier had been ordered to march his Army south for the chastisement of the Eternal City. His progress had been rapid and the news was circulating that he had entered Rome on February 13th without meeting opposition.

On the Friday morning, after reporting to his General, Roger arrived promptly at nine o'clock at the fine mansion in the Rue du Bac, now occupied by the Minister of Foreign Affairs. Talley-rand received him like a long-lost brother and ushered him into a small, private dining room, where a breakfast in keeping with wealthy households in that age was served. There was a wide choice of hot dishes, with cold game, Westphalian ham and hot-house fruit to follow. While they ate, a *sommelier*, wearing his silver chain of office, kept their glasses filled with a Château Latour that had lain for twenty years in a bin.

As soon as they were seated Talleyrand asked for an account of Roger's narrow escape from execution. When it had been given him he murmured, " I find this exceedingly diverting, in view of the fact that the magistrates in Boulogne were entirely right in supposing you to be—well, you will understand what I mean.'

'On the contrary,' Roger replied quickly, 'they were grossly wrong in their assumption of both my nationality and my intent.'

'You imply that you have taken out naturalization papers. How wise of you. When did you do that? '

'I have not done so. Such a step would result in endless fuss. Meanwhile, I would probably be deprived of the right to serve the country of my adoption.'

'That, from what I have learned in the past few days, would be a grievous loss. General Bonaparte thinks very highly of you.'

'I am most gratified to hear it. I have the greatest admiration for his talents and am devoted to him.'

'Yes, he has an amazing capacity for inspiring devotion,' Talleyrand agreed. 'Shortly after I took office he sent Monge— you remember Monge, the scientist and the last Minister of the Navy under our late King—back from Italy with Berthier, to report on his intentions with regard to the future of northern Italy. I was immensely impressed by the way in which they spoke of him. After talking with them I came to the conclusion that here at last was the man France needed to rid us of these incompetent rogues who now govern the country and to make her once again respected among the nations. I then wrote to him, offering him my friendship and my support in any measures he might propose for the betterment of our affairs.'

'I know,' smiled Roger. 'I read your letter. I was much amused by the flattery you used to tickle his vanity and win him as your ally. I even recall your most telling phrase: " In our negotiations the very name of Bonaparte is a help that should smooth over all our difficulties."'

For the fraction of a second Talleyrand, arch-diplomatist though he was, disclosed that he was taken aback. 'You . . . saw my letter? Pray, how did that come about? '

'It so happens,' Roger replied lightly, 'that I am not only

accounted a passable swordsman—an attribute that I share with the majority of Bonaparte's other Staff officers—but I am also capable of drafting a lucid despatch, or making a reliable précis of a long report. Most of these bravos would rather face charging cavalry than undertake such work; so Bonaparte employed me while at Montebello as an assistant to Bourrienne.'

Talleyrand slowly drank a little of the superb claret, then he murmured, 'Then you are privy to all our secrets?'

'Certainly, my dear Minister, and I have deserved this confidence. Moreoer, as we have long been allies with no secrets from one another, I will let you into a confidence that I would disclose to no one else. Bonaparte never had any intention of making a descent on England this year, and he is set on leading an Army to win glory in the East.'

It was Talleyrand's turn to smile. 'I am already aware of that, and gather it has long been his ambition. In fact, I have done my best to smooth his path to its accomplishment. As far back as July I addressed a memorandum to the Institute, pointing out France's need for colonies and urging that, since we had lost nearly all our possessions in the West Indies to the British, we should now turn our eyes east and make a bid for a great part of the decaying Ottoman Empire. I have since made two confidential reports to the Directors, one on January 28th and another as recently as February 15th in which I have pointed to Egypt as the vulnerable spot because, although they are technically subject to the Sultan, the Mameluke Beys who rule there flout his authority and so might be subdued by France with the Sultan's connivance.'

Roger shook his head. 'To me it sounds a crazy project. Bonaparte might well find himself cut off there, and from lack of supplies have his whole Army founder in the desert sands, as happened with Cambyrer the Persian. As far as I personally am concerned, I'll have no part in it. Should he persuade the Directors to agree to his plan, I shall feign sickness or resort to some other ruse to evade having to accompany him.'

'You said but now that you were devoted to him.'

'Indeed, I am. But not to the point of risking dying of thirst without rendering him any useful service. A year ago I was in Egypt, also in India. That is a major reason for Bonaparte's regard for me. At Montebello, having no campaign to direct and being bewitched by these countries, he made me give him descriptions of them that lasted for hours. But, having been to Egypt and seen something of its deserts, I've no mind to die in one of them.'

'Why then did you further excite his imagination concerning these countries, as you obviously must have done to hold his attention for so long, rather than leave him to pursue the obvious course—a descent on England?'

'Because anything would be preferable to that,' Roger replied boldly. 'The chances of getting an Army ashore with its artillery without interference by the British Navy would be negligible. But, that apart, a direct attack upon their homeland would antagonize the English to such a degree that there could never be any reconciliation in our lifetime. And you know as well as I do that nothing short of a peace between France and Britain can bring about a permanent settlement of the upheavals that have disrupted the Continent these past eight years.'

'You are right in that,' Talleyrand agreed, 'and it has ever been my ambition to bring the two nations to a friendly understanding. But you are wrong in regarding Egypt as a death-trap and supposing that its conquest would not greatly benefit France, as well as gild Bonaparte's laurels. Once there I am confident that he would manage to establish himself; and to seize Egypt for France is no new idea. Over a hundred years ago Libniz proposed it to Louis XIV. In Louis XV's time the Duc de Choiseul actually drew up a plan for the sending of an expedition and, only a few years before the Revolution, it was revived by Saint-Priest, who was then our Ambassador in Constantinople. Talking of which, I will let you into a little secret. I have promised Bonaparte to get myself appointed Ambassador to the Porte, with the object of persuading the Sultan to agree to France replacing the Mamelukes in Egypt.'

'You really believe, then, that Bonaparte could succeed in maintaining himself there?'

For a moment Talleyrand was silent, then he said thoughtfully, 'Provided the English do not become apprised of our plan and send a Fleet into the Mediterranean, I do not see why he should not. And if he does the project should pay us immense dividends. Unlike France, whose main source of wealth lies in her agriculture, that of Britain is derived from commerce. If we held Malta and both ends of the Mediterranean we could ruin her great trade with the Levant. Moreover, consider Egypt's geographical position. She is readily accessible from Europe and is a bridge-head into both Asia and Africa. As a base for further operations, followed by a great increase in our trade with the East, she is, therefore, invaluable. Expeditions mounted there could sweep north through Syria and overrun the huge territories of the decadent Ottoman Empire, or be despatched against India with equal ease. One can hardly put a limit to what Bonaparte may achieve if the Directory let him have his way.'

'Do you think they will?'

'You may count it as certain. They are terrified of him, and would consent to anything to be rid of him.'

'They really fear, then, that he may stage a *coup d'état* and throw them out?'

'I doubt if he yet feels strong enough to attempt it. He would be content, for the moment at least, if he were made a Director. However, there is a law stipulating that no Director shall be less than forty years of age, and he is not yet twenty-nine. He is pressing for the law to be altered, but it is most unlikely they would agree to that. To have him among them would mean that they would become no more than his lackeys.'

For a moment Talleyrand paused, then he continued, ' However, if he survives his Egyptian venture I have little doubt the day will come when he will sweep them away. His ambition is unbounded. At our first meeting he said to me, "You are a nephew of the Archbishop of Cambrai, who is now with Louis XVIII at Mitau." Note, he referred to the royal exile not by the only title Republican France accords him—the Comte de Lille—but as " King ". Then he went on, " I also have an uncle who is an Archdeacon in Corsica. He brought me up. In Corsica, you know, an Archdeacon is the same as a Bishop in France." I was secretly a little amused by his anxiety to show that he also was a gentle-man. But the way he spoke gave me furiously to think. It struck me that within a year or two he may well be talking of " we nobles " and that perhaps a time might even come when he will be referring to Louis XVI as " my poor uncle ".'

Roger laughed. 'Oh, come! That is going a little far.'

'Well, we shall see,' smiled the diplomat. 'In the meantime there is another reason why the Directors must get him out of France. The war with Austria is over, and they are left with an enormous Army on their hands. They dare not disband even a half of the two hundred and fifty thousand men now under arms and allow them to return to France without pay or employment.'

'I agree,' Roger nodded. 'To do so would be to invite anarchy and another revolution more bloody than the first.'

'Then, since they cannot be sent against England, they must be employed elsewhere. Even as things are, the Government is at its wits' end where to find the money with which to continue to pay them.'

'What, after receiving all the hundreds of millions that Bonaparte sent to the Directory from Italy?'

'Yes. France is bankrupt. That is why General Ménard has been sent into Switzerland. A Republican Party hardly exists there. Those petitions asking for our protection are a farce and carry only a few score names. But the Swiss are a wealthy people. Incidents must be provoked, so that we have an excuse to intervene, and, having presented a bill for restoring order, loot the rich treasuries of the Cantons. Thus we shall get the millions to pay our troops.'

Roger sighed. 'What a disgraceful and revolting business! But where have all the millions gone that were looted from Italy?'

'No doubt you have been to one of Barras's receptions at the Luxembourg. They take place every night. Scores of other Government officials have poured the money away to only a slightly less degree. Then there are the Army contractors. They are like a swarm of locusts and the whole administration leaks gold like one vast sieve.'

With a little smile, Talleyrand went on, 'In this I am happy to think that my own hands are clean. Immediately I was appointed Foreign Minister I determined to make my fortune out of the post, because to live well is the breath of life to me. And I'm doing none too badly. But at no cost to France. I take only foreign money, for greasing the wheels in our negotiations with foreign Powers. That is a perquisite which Foreign Ministers in every country have always enjoyed.'

For a moment they were silent, then Talleyrand said casually, 'But about yourself, my dear fellow. How long is it since you decided to become a Frenchman?'

Roger knew that the critical moment had come, but he answered with equal casualness. 'Quite recently. Last autumn, in fact. You will recall that when first we met I told you of how I had run away from home to France, rather than enter the Navy as my father wished. For that he has never forgiven me. In consequence, I have neither patronage nor fortune in England. In '94 I decided to try my luck in the West Indies, as my cousin had recently been made Governor of Martinique. But we had quarrelled when young, and he still held it against me; so I returned to England. Then in '96 I sailed to India, having heard that fortunes could be made there swiftly. Unfortunately, I am not suited to trade and succeeded only in getting myself into debt.'

Talleyrand smiled. 'In that we are birds of a feather. I attempted to repair my fortune while in America by dabbling in commerce, and I had no luck. But please continue.'

'Finding myself at the end of my tether, I saw no point in remaining in a country rendered uncongenial by intense heat and poisonous reptiles. So I got together what money I could and returned to Europe by way of Egypt. In Venice I again met Madame Bonaparte, who was already a good friend of mine, and she took me to the General's headquarters at Montebello. I served with him at the siege of Toulon, and was also with him on 13th *Vendemiaire*. We had also, on numerous occasions, discussed matters of strategy and, evidently feeling that I could be useful to him, he offered me a post as one of his aides-de-camp. It was then that, seeing no possible future for myself in England, I decided to cut myself off for good from the country of my birth and follow the path of fortune that had been opened to me in France.'

'Your decision was very understandable,' Talleyrand said. 'Yet I seem to recall that, when I was on a diplomatic mission in London in '92, you came to me and I briefed you before you proceeded to France as a secret agent for Mr. Pitt.'

'True,' Roger agreed. 'Yet even then I was acting not against France, but only against the terrorists who were deluging the country in blood. And you gave me your help willingly.'

'Indeed, yes; because our interests were then identical. But what guarantee can you give me that you are not still acting as an agent for Mr. Pitt?'

'None,' Roger laughed. 'But surely if the Bastille still existed you would not clap me into it?'

'The Temple would serve equally well,' Talleyrand replied smoothly, 'and there you would have the company of a most adventurous fellow: one quite after your own heart. I refer to a Captain Sidney Smith. Although an officer of the British Navy, I am told that he fought as a volunteer with the Swedes in their war against Russia. He also acted as a spy when the British threatened war against the Emperor of Morocco and, disguised as an Arab, made a reconnaissance of that country. He can pass as a Frenchman, too, as he lived for two years in France before the Revolution. But a year or so ago he let his zest for adventure tempt him once too often. In an entirely private venture, of which his Admiralty knew nothing, he attempted to land a party, with the object of blowing up our docks at Le Havre. He was captured and has since remained a prisoner. I could arrange for you to be allowed to see one another, and I am sure you would find him a most entertaining companion.'

'But surely——' began Roger with a startled look.

With a laugh, Talleyrand raised his hand and cut him short. 'No, no, my dear fellow, I was but joking. I would not even dream of treating you so scurvily. I owe to you not only the preservation of my little house at Passy, with all its treasures, from despoliation during the dark days of the Terror, but also my life. It would be an ill return to have you locked up behind stone walls.'

Roger breathed again as the quiet, cultured voice went on, 'Yet, now that I am an official of the French Government, I cannot altogether ignore what I know of your past. I must at least request from you your word as a gentleman that, while you remain in France, you will not give way to any impulse you may feel to communicate in any way with your English relatives or any other British person.'

Had Roger hesitated, even for an instant, it would have disclosed to the agile mind that was seeking to probe his that he had lied when declaring that henceforth he intended to give his whole allegiance to France. So he replied at once:

'I give it willingly.'

'I thank you.' Talleyrand gave a little bow. 'And now there is just one other point. I must request you to change your mind and accompany General Bonaparte to Egypt.'

8

The Liberators

TO TALLEYRAND'S first demand, couched though it was as a polite request, Roger had had no option but to accede at once; but this was another matter. For the past few days he had been dwelling on his future with most pleasurable feelings. Once Bonaparte had set sail for Egypt he would no longer constitute a menace either to the Directory or on the Continent of Europe. With no prospect of a *coup d'état* establishing a new Government with, probably, a drastic change in French policy or of a renewal of the war with Austria, there would have been no advance information of importance that Roger could hope to collect by remaining in Paris. He had therefore been envisaging an early return to England with the possibility, remote though he feared it to be, that he might persuade Georgina to marry him. But if he agreed to go to Egypt that would put a definite end to any such prospect.

After a moment he said, 'No, no! As I have already said, I have no mind to commit myself to an adventure which may keep me out of Europe for several years, or to risk a futile death by thirst. And why should you ask it of me?'

Talleyrand smiled. 'For one reason, my friend: because I have your interests at heart. You have told me of your new resolution to make a career for yourself in France. What better first rung on the ladder to fortune could you desire than to have become one of Bonaparte's aides-de-camp? Fate has enabled you to hitch your wagon to a star. Should you excuse yourself from accompanying the little Corsican he will never forgive you, so you will find yourself finished here when you have scarce begun. Besides, unless my judgment is much at fault, he will not remain away from France indefinitely. Whatever inducements the East may appear to offer,

123

the real prize lies here, as Dictator, and he is well aware of it.'

'There is much in what you say,' Roger admitted reluctantly, 'and, of course, I am devoted to him. But, even so . . .'

'So you have said. But you must forgive me if I remark that if you are prepared to deprive him of your services at this turning point in his career I should be bound to feel some slight doubt about your devotion being genuine.'

'Oh, come! If he asked me I'd risk my life in his service anywhere in Europe. It is just . . . well, that having been to Egypt I am extremely loath to return to that sweltering and disease-ridden country.'

'Yet I fear you must.' Talleyrand gave a mock sigh. 'You see, my dear fellow, eager as I am to believe every word you have told me, you have given me no proof of this change of heart which you have recently experienced. I am, alas, cursed with a suspicious nature. You say that you have now abandoned all ties with England and have become, er . . . in all but the formalities . . . a Frenchman. More, you are now a soldier of France. If, therefore, you wish to convince me, once and for all, that you have told the truth, you must prove it by going where your duty calls you.'

Roger knew that he was trapped. He had counted too highly on established custom concerning foreigners in an enemy country. Up to and at that date wars were regarded as a matter for governments and their fighting forces. Civilians of one nation were courteously permitted to travel through or continue to reside in countries with which their own countries were at war. It was not until Napoleon became Emperor of the French that a new era was introduced by his having all enemy aliens rounded up by his police and thrown into concentration camps. Moreover, there was nothing at all unusual in a man of one nationality making a career in the Army or Navy or another. For that matter, Bonaparte was himself more Italian by blood than he was French, and the Englishman Tom Paine had been a Deputy in the French Convention.

Banking on Talleyrand's friendship, Roger had not expected that the diplomat would treat him as an exception to the prevailing rule. That might well have proved the case had he been in France as a civilian, or even had Talleyrand not known of his past association with Mr. Pitt. Belatedly he realized that it had been too much to expect the Foreign Minister to allow him to retain his status as a French Colonel in Paris with access to military secrets. No alternative had been suggested; but Roger felt certain there would be one, and one which might well put a permanent end to his activities as a secret agent. Once more he felt that there was nothing for it but to agree; so with as much cheerfulness as he could muster he replied :

' So be it, then. Since you insist on my giving you this evidence of my good faith, I'll go to Egypt; but if I die there my blood will be on your head.'

' God forbid that either of us should be called on so to suffer,' smiled his host. ' And now that everything is settled between us in such an amicable manner let us drink to your safe return. That the peaches are somewhat short of perfection you must forgive, but at this season I have to have them brought by courier from hothouses in the south of France. I assure you, though, that the Château Yquem that goes with them is near as old as myself and could hardly be bettered.'

It was not until half an hour later, as Roger walked away from the Rue du Bac, that he had a chance to take serious stock of his new situation. He still felt that the account of himself which he had given was sufficiently plausible for Talleyrand to have at least half believed it, but the fact that he had not swallowed it hook, line and sinker. Instead, he had not only extracted a promise that Roger should not communicate with his country but had also taken steps to see that he would shortly be transported to a distant shore where, for a long time to come, even if he ignored his promise, he would be in no position to send information to England about such plans as the Directory might be making.

On one point Roger took an immediate decision. It could be taken for granted that during the six months the Foreign Minister had been in office he would have established his own service of secret agents. That being so, if he did suspect that Roger was still acting for Mr. Pitt, he would be kept under constant observation from now on until he was safely out of Paris. Therefore, it would be tempting Fate to pay another visit to the secret post-office and hand in his despatch.

That did not particularly worry him. He was in fact relieved that circumstances should prevent his having to carry out a duty at the cost of breaking his word to a friend. He regarded it as a good thing that preparations to resist invasion should continue to be made in England at high pressure; for, although Bonaparte had refused the gamble, the Directory were so eager that the operation should be undertaken that it was quite possible that during his absence they might persuade Moreau or some other General to undertake it.

As far as the expedition to Egypt was concerned, its preparations would take many weeks, if not months, and must be on such a scale that other British agents could hardly fail to learn their purpose. It was annoying to have acquired this important piece of information long before any other agent was likely to do so, yet be deprived of the kudos for passing it on. But it was better to be safe than sorry, so he quickly resigned himself to leaving it to someone else to report.

That brought him to the all-important question—should he or should he not accompany Bonaparte? If he backed out, it was certain that the clever Talleyrand would think of some way of thoroughly discrediting him without actually bringing him into danger. It would then be useless for him to remain in Paris. Moreover, as Talleyrand had pointed out, to resign his appointment at such a juncture would cost him for good the place he had won in Bonaparte's confidence and, if the General did return safely from his Eastern venture, there could be little doubt that he would prove the dominant figure in the French politics of the future.

Having reasoned so far, it became apparent to Roger that he was faced with clear-cut alternatives—either he must go to Egypt or slip quietly away to England with his tail between his legs and confess to Mr. Pitt that he was finished as a secret agent.

Could he have been certain that Georgina would marry him, he would have been prepared to take the latter course; but he knew that for her to change her mind after all these years was very unlikely. That being the case, there would be nothing to console him for retiring from the ringside seat from which he had observed, and sometimes influenced, High Policy in Europe for so long. Moreover, it was a bitter thought that he would end on a note of complete failure the career he had followed for the past ten years with such outstanding success.

The alternative, too, offered extremely high dividends. By going to Egypt he could convince Talleyrand of his bona fides, and so even win his confidence. He would retain Bonaparte's goodwill and if, as Talleyrand predicted, he returned sooner than might be expected to assume dictatorial powers, his goodwill would then be invaluable.

There were two other smaller points, though important ones to Roger. First, he had promised Talleyrand not to communicate with England only while he was in France. Once outside the country he would again be free to do so by any means he could devise without any feeling of shame at having broken his word, even though it were in the service of his country. Secondly, although he might leave France with Bonaparte, it did not follow that he would remain with him indefinitely. An occasion might well arise by which, while still retaining the General's goodwill, he could manage to get back to Europe long before Bonaparte.

By the time he was crossing the Place du Louvre towards La Belle Étoile he had decided that Talleyrand had, for the present, cornered him; so he must accept the challenge and play the game out or lose all respect for himself. On reaching the inn he went up to his room, lifted a loose floor-board, took the despatch he had written from its hiding place and burned it. Then he resolutely set about accustoming his mind to the fact that he would soon be leaving Europe and might not see his own country again for a long time to come.

During the weeks that followed he spent his time much as he had since his arrival in Paris. The Directory had not yet given its official consent to the expedition to Egypt so no overt preparations for it could be made; but Bonaparte had begun to draw up lists of his requirements, and from time to time used Roger to make discreet enquiries about the availability of different items. Apart from that he continued with his social round, which was rapidly making him one of the best-informed men in Paris. This round included attendance at all receptions given by members of the Bonaparte family, the older members of which he had met in Italy.

The General's mother, Madame Letizia, entertained rarely, but Roger saw her occasionally at the houses of her children. She was a tall, angular woman and had inherited from her peasant ancestors both the best and worst of their qualities. Her husband had died in '85, leaving her far from well-off and with a brood of seven children, ranging from one to seventeen years of age. During the upheavals that had shaken Corsica in the years that followed she had often been in dire straits to support her young family, but had faced every hardship with immense courage and, while treating her children with great strictness, had succeeded in bringing them up in the best traditions of the *petit-noblesse*.

She was devout, high-principled and unspoilt by her second son's rise to greatness. But she was extremely mean, owing to a belief that such prosperity could not last and that a day would come when to help her extravagant children she would need all she could save from the generous allowance the General made her.

Joseph, her eldest son—now aged thirty—had recently returned from being Ambassador at Rome. He had studied law at Pisa and was a virtuous, good-natured, intelligent man. After the family left Corsica and settled in Marseilles as refugees he had married Julie Clary, the daughter of a wealthy merchant there. She made him an excellent wife and was regarded by all as an angel of goodness, owing to her tireless activity in every form of charity. They had a pretty house in the Rue du Rocher, to which Joseph had brought back with him from Rome his wife's sister, Désirée. She was a great, if somewhat insipid, beauty and some years earlier had inspired Bonaparte with a most tender passion. At the moment she was in deep mourning for General Duphot, for she had become engaged to him before his untimely death in Rome the previous December.

Between Napoleon and Lucien, Letizia's third son, there was a gap of six years. Physically he bore little resemblance to the others, for he was tall, ill-shaped and had a small head and long thin limbs like those of a spider. In addition, he was so near-sighted that he was always peering at people with his head thrust forward and eyes half-closed. After Napoleon he was the most talented and independent-minded of the family, and its firebrand. As a dyed-in-the-wool Republican, he had been imprisoned as a Robespierrist at the end of the Terror, although he was only nineteen at the time. His brother Napoleon had had some difficulty in securing his release. He then got himself work as a storekeeper in St. Maxim and while there had married Christine Boyer, the daughter of the village innkeeper.

It was in keeping with Lucien's Republican principles to have married a barmaid; but the news drove his brother, then in Italy, into a frenzy of rage, for the young General-in-Chief was already visualizing himself as the head of a powerful family and planning for his relatives to marry far above their social status. Christine proved to be a good-looking, but undesigning, sweet-natured girl, and she soon won the love of all her husband's family, with the one exception of the General. She very soon adapted herself to her new circumstances and on coming to Paris was much admired for the elegance with which she displayed on her tall figure the latest creations of the fashionable dressmakers Leroi, Despaux and German. Even so, it was a long time before the disgruntled Napoleon would receive her, although, to enable the couple to support themselves, he procured for Lucien a post as one of the Commissioners with the Army in Germany. From this post they had just returned to Paris and Lucien was about to enter the Assembly as Deputy for Corsica.

Élise, the General's eldest sister, was just twenty-one. She was the least good-looking and least attractive of the sisters. Having been sent at an early age to Madame Campan's Academy for the Daughters of the Nobility as a charity pupil, supported by the late Queen, she always endeavoured to conceal the fact that she owed her excellent education to Marie Antoinette, and gave herself airs far above those to which a member of a poor Corsican family could pretend. Nevertheless, in the previous May she had married Felice Bacciochi, a Corsican landowner of little better birth than herself. This marriage, too, had infuriated her ambitious brother, as he had by then already established his Court at Montebello, and it had been contracted without his knowledge. However, Madame Letizia had been privy to the match and had sponsored it, from the belief that a solid Corsican with a little land would make Élise a better husband than some sprig of the Italian nobility selected for her by the General. Even so, he provided the Bacciochis with a house in the Grande Rue Verte and enabled them to entertain lavishly; but Élise showed him little gratitude and the ambitious intrigues that she conducted with considerable skill were often a cause of annoyance to him.

Louis, some eighteen months younger, came next. He was a mild, easy-going young man, lacking both the robust health and quick intelligence of his elder brothers. Yet he was the General's favourite, because he had been personally brought up by him. At the time when Napoleon was a near-penniless officer, studying at the Military College in Paris, he had sent for Louis, shared his attic with him, taught him at night by candlelight and made great sacrifices to clothe and feed him. At the age of seventeen Louis accompanied the General to Italy as one of his aides-de-camp and had acquitted himself creditably during the campaign. As he still held this appointment, Roger saw a lot of him.

Pauline was still only seventeen. She was the beauty of the family—gay, amusing and always surrounded by young men. She, too, had married in the previous summer, but a man of her brother's choice: the handsome young General Leclerc. She was Napoleon's favourite sister and, although like the others, ambitious and grasping, she showed him more affection and loyalty than they did. She and her husband were now installed in a house in the Rue de la Ville l'Évêque.

Caroline, aged fifteen, and Jerome, aged thirteen, were still completing their education. These two were as yet too young to have joined in the family feud; but the rest, however much they might quarrel about other matters, were united in one thing—their hatred of Josephine. The puritanical Madame Letizia considered her daughter-in-law little better than a whore, while the others were riddled with jealousy and intensely resented Josephine's failure to reprove flatterers who insinuated that as she was better born than Napoleon she had done him a favour by marrying him.

Since Josephine, between her two marriages, had sunk to the status of a titled *demi-mondaine*, dependent for money on such presents as her men friends gave her, and had been no longer received by ladies of good reputation, Roger appreciated the point of view of the Bonaparte family. But Josephine had always shown him such unfailing kindness that, without going so far as to champion her against her detractors, he endeavoured, whenever the opportunity arose, to make them think better of her.

In all the salons Roger attended the talk, when not concerned with the latest scandals, was of events in Italy and Switzerland. In the latter country the declaration by the Directory at the end of December that France would give her protection to the Republicans of the Vaudois had led to a general war. The mobs in Zürich, Basle and Geneva had taken up the agitation for equality. General Schaumberg was ordered to march a Division of the French Army of the Rhine into Switzerland, and General Brune another Division from the Army of Italy. The Bernese aristocracy had, meanwhile, told their people in the cantons that the French were bandits and atheists who would rob them and deprive them of their religion, upon which twenty thousand stalwart mountaineers banded together in defence of their property and beliefs.

Numerous bloody engagements followed and, unfortunately, the Swiss, having on two occasions been compelled to retreat, believed that they had been betrayed by their officers. So they murdered many of the best among them, including the Bernese General, Erlach. Compelled to give way before the disciplined assaults of the French, the Swiss patriots had fallen back on Berne. Women, old men and young boys heroically threw themselves on the bayonets of the enemy in an endeavour to defend the city, but to no avail. On March 5th, after a most bloody massacre, General Brune entered it as a conqueror.

Soon afterwards, having arbitrarily annexed the city of Geneva, the French renamed the Swiss Confederation, calling it the Helvetic Republic, and installed a Government on similar lines to that in France. They then set about realizing the intention which had inspired their unscrupulous decision to bring murder, misery and ruin to this peaceful people—namely, the systematic looting of the country from end to end.

While hundreds of priests were being dragged from their hiding places and shot, and bands of Christians who still resisted were being hunted through the mountains until they could be cornered and massacred, the French Commissioners were sending back to France millions of gold francs looted indiscriminately from the treasuries of the cities and the private savings of individuals.

These doings caused Bonaparte considerable anxiety, as France's unprovoked attack on the Swiss cantons had alarmed many of the German Princes. With good reason they felt apprehensive that they might become the next victims of the rapacious Republic and that their best means of protecting their territories lay in combining their forces under the leadership of Austria and urging the Emperor to renew the war against France. A fresh outbreak of hostilities on the Continent would have led to many of the best regiments, which Bonaparte had earmarked for his Egyptian expedition, being sent to the Rhine. That was the very last thing he wanted; so he was doing his utmost to restrain the republican belligerency of the Directors and manœuvre them into taking steps calculated to reassure the Germans.

Nevertheless, no man was more guilty of this bloody plundering of a nation than Bonaparte. When in Italy he had already been dreaming of himself as the Conqueror of the East and, without disclosing their object, making certain preparations which would facilitate his great design. One had been to send a million francs to the authorities at Toulon, to enable them to repair certain warships and thus strengthen the Fleet he would need to escort his transports. On learning of this the Directors had promptly seized the million for their own use. Angry as he was, Bonaparte had not at that time felt himself strong enough to join issue with them; so the warships remained unfit to put to sea.

Then, on his return from Italy via Switzerland, he had seen the wealth of the latter country and decided that she should pay for fitting out his armada. It was he who had conferred in Berne with the Swiss agitator Peter Ochs, encouraging him to create disturbances at the head of mobs calling for 'Liberty', and promising him the protection of France. He well knew that intervention would automatically be followed by conquest and a stream of Swiss gold flowing to Paris.

Now that he was in Paris he knew that the Directors would think twice before they dared to countermand any measures he took, and he was complacently reaping the fruits of his infamy. Roger had seen a letter from him that was to be despatched to Lannes, who had been sent to serve under Brune in Switzerland. In this letter Bonaparte instructed the Brigadier to have three millions of the stolen gold sent at once to Toulon.

Meanwhile in Rome things had been going far from well. Berthier's entry into the city on February 13th had been the signal for the Republican leaders there to raise the mobs against the nobility and the Vatican. Berthier, installed in the Castle of St. Angelo, overawed the Papal troops and so ensured the rabble a free hand. Two days later, amid scenes of great excitement, the Pope was deprived of his temporal powers by public acclamation and Rome was proclaimed a Republic.

Bonaparte, although in Paris, was still technically General-in-Chief of the Army of Italy, and it was he who had sent Berthier his orders. On receiving them, the ugly little Chief-of-Staff had replied, 'In sending me to Rome you appoint me treasurer to the Army of England.' And he set about this welcome task in no uncertain manner.

The treasures that Bonaparte had blackmailed the Pope into yielding up the preceding year as the price of saving his city from occupation were a bagatelle when compared to the new plundering that Berthier and the French Commissioners undertook. They stripped the Vatican bare of its valuables and treated in a similar manner the scores of palaces of the Roman nobility, except in such cases where their owners could raise huge sums to bribe those who ordered the looting to refrain. Inside a month the French 'bringers of Liberty' had made off with no fewer than sixty million francs in gold and, in addition, works of art that in value equalled that sum.

Moreover, they had treated the eighty-year-old Pope Pius VI with revolting barbarity. He had consistently offered a passive resistance to their threats and extortions and refused to leave Rome. Thereupon the French Commissioner Haller had snatched his pastoral staff, torn his ring from his finger, bundled him forcibly into a carriage and sent him under guard to Siena, without baggage or attendants.

This violent act, and the sack of Rome, soon produced serious repercussions. Christians everywhere were horrified at the brutality shown to the aged Pontiff, and in many countries the feeling strengthened that the French Republic was a menace to civilization and must be fought and overcome.

Another result which the French had not foreseen arose from the distribution of the looted millions. No doubt a great part of them reached the Directory; but Berthier, his Generals and the Commissioners retained great fortunes for themselves, whereas the junior officers and troops were given little or nothing. Resentment at having done the work while their superiors strutted about smothered in stolen jewels led to serious unrest in the Army.

Berthier, sensing trouble from the petitions presented by his ill-paid, half-starved troops, promptly retired to the Cisalpine, leaving General Masséna in command in Rome. No sooner had Berthier departed than a mutiny broke out. During the Italian campaign Masséna had shown himself to be one of Bonaparte's most able Generals, but his courage in the face of troops refusing to obey orders did not equal that he had displayed on the battlefield. He, too, promptly left Rome, handing over his Command to an unfortunate junior General named Dallemagne. Upon this the workers of Rome, by then disillusioned about the benefits of 'Liberty' brought to them by the French, rose in revolt and attempted to drive the French Army from the city.

In northern Italy the indignation at the behaviour of the French in Rome was intense, and the Councils of the Cisalpine Republic refused to ratify a treaty that their envoy had been bullied into signing in Paris. By this treaty they would have had to support twenty-five thousand French troops, make a big contribution to the French war loan and virtually bind themselves to France as a satellite. All classes were now regretting bitterly that they had thrown off the light yoke of Austria to replace it with a tyranny that respected neither God, honour, property nor morals, and the people were ripe for an attempt to drive out the French. On March 20th Berthier's troops purged the Councils, forced their rump to sign the treaty and overawed the populace with their cannon. Thus the Cisalpine Republic was robbed of the independence guaranteed it by the Treaty of Camp Formio; but it remained a cauldron seething with unrest.

In April there came trouble in Vienna. At Rastatt Austria had agreed to cede to France the left bank of the Rhine, but the uncouth brigands sent to the Conference by the Directory as its representatives were behaving in such an aggressive and high-handed manner that, angered by their gratuitous insults, the German plenipotentiaries had come near to refusing to continue the negotiations.

The Directory then poured fuel on the fire by sending as its Ambassador to Vienna General Bernadotte. No choice could have been worse, as he was an unscrupulous, fierce tempered Garçon and a red-hot revolutionary. His Division had been sent from the Rhine to reinforce Bonaparte's Army in Italy, and several score of his officers and N.C.O.s had fought duels with their compatriots rather than submit to Bonaparte's innovation that the term 'Citoyen' should be dropped and the old form of address, 'Monsieur' be revived.

Now, to flaunt his revolutionary principles in the face of the Viennese, Bernadotte, on the eve of a patriotic festival, displayed an enormous tricolour flag over the gate of the Embassy. The Viennese were so furious that they tore the flag down and threatened to burn the mansion about his ears. He declared that the French Republic had been insulted, demanded his passports and returned to Paris, thus bringing the two countries once again to the brink of war.

In was only on April 12th—three days before the incident in Vienna—that Bonaparte had at last succeeded in getting from the Directory a definitive directive for his expedition. In brief, it was that he should take possession of Egypt, chase the English from all their possessions in the East that he could reach, establish bases in the Red Sea, have the Isthmus of Suez cut through and, as far as he could, maintain good relations with the Sultan of Turkey.

His fury, therefore, can be imagined when news arrived of Bernadotte's provocation of the Austrians, with the renewed threat that another outbreak of war in Europe might, at the eleventh hour, prevent his carrying out his cherished design. For a few hours his future hung in the balance; but by a combination of tact, sound reasoning and browbeating he succeeded in persuading the Directors to swallow the insult to the French flag, thus preventing a resumption of hostilities.

Although the object of the expedition continued to be a closely guarded secret, the fact that a great force was assembling in the Mediterranean ports, under French control, could no longer be concealed. From Marseilles right round to Civitavecchia every ship was being examined for seaworthiness, repaired when necessary and listed with the number of troops she could carry. Picked regiments from all quarters were also on the march, converging on the ports, and vast quantities of supplies were being sent to them.

Bonaparte worked tirelessly, often for more than eighteen hours a day, dictating hundreds of letters and personally supervising the ordering of the smallest details. Berthier, whom he had recalled from Italy, worked even longer hours. People might laugh behind Berthier's back at his vanity and his assumption that brilliant uniforms could disguise his ugliness, but he had a capacity for work which no other Staff officer could rival. He could carry on at a time of crisis for three or four days without any sleep at all, and his memory for facts and figures concerning the Army was prodigious.

From the latter part of March, Roger and his fellow aides-de-camp had little leisure. As the chosen band who, with a few of Bonaparte's most trusted Generals, were alone in the great secret, they were called on to carry out a thousand errands needing firmness coupled with discretion. By the end of April the General-in-Chief's demands on them had increased to such an extent that they had to forgo all social activities and were lucky if they could drop into their beds by the early hours of the morning.

On May 1st Roger and several other Staff officers quietly left Paris. On May 9th Bonaparte joined them in Toulon. Everything was now in readiness. The expedition had by then been organized as four sections. The largest, concentrated on Toulon and Marseilles, was under Bonaparte's personal command. Another from Genoa under Baraguay d'Hilliers, a third under General Vaubois, was to sail from Ajaccio, and the fourth under Desaix from Civitavecchia.

When united, the armada would consist of thirteen ships-of-the-line, fourteen frigates, seventy-four smaller war vessels and between three and four hundred transports. On board there were some forty thousand troops, ten thousand seamen and several hundred civilians whom Bonaparte had decided, for a variety of reasons, to take. The Senior Naval Officer was Admiral Brueys; but he had been placed under the orders of the General-in-Chief, who accepted full responsibility for the direction of the expedition.

For some weeks rumours had been rife about the destination of this great concentration of troops and shipping. Some people believed that the intention was to seize the Sultan's dominions in Europe and free the Greeks and other Christians from the Mohammedan yoke. Others thought that the armada would sail round the Cape of Good Hope to wrest India from the British. A few rightly guessed that its objective was Egypt. But the majority were of the opinion that it was to be a follow-up, on a far greater scale than had ever before been attempted, of the old plan to land an Army in Ireland.

On arriving in Toulon, Bonaparte gave added credence to this last belief by a stirring proclamation addressed to his troops in which he termed them the 'Left Wing of the Army of England', the inference being that the right wing had mustered in the Channel ports and that, when the two French Fleets had united to destroy that of Britain, both Armies would descend on the hated English.

Bad weather delayed the sailing and, during the days of waiting, Josephine, who had accompanied her husband to Toulon, begged him repeatedly to allow her to sail with him. She argued that since she had been brought up in Martinique she would find the heat of Egypt pleasant rather than exhausting. Feeling that her presence would distract his thoughts he refused, but at length relented to the extent of agreeing that she should follow him in a few weeks' time.

On May 19th the bad weather at last abated, so it was decided to put to sea. Roger, with the rest of Bonaparte's Staff, was in the hundred-and-twenty-gun *L'Orient*, the largest warship afloat. In the great ship were also most of the senior Generals and a considerable number of distinguished intellectuals whom Bonaparte was taking with him to unravel some of the mysteries of the East. Roger had been allocated a bunk in a fairly spacious cabin, which he shared with three other aides-de-camp, and it was quite near to that which had been given to Bourrienne.

Shortly before anchor was weighed Roger looked in on the *Chef de Cabinet*, who had already settled down to work.

Glancing up at him, as he stood in the narrow doorway, Bourrienne handed him a paper and said, 'What d'you think of this? I received it only as the last crates of chickens were being hoisted aboard.'

It was an intelligence report and read:

Government in London still believed to credit Deception Plan and assume armament assembling in Mediterranean ports has as object (1) combination with Brest Squadron and Army of the North for descent on England or (2) possibly invasion of Ireland. Reliable information recently received that on April 20th Cabinet decided to send powerful squadron into Mediterranean with object of intercepting French expedition before it can enter Atlantic and combine with Franco-Spanish forces there. Above now confirmed by squadron detached from Lord St. Vincent's fleet passing Straits of Gibraltar under command of Rear Admiral Sir Nelson.

Roger had been wondering when he would manage to get back from Egypt. As he returned the intelligence report to Bourrienne, he began to wonder if he would even get there.

9

'Who wouldn't be a Soldier, ah! It's a shame to take the pay'

THE activities in the Mediterranean ports during the past two months had been so exceptional that Roger had felt certain that news of them could not have failed to reach the British Government. But it came as a surprise to him to learn that, after having been compelled to withdraw from the Mediterranean eighteen months before, the British should again have taken the initiative.

He promptly reasoned that the assumption in the intelligence report—that the British Government still credited the Deception Plan—was wrong and that, although he had been unable to send home information of the expedition's destination, they had learned from some other source that Bonaparte intended to invade Egypt. Otherwise, surely St. Vincent would have waited until the French armada was well out into the Atlantic and so far more vulnerable to attack.

In any case, it was incapable of defending itself against a strong British Squadron; and Admiral Brueys had made no secret of it to Bonaparte's Staff that, should he be attacked, he was far from happy about his chances of convoying the Army safely to its objective. The French Navy was still suffering seriously from the effects of the Revolution. During that time nine-tenths of its experienced officers had either been sent to the guillotine or gone into exile and all offences still had to be tried by jury, which meant that discipline was almost non-existent. Three of the battleships were old and rotten, many of the transports were barely seaworthy, cables and sails were of poor quality, much of the equipment was badly worn and there were very few spares of any kind. In consequence, if an Admiral with the dash and determination of Nelson came up with the armada the result must be a massacre.

As an Englishman, Roger was naturally pleased to learn that there was now a good prospect of his country gaining a resounding victory and destroying the flower of the French Army at one blow. However, as he was at present with that Army and in a ship from which there was no possible means of escape, he had to face the unnerving fact that he might well be destroyed himself.

Actually his fears were, for the time being, groundless; for Nelson had entered the Mediterranean a few days earlier, with only three ships-of-the-line and five smaller craft, his instructions being to reconnoitre the French coast and, if possible, find out the intended destination of Bonaparte's armada. This latter fact was not, as Roger supposed, known to the British. It was not until some days later that Earl St. Vincent received orders from London to send a strong Squadron into the Mediterranean and despatched, to come under Nelson's command, a further fourteen ships-of-the-line, whose Captains were some of the ablest officers in the British Navy.

Moreover, when the armada had been only one day at sea a tempest sprang up and, while the French Fleet escaped with a severe tossing, Nelson's ships were caught in the centre of the storm. His own ship was dismasted and he had to take refuge under the lee of Sardinia to refit, thus losing his first chance of intercepting the French expedition.

Roger was seasick, as he usually was in bad weather; but even his miserable condition did not prevent his constantly coming up on deck to gaze anxiously in all directions, fearing at any time that Nelson's ships would appear on the horizon, heralding for him the horrible possibility of being killed or drowned within the next few hours.

When, after some days, the weather improved he was able to distract his mind from his fears somewhat by mingling with his fellow-passengers, and rarely can such a galaxy of brains, talent and gallantry have been assembled for a long voyage in one ship. Bonaparte was taking to Egypt Kléber, Desaix, Bon, Menou and Reynier as his Divisional Commanders; Alexandre Dumas to command the cavalry, Dommartin the artillery and Caffarelli the engineers; Lannes as Quartermaster-General, Berthier as Chief-of-Staff and fourteen other Generals, including Marmont and Pauline's husband Leclerc. Murat, Junot, Davoust, Bessières, Rapp, Savary, Duroc and Eugéne de Beauharnais were also included. All of them were to win glory and ten of them were destined to become Princes, Dukes and Marshals of the Empire.

Many of these *beaux sabreurs* sailed with Bonaparte in the mighty *L'Orient*. Also on board were Monge, Berthollet, Denon and a number of other distinguished intellectuals. Even Bonaparte's triumphs in Italy had given him scarcely more pleasure than having been elected to the Institute on his return to Paris. So proud was he of the honour that he even signed his letters, ' Member of the Institute and General-in-Chief '. His interest in science was hardly less than that in military affairs, and his intention was that, while he conquered Egypt, these civilian members of his entourage should delve into the secrets of the past and bring France honour by revealing to the world much that was still unknown about the ancient civilizations of the East.

To assist them in their labours and for employment with the Army, Bonaparte had enrolled a considerable number of interpreters who spoke Arabic, Turkish or Greek; and in the hold of *L'Orient* there lay several printing presses, with founts of type in these languages, so that declarations and propaganda could be printed without delay.

Roger had a flair for languages and on his long voyage to India in '96 he had learned Persian—the diplomatic language of the East—from one of the India Company's officials. Then, on his return to Europe, via the Red Sea, he had mastered colloquial Arabic. Now he took the opportunity to brush up his Arabic by spending an hour or two each day with one of the interpreters, and also learned from him a few phrases of Turkish.

The main convoy from Toulon and Marseilles sailed first to Genoa then to Corsica, to pick up its other contingents, but it failed to make contact with the fourth flotilla which had assembled at Civitavecchia. It was not until they were off Malta that Desaix succeeded in reporting with it.

Owing partly to contrary winds, and partly to the difficulty of keeping together such a great number of ships, the speed of the armada averaged only fifty miles a day; so it was nearly three weeks later, and June 9th, before they sighted the island stronghold that had for centuries been held by the Knights of St. John of Jerusalem.

Bonaparte had declared when he was in Italy that any Power holding Corfu and Malta could control the Mediterranean. Already nurturing secret designs against the East, he had robbed Venice of the Ionian Isles, after installing a French garrison in Corfu by a shabby trick. For Malta then being beyond his military orbit, he had resorted to other methods. A certain M. Poussielgue, who was Secretary of the French Legation in Genoa, had relatives living in Malta. Learning this, Bonaparte sent for him and despatched him on a mission to the island, ostensibly to increase its trade with France, but secretly to undermine the discipline of the Knights and bribe a number of them.

The Knights' original function had been to protect pilgrims on their way to the Holy Land; but with the ending of the Crusades this duty fell into abeyance, so the Knights had undertaken that of protecting Christian shipping in the Mediterranean from the Barbary pirates who infested the coast of North Africa. However, for more than a century past they had become decadent, leading a life of luxurious ease and licentiousness. The only vessels they now possessed were a few half-rotten warships that never put to sea and some gaily painted galleys that they used for water festivals.

On arriving before Valetta, Bonaparte asked permission for his Feet to enter the great harbour to take on water. The Grand Master replied that by custom only two warships of any nation were allowed into the harbour at one time. Bonaparte then summoned the island to surrender and ordered Admiral Brueys to begin bombarding the forts.

These were immensely strong and Valetta had long been regarded as impregnable. It could certainly have withstood a siege for many weeks. But Poussielgue had done his work well. Only a few cannon were fired in reply. The French Knights betrayed their Order and led the native Maltese, who were little better than their slaves, in a revolt which put an end to further resistance. So in a single day the Conqueror of Italy became the master of one of the greatest strongholds in Europe.

Yet he and France were soon to pay dearly for this cheaply bought victory. Fearing an aggression that they were too supine to resist on their own, the Knights had recently offered the Grand Mastership of their Order to Paul I of Russia. The Czar, in due course, joyfully accepted, as he saw in Malta a naval base which would be invaluable to him in his ambition to dismember the Empire of Russia's hereditary enemies, the Turks. With childish vanity he began preening himself in the colourful robes of a Grand Master as the champion of Christendom. When he learned that Bonaparte had robbed him of the romantic role which he had expected to play his anger knew no bounds and from that moment he became one of France's most deadly enemies.

Bonaparte stayed only seven days in Malta, but during that time he carried out as many reforms as would have taken most administrators a long term of office. He abolished the Order, compensated the French Knights, gave the people a Constitution, revised the taxes, customs and octroi dues, ordered certain streets to be broadened and public fountains to be installed, decreed a new curriculum for the university and reorganized the hospitals and the post-office. In addition, he naturally suppressed the religious houses, stole their funds and made off with all the bullion, jewelled chalices, crucifixes and other treasure he could lay his hands on. Only the solid silver gates at the Church of St. John escaped him because they happened to have been painted over.

With a Republican Government installed under a French military dictator, and the pillaging of Valetta completed, the armada sailed again, this time for Egypt. Life in *L'Orient* was resumed on the lines it had taken soon after the departure from Toulon. On Bonaparte's instructions Bourrienne had selected a considerable library of books for him to read on the voyage. Knowing his master's tastes, the *Chef de Cabinet* had included a hundred and twenty-five volumes of history both ancient and modern, the best of the Roman poets, the masterpieces of the French theatre, a few books of travel and some forty novels, most of which were translations from the English. To complete this comprehensive assortment he had added a Bible, a Koran, the Vedas and several other books dealing with Eastern customs and religions.

Bonaparte showed particular interest in these last, as he was anxious to familiarize himself with the ways of the people in the countries he intended to conquer. For the greater part of each day he lay on the bed in his big cabin engrossed in these books or in accounts of the campaigns of Caesar, Hannibal, Marlborough and Louis XIV. But every evening he summoned to his cabin a selected company with whom he carried on animated discussions far into the night. In his insatiable thirst for knowledge he bombarded the savants with an endless stream of questions on an immense variety of subjects, and often propounded some debatable philosophical or religious belief for the pleasure of seeing them argue hotly about it.

Off Crete, those aboard the armada remained blissfully ignorant that it had been missed by Nelson by only a matter of hours; but when approaching Egypt the frigate *Junon* was sent on ahead to Alexandria, and returned with the alarming news that the British Squadron had put in there the previous day. Roger again began to scan the horizon with acute anxiety, but the General-in-Chief showed no trace of dismay. He ordered Admiral Brueys to continue on course, and his lucky star was in the ascendant. Nelson, having revictualled his Fleet at Naples, had guessed that Bonaparte's probable destination was Egypt, so he had made all sail there. Not finding the enemy he had turned north, now believing that the French had made their landing in Syria. On July 1st, the topmasts of his ships disappeared below one horizon only as those of the French armada began to appear over the other.

The French Consul at Alexandria, who had been taken on board the *Junon*, declared that any attempt to enter the harbour would certainly be opposed, so Bonaparte ordered sail to be set again for Marabout, some nine miles along the coast. It was nightfall when they arrived there, the hundreds of transports were scattered over many square miles of sea, and a gale had arisen driving them on to a lee shore. Nevertheless, the General-in-Chief gave orders for an immediate landing. Brueys protested that such an attempt would be suicidal; but Bonaparte, now harassed by the thought that at any hour Nelson might return and catch him at a terrible disadvantage, overruled his Admiral and was the first to step into a boat.

A night ensued of desperate effort, terror, and death for many. The shore of the creek was lined with reefs upon which the sea broke furiously. The howling wind frequently drove the boats from their course or piled them up on rocks. Bonaparte had brought only a limited number of horses, counting on mounting the bulk of his cavalry on animals procured in Egypt, but it was important to land a few dozen for scouts and despatch riders. The poor brutes were lowered by slings into the heaving sea, and men in the boats then grabbed their bridles to tow them ashore.

Terrified and, except for their heads, totally submerged, many of the horses dragged the men from the boats so that they drowned with them, but others swam gamely and survived the ordeal. In the darkness on the beach there was hopeless confusion. The night was cold and everyone was drenched to the skin, yet Bonaparte would not allow any attempt to form a camp. By dawn he had some five thousand troops ashore and ordered an immediate advance on Alexandria.

Wet, cold and hungry, but inspired by his indomitable purpose, his soldiers began their first march across the sands of Egypt. The horses so far landed were so few and in such poor shape that he and his Generals marched with the men. On their way they were fired on by a few mounted Arabs, but no serious resistance was offered until by mid-morning they came within musket shot of the walls of the city, beyond which rose the domes of mosques and the slender towers of minarets.

There he divided his force into three columns. One was to be led by Bon against the Rosetta Gate, another by Kléber against the Gate of the Pillar and the third by Menou against the Gate of the Catacombs. The Turkish garrison maintained a steady fire with both muskets and antiquated cannon, whereas the French had so far been unable to land any of their artillery. But now, suffering for the first time under a blazing sun from acute thirst, their desperate need for water inspired them with a fierce determination to break into the city. After a number of bloody assaults, in which both Kléber and Menou were seriously wounded, they forced a breach in the crumbling walls, poured through it and drove the defenders back in confusion through the narrow streets.

A Turkish Captain who had been captured realized that further resistance was useless, and offered to act as intermediary. Bonaparte then produced a proclamation which he had prepared and sent him with it to his Commander. In this proclamation the wily Corsican declared that the French had come only to liberate the Egyptian people from the tyranny of the Mamelukes and prevent their further depredations on French commerce. He guaranteed respect for property and the Mohammedan religion —pointing out that it was France that had destroyed the Pope and the Knights of Malta, who had for centuries waged war on the Muslims—and promised to support the Sheiks, Cadis and Imams in a continuance of their duties to the glory of the Sultan.

These specious promises had the desired effect. A cease-fire was ordered and by four o'clock that afternoon he was master of Alexandria.

Yet when the French Army took possession of the city the troops were bitterly disappointed. Thousands of them were veterans of Bonaparte's Italian campaign, during which they had lined their pockets and had hoped, on returning to France, to buy pleasant farms or little businesses and settle down to a peaceful life of domesticity. Thousands of others were conscripts who had been forced to leave their homes in order that regiments might be brought up to full strength. The reluctance on the part of both veterans and conscripts to leave France had been over-come after the armada had sailed by a rumour put about amongst them that they were on their way to the East, where riches were inexhaustible, and that every man of them would return with a fortune.

Now, as they marched through the streets of the ancient city where Cleopatra had ruled in splendour, and which had been famous for centuries for its luxury, they saw only half-ruined mosques, palaces long since fallen into disrepair and squalid slums inhabited by poverty-stricken people.

This was no surprise to Roger, as he had spent several days in Alexandria during the previous July. He knew that, apart from the residences of the Mameluke Beys, the only well-furnished, comfortable houses were those occupied by Greek merchants in the so-called ' new town ' which lay outside the city.

One of them was the property of a Greek banker named Sarodopulous, who had been most helpful to Roger and, more-over, had him invited to stay until he could get a passage to Crete. This now presented Roger with a problem, as he had been travelling as an Englishman and Sarodopulous's principal reason for entertaining him so hospitably was because Mrs. Sarodopulous had been born an Englishwoman. If Bonaparte remained long in Alexandria it seemed highly probable that, since the banker was one of the town's wealthiest citizens, he and Roger would meet; and the Greek was going to be very surprised at finding that the Englishman he had entertained had in a few months been trans-formed into a French Colonel.

The thought of such a meeting did not cause Roger any great anxiety because, unlike Talleyrand and the despicable Fouché— who appeared to have sunk into oblivion—the Sarodopulouses

F

had only the story he had given them himself to go on. He could, therefore, simply repudiate it; and, should Bonaparte learn of the encounter, he would accept without question Roger's explanation that while in Alexandria he had posed as an Englishman in order to secure as much information as he could about the enemies of France.

Now that the Army of Egypt had established itself on land, Roger knew that he was likely to be very fully employed. His appointment by Bonaparte as his Aide-de-Camp-in-Chief had, of course, not matured, as the appointment had been dependent on the invasion of England and had been announced only as one of many little bluffs which would help give credence to the deception plan. But Bonaparte's reason for making Roger one of his aides-de-camp when in Italy had been because he was already dreaming of conquering the East and, as Roger had just returned from travelling in India and Egypt, he had decided that an old companion-in-arms with such experience would be of value to him on his Staff.

As usual, the General-in-Chief lost no time in putting to use any asset he had secured and that morning, much to Roger's relief, he had kept him out of the battle, but told him to arrange for suitable quarters as soon as the city surrendered.

It was Géraud Duroc, one of Roger's companions in Italy, who now held the appointment of Aide-de-Camp-in-Chief. He was a Republican and puritan but a man whose gentle charm made him beloved by all, and he now lived only to serve Bonaparte. Roger set off with him and an escort from Bonaparte's pet regiment of Guides and in the course of an hour they visited several palaces. Had Roger been in his master's shoes he would have taken up his quarters in one of the fine villas in the ' new town ', but he knew that the General-in-Chief would be extremely angry if he were not installed in one of the most imposing buildings in the city. There was also the point that he had given strict instructions that there was to be no pillaging and that the inhabitants were to be put to a minimum of inconvenience in accommodating his troops. They were, therefore, fortunate in finding a palace owned by a wealthy Pasha who had fled with his family on learning of the approach of the invaders.

Roger did all the talking, while Duroc made certain suggestions about the allocation of rooms for various purposes. The water carts were sent for, so that there would be ample for all purposes, extra divans brought in for junior members of the Staff and a lavish supply of food procured from the nearest market. In due course Bonaparte arrived with his entourage. They ate a hearty meal then, utterly exhausted from their night and day of strenuous effort, threw themselves, still in their clothes, on the divans and slept.

Soon after Roger awoke next morning his mind turned again to Sarodopulous. He decided that it would be sound policy to go to see the banker and give an explanation to him in private, rather than leave their meeting to chance when the odds were that other people would be present.

Immediately they had broken their fast Bonaparte set to work with Bourrienne, and kept all his aides-de-camp hurrying hither and thither on a score of errands; but during the morning Roger managed to get a word with Lannes and offered his help to the harassed Quartermaster-General in one of that functionary's most important responsibilities. Lannes gave the idea his blessing and passed him on to Andréossi, who readily accepted the proposal. That evening Roger got his master's permission to ride out to the 'new town'.

Sarodopulous's handsome white villa had a terrace on the seaward side with a splendid view over the beautiful bay and as Roger trotted up the road he saw the banker sitting alone on the terrace; so, instead of riding round to the front door of the villa and having himself announced, he dismounted, hitched his horse to a stone pillar and walked up the steps.

As he approached the table at which Sarodopulous was sitting, the banker stood up, eyeing Roger's uniform with some apprehension. Then his dark eyes opened wide and he exclaimed in English:

'Why! If it isn't Mr. Brook.'

'Colonel Breuc, aide-de-camp to the General-in-Chief of the Army of Egypt,' replied Roger, keeping his face expressionless as he made a formal bow.

'But . . . but . . .' stammered the Greek.

With a laugh, Roger held out his hand. 'But the same person to whom you extended much kindness when last in Alexandria. You will recall that I came to your office to cash a draft on Hoare's bank. As it was drawn on London and I am bilingual, you naturally took me for an Englishman; then, your wife being English, you invited me to become your guest. I had travelled for

many months and was positively starved for civilized society, so
I gave way to the temptation to accept your hospitality under
false pretences. I can only hope that you will not think too harshly
of me.'

Sarodopulous stroked his greying, curly beard and smiled.
'Why, no. Since you had come all the way from India, with only
Asiatics for companions, I can understand how you must have
felt. Personally, too, it would have made no difference to me had
you declared yourself a Frenchman. As an international banker,
my relations with French and British merchants are equally
good. But I fear my poor wife would not have agreed to receive
you.'

'Do you . . .' Roger's face suddenly became grave, 'do you
mean . . . ? '

The Greek nodded. 'Alas, yes. Last January. You will recall
her fondness for the pleasures of the table. Nothing could
restrain her, and her weight became too much for her heart.
Going upstairs one evening . . . I miss her greatly, but it is some
consolation to me that it was all over very quickly.'

Roger well remembered the enormous bulk that the one-time
Suffolk girl had acquired from her love of rich foods, and the
gargantuan meals she had pressed upon him. Sorry as he was
for Sarodopulous, he could not help feeling some relief at her
demise, as she had remained fanatically patriotic and he had
feared that she would prove an awkward stumbling block in his
resuming good relations with the banker. Having expressed his
sympathy with the bereaved husband he went on:

'You will, no doubt, have been informed of General Bonaparte's proclamation, announcing that the French have come to
Egypt only to drive out the Mameluke tyrants and that they wish
to establish most cordial relations with the Egyptian people. He
does not, therefore, come here as a robber, but intends to pay for
the great quantity of supplies he will need for his Army. To do
so we shall require large sums of local currency. Having in mind
your past kindness to me, and knowing you to be an honest
broker, I had a talk with General Andréossi this morning. As our
Paymaster-General he will be responsible for obtaining Egyptian
money in exchange for gold. On my recommendation he has
agreed that you should be appointed our principal agent.'

Sarodopulous's dark eyes opened wide, and he exclaimed,
'But Mr. . . . I mean Colonel Breuc, how can I ever thank you!

I give you my word that General Andréossi shall have the best rate of exchange that can be procured in Alexandria. Yet, even so, to act as agent for the French Army will bring me a fortune. But come; we are still standing. Be pleased to sit down while I order wine. Then you must tell me about yourself and this amazing General on whose Staff you are. And you will honour me, I hope, by staying to supper.'

For the next hour Roger said little of his own doings, but talked freely about other matters, and gave a graphic description of the hazardous landing of the Army. He was then introduced to the banker's widowed sister-in-law and her son Achilles, who had been living with him since his wife's death. This Greek lady must have been a beauty when young. in spite of her face being somewhat marred by smallpox, and her son—a tall, well-built young man of about twenty-five, who had recently been made a partner in the family firm—was strikingly handsome. After a most excellent meal with these charming and intelligent Greeks, Roger rode back to the old city, well content with the outcome of his visit.

The following day proved another of feverish activity at Bonaparte's headquarters. Having sent for Sheik Koraim and other principal officials of the city, he spoke at great length of the benefits the French Republic was bringing to the world through its systematic destruction of all tyrants, and particularly the religious tyranny long wielded by Rome and her Christian priests. He even went so far as to say that he personally thought more highly of the Mohammedan faith, and quoted at them extracts from the Koran that he had learned by heart during the voyage.

Roger, who was present at this performance, thought it unlikely that the Sheiks and Imams would believe in the sincerity of these statements; but they were at least favourably impressed and willingly agreed to form a new Council to maintain order in the city and to co-operate with the French military authorities.

To have gained their goodwill was an important asset, as Bonaparte intended to push on as soon as possible to Cairo and he could afford to leave only a limited garrison in Alexandria. He would, however, have probably secured it without great difficulty in any case, owing to the very exceptional conditions maintaining in Egypt.

The country had for long been a part of the Turkish Empire

and, in theory, was ruled by a Pasha appointed by the Sultan. But as Egypt was so far from Constantinople the Sultans had feared that one day an ambitious Viceroy might repudiate their authority and make himself Sultan of Egypt. To guard against such an eventuality they had appointed twenty-four Mameluke Beys, each with a following of several hundred men, to act as Governors of the provinces, independently of the Viceroy. In this they had been too clever, as it was the Beys who had repudiated the authority of Constantinople and had for centuries treated Egypt as a flight of vultures would have treated the carcass of a dead horse.

These Mamelukes formed a caste apart, dating from the time of Saladin. They were fair-skinned, often blue-eyed, Circassians, hand-picked as the handsomest and fittest small boys in the Caucasus, bought as slaves and shipped to Egypt. There they were brought up under the strictest discipline, and in ignorance of their origin, to the profession of arms. Each Bey owned five or six hundred of them, and each Mameluke had two native Copts to groom his horses and care for his weapons. They lived in camps and had no relations with the population, other than to plunder it at the order of their masters. They were magnificently equipped, the finest horsemen in the world and lived only for fighting. The Beys were far stronger than the Turkish garrison; so they treated the Sultan's officials with contempt, while terrorizing the Arabs and the wretched Copts who formed the greater part of the population. Often they fought among themselves for the control of greater areas of territory; and at this time two of them wielded authority over all the others. The elder, Ibrahim Bey, was crafty and powerful; his rival, Murad Bey, was valiant and ambitious.

So eager was Bonaparte to continue his conquest of the country that the remainder of his men, with the guns and horses he had brought, having been landed at Marabout on July 2nd, on the night of the 3rd he despatched Desaix's Division to Rahmaniyeh, about thirty miles up the Rosetta mouth of the Nile to act as advance guard of the Army. Any other General would have sent them up to the coast to Rosetta, then along the inhabited banks of the river, but that would have meant their marching nearly double the distance. So impatient was he that he ordered Desaix to head straight across the desert and Reynier's Division to follow the next day. On that day, too, he ordered Menou to march up the coast, capture Rosetta, form a flotilla there and proceed up the Nile to rendezvous with Desaix at Rahmaniyeh. On the 6th, having completed his arrangements in Alexandria, he left the wounded Kléber in command of three thousand men to garrison the city and himself led the rest of the Army along the desert trail that the gallant Desaix had blazed.

During the next few days Roger's worst forebodings were nearly realized. The reports already sent back by Desaix were harrowing. Scorched and blistered, his weary men were staggering across miles of shifting sands. They had met with no serious opposition, so it was evident that the Mameluke strategy was to draw them as far as possible into the desert before attacking; but during the march they were constantly pestered by Bedouin, who skirted the flanks and rear of the column, occasionally firing at it and falling upon and butchering all stragglers.

Fear of these Arabs was the main factor that kept the column together, for the suffering of the men from thirst was terrible and, as discipline had gone to pieces, small parties of them would have blundered off in all directions in a desperate search for water. Every well they came to had been filled in with sand by the Arabs, and even when they had frantically cleared away the sand there was not enough water in the holes to quench the thirst of more than a few dozen of them. Reynier's Division, following a day's march behind, suffered even worse, for on arriving at well after well they found them completely dry.

On the 7th both Divisions reached Damanhûr. They had been told that it was one of the largest towns in Lower Egypt, but found it to be only a huddle of tumble-down houses and mud huts, enclosed with walls that were falling to pieces. There was not sufficient food in the place to be worth commandeering, and they had nearly exhausted the hard biscuit they had brought with them from Alexandria. Almost at the end of their tether, they took such consolation as they could from the small ration of water that was available and the palm and pomegranate groves outside the town, which provided the first blissful shade they had encountered since starting on their terrible march.

The General-in-Chief caught up with them there on the following day, and the march of the other Divisions which accompanied him had been no less gruelling. Their route had lain along a canal dating from the Roman occupation. Having been abandoned for fifteen hundred years it was now no more than a series of

elongated depressions, which filled with water each year only
when the Nile flooded. As that took place in August or September,
and this was July, the very little water left in it lay in small,
stagnant pools, overgrown with moss and alive with horrible
insects. In spite of that, every time the men sighted one of these
greenish patches they rushed down to it and fought among themselves for the temporary relief afforded to those who succeeded
in getting their mouths into the brackish filth and sucking it
up.

There were water and cooks' carts with the Headquarters
Staff, but after the first day there was nothing to cook; so the
Staff also had to make do on hard biscuit. Bonaparte, ever a
father to his men, kept his officers on an absolute minimum of
water, so that all that could be spared should be given to wounded
or ailing soldiers.

Roger survived this nightmare trek in better shape than the
others. Knowing what he might be in for, he had abandoned all
his belongings except his weapons, so that he could take a dozen
water-bottles with him. Yet even so he suffered grievously, as
from dawn to dusk there was no protection from the blazing sun,
and he drank only sparingly so that he might share his wealth
in water with the worst stricken among his companions.

At Damanhûr they learned that Desaix had met with another
form of misfortune. In the desert at night there had been nothing
to which to tether the horses. A sentry had panicked and had
fired at what he believed to be Arabs, with the result that most
of the horses had bolted and in the pitch darkness it had proved
impossible to recapture them.

By this time the troops, who had been told that Egypt was
' more fertile than the plain of Lombardy ', and had been promised
six acres per man, were verging on mutiny. The officers, too, who
had become accustomed to rich living, openly showed sympathy
with them. Bonaparte was accused, even within his hearing, of
having wilfully deceived them and led them to their destruction.
Lannes and Murat, of all people, actually threw their Generals'
hats on the ground and stamped upon them in their fury of
disillusion and despair.

Yet the little Corsican rode out the storm. He was the only
man in his Army who appeared unaffected by the terrible heat.
Wearing the green uniform of his Guides, buttoned up to the
chin, he walked as often as he rode. To every complaint, whether

from officers or men, he made a swift, tart rejoinder, abusing them roundly for lack of faith, lack of stamina, lack of courage. His thin, bony frame rigid with indignation at their grumbling, his enormously broad jaw thrust out in unshakable determination, he forced them, by sheer will-power, to continue onward across the burning sands.

There followed two more appalling days, during which the main Army, now about thirty thousand strong, continued to stagger across the desert. Their only food now a few handfuls of corn per man, acquired in Damanhûr, and water was absolutely unobtainable, except for the few who carried a small hoarded supply. It had become literally worth its weight in gold, and the richer of the sufferers were offering those who had it *a louis d'or* for a small tin cupful.

The Bedouin continued to harass the column from its flanks and frustration added to the torments of the troops, for there was no ammunition apart from what each man carried, and that had to be husbanded against a pitched battle with the Mamelukes, so they were under strict orders not to return the Arabs' fire. Now and again men screamed with agony as they were stung by scorpions and a number of the weaker actually died of thirst or sunstroke.

At last, parched, blistered, their skin drawn taut over their cheek-bones and their eyes starting from their heads, they reached Rahmaniyeh and the Nile. Croaking and delirious, they swarmed down the bank to lap up the blessed water; some flung themselves fully clothed into the river and were drowned.

For a few days Bonaparte allowed the Army to rest at Rahmaniyeh. While there, its lot was somewhat ameliorated by limitless water and great quantities of both luscious water-melons and wheat, although there were no mills to grind the corn into flour. On the 13th, learning that the Mamelukes were massing further up the river, Bonaparte ordered a resumption of the march. On the following day they reached the village of Chebreïss.

There the Army had its first serious encounter with the enemy. Murad Bey had assembled some three thousand of his cavalry on the left bank of the river up which Bonaparte was advancing. The Bey had also posted forces of his auxiliaries on both banks and had brought seven Turkish gunboats down from Cairo. The French flotilla, that had come up from Rosetta under a naval officer named Perrée, had on board, in addition to the unmounted cavalry, all the non-military personnel, and had been ordered to keep pace with the march of the troops on land. However it got too far ahead, so was first in contacting the enemy, and was so roughly handled by the Turkish gunboats that it was forced to retreat.

Bonaparte then arrived on the scene with his five Divisions. Each was marching in a square, with infantry six deep on all sides, the artillery at the corners and such mounted men as there were in the centre. As the Mamelukes drew near, the squares halted in positions enabling them to support one another by flanking fire. In great clouds of dust, yelling like fiends, Murad's splendid cavalry charged the squares, first discharging their pistols, then waving aloft their flashing scimitars. But the disciplined fire of the French was a thing they had never before met. Many of them went down in the first charge, the remainder rode round the squares in confusion, small bodies of them attacking again and again with great bravery; but they were driven off and, after this one bloody encounter, they retired into the desert, having lost over three hundred men.

The French were greatly heartened, for they had withstood the terrible onslaught yet sustained very few casualties. But when the march was again resumed a renewal of their hardships caused fresh outbreaks of discontent. It began to be generally said that Bonaparte had allowed himself to be made a fool of by the Directors; that they had fired his imagination with lying tales about the riches of Egypt, in order to get rid of him; that the fabled Cairo did not exist, except perhaps as a collection of mud huts.

Now that they were marching up the bank of the Nile at least there was no shortage of water, and they could cool their weary bodies each evening by bathing in the river when the column halted. But the more water they drank the more they sweated, so that the dye from their uniforms began to stain their skins. Food for such numbers also continued to be a terrible problem, for meat was almost unobtainable and melons gave no sustenance. The only thing procurable in quantity was wheat, but there were neither mills to grind it nor ovens to bake it into bread; so they were reduced to pounding the grain on stones with their musket butts, making a mash by adding a little water and chewing the resulting uncooked mess.

The sands they trod seemed red hot. Out of a brassy sky the sun blazed down on their backs, myriads of flies appeared from nowhere and crawled over their sweating faces, the dust raised by thousands of marching feet choked and blinded them. Roger cursed the name of Talleyrand for having caused him to come on this ghastly expedition; the rest of the Army cursed that of Bonaparte.

On July 21st, after seven consecutive days of tramping through this living hell, they came in sight of the minarets of Cairo and the Pyramids. The city lay on the opposite bank of the river, the Pyramids some miles ahead of them and a little to the right. Between them and the triangular man-made mountains of stone lay Embabeh, a village that had been converted by the Mamelukes into a great, entrenched camp that ran down to the river bank. There, Murad Bey had mustered his whole force to give battle.

His rival, the crafty Ibrahim, had assembled his legions on the city side of the river. Later he said that he had expected the French to attack up both banks, but it was thought possible that he had hoped that Murad's men and Bonaparte's would each destroy so many of the others that he would become master of the situation without having fired a shot.

Nevertheless, even without his jealous compatriot, Murad's force was truly formidable. It consisted of not fewer than ten thousand Mameluke cavalry, their twenty thousand Coptic helots and several thousand Arab auxiliaries. In addition the Turkish Viceroy, refusing to believe Bonaparte's declaration that he had come to Egypt as the Sultan's friend only to oust the Mamelukes, had sent his Janissaries to Murad's aid.

The seething mass of helots had been armed and, twenty deep, formed a living barrier behind the shallow earthworks that had been thrown up in front of the village. At frequent intervals along the line were cannon, brought out from the city and manned by the Turks. The Arabs, on their racing camels, were stationed on the inland flank with their backs towards the Pyramids, ready to come in and massacre the wounded. In the centre, a mile-long host of the Mamelukes—the lineal descendants of Saladin's chivalry who had driven the Crusaders from the Holy Land—cavorted on their splendid Arab steeds, their bronze casques, scimitars and rich equipment glittering in the sun. Each man was armed with a pair of pistols and a dagger in his girdle, a second

pair of pistols in his saddle holsters, a battle-axe hanging from
the saddle and a scimitar ground to such sharpness that it would
cut a thread of silk.

The five Divisions of the French Army again advanced in
squares. That of Desaix on the extreme right faced the Pyramids.
Then came Reynier's; Dugua's was in the centre and those of
Vial and Bon were opposite Embabeh. The General-in-Chief and
his Staff occupied the middle of the centre square. Galloping up
and down, his eyes flashing with the light of battle, Bonaparte
strengthened the morale of his troops by crying to them,
'Soldiers! Remember that from the summit of the Pyramids
forty centuries look down upon you.'

While still out of cannon shot he then surveyed the enemy's
positions through his telescope. Noting that the Turkish guns
were fortress pieces without wheels, so could not be manœuvred
during the battle, he temporarily held back his left and ordered
his right to advance, with the object of outflanking Murad and
driving his cavalry back so that it should mask the Turkish
cannon. Desaix's Division, supported by Reynier's, went forward
at the quick step towards a cluster of palm trees with some mud
huts among them. But Murad proved no mean opponent. Realizing Bonaparte's intention, he launched eight thousand of his
cavalry upon the right flank of the French Army. Next moment
the ground shook to the hunder of thirty-two thousand hoof-
beats.

Officers who were there that day and lived to fight through all
Napoleon's campaigns afterwards declared that no cavalry charge
before or since ever equalled the onslaught of the Mamelukes.
The belief that those who die in battle go straight to the delights
of Allah's Paradise made them completely fearless. Although the
foremost fell by the hundred, mown down by the musket balls
and grape-shot from the guns of the French, the following ranks
leapt their horses over the great swathe of dead and dying and
flung their mounts and themselves upon the squares. They gave
no quarter and expected none. Yet their valour was in vain. The
French stood firm and neither square broke.

As the survivors wheeled away Desaix and Reynier advanced
to carry out the turning movement. Bonaparte then ordered Vial
and Bon to attack the entrenchments. Elated by their comrades'
heroic stand, the two Divisions formed column and streamed
forward cheering wildly. The Turkish cannon were old and ill-

aimed, several of them blew up. The enormous rabble of helots, the majority of whom were armed only with spears, flails and billhooks, read death in the fierce faces of the veterans of Italy. Flinging down their weapons, they fled. There ensued a massacre. Many of the remaining Mamelukes were driven in upon the terrified helots and, rather than surrender, at least a thousand of them rode their horses straight into the river where, weighed down by their heavy equipment, they were drowned.

The Battle of the Pyramids lasted barely half an hour. During it Bonaparte had sat his horse impassively in the centre of the square formed by Dugua's Division. He had not found it necessary to employ it. Not a man in it had done more than fire a few shots.

The loot collected from the corpses on the battlefield was enormous. The scimitars and daggers of the Mamelukes were beautifully chased and inlaid with gold, while many were set with precious stones. Their casques, girdles and the harness of their horses were also embellished with gems, and their pistols had silver barrels. As a protection against sabre cuts, each man was wrapped in layer after layer of rich silk shawls and, as they always carried their wealth with them, there were, in their saddle-bags, purses containing anything up to three hundred gold pieces. The French despoiled such dead as were to be seen and then for days afterwards fished in the river with stout hooks to draw up other bodies, for it was reckoned that on average the equipment of a Mameluke was worth ten thousand francs.

Bonaparte was naturally pleased that after the demands he had made on his men they should reap this rich reward, but he was even more pleased at the capture of many hundred magnificent horses on which to mount his cavalry, and about the same number of camels which would be useful for a baggage train. His casualties, too, had been amazingly light. Owing to the squares having held, only thirty men had been killed and some three hundred wounded.

The gallant Murad Bey had been wounded in the face but had succeeded in getting away a part of his Army, although their numbers were insufficient to menace the French further for the time being. Ibrahim Bey's force was still intact on the other side of the river and at present Bonaparte had not the means to cross it; so he decided to encamp at Ghizeh. There he occupied Murad's country house, a delightful airy mansion in which his Staff were surprised to find divans and scores of cushions covered in the finest damasks and silk from Lyons. In the cool of the evening they celebrated their victory in the beautiful garden which was planted with many ornamental trees and with vine-covered arbours on which hung grapes as fine as they had ever seen.

Meanwhile in Cairo anarchy had broken out. Ibrahim Bey, having no mind that his force should suffer the fate of Murad's, decided to retire towards Syria, and the Turkish Viceroy fled with him. Upon this the long-oppressed Copts streamed out of the slums and set about attacking the palaces and houses of the rich. Unlike Alexandria and the towns the French had so far seen, Cairo was a city with a population of three hundred thousand. Living there were hundreds of wealthy merchants of many nationalities, who owned fine mansions, big harems and scores of slaves. Finding themselves in peril of their lives, many of them mounted on camels and, with their households and most valuable possessions, endeavoured to escape the mobs by leaving the city. Others barricaded themselves in their houses and, with their retainers, strove to defend them. There ensued a night of terror, looting, rape and murder.

The following day the subordinate Pasha—left behind without instructions by the Turkish Viceroy—the leading European merchants and the Sheiks of the Mosque of Jamil-Ayer met together and agreed to save themselves by entering into negotiations with the French. Bonaparte, delighted to acquire the city without having to fight for it, received most graciously the deputation they sent to him, and terms of surrender were quickly agreed.

A number of boats were procured and on the 23rd General Dupuy was sent across the river with half a Brigade, to accept the formal surrender of the city. Roger accompanied him. He found the palaces of both Ibrahim and Murad had been partially looted and, considering the latter the finer of the two, he took possession of it for the General-in-Chief. With him he had brought the soldier who had acted as his servant since leaving Toulon, a cheerful young Provençal named Jean Marbois. Together they then looked round for accommodation that would suit Roger, should Bonaparte decide to make Cairo his headquarters for some time.

In a nearby street they found a pleasant but unpretentious three-storey house. The owner, an Arab merchant, had fled and his four servants were making merry there. Roger informed them sharply that he intended to occupy it and would employ them at the wage they had been receiving, but if they left the place he would have them hunted down and thrown into prison. Then he left Marbois in charge and returned across the river to make his report.

On the 25th Bonaparte entered Cairo and took up his residence in Murad's palace with Bourrienne, Duroc, Eugène de Beauharnais and several other members of his Staff. Meanwhile, Lannes had arranged suitable accommodation for the other senior officers and for billeting the troops in the now-empty barracks of the Janissaries and other large buildings.

As Cairo had surrendered it had, by the laws of war, escaped the horror of being given over to the troops to sack. Moreover, Bonaparte was most anxious to conciliate the Mohammedan citizens so he had ordained that their mosques, religious customs and their own laws were to be respected. All the same, to instil fear into any of the inhabitants who might be tempted to question the status of the French as their masters, in the principal square he had the heads lopped off of a score of those who had shown themselves to be unwilling hosts, and declared that, after all his soldiers had been through, it would be unreasonable to put too severe a restraint upon their enjoying a fair degree of licence during their first few nights in Cairo.

It was on the second evening of the occupation, the 26th, after Roger had supped at the General-in-Chief's headquarters and was strolling back to the house he had taken over for himself, that he heard screams coming from a *cul-de-sac*, the entrance of which he was about to pass. There was nothing particularly arresting in that; for, although the troops were not allowed to break into houses, no restraint was put upon them with regard to any women they might come upon in the streets. Ordinarily he would have taken no notice and walked on, but it suddenly impinged on his mind that the woman who was being assaulted was shouting for help in French.

Quickening his pace, he turned into the *cul-de-sac* and strode swiftly down it. Fixed in the wall at its far end there was a lantern; beneath it was a struggling group of six men and two women. Hurrying towards them, he cried loudly:

'Hi! what goes on here?'

Momentarily the struggle ceased. The men turned and scowled at him. One of the women, taking advantage of their attention being temporarily diverted, tore herself from the grasp of the man who was holding her. Before she could run two steps the man grabbed her by the hair and pulled her back. In her attempt to escape she had swung round face to face with Roger, and he found himself staring at one of the most beautiful young women he had ever seen in his life.

10

Love at First Sight

THE girl—for Roger judged her to be not more than seventeen—
was swathed from chin to feet in voluminous black garments that
gave her the appearance of a bundle, so it was impossible to get
any idea of her figure; but her hood had been ripped from her
head and her yashmak from her face, so that the light from the
lantern showed her features clearly.

They were, at the moment, distorted by pain from her having
been brought up short by the soldier's violent tug on her hair.
It had come uncoiled and now showed as a dark mass at the back
of her neck, framing her tight-stretched throat and upturned face.
Her forehead was low but broad, the hair growing down in a
widow's peak. Her eyebrows resembled the wings of a sea-gull
curving gently upwards at the ends. Her eyes, now wide from fear
and pain, were enormous and fringed by dark, curling lashes. Her
mouth, too, was open from the gasp she had given, revealing two
rows of even, shining teeth. Her cheek-bones were high and her
chin rounded, with a cleft in the middle. Below it her throat was
a firm, slender column, disappearing into the folds of her shape-
less garments.

Roger drew in his breath, then said sharply to the man who was
holding her, 'Let go this woman's hair. You're hurting her.'

With a sullen look, the soldier obeyed. The girl instantly made
to dart off up the alley, but a Sergeant who was standing near her
grabbed her arm, pulled her back and growled, 'Not so fast, my
pretty.' Then he turned to Roger and said in a belligerent voice:

'We're not on duty now, Colonel. You'd best mind your own
business and leave us be.'

Roger knew then that if he meant to rescue the girl he was

going to have his work cut out. The Sergeant and at least three of the other five men he judged to be veterans of the Italian campaign. There the troops had been allowed full licence on scores of occasions, to loot and rape at will when they had captured cities, towns and villages. Husbands who had endeavoured to protect their wives, or fathers their daughters, had often been beaten insensible or even killed, but no disciplinary action had been taken. Many of the men were ex-*sans-culottes* who clung tenaciously to the doctrines of the Revolution. They would obey their officers in all matters to do with war, but treated them as equals on other occasions. None the less, he replied firmly :

'It is my business. The General-in-Chief has given strict instructions that the inhabitants of the city are to be treated with respect.'

The Sergeant sniffed. 'Yes. No breaking into houses; that's the order. And a bloody shame it is, seeing what we've been through this past month. But you can't tell me the "Little Corporal" means to deprive us of any woman we can get our hands on.'

Roger had no doubt at all that the Sergeant was right about that. As happened with seaborne expeditions sent out by every country, the sailors had managed to smuggle a few molls on to each ship; but Bonaparte had cut down ruthlessly on camp-followers, and only a small part of the Army had, for a few days, actually occupied Alexandria, so it was getting on for three months since the great majority of the men had had any commerce with women. As it was every General's business to keep his men as contented as possible, and as Bonaparte himself was far from being a puritan, Roger felt certain that the declaration about the troops being allowed a fair degree of licence would cover their taking, by force if necessary, such women as they could find in the brothels, streets and other public places. Even so, he proceeded to argue the point and said :

'That's all very well. Ordinarily I would not think of interfering with you; but this girl is no woman of the streets. I heard—'

'Who cares what she is, or this one either?' cried a be-whiskered giant who was holding the other bundle of black garments against his chest by an arm crooked round the front of her neck. 'They're women and ours by right of capture. That's all that matters.'

Ignoring the man's insolence, Roger replied quickly, 'I was about to say that I heard one of them call for help in French.'

'Us, too; and all the better,' interrupted the Sergeant. 'It was this one here. When she's danced a jig on her back for us we'll make her sing us a song.'

Suddenly the girl he was holding burst out in a husky voice to Roger, 'I am French! My father is a French merchant! Monsieur, I implore you to save us from these men and take me and my maid to his house.'

'There!' Roger declared triumphantly. 'You heard what she said. She is a Frenchwoman. I refuse to stand by and let you treat her as though she were an Arab street-walker.'

'Then do the other thing,' retorted the Sergeant roughly. 'Stop acting like a creeping Jesus instead of one of our Colonels, and get out.'

For a moment Roger was silent. He was one of the finest swordsmen in that Army of fine swordsmen. Had there been only two, or even three, of them, he would have whipped out his blade and scared them into submission by swiftly pinking them in the arm or leg, while threatening worse if they dare attack him. But six men could not lightly be wounded by one in a matter of a few seconds. If all six of them set on him simultaneously it was certain that he would be overcome and, perhaps, seriously wounded.

An alternative was to endeavour to attract the attention of one of the squads that had been ordered to patrol the streets as a protection against looting. But the nearest might be half a mile away and, even if his shouts were heard and a patrol arrived on the scene, there was no legitimate charge upon which he could have the Sergeant and his cullies arrested. Only at a direct order from one of their own officers, if he could be persuaded to give it, were they likely to release the two women.

As Roger gazed at the beautiful, anxious face within a yard of his own he decided that anything was worth trying. Expecting that the men meant to take their captives back to their barracks, he asked, 'Where are you quartered?'

The Sergeant jerked a thumb over his shoulder at a small, dark house behind him. 'Why, here. It's empty. There's not a stick of furniture in it. But they say the Army will be in Cairo for a while, and when we come on it this afternoon I thought it would make a better home from home for me and my mates than the lousy stable we'd been given; so I got my officer's permission for us to occupy it.'

'Come on!' growled the bewhiskered giant. 'Let's get moving. With all this argument we're wasting half the night.' Then he began to push the woman he was holding towards the rickety door of the house.

'One moment!' cried Roger. 'One moment!' Yet he could not think of anything more to say. He was now wondering desperately if he could possibly overcome them by a sudden attack without becoming liable for the death of one of them or being struck down himself.

His reluctance either to fight or quit showed in his expression. Noticing it a young, snub-nosed soldier said with a laugh, ''E can't bear to take 'is eyes off 'er, Sarge. Tell yer what 'is trouble is. 'E wants a go wiv her 'imself.'

The Sergeant shrugged and gave a grunt. 'If that's the case, I've nothing against his taking his turn with us. We're all made the same, aren't we? Liberty, Equality and Fraternity. That's what we fought for in the Revolution and share and share alike has always been my motto. Although,' he added, somewhat illogically, 'he'll have to pay us for letting him see the colour of her heels. How about it, Colonel?'

Seized with a sudden inspiration, Roger replied, 'You're right. I've taken a fancy to this girl. But I've no mind to have her on the bare boards in a hovel. I want her to myself in my own lodging, so I'll buy her from you.'

'No you won't,' growled a thick-set man who had not so far spoken. 'I haven't had a plum like her since I was a jailer at Nantes, way back in '93, and made a little Countess jig with me in prison before Carrier sent her to be drowned. The floor is good enough for us and it's good enough for you.'

'You shut your trap,' snapped the Sergeant, rounding on him. 'This might be good business. What'll you give for her, Colonel?'

Roger decided that a gold piece per man with something extra for the Sergeant should do the trick, so he said, 'Ten louis.'

The Sergeant spat. 'Then your luck's out. She's worth twenty times that. Just look at her, and think what she'll be like when you've got her clothes off.'

'All right. Twenty-five, then.'

'You're wasting my time, Colonel. When we've had our fill of her we'll bring the other lads along. Plenty of them will cough up ten francs a go to put her on her back. She'll earn us twice that in a week, and more.'

It had not occurred to Roger that they would force the girl to prostitute herself to every man who wanted her, but he now recalled hearing that some of the troops had done that with good-looking girls they had got hold of in Italy. And the Sergeant was right. Many of the men had pockets full of money, taken from the bodies of the Mamelukes. When the news got round that such a ravishing beauty was to be had they would queue up for her and she would be lucky if she did not die from exhaustion.

'There's something in what you say,' he admitted reluctantly. 'But, remember, the General-in-Chief is not given to standing still. It's quite on the cards that you'll be ordered out of Cairo within a few days and you won't be allowed to take her with you. The odds are that you won't be here long enough for her to earn you more than twenty-five; but I want her, so I'll make it fifty.'

'Why should we sell her?' growled the thick-set man, appealing to his companions. 'We've got money enough, Comrades, and what better could we buy with it than this wench? I'm for sending the Colonel about his business.'

Again the Sergeant rounded on him. 'Keep your big mouth shut, Vachot, or I'll shut it for you. We'll still have the other filly and one pair of girls' legs is as good as another in the dark.' Turning back to Roger, and now obviously delighting in his role of Oriental slave-dealer, he went on:

'Come now, Colonel. Fifty's not enough by half, and you know it.' Tears were now welling from the girl's eyes, and her head hung down; so he thrust a hand beneath her chin and turned up her lovely face. 'Just look at her! Why, she's fit meat for the " Little Corporal " himself, God bless him. I wouldn't be surprised if she was a Sultan's daughter. Yes, that's what she is, a Sultan's daughter. Must be from her looks and the rings we took off her fingers. Don't take no notice of what she said about her father being a French merchant. That's just eyewash because she's afraid we might ask a fortune for her ransom. She's an aristo' to her fingertips. Anyone could see that. But I'll let you have her for a hundred louis. Just think what a night you'll have with her. And maybe you could get your money back a hundred-fold by returning her to the Sultan afterwards.'

Roger hesitated only a moment. Two of the others had muttered approval of Vachot's protest against relinquishing the girl for money. The sum was far more than he had meant to pay, but if he did not clinch the deal now he might still lose her. And apart from his natural unwillingness to abandon her to weeks of suffering at the hands of the brutal soldiery, he did not disguise from himself that the reason his heart was beating so quickly was because of his eagerness to have her for his own mistress.

'Very well,' he said. 'I'll pay your price. Wait here till I get out my money.'

Turning his back he walked a few paces away, undid the clothes about his middle and began to fish coins out of the pockets of his money-belt. Counting them as he did so, he stuffed them into the side pocket of his uniform coat. By the time he had transferred a hundred the weight of the belt was reduced by half; but that did not worry him, for he could draw more pay from Andréossi. Moreover in one of the pockets of the belt reposed a packet of small diamonds, some of which he could always sell in an emergency. Returning to the Sergeant, he counted the gold out into his eager hands under the light from the lantern.

The girl stood by, limp now, but her face expressed intense relief. When the counting was done she said to Roger in her husky voice, with the strange French accent, 'May Allah bless you, my Lord, for all your days, and give you many splendid sons as a reward for what you have done this night. But will you not also please buy my maid? For her, I feel sure, they would accept a far lower price.'

Knowing that even if he were willing to part with another considerable sum the men would never agree to give up altogether the night of licentiousness to which they were looking forward, he replied shortly, 'No, I regret; but that cannot be done. Come now.'

As he took her by the arm and led her away down the *cul-de-sac,* the maid cried in Arabic, 'Lady, I beg you not to forsake me.' But her plea was half drowned by the Sergeant and his men shouting after them, with much laughter, bawdy jests and obscene instructions on how they should spend the night.

When the shouts had died down Roger said, 'I'm sorry about your maid; but our soldiers have been starved of women for many weeks, and they would never have let her go.'

The girl beside him shrugged. 'No matter. She is country bred, strong and no longer a virgin; so she will come to little harm and may, perhaps, even enjoy herself. Had not my . . . my father bought her, she might well have been sold into a brothel.'

Her attitude struck Roger as, to say the least, unfeeling; but her looks had already so bewitched him that he was eager to make allowances for her view of life being very different from his own. Although she was light-skinned and spoke French fluently she had a marked accent, and the words with which she had thanked him for saving her had disclosed that she was a Muslim. Every Mohammedan of standing owned slaves, and he knew that many regarded them as little better than valuable cattle.

He had no time to ponder the matter further, for they had reached the entrance to the street and she made a move to turn left.

Tightening his grasp on her arm, he drew her back and said, 'That's not the way. We turn right here.'

'It is the way to my home,' she replied. 'Please escort me to it.'

Smiling down at her, Roger shook his head. 'No, no; we are going to my lodging, and it lies in the opposite direction.'

For a moment she stared at him, then she said, 'Just now you behaved like a true Effendi, with . . . what is the French word . . . yes, with chivalry. I beg you, do not now disappoint me. Take me to my home and . . . and if you wish you shall be well rewarded.'

'The only reward for which I wish is your company,' he returned smoothly, 'and that I can best enjoy in my own lodging.'

Her mouth hardened and her eyes darkened angrily. Suddenly, she attempted to pull away from him.

Jerking her back, he said sharply, 'Stop that! No nonsense now! You will come with me quietly. If not I'll return you to the Sergeant and his men. I've not a doubt that they'd be willing to give me back half the money I paid for you.'

The threat had its effect. She wilted and obediently accompanied him. But she ignored several questions he asked her as they walked along, and maintained a sullen silence until they reached the house he had taken over.

Inside the entrance there was a small, open patio in the sunken centre of which a little fountain tinkled into a stone basin. Outside the July night was sweltering, but here it was reasonably cool. In the four corners of the patio there were low stools, piled with cushions. Motioning the girl to one of them, Roger took off his coat, mopped the sweat from his face with a handkerchief, sat down on another stool and had a good look at her.

In the full light of the hanging lamps that had been left burning by the servants he saw that, although her hair was dark, her skin was even fairer than he had expected. Unlike so many women in the East it had not a single pock-mark, and her complexion was flawless. Her eyes were not black but tawny. There were traces of kohl under them but she must have rubbed most of it off in an absurd attempt to make herself less attractive, since the little that was left had been insufficient for her tears to cause it to run enough to disfigure her cheeks. As he studied the marvellous head that rose so incongruously from the black draperies, he thought, ' Stap me, but that Sergeant was right. She looks every inch a Sultan's daughter. Although she isn't, no Commander of the Faithful could ever have had a lovelier one.' Then he said :

' Mademoiselle—or perhaps I should address you as madame— to maintain this silence is stupid. I make no promise to return you to your father either now or later. But I'll not even consider doing so unless you tell me about yourself. What is your name? '

For a minute she regarded him speculatively with her enormous tawny eyes, then she answered. ' Since you insist on knowing, *Monsieur le Colonel,* it is Zanthé. And I am unmarried.'

' Well,' he smiled, ' that is a start. Now, how did it come about that you were caught by those soldiers? '

' As you must know,' she told him, ' after the great battle on the other side of the Nile the mobs of Cairo swarmed out of their dens. The Janissaries who would have put them down had died fighting or had fled. There was no one to defend the mansions of the wealthy except the men of the households. Many were broken into and their inmates murdered. We succeeded in defending ours; but my . . . my father feared that the riots would grow worse the following night, so it was decided that we should leave the city. By day things were fairly quiet; but unfortunately there were delays, owing to our wishing to take with us many valuable belongings. It was evening before we left, and the sun was setting behind the Pyramids. Near a village a few miles outside the city our caravan was attacked by marauding Arabs. There was a fight, my father was killed . . .'

' Mademoiselle, I am truly sorry,' murmured Roger.

She gave a little shrug. ' It was the will of Allah. I feel no great grief for him. He was no longer young and was at times a very cruel man.'

'What happened then?'

'When they saw my father fall dead the men of our escort panicked and fled. All the other women of the seraglio were riding on camels, so I suppose they and the baggage were carried off by the Arabs. I was on horseback. Beside me Ali, my father's falconer, was riding with my maid mounted behind him. Ali seized my bridle and turned my horse. We galloped off and got away in the darkness. A few minutes later we found ourselves back in the village. Fearing to return to Cairo I decided to seek refuge there, and we were hidden by a farmer in his barn.

'This morning I found that the French had entered Cairo and had restored order, so I thought it would be safe to go home. But shortly before we were about to set out a further misfortune befell us. A party of French soldiers arrived in the village. I hid again; but it was horses they were seeking and they took every animal they could find, including ours. Our only course was to walk. That is why we did not reach the city until after dark. When we got to my home we found it had been broken into and partly looted. I was very tired, so rested there for some time while Ali got us a meal. But with all the locks broken I feared to stay the night there, in case marauders returned to carry away more loot, and I decided to seek shelter with relatives. It was while on our way to . . . to my uncle's house that we were attacked by the Sergeant and his men. They threw poor Ali down, beat and kicked him and left him, perhaps, dead. Then they dragged my maid and me down into that *cul-de-sac* where you found us.'

In the main her story had the ring of truth. During the French occupation of Venice no woman had been safe in the streets at night, even when accompanied by a man. Bonaparte's fierce troops had pitched many such Italian escorts into the canals; so Roger knew that the Sergeant would not have hesitated to set his men on the unfortunate Ali. Her account of her flight from Cairo also sounded highly plausible. Yet there were certain discrepancies in her story that he meant to plumb. For the moment, he said only:

'You have certainly been through a terrible time these past few days, and particularly tonight. Although you rested and fed a few hours ago, no doubt you would like some refreshment.'

'I am not hungry, monsieur,' she replied, 'but I would like something to drink, provided it is not wine.'

Leaving her, he went out to the back of the premises. The previous day he had led a party to find and purchase by order, at any price he chose to fix, various delicacies for the Headquarters Mess. In a few houses owned by rich Copts he had found cellars of wine and had had the bulk of them transported to Murad's palace. But he had reserved several dozen for himself, and he now opened a bottle of rich Kamiros wine from Rhodes. Then he hunted round until he found some sherbet for his guest.

As he handed her the sherbet he said, ' Mademoiselle, from several things you have said, and your refusal of wine, it is clear to me that you are a Muslim. Yet you told me that you were the daughter of a French merchant. I find that strange.'

After hesitating a moment she replied, ' I said that because I thought it would carry more weight with you and those men. But it is my mother who is French and taught me that language.'

' What happened to her? Was she captured by the Arabs with the other women? '

' No, monsieur. Fortunately she was not in Cairo. She . . . she was divorced by my father and married again. She lives in . . . in Syria.'

' But as a Frenchwoman, your mother was surely a Catholic. And, even if repudiated by her husband, her faith would not permit her to remarry.'

Zanthé looked away quickly. ' Things are different in Mohammedan countries. Everything was . . . well, arranged for her.'

Roger felt sure that his beautiful captive was lying, and not very cleverly, for she could quite well have said that her mother had become a Muslim. As he was wondering how best to get the truth out of her, she drank up her sherbet and said, ' I am tired now, and would like you to take me to a room where I can sleep.'

Nothing loath, Roger finished his glass of wine and stood up. ' We will go upstairs then. This house is not large, but it is comfortably furnished, and I will leave nothing undone to assure you a sound sleep.'

Taking with him his glass and the bottle, which was still two-thirds full, he led her up to the best bedroom of the house. The two oil-lamps in it had been left burning by his servant, and shed a gentle glow round the room. Its main feature was a huge divan bed. Setting down his bottle and glass on a small Moorish table inlaid with ivory, he locked the door.

'What are you about?' Zanthé exclaimed, her eyes widening. 'You cannot remain here, monsieur!'

'Indeed I can,' he smiled. 'This is my bedroom.'

'Then you must take me to another.'

His smile deepened. 'That would not be hospitable. Since you have lived in a harem, you are not used to sleeping alone; so you might wake up in the night and be frightened, and this divan is more than big enough for both of us.'

'I refuse!' she cried. 'I refuse to sleep in the same room with you.'

'My beautiful Zanthé, I fear you have no choice. I am loath to remind you of it, but you are now a slave, bought and paid for by me, and you will henceforth do as I tell you, without argument.'

'Then . . . then, monsieur, I demand that you respect me.'

Roger made no direct reply, but asked her, 'How old are you?'

'I am seventeen.'

'Excellent. I guessed you were somewhere about that. And now I will tell you something. In Mohammedan countries no girl as beautiful as you remains unmarried after she is fifteen. She is a valuable chattel and her father sees to it that by giving her to one of his friends he forms a useful alliance for his family.'

'That . . . that is true in most cases. But I . . . I am an exception. My father allowed me to remain unmarried because . . . because I am half French. I am still a virgin. You cannot——'

'Were that so, I might have scruples. But even in France all pretty girls are married at your age. As to your virginity, there is an easy way by which I can find out.'

'You would not dare!' she gasped.

'I certainly would,' he retorted quickly. 'And I will tell you another matter on which I believe you lied to me. All you told me about your father really applied to your husband. Come now. Am I not right? And, remember, you are my prisoner. Tomorrow I can set enquiries going about you, and in a few days a description of anyone so beautiful as yourself is certain to reveal the truth.'

Her angry eyes fell before his. 'Well . . . yes. It seems I must admit it.'

He smiled again. 'You also said he was no longer young, and was at times cruel; so it is clear that you can have had little love for him. That is a relief to me, for I should be reluctant to force a widow of a few days who was grieving deeply for a much-loved husband.'

'So you mean to force me!' she flared.

'I trust not. Must I remind you that barely an hour ago I saved you from a most terrible ordeal at the hands of six ruffians, who would later have hired you out to scores of their comrades. Since you are a fully experienced woman, I should have thought you would be happy to reward me.'

'You did only what any decent man would have done. It was Allah, blessed be the name of His Prophet, who saved me. The fate of every one of us is bound about his brow, and I was not born to be taken like an animal by any man who wants me.'

'Listen, madame,' Roger said earnestly. 'It was no doubt the will of Allah that brought me, and no one else, to your rescue. Had you been some other woman the odds are that I would have left you with those men. But if one can fall in love at first sight then I did so with you. I am an officer on the Staff of the General-in-Chief, so I can protect you. And now that your husband is dead you need a protector. I am also rich enough to give you everything in reason that you want. While I remain in Cairo this pleasant little house will make a charming home for us. When I have to leave I will arrange with the Garrison Commander for a continuance of your protection. Other women have accounted me a good lover and a kind one. I do not threaten now, but beseech you. Will you not accept my homage, allow me to become your slave instead of your being mine, and grant me this night that which is now my dearest wish?'

Coming from as fine a man as Roger, it was a declaration that would have flattered any woman. Few, had they been under such an obligation as Zanthé was, would have hardened their hearts against such an appeal. But she violently shook her head and cried:

'No! No! No! Even if I believed all you said I would not be willing. To give myself to you would be to disgrace my blood. You are an enemy. Nobody believes the lies told by your General—that he has come here as the friend of Turkey and only to chastise the Mamelukes. We are not ignorant of what he did in Italy: of how he snared the people into believing that he was bringing them liberty, then trampled on them and robbed them of all they possessed. That is what he means to do here. He comes as a conqueror, to despoil our country and make us into slaves. And you, *Monsieur le Colonel,* have admitted to being on his Staff; so you must lend yourself willingly to the evil that he does. No! If it be my fate to be taken against my will I would rather it should be by an honest Arab bandit.'

Roger listened with amazement to her outburst. It had not occurred to him that she would regard him in such a light, and he was half inclined to think that she was making a show of patriotism only as another excuse for repulsing him. After a moment he said with a frown:

'Madame, I fail to understand you. This is neither the time nor place for us to enter on a discussion of General Bonaparte's principles. At least no one can deny that he is a great soldier and that his victories have brought glory to France. Since you are half French one would expect you to be no less than neutral and have some admiration for him. But all this is irrelevant to our situation. I give not a damn how you feel on such matters. The night grows old and I have no mind to parley with you further. Under the age-old usages of war you are now mine, to do with as I will, and I have made clear my intentions. Oblige me by getting yourself undressed.'

Her tawny eyes flashed. 'I refuse! I refuse to display myself naked before you.'

'About that we shall see,' he said grimly. Then he began to take off his clothes.

As he did so, he was thinking with distress of how the delightful visions he had had of what would happen when he got her up to the bedroom had been rudely shattered. An Eastern beauty of seventeen was the equivalent of a woman of twenty-five in Europe; so he had felt certain that she must have been married for some years. That being so, in view of what she owed him he had not expected to have any trouble with her. A becoming display of reluctance, no doubt, soon overcome by a little playful teasing. Then an acceptance of the will of Allah, followed by a sweet rhapsody of passion.

Instead he would now have to take her by force; and he had never had the least inclination for that sort of love-making for, to him, it robbed the act of the major part of its pleasure. He had taken a woman that way only once—the cynically promiscuous but beautiful Natalia Androvna—and then only to teach her a lesson for having given him a rendezvous and, instead of keeping it, having had him set upon and whipped for her amusement.

Yet he meant to take the lovely Zanthé. It was getting on for six months since he had parted from Georgina. He had lived with her only for six weeks and before that had endured a period of continence of ten months since the tragic death of Clarissa. As a very virile man his need for a woman was, therefore, great, and all the greater now that he had found one who satisfied his exceptionally high standards. He felt not the faintest scruple about the morality of the matter. He was doing no more and no less than hundreds of soldiers were doing that night in Cairo, and had done all over the world in conquered countries from time immemorial.

Having stripped to the buff, he slipped on a silk robe that he had bought the previous day, and poured himself another glass of wine, drank it off and advanced on Zanthé. She had been standing by the big divan with her back half turned, so as to avert her eyes from him while he was undressing. In a final effort to render her complaisant he said:

'My very dear and beautiful Zanthé. Once more I beg you to be reasonable. As you have been married you know what to expect and have naught to fear. Your husband is dead and you had no love for him. As a woman of French extraction you cannot really regard me as an enemy. Were it not for me you would now be going through hell upon bare boards, under a succession of filthy, brutal ruffians, and——'

'I should not,' she cut him short. 'I should have killed myself.'

'Oh, come!' he protested. 'That is easier said than done; unless you have a swift poison on you.'

'No!' she cried. 'With this!' And, with a sudden movement, she whipped out a razor-sharp, jewel-hilted stiletto from under her black robes.

Roger took a swift pace back. 'I see!' he exclaimed. Then he laughed. 'Now that gives me real pleasure. The fact that you are armed removes my last scruple about using force upon you. If you can protect yourself with that ugly weapon, even should you wound me seriously I will have you escorted to your home in the morning. If not you must submit to being ravished and delight in it, as did primitive woman with primitive man after he had fought with her and dragged her to his cave.'

Zanthé made no reply. She was breathing fast, but her eyes

were now narrowed and fearless; and she held her dagger well back, ready to plunge it into him.

For a moment they eyed one another cautiously. Then he snatched up a cushion and threw it at her head. She ducked and glared at him. He laughed and threw another. Again, with an agile movement, she swayed her body sideways, so that it passed over her shoulder. Turning away he poured the last glass of wine from the bottle with leisurely inconsequence. Returning, he confronted her and said, still smiling, ' You enchanting little fool. It is quite futile for you to exert yourself.' Then he raised the glass to his lips and drank again.

Seizing the advantage he had given her by tilting back his head, she raised her dagger and, her eyes blazing at his provocation, leapt at him. But he was ready for her. Instantly his glass came down and he flung its remaining contents straight in her face. Temporarily blinded by the wine, her rush ended in a stumble. Dropping the glass, he seized in one hand the wrist that held the dagger, twisted it from her with the other and flung it behind him to the far end of the room.

As she reeled back, still blinded, he gave her a violent push, his mouth now set in a hard line. The backs of her knees came in sharp contact with the edge of the divan. Her feet shot from beneath her and she fell prostrate upon it. Next moment, ignoring her screams for help, his hands were tearing at her black garments, wrenching them off, to reveal first her bosom then her torso. Beneath her outer garments she was wearing a belt of gold net, set with precious stones, and a pair of voluminous red silk trousers, caught in at the ankles with gold bands. Holding her down with one hand, he tore those away with the other until she had not a vestige of clothing left on her.

For a moment he stood back while, panting and gasping, she tried to get the stinging wine out of her eyes by rubbing them with her knuckles. Staring down at her naked body he saw with delight that it was as perfect as her face. Her breasts were full and stood up proudly, her hips were beautifully rounded and her legs were longer in proportion to her body than those of the average woman.

' Now! ' he cried breathlessly. ' Now, will you give in? '

' No! ' Her voice came in a hoarse shout. ' Never! Never! '

His response was to fling himself on her. For a few minutes she struggled wildly, endeavouring to claw his face and bite his

chin. But he jerked his head away and beat down her hands.
Suddenly her body contracted beneath him and she gave a sharp
scream. Then, just as suddenly, her limbs relaxed and she began
to moan. He had often heard women moan like that and knew
that it was from pleasure. Another few moments and she became
as wild with passion as himself. Her arms came round him and
clasped him in a vice. In Turkish she cried out some phrase to
Allah that he could not interpret. Then it was all over.

Exhausted by their transports, they lay side by side, his arm
encircling her neck. After a while she pulled away from him,
turned her face to the wall and began to cry quietly. He knew
the reason for her tears, and felt badly about them. In one thing,
at least, she had not lied to him. She had, after all, proved to be
a virgin. That accounted for the prolonged resistance she had put
up, and it seemed evident now that her husband must have been
a homosexual. But nothing could now undo what had been done
and Roger endeavoured to comfort himself with the thought that
she had suffered little by comparison with the fate that would
have been hers at the hands of the men from whom he had
rescued her. The dawn was already filtering through the curtains,
and he fell asleep.

It seemed that he had scarcely closed his eyes when he was
roused by Marbois knocking on the door. Bonaparte was an early
riser and expected his Staff to be in attendance the moment he
was ready to transact business. Roger would have given a great
deal to have been able to remain, comfort Zanthé with sweet
words and, perhaps, make love to her again. But he dared not
linger. She was lying on her side in a deep sleep; so he crept out
from under the light coverlet he had pulled over them before
going to sleep, dressed very quietly and left the room, locking the
door behind him.

Downstairs he drank the coffee that the servants had prepared
for him, and ravenously demolished a plateful of sweet cakes.
Then he called for Marbois and said to him, 'I brought a lady
home with me last night. She is up in the bedroom still asleep.
Do not disturb her; but wait till she calls, then take her up anything she may ask for to break her fast. But on no account is she
to be allowed to leave the bedroom or speak to the native
servants. Keep her locked in, and I'll be back as soon as I can.'
Buckling on his sword, he hurried round to headquarters.

For an hour he stood about with several of the other aides-de-camp in the ante-chamber, then Bonaparte asked for him. After giving him one swift glance, his master proceeded to stuff some sheets of paper, covered with close writing, into a thick envelope and seal it while he said:

'I have already sent a despatch to the Directors, describing the Battle of the Pyramids. This is another, reporting my occupation of Cairo. I have selected you to carry it because, as you speak Arabic, you should meet fewer impediments to speed in the towns and villages through which you must pass. I have, several times, already pointed out to Admiral Brueys the folly of risking an encounter with the British Fleet by remaining on the Egyptian coast, and have urged him to seek safety by returning to Toulon; or, at least, under the guns of Malta. I hope that by the time you reach Alexandria you will find that he has sailed. If so, he will have left several frigates there to carry despatches to France. In that case, give the despatch to the Captain of one of them and tell him to have it forwarded with all speed from the first port under French control that he can reach. Should Brueys still be loitering there, give it to him and tell him from me to delay no longer but be gone. Take any escort you desire and leave immediately.'

'*Mon Général*, you may rely upon me,' replied Roger promptly. Then he took the despatch, saluted smartly and, with rage in his heart, marched from the room.

Having given orders for a horse for himself, and a half-troop of Guides as escort, to be got ready at once, he hurried back to his lodging, still almost exploding with pent-up fury. He had long since come to the conclusion that the embraces of women were like olives out of a bottle; the first could be got only with difficulty but the rest came easily. From the moment he had been woken he had begun to look forward with intense delight to the second night that he would spend with Zanthé. Now that this mission had been thrust upon him it would be more than a week before he could hope to possess her again.

Arrived at the house he called loudly for Marbois and, when the young Provençal came hurrying from the back premises, Roger gave him his orders in a succession of swift, staccato sentences. 'I have been ordered away on a mission. I expect to be away for at least a week. You will remain here and consider yourself as confined to barracks. In short, you will not leave the house. Have the servants buy anything the lady upstairs may ask

G

for. But you will take up her meals yourself, and she is to be kept
under lock and key. Neither the servants nor anyone else are to
be allowed to communicate with her. If she asks you to take any
message or letter for her you will accept it but not deliver it.
Keep it until my return. Is that clear? '

'Yes, *Monsieur le Colonel*,' replied Marbois, drawing himself
up. 'I understand your wishes perfectly.'

'Good,' said Roger. Then, thrusting some money to cover
expenses into the young soldier's hand, he wheeled about and
hurried back to headquarters.

Even by taking the short cut from Rahmaniyeh across the
desert, the journey from Cairo to Alexandria was the best part of
a hundred and fifty miles. The roads were no more than tracks,
the heat was almost unbearable and, as no remounts were available *en route*, the strength of the horses had to be husbanded.
So, although Roger left Cairo on July 27th and made the best
speed possible, it was not till the morning of August 1st that he
reached Alexandria. He had rested his troop the previous night at
Damanhûr, and had done half of the last thirty miles before
daylight; so after five days of most exhausting travel he was very
tired. Even so, he decided to accomplish his mission that day,
sleep the night in Alexandria and set off on his return journey
early the following morning.

After a talk with that tough veteran General Kléber, to give
him the latest news, and having learned that the Fleet had not
yet sailed, Roger secured a new mount and, in spite of the midday heat, rode on to Aboukir. There he found the line of three-
deckers at anchor in a long, shallow bay with rocks and an island
at its far end. A boat took him off to the mighty *L'Orient* and,
when the Officer of the Watch had sent his name to the Admiral,
Brueys at once received him.

Having handed over his despatch Roger gave the Admiral
Bonaparte's verbal message, upon which Brueys replied with a
nod, 'I am well aware of the General-in-Chief's view of the
matter. It was originally planned that I should take the Fleet
into the harbour of Alexandria, where it would have been safe
from attack; but it was found that the harbour mouth was too
shallow for my largest ships to enter. He then urged me to make
for Corfu. But what sort of a Frenchman would I have been to
turn my back on him at such a time?

' We all know that he has unshakable faith in his star; but had things gone wrong and our Army been defeated, its plight, marooned here in a strange land without either reinforcements or supplies, would have been too terrible to think upon. I could not possibly reconcile myself to any other course than to remain here, so that, did the worst happen, I might take off what remained of the Army and so save it from complete destruction.'

Roger smiled. 'Pray accept my compliments on your decision, *Monsieur l'Amiral*. It was in the highest traditions of your Service, and thousands of us soldiers might well owe our lives to you. But now the Mamelukes have been signally defeated, their remnants scattered and the General-in-Chief is firmly established in Cairo; the situation is very different.'

'Indeed, yes; and I thank God for it. Yet we are desperately short of supplies, for we have been supplying General Kléber this past month instead of he us. We'll still have to secure a sufficiency of food and water, but once that it done I'll feel no scruples in setting sail for Malta. I see, though, Colonel, that you have obviously ridden hard and need rest and refreshment. It is just on our dinner hour. You must join us and afterwards I'll have a cabin prepared for you so that you can spend the night on board.'

'I thank you, Admiral,' Roger replied. 'I should be most happy to dine, but I am promised to sup with General Kléber and intend to start back for Cairo in the cool of the early morning.'

By now his appearance was very different from the gallant figure he had cut in Paris. His fine uniform had become sadly stained during the campaign and after his recent journey he looked like a scarecrow. He was covered with dust from head to foot, his hair was a bush and his face begrimed. But a marine was detailed to brush his clothes while he had a good wash and a quarter of an hour later, when he was conducted to the spacious stern cabin, he looked fairly presentable.

With the Admiral now were Commodore Casabianca, the Captain of *L'Orient*, and a number of other officers. When Roger had been presented to those he had not met on the voyage out they sat down at the big oval table to dine. During the early part of the meal Brueys and the others asked him many questions about the campaign, and listened eagerly to his accounts of the desert march, the Battle of the Pyramids and fabulous Cairo. But soon after two o'clock this pleasant party was suddenly interrupted. The door burst open and a young Lieutenant tumbled into the room, shouting:

' *Les Anglais! Monsieur l'Amiral! Les Anglais!* ' It then transpired that Nelson's Fleet had just been sighted and was bearing down upon them.

Chairs were thrust back, and with Brueys leading, they all rushed up on deck. There a hundred eyes were glued to telescopes. Roger followed the Admiral up to the poop and shaded his eyes with his hand to cut out the glare of the brilliant sunlight. Even without a glass he could make out, just above the distant horizon, the tips of more topmasts than he could count. It was no false alarm. After his ten-week fruitless search back and forth across the length and breadth of the Mediterranean Nelson had, at last, run the enemy to earth.

Roger stood there, cursing himself. If only he had started an hour earlier from Damanhûr that morning. If only he had ridden straight on to Aboukir, instead of stopping in Alexandria to talk with Kléber. If only he had refused Brueys's invitation to dinner. Had he done any of those things he would be safely back on shore by now. But here he was, in the French flagship, with battle imminent; and, above all, a battle against his own countrymen. To ask to be put ashore now would look like rank cowardice. Yet he considered it, Perhaps it would not appear too bad if he said that it was imperative that he should rejoin the General-in-Chief with the least possible delay. But he was not taking back any despatch, so such an excuse for turning tail would not be looked on as valid. While his mind was still racked with awful indecision, Brueys settled the matter for him by saying:

' Of course, Colonel, you will now wish to remain with us, to share our dangers and our glory. I shall be happy to count you as a military member of my personal Staff.'

11

The Battle of the Nile

RARELY had Roger spent a more miserable afternoon. There had been no possible reply to Brueys other than 'I am honoured, *Monsieur l'Amiral*, and will do my utmost to be of service.' After that there was nothing for him, as a landlubber, to do but await the battle, and he had a horror of such desperate encounters.

It was not that he lacked courage. At Sherborne he had several times fought George Gunston, the bully of the school, although each time he knew he would get a licking. He had fought duels with sword and pistol, taken part in many affrays and would not have hesitated to fight anyone on any grounds that justified a resort to weapons. It was the terribly impersonal nature of battles that he hated: to be one of a group of men firing at and being fired at by another, without the faintest knowledge of the man you might wound or be wounded by; or to be cut in half by a bounding cannon ball, fired by an artilleryman whom you could not even see and who, if you had met him, might have proved to be the most charming fellow. Indeed although every Frenchman was technically his enemy, he counted many friends among them and there were several to whose rescue he would have gone at the peril of his life. He would have been the last man to suggest that his country should not go to war in defence of her liberty and rights, but that did not make the indiscriminate slaughter involved any the less horrifying to him.

He had been lucky in the present campaign, as Bonaparte and his Staff had come under fire only during the brief skirmish at Chebreïss and had not even participated personally in the great Battle of the Pyramids. But now he was fated to spend several terrifying hours and, perhaps, meet his death in a head-on clash between some twenty thousand men, the majority of whom passionately hated each other's country and were thirsting for one another's blood.

And it was not even as if it were to be a land battle. Roger would have defended a post to the last if he had been charged with doing so; but, as a general principle, he was a great believer in the old adage, 'He who fights and runs away lives to fight another day.' In a conflict on land one could at least add to the chance of survival by using judgment about when to lie down and when to stand up. If things went badly, it was generally possible, by keeping one's wits about one, to avoid getting mixed up with any mass of routed infantry that would attract the enemy's artillery fire or pursuing cavalry. It was also possible to sham dead and lie in a ditch until the coming of night enabled one to creep away from the battlefield.

But none of these ruses to save oneself was possible in a naval battle. A man was just as liable to be wounded or killed whether he stood up or lay down. And it was not only the enemy's cannon balls that were to be feared. A falling mast or yard might shatter his head like an eggshell and, as the shot crashed through bulwarks and decks, great splinters of jagged wood, which could cause the most ghastly wounds, whizzed through the air to right, left and centre. Last but not least, if the ship he was in got the worst of the action there could be no galloping away from her, and it was pointless to lie in the scuppers pretending to be dead. If badly holed below the waterline she would sink, carrying him down with her to Davy Jones's Locker, or, if she had been set on fire, blow up. In either case there would be no morning after.

Roger knew the composition of the French Fleet without having to run his eye down the line of ships. Apart from four frigates and other smaller craft, Brueys had *L'Orient*, the mightiest ship afloat, with one hundred and twenty guns, three eighties and nine seventy-fours. That made a total of over one thousand guns, in comparison with which the one hundred and seventy-four pieces of artillery that Bonaparte had brought for his land battles were a mere pittance. Roger thought it reasonable to assume that Nelson's Fleet carried about the same number as the French. That means that as soon as battle was joined some two thousand cannon would be blazing away as fast as men could load them. Even at only twenty rounds per gun, forty thousand murderous lumps of iron—not to mention innumerable bullets from muskets

—would be flying in all directions; and he was in the flagship, to which it was certain that the enthusiastic British would give their very special attention.

He would have felt even gloomier about his chances of survival could he have known of Nelson's declaration to his Captains, When we do come up with the enemy I'll not be content with victory. It must be annihilation.'

During the afternoon there was nothing he could do but watch, while officers, marines and sailors bustled about the decks preparing for action. Had Brueys's Squadron been caught while transporting the Army, it could not possibly have driven off the enemy. Despite the Admiral's protests, such a mass of equipment —field guns, wagons, crates of saddles for the dismounted cavalry, officers' baggage, ammunition and other stores—had been stacked on the decks that it would have proved next to impossible for his ships to run out and fight their guns.

In consequence, it had been decided that if the British came upon the armada the French should endeavour to close with and board them, as all Brueys's ships-of-the-line had at least three hundred and fifty troops packed like sardines in them; it was hoped that they, by sheer weight of numbers, would overwhelm the enemy.

Now, there were no soldiers in the ships; but at least they had been disembarrassed of a great part of their strangling top-hamper, so they could have put to sea and met the British in a battle of manœuvre. For some while Brueys discussed the possibility with his senior Captains; but the prevailing opinion was that they would do better to remain where they were because the seamanship of the men was so indifferent, and they had neither food nor water aboard for a cruise of more than a few hours.

The northern end of Aboukir Bay, in which the French lay, ended in a hook, on the point of which stood a small castle. From the point a shoal ran out to Aboukir Island and some way beyond it. Brueys's ships were anchored in a long line behind this protection and, moreover, in the bay itself there were many other shoals and shallows. It was thought most unlikely, therefore, that Nelson would risk bringing his ships into such dangerous waters after dark and, although they had been steadily approaching all through the long, hot afternoon, they still had some distance to cover.

Nevertheless, preparations for action went ahead. Bulkheads were taken down, cannon balls and powder charges brought up, buckets of water placed beside the guns, hoses coupled to pumps ready for fire-fighting, and all the supplies, crates, bales and boxes that remained on deck shifted to the landward sides of the ships because it was taken for granted that no sane Admiral would risk sending his ships into the shallows that lay between the French Fleet and the shore.

As the British rounded the distant point it became possible to assess their strength accurately. There were eleven seventy-fours, one fifty-gun ship and a brig. Then, to the delight of the French, it was seen that one of the seventy-fours had gone aground on the hidden sandspit beyond Aboukir Island, thus making the odds—by this reduced to less than nine hundred guns against over a thousand—still further in their favour.

At about five-thirty the British began to form line of battle, showing that, although twilight would soon be falling, they did intend to attack that night. Majestically, under full sail, they came on in an irregular line, Captain Sam Hood in *Zealous* and Captain Foley in *Goliath* striving to out-distance one another for the honour of being the first to enter the battle.

Goliath won and, to Brueys's horror, came up on the inshore side of his vanguard, followed by four other British seventy-fours. Nelson and his leading Captains had swiftly realized that, as the French ships lay to the wind, there must be at least their own length of water deep enough to keep them afloat when, still at anchor, they swung with their sterns to the shore. Where one seventy-four could swing another could pass without running aground. As the guns of the French ships on the shoreward side lay under piles of impedimenta, they could not be fired.

After firing a broadside into *Guerrier*, the ship at the head of the French line, *Goliath* overshot her and came to anchor opposite the second French ship, *Conquérant*. But *Zealous* anchored opposite *Guerrier*, while *Orion*, *Theseus* and *Audacious* sailed on, pouring broadsides into *Guerrier* and *Conquérant* as they passed, then concentrating their fire on the next in line; *Spartiate*, *Aquilon* and *Peuple Souverain*.

Nelson's orders had been to attack the French van and centre, and now he came up in his flagship *Vanguard* with the remaining six British ships on the seaward side of the French line. Caught between two fires as the sun sank below the horizon, the five enemy ships first to be attacked suffered terrible damage.

The French line was nearly two miles long, and *L'Orient* was stationed exactly in the centre of its thirteen ships; so little could be seen from her during the first part of the action except dense clouds of smoke. But by seven o'clock it was fully dark and every minute the smoke pall was stabbed by the bright flashes from hundreds of guns. Slowly but inexorably, like a vast burning taper, the smoke and fire spread along the line as ship after ship came into action.

Vanguard was the first ship to anchor outside the enemy line, and Nelson had her brought to within pistol shot of *Spartiate*, which was being attacked by *Theseus* on her other side. Even so, the flagship was hard pressed until *Minotaur* came up and drew the fire of *Aquilon*, which had also been engaging *Vanguard*. Meanwhile, losing station owing to the smoke and darkness, *Majestic* and *Bellerophon* had got too far ahead. The latter, finding herself opposite *L'Orient*, took on alone this mighty ship-of-war which had nearly double her own gun-power.

Now, after some five hours of dread anticipation, Roger experienced all the horrors of a great naval battle. While the French Fleet had been convoying Bonaparte's Fleet of transports to Egypt, Brueys and a number of his senior officers had feared that, discipline being so bad, many of the pressed sailors might, if attacked, refuse to fight at all and seek a false security by hiding themselves below decks. But now those fears were proved ill-founded, largely perhaps because the men realized that their Admiral had a superiority in ships and an even larger superiority in guns and also because the victories of the Army on land had made them feel that they must not digrace the flag to which their comrades had brought so much glory.

The seamen in all the French ships so far attacked had shown admirable courage, and those in *L'Orient* proved no exception. With shouts and cheers they laboured at the guns, greatly encouraged by the fact that their part in the battle appeared to be only a single-ship duel with a much inferior enemy. This eager handling of their guns, and *L'Orient*'s weight of metal, soon began to tell. At the price of comparatively few casualties all three of *Bellerophon*'s masts were shot away and, to the cheers of the French, she drifted, helpless, out of the battle.

Meanwhile *Majestic* had attacked *Heureux*, still further down the line, and had run her jib-boom into the French ship's rigging. She was also exposed to the fire of *Tonnant*. Her Captain was killed and she suffered terrible casualties. But her First Lieutenant succeeded in getting her free and continued to fight her with great gallantry, attacking, unsupported, *Mercure*, the fourth ship from the French rear.

Unable to see what was happening, except in his immediate vicinity by the orange flashes of the guns, Roger now had depression added to his personal fears; for he could judge the progress of the battle only by the crushing defeat of *Bellerophon*. He would have been even more depressed had he known that at about eight o'clock. Nelson had been struck on the head just above his old wound by a piece of the chain shot used by the French to cut through enemy ships' sails and rigging. The metal cut the Admiral's forehead to the bone, causing a long flap of flesh and a stream of blood to come down over his good eye and blind him completely. Believing that he had received a mortal wound, he sent last messages to his wife and several of his Captains.

Plunged into total darkness, he could not be persuaded, even by his Principal Surgeon, that the wound was only superficial. Yet if he had died then it would have been as he had always wished, for he had hardly been taken to the cockpit when news that victory was assured was brought to him. The ships in the French van, dismasted and with huge, gaping holes in them, had been reduced to corpse-littered hulks. *Conquérant* had been the first to strike her flag, *Guerrier* followed at eight-thirty, *Aquilon* soon after. *Spartiate* had ceased to fire and *Peuple Souverain*, having broken from her moorings, had drifted ashore in flames. The French centre—*Franklin, L'Orient, Tonnant* and *Heureux*—were now surrounded by a superior concentration of British ships that was pouring broadside after broadside into them and, as the night wore on, must be pounded into surrender.

L'Orient had *Alexander* on one side of her and *Swiftsure* on the other. White to the gills, Roger remained on the poop of the flagship, expecting every moment that a cannon ball would cut him in half or take off his head. In the heat of battle Brueys had found no use for him; so he could only stand there with his eyes smarting and half choked by the acrid fumes from the gunpowder. Through gaps in the smoke he caught glimpses of the deck. In places the bulwarks had been shot away; here and there cannon had been overturned. Broken spars and cut ropes fallen from aloft were inextricably mixed with scores of dead and dying. The screams of the wounded rent the air every moment, making the night hideous. There was blood everywhere.

At a little before nine o'clock a longboat not far from Roger caught fire. He had been helping to bandage a wounded sailor. The man suddenly jerked his head forward, spewed blood and died; so Roger let the body fall back. Running to the burning boat, he helped several other men cut her away. When he returned to the poop someone told him that the gallant Brueys had been killed by a cannon ball. *Audacious* had now joined in the attack on *L'Orient*; so broadsides from three ships were raking her, while musket balls fired by marines in their fighting tops came whistling down at a sharp angle to take their toll of the exposed French sailors. Her upper decks were now a shambles, nearly all the guns on them having been put out of action, but the greater part of those on her lower decks continued to fire and her surviving officers had no thought of surrender.

Two more of her boats were set alight and extinguished, the fire then started on the poop. While lying inactive in the bay she had been painting ship, and much of the paint on her stern was still wet. The flames caught it and ran quickly up the tarred rigging. An attempt was made to put out the fire, but British cannon balls had destroyed the nearest fire-fighting appliances and rows of water-buckets and were crashing through the stern rails every moment. By half past nine the after part of the poop was well ablaze, lighting up a scene of most appalling carnage and confusion. In the lurid glare of the flames Roger caught sight of Commodore Casabianca. He was lying wounded and near him the deck was burning but his ten-year-old son, who had come on the voyage as a cabin-boy, was clinging to his hand, refusing to leave him.

Suddenly Roger took a decision. Two-thirds of the ship's company were now either dead or wounded. By a miracle, as it seemed to him, he was one of the remaining third. But his immunity could not last much longer. With Brueys dead and no one knowing any more what his neighbour was doing, why should he remain to be slaughtered? Better to go over the side and take his chance in the water. Stumbling through the blinding smoke, he found one of the poop ladders and slithered down it into the well of the ship.

Tripping over a legless corpse, he was thrown against an overturned gun. Beyond it was a great rent in the bulwark, where the gunport had been. Heaving himself up, he lurched towards it. At that moment a thought struck him. Bonaparte's despatch!

During the five and a half months since he had left England he had been unable to send home a single report or piece of intelligence of any value. Perhaps even worse in Mr. Pitt's view, instead of carrying out his instructions to do anything he could to hamper Bonaparte's success and rise to power he had, in small ways, rendered him many useful services. Here was a chance to make good his apparent negligence and to serve his country to some purpose. It was very probable that in the despatch Bonaparte had not only described his occupation of Cairo but had also informed the Directors of his future intentions.

Swinging round, Roger stepped over the legless body, jumped another, slipped in a pool of blood, fell, picked himself up and made for the entrance under the poop that led to the dead Admiral's cabin. The passage was in darkness, except for the flickering light of the still-thundering guns. He groped his way along it and into the great stern cabin where, eight hours before, he had been laughing and talking with Brueys and his officers round the big dining table. It was bright as day inside the cabin, for the fire had already caught the woodwork of the stern galley outside the semi-circle of tall, sloping windows.

Adjacent to the big cabin was a smaller one that Brueys used as an office and in which he had received Roger. As Roger thrust open the door he heard a sudden movement, then saw that a terrified man was crouching in one of the far corners.

He was dressed as a civilian, so Roger guessed him to be either Brueys's secretary or a super-cargo. The one thing he could not afford was for a Frenchman to be able to identify him afterwards and state that he had made off with the despatch, and there was just a possibility that this man might survive the battle. His own life might be forfeit if he let the man live; so he pulled a pistol from his sash, intending to kill him.

'What . . . what are you about to do, monsieur?' gasped the trembling wretch.

The idea of pistolling a defenceless man in cold blood went

horribly against the grain with Roger and a way of making his theft appear a commendable action suddenly occurred to him. With a frown he said, ' For lurking here like a coward I ought to shoot you. But I fear *L'Orient* must soon surrender, so I have come here to prevent a despatch that I delivered to Admiral Brueys this afternoon from falling into the hands of the English.' Then, turning his pistol on the lock of a stout cabinet in which he had seen Brueys put the despatch, he fired it.

The lock was shattered and after a sharp pull the doors of the cabinet came open. Inside there were rows of pigeon-holes filled with papers. Roger soon recognized the despatch from its size and unbroken seals. Quickly he undid his tunic, thrust the despatch inside and, without another glance at the poor devil he had spared, left the cabin.

Out on the open deck the scene was even more ghastly than when he had left it, for during the past five minutes the fire on the poop had trebled in size and now had the mizzenmast, with its yards and gear, burning like a huge candle. The fierce light of the flames lit a much greater area of the ship and the writhing figures half obscured by smoke might well have been in Dante's Inferno. But Roger's only thought now was to save himself.

Noticing a rope that led out through a gap in the bulwarks, he grabbed it with both hands, gave a quick look to make certain there was no wreckage in the sea below the gap, then sat down, turned on his stomach and thrust himself outward. The rope, having been cut, was not secured to anything on board. In consequence instead of his being able, as he had hoped, to clamber down it, he went hurtling down, hit the bulge of the ship's side with a most frightful thump, bounced off it and landed with a great splash in the sea.

For what seemed an age he went down, down, down, until he thought that his lungs would burst. But at last he began to rise and surfaced, gasping and gulping. As soon as he had shaken the water from his eyes, he got his bearings. There, within twenty feet of him, towered the gargantuan *L'Orient*, many of her lower guns still belching fire and smoke, but her stern now ablaze. Turning, he struck out for the nearest British ship.

She was no great distance away, and he was a strong swimmer. In spite of being weighed down by his sodden clothes, he reached her after ten minutes of steady effort. But it was another matter to get aboard her. Had he had the voice of ten men and shouted himself hoarse he would still have been unable to make himself heard above the deafening thunder of the guns. Even if he had, her crew, giving every thought to their duties at their action stations, would not have left them to throw him a rope.

After swimming half round the ship he found himself facing her anchor chain. Gratefully, he grasped and clung to it, praying that, until some chance arose of his getting into the ship, he would not be hit by a stray bullet or flying piece of debris. Fortunately, as it was the height of summer, the sea was warm; so he stood no risk of having to let go the chain from numbed limbs and hands.

For the next half-hour, from sea-level, he watched the battle. The British ships continued to fire relentlessly on their foe. Fewer and fewer guns from *L'Orient* replied, and the whole of her stern became a raging furnace. Soon after ten it was evident that orders had been given to abandon ship, as those of her crew who still survived began to jump into the water. At ten-fifteen the flames reached her main magazine and she blew up. The explosion was so terrific that it was heard as far away as Alexandria. Masses of burning debris were shot hundreds of feet into the air, to descend on the decks of the British ships that had brought doom upon her, or to hiss fiercely in the water.

The blast and a great tidal wave wrenched Roger from his hold on the cable. He was again submerged and had to fight his way to the surface. When he came up it was pitch dark and utterly silent. The magnitude of the explosion had so shaken the combatants on both sides that they spontaneously ceased to serve the guns. It was not until nearly ten minutes later that a French ship resumed the battle by again opening fire.

Had *L'Orient* not blown up she would have proved the most valuable prize ever taken by the British, for in her hold she carried £600,000 in ingots of gold looted from the new Swiss and Roman Republics and, in addition, the huge treasure in gold and gems that Bonaparte had stolen from the Knights of Malta. These were to have been his treasure chest for the conquest of the East; so it was a shattering blow to him that the whole of this great wealth should have gone down with *L'Orient* to the bottom of Aboukir Bay.

But Roger was thinking only of his own survival. Swimming round and round in the darkness he again, at length, hit the anchor cable and clung on to it. Soon after, fires ignited by the flaming debris falling on to British ships, and a renewal of the firing, intermittently lit the scene.

Some three hundred of the survivors in *L'Orient* had jumped into the sea before she blew up; upon which *Audacious*, to the cable of which ship Roger later earned he had been clinging, put out several boats to pick up as many as they could. Seeing this, Roger swam to the nearest boat and, to his immense relief, was hauled aboard. A quarter of an hour later he and a number of others who had been rescued were hoisted in through the lower ports of *Audacious*, herded to one end of her tier deck and, under guard, kept there for the remainder of the night.

The battle continued sporadically until 3 a.m., and was resumed for a while after dawn. Vice-Admiral Villeneuve in his flagship, *Guillaume Tell*, one other ship-of-the-line, *Généreux*, and a frigate, made sail and got away. It was later said that they would not have escaped had Nelson not been temporarily incapacitated by his wound, and so unable to direct the later stages of the battle. As it was, despite *Zealous*'s crippled state, gallant Sam Hood gave chase, but no other British ship was in a condition to support him; so he was recalled.

Daylight revealed the fruits of victory. Eleven of the thirteen French ships-of-the-line had been captured or destroyed. Out of some eight thousand French sailors, over five thousand were dead and the majority of the remainder were prisoners. It was possibly the most bloody sea battle ever fought and the greatest triumph for British sea power since the defeat of the Spanish Armada. It made the Mediterranean henceforth, for over a century, a British lake; and the French Navy was so completely shattered that seven years elapsed before, in combination with a large Spanish Fleet, it again dared challenge Nelson at Trafalgar.

During that night Roger had no inkling of all this, apart from the knowledge that his countrymen had proved victorious. He had mounted his horse long before dawn that morning at Damanhûr, ridden thirty miles to Alexandria, talked with Kléber, ridden on to Aboukir, gone aboard the flagship, delivered his despatch to Brueys, sustained over five hours of appalling anxiety and a further three of hideous battle.

When going overboard he had hurt himself badly and the exertion of swimming and clinging to the cable had drained away his last reserves of strength. He was hardly able any longer to think coherently, yet sufficiently able to realize that he was in

some danger: for in no circumstances, while he remained among
the French prisoners, must he give away the fact that he was
English. Wondering vaguely what new problems and perils he
might have to face next day, he slumped down on the hard deck,
utterly exhausted, and, almost instantly, was asleep.

12

The One Who Got Away

THE personnel of *Audacious* were so fully occupied preparing the
dead for burial, tending their wounded, clearing away wreckage,
and stopping holes torn in the side of the ship by French cannon
balls, that it was mid-morning before they had time to give any
attention to their prisoners. Roger was roused by movement all
round him and found that half a dozen Jack-tars, supervised by a
Lieutenant, were serving out a ration of ship's biscuits and a
drink of water, dipped from buckets.

He eagerly swallowed the few mouthfuls of brackish water, but
was not sufficiently hungry to tackle the biscuits. It was very cold
down there on the tier deck; so his clothes had not yet dried out,
and his right arm and hip, with which he had hit the bulge of
L'Orient when going overboard, were stiff and painful.

Looking about him he saw in the dim light some fifty officers
and men in the same wretched state as himself: their clothes torn
and sodden, their faces begrimed and their hair in rats'-tails. With
some twenty others, who had been picked up and taken to other
ships, they were the only survivors of the eight hundred men who
the day before had manned the mighty *L'Orient*.

When the ration had been served the Lieutenant sat himself
down on an upturned barrel and, using a crate for a table, produced some sheets of paper. A Petty Officer then marshalled the
prisoners into a queue for examination. The Lieutenant spoke
little French, but all he asked each man was his name, rank and
ship; then he wrote them down. When Roger's turn came he drew
himself to his full height and replied in French:

'Breuc, Colonel on the Staff of French Army headquarters,
Cairo, and aide-de-camp to the General-in-Chief.'

The Lieutenant gave him a surprised look, took down what he had said and put a large cross against his name, then told him to stand aside with another French officer who had been singled out from the ratings. By the time all the names had been taken, the group of officers numbered five, with one Midshipman. A Sergeant of Marines beckoned them to follow him and took them to the bread-room, where they were locked in.

There, while agreeing that they were lucky to be alive, they commiserated with one another on the defeat their Fleet had sustained and speculated gloomily about their future as prisoners-of-war. Roger produced his share of apparent despondency, but inwardly he was now in excellent spirits. Apart from his right arm and side being badly bruised and aching, he had come through the terrible night unscathed and rosy prospects lay ahead of him.

He had known that he had to do no more than say he was one of Bonaparte's aides-de-camp to ensure his being brought before a senior officer for questioning. From that it should be only a step to securing a private interview with Admiral Nelson, to whom alone he was prepared to disclose his true identity. None of the prisoners had so far been searched, presumably because it was thought that they would have only small, private possessions on them. He still had the despatch concealed under his tunic and even should it be taken from him before he got to the Admiral that would not prevent it from being sent to Nelson with him. All he had to do was guard against anyone, French or British, finding out that he was an Englishman, and that should present no great difficulty.

Then, once he had had his interview with the Admiral, good-bye to Egypt. Kléber would report that he had left Alexandria to deliver the despatch to Brueys on the afternoon that the British Fleet had been sighted. Bonaparte would assume that he had been either killed or captured during the battle, and what more perfect explanation could there be for not returning to him? Now that he had captured Cairo and had virtually subdued Egypt, it was certain that he would proceed with his ambitious schemes. The Directory had ordered him to occupy the Red Sea ports, and it was highly probable that, having secured them, he would use them as bases for a descent on India. Alternatively, he might first turn north to conquer Syria. But, whichever he did, India would be his ultimate objective, and to conquer the whole of the East must take him several years.

Roger had had more than enough of deserts and battles, and now he could get Nelson to send him home, either as an important prisoner who would be well treated, or under another name in a merchant ship. Even if at a later date he wished to return to France he would still be able to do so with a clean bill as a Frenchman, because he could say that he had been held as a prisoner in England. Even Talleyrand could have no reason to suspect that his capture had not been genuine.

One thought only marred his delight at chance having provided him with a way to escape further service in the East: that was of Zanthé. There she was—the most breathtaking beauty he had seen for years, lovely to look at, lovely to touch and, with her rich, deep voice, lovely to listen to—his captive in Cairo. Not to return to her seemed the height of ingratitude to those generous, joy-loving gods of Olympus who had sent her to him. To have done so, then immediately to have placed him in a position where every other interest demanded that he should sacrifice her, was harsh indeed. But one of the reasons why Roger had survived so many perilous situations was his ability to face facts squarely and weigh their pros and cons.

To return to Zanthé might bring him delirious happiness, but for how long? At the best for a few months, while Bonaparte fully established a new administration throughout Egypt. He was such a dynamic worker that it was quite possible that, having set the pattern, after a few weeks, he would leave someone else to do the administering and himself march on to new conquests. Still worse, as Roger spoke Arabic, his master might any day take it into his head to pack him off on some mission to a desert Sheik or the Red Sea ports, and he would not be able to take Zanthé with him.

There was, too, the most potent reason of all for not returning to Cairo. It was most unlikely that any opportunity such as this to get back to England would occur again, so he would be tying himself to Bonaparte for an indefinite period. And now the French Fleet had been destroyed, the Army was cut off. This meant that should disaster befall the adventurous Corsican he would be unable to take his Army back to France. He and all those with him would become slaves of some Eastern potentate or perish.

On the other hand, there beckoned England, Home and Beauty in the form of his beloved Georgina and, however passionately he might be attracted to other women, he always had loved and always would love her above all, for she was his true female counterpart in heart and mind as well as body.

Regretfully, but without hesitation, he put from him the lure of Zanthé.

Early in the afternoon the Sergeant of Marines unlocked the door and beckoned Roger out. With a gloomy grimace for the benefit of his fellow-prisoners, he stepped into the passage, then followed the Sergeant up on deck, happily confident that he was about to take the first fence that would put him on the way to England.

The Captain of *Audacious,* telescope under arm, was pacing his quarter-deck, while keeping an eye on the working parties labouring on the most urgent repairs to spars and rigging. Roger was marched up to him, then halted and made a graceful bow. The Captain returned it courteously and asked in poor French:

'Is it true that you are one of General Bonaparte's aides-de-camp?'

Roger bowed again. '*Oui, Monsieur le Capitaine.*'

'How long is it since you left the General?'

'Six days. I am, as you say, direct from Cairo and became mixed in battle,' Roger replied with a strong accent and deliberately distorting his English.

The Captain nodded and spoke in English himself. 'In that case I feel sure Sir Horatio Nelson would like to speak with you. I have ordered a boat and am sending you across to his flagship.'

'It is great honour.' Roger bowed once more, now with a smile at having achieved his object without even having to use the bait he had prepared to get himself sent to the Admiral.

A well-grown Midshipman, who was standing by, was given a message about Roger for the Officer of the Watch in *Vanguard.* Roger was then taken to the ship's side, where a rope ladder led down to the waiting boat.

It was then that he had his first sight of the destruction wrought by the battle. Twenty-five ships lay at anchor scattered about the long, shallow bay. *Culloden* alone among them showed no sign of damage. Despite herculean efforts, and hours of cursing by her unfortunate Captain, Troubridge, who was one of Nelson's most able officers, it had proved impossible to get her off the

sandspit beyond Aboukir Island, where she had run aground
while still out of range of the enemy. There was hardly another
ship that had not lost a mast, and several had had all three shot
away. Most of the French ships had been reduced to no more
than floating hulks and two, having been burnt out and sunk,
had disappeared. From the masts still standing in the British
ships many of the sails still sagged in tatters. For miles round the
gently heaving sea was strewn with wreckage, barrels, crates and
hundreds of bobbing corpses, while scores of boats went to and
fro among them picking up anything that appeared worth
salvaging.

Through this watery charnel-house Roger was rowed to *Vanguard*. On board her the 'Middy' gave his message and, after a
wait of ten minutes out on the deck, Roger was taken in under
the poop to Berry, Nelson's Flag Captain.

After greeting him courteously, Berry said in French, 'Since
you have come from Cairo it is to be assumed that your Army
has captured that city.'

'Yes,' Roger replied in the same language. 'On the 25th
General Bonaparte took possession of the capital, after inflicting
a crushing defeat on the Mamelukes four days earlier on the left
bank of the Nile.'

'We picked up a rumour,' Berry said, 'that there had been a
battle in which your Army was victorious, but we have had no
particulars. Would you be agreeable, Colonel, to describing these
events to my Admiral?'

Roger drew himself up and put his hand on his heart. 'You will
appreciate, Captain, that it would not be in keeping with the
honour of a soldier of France to disclose the strength of our
forces, or their situation with regard to supplies. But I should be
happy to describe to your Admiral the actions in which the Army
has been engaged.'

Berry bowed. 'I thank you, Colonel. Sir Horatio has been
wounded, although, thank God, not seriously; and he is at
present much occupied. But I feel certain he would wish to hear
an eyewitness account of these events. Be good enough to wait
here.'

The Flag Captain left him and returned after a few minutes to
take him along to a larger cabin. Nelson was seated behind a
desk littered with papers. Roger had heard a great deal about
this quite junior Admiral whose heroic exploits had already led

the British people to take him to their hearts, but he had never before seen him.

Nelson had still two months to go before his fortieth birthday, but the pain he had suffered from severe wounds had made him look much older and had turned his hair grey. Roger was surprised, too, at the Admiral's frailty. With his thin, lined face and small body he looked a mere wisp of a man, and the loss of his right arm at the shoulder, with the sleeve pinned tightly across his chest, made him look even smaller. His head was bandaged and he was not wearing a shade over his misty eye, the sight of which he had lost during the taking of Corsica, but his 'bright' eye gleamed as alert and purposeful as ever.

After the Peace of '83 he had taken six months' leave to go to France, with the intention of learning the French language, because few officers then spoke it and while in the West Indies he had found it frustrating to have to rely on indifferent interpreters when questioning the personnel of French prizes he had taken. He had no gift for languages, so had never succeeded in fully mastering French, but he spoke sufficient of it to greet Roger in that tongue.

Politely coming to his feet, he said, 'Colonel, may I offer you my commiserations on having become a prisoner-of-war; but be assured that we shall treat you with the respect to which your rank entitles you. Pray take a chair and tell me all that you feel you can in honour disclose about the remarkable prowess of your Army.'

Roger bowed and replied, '*Monsieur l'Amiral,* the prowess of your Fleet equals, if not exceeds, that of our Army. I am greatly honoured that you should receive me. Since I must be conveyed to England as a prisoner there is one favour I would ask. Would you be so kind to inform Sir Christopher Brook of it?' Then he calmly accepted the invitation to sit down, and crossed his long legs comfortably.

'Chris Brook!' exclaimed Nelson. 'Why, he is an old friend. I served under him in the Indies. How comes it that you are acquainted with him?'

Roger cast a glance at Berry, who was standing in the doorway, and replied, 'Our association was of a distinctly private nature; but if I had your ear alone . . .'

'You intrigue me greatly,' said Nelson. Then he added to

Berry, 'I know you have much to do. Get on with it and leave me with the Colonel for a while.'

As Berry hesitated, the little Admiral pulled open a drawer in his desk, took a small pistol from it and pressed one of the triggers, upon which a miniature bayonet shot out from below the barrel. With a smile he said to Berry, 'Dear friend, I can see you fear that if you leave me alone with the Colonel he may do me an injury. Put your mind at rest. He is unarmed and, big fellow as he is, should he attack me I will stick him full of holes with this.'

When the Flag Captain had reluctantly withdrawn, Roger said in a low voice in English, 'Sir, I have spent much of my life in France, and it is true that I am one of General Bonaparte's aides-de-camp. In France I am accepted as a Frenchman who has some English blood, and a number of people there believe me to be a cousin of one Roger Brook. The fact is that I am Roger Brook, son to Admiral Brook, and for the past ten years I have served my country in secret as an agent of Mr. Pitt.'

'What's that you say!' cried the Admiral. 'That you are a Staff Officer of Bonaparte's, yet an Englishman and Chris Brook's son! I can scarce believe it.'

'Here is the proof,' smiled Roger, undoing his tunic and producing the despatch. 'General Bonaparte charged me to deliver this to Admiral Brueys for forwarding to the Directory. I did so yesterday afternoon, then could not escape remaining in *L'Orient* for the battle. After Admiral Brueys had been killed and the ship took fire, I went to his cabin, retrieved the despatch from a cabinet in which he had locked it and went overboard in the hope of bringing it to you. Under God's protection, I have succeeded.'

His good eye glittering with excitement, Nelson took the despatch and ripped it open. After a glance at the closely written pages he threw them back to Roger and said quickly, 'Your French must be far better than mine, Mr. Brook. Pray translate it for me.'

To Roger the request presented no difficulty. For the next five minutes, pausing only now and then to render the sense exactly, he gave a version in English of the despatch. In a series of the abrupt, dogmatic statements that were typical of Bonaparte's address, either in speech or writing, it gave an account of his occupation of Cairo and his intention when he had fully subdued Egypt to march north and conquer Syria.

'Shiver my timbers!' Nelson exclaimed, when Roger had done. 'This is indeed valuable intelligence, Mr. Brook. In obtaining it for us you have been of as much service to your country as an extra frigate would have been to me these past two months. 'Twas only the lack of sufficient of those eyes of the Fleet that prevented me from receiving intelligence of the whereabouts of the French weeks ago and coming up with them to destroy them utterly. Owing to your courageous conduct, we now know Syria to be the next victim on this horrible young Corsican's list.'

Roger shook his head. 'Permit me to remark, sir, that General Bonaparte does not merit the opprobrium of the word " horrible ". He is, like all the French who have risen to power since the Revolution, a thief on a grand scale. He is, moreover, completely unscrupulous. Daily he makes promises that he has no intention of keeping and, at any time, to gain his ends he will tell a bare-faced lie.

'Yet, as a person, he possesses great powers of attraction. At times he falls into ungovernable rages, but they are brief and the smiling amends he makes afterwards, if his fury has had small justification, leave their victim more devoted to him than before. He is extremely generous to those who have served him well, and particularly to his family who have done little to deserve it. He has no thought of amassing a fortune for himself, which he could so easily do, but seizes treasure only to fill the empty coffers of his country.

'He is most loyal to his friends, invariably treats women with great courtesy, has an excellent sense of humour and delights in simple games. When I was living at the Court he formed in Italy, after the Armistice of Leoben, he would partake in the evenings, like any schoolboy, in charades with his family and friends, and in other pastimes, too, in which, at times, he willingly made himself a laughing stock.

'And he has yet other sides. Although not trained to law, he is a great administrator. Although not schooled in science, he can hold his own with the finest intellects and his thirst for know-ledge is insatiable. He has brought with him to Egypt more than a hundred distinguished civilians—archaeologists, architects, artists and others—for the purpose of revealing to the world the truth about the country's ancient civilization. No, sir, I assure you the word "horrible" is not applicable. I am even of the opinion that if given peace and power he would become a great and just ruler, bringing to France a new era of true liberty, toleration and prosperity.'

Nelson shook his head. 'Indeed, Mr. Brook, I find this personal account by one who knows Bonaparte well of the greatest interest, and you have made out a good case for him. But it is the duty of both of us to do our utmost to destroy him and all the other blasphemous atheists who now make the French race anathema to us. My most earnest prayer is that I may be permitted to continue helping in God's work and live to see this done. Please tell me now of your hazardous landing, the desert march and the great battle outside Cairo.'

For half an hour Roger described the scenes through which he had lived during the past month, Nelson interrupting him only occasionally to ask swift, shrewd questions. When he had done the Admiral said:

'And now, what of your future plans?'

Roger laughed. 'Why, sir, I could not have a happier outlook. Being captured gives me the perfect excuse for returning to England, and I am counting on your good offices to have me conveyed thither.'

Nelson looked thoughtful, then he said, 'But did you not tell me that you are employed by Mr. Pitt?'

'Not in the ordinary sense, sir. I have undertaken certain special missions for him, but I remain my own master. When I last saw him I was not charged with any specific task. I volunteered only to return to France and do my best to keep him informed of the future intentions of the Directory. I will not trouble you with particulars of the event which led to my accompanying General Bonaparte to Egypt. It suffices to say that I had no wish to do so, but was compelled to it, lest suspicion fall upon me of my intentions in France.'

'Yet coming to Egypt enabled you to provide us with an invaluable piece of intelligence—this despatch. Your position as an Englishman on Bonaparte's Staff is unique. If you remain here similar opportunities may well arise. Moreover you were previously cut off from sending regular reports, whereas now that the French Fleet is destroyed I shall blockade the coast. There will be British ships constantly patrolling these waters. We could arrange for boats to be sent ashore to lonely places at certain times to pick up anything you could send. Even a general outline once a month of what is going forward at Bonaparte's headquarters would be worth its weight in diamonds to us.'

Roger gave the Admiral an uneasy look. 'There is much in what you say, sir. But Cairo is all of five days' ride distant, and I could not leave my post at will. It would be near impossible to find a safe hand by which to send such reports to the coast and, did one go astray, it would cost me my life.'

'I appreciate that; but even so I think you should remain. Leaving aside the question of regular reports, you might well become privy to some major decisions by Bonaparte which could mean the success or failure of an entire campaign. It would then be worth while for you to leave your headquarters without permission in order to inform us of it.'

As Roger listened, black misery descended on him. It now looked as though his happy dreams of the morning were to be shattered completely. Suddenly revolting against the course the Admiral was seeking to force upon him, he exclaimed:

'But damme, sir! I've already done enough to justify my request for a passage home. Owing to your great victory, the French are now cut off. Even should Bonaparte wish to take his Army back to France he cannot. So maybe for years to come I'd be stranded in the East.'

Nelson's thin, lined face grew stern. 'Must I remind you, Mr. Brook, that our country is at war? On that account many of my brave men gave their lives this past night; whereas you are called on only to return to Cairo, and by so doing may render a service far greater than lay in the power of any one of them to perform.'

Roger suppressed a groan, then shook his head. 'I cry you mercy, sir! I am no coward. Time and again, during these past ten years, I've risked my life; but there's a limit beyond which——'

'Mr. Brook!' the Admiral cut in, 'there is no limit to the duty we owe our King and country. And in these very special circumstances I do not consider it consonant with mine to find you a passage home.'

With fury in his heart, Roger stared at the frail, tense figure on the far side of the desk, then burst out, 'If you think the last would deter me, you have misjudged your man. Had I a mind to it, I would unaided reach China or Peru. Aye, or still in the guise of a French Colonel break prison and, despite your damned blockade, reach home.'

A smile twitched at Nelson's lips and he said quietly, ' You are wrong, Mr. Brook. I have not misjudged my man. There spoke the son of my old comrade-in-arms. You could not have proved better to me that you are a real chip off the old block and a true Englishman. And that is why you will return to Cairo.'

Roger slumped back in his chair with a heavy sigh. Then, suddenly, he smiled. ' I had meant to, sir, to give you joy of your great victory. Now I give you joy of two, although the latter is a very minor one. I give you best, and will do as you wish.'

' Well said! I felt assured you would.' The Admiral's bright eye now beamed with approval. ' With my next despatch I'll enclose a letter for your father's eye only, thus giving him the joy of reporting to Mr. Pitt the fine service rendered by his son. And now, how shall we set about returning you to Bonaparte? '

This was no simple matter; for the thunder of the cannonade had brought hundreds of Arabs to the beach, and since dawn they had been murdering and stripping such French sailors as had managed to swim ashore. Even if it had been safe for Roger to land he could not be provided with a horse and it was over ten miles to Alexandria. Then, since he insisted that none of Nelson's men should be allowed into his secret, they must continue to believe him French, yet some way must be devised by which he could escape.

After ten minutes' thought and discussion a way was found. Nelson recalled his Flag Captain and said to him, ' Berry, the Colonel is a most sensible man. Naturally he dreads the possibility of being held a prisoner for several years. Therefore, in return for a certain service—although I could not allow him to return to Bonaparte—I have agreed that we will put him ashore as a free man in Crete, Italy or Sicily, as may prove convenient. The service he will render us is to go in a boat with you to the outskirts of Alexandria and point out to you the position of certain concealed batteries the French have mounted along the coast. As the Colonel has not yet broken his fast, be good enough to take him to your cabin, have a meal and a bottle of Marsala sent there and then, while he eats, return to me.'

Berry gave Roger a look that barely disguised his contempt for such a traitor, then beckoned him to follow. He bowed his farewell to the little Admiral, with the faintest hint of a wink, and ten minutes later was hungrily disposing of a meal of salt pork washed down by good wine in the Flag Captain's cabin.

When Berry returned to his Admiral, Nelson said, 'Don't be deceived, my dear fellow, by our Colonel. He is no traitor, but a brave man and a slippery customer. I feel certain that he suggested this betrayal of the batteries outside Alexandria because he knows that twilight will be falling by the time a boat can take him there, and that it will have to go close inshore. I'd wager a guinea to a penny that he means to jump out and swim for it.'

'Should he attempt it,' Berry growled, 'I'll put a pistol bullet through his head.'

The Admiral laughed. 'Nay, nay; you'll do nothing of the kind. He gave the impression that he was talking very freely, and so did I. In short, I trust that I matched his cunning with my own. I've given him a main-sail full of false information and I wish him to convey it to that scoundrel Bonaparte. A mile or two before you come opposite Alexandria have the boat pull close inshore. Should I prove right, and he jump for it, let him. And beforehand you must give orders to the boat's crew that they should fire after him but in no circumstances hit him. Is that clear?'

'Aye, aye, sir,' Berry grinned. 'What a good jest, to use him to deceive the Frog-eaters.'

Roger had no sooner finished his meal than the Flag Captain escorted him down to a longboat, the crew of which had already received their instructions. Again he looked from side to side at the scene of terrible devastation and, as the sailors bent to their oars, the boat nosed its way between wreckage of all kinds and bloated corpses.

Half an hour's strenuous pulling brought them to seaward of Aboukir Island and, passing over the sandspit, they rounded the promontory. After another hour and a half, that seemed far longer to the anxious Roger, they were within a few miles of Alexandria. By then it was half past six and the sun was sinking low on the horizon. The boat was no more than a hundred yards from the shore and Roger felt that the time had come for him to make his breakaway.

In the stern of the boat Berry was sitting on the landward side of the coxswain and Roger on the seaward side. Praying that Nelson had given his instructions clearly, and that they would be obeyed to the letter, Roger pointed to a mound at no great distance from the beach, and said :

'*Regardez, Monsieur le Capitaine la première redoute . . .*'
Then, jumping up, as Berry turned to look shoreward, he gave him a sharp push sideways and leapt over the gunwale into the water.

As his head came up he heard shouts and oaths. Ducking swiftly, he swam a dozen yards under water. When he came up a second time he heard shots and several pistol bullets sang over his head. Swimming strongly he got halfway to the shore, then looked back. The coxswain was yelling at the crew of the boat and turning her to come after him. Berry was standing up in the stern, reloading his pistol. The shelving shore was shallow. Next moment Roger's feet and knees struck sand. Half wading, half swimming, he floundered on, looked back again and saw that the boat had run aground.

Two more pistols cracked. Fearful that he might yet be hit by a bullet, he stood up and splashed his way ashore. By the time his boots were squelching on dry sand the firing had ceased and two of the boat's crew, having poled their oars, were endeavouring to push the boat off into deeper water. He covered another hundred yards at a lurching run, then flopped down behind the nearest of a group of palm trees.

The only rest he had had since setting out from Damanhûr, nearly forty hours earlier, had been his sleep of exhaustion on the hard tier deck of *Audacious*. He would have given a great deal to scoop out a hole for his hip in the warm sand and spend the night where he was. But he dare not, in case marauding Arabs came upon and killed him. After twenty minutes to recover from his exertions, he got to his feet and set out on the two-mile trudge to Alexandria.

By the time he reached the most advanced French picket it was fully dark and, when challenged, as he did not know the password, he could only shout that he was a French officer who had escaped from the English. Giving him the benefit of the doubt the sentry called his Sergeant and, as soon as the N.C.O. was satisfied, he could not have been more helpful. From somewhere he produced an Arab with a donkey cart and Roger was driven in it to Kléber's headquarters.

There he told his story to the General, who had already heard of the disaster to the French Fleet but was anxious to have a full account of it. Roger did his best to oblige him for some twenty

minutes, then declared that he was so exhausted that he must go
to bed. Kléber, loudly commending him for the wit and courage
he had displayed in fooling 'those pigs of English' and making
his escape, took him up to a bedroom, and a quarter of an hour
later he was fast asleep.

In the morning he woke with his bruised arm and side still very
sore and, anxious though he now was to get back to Cairo, he
decided that it would be foolish to set out on the long journey
without having taken at least twenty-four hours to become in
better shape. He took his time in getting up, washing and cleaning himself, while one of the Guides he had brought as escort
sponged and pressed his now faded and tattered uniform.

Shortly before midday he went to Sarodopulous's office and
asked the banker if he might spend the rest of the day and a night
at his villa. The bearded Greek was delighted and told his handsome nephew, Achilles, to accompany Roger out to the villa and
see that he had every comfort.

Roger spent a lazy afternoon on the terrace overlooking the
bay. Shortly before dusk his host joined him and gave him the
bits of news that he had received from correspondents in several
countries, or had picked up from merchant captains who put in
at Alexandria. Most of the news was months old, but it often took
many weeks for happenings in Western Europe to become known
in Egypt.

In May, Count Cobenzl had replaced the less urbane Baron
Thugut as Austrian Foreign Minister, and a defensive Treaty had
been signed between Austria and Naples.

Towards the end of May there had been a rebellion in Ireland.
Disappointed of French support, but encouraged by the London
Corresponding Society, some thirty thousand United Irishmen
had taken up arms in Kildare and Westmeath. But the plot
had been leaked, a number of the leaders had been arrested
in Dublin just before the signal for the rising had been given
and, after a limited amount of fighting, the revolt had been
suppressed.

The most astounding news to Roger was that his real master
had fought a duel. Apparently an Irish Member of Parliament,
named Tierney, had so consistently sought to thwart him on
questions of defence that in the House Mr. Pitt had publicly
denounced him as a traitor and had refused to withdraw his
words. Tierney had thereupon challenged him and, although frail

'Billy' Pitt had never fired a shot in anger, he had at once accepted. On Whit Sunday, May 27th, they fought with pistols on Wimbledon Common. In the first discharge neither was hit. In the second Pitt fired into the air, and Tierney then refrained from firing, declaring himself satisfied. But that the brilliant, high-minded Prime Minister—the very soul of all that was best in Britain and the keystone of her resistance—should have felt in honour bound to expose himself to possible death at the hands of a cantankerous, unpatriotic bully had profoundly shocked all decent people.

One other piece of news gave Roger pleasure. The personally charming but utterly irresponsible Charles Fox, wedded with the years ever more closely to the principles of the French revolutionaries, had, at a birthday dinner given in his honour, argued that two thousand good men might do as much in Britain as Washington had done in America, and later proposed the toast, 'To our Sovereign, His Majesty the People'. For that the King had struck Fox's name from the members of the Privy Council.

Sarodopulous then asked Roger how he was placed for funds. Roger thanked him and replied that he had sufficient for his immediate needs and could obtain more from the Paymaster-General in Cairo.

Sarodopulous smiled at him. 'Perhaps that may not be as easy as you think now that *L'Orient* has gone down with the treasure that was to pay the French Army. Do not look surprised at my knowing about that, or of your capture and courageous escape, although you made no mention to me of it. As a banker it is my business to be well informed on such matters. All I wish to say is that owing to your introduction I have made a great deal of money, even though charging only the normal rate of exchange. Therefore should you at any time find yourself short, you have only to draw upon me and I shall be happy to honour your draft.'

Roger thanked him heartily and said that, while he hoped it would not be necessary, he would avail himself of the banker's generous offer should he find himself embarrassed for funds.

The Greek then drew from his pocket a little sack made of soft leather. Opening it, he tipped into his hand a finely worked gold neck-chain which had a single medium-sized but very fine blue diamond hanging from it. Handing it to Roger, he said:

'This at least I insist that you accept as an immediate token of my gratitude. In France a man like yourself must know some lady whom it would not be unfitting to adorn.'

When arranging for Sarodopulous to become financial agent to the French Army in Alexandria, Roger's only thought had been to make a return for the banker's past kindness. However he was well aware that not only in France, where there was now no limit to corruption, but also in England it was still general practice to receive a suitable present for such a service. In consequence, having expressed his delight at this beautiful jewel, he willingly accepted it, thinking meanwhile how well it would look between the breasts of his beautiful Zanthé.

Roger enjoyed an excellent meal with the banker, his sister-in-law and Achilles, then went early to bed, for he had ordered his escort of Guides to report at the villa at four o'clock the following morning; so that by an early start he might cover the thirty miles back to Damanhûr before the great heat of the day.

It was on August 4th that he set out for Cairo. Having resigned himself to accept Nelson's arguments, he did so without reluctance. However uncertain and dubious the future to which he was again committed, for the moment he was more than consoled by the thought of the immediate joys that lay ahead of him. Fate had decreed that he would not, after all, have to sacrifice the delight of having the beautiful Zanthé for his mistress.

He felt no regrets for the way in which he had taken her. Any young woman in a country that had been invaded, who fell into the hands of its conquerors, would have been amazed had she been treated in any other way. The best she could hope for was that an officer would find her attractive and become her protector. To his mind, Zanthé had been exceptionally fortunate. Not only had she been saved from most brutal usage, by being bought by a man who was in a position to keep her in safety and comfort, but this man was one whom Roger—never having been given to false modesty—considered with some justification to be as fine a fellow as any she could have found in Cairo.

Her resistance, as it had transpired, had not been on account of any personal repugnance to him, or because he was one of the invaders of her country, or because she was in love with someone else; for, clearly, there had been no love between her and her husband, and Eastern women of good standing were given no opportunity to carry on love-affairs outside their homes. It had been due simply to the normal fears of any girl lacking all experience and about to be taken by a man whom she had known for little more than an hour. Had he realized that, he would have refrained from pressing her and given several days to wooing her into willing submission.

Yet, on consideration, he felt that it was just as well that things had happened as they had. After all she was not a young girl in the accepted sense, nor frigid from some inhibition, but a fully grown woman, capable of intense passion, as he had soon discovered. Moreover in addition to her devastating physical attractions, she was obviously a cultured woman and spoke French fluently. That promised many hours of delightful conversation in which he would not have the labour of translating his thoughts into Arabic. Knowing the fatalism that was such a strong feature of all Eastern minds, he was in good hopes that when he got back to her she would receive him without rancour, having decided to accept her new situation. If she did still harbour resentment, when he presented her with the beautiful jewel that Sarodopulous had given him she could hardly fail to be pleased with such a splendid peace offering. But the more he thought about it the more confident he became that, having had close on a fortnight to ponder what would have been her fate had he not rescued her, she would have realized how fortunate she was and now be anxious to show her gratitude.

Eager as he was to behold her again, his bruised arm still pained him and he did not make any better speed than he had on his outward journey; but during the five days that it took him to get back to Cairo visions of Zanthé filled his mind to the exclusion of all else. He had to tell himself repeatedly that he must not let her make a slave of him, yet he knew that he was more passionately in love than he had been for a very long time.

Late in the afternoon of the 8th he entered Cairo and, in duty bound, rode straight to Bonaparte's headquarters to report his arrival. News of the annihilation of the French Fleet had reached the capital from Kléber by fast courier three days earlier, so the first shock and sense of despair felt by Bonaparte's Staff on learning that there could be no return to France had worn off. But when Roger entered the General-in-Chief's ante-room he was surprised to find that his own escape had been reported by another courier the previous day.

His fellow aides-de-camp and his old friend Junot, now a

H

General, who happened to be there, all hailed him with delight, crowding round to embrace and congratulate him. He was even more surprised when he heard the account they had received of his escape. It was believed that when being taken from one ship to another in a boat he had fallen upon the officer-in-charge, snatched both his pistols, shot him with one and the coxswain with the other, then dived overboard and swum through a hail of musket balls to the shore.

It was not uncommon for acts of bravery to be magnified in this way by inaccurate information and, as no one could prove to the contrary, Roger decided not to disillusion his admiring companions. It tickled his sense of humour that he should be acclaimed a hero for an exploit he had planned himself and carried out at little risk, and it was also pleasing to know that it would add considerably to the already high regard that Bonaparte had for him.

A few minutes later the General-in-Chief received him with great cordiality, patted him on his bruised arm, tweaked the lobe of his ear painfully—a favourite, if peculiar, way he had of showing his approval of those who had performed brave deeds—then made Roger sit down and give him a description of the battle, as he had so far had reports of it only from people who had not been present.

Bonaparte was still furious with Brueys for having failed to obey his instructions to seek safety under the guns of either Malta or Corfu, and thus losing his Fleet; but he did not seem at all dismayed at his Army now being cut off in Egypt, and he was intensely interested in the tactics used by the British Fleet. Anxious as Roger was to get to Zanthé, it was over an hour before his master, giving Roger's ear another sharp tweak, allowed him to depart.

As he reached the door Bonaparte called after him, 'You have returned just in time to accompany me on an expedition. That crafty old rogue, Ibrahim Bey, is still lurking, with several thousand Mamelukes, two or three days' march east of Cairo. Reynier, whose Division I sent in pursuit, does not appear able to overcome him, so I must go myself to drive him out of Egypt. We leave at four o'clock tomorrow morning.'

Roger's breath caught in his throat. Turning, he stared at Bonaparte's back, his face a picture of dismay. His first delight in Zanthé had been all too brief. Now he was to be torn from her arms in the middle of the night and might not see her again for weeks. To protest at an order of Bonaparte's could bring on one of those furious rages and even lead to dismissal. Yet he felt he must risk it. After a moment he said:

' *Mon Général*. You know well that I would willingly go with you anywhere at any time. But should I collapse, I would only be a burden to you. During the past fourteen days I have had little sleep and in getting clear of the burning *L'Orient* my arm and side were bruised black and blue. One more day in the saddle and I fear I'd fall from it from sheer exhaustion.'

Bonaparte was already busy with some papers. He did not turn his head, but said, ' I had temporarily forgotten what you have been through. Get to bed, then, and I'll see you on my return.'

Nearly overcome with relief, Roger thanked him and stumbled from the room. On leaving the headquarters he almost ran the short distance to his little house. The door was standing open. Hurrying inside he noticed that, although the fountain was still playing in the small open court, the piles of cushions had been removed from the corners. Vaguely he wondered why. Running upstairs, he found the door of the principal bedroom also open. There was not a stick of furniture in it. Frantically, he yelled for Marbois. There came no reply. The house was empty, and Zanthé gone.

13

The Loves of the Exiled

SCARCELY able to believe his eyes, Roger stared about him. Empty
of furniture, the room seemed larger than when he had last been
in it. For an instant he thought that he might have entered the
wrong house; but he had not. He recognized the intricate pattern
of the lace-like woodwork of the enclosed balcony that protruded
over the narrow street.

Swinging on his heel, he again yelled for Marbois, then for the
Arab servants. The echo of his voice came back to him, but no
other sound broke the stillness. Pounding down the stairs three
at a time he rushed through to the kitchen quarters. There was
no one there, the fire was out, the cooking pots had gone and the
cupboards stood open. Only some decaying vegetables and a little
spilled fat on a stone slab, both now black with flies, showed that
the place had ever been occupied.

Still he could hardly credit that he was not suffering from
an appalling nightmare. The mental pictures he had been con-
juring up of his return to Zanthé were still so clear in his mind
that it fought desperately against accepting the fact that he had
lost her. After a few minutes he persuaded himself that she would
not have fled from him deliberately, and that there must be some
other explanation for her disappearance.

Although already subconsciously aware of it, the thought that
Marbois had also disappeared suddenly became uppermost in
his mind; and Marbois must know what had happened. Next
moment Roger was out in the street and running hard in the
direction of a Hamam in which his servant's Company had been
quartered. On reaching it he controlled himself with an effort,
broke into a swift walk and strode inside.

212

There, amid a splendour of Moorish arches, tiled walls and bathing pools, some fifty soldiers were lounging, playing cards, polishing their equipment or simply dozing on straw-filled palliasses.

Marbois was among them. On seeing Roger enter, he stood up then, suddenly white-faced and apprehensive, came hesitantly towards him.

'What are you doing here?' Roger demanded. 'I ordered you to remain in the house until my return.'

'I . . . I left it only because it was empty, *Monsieur le Colonel,*' stammered the young Provençal.

'Empty!' cried Roger. 'What the hell do you mean? Who emptied it? Explain yourself this instant!'

'The people who owned the house,' replied the trembling Marbois. 'They came back two days after you left Cairo. A father and three younger men that I took to be his sons. They talked for some time with the Arab servants, then went away. That night they came back with carts and carried all the furniture out to them. . . .'

'And you let them?' Roger blazed. 'You, a soldier of France, allowed these people to render my lodging uninhabitable and put you out into the gutter!'

'Monsieur, I was one and they were many. They set on me and tied me up, then emptied the house and left me there. It was morning before I managed to free myself and report what had happened.'

'To whom did you report?'

'To the Commander of my Company, Captain Lestrange.'

'Very well. Get back to the house. Beg, borrow or steal something for me to sleep on tonight and food for the morning.' Abruptly, Roger turned on his heel and, followed by the amused glances of a score of soldiers who had listened in silence to his outburst, stalked from the baths.

It took him an hour to run Lestrange to earth and when he did he received scant satisfaction. The Captain agreed that an assault on a French soldier was punishable by death, but pointed out that justice could not be done on the culprits when their identity was unknown.

Roger angrily demanded why he had neglected to find out the name of the owner of the house and have him searched for. Lestrange excused himself by saying that it was not as though

Marbois had been murdered; he had many other duties to attend to, and surely now that Roger had returned to Cairo he could easily find himself another comfortable lodging.

Roger did not care a fig about having been left with an empty house. It was the loss of Zanthé that was driving him almost berserk. But nothing could be gained by telling the Captain about her, and what had occurred was already clear to him. Like hundreds of other well-to-do citizens of Cairo, the owner of the house had fled owing to the riots that had followed the Battle of the Pyramids. Some days later, learning that Bonaparte had restored order in the city, he had returned to resume possession. Finding that it had been taken over by a French officer, and realizing that he had no hope of turning him out, he had decided to make sure that he was at least not robbed of his belongings. So he had removed everything and had taken Zanthé with him.

Hurrying back to the house Roger questioned the people who lived on either side of it. At first they denied all knowledge of their neighbour, but eventually admitted that his name was Hassan ben-Jussif and that he was a dealer in precious stones. However, neither threats nor offers of money would induce them to give any information about his relatives, or suggest where he had gone.

By then it was dusk, but Roger would not yet give up. He spent another hour and a half seeking out the Provost Marshal. Having described what had taken place, he asked that an intensive search be set on foot for both Hassan ben-Jussif and Zanthé. But he had been able to secure only a very vague description of the former, and when he attempted to give a word picture of Zanthé that would make her identifiable he found it far from easy.

To his intense annoyance he now realized that he had not troubled to ask her full name or that of her dead husband. He could only say that she was about seventeen, of medium height, dark-haired but fair-skinned, had a well-developed figure and a beautiful face, with tawny eyes, eyebrows that turned up at the ends, a full mouth and gleaming white teeth.

The Provost Marshal shook his head and said, 'I'll do what I can, my dear fellow, but I cannot hold out much hope of tracing these people. Cairo has a population of near half a million and there are a thousand streets and alleys in it. As ten days have elapsed since this occurrence, any trail they may have left has gone cold by now. There are hundreds of places in which this man ben-Jussif might remain concealed for months without my police obtaining word of him. As for the girl, she will have been put in some harem or other and is unlikely to emerge again. Besides, the fact that you bought her from some soldiers for a hundred louis gives you not a jot of title to her under Mohammedan law. And you must know the orders that the General-in-Chief has given. He is so anxious to woo these people that it has been made a crime to molest them in any way. He allowed the troops a limited licence for those first few nights in Cairo, but now my instructions are that even street women must be treated with reasonable decency.'

With this cold comfort, and now ready to drop with fatigue, Roger once more returned to the house. Marbois had, meanwhile, made him up a shake-down in the big bedroom. Gazing round its echoing emptiness with lack-lustre eyes, he thought bitterly of the scene that during the past few days he had so consistently envisaged as taking place there; then he threw off his clothes and, almost crying with distress, fell asleep.

Next morning he gave Marbois money to buy new pots and pans and told him to engage a houseman and a cook. Then he went out himself and bought divans, cushions, handwoven rugs and other items, sufficient to furnish about one-third of the house, which was all he intended to occupy. Having completed his purchases he went to headquarters and sought out Bourrienne, in order to learn from him what had been taking place recently in Cairo.

Industrious as the *Chef de Cabinet* was by nature, his master's departure from Cairo had eased the pressure of business; so he was pleased to see and talk with his one-time assistant. He said that during the fortnight that the General-in-Chief had spent in the Egyptian capital he had displayed more than ever his extraordinary ability to tackle scores of problems with sound judgment and despatch.

General Bon, with his Division, had been permanently installed in the great Citadel outside the city, to overawe such groups of malcontents as remained in it, and, as a warning to possible trouble-makers, Bonaparte still had the heads of half a dozen men who were guilty of small offences cut off publicly in the streets every evening. On the other hand, he had been greatly impressed with the bravery of the Mamelukes, so was now forming those taken prisoner into Companies, to be incorporated into the French Army and, as a mark of his confidence in them he had taken two, Roustan and Ibrahim, into his personal service.

Without waiting a day he had appointed nine prominent Sheiks to form a Divan, invested with authority to keep order in the city. Two days later he established four similar Divans in the provinces of Alexandria, Rosetta, Ghizeh and Kelyoub. Thus he gave the inhabitants the illusion that they were to be governed by men of their own race, while in reality he kept local control himself and vested it in the provinces in Kléber, Menou, Belliard and Murat. He had also appointed Intendants, to collect for him all taxes formerly paid to the Mamelukes, had done much by a series of proclamations to get the wheels of commerce turning normally again and had given an order that wherever the victorious Tricolour of France was flown, the Crescent of Islam should be hoisted to fly beside it.

He had, too, lost no time in informing the Directory of his immediate needs to convert Egypt into a pleasant and thriving French colony, and Bourrienne showed Roger a copy of the list he had sent. It read: a company of actors, a company of dancers, four marionette shows, a hundred Frenchwomen, the wives of all the married men in the Army, twenty surgeons, thirty apothecaries, ten physicians, some founders, some distillers and dealers in liquor, fifty gardeners and their families and seeds of every kind of vegetable, a hundred thousand litres of brandy, thirty thousand ells of blue and scarlet cloth and a supply of soap and oil.

Roger thought the priorities somewhat strange but, as he handed the list back, his only comment was, 'I fear it will be a long time now before we see either the marionettes or the whores.'

Bourrienne gave a wry smile. 'Yes. This, of course, was sent off before we heard about the destruction of our Fleet. That is a terrible blow to us. When I received the despatch our little man was out in the desert, and I sent it on to him. Temporarily, I think, he was quite shattered, but he has remarkable resilience. In no time, he was going about saying such things as, "This is the moment when characters of a superior order assert themselves. The English have compelled us to do greater things than we expected" and "We must now die in this country or come out of it as great as the Ancients."'

The last sums up our situation in a nut-shell,' remarked Roger gloomily.

' But think of the countries we shall see, if we survive. Having secured our rear by conquering Syria, we shall descend the Red Sea, invade and subdue India, turn north-west through Persia, overrun Turkey and arrive home by way of a crushed Austro-Hungary.'

' Heavens above! Can you mean this? '

' Not seriously,' Bourrienne smiled, ' but at times that is the way our master talks. Personally, I think the duration of our ordeals in the East depends upon events in France. Although he fancies himself in the role of another Alexander, it is upon France that his eyes are really fixed. By leaving the stage there he has given the Directors enough rope to hang themselves, and as soon as they are ripe to swing he will somehow manage to return.'

' What! And leave us in some damned jungle to be eaten by cannibals? '

Bourrienne laughed. ' I don't think he would leave me, but he would have to leave a lot of other people and, perhaps, you would be among them.'

' Enough! ' Roger cried, standing up. ' I've ample to depress me without listening to prognostications of so black a future.' And, leaving his friend, he went back to his lodging to superintend the installation of the new furniture he had bought.

During Bonaparte's absence the gallant Desaix had been left in command in Cairo. Roger, in an attempt to take his mind off the loss of Zanthé, attached himself temporarily to him. As Desaix had his own aides-de-camp, Rapp and Savary, Roger was given no special tasks, but he attended the General on an interesting inspection of the Citadel. There was a magnificent collection of armour in it, taken from the Crusaders. Some of the helmets hung outside one of the great interior gates of the fortress and, although they had been there for six hundred years, owing to the dry climate of Egypt they showed little sign of deterioration.

He also rode out with Desaix and some hundred others to the Pyramids. There they marvelled at those vast monuments formed from great blocks of stone, so perfectly aligned that one could not put even the blade of a dagger between them. With a dozen or so of the younger officers, Savary and Roger climbed to the top of the Great Pyramid. It was a most exhausting exploit; but when they reached the summit they found that the apex of marble casing had been torn away, so there was plenty of room to sit down and enjoy the stupendous view.

Yet these distractions failed to keep Roger's thoughts for long from Zanthé. Every morning he harried the Provost Marshal with fruitless enquiries for news of ben-Jussif. Whenever he walked the streets he peered at the face of each woman, however poorly dressed, hoping that above her yashmak he might recognize the lovely, tawny eyes that still haunted his daydreams.

After a week's absence Bonaparte returned. On August 11th he had met and defeated Ibrahim Bey's force at Salahiyeh and had driven the remnants of it back to the Syrian frontier.

On the 18th the Nile was declared to have risen to the maximum height it could reach that year and Bonaparte, desirous of gaining the goodwill of the people, joined with his Staff in the annual rejoicing. Two days later there fell the great festival of the Birth of the Prophet. The Sheiks and Imams, now anxious to propitiate the weedy little Corsican who had been clever enough to endow them with a semblance of power and before whom they now bowed low, addressing him as 'The Exalted One', invited him to attend the celebrations.

Accordingly, accompanied by several Generals and the principal members of his Staff, he went to the house of the Sheik El Bekri. Like the hundred or more Sheiks assembled there, they sat down on carpets, with their legs crossed. The Sheiks then recited many verses from the Koran recording the life of the Prophet and, as they uttered their sing-song litany, swayed their bodies to and fro rhythmically. Afterwards a great supper was served of foods, mostly very highly spiced, and an abundance of sweetmeats. Everyone used his fingers to eat with, which surprised most of the French guests; but Roger, having travelled in the East, was used to this custom.

Through his interpreter, Bonaparte made it clear that he thought more highly of the Mohammedan than the Christian religion; so he was pressed by the Imams to become a convert to their faith. With his usual duplicity he led them on by saying that he would like to do so, but did not feel that he could submit to circumcision or give up wine, which was a necessity to people who had been reared in a cold country.

His objections gave the Imams much to wrangle over during

the months that followed. They eventually agreed that circumcision could be dispensed with and that wine might be drunk in proportion to the good works accomplished by the drinker. But by that time Bonaparte had other fish to fry and, in any case, he had never had the least intention of antagonizing the millions of convinced Christians in Europe by becoming a Muslim.

The nearest he ever got to that was to have a Turkish costume made for himself and appear in it one morning at breakfast, to amuse his officers; but he soon found it so uncomfortable that, having had his joke, he threw it off.

On August 22nd he founded the Institute of Egypt on the model of the famous *Institut de France*. It had four Sections—Mathematics, Physics, Political Economy, and Literature and Art. Monge was made President, Bonaparte modestly reserving for himself the Vice-Presidency. Berthollet, Denon and all the other intellectuals who had accompanied him to Egypt made up the membership. Also included was a number of his officers, selected by him in this instance only on their standard of education. Caffarelli —his one-legged, highly gifted Chief Engineer—was among them, and Bourrienne; also Roger, on account of the many languages that he spoke and the fact that his general knowledge far surpassed that of his courageous brother aides-de-camp.

At the very first meeting of the Institute Bonaparte requested its members to deliberate and report on: how to improve the baking ovens of the Army; could any substitute for hops be found for making beer; were there any means of purifying the waters of the Nile; would windmills or watermills prove more serviceable in Cairo; could saltpetre be found in Egypt, or some other ingredient that would enable gunpowder to be made locally. He also charged the Institute to examine measures for improving the education of the natives and to bring out a newspaper every ten days, in French, to be called ' *Décade Egyptienne* '.

The Institute was housed in a palace of one of the Beys. All the machines and technical instruments brought from France were set up in it, a big laboratory for chemical experiments was installed and soon a number of rooms began to be filled with objects of interest dug up by the archaeologists. Some of them measured the Pyramids and the Sphinx, others made drawings of temples, statues and mummies. Others again set themselves the colossal task of translating the hieroglyphics.

Meanwhile Bonaparte set up scores of small factories—a mint, foundries, distilleries, gunsmiths, shoemakers, clothiers, saddlers, ropemakers and others—in which he employed all the tradesmen of his Army. Rarely, if ever, has so much been accomplished with so little by one man in so short a time.

Yet, after a month in Cairo, the Army was seething with discontent. Both officers and men found Egypt far from being, as had been depicted to them, the fabled land of the Ptolemies. Food was short and monotonous. No man might go out alone in the streets at night or wander far from a camp in the desert without risk of being set upon and killed. They were not even allowed the consolation of robbing the native traders and making free with their women. Wine was unobtainable, and strong liquor far beyond the price they could afford. Above all, they were now cut off from their homes and beginning to fear that they would never see them again.

The resentment of some of the senior officers at Bonaparte having got them into this situation was still more bitter than that of their juniors, for many of them had made fortunes during the Italian campaign and now they saw no prospect of ever getting back to France to enjoy them. Even Generals such as Lannes, Bessières and Murat, who owed everything to Bonaparte, criticized him openly in his presence until, on one occasion, he was stung into rounding on them and snapping at the huge mulatto, Dumas:

'Enough of your seditious parleys! Take care that I do not perform my duty. Your six feet of stature shall not save you from being shot.'

Very few officers were prepared to stand up for their General-in-Chief, but among them was the faithful Junot, whom he had picked out when a Seargeant at Toulon and made his very first aide-de-camp. Junot heard one of his brother Generals, Lanusse, make some disparaging remarks about their master and promptly joined issue with him. Murat was also present and, wishing to reconcile them, invited them both to dine with him that day. Bessières, Lannes, Lavalette, Leclerc, Roger and several other officers were also invited. After dinner they sat down to cards. Junot was the biggest winner and after a time had a pile of gold pieces in front of him. Lanusse, having lost heavily, asked him for the loan of ten louis, upon which Junot replied, 'I'll not lend money to a traitor like you.'

Instantly everyone was on his feet. Lanusse retorted that Junot was a scoundrel. The others endeavoured to pacify them, but it was useless. Although duels were forbidden they insisted on fighting at once, and that it should be a duel to the death.

Lanusse, being the challenged party, had the choice of weapons and chose pistols. It was an insane choice because Junot was the best pistol-shot in the Army and at twenty-five paces could cut a bullet in two on the blade of a knife. With great generosity he refused to fight with pistols and, despite the protests of his friends, insisted that it should be swords.

The palace occupied by Murat had a pleasant garden sloping down to the Nile, and they trooped out there. By then it was nine o'clock and darkness had fallen; so their host tried to stop the duel on the pretext that they could not see well enough for it to be a fair fight. But Lanusse shouted some offensive expressions about Bonaparte, and Lannes cried with an oath, ' Hold your tongue! You're going to cut one another's throats. Isn't that enough? '

Torches were fetched and by their light the two Generals threw off their coats, then sparks flew from their sabres as each tried to cut down the other. The impetuous Junot delivered a stroke that would have killed Lanusse had he not been wearing his hat. As it was, the hat saved his head and the point of the blade laid open only his cheek. In delivering the blow, Junot had exposed himself and, Lanusse being the better swordsman, brought his sabre round in a back-hander that inflicted a terrible wound eight inches long right across Junot's stomach.

It fell to Roger, the following morning, to break to his master the news of the affair and that Junot was lying at death's door. Bonaparte's first words were, ' My poor Junot! Wounded for me! But the idiot; why did he not fight with pistols? ' Then, seized by one of his terrible rages, he cried:

' Why am I cursed with such Generals? Have they not enough to do with the Mamelukes and the Arabs, that they must go into the reeds of the Nile and cut each other's throats among the crocodiles? For this Junot deserves putting under arrest for a month as soon as he gets well.'

Another General who was constantly whining to get home was Berthier. While in Rome, the ugly little man had fallen in love with the beautiful Madame Visconti. So consumed with passion for her was he that during the campaign his Staff-work had gone all to pieces, and Bourrienne had actually come upon him in his tent, kneeling on the ground and praying before a portrait of his lovely mistress.

Roger could sympathize with him, as his own craving for Zanthé continued unabated. The Provost Marshal's police had completely failed to trace ben-Jussif; but towards the end of August chance led to Roger's seeing her again.

Among Bonaparte's endeavours to render the garrison of Cairo more content had been the organizing of the Tivoli Garden. A number of cafés had been opened there, at which officers and men could drink, play cards and discuss the news that came in from the Divisions that were still carrying on a guerilla warfare in the desert. It was also frequented by the few Frenchwomen who had succeeded in smuggling themselves on to the ships of the armada, or had since managed to reach Egypt on other vessels, the wives and daughters of the European merchants established in Cairo and of those wealthy Copts who were not, like the Moslem ladies, confined to harems.

In the cool of the evenings, except that it was graced with palms instead of chestnut trees, it had become more or less a replica of the garden of the Palais Royal in Paris. Zanthé was half French, and Roger had a faint hope that one evening she might come to the garden; so he often frequented it; but it was not there that he was destined to meet her.

Other diversions instituted by Bonaparte were duck-shoots in the early morning in the marshes of the Nile, and boating parties on the river later in the day. One afternoon Roger, Duroc and Lavalette decided to go on a boating expedition, so went down to one of the wharves. Two handsome palanquins had been set down on it. They obviously belonged to someone of importance, for not only were there negro bearers lounging beside them but also an escort of Turkish Janissaries.

While Roger and his fellow aides-de-camp were waiting for a boat, a beautiful gilded barge pulled in to the wharf. Two more Janissaries sprang out of it and proceeded to help ashore half a dozen Muslim ladies. All of them were wrapped in voluminous robes of silk and wore yashmaks which concealed the lower parts of their faces. The first of the group was obviously elderly and, as she passed the French officers, she lowered her eyes to the ground; but the second gave them a quick glance and Roger caught it. He would have known those wonderful tawny eyes anywhere.

' Zanthé! ' he cried, springing forward.

The startled look in her eyes showed that she had already recognized him but, instantly, she switched her glance away and hurried after the leader of the group towards the more richly decorated of the two palanquins. At Roger's cry, the Janissaries gave him an angry stare and closed round the ladies. Duroc, meanwhile, had grabbed him by the arm, pulled him back and demanded:

' What are you about? '

' That lady . . .' Roger stammered. ' I know her! Let me go! I must speak with her.'

Still gripping his arm, Duroc exclaimed, ' You cannot! Are you mad? You know the General-in-Chief's orders. These people are Turks, and of high standing. They are our allies, and he'll have your head off if you interfere with one of their women.'

' She's not a Turk; she's French! Or half French, anyway,' Roger protested. But Duroc continued to cling to him, while the six women mounted into the palanquins and were borne away.

For a further few minutes Roger and Duroc wrangled, then, on Roger's giving his word that he would do nothing rash, Duroc let him go. Hurriedly he set off after his beloved until he came up to within a dozen paces of the rear palanquin, and he followed it at a slower pace. For a quarter of an hour the little cavalcade wound its way through the tortuous streets of the old city, then entered the courtyard of a large palace that Roger instantly recognized. It was that of the Sultan's Viceroy, who had fled, and it had since been occupied by the Pasha whom he had left behind as his deputy.

Far from being elated at having at last discovered where Zanthé now lived, Roger was cast into further depths of misery. Violent jealousy was now added to the torment of his loss, for it seemed obvious that Zanthé, having lost her husband, had been taken as a concubine by the powerful Pasha. The thought of her in the arms of that grossly fat, cunning Oriental, whom he had seen on several occasions, nearly drove Roger into a frenzy. Blinded by rage he stalked the streets, heedless of where he was going, and it was over an hour before he had cooled down sufficiently to think clearly.

Returning to the palace, he made a careful reconnaissance. In his fervid imagination he was now visualizing himself breaking in and rescuing Zanthé from the horrible fate that he felt certain must have been forced upon her by her family. The entrance to the courtyard was guarded by Janissaries and on either side it was flanked by other palaces; so he walked through several narrow, zigzagging alleys until he judged that he had got behind it. Some minutes elapsed before he was able to make quite certain of his bearings; but at length he satisfied himself that a long, eighteen-foot-high wall, with iron spikes on top and the fronds of palm trees showing above them, must screen from sight the bottom of the spacious garden of the palace.

In the wall there was a single, low doorway of stout wood bound with iron. It was barred on the inside, and one glance at it was sufficient to tell him that it would be difficult to force short of blowing it open with gunpowder. It reminded him of a similar door that he had blown open in India, also with the intention of rescuing a lovely lady from a harem.

But the circumstances had then been very different. He had had British troops to aid him, the girl inside had been English and, in all but name, his wife; for they had planned to marry as soon as they could get home. Now, even if he procured a bag of gunpowder and blew in the door, how could he hope to overcome single-handed the score or more of Janissaries that the Pasha retained as a bodyguard?

A further thought then cooled his ardour. Could he even count on Zanthé being willing to let him carry her off? It was possible that, as an Eastern woman, brought up in the Mohammedan traditions, she had never expected to have a young and handsome husband. As the daughter of an Arab merchant she might even count herself lucky to have become—as her beauty would ensure —the pampered favourite in a wealthy nobleman's seraglio.

Loath to give up his wild idea of regaining possession of Zanthé by force, he spoke to a man who was sitting in a doorway of one of the houses facing the wall. On the flimsy excuse that he was feeling faint from lack of air, he offered the man a piece of money to be allowed to go up and sit for a while on the roof of his house. The man, who was a leather merchant, readily agreed and led him through his shop, up two flights of rickety stairs on to the roof. Like nearly all the roofs in Cairo it was flat and, the house being a two-storey one, only a few feet above the level of the wall opposite.

From there Roger could see, two hundred yards away, the upper storeys of the back of the palace and the domes of its roof, but his hopes of seing into the garden were disappointed. Immediately inside the wall a double row of palm trees had been planted, so that their interlaced fronds rose for another dozen feet above the wall, thus securing the privacy of the garden from the gaze of the occupants of the dwellings outside it. If he came and sat there for hours every day, there still would be no chance of even catching a glimpse of his divinity.

Returning to his house he refused the meal that had been prepared for him and spent a miserable evening thinking of plans to get speech with Zanthé, only to reject them. Had she been living in the house of her former husband, he might have got into it by disguising himself as an Arab pedlar of silks, fans or perfumes, or he could have kept observation on it until, as sooner or later must prove the case, she would be carried from it in a litter to visit friends or go shopping in the bazaar. But, even if he could get into the palace, he knew that he would never be allowed into the seraglio, and any attempt to waylay her when she left would be equally hopeless, as it was certain that she would be accompanied by a guard of Janissaries.

Next day, almost ill with longing for her, he resumed his duties. But he was not the only one mooching round headquarters in a state of sullen depression, although the others had different reasons. The situation of the Army was going from bad to worse. Many of the men had become victims of venereal disease, contracted from the coloured street-women, and several hundred were suffering from acute ophthalmia, caught while bathing in the polluted waters of the Nile. Food was becoming scarcer than ever and from Alexandria and Rosetta Kléber and Menou both reported actual famine; because Nelson, realizing how short the French were of supplies, had deliberately put ashore the three thousand sailors he had captured at Aboukir, to deplete further their scant reserves.

In spite, too, of all Bonaparte's blandishments, the half-million population of Cairo were becoming increasingly restless. They were finding, as had other people whose countries he had occupied, that 'liberation' by the French had to be paid for in no uncertain manner. Not only were taxes exacted as heavy as they had had to pay under the brutal oppression of the Mamelukes, but the French, having lost their own treasure in *L'Orient*, were now seizing hoards of gold wherever they could find them, in order to pay their troops. The number of French soldiers murdered increased weekly, and even the Turkish officials would no longer co-operate with their 'allies' except when practically forced to do so.

Bonaparte continued to work like a demon and showed no lack of confidence in the future. But at about this time he received a terrible personal blow, about which Roger heard from Bourrienne.

The letters that now got through from France were very few, but one had reached Junot. Among other news, it stated that Josephine was being unfaithful to her husband and that her infidelities were so flagrant that they were the talk of Paris. Junot, who regarded Bonaparte as a god, could not endure the thought that his wife should betray him. He became so enraged that he committed the shocking indiscretion of showing the letter to his beloved master.

Bonaparte had good cause to suspect that Josephine had already been unfaithful to him within a few weeks of their marriage. He had had to leave her in Paris after a single night's honeymoon to set off on his Italian campaign and, despite his passionate appeals by letter to her, many months had elapsed before he could persuade her to join him in Italy. Now that he was convinced of her infidelity his rage and despair knew no bounds.

Some days later, in the hope of getting Josephine out of his mind, he ordered Duroc to arrange an entertainment for himself and his Staff at which he could inspect a number of Eastern beauties. Duroc, being puritanical by nature, was not the man to have been charged with this commission, and he bungled matters badly, probably by simply ordering an Arab slave-dealer to select the beauties for him. In any case, those produced at the Haman where the party was held were to the Arab and not the European taste. They were quite young, but had been specially fattened by a régime of idleness and gorging great quantities of sweet-meats. Their breasts were huge and their bottoms enormous. In vain they sang a monotonous chant in shrill voices, twanged their lyres and wagged their naked stomachs in a Nautch dance. Bonaparte looked on sourly for a while, then stood up and stalked out in disgust.

Yet, a few days later, his interest was really caught, and by a Frenchwoman he chanced to see in the Tivoli Garden. Roger, who happened to be with him, was promptly charged to find out who she was. As Roger had once before played ponce, in the service of his country, to Bonaparte, he had no objection to doing so again in the hope of cheering up the unhappy little Corsican and rendering the atmosphere at headquarters slightly less sultry.

The following evening he was able to report that the lady's name was Marguerite Pauline Fourès, and that she was the wife of a Lieutenant in the 22nd Infantry of the Line. They had married only just before the expedition had sailed for Egypt and were so loath to part that, disguised in the uniform of a soldier, she had accompanied her husband on the voyage. Bonaparte then told Roger to arrange a little dinner party, at which the lady would be present.

Using General Dupuy, who was then Commander of the Cairo garrison, as his willing stalking horse, Roger arranged for the party to be held at the General's house. He then got together half a dozen other senior officers whose wives had, in one way or another, succeeded in reaching Cairo, and had an invitation sent to Madame Fourès, which did not include her husband. In spite of that the lady, doubtless flattered by this attention from the High Command and even, perhaps, hoping to advance her husband's prospects, accepted.

After dinner the General-in-Chief dropped in. With his usual directness he stared at Marguerite Pauline as though he meant to eat her, and nobody could deny that she was worth staring at. She was small, had a lovely figure, big violet eyes and such an abundance of fair, golden hair that it was said that it would make a cloak for her whole body. To these personal charms were added great vitality, a bubbling sense of humour, a silvery laugh and a voice which would have enabled her to earn her living as a professional singer.

That evening Bonaparte attempted nothing, but told Roger that he must arrange another dinner party, and soon. Roger obliged and, before hand, received his master's instructions. This time the General-in-Chief attended the dinner, sitting on one side of Pauline while Roger sat on the other. The meal had hardly started when Roger, carrying out his orders, clumsily spilt his soup into Pauline's lap. His master jumped to his feet, abused him roundly and, taking Pauline by the arm, hurried her off into another room to help her repair the damage. To the considerable embarrassment of the rest of the party they were away for two hours.

The next move was to get rid of Pauline's husband. Bonaparte sent for him and said that he had heard such excellent reports of him that he had decided to do him a signal honour. Handing him a bulky despatch, he told him to return to France and deliver it to the Directory. The astonished Lieutenant, believing that his fortune was made, hurried off to Alexandria and went aboard a merchant ship. As the wily Corsican had expected, the ship and Lieutenant Fourès were promptly captured by the English.

By then, Bonaparte had installed the gay and charming *La Belilotte*, as Pauline was nicknamed, in his own palace and, with the utmost cheerfulness, was parading her about Cairo openly as his mistress. The British had many spies in Cairo and the Commodore in charge of the blockade had learned of the French General-in-Chief's infatuation; so he decided to play him a scurvy trick. He told the gullible Fourès that his ship had been ordered to the Pacific and that it would be inconvenient to have a prisoner on board for many months. Then he courteously put him ashore.

Fourès hurried back to Cairo, was amazed to find his wife absent from their lodging and, after receiving many evasive replies from people whom he questioned, at last learned what had happened. Against everyone's advice he forced his way into her apartment and a stormy scene followed. But Pauline was far too honest and much too pleased with her good fortune to beat about the bush. She sent him packing. Next day, on the orders of the General-in-Chief, the Commissary-General of the Army pronounced the Fourès divorced, and the Lieutenant passed from the pages of history.

Glamorous, amusing, kind-hearted Pauline then settled down to enjoy herself thoroughly. She was beloved by everyone and in the afternoons, when she drove round the city in a carriage and pair, always escorted by two of her lover's aides-de-camp, the troops all greeted her with cries of ' Good luck to you, Cleopatra! ' and ' Long live the little General! '

The only person who disapproved of the arrangement was seventeen-year-old Eugéne de Beauharnais who, much as he admired his step-father, had the boldness to protest at this infidelity to his mother. But the young man had not a leg to stand on, and the only satisfaction he got was to be relieved of his turns at escorting *La Belilotte* on her afternoon drives.

Throughout September, in all else things went no better for Bonaparte. He was still doing his utmost to persuade the Turks that he had taken over Egypt in the interests of their master the Sultan. In the hope of furthering this policy he despatched a letter in most cordial terms to Djezzar, the Pasha of Acre. This Pasha had a most unpleasant reputation for craft and extreme cruelty; but he ruled all Syria and, although nominally the Sultan's Viceroy, had made himself virtually independent, so he would have proved a powerful ally. But he contemptuously ignored Bonaparte's overture.

In mid-October good news came in from the south. Desaix had been despatched, with some three thousand men, up the Nile to deal with about the same number of Mamelukes, who were still under arms with Murad Bey and continued to menace the peaceful settlement of the country. On the 7th Desaix had inflicted a severe defeat upon them, which rendered them incapable of doing further serious harm.

But Cairo was growing ever more restless and, unrealized by the French, the Imams who went up to the minarets every evening to call the Faithful to prayer had begun instead to call upon the whole country to revolt and massacre the invader. Bands of armed men were being secretly organized in the city, Bedouin Sheiks were mustering their forces outside it, and the Turks were turning a blind eye to these preparations for a Holy War.

The signal for the outbreak was the massacre of a convoy of French wounded who were being brought up from Salahiyeh. When news of it was received on the night of October 20th the word was given by the Muslim ringleaders for the revolt. In the early hours of the 21st, thousands of turbaned fanatics streamed out into the streets and set about killing every Frenchman they could find.

Roused by the clamour, Roger and Marbois hastily pulled on their clothes and ran outside. At the entrance to the main street a group of half a dozen Muslims rushed at them, screaming ' Death to the Unbelievers.' Roger halted, took careful aim with his pistol, fired and dropped their leader dead in his tracks. The others, being no braver than the average slum rat out for easy plunder, halted, gave back and took refuge under an archway. But the shouting from nearby streets, and that such a rabble should have dared to attack him, was quite sufficient warning for Roger. Turning, he grabbed Marbois by the arm and together they ran at the best pace they could make to headquarters.

Bonaparte had just come downstairs. No one knew what was happening. News came in that General Dupuy had been killed in the street by a lance, then that a company of Bedouin Arabs were endeavouring to force their way into the city by the Bab-el-Nasser gate. Bonaparte told Sulkowsky to take half a company of Guides and reinforce it. Sulkowsky was a good friend of Roger's; so when Roger heard this he went to the General-in-Chief and reminded him that Sulkowsky had only just recovered from a wound he had received in August in the battle at Salahiyeh. Then he asked to be allowed to relieve his brother aide-de-camp.

'Very well,' said Bonaparte. 'Take another fifteen Guides, follow and send him back with an escort, then take charge of the gate yourself.'

When Roger reached the gate it had already been broken open and, to his great distress, he found Sulkowsky dead. But his men had poured a murderous fire into the Arabs and they had fled.

Suddenly it dawned on Roger that this great disturbance in the city was the very thing he had unconsciously been waiting for. Swiftly he had the gate firmly secured, then placed a Lieutenant of Guides in charge of it, leaving him sixty men. Ordering the rest to follow him, he set off for the Pasha's palace.

On the way they had several skirmishes with the insurgents, but a volley of musketry scattered them on each occasion and Roger lost only two men. A quarter of an hour later they reached the little door in the great wall at the end of the palace garden. A score of musket balls aimed at the hinges weakened it considerably; a battering with musket butts did the rest. In ten minutes they had forced it back far enough to squeeze through.

As they approached the palace through the garden, one of the Janissaries gave the alarm. There ensued a short, sharp conflict, but the Turks were soon worsted by the veteran French. Six or more Turks fell, killed or wounded; the remainder fled.

When the firing had ceased, the corpulent Pasha, accompanied by several of his civilian staff, came out on to a terrace at the back of the palace and waved a white cloth in token of surrender. Wasting no time, Roger ordered him to lead the way to his seraglio. The Pasha broke into violent protests. Roger jabbed a pistol barrel into his stomach and told him that if he wished to live he had better not argue.

The sweating Pasha gave in and led Roger, followed by his men, along a tiled corridor to a series of arcaded rooms that opened on to the garden and were plentifully furnished with colourful divans. In one lofty room some two dozen women were assembled, most of them huddled together in a corner, some clutching children and others staring over their yashmaks with big, frightened eyes at the French soldiers.

At the first glance Roger identified Zanthé. She was not among the group, but was seated on a divan beside the elderly woman who had come off the barge in front of her, whom he assumed to be the Pasha's principal wife. Bowing to them he said:

'Ladies, I apologize for this intrusion but, as you must know, the population of Cairo is in revolt. As was the case when that last happened, the mob may break into the palaces and do their inmates grievous injury. Have no fear. I am here to protect you. However, as it appears that the Turkish authorities have taken no steps to suppress the insurrection, they must have countenanced it. Therefore it is my duty to take two hostages.' After pausing a moment he waved a hand towards Zanthé and added, 'They will be His Excellency the Pasha and this lady.'

At that moment a hoarse voice exclaimed behind him, 'Why, blow me, if she ain't yer old love, the Sultan's daughter.'

Swinging round, Roger recognized the Sergeant who had sold Zanthé to him. Scowling, he demanded, 'What the devil are you doing here?'

'No offence, Colonel,' replied the veteran with a grin. 'I was among the guard at the Bab-el-Nasser gate. Seein' you had taken over and left it secure, I thought it would be more interestin' and there'd be a bit of loot, perhaps, if instead of staying there I came along to give you a hand.'

Meanwhile Zanthé had come to her feet. Her splendid eyes flashing, she cried in French, 'How dare you pursue me! This is an outrage! I refuse to become your hostage.'

Roger ignored her and counted up his men. He found that they numbered twenty-two, including a Lieutenant, the Sergeant, Marbois—who had been with him throughout—and two Corporals. He ordered the Lieutenant, with one Corporal and nine men, to remain there and, with the help of the surviving Janissaries, to protect the seraglio. The other Corporal he told to act as escort to the Pasha. Then, turning to the Sergeant and motioning to Zanthé, he said:

'Sergeant, you have taken charge of this lady before. This time you will be more gentle with her; but, even should she struggle, you will persuade her to accompany us.'

Realizing that it would be futile to put up a fight, Zanthé, angry-eyed but passive, allowed the Sergeant to take her by the arm, and the terrified Pasha offered no resistance. Surrounded by the remaining half of his men, Roger led the way from the palace across the garden, out through the wall gate and round to his little house. There he again divided the party. He could not possibly take Zanthé back to headquarters; but he was already convinced that the rising was only a matter of dangerous mobs which could be put down by disciplined soldiers in a matter of hours. His small house was, therefore, very unlikely to be attacked, provided it was suitably garrisoned.

When they reached it, he had Zanthé taken up to the bedroom and locked in. He had decided to leave the Sergeant there, with the Corporal, Marbois and three men. To the Sergeant he said:

'My servant will provide the lady with anything she may require. You will remain here and, should the house be attacked, defend it to the last bullet. But I think it improbable that you will be called on to do more than sit here for, perhaps, twenty-four hours. One warning I must give you. Get no ideas with regard to the lady. When I return, should I learn that you have so much as laid a finger on her I'll cut off your ears and stuff them your throat.'

The Sergeant grinned and touched his forelock. 'That's the sort of orders I like to hear, *mon Colonel*. Shows you're made of the right stuff and worthy to be on the Staff of the " Little Corporal ".'

Roger would have given practically anything to be able to spend the next half-hour simply talking to Zanthé and endeavouring to persuade her that he had acted as he had only because of his intense love for her. But he dare not delay reporting back to the General-in-Chief.

Followed by the remaining five men, who escorted the Pasha between them, he made his way back to headquarters. There he learned that the General-in-Chief had wisely decided not to expose his troops to street fighting, during which they would be shot at from roof-tops, and that all French forces were being withdrawn to the Citadel.

Three-quarters of an hour later he reported Sulkowsky's death to his master, and informed him that he had brought in the Turkish acting Viceroy as a hostage. Bonaparte had been greatly attached to his Polish aide-de-camp; so he was very distressed at Roger's news. But regarding the Pasha, he said:

'You have anticipated my wishes, Breuc. These Turkish officials have shown themselves to be untrustworthy; so I have already issued orders for the arrest of the principal ones among them. But we must not treat them harshly, and must still endeavour to win their goodwill, otherwise the Sultan might declare against us and that would make the establishment of a colony here far more difficult.'

For two days, from the heights above Cairo, Bonaparte rained cannon balls and grape-shot upon the city. His principal target was the Great Mosque which was believed to be the headquarters of the rebellion. This cannonade completely quelled the ill-organized attempt to dispossess the conquerors. Forty-eight hours after the trouble had started the streets were silent and the French began to infiltrate back, unopposed, to the barracks and palaces they had previously occupied.

Accompanied by a squad of dismounted Guides, Roger hastened down to his house and found all well there. The small garrison had suffered only from a shortage of food. Having sent some of them out to procure supplies, Roger went upstairs, unlocked the door of the room in which Zanthé had been confined and confronted her.

She was sitting on his bed, her eyes cast down. Throwing himself on his knees before her, he seized her hands and cried, ' My beautiful Zanthé, I deplore these past two days in which you must have suffered much discomfort. It was through no fault of mine. Now that the trouble is over I swear to you that I will leave nothing undone that will make you happy.'

After a moment, her eyes still cast down, she replied, ' I am your captive. You are strong and virile. If you force me again I shall not be able to resist you. But how can a woman feel love for any man who behaves in that way towards her? For what you did to me, I hate you. And should you repeat it, given the least chance I will kill you.'

Her bitter words dissipated all Roger's hopes that, having once submitted to him, she would accept his further love-making without resistance and, perhaps, with pleasure. He realized now that his only hope of softening her heart was to woo her, if need be for several weeks. He had no hesitation in deciding to do so, because he felt that such a glorious prize would be well worth any restraint he would have to put upon himself.

With his usual practicability, he stood up and said with a wry smile, ' Well, at least we will dine together and discuss the matter further.' Then, realizing that there was nothing fit to eat in the house, he left her, collected Marbois and went out with him to see what delicacies could be procured in the market, which had opened again after being closed for two days.

Only a limited number of stalls displayed goods for sale, and those they had to offer were, for the most part, very indifferent. Roger spent over an hour hunting round before he found a fresh-killed duck, zucchini, green almonds, lemon curd and a rose-scented Rahat Lacoum, that he felt were adequate for setting before Zanthé at their first meal together.

When he arrived back at the house, he was very surprised to find Duroc in the little fountain-court and Zanthé down there with him, sitting cross-legged on one of the piles of cushions. With an unhappy look on his sanctimonious face, the Aide-de-Camp-in-Chief drew Roger aside and said in a low voice:

'Breuc, how could you be such a fool? I warned you when we saw this woman at the landing stage not to interfere with her. The Pasha complained that you had carried off a lady from his seraglio, and I felt sure that I would find her here. In spite of the treachery of these Turks you must know that our master is still anxious to propitiate them. He is furious with you. I have been ordered to escort the lady back to the Pasha's palace and place you under close arrest.'

14

Pastures New

ROGER stared aghast at Duroc. It took nearly a minute before he realized, as seen through other eyes, the enormity of the thing he had done. His passion for Zanthé had blinded him to all else than the craving to have her again in his keeping. He had ignored the fact that she had recently become the concubine, or perhaps even a junior wife, of the most important Turkish official south of Constantinople. He had ignored this in spite of Bonaparte's declaration that everything possible must be done to keep the Turks from openly siding with France's enemies.

Had Zanthé still been the lone widow of a merchant he might possibly have justified taking her under his protection, to save her from molestation while the city was in a state of riot. But he had left a garrison in the Pasha's palace to protect the other women in the seraglio; so he had no excuse for having removed her from it.

His brief conversation with her an hour earlier flashed back into his mind. She had then made plain her intense resentment at his having carried her off; so it was not even as though he could plead that a mutual passion had made her a willing accomplice in his act and that he had rescued her from a situation that she detested. There was nothing for it but to pay the price for the rashness into which his obsession had led him.

Drawing a sharp breath he unhooked his sword, handed it to Duroc with a bow and said, ' Monsieur, I surrender myself your prisoner.'

Duroc returned his bow, took the sword and replied, ' Monsieur, I have to escort this lady back to the Pasha's palace. Be good enough to proceed to headquarters and await my return there.'

Roger gave one quick look at Zanthé. Her yashmak masked her mouth, but her tawny eyes held a mocking smile. He made her a formal bow and said, ' Madame, my love for you is the only excuse that I can offer for such inconvenience as I have caused you. It seems that I am about to pay heavily for it; but let me assure you that I am unrepentant. Given another chance, I would do the same again for an hour in your company.'

The smile left her eyes and astonishment took its place, but she made no reply. Turning on his heel, he marched out of the house.

Half an hour later Duroc joined him at their old headquarters and there condoled with him on the result of his folly. It then transpired that the General-in-Chief had expressed no wish to see him immediately; so they went upstairs together. Roger was allotted an attic room in the palace where, being under close arrest, he was to remain until sent for. Duroc said that he would arrange for Marbois to bring Roger's things round and look after him. His meals would be sent up from the mess. Duroc also promised that later in the day he would bring up some books; he then left Roger to his extremely distressing reflections.

To start with, he had lost his beautiful Zanthé—this time, as it seemed, for good. That was bad enough in all conscience, but very far from being the end of the matter. If a Turkish gallant had carried her off the outraged Pasha would, no doubt, have insisted on having his head brought to him on a charger; so if Bonaparte wished to retain this Oriental potentate's goodwill he would have to demonstrate publicly his extreme displeasure by taking some really drastic action against the culprit.

Roger did not think it likely that his master would go to the length of having him put in prison. On the other hand, it seemed improbable that open arrest for a month or more would be thought sufficient to meet the case. In Italy, in one of his ungovernable rages, Bonaparte had, on the spot, reduced a General to the ranks because he had allowed the Austrians to push him out of the castle of Castiglione; so Roger did think it possible that he might shortly find himself drilling with a musket and being cursed by a Sergeant-Major. In any case, it seemed certain that he would be deprived of his aide-de-campship, which would put an end to the prospects, so enthusiastically envisaged by Admiral Nelson, of further serving his country by passing on some vital piece of information about Bonaparte's future intentions.

Later in the morning Marbois arrived with the prisoner's

personal belongings and in the afternoon Duroc brought him half
a dozen books; but his mind was too agitated by dismal speculations about his future for him to do more than glance at them.
Evening came without his being sent for to face the wrathful
Corsican, then ensued a night of troubled sleep. By midday next
day still no summons had come; so he sent Marbois round to the
house to fetch some of his wine and some cushions with which
to make the attic somewhat more comfortable. Then, by hard
concentration, he succeeded in interesting himself in the Abbé
Prevost's romance *Manon Lescaut*.

It proved as well that he had books and wine to solace his
solitary confinement, for it was not until October 27th, the fourth
day after his arrest, that Duroc came for him. Having escorted
him downstairs and announced him to the General-in-Chief the
aide-de-camp hastily withdrew to avoid becoming involved in
the expected tempest.

Bonaparte was pacing up and down the big room, his hands
behind his back. Halting suddenly, he swung round. His dark eyes
flashed angrily and he demanded:

' Well, what have you to say for yourself? '

' Say! ' Roger cried indignantly. ' *Mon Dieu*, I have a lot to
say! You do some strange things at times, but I have always stood
up for you. I tell people that you are a genius—not an ordinary
man, but one inspired by God—sent to us to restore the glory
of France. I say that they must make allowances for your follies
and take no notice of the small, silly things you sometimes do,
because your mind is always occupied by far greater matters that
will alter the fate of nations. And what is my reward? What is my
reward? To have my property stolen and to be shut up for four
days like a criminal. I will not be——'

The thin little Corsican, his enormously broad jaw thrust out,
stared at him in amazement then shouted, ' Stop! What in
thunder do you mean? '

' I mean,' Roger stormed, ' that I will not be treated like a pick-
pocket. Because your mind is set on conquering half the world
you cannot with impunity jump on the faces of your loyal
servants. I, for one, will serve you no longer. You already have
my sword. Take my rank badges and my sash. I have no further
use for them. I will become a waiter or a brothel-keeper, since
you seem to think I am fit for naught else. Do with me what you
please! You have the power! Abuse it as you will! But under-

stand one thing. After the scurvy way in which you have treated me I am finished with you.'

For a moment Bonaparte was silent, then he said harshly, ' Have you gone mad? I have the right to demand an explanation from you, yet you have the insolence to pretend that it is you who are aggrieved. A clever move, but one which will not serve you.'

' I did not expect it to. You are too wrapped up in your own daydreams to care what happens to others.'

' That is untrue! I am the father of my soldiers.'

' Of your soldiers, yes. But not of your friends. Why, you had not even the decency to visit poor Junot in hospital after he had had himself half killed out of love for you.'

' Discipline must be maintained.'

' And who maintained it for you except loyal friends like Junot and myself—we who are prepared to draw our swords even upon our seniors when they openly proclaim you to be a madman? '

' Enough! Enough! All this is beside the point. In defiance of every instruction I have issued you violated the seraglio of the acting Viceroy and made off with one of his women.'

' And why not? She was not his, but mine. I had bought and paid for her.'

' You had bought her from him? I do not believe it. To lie in this fashion can only make your case worse.'

' Do not judge others by yourself,' Roger snapped back. ' You needs must——'

' How dare you! ' roared the Corsican, his normally pale face turning dead white. ' I'll not be spoken to like this! I . . . I . . . I'll . . .' He choked and looked as though he were about to have an apoplectic fit.

' You needs must lie for political reasons,' cut in Roger, finishing the sentence he had begun. ' But I do not have to. As for saying to you what I have—do not think that because others lack the courage to tell you the truth about yourself that applies also to me. You cannot do worse than have me shot, and I'll say to you what I damn well please.'

He knew that he was taking a desperate gamble; but he had had four days in which to decide on the way in which he would meet his master's accusations. Tame acknowledgement of his guilt could have led only to dismissal and punishment. In the past he had defied people greater than Bonaparte had yet become, and he felt that his one hope of saving himself lay in using the Corsican's own favourite tactics of violent, relentless attack.

Taking a quick breath he hurried on, 'I tell you I bought this woman. The fact is that I came upon her in the street, the night after we entered Cairo, surrounded by half a dozen soldiers. They were about to drag her into a house and rape her. To save her, I bought her from them for a hundred louis.'

Still trembling with fury, Bonaparte stared at him and muttered, 'Is this the truth? Do you swear it?'

'Indeed I do, and should you still doubt me you have only to have her questioned. It was my misfortune that the very next day you sent me with a despatch to Alexandria. On my return I found that the owner of the house in which I had installed myself had emptied it of its furniture and taken her away with him. The Provost Marshal has been hunting her on my behalf for weeks, but without success. Then, four days ago, while the revolt was at its height, I seized the Pasha for you as a hostage. In his palace I found her. She was mine by right of purchase; so naturally I took her away with me. What else would you expect me to have done?'

By one of the extraordinarily swift changes of mood to which Bonaparte was subject he had, while Roger was speaking, become quite calm. Resuming his pacing up and down, he said:

'Breuc, I have a considerable esteem for you, because you are as brave as any of my *beaux sabreurs*, yet, unlike most of them, you have the wit and temerity to defend yourself when accused. But this will not do. Had you paid ten thousand gold louis for this woman that would still give you no title to her. She is no slave-girl but a lady of high birth and breeding.'

Roger refrained from contradicting this assertion. Secretly, he was now greatly elated at his success in having manœuvred his master from pronouncing summary judgment on him and having persuaded him to a discussion of his case. With a shrug he said:

'She is beautiful enough to be a Sultan's daughter, but she has no claim to nobility. She is half French and told me herself that she had recently lost her husband, who was no more than a merchant.'

Bonaparte swung round upon him. 'Then she deliberately deceived you, probably because she feared that if you knew the truth you would have demanded a great sum for her ransom. She is no merchant's relict, but a widow of the Commander of the Turkish garrison. He was killed in the battle of Embabeh.'

It was Roger's turn to stare. After a moment he said, 'I understand now, *mon Général*, why you look on my action with such displeasure. I naturally supposed that the Pasha had taken her as one of his concubines; so I felt that my right to her, as her previous owner, was better than his. But if, as you say, she is of noble birth I take it he must have made her one of his wives.'

'She is neither the Pasha's wife nor his concubine,' Bonaparte replied testily. 'It is simply that, having been widowed and with the city in a state of unrest, she took refuge in the Pasha's seraglio; just as a woman of our own race, in similar circumstances, might seek refuge in our Embassy. But that makes what you have done no less reprehensible. You, one of my personal aides-de-camp, forcibly abducted this woman and all Cairo knows about it.'

'It distresses me greatly to have caused you embarrassment in this way,' Roger said with apparent contrition.

'Apologies are not enough.' Bonaparte's voice became harsh again. 'In Muslim eyes it is a most heinous crime to break into a seraglio. It is not to be wondered at that the old Pasha is calling for your blood. Apart from that, you have given me cause to deal severely with you. You seem to think you had a right to carry off this woman. Had she in fact been only a merchant's wife—a woman of no particular account—whom, by some trick, you could have lured to a rendezvous and so secured her again, I would not have held it against you. But by openly using violence you showed a flagrant disregard for my expressed wishes regarding our treatment of the population. As matters are, I've no alternative other than to make a public example of you.'

Roger shrugged. 'If your prestige will be enhanced by so doing I willingly accept anything you may decree.'

'In the circumstances I cannot possibly retain you as one of my aides-de-camp.'

'I understand that, *mon Général*. All the same I find it regrettable; because I think in that capacity I have been of some value to you, whereas I can be of little use in any other.'

'You mean that you have never served as an officer in a regiment or even been trained as a soldier.'

'Exactly. I know next to nothing of military evolutions or procedure. Doubtless after a few months I would have picked up enough to be capable of commanding a Company. But what then? I'd still not be worth as much to you as hundreds of others who have had years of experience.'

' Yes, yes, I realize that,' Bonaparte replied impatiently, ' and in other ways you are a man of exceptional abilities. I find it difficult to contain my anger at the thought that through your folly I shall have to deprive myself of your services. Yet I see no alternative.'

' Is that really so? Could you not appease the Turk by cashiering me, then, as a civilian, making me Bourrienne's assistant? '

Bonaparte shook his head violently. ' That is out of the question. It would be known at once that I had slapped you on one cheek and kissed you on the other.'

Roger had felt it certain that his suggestion would be rejected, and he had made it only to lead up to another. Now, his heart beating a little faster, he introduced the bold and subtle idea that had come to him during his confinement by asking:

' How long is it since you have had authentic news of what has been happening in Paris? '

As he expected, his question provoked a new explosion. Stamping his foot, the little Corsican cried angrily, ' Paris! It might be as distant as the moon for all I know of what goes on there. It is now months since I had a despatch from those miserable Directors. Some despatches may have been intercepted by the English, but that could not apply to all did they write to me regularly. Having, as they think, got me out of the way, they are deliberately keeping me in ignorance. No doubt they fear that if things were not going well there, and I knew it, I'd return and pitchfork them out of the Luxembourg into the gutter. And so I will, should an occasion arise when it suits me to do so. But this has naught to do with my future employment of you.'

Drawing a deep breath, Roger launched his project. ' It might, if you have a mind to make the best possible use of me. Why not send me back there to——'

Again Bonaparte stopped his pacing, swung on his heel and repeated, ' Send you back there? '

' Yes,' Roger hurried on. ' To find out for you what those fellows are up to. Since I can pass as an Englishman I'll have no difficulty in getting through the blockade. With luck I could be in Paris in a month. Talleyrand is your friend and has been mine for many years. He misses nothing and in an hour could give me a

I

correct appraisal of how matters are going with both your friends and your enemies. I could return as easily as I went, and be back here soon after Christmas with a mass of information that you could obtain in no other way.'

'*Ventre du Diable*; this is an inspiration! ' The Corsican's dark eyes lit up, he gave a sudden laugh and, stepping up to Roger, slapped him on the shoulder. 'Breuc, I have always said you would be worth a Division to me. I would have been mad to have turned you into a cavalryman. If I march against Syria, as is my present intention, I'll not start towards the end of January. Unless the weather proves most unfavourable you should be able to rejoin me before that. Then on what you have to report I can form a decision whether to adhere to my plan or . . . or adopt some other.'

Roger beamed. 'You may rely upon me, *mon Général*, to use the utmost despatch. When do you wish me to start? '

'I would say this instant, but you must carry letters for me to Talleyrand and to my brother Joseph. I shall give out, of course, that I have dismissed you, and sent you to kick your heels on garrison duty in some small fort on the coast. Go now. See Duroc. Pull a long face and tell him that, then say I have authorized him to return your sword to you. Bourrienne alone will be in our secret. Collect my letters from him at four o'clock and be ready to set out immediately afterwards.'

'These letters,' Roger said. 'Making the voyage to Italy or Spain as an Englishman it is unlikely that I shall be searched, but it would be wise to guard against that hazard. I suggest they should be written on thin paper, so that I can conceal them in the lining of a coat.'

'You are right. Bourrienne keeps some special paper and fine pens for such missives. I will tell him to use these.' Bonaparte stretched out a hand and gave Roger's ear a swift tweak. 'Go now and good luck to you.'

During the hours that followed Roger found it extremely hard to conceal the delight he felt at having succeeded in his great coup; but he did his best, when saying good-bye to Duroc and his other friends, to pretend disgust at the way in which his master was sacrificing him to the Pasha. They all condoled with him and tried to cheer him by saying they felt sure that Bonaparte, having made the gesture, would soon recall him, and the lovely, violet-eyed little *La Bellilotte*, touched at the thought that he had lost his post on account of a love-affair, said she would do her utmost to soften the heart of her all-powerful lover.

Roger drew his pay to date, had Marbois pack his few belongings, arranged for an escort and at four o'clock went to Bourrienne's office. The *Chef de Cabinet* greeted him with a smile, then said enviously:

' My compliments, *mon vieux*. After such outrageous behaviour you should by now be Trooper Breuc and sweating in some fatigue party. Instead you've won the boon of leaving this devilish country. In a few weeks you'll be back in our beloved France.'

Roger grinned at him. ' Better to be born lucky than rich.'

' Luck alone is not enough. One must have the brains to use it. And you are as clever a devil as ever wore a pair of field-boots.'

' Nay. It's our little man who is clever. He saw on the instant that to dismiss me would be only cutting off his nose to spite his face. Have you any personal commissions that I can carry out for you? '

Bourrienne nodded and produced three letters. ' Here are the despatches for Talleyrand and Brother Joseph. The third is for my wife, if you would be so kind.'

' With pleasure.' Roger pocketed the three flimsies. He had asked for the letters to be on thin paper only because it would look well to do so, for he had no intention of going to France and delivering them. But he was determined to have Bourrienne's letter forwarded somehow. He then took leave of his friend, left the building and set out on his journey.

The first stage was uneventful and he reached Alexandria early on the morning of November 2nd. Leaving his escort there, with orders to start back to Cairo on the following day, he rode straight on to Sarodopulous's villa, arriving in time to join the banker and his nephew for breakfast.

Over the meal Roger told them that he had been ordered to return to France and intended to pass the blockade by posing as an Englishman. He then asked their help in securing a passage in any merchant ship shortly sailing westward and in acquiring an outfit of civilian clothes. The banker willingly promised to arrange matters and said how pleased he would be to have Roger as his guest while he was waiting for a ship.

Roger spent a lazy day at the Villa recovering from the fatigue of his journey. After the siesta hour handsome young Achilles Sarodopulous returned, accompanied by a trader with a collection of European clothes. Only second-hand garments were available and it was an odd assortment. However, there were items among them good enough for a passenger who did not wish to appear ostentatious and Madame Sarodopulous said she would have those selected by Roger disinfected by baking them in the fierce sunshine.

That evening when the banker got home he told Roger that, as the war had seriously interfered with merchant shipping, he had provisionally booked a passage for him in a local grain boat which was leaving for Crete in four days' time. It was in this way that Roger had sailed from Egypt the previous year on his return from India, and he felt confident that he would have no difficulty at Candia in picking up a neutral ship sailing for one of the Italian ports; so he asked his host to confirm the booking.

After dinner they had a long talk about international affairs. The big news, that had not yet filtered through to Cairo, was that the Sultan had declared war on France over a month ago. This caused Roger to smile wryly, for, had Bonaparte known of it, he would certainly never have sacrificed one of his aides-de-camp to the Turkish Pasha. But, on balance, Roger felt he had no cause for regret that the news had not reached Cairo earlier. Although he had lost his beautiful Zanthé, he was finished with deserts sunburn, snakes, mosquitoes and the danger of being knifed in the street one night on his way home.

Continuing, Sarodopulous told him that, at long last, towards the end of August, a French force under General Humbert had landed in Ireland to give the malcontents there a stiffening of regular troops. Believing the French to be in much greater numbers than they were, the United Irish had again risen. But Humbert had barely a thousand men; so the Marquis of Cornwallis, who had been sent to take command in Ireland, had soon routed the rebels and forced the small French contingent to surrender.

The French had now gained control over all but the more mountainous parts of Switzerland. In those districts bands of peasants were still fighting to the death to defend their liberties and religion. The terrorist Director Rewbell had sent his brother-in-law, Rapinat, as Chief Commissioner to the newly formed Helvetic Republic and, by massacres, rapine and burning churches filled with men, women and children, this unspeakable brute was endeavouring to crush all resistance.

The same ghastly scenes were being enacted in Piedmont. Backed by the French, a rabble from Genoa had invaded the King of Sardinia's mainland territories. Behind them as they advanced they left a chain of village churches in flames, with their pastors and congregations locked inside them.

In Bonaparte's pet creation, the Cisalpine Republic, everything had fallen into hopeless disorder. Owing to his wholesale looting of the treasuries of the cities the finances were in a state of chaos. General Brune had succeeded Berthier there and could keep the people down only by overawing them with displays of force. The pay of his troops was months in arrears; so he had to turn a blind eye to the beating, torturing and murdering of Italians by his officers and men, in an effort to extract money from them. Throughout all Italy everything connected with France had become a symbol for hatred and it was reported that the masses were only awaiting a signal from some bold hand to rise and slit the throat of every French robber in the peninsula.

On November 6th, having enjoyed four days of blissful relaxation, Roger took leave of his good Greek friends. After clearing the port of Alexandria the grain ship, by arrangement between Sarodopulous and her Captain, dropped round into the bay and Roger went off to her in a dhow. An hour later she was challenged by a British sloop-of-war and boarded by a small party, commanded by a Midshipman.

As the grain ship traded regularly to Crete, returning with cargoes of olive oil, the vessel was searched only perfunctorily. Roger, when questioned, said his name was Robert MacElfic, that he had represented a firm of Scottish merchants in Alexandria and that the French occupation had ruined his firm's trade with Egypt; so he had decided to return home. His mother had been a MacElfic and had always retained something of her Highland accent; so he had never had difficulty in imitating it. He soon convinced the ' Middy ' of his *bona fides.*

Roger knew, from his previous voyage, that the food and accommodation in a grain ship would be very primitive; so he had brought with him a supply of provisions. Philosophically, he resigned himself to possibly a week or more of considerable discomfort; but the weather and winds proved favourable, the crossing took only five days and he landed at Candia on the 11th.

He had decided on Naples as the next stage in his journey, as it had now become the principal British naval base in the

Mediterranean. He was certain that there he would be able to find a ship to carry him home, and it was home that he meant to go. Even Admiral Nelson, he felt, could not now consider him unpatriotic for deciding to give up his dangerous role as a secret agent. It would have been pointless to remain in Egypt as a cavalry officer. As it was he had come away with two further despatches from Bonaparte which, having read them within a few hours of receiving them, he knew would prove of considerable value. Moreover, he was in a position to give a far more detailed account of the French Army's situation and resources in Egypt than the British Government could possibly receive from other agents.

In the squalid little Turkish-ruled town of Candia he had to wait six days before he could get a passage to Naples, and then it was on a Turkish brigantine manned by Greek sailors. Again he took aboard a store of provisions, but they ran out long before he reached his destination. After leaving Crete the ship sailed smoothly up the Greek coast for four days, but on the fifth she was hit by one of the fierce storms that are apt to arise suddenly in the Mediterranean during winter. The Greeks, being good sailors, handled the brigantine well in the circumstances, but she lost her foremast and, despite all their efforts, was driven right off her course far up into the Adriatic.

Roger, as usual in bad weather, was wretchedly ill and spent three days of utter misery, unable to keep down even a few mouthfuls of biscuit. The thought of returning to England via Gibraltar, and probably having to endure another such prolonged nightmare while crossing the Bay of Biscay in December, caused him to alter his plans. He decided that he would instead travel up Italy and go home by way of France. With this in view, he asked the Captain to land him at Bari.

To his intense annoyance, the Captain refused to oblige him. Neither could he be bribed by a sum which Roger felt was as large as he was prepared to offer, since he could go home overland from Naples as easily as from Bari. He would now be losing only a little time, and time was now of no great importance to him.

Better weather came again, enabling the brigantine to beat round the heel of Italy and up through the Straits of Messina to Naples, where Roger landed on Monday, December 3rd.

In September, '95, he had been sent by Mr. Pitt on a mission to the Prince de Condé, who commanded the Royalist Army, and to General Pichegru, who commanded the Republican Army, both of which were on the Rhine. It was then that he had decided to assume a third identity as a non-existent nephew of his mother's, for which he took the name of Robert MacElfic; for he feared that, if he went to Condé as Roger Brook and to Pichegru as Citizen Representative Breuc, his two identities might become linked. Previous to that mission, while crossing the Atlantic, he had let his beard grow; so to fit himself for the part he had retained this slight alteration to his appearance.

The situation in Naples would, he knew, be very different from what it was when he had last visited the city early in the autumn of '89. Then, the doctrines of the French Revolution and Bonaparte's descent on a land of peace and plenty had not disrupted life throughout the peninsula. Now, although the Court of Naples was fanatically anti-French, many of the nobility and a large part of the bourgeoisie were said to hold strong Republican views. Numbers of them would have travelled in France; besides which it was certain that the French Embassy would be employing scores of secret agents in the city. Thus Naples had become another no man's land in which Brook might be linked with Breuc, and it was this which had decided Roger again to become MacElfic. Since leaving Egypt he had, therefore, again allowed his beard to grow; so after four weeks his cheeks and chin were now covered with short, crisp, slightly curly, brown hair.

On landing, he secured a *carozza* and told the driver to take him to Crocielle's Hotel. They had hardly set off along the waterfront before he saw that all the buildings were decorated with flags; so he called up to the man, asking the reason for this gay display. Turning on his box the driver replied cheerfully:

'Have you not heard, signor? We are celebrating our victory over those pigs the French. Tidings arrived yesterday that our good King Ferdinand entered Rome in triumph four days ago.'

This was surprising news indeed to Roger and he was even more surprised when he learned that the Neapolitan Army had invaded the Roman States only six days before it had captured Rome. Either the Italians must have shown most unusual dash or the French had suddenly gone to pieces.

At the hotel Roger learned further particulars of this new war that had broken out only while he was being desperately seasick in the Adriatic. Britain was said to be supporting it enthusiastically and Nelson was the hero of the hour. He had sailed on

November 22nd—the day before war had been declared—for Leghorn, with five thousand Neapolitan troops on board, to support the Grand Duke of Tuscany, a nephew of the Queen of Naples, in an attempt to throw the French out of his dominions. Austria, on the other hand, having only a defensive alliance with the Kingdom of the Two Sicilies—of which Naples was the capital—had not yet come in, although the Emperor—another nephew and also son-in-law of the Queen—had sent on loan his veteran General Mack to command the Neapolitan Army.

While eating the first enjoyable meal he had had for a month, Roger considered this entirely new situation which suddenly appeared to threaten the dominance of the French in Italy. He would have been delighted by it had he not had distinct misgivings about the outcome.

Admittedly the French forces were stretched to the limit, garrisoning Holland, Belgium, the ex-German provinces west of the Rhine, Switzerland, all northern and central Italy, Corsica, Corfu, Majorca and Malta, in addition to which their greatest General and finest regiments were marooned in Egypt. But, even so, how could a second-class Power like the Two Sicilies possibly hope, unsupported by any other nation, to defeat the mighty Republic?

It was, too, only in recent years that the Sicilies had ranked even as a second-class Power. The kingdom was theoretically a fief of Spain. The Bourbon King of Spain, Philip V, had given it to his second son, Carlos, and had won the goodwill of the Neapolitans by a promise that the two crowns should never be united. In 1759 Carlos had succeeded his father as King of Spain, so had resigned Naples and Sicily to his son, the present King Ferdinand, who was then only eight years old.

During the boy's minority a Tuscan Minister, Bernardo Tenucci, had ruled in his name at the dictation of the Court of Spain; but at the age of seventeen Ferdinand was married to Caroline, the eldest daughter of the Empress Maria-Theresa of Austria, and from that moment the influence of Spain had begun to wane.

The young couple could hardly have been more ill-matched. Ferdinand was a boisterous, easy-going fellow, with no interests other than outdoor pursuits. What very little brain he possessed had been criminally restricted in its development by Tenucci, who had seen to it that his education should be rudimentary so that when he grew up he would be incapable of interfering in politics. Caroline, on the other hand, had an ungovernable temper, was well-educated, religious and inordinately ambitious.

Although the masses in both the Kingdom of Naples and the island of Sicily lived in the direst poverty and under the severe repression of corrupt officials, they never blamed this on King Ferdinand. On the contrary they adored him, because his simple pleasures brought him into intimate contact with them. Dressed in a jersey, woollen cap, coarse trousers and seaboots, he often spent the night fishing. In the morning he would sell his catch in the market, haggling like any other huckster for the best price he could get for each fish from a crowd of laughing housewives. Then he gave away the money he received. But the strongest hold he had acquired over the riff-raff of Naples was through having accepted the office of Master of the Guild of the *Lazzaroni*. This Guild consisted of literally thousands of professional beggars and petty criminals, who made a living by preying in a hundred ways on the better-off part of the population. Ferdinand encouraged and protected them and delighted in the nickname the people gave him of '*Il Rè dei Lazzaroni*'.

His other main interest he termed 'hunting'. It consisted only of standing in a stone sentry-box, while hundreds of beasts and birds were driven past him. With an indefatigable lust for slaughter he stood there hour after hour, shooting them down. He was also a great practical joker and from time to time found it most amusing suddenly to decree that some staid visitor to his Court should be tossed in a blanket.

While this young moron was harmlessly enjoying himself, or bellowing with laughter at his sadistic pranks, Queen Caroline had been intriguing without pause to get the Government of the country into her own hands. Whenever Ferdinand put up the least opposition to her proposals for innovations she flew into such violent tempers that he was only too glad to escape from her at the price of giving way. Even when at table she screeched at him like an angry eagle, and on one occasion actually bit him. In due course she had succeeded in getting rid of Tenucci and replacing him with a Minister of her own choice.

This was General Sir John Acton, the son of an English physician who had settled in France. At an early age Acton had joined the French Army, but later left it for the Court of Tuscany. In '75 he had greatly distinguished himself while commanding a

Tuscan frigate in an expedition to suppress the pirates of Algiers. Four years later Queen Caroline had persuaded the Grand Duke to let her have Acton to reorganize the little Neapolitan Army.

The newcomer had at once set about building a Fleet out of all proportion to the resources of the country. To secure enough money for this he had to be made Minister of Finance, as well as of Marine. To these posts he had soon added that of Minister of War and, finally, Prime Minister. He was now sixty-three and for the past twenty years he and the Queen had run the country. Naples now had a Fleet of one hundred and twenty ships and, on paper, an Army of sixty thousand men, so had become a Power of some importance. But the effort had virtually bankrupted the country.

On the credit side, as Roger naturally regarded the matter, Acton was the firm friend of Sir William Hamilton, who had been British Ambassador in Naples for the past thirty-five years; while an even stronger tie existed between Sir William's wife, the beautiful Emma, and Queen Caroline. Working hand in glove, these four had weaned the Kingdom of the Two Sicilies away from Spain and France into the orbit of Austrian, and British influence. Above all, the triumph of Sir William's long career had been the securing for Britain of the magnificent harbour of Naples as a naval base, from which her sea power could command the Mediterranean.

Having finished his meal Roger decided to lose no time in calling on Sir William. He took a *carozza* up the hill to the beautiful Palazzo Sessa, which housed the British Embassy. Giving his name to the footman as Robert MacElfic, he added that he was a cousin of the Earl of Kildonan and that he would be grateful if the Ambassador could spare him a few minutes on urgent business.

He was kept waiting in the big marble hall only long enough for him to admire some of the ancient statues which formed a small part of the priceless collection of Roman remains that the Ambassador had acquired during his long residence in Naples; then the footman returned and showed him into the splendid library.

The elderly Ambassador rose courteously from behind a big desk to receive him, shook hands and waved him to a chair. He then raised his quizzing glass, looked at Roger again and said,

Your face is vaguely familiar to me, Mr. MacElfic. Surely we have met somewhere before? '

'Indeed we have, sir,' Roger replied with a smile. 'I had the pleasure of being your guest here for a week in the autumn of '89. But you knew me then by my real name, Roger Brook.'

'Then why use any other?' Sir William asked. 'And why make free with that of my Lord Kildonan? '

'Since His Lordship lives much in Rome, I thought it fairly certain that Your Excellency would know him and that might induce you to see me without delay.'

'That was a shrewd move,' Sir William remarked. 'I do know him slightly and it is to that you owe my prompt reception of you.'

Roger smiled. 'He is in fact my cousin, although I have never met him. My mother's family were all fanatical Jacobites. When she ran away with my father, who is a loyal servant of the Hanoverian line, they cut her off from them entirely. But to come to the point of my visit—you may perhaps recall that when I was last in Naples it was on behalf of Queen Marie Antoinette. I came to enquire if Queen Caroline would give her nephew the Dauphin asylum here, should the safety of the Royal Family in France become threatened by the revolutionary movement.'

'I do recall the matter. Queen Caroline and King Ferdinand agreed to receive the boy, but that poor, woolly-minded man Louis XVI later conceived the notion that his son belonged to the people; so he would not allow him to leave France.'

'Alas, yes. And now what I have to add is for Your Excellency's ear alone. On that occasion there was no reason against my using my own name. But since then I have spent long periods in France as an agent of Mr. Pitt, and I am known there as Colonel Breuc. I am, moreover, one of General Bonaparte's aides-de-camp, and——'

'What's this you say! ' exclaimed the Ambassador.

'Surprising as it may sound, it is the truth,' Roger laughed, 'and only this morning I landed here from Egypt. With me I have brought two despatches that General Bonaparte charged me to deliver in Paris. May I request that you have copies of them made by a safe hand and despatch them at the earliest opportunity to London?'

'Indeed I will! ' Sir William cried enthusiastically. 'And a copy for our dear Admiral, Sir Horatio Nelson, as I've not a doubt but that the contents of these despatches will be of value to him, too. But about yourself—this feat of yours is of surprising interest. Pray tell me more, and of what that terrible young Corsican bandit is up to in Egypt.'

For the next half-hour the Ambassador sat enthralled, while Roger gave him an account of his doings since leaving England. Then he said, 'From all this you will appreciate why I arrived here as Robert MacElfic. As Roger Brook I might well have been identified as Colonel Breuc by some Frenchman, or by some Neapolitan who sympathizes with the Revolution and who, having been in France, might have met me there.'

'It was a wise precaution. And, alas, it is true enough that many Neapolitan intellectuals have allowed themselves to be contaminated by these pernicious doctrines. But now that Naples is at war with France Queen Caroline will soon take steps to deal with such traitors.'

'On landing I was very surprised to hear that Naples had challenged the Republic, and of the first splendid successes of her Army.'

Sir William smiled. 'The news could not be better. But we expected it. When General Mack inspected the Army before leading it against our enemies he said that he had never seen a finer body of men.'

'I seem to recall hearing, sir, that when young you were an officer of the Foot Guards. May I ask if that was also your opinion?'

'Well, er . . . I could hardly say that. One must allow for the fact that the majority of them are peasants only recently called up. But their enthusiasm for a war against those atheists and robbers was unbounded.'

'Do you then count enthusiasm enough? I am no soldier, but I have seen enough of war to know how greatly experience of being shot at matters. Every French battalion has its leaven of old soldiers; not only men who fought under Bonaparte in Italy, but also under Dumouriez, Kellermann, Moreau, Jourdan, Pichegru, Hoche and other Generals during the long years of the Revolutionary Wars. At the Battle of the Pyramids, had there not been many such to show an example of calmness to the conscripts it is certain that the sight alone of the Mamelukes' ferocious onslaught would have been sufficient to cause the squares to break, and every man in them would have been massacred. Brave fellows as the Neapolitan levies may be, have you no fear that when the French have had time to concentrate their forces King Ferdinand's Army may suffer a terrible reverse? '

'Not with General Mack to plan their dispositions. He has had many years' experience of war, and is as wily an old fox as ever put on a uniform.'

Roger shook his head. 'Old, yes. Too old, in my opinion, and set in the military tradition of the past. Such Generals, who wait to strike until an opportunity arises for them to engage in set-piece battles on ground favourable to themselves, can stand little chance in the new wars of swift manoeuvre that Bonaparte has initiated. If Austria had sent the Archduke Charles I'd regard King Ferdinand's chances of continued victory as far better.'

The Ambassador nodded. 'You may be right in that. He is certainly their best General. I imagine that the Emperor is reserving him to lead his own forces.'

'You think, then, that Austria will come in? '

'We feel confident of it. Mr. Pitt is doing his utmost to form a Second Coalition against the French. Turkey, as you will know, is already in. The Czar Paul has accepted the Grand Mastership of the Knights and, outraged by the French seizure of Malta, is sending a Fleet into the Mediterranean. Naples, although a comparatively weak Power, has had the courage to lead the way. It is unthinkable that Austria should not follow.'

'We must certainly hope for that. But would it not have been sounder policy to ensure first that before Naples challenged the might of the Republic she could rely on Austria's support? I cannot help feeling that the Court of Naples has acted with great rashness and I was very surprised to learn, if rumour be true, that the British Government encouraged her to it.'

For a moment Sir William hummed and hawed, then he replied, 'Between ourselves, Mr. Brook, Whitehall did urge caution on us. But I received the despatch only after the die was cast. Admiral Nelson, as you no doubt know, regards the French as devils out of hell who, for the salvation of Europe, must be utterly destroyed. In fact, he looks upon himself as a weapon forged by God to bring about that end. He holds that we should strike at them continuously and relentlessly, anywhere and everywhere, without thought of how great may be the odds against us. His views coincide with those of Queen Caroline,

General Acton and, for that matter, myself. It was largely Admiral Nelson's optimism and unbounded enthusiasm which launched Naples against France. He pointed out to us that after his great victory at the Nile he was free to give us the entire support of his splendid Fleet, and also how thinly the French are spread in Italy now that their Army has to hold down so many conquered peoples. We all felt that his arguments were unanswerable, and now we can only pray that his optimism was justified.'

'I wholeheartedly echo that prayer,' Roger said seriously. 'He may well be right, for he is a born leader. The assurance with which he sailed in and annihilated the French Fleet at the Battle of the Nile could not have been surpassed even by Drake. And his personal magnetism and charm are amazing. As I have told you, although I felt no obligation to go back into Egypt and to do so was against my will, he persuaded me to it.'

Sir William nodded. 'That brings us to the present. What have you in mind to do now?'

'Why,' Roger laughed, 'having pulled the chestnuts out of the fire a second time, to go home.'

'I assumed as much. Well, in the course of the week a frigate will be sailing for Gibraltar and from there you should have no difficulty in securing a passage to England. I will arrange for accommodation in the frigate to be reserved for you.'

Roger shook his head. 'I thank Your Excellency. Let the frigate carry copies of the despatches, also a full report that I must write for Mr. Pitt which I will let you have tomorrow; but I have no mind to voyage in her. I am the worst sailor that ever was and the very thought of the weather which a ship may meet with in the Bay of Biscay makes my poor stomach turn over. I intend to travel overland up Italy and through France, becoming again Colonel Breuc when the need arises; then I shall get a smuggler to run me across the Channel.'

The Ambassador held up a slim hand in protest. 'No, no! I implore you not to attempt that. As a lone traveller without escort the odds on your coming to grief would be a hundred to one. The whole peninsula is now in ferment. No laws can any longer give you a shadow of protection. Swarms of French deserters and Italian bandits infest every highway. It is said that there are over a hundred thousand of them. No matter whether you travelled as Englishman, Frenchman or Turk it is a certainty that one of these bands would waylay, rob and murder you.'

It would have been the height of folly to ignore such advice; so Roger was forced to reconsider the matter. After a moment he said, 'If King Ferdinand succeeds in continuing his advance and the Tuscan revolt against the French proves successful, so that they join forces above Rome, a few weeks may see the country more or less pacified, at least as far as communications from Naples to the north are concerned. I should then be able to get through without undue risk.'

'That is a possibility,' Sir William agreed. 'But even given complete victory over the French a considerable time must elapse before these bands can be suppressed and travel becomes reasonably safe again. After all, what are a few days of seasickness? Since you wish to get home, surely it would be better to face the possibility of bad weather and sail in the frigate?'

Roger's mouth set in a hard line. His memories of his frightful sufferings in the Adriatic were so recent that he could not bring himself to agree to Sir William's suggestion. 'No,' he said after a moment, 'I prefer to remain here for a while and see how the war develops.'

It was a decision that before he was much older he was bitterly to regret.

15

The Looker-on sees most of the Game

SIR WILLIAM HAMILTON urged Roger to become his guest, but he regretfully declined. It was only just over ten years since the Young Pretender had died and a number of the Jacobite nobles who had made up his little Court-in-Exile in Rome still had apartments there. As Roger pointed out, although he might pay his respects to British Ambassadors when in foreign countries, it would not be in keeping for him, while he remained a MacElfic, to stay at the Embassy of the Hanoverian King.

It was agreed, therefore, that he should deliver his despatch late the following night and come again to the Embassy only once a week, to the Ambassador's official reception, as long as he chose to stay in Naples.

Returning to his hotel he procured ink, paper, quills and sand, and took them up to his room. There he spent several hours covering page after page with fine writing, giving Mr. Pitt every particular he could think of concerning the situation in Egypt.

Next morning he went out to renew his acquaintance with the city which, after Paris, was the largest in Europe. Superficially he found it unchanged. The waterfront spread along the northern end of the vast bay which ran out westward to the peninsula of Pozzuoli. Beyond the point lay the islands of Procida and Ischia. Inland from the centre of the bay the great cone of Vesuvius, with its plume of smoke, towered up against the blue sky. In the distance to the south the other arm of the bay curved seaward, forming the twenty-mile-long peninsula of Sorrento. A few miles beyond its tip could be seen the island of Capri. Under a wintry sun the prospect was as beautiful as ever, and the narrow, smelly streets behind the waterfront still teemed with bronze-skinned men and sloe-eyed women.

Yet before the day was out he found that the atmosphere and spirit of Naples had become utterly different. His memories of the week he had spent there in '89 had always caused him to think of it as a Paradise on earth. That, perhaps, was largely due to his having found there again the beautiful Isabella d'Aranda, who had refused him her favours as a maid but, as a neglected wife, had given herself to him willingly. He had stayed with Sir William, who had proved the perfect host; and who had nick-named his Embassy 'The Royal Arms', in token of the fact that he liked his constant stream of guests to regard themselves as absolutely free to take their meals there only when they wished and to come and go at any hour they liked. That had enabled Roger to spend the greater part of each night with Isabella, and a good part of each day as well.

But it was not only this love-affair that had made the week pass for him in such a haze of happiness. Isabella had introduced him to many of her friends among the Spanish-Neapolitan nobility. All of them owned charming villas outside the city and every day they made up parties of pleasure to drive out and dine at one or other of them, then spend the long afternoons strolling or love-making in enchanted gardens made beautiful with grottoes, arbours, fountains, waterfalls and ancient statues. The only things they thought about were making love, acting charades, reading poetry and carrying on their love-affairs at dances or the opera.

Even the masses in the poorer parts of the city had radiated cheerfulness. They had little money and most of them were dressed in rags, but there was an abundance of fish, fruit and vegetables which could be bought for a few coppers. For the greater part of the year they were warmed by the sun; frequent saints' days provided an excuse for idling and jollification; and wherever one went they were always to be seen laughing and cracking bawdy jokes.

Now they were ominously quiet and sullen. Sir William might be right about the deeply religious peasantry having marched off full of enthusiasm to fight the atheist French; but great numbers of the city-dwellers had been taken too. Their families were anxious for them and in thousands of cases had been deprived of their breadwinners. The price of fish had never been so high, because the fishermen had been pressed to man the Fleet. The supplies of vegetables coming in from the country had also been greatly reduced. In the old days scores of gaming houses and brothels had done a roaring trade; now, owing to the lack of money, two-thirds of them were closed, so that hundreds of pimps and prostitutes were starving.

Roger also found that the carefree social world of Naples had ceased to exist. At his hotel and in the cafés whoever he spoke to would now converse only on two subjects—the war and politics. Elated as the Neapolitans were at their King having entered Rome, many of them expressed dark forebodings about the future. For years past they had heard accounts of French victories and the way in which the French viciously despoiled the territories they conquered. Alone in Italy, the Kingdom of Naples had so far escaped. But could it continue to do so if the French succeeded in concentrating a great Army north of Rome and marched south? Roger found too that, as he had supposed, a large section of the population had become obsessed with revolutionary ideas.

Although they spoke guardedly at first quite a number of them, on learning that he was British, said how greatly they wished that Naples might become a limited Monarchy like that of England, with the final say being with the elected representatives. They added that this was impossible to hope for under their own King, so their country could be saved from disaster only by making it a Republic.

From these conversations he learned that Queen Caroline and her Minister, Acton, were universally hated. All through the '90s the poison of the Revolution had been filtering down through Italy, and the Government had used ferocious measures in a futile attempt to check it. Scores of lawyers, doctors and intellectuals had abandoned their old interests to write about and preach ' The Rights of Man '. Many of the nobility had encouraged them and had striven in vain to bring about long-overdue reforms. One after another they had been seized and thrown into prison without trial. Hundreds of these idealists, among them many of the most respected men in Naples, were now rotting in prison.

Sorry as Roger was for them as individuals, he could not sympathize with the attitude of mind that had brought upon them such a fate. Having lived through the Revolution in Paris, he knew only too well the course taken by such political upheavals. Had those Neapolitan Liberals ever succeeded in getting control of the Government, within a year they would have been replaced by extremists and all the horrors of mob rule would have ensued. Even as things were they had helped, by preaching revolution, to reduce Naples from a city of delight to its present miserable state; although the buffoon of a King and his tyrannous Queen had been as much to blame, for neglecting the welfare of their poorer subjects and failing to make use of the talented men who could have brought a greater prosperity to their country.

At midnight Roger went to the Palazzo Sessa. This time he was shown into one of the small drawing rooms, and there he found Sir William with his beautiful wife Emma.

She had started life as a nursemaid, then had become an artists' model and the mistress of several gay bloods in London. Sir William had acquired her from his nephew, although when she accepted an invitation for herself and her mother to come out and winter in Naples as the guest of the already-elderly Ambassador she was not aware that he had bought the right to attempt to make her his mistress. Her mother, Mrs. Cardogan, had been given the post of housekeeper and, although Emma was still in love with the nephew, when the truth was gently conveyed to her she had offered little resistance to the charming uncle's advances. The whole affair had been conducted most decorously. Emma took up painting and dancing with considerable success. When, in due course, she was presented to Queen Caroline the Queen had taken an immediate liking to her. That liking had soon become such a passionate attachment that hardly a day passed without their seeing one another and, in addition, exchanging gushing letters, sometimes as often as three times a day.

When Roger had visited Naples in '89 Emma, although already established as the hostess at the Embassy, was not then married; but for the past seven years she had been Lady Hamilton. She was now thirty-three, a Junoesque beauty with chestnut curls, a cupid's-bow mouth and big, blue eyes. Her attraction lay in her brilliant colouring, great vivacity and kindness of disposition, but Roger personally preferred ladies with a more moderate size in limbs.

Finding her with Sir William caused him considerable annoyance, for coming upon her in private like this made it awkward for him to pretend that he had never met her; nor was he any better pleased when the Ambassador said:

'Mr. Brook, you will remember my wife. I have been telling her of the fine service you have rendered us and something of your adventures. But when you come to our receptions she will, of course, receive you as Mr. MacElfic and you need have no fears that your secret will not be safe with her. She is in all our secrets.'

Roger was not surprised to hear that; but he would have much preferred for her not to be let into this, as he knew her to be a born gossip. Although she might be discreet about important matters he thought it certain that she would talk to her crony the Queen about him, if to no one else.

However, the damage was now done and nothing was to be gained by looking sour about it; so when making his bow he gave her his most charming smile. Rising from a stately curtsey, she swayed gracefully forward, took both his hands and exclaimed theatrically:

'Mr. Brook, the despatches you have brought, writ by the infamous Bonaparte, will prove invaluable to our brave Admiral. It is God's work that you have done, for Sir Horatio is His instrument, and God will reward you.'

Roger had not seen matters in quite that light, although he had already gathered that in Naples Admiral Nelson had more or less taken the place of God, at least in Court circles. Bowing over the statuesque Emma's hands, he raised the right one to his lips and murmured, 'The small service I have rendered is as nothing compared to those of Your Ladyship. I am told that it was entirely due to you that our Fleet was allowed to victual and water at Naples, although it was then a neutral port, and that, had it not been permitted to, then there could have been no Battle of the Nile.'

Emma turned her big blue eyes up to heaven. 'Indeed, sir, too much has been made of that. It was my privilege to cast myself at the feet of our sweet Queen Caroline. She is an angel and, knowing our sainted Admiral's dire need, assented to the prayers of his handmaiden.'

These civilities having been exchanged, Roger produced his report for Mr. Pitt and handed it to Sir William. Pouring him a glass of Marsala, the Ambassador said, 'I am told that a British sloop will be sailing for Gibraltar in three days' time. Bonaparte's despatches and this report will go with it in the Embassy bag. I propose, however, to have it copied by a safe hand for our paladin, Sir Horatio; for it is certain that he will find much of interest in it.'

'By all means, sir,' Roger agreed. 'I must ask, though, that you will return General Bonaparte's originals to me. As a precaution against the copies being lost at sea I intend to carry the originals myself to London.'

'Certainly you shall have them. But are you still determined to travel overland? '

'I am. Having got off copies of the despatches and my report, there is no urgent reason for me to start for home. Rather than go by sea, I'll dally here awhile in the hope that in another few weeks it may become less dangerous to travel up the peninsula.'

Sir William nodded. 'I trust your hopes may be fulfilled. In any case the decision lies with you. Reverting to your despatches, one of them was addressed to Talleyrand. Did you know that last July he was deprived of his post as Minister of Foreign Affairs? '

Roger raised his eyebrows. 'No, I did not. Has Your Excellency information as to why he was deprived of his portfolio? '

'I have indeed,' the Ambassador smiled. 'The Directory and sycophants who serve it are the most venal crowd unhung. One could not have supposed that any one of them could possibly have over-reached himself; yet that blackguard Talleyrand did. He demanded of an American delegation so huge a bribe to favour a new commercial agreement with the United States that, rather than pay it, they complained to the Directory. And the Directors threw him out.'

'That is bad news,' Roger commented seriously. 'I know de Talleyrand intimately, and I can assure you that secretly he is a friend of Britain. Were he allowed to have his way——'

'I cannot believe it,' Emma broke in impetuously. 'He was a priest, a Bishop even. Yet he has denied his vows and willingly serves the spawn of hell that now rule France. He has covered himself with infamy, and is a declared atheist. How could he possibly be the friend of a God-fearing people? '

Roger shrugged. 'Permit me to remark that to confuse religion with politics can often lead to grave errors of judgment. Knowing as I do the men who now rule France, I can assure Your Ladyship that, since Talleyrand has gone, all the odds are that he will have been replaced by a man who will be less inclined to have a true appreciation of Britain's power and vital interests.' Knowing that it was pointless to defend Talleyrand further, or attempt to present Bonaparte as a human being, he asked, 'What other news is there out of France?'

'A law has been passed which will greatly increase the size of the French Armies,' Sir William replied. 'It was proposed by General Jourdan that the whole manpower of France should be subject to conscription. All young men between the ages of twenty and twenty-five are now liable to military service. They are to be registered by their Departments and, in groups from the age of twenty, will be called up as required.'

'That can mean no more,' Roger suggested, 'than the *levée-en-masse* that Carnot instituted when France was hard pressed by the Monarchies during the early years of the Revolutionary Wars.'

'I think it does,' the Ambassador countered. 'That was only an emergency measure, whereas this is a piece of permanent legislation. It is the first time that the youth of a nation has been required, upon reaching a certain age, to report automatically for military service. That is an entirely new conception of the duty a man owes to his country. It may well spread to other nations.'

'What of the Directory?' Roger asked. 'Is the personnel the same?'

'There has been no change since last May. In the middle of that month François de Neufchâteau drew the retiring ballot and was replaced by an ex-member of the Regicide Convention named Treilhard. At the same time the Directors again declared several Deputies newly elected to the Assembly, to be Royalist conspirators, and arbitrarily threw them out. But I expect you will have heard about that.'

Roger shook his head. 'Word of Treilhard's appointment failed to reach us before we sailed from Toulon on May 19th; and since then little news has trickled through to Egypt. I take it that matters are no better with the unfortunate Swiss or the people of Piedmont.'

'Alas, no. The brave Swiss are suffering an appalling martyr-dom at the hands of those pitiless fiends. As for Italy, as I told you yesterday it is a seething cauldron of strife from Rome northwards. The larger cities are still held by the French, but the country outside them is in a state of complete lawlessness.

Men, women and even bands of precocious children fall upon
solitary travellers and tear them limb from limb to get hold
of their money and such provisions as they may have with
them and, if they secure nothing better, they cook and eat their
horses.'

For a further half-hour they talked on then Roger took his
leave, having promised to attend the Monday reception at the
Embassy. He accepted out of curiosity to see who among the
Neapolitan aristocracy remained friendly to the British, or deemed
it expedient to continue to court them. Now that he had grown a
beard and could be introduced as Robert MacElfic, he regarded
as neglible the risk of anyone he had met ten years ago in
Naples identifying him as Roger Brook.

Next day, December 5th, *Vanguard* entered the bay, bringing
Nelson back from a bloodless victory. When he had appeared with
his Squadron off Leghorn and had threatened to bombard the
port, the pro-revolutionary Municipal Council had promptly surrendered and, accompanied by its French 'advisers', fled. The
five thousand Neapolitan troops had been landed with their
cannon and baggage and would, it was hoped, enable the Grand
Duke to clear the French out of Tuscany.

But the gallant little Admiral's reception was very different
from that which had greeted him on September 22nd when he had
arrived with his Fleet from the Battle of the Nile. Then King
Ferdinand, clad in gala attire, had done him the unprecedented
honour of sailing three leagues out into the bay to greet him.
Neapolitan bands had learned to play 'Rule, Britannia' and
'See the Conquering Hero Comes' for the occasion. Every ship
for miles along the coast and the whole waterfront had been
decked with flags and they were crammed with a hundred
thousand cheering people. Emma, who naturally accompanied
the royal party, had flung her arms round the Admiral's neck
then collapsed weeping with happiness on the deck. The King
and Queen had declared him to have been sent by God to save
Italy, and their young son had said that every morning he would
stand in front of a portrait of the hero and pray to grow up like
him.

Now the Fleet was scattered. One Squadron under Troubridge
was blockading the Roman coast, another under Bell was blockading Malta and the remainder under Hood were still blockading
Egypt. There was no reception of any kind; no thunder of salut-

ing cannon, no flags, no cheering thousands. The Admiral went ashore and, almost unnoticed, made his way up to the Palazzo Sessa.

There, as Roger learned later, he was met by most disturbing news. A rumour had come in that Mack's Army had suffered a severe defeat and that the General himself had been made a prisoner.

During the following two days the fact that things were going wrong became common knowledge in the city. Scores of Neapolitan gentry who, although knowing nothing of war, had gaily gone off in beautiful uniforms to fight now suddenly reappeared in civilian clothes making every sort of specious excuse for having left the Army. The accounts they gave of the campaign showed that it was being hopelessly mismanaged. Even during the victorious advance the organization had been so bad that for three days the majority of the troops had been without rations, and the King himself had lacked food for thirty-six hours.

To escape from this atmosphere of uncertainty and depression, Roger spent the Saturday revisiting Pompeii; but his excursion did little to cheer him. Memories of his previous visit provided too great a contrast. Then, with Isabella and a gay party, he had picnicked there and they had had Sir William—a great authority on Roman civilization—to give them a graphic description of the city as it must once have been, and of the terrible eruption that had overwhelmed it.

On Sunday he made another excursion, this time up to the crater of Vesuvius. He thought the huge bowl of lava, with its crisp crust of snow round the edge, tremendously impressive, but despite the wintry sunshine it was terribly cold up there; so he was glad to get down again to the shelter of trees and houses. It was only when he was among them that he realized he had hardly looked at the magnificent view over the bay, as his mind during the long trudge had been almost entirely occupied by gloomy speculations about what might happen if the Neapolitan Army had actually been defeated.

When Monday evening came he attended Sir William's weekly *conversazione*. Instead of the two hundred or more people usually to be seen at these gatherings, bowing, curtseying and chattering over wine and delicacies, the fine, pillared salon and the adjacent rooms were almost empty. There was barely a score of people present and nearly all were men with anxious faces;

but among them was Nelson, who when in Naples always made the Embassy his headquarters.

Emma received Roger most graciously and, after they had exchanged a few platitudes, asked for his arm to lead her to the buffet. On the way there she raised her fan and whispered to him behind it, 'Our slayer of dragons wishes to speak with you. At the moment that tiresome Prince Pignatelli is monopolizing him, but we will break in upon them.' Then she changed direction slightly and bore down on the Admiral.

When she had curtseyed and the three men had exchanged bows she said, 'Permit me to present to you, dear gallant Sir Horatio, and to Your Highness, Mr. Robert MacElfic who is on a visit to Naples.'

There were more bows and the elderly Prince smiled at Roger. 'I fear, Mr. MacElfic, you have chosen a most unfortunate time to visit our beautiful city.' Then he added, with the unfailing hospitality of the Italians, 'Nevertheless, if I can assist you to see something of it I shall be most happy to do so.'

As Roger thanked him, Nelson asked with his usual impetuosity, 'Where are you from, Mr. MacElfic, and how long is it since you arrived here?'

'I have been in Naples a week, sir, and have come from Crete.'

'Ah, Crete!' exclaimed the Admiral. 'You are just the man I wish to see, then. Now the Turks have become our allies I am anxious to know how their preparations for war are going forward in that island.'

'Come, Prince.' Emma tactfully laid her hand on Pignatelli's arm. 'Pray take me to the buffet and find me a glass of wine.'

As they moved away, Nelson said to Roger, 'We'll be less likely to be interrupted in one of the smaller rooms.' Then he turned abruptly and, with Roger beside him, walked quickly through a doorway into a drawing room panelled in yellow satin.

Halting in front of the marble mantelpiece, he turned, his drawn features flashed into an enchanting smile and he said, 'Now, Mr. Brook, my thanks and heartiest congratulations. You see how right I was to persuade you to return to Cairo? The despatches you secured for us are invaluable.'

Roger returned the smile. 'I am glad, sir, though my obtaining of them was largely due to luck.'

'Luck, maybe; but courage and resource must also have been needed to get away with them. My old friend Chris must be proud to have such a son. Your long report, too, I read with the greatest interest, although I must admit that I was very disappointed by it.'

'In what way, sir?'

'Why, I had hoped that a good half of those atheist dogs in Cairo were by now dead of starvation, the Arab pox or the plague. Instead, you tell us they are erecting windmills to grind the corn, planting vineyards and even amusing themselves by opening cafés like those they have in Paris.'

'I would I had better news for you. But the French are determined to surmount the difficulties which have arisen from your having cut them off, and their Army shows no sign of disintegrating. It is, of course, General Bonaparte's genius for administration which accounts for their still-high morale.'

'That emissary of the Devil!' Nelson's bright eye flashed angrily. 'But I forgot. At Aboukir you made it plain to me that you have a sneaking admiration for . . . for this man that I can think of only as the very personification of Evil.'

Roger had the temerity to smile. 'It is said, sir, that one should give the Devil his due. If General Mack had a one-hundredth part of Bonaparte's organizing ability the Neapolitan Army would not be in its present alarming situation.'

The Admiral's smile suddenly returned. 'Well said, Mr. Brook. You have certainly made your point there.' After a moment he added, with a shake of the head, 'Everything seems to have gone awry and I am bitterly disappointed. Until my return here last Wednesday I had the greatest hopes for this new war against those devilish French.'

'It is said, sir, that you encouraged the Neapolitans to enter on it, though I could scarce believe that.'

'Why so? We had good reason to believe that the French were planning the conquest of King Ferdinand's territories, and I told His Majesty roundly that either he must attack while the French in middle Italy were still weak or stand to lose his throne.'

'Since the French were unlikely to be reinforced for some time, would it not have been wiser to wait until Austria was fully committed to make war again on the Republic?'

The little Admiral drew himself up and said haughtily, 'Do you presume, Mr. Brook, to question my judgment?'

'Sir,' Roger replied, 'I have on occasion questioned the judgment of Mr. Pitt and, hate Bonaparte as you may, that of the greatest soldier of our age. I had, therefore, thought that I might speak my mind to the greatest sailor of our age. But if I have presumed I pray your pardon.'

Nelson, ever susceptible to flattery, instantly relaxed. 'I see now how you have achieved your extraordinary position. It takes more courage to criticize one's superiors to their faces than to stand up to shot and shell. You consider that I acted rashly. Well, perhaps I did. But a great part of the success with which God has blessed me has been due to my attacking the enemy without counting the odds. In this case the odds favoured Naples by four to one, and by swift action I felt they stood a good chance of throwing our enemies out of a large part of Italy. Remember, the French nation has become a hydra-headed monster and, if our Christian civilization is to be saved, we must seek at all times to destroy a part of that monster with every means that becomes available. That is my doctrine and no considerations will ever deter me from practising it.'

Roger bowed. 'It is that, sir, which has earned you the love and admiration of our whole nation. But about the present. A hundred rumours are running round the city. Would you do me the favour of telling me to the best of your knowledge how matters really stand?'

'Willingly,' came the prompt reply. 'It is only right that men like yourself should know the truth and what we may expect. The rumour that General Mack has been taken prisoner is unfounded. But the French have driven back the right wing of his Army and captured all its artillery and baggage. Most of its officers have shamefully deserted and it has now become a rabble. At Castellana the French are holding a strong position with thirteen thousand troops, and Mack is said to be moving against them with twenty thousand. Should he prove successful, all is far from being lost. He might then still hold the fortified line of the frontier; but, frankly, I have grave doubts of his ability to defeat the French.

'Shortly after my arrival I was received by Her Gracious Majesty, Queen Caroline, whose splendid courage is our main support in our endeavours against the enemy. I found her heartbroken at the shocking performance of the Neapolitan Army. God knows, the officers had not much honour to lose, but they

lost any they had. Her Majesty told me that the Divisions of
Generals San Filippo and Micheroux had turned and run thirty
miles at the mere sight of the French. San Filipino, instead of running, saved his skin by going over to the enemy. The Prince of
Taranto displayed such cowardice that King Ferdinand tore his
epaulettes from his shoulders with his own hands. I have always
found that Italians are brave men individually but when regi-
mented as soldiers they seem to go all to pieces. To be honest, I
now fear the worst.'

'Should what remains of General Mack's Army be driven in
upon the city, do you think there is any hope of holding it?'
Roger enquired.

The Admiral shook his head. 'The three great fortresses are
considered impregnable, so they may hold out. But the city has
no walls, so it cannot be defended. I shall, of course, evacuate all
British nationals who are resident here and the Royal Family,
should they decide to retire to Sicily. You may count upon my
finding a place in *Vanguard* for you.'

Roger, having been once bitten by this small, vital man who
lived only to scourge the French, was twice shy; so he replied, 'I
thank you for the offer, sir. However, as the Jacobite MacElfic, I
am regarded as more or less a neutral here, and I feel that I could
possibly prove of more use by remaining on in the city.'

'You may well be right in that,' the Admiral agreed, and
shortly afterwards they returned to the big salon.

For a while Roger talked with several of the gloomy Neapolitan nobles there; then, as he took his leave, Sir William said,
'Next Thursday, the 13th, is my birthday. We have always celebrated it with a big party here. Invitations were sent out over a
fortnight ago, but I trust you will not mind a belated one. Eight
o'clock and silk stockings. I shall look forward to seeing you.'

Roger accepted, although he could not think that a party of
any kind could prove a success in the present state of Naples,
and he concluded that the Ambassador meant to give it only as a
gesture to show that, in spite of General Mack's reverses, the
British were still confident that the Kingdom of the Two Sicilies
would emerge victorious from the war.

But the party never took place. On the morning of the 13th
Roger received a note from Sir William to the effect that, the
situation being so uncertain, he felt that this was no time for any
celebration and was cancelling all invitations.

On the following day, the 14th, the great blow fell. Like so many of his officers, King Ferdinand had fled from the enemy and arrived back in Naples. The whole Neapolitan Army was in full retreat. The French under General Championnet and headed by two future Marshals of the Empire, Macdonald and Ney, were advancing at full speed upon the capital.

16

No 'Happy New Year'

FOR four days King Ferdinand had lorded it in the magnificent Farnese Palace in Rome, thundering forth boasts about what he would do to the godless French when he came upon them. But at the first move by the French Commander, General Championnet, he was seized by panic. So fearful for himself was he that he insisted on changing clothes with one of his officers so as to make himself less conspicuous. Helped on to a horse, he rode it at full gallop until, under his weight, the animal had nearly collapsed. Then Ferdinand took to a coach and, clinging to the hand of one of his nobles, had himself driven as fast as possible to Naples.

His laments, and those of the Queen and the Hamiltons, about the conduct of the French were loud and long. Apparently, Championnet had left a letter for General Mack, stating that he was withdrawing his forces from Rome to save the civil population from the horrors of street fighting. The naive Neapolitans had taken this to mean that he had surrendered Rome to them. In fact, as an experienced soldier, Championnet had simply withdrawn a garrison too weak to hold the city until he could concentrate his widely scattered forces and reoccupy it. But nothing would persuade his deluded enemies that he had not acted with diabolical treachery.

In spite of Ferdinand's cowardly behaviour, his *lazzaroni* remained entirely loyal. A great multitude of them crammed the square in front of the royal palace yelling for him. When at length he appeared on a balcony with the Queen, they made him swear that he would not leave Naples, then shouted that, with the aid of their patron saint, Geronimo, they would defend him to the death.

That afternoon Roger received a note from Sir William Hamilton asking him to come up to the Embassy. When, in the evening, he did so, he found a small army of workmen busily crating the most valuable items from the Ambassador's collection of antiques. He told Roger that their loyal and generous friend, the heaven-sent Admiral, had already had shipped to Gibraltar, simply as a precaution, the best pictures in the collection. But now the time had come when as many other treasures as possible must be got away, as an insurance against their falling into the hands of the unspeakable French.

When Roger enquired why he had been summoned, Sir William said:

'You are under no obligation to me, but I mean to ask a favour of you. In my files I have many hundreds of letters relating to my diplomatic activities. Some of them make mention of secrets that could be damaging to British prestige, if known to the enemy. I have so many urgent matters to attend to that I have not the time to go through them. No one could be better entrusted with this task than yourself. I beg you, therefore, to undertake it. My wish is that all documents of importance should be preserved for me to take with me should we be compelled to evacuate the Embassy, and that the others should be burnt.'

Far from thinking of refusing, Roger was only too glad to have some useful work to occupy him during the emergency, and early next morning he set about the formidable task of scanning and sorting Sir William's correspondence.

King Ferdinand's return had brought about a new situation in the city. He had cordially endorsed his loyal *lazzaroni's* determination to defend Naples and, the Army having failed so lamentably, the leaders of the *lazzaroni* took matters into their own hands. Large bodies of them picketed all the approaches to the city, seized the returning deserters and took their arms from them. But the King's resolution to rely on this vast rabble of petty thieves and professional beggars did not last for long.

Queen Caroline had a deep-seated distrust of mobs. In the fact that the Royal Family had been forced to show themselves on the balcony of the palace a few hours after the return of the King had leaked out, she saw a repetition of the scene at Versailles in '89 following which Louis XVI and Marie Antoinette had been forced by the mob to accompany it, virtually as prisoners, back to Paris. Fearing that she might suffer the same fate as her sister, Caroline had at once begun to urge upon Ferdinand that their only certainty of safety lay in flight to Sicily.

A few days of her nagging had been sufficient to weaken the King's resolution. Then, on the 18th as Roger learned from Sir William, a despatch was received from General Mack. He reported that what remained of his Army had disintegrated into a rabble and besought Their Majesties to escape from Naples before the French entered it. That settled the matter. For the next few days frantic preparations for the evacuation were made with as much secrecy as possible.

Already, from the 15th, Queen Caroline had been sending each night to the Palazzo Sessa boxes and bundles of every description for transfer to Nelson's flagship. Emma sat up till daybreak, receiving and repacking everything from a fortune in diamonds to nappies for the royal babies.

The flight was fixed for the night of Friday 21st. But recently the weather had broken, and on the Friday morning such a storm blew up that it was feared that it might be found impossible for the barges to convey the fugitives from the quay to *Vanguard*. During the day half a dozen contradictory messages reached the British Embassy from General Acton about possible postponement of the venture, but when evening came it was decided that the risk should be taken.

At half past eight Nelson landed at the Arsenal steps and proceeded to the palace by way of a long, subterranean tunnel. He then escorted the royal party and their principal courtiers back along the tunnel and transported them safely, but in sheeting rain, to his flagship. Roger, still in charge of the important documents he had saved from the Embassy files, went off in another boat an hour later. He had an awful tossing and was at length hauled aboard *Vanguard* soaked to the skin.

He found the decks piled with royal possessions that there had not as yet been time to stow away—pictures, furniture, statuary and innumerable bales and boxes. It looked as though Sir William's estimate, that they had succeeded in carrying off between two and three million pounds' worth of goods, might not be too high.

The great stern cabin was crowded with people. Queen Caroline was weeping in Emma's large, protecting arms; Nelson, behaving no longer like an Admiral but like a schoolboy besotted with calf-love, was exclaiming to everyone how courageous and angelic Emma was. The royal children were also in tears. General Acton, the Court Chamberlain Prince Belmonte, Prince Castel-cicala and the Austrian Count Thurn stood grouped in a corner, looking as glum as though they were about to be sent to the guillotine. A score of other notabilities, male and female, were seated on the deck, clasping their most precious belongings which, at short notice, were all they had been able to bring with them. Some of them were already being seasick from the rolling of the vessel.

Pushing through the crush, Roger found Sir William and gave him the weighty leather satchel crammed with papers. Having thanked him the Ambassador said, 'Why not come with us? I pray you, do. With the King gone, anything may happen. It is certain that there will be riots and you might well be killed in one, or during the fighting when the French force their way into the city.'

Roger shook his head. 'No. It is good of Your Excellency to suggest it; but things can hardly become worse than they were in Paris during the Revolution, so I expect to be able to take care of myself. And when the fighting is over I still hope to make my way home overland.'

Very distressed at the sight of so much misery, Roger went out on deck, in spite of the rain, and huddled against a bulwark until he could get a boat to take him ashore. The inward trip was even worse than the outward one and the boat tossed as though a bucking stallion were beneath her. Before reaching the wharf Roger was violently sick, which strengthened his conviction that he had been wise to refuse Sir William's invitation to accompany the royal party to Sicily.

The next two days gave him still greater cause to be glad that he was safe on land. On the 22nd a gale of such ferocity raged that Nelson's ships could not set sail and, buffeted by huge waves, rolled back and forth as though they were barrels. On the morning of the 23rd they did set sail; but the wind and seas were still so high that the ships could not round the island of Capri, the topsails of *Vanguard* were blown out and, when night came down, the Squadron was still helplessly beating about the bay.

Later it was learned that the sufferings of the passengers had

K

been appalling. The majority of the Italians remained night and day on their knees, alternately vomiting and offering up last prayers. Count Esterhazy, in the hope of appeasing the sea, threw into it a diamond-encrusted snuff-box with a portrait of his mistress on the lid. Sir William sat on his cot holding a loaded pistol, having determined to shoot himself at the last moment rather than drown. Alone among the women Emma, to her eternal honour, refused to succumb. All the royal servants were incapacitated; so she looked after the whole family, gave away her own bedding and could not be persuaded even to lie down until *Vanguard*, with considerable difficulty, got into the harbour of Palermo on the 26th. But even her devoted care could not prevent Prince Alberto, Queen Caroline's six-year-old son, from dying in her arms on the second day of that terrible voyage.

Meanwhile panic, confusion and mutiny reigned in the bay. On the morning of the 22nd, as soon as it became known that the Royal Family had abandoned Naples, hundreds of other families made up their minds to flee from the French. Sir William had sent word to the British residents, the majority of whom had been accommodated during the previous night in three transports. Nelson had made arrangements for two Greek polacres to take off the French Royalist exiles; but from first light onward, in spite of the raging storm, a large part of the Neapolitan nobility put out in a swarm of boats and begged to be taken on to the heaving ships.

There was trouble, too, in the Neapolitan Navy. The Commander, Commodore Caracciolo, naturally felt aggrieved that his King should have taken refuge in a British ship rather than in one of his own. To add insult to injury, a part of the royal treasure that had been sent aboard his flagship was later removed to the ' greater safety ' of *Vanguard*. But Queen Caroline did not trust the Neapolitans, and neither did Nelson.

They had some reason for that. As soon as Caracciolo's sailors learned that the Fleet was to put to sea, the majority of them refused to abandon their families and went ashore. Caracciolo reported that he had sufficient men to handle his flagship, and accompanied the exodus to Palermo—although only to be hanged from the yardarm by Nelson six months later on somewhat dubious evidence that he had turned traitor. But what was to be done about the other ships of the Neapolitan Navy that could not weigh anchor?

Nelson was in favour of sinking them there and then; but the King, the Queen and Acton, having almost bankrupted their country to build their Fleet, implored him to spare it. He was prevailed upon to do so, but left behind Commodore Campbell, who was in command of three Portuguese frigates, with strict instructions that in no circumstances was any part of the Neapolitan Navy to be allowed to fall into the hands of the French.

Ashore there was general turmoil. Before sneaking out of his palace, Ferdinand had sent for General Prince Pignatelli. When the General arrived he found no King but a document, left carelessly on a table, appointing him Regent of Naples. Unfortunately he was both a weak and a stupid man, and hopelessly incapable of handling the situation. He took no steps whatever to place the city in a state of defence and when the *Eletti*, as the Municipal Council composed of nobles was called, urged him to form a National Guard for the maintenance of order he told them that such matters were nothing to do with them.

Had Pignatelli been a brave and able man it is quite possible that Naples might have been saved from the French, for their advance was being checked in a most unexpected manner. Now that the Neapolitan Army had been disembarrassed of its cowardly officers, the many thousands of soldiers who still remained in the field suddenly began to fight. The war they waged was entirely un-coordinated but, often led by fanatical village priests, they fell upon the French with extraordinary ferocity wherever they could find them. The French were very inferior in numbers and were forced to concentrate in solid bodies and, instead of advancing further, defend themselves in villages.

But no advantage was taken of this unlooked-for respite. On the contrary, matters in Naples went from bad to worse. Pignatelli, presumably on the King's instructions, endeavoured to set fire to the Arsenal. He was prevented by the *Eletti*, but they failed to stop him on December 28th from burning the hundred gunboats that were anchored off Posilipo and having the great store of powder and shot kept at Mergellina thrown into the sea. Ten days later Commodore Campbell, by then convinced that the Regent meant to hand over Naples to the enemy without striking a blow, turned the guns of his Portuguese frigates on the helpless Neapolitan vessels and sank all the bigger ships of the Fleet.

In defiance of Pignatelli, the *Eletti* decreed the calling up of fourteen thousand citizens; but the move proved abortive, as the Regent refused to release more than two hundred muskets from the castles. He declared his policy to be to do nothing to increase the enmity of the French but to levy a huge tax and use the money to bribe them to concede an armistice.

He appeared to be successful in this. On January 11th General Championnet agreed to spare Naples for two months on condition that various strong places and a great area of territory were ceded, that the ports of the Two Sicilies were declared neutral and that, within the current month, Naples paid an indemnity of ten million francs, half of which was to be forthcoming within the next three days.

During this fortnight of confusion and anxiety Roger played no part in events. Having sent off his despatches, he was free of all responsibility and he had no urgent reason for endeavouring to get home. With such patience as he could muster he continued to hope that in another month or so the peninsula would have been sufficiently pacified for him to risk setting out for France. In the meantime he kept himself occupied by riding every morning, practising in a fencing school near his hotel for an hour or so every afternoon and picking up the rumours of the day in cafés in the evening.

But the news of the armistice seemed to give him the sort of chance for which he had been waiting. Before that it would have been suicidal for him to attempt to join the French. To increase the strength of his Army, King Ferdinand had released all the criminals from the Sicilian jails and had formed no fewer than sixteen battalions with them. With thousands of such desperadoes roving the countryside, no solitary traveller could possibly have hoped to get through to Rome. But now the French would be sending emissaries to Naples, and Roger planned to get in touch with them. If, on some excuse or other, he could have himself sent to General Championnet, the rest should prove easy. After Bonaparte's letters had been copied he had retrieved them from Sir William. He would only have to show them and declare himself as Colonel Breuc to be provided with an escort that would see him safely back to France.

On the 12th, in accordance with the armistice terms, the Neapolitans handed over Capua. General Mack, now scared that his own soldiers would kill him, sought the protection of the French.

When he was about to surrender his sword Championnet said contemptuously, 'Pray keep it. My Government does not allow me to accept presents of English manufacture.' Then he told the old man to go home.

On the evening of the 14th the French Commissioners arrived to collect the first half of the indemnity. It had been got together only with great difficulty as Ferdinand had emptied the national treasury before his departure, carrying off twenty million ducats. But the French never got their money. A seething mob of *lazzaroni* refused to allow it to be handed over and attacked the five carriages in which the Commissioners had arrived. They were rescued only with difficulty by the National Guard, kept in protective custody for the night and departed the following morning vowing vengeance for the insults to which they had been subjected.

Roger found it impossible to get anywhere near them and, as the action of the *lazzaroni* had put an end to the armistice, he was left in the same frustrating situation as before.

Within the next twenty-four hours it became clear that the *lazzaroni* were now the real masters of the city. For the past three weeks they had, in one way or another, been acquiring arms and, just in time, a great quantity of weapons became theirs for the taking. The five thousand troops whom Nelson had conveyed to Leghorn returned with their tails between their legs. The Grand Duke had, after all, proved too frightened to launch an attack from Tuscany on the French and had packed the Neapolitans back into their transports. On their arrival at Naples, hordes of *lazzaroni* swarmed aboard the vessels and seized every weapon in them.

Elated by their success, they proceeded to attack the Castel Nuovo. Pignatelli sent orders to the Commander to defend the castle but not to fire upon the mob. As it was an impossibility to do one without the other, the unhappy officer allowed the *lazzaroni* to take possession. By similar means they secured the great fortress of Castel Sant'Elmo, up on the heights, and the other great Castel dell'Uovo, down on the harbour.

They then began a witch-hunt for 'Jacobins', as Neapolitans with revolutionary leanings were termed. Anyone believed to have French sympathies was dragged into the street and murdered, then his house was pillaged. This led many hundreds of the lesser nobility and bourgeoisie with Liberal leanings to decide that the only hope of saving their lives lay in siding with the French and, if possible, helping them to capture the city. A number of them banded themselves together and, by a trick, succeeded in gaining possession of the Castel Sant'Elmo, where they shut themselves up.

Meanwhile the *lazzaroni* had broken open all the prisons. The intellectuals who had been locked up in them, on Queen Caroline's orders, as Jacobins were butchered, but the criminals were let loose to join in the orgy of murder and destruction that was now taking place.

On the night of the 17th Pignatelli fled to Palermo. By that time the mobs were no longer bothering themselves about the politics of the wealthier citizens, but were breaking into and looting every house in which they thought they would acquire plunder easily. A hundred thousand male and female cut-throats were storming through the great, wealthy city and its state of anarchy had become worse than that in Paris during the most terrible days of the Revolution.

Roger, now considerably alarmed for his own safety, remained in his hotel; but even that did not save him from a most unpleasant experience. On the night following Pignatelli's flight the hotel was attacked by a mob howling for blood. He had only just time to jump out of bed, snatch up his weapons and money-belt, pull on his travelling coat and get out of his bedroom window on to the roof of a verandah at the back of the building.

Climbing down to the ground, he made off through a side door in the courtyard and along several alleys until he could no longer hear the shouts and screams coming from the hotel. It was bitterly cold and he spent the rest of the night huddled, shivering, in a doorway, praying that Hell might open and swallow Ferdinand and Caroline for the horror they had brought upon their capital.

By dawn he had decided that Naples had become too hot to hold him. Tempests or no tempests, he must get out of this inferno before he was murdered; so he must go home by sea. As soon as there was light enough, he set out along the waterfront and trudged the five miles or more south along the bay to the little fishing port of Portici. There he talked cautiously with some fishermen and, selecting one of whom he liked the look, drew him aside. After ten minutes' haggling he persuaded the man, for a considerable sum in gold, to find him some warm clothes, then run him down the coast and across the straits to Messina.

Soon after midday, warmed by a good meal of fish soup and rough wine, and wearing coarse woollens under his travelling coat, he went aboard the fishing smack. The crew consisted of the owner and his two stalwart sons. Roger had little fear that, having such odds in their favour, they might set upon and rob him, since they seemed very decent folk and, moreover, he was armed with two pistols as well as his sword.

The weather continued to be cold with occasional squalls of rain, but, for the most part, it was sunny and, after the nightmare happenings in Naples, he found it a great relief to sit day after day in the stern of the boat, free from all anxiety. After rounding Capri they kept within a mile or so of the coast, now and then putting in to fishing villages to replenish their stores. Tacking slowly south, the three-hundred-mile voyage took sixteen days and Roger had become so used to doing nothing, except steer the boat occasionally or help with the sails, that he was almost sorry when on February 4th they landed in Sicily.

In Messina he spent three nights in a bug-ridden hotel, but there was no better accommodation to be had. After purchasing the best suit of clothes he could find, he set about making preparations for his journey to Palermo. The Sicilian capital was a hundred and fifty miles distant, and the only way to reach it was by a road following the northern coast of the great island. Long stretches of this road were little better than cart-tracks, the so-called inns along it were no more than hovels, and it was said to be infested with brigands. On hearing this, Roger decided that the only way to make the journey with a minimum of discomfort and a reasonable degree of safety would be to hire a travelling coach, in which he could sleep at night, and engage armed outriders for his protection.

The standard of living in the island was so low that men could be hired for any purpose for quite a small sum, but the total cost of such an expedition was considerable and his store of gold was now running low; so he sold a few of his small diamonds to a Spanish Jew who happened to be staying at the inn.

On the morning of the 7th, escorted by four villainous-looking mounted men armed to the teeth, he set out. Stoically he endured the jolting, while deriving such consolation as he could from the beauty of the scenery. To his right there was an endless succession of bays enclosed by wooded promontories and to his left, for the first three days, the magnificent cone of Etna continued to dominate the north-east of the island. On the afternoon of the 13th he reached Palermo.

The walls of the ancient city were most impressive but he found the city within them composed almost entirely of slums, many of which dated back to the occupation of the city by Saracens and Normans. The British Embassy, he learned, had been established in the Villa Bastioni, and he went there as soon as he had paid off his escort. He found it to be a handsome mansion overlooking the Marine Promenade and adjacent to the beautiful Flora Reale gardens, but it soon transpired that the occupants were far from happy in their new home.

Sir William and Emma received him most kindly, but had a sad story to tell. In addition to bemoaning the loss of their fine Neapolitan properties and a great part of their possessions, they had found Palermo most disappointing. The Royal Family had never previously stayed there, except in summer, and then only at long intervals. In consequence, none of the palaces had fireplaces and most of them had fallen into disrepair. As the weather had been very inclement the refugees had suffered severely from the cold and Sir William had spent several weeks in bed with a fever. The King and Queen had installed themselves in the only habitable rooms in the Colli Palace and the Queen, still terrified of assassination, constantly moaned about it being two miles from the harbour, which would make it difficult to escape if the mob took it into its head to follow the example of that of Naples.

As it had taken Roger nearly four weeks to reach Palermo, the Hamiltons had much more recent news of Naples than he had, gleaned from refugees who had continued to arrive by sea. The disciplined French columns had forced their way through the rabble remnants of the Neapolitan Army and launched their attack on the capital on January 23rd, upon which the Liberal nobility in the Castel Sant'Elmo ran up the hated tricolour flag. The *lazzaroni* resisted the French with extraordinary ferocity. Thousands of them were killed as they defended every street and every house, but again French discipline triumphed. After several days of desperate fighting they crushed all opposition, and on February 4th General Championnet proclaimed the Kingdom of Naples as the Parthenopean Republic.

The news from northern Italy was no better. The French,

infuriated by the Grand Duke of Tuscany's half-hearted attempt
to move against them, had taken over in Florence; so the Duke,
too, had to seek safety in exile. The Genoese of the Ligurian
Republic had penetrated to Turin and had roused the Republicans
there against their King, Charles Emmanuel IV. On December
9th he was forced to abdicate the throne of Piedmont and took
refuge in his other kingdom, the island of Sardinia. This last
event, although apparently a minor one among the upheavals
that the French had caused over such a great area of Europe,
was, a year later, to have consequences that altered the fate of a
dozen nations.

On the credit side the beginnings of a Second Coalition against
the French had at last matured. In the New Year of '99 Britain
had signed an alliance with Russia and Turkey and it really
looked now as if Austria meant to join them. Nelson's victory of
the Nile had already established British supremacy in the Mediterranean and the capture of Minorca towards the end of the preceding year had provided the Admiral with another base. The
addition of Russian and Turkish, as well as Portuguese, Squadrons now enabled the Allies to enforce a strict blockade on all
enemy ports.

When Roger enquired after the gallant Admiral, Sir William
pulled a long face and said, ' Since making Palermo his headquarters, our beloved hero has been much under the weather.
Soon after our arrival here it was my most unhappy duty to
hand him a despatch from an officer named Sir Sidney Smith. The
despatch stated that Their Lordships of the Admiralty had
charged Sir Sidney both to take over all negotiations with the
Turks and to conduct all future operations in the eastern
Mediterranean.'

' The name rings a bell,' Roger remarked. ' Surely he must be
the man whom Talleyrand mentioned to me when I was last in
Paris as being a prisoner in the Temple.'

' You are right; but he succeeded in escaping, with the aid of a
French Royalist: one Colonel Phélippeaux. He subscribed his
letter in most pretentious terms, as Knight of the Royal Swedish
Order of the Sword, Minister Plenipotentiary to the Grand Turk
and Chief of Operations by Land and Sea in the Levant. It is, of
course, true that his younger brother is our Minister at the
Porte, which should greatly assist his negotiations there, but——'

' But the insult! ' Emma broke in passionately. ' To deprive of one of his Squadrons the greatest sailor England has ever had and allow this popinjay to reap the glory of finishing off Bonaparte. The humiliation of it is beyond bearing. One can only suppose that their Lordships are gone mad.'

Roger would have given pride of place to no man in his admiration for the little Admiral's grasp of all naval matters, initiative and great personal courage, and he was shocked by this most ungenerous treatment of him. All the same, he thought that there was a possible reason for it. Although, as far as Nelson was able, he had for the past five months continued to control his distant Squadrons operating against Egypt, Malta and the Balearics and in the Gulf of Genoa, he had devoted his own energies entirely to the affairs of Naples. He had even promised that in no circumstances would he abandon Their Sicilian Majesties. The reason for that was not far to seek and was so generally known that tidings of it would long since have reached London. In Whitehall it might well be thought that, instead of remaining inactive in Palermo, he ought by now to be back in the Levant, doing his utmost to hamper the advance up the Syrian coast which it was known Bonaparte intended to undertake in the New Year. Therefore a more singleminded man had been sent to do it for him.

Naturally, Roger made no mention of his plausible speculations and Sir William was going on, 'You will appreciate how aggrieved was so sensitive a soul as Sir Horatio by this belittling of him. He wrote at once both to Earl Spencer at the Admiralty and to St. Vincent, as his Commander-in-Chief, stating that he could not support having Captain Hood's Squadron taken from him by an officer junior to himself, and asking to be relieved of his Command.'

'I pray God they are not such fools as to allow him to give it up,' Roger said with all sincerity. Then he asked if Sir William would secure him an interview with the Admiral.

'He is residing here as our treasured guest,' said Emma, 'and we should be happy to have you, too, with us if you will forgive our putting you in a small room at the top of the house.'

Sir William added, with a sad little smile, 'It's that, or the company of bedbugs and rats. Palermo is now choc-a-bloc with refugees of a dozen different nationalities. The only passable hotel is full to overflowing and every moderately sanitary building is packed to the roof-tops.'

Roger's reason for not accepting the Hamiltons's hospitality in Naples did not pertain in Palermo, so he gratefully accepted and was shown up to an attic room. At supper that night there were some twenty people, the majority of whom were now penniless and living on Sir William's generosity although he had lost a great part of his fortune. A number of them seized upon Roger, as a newcomer, to pour out the tale of their misfortunes; but later in the evening the Ambassador took him to a room that had been set aside as an office for Nelson.

The Admiral, pale and ill-looking, was doggedly working in his left-handed scrawl through a pile of correspondence, as he now had half a dozen allies with whom to deal in addition to the scattered ships of his Fleet, and was preparing to defend Messina from attack by the French. After greeting Roger courteously but abruptly, he asked in what way he could be of service to him.

Determined to give the little fire-eater no grounds for inveigling him into further work as a secret agent in the Mediterranean, Roger cannily refrained from asking directly for a passage home. Instead he said that, having got as far as Naples, he had intended to return overland to France but, as that had proved impossible, his only alternative was to go home by sea. Then he could slip across the Channel to deliver Bonaparte's despatches and resume his secret activities in Paris.

The Admiral wasted no words, but said glumly, 'I myself may shortly be sailing for England. In that case I will take you with me. In any case I will arrange matters for you. Pray excuse me now.'

Roger had not long to wait. Two days later a corvette arrived from Gibraltar. She carried a despatch for Nelson and a few hours later Sir William joyfully passed on its contents to Roger. Owing to a misunderstanding the 'Great Plenip' as they had derisively nicknamed Sir Sidney Smith, had taken more upon himself than had been intended. Nelson was still Commander-in-Chief for the whole of the Mediterranean. Hood's Squadron would continue to act under his orders, as also would the pretentious Commodore. The Admiral was writing a despatch for the corvette to carry and, having watered, the ship was to proceed again to sea the following evening. Roger was to sail in her.

On the afternoon of the 16th Roger said good-bye to the kindly Hamiltons, then went aboard the corvette *Firefly,* whose Captain was a Lieutenant Shotter. The Lieutenant, a big, middle-aged, cheerful man, welcomed Roger aboard and showed him to a small cabin. Having stowed away his few belongings, Roger went on deck and, as the early dusk of the February evening fell, watched Palermo fade away in the distance.

That night as he settled down in his narrow cot he sighed with satisfaction. After twelve months away from England he was at last on his way home. It might be another two months or more before he got there and, at this time of year, it was certain that there would be periods of bad weather during which he would suffer from seasickness. But that was a small price to pay to escape for good from the perils he had had to face for so long. Once home, he was now determined never to go abroad again until peace was restored.

When he went on deck next morning he found that, during the night, favourable winds had enabled the corvette to cover the sixty miles along the coast to the north-west tip of Sicily and that she was now off the little port of Tripani. By noon she had rounded the islands lying off the peninsula and was heading south. After a pleasant meal with the cheerful Lieutenant Shotter, Roger went below again for an afternoon nap.

Roused by the striking of eight bells, he went up and joined the Lieutenant on the poop. The weather was cold but fine and, after a few minutes, he noticed that the declining sun was almost directly astern. Turning to Shotter, he said:

'Am I crazy, Lieutenant, or are your methods of navigation most unusual? The sun is behind us, so we must be sailing east; whereas for Gibraltar we should be proceeding west.'

The Lieutenant gave him a slightly pitying smile. 'I'm sorry to have to disillusion you, Mr. MacElfic, but we are not going to Gibraltar. My instructions are to take *Firefly* to Egypt.'

17

Shanghaied for Further Service

ROGER'S blue eyes grew dark with anger. Suddenly he found his voice and demanded, 'What the hell is the meaning of this?'

'I can hardly make my meaning plainer, sir,' replied the Lieutenant. '*Firefly* is bound for Egypt.'

'There has been a mistake,' Roger rapped out. 'An absurd misunderstanding. Admiral Nelson promised me a passage home. I must request you to put about at once and land me at the nearest Sicilian port.'

'I'm sorry, sir, but that is out of the question.' Shotter remained quite unruffled in the face of Roger's angry stare. 'The misunderstanding must be on your part. Sir Horatio gave me my orders personally and they were to take you to Egypt.'

'Were they, by God! Then he's tricked me and——'

'I don't like to hear you say that, sir,' the Lieutenant interjected swiftly.

'I don't give a damn what you like,' Roger roared. 'The Admiral has no right whatever to dictate my movements. I am not his servant, but Mr. . . . . Well, no matter. But I have friends powerful enough to have you dismissed the Service. Do you refuse to put about and land me it will be the worse for you.'

'Mr. MacElfic, I'm sure you don't mean that, because you know that I must obey the orders I've been given. If you thought you were on your way home I sympathize with you; but you're not, and it will make things much more pleasant for both of us if you act sensibly.' As he spoke, Shotter drew a letter from his

285

pocket and added, 'Sir Horatio said that, when you learned our destination, you might be somewhat upset and he told me to give you this. No doubt it will explain matters.'

Seething with rage, Roger took the letter, broke the seal and read:

Mr. Brook,

I trust you will not think too badly of me for the small deception I have practised upon you. Sir William Hamilton will have informed you that I am still responsible for the conduct of operations in the Levant. Owing to the extraordinary position you have created for yourself as the confidant of Bonaparte, I am convinced that you can be of far greater service to your King and Country by returning to him than by going to Paris. In any case, I cannot find it in me to deprive my Command of such a valuable source of intelligence as you have in your power to provide. I am, therefore, sending you to my subordinate, Captain Sir Sidney Smith, with instructions to him to make use of you as he sees fit.

I am, etc.
Nelson

After what Shotter had said the contents of the letter were more or less what Roger had expected; but that did not lessen his rage. When he had read it through the Lieutenant said:

'Now, sir, may I suggest your showing that you bear me no personal ill feeling on account of your situation by coming below and joining me in a glass of wine.'

Roger shook his head. 'I appreciate your offer, Lieutenant, but for the moment I am in too churlish a state to do justice to any man's hospitality. However, in an hour or so, if you will permit me?'

For a good hour he remained in his cabin in a positively murderous mood at the thought of the way in which he had been trapped. But his anger gradually subsided and at last he could even appreciate the grim humour of the turn events had taken. He had thought of himself so clever in lying to the little Admiral about wishing to get back to Paris, but it was Nelson who had had the last laugh. All the same, Roger was not prepared to submit tamely and he felt that an occasion was almost certain to arise when he could leave *Firefly* long before she arrived off the coast of Egypt.

He was soon disillusioned in that hope. When he joined Lieutenant Shotter in his cabin the Lieutenant filled two glasses from a decanter of Canary Sack then said, 'There is just one point, Mr. MacElfic, which I think we should settle right away. We can then leave this unhappy subject for good and, I hope, prove pleasant company for one another on the voyage. However favoured we are with the weather, we shall have to look in at Crete to pick up fresh victuals and water and, should we be blown badly off our course, perhaps at other places. I trust you will not attempt to jump ship.'

'Do you mean that I am your prisoner?' Roger asked, his ire again beginning to rise.

'I should prefer not to put it like that,' the cheerful Shotter replied. 'It is simply that I am under orders to deliver you to Sir Sidney Smith. My Admiral was most positive about that. Therefore I must ask you to give me your parole or, if you will not, I shall have to take the precaution of putting you under guard whenever we are within swimming distance of the shore.'

For a moment Roger considered. Had he been in an enemy ship he would have refused to give his parole, and backed himself to escape. But to do so from a British ship while under guard would be almost impossible without seriously injuring one or more of the British sailors; and that he was not prepared to do.

With a nod he said, 'Very well, then. I'll make no attempt to escape until you have carried out your orders with regard to me.'

They then shook hands on it and drank 'good luck' to the voyage in their first glass of wine.

The voyage of *Firefly* proved uneventful, except that she was twice blown back and forced to shelter for a few days under the lee of Crete. Having escaped being caught in the open she evaded the worst of the storm and Roger, although distinctly queasy, managed to survive the week of bad weather without being seasick. Just under three weeks after leaving Palermo they sighted Alexandria.

They received the latest intelligence from a blockading frigate. Bonaparte had adhered to his plan and, early in February, had launched his invasion of Syria. On the 20th, after a twelve-day siege, the powerful fortress of El Arish had surrendered to him. The French had then proceeded up the coast and were now laying siege to Jaffa. Having learned this, the new Commander in the Levant had left Alexandria to succour the besieged city. Shotter promptly rehoisted sail and set off after him.

Three days later *Firefly* was off Jaffa. There was no sign of Sir Sidney Smith and tricolour flags were flying over the city; so it had evidently been captured. They hailed an Arab dhow that was lying half a mile out from the harbour and, as Roger was able to act as interpreter, secured an account of what had taken place.

The French had appeared before the great walled city on March 3rd. The garrison, which was said to have numbered over four thousand men, had made several determined sorties, but had been driven back. After two days of severe fighting the French artillery made a big breach in the walls. Bonaparte, presumably to save his Army from the casualties inseparable from an assault, sent a messenger under a flag of truce to offer terms. But the ferocious Djezzar Pasha, who, from Acre, ruled all Syria, had ordered the messenger's head to be cut off and sent back to Bonaparte. The French then carried the city by storm. Djezzar succeeded in getting away but the greater part of the garrison surrendered.

It was then discovered that some two thousand of them were from the garrison of El Arish. Apparently, not wishing to be burdened with so many prisoners, Bonaparte had, after taking the great fortress, freed them on condition that they would take no further part for a year in the war between France and Turkey. However, they had promptly broken their word and marched off ahead of him to strengthen the garrison at Jaffa. On March 9th, two days after the fall of Jaffa, Napoleon had had the whole two thousand taken out to the sand-dunes and shot.

When Shotter heard this his language about the French became unprintable. Roger, too, was profoundly shocked and felt that such an appalling massacre must always remain a stain on Bonaparte's name.

Proceeding up the coast on the following day, March 12th, *Firefly* came up with Sir Sidney Smith's Squadron. It consisted of two frigates: *Tigre*—in which Sir Sidney, having promoted himself, was flying the broad pennant of a Commodore— *Theseus*, and a number of smaller vessels. A boat was lowered and Shotter went aboard *Tigre*. Three-quarters of an hour later he returned and called up to Roger to come down and join him in the boat, which then made a second trip to *Tigre* and they both went aboard.

Sir Sidney received them in his stern cabin. He was a fine-looking man of thirty-four, very richly dressed and wearing the sash and diamond-encrusted Grand Cross of his Swedish Order. When the introduction had been made he said to Shotter, 'I thank you, Lieutenant. You may leave us.'

During the three and a half weeks of *Firefly*'s voyage, her Captain and Roger had become firm friends; so as Shotter was about to leave the cabin, Roger wrung him firmly by the hand, thanked him for his many courtesies and said he hoped they would meet again. Shotter warmly reciprocated the hope and closed the cabin door behind him.

Sir Sidney then tapped a letter that was lying on his table and said, 'Mr. MacElfic, do you know the contents of this?'

'No,' Roger replied coldly, 'but I can make a good guess. It is from Admiral Nelson and in it, without any warrant to do so, he places me at your disposal as a secret agent.'

'It does much more than that. Sir Horatio informs me that for several years you have been in the service of the Prime Minister, and may be entrusted with both military and diplomatic secrets of the highest order. It also states that you performed the extraordinary feat of getting yourself appointed one of General Bonaparte's aides-de-camp. You must be a very exceptional man, Mr. MacElfic, and I am honoured to have your company on this station.'

Considerably mollified by this welcome, Roger replied, 'I thank you, sir. I am much relieved to feel that, from what Admiral Nelson has said of me, you are not likely to request me to risk my neck counting the guns in a fort for you, or finding out if some local Sheik can be bought for a small sum of money. For my part, since I have been sent here against my will, I am at least consoled that it should be to an officer so distinguished for his brains, initiative and daring.'

Sir Sidney smiled. 'That was generously said. But Sir Horatio says nothing of your having been reluctant to join me. Perhaps you would clarify the point.'

'Put briefly, Admiral Nelson decided that my connection with General Bonaparte could be used to inflict greater damage on the French than would allowing me to return to Paris. So having promised me a passage to Gibraltar he virtually shanghaied me and put me on a ship bound for Egypt.'

'Then I can sympathize with your resentment. But the little man will stick at nothing that he feels may help discomfit our enemies, and I am the gainer. When, pray, were you last in Paris? '

'In early May. I sailed with Bonaparte to Egypt. But in March we might well have met.' Roger gave a sudden laugh. 'There was an occasion when I was threatened with being sent to join you in the Temple.'

'Indeed! Well, you may thank your stars that you did not. I spent two years in that damnable prison, and during them I nearly died of frustration.'

'That I can well believe, sir, knowing your zest for action. I, too, know that gloomy prison, though not as a prisoner. I penetrated it several times during an abortive attempt to rescue poor Queen Marie Antoinette.'

'Did you now! Perhaps, then, you knew a most devoted servant of the Queen and dear friend of mine—a Swedish nobleman, Count Axel Fersan? '

'I knew him well,' Roger smiled. 'And that brings us to Sweden. We might well have met there for I, too, served King Gustavus in his war against Russia; and, for a special service I was fortunate enough to render him, he did me the honour to confer on me the Order that you wear. But, alas, I had to bury my Star beneath the foul straw of a cell in the fortress of Schlüsselburg, for had it been found upon me it would have cost me my life.'

Holding out his hand, the Commodore shook Roger's and said enthusiastically, ' Mr. MacElfic, I can see that we are birds of a feather, and shall delight in one another's company. You must dine with me and we shall find a thousand things to talk about.'

Roger was shown to a cabin, where he found that his few things had been brought over from *Firefly*. For an hour or so he lay down in his cot and considered his situation. Pleased as he was with his reception, he was still extremely loath to rejoin Bonaparte and again face deserts, thirst, a plague of flies and the many hazards inseparable from a campaign in Syria. Yet, short of flatly refusing to serve Sir Sidney, he saw no alternative. He could only hope that he might be able to strike some sort of bargain, then pray that his luck would hold.

When they met again for dinner, at which only the two of them were present, Sir Sidney opened the conversation by remarking, 'I fear we can scarcely look on this as a celebration, because in the despatch referring to yourself I also received notice of my demotion. But perhaps you were told about that before you left Palermo?'

'Sir William Hamilton did tell me that there had been some misunderstanding,' Roger replied tactfully.

'Let us call it that. The fact is that our little Admiral, although rightly weighed down with all the laurels he can carry, is still jealous of anyone else gaining a single leaf from that honour-bestowing shrub. With him three weeks' sailing distance away in Palermo, dancing attendance on a buffoon King and a terror-crazed Queen, it is only sensible that the Levant should be an independent Command. But since the Nile, he has become raised to such heights by the adulation of the people that his superiors no longer dare cross him. In consequence, our strategy must suffer.

'He has ordered me to strike my broad pennant and revert from the rank of Commodore to that of Captain. That I shall not do, because it would be bad for discipline for my Squadron to see their Commander receive such a slap in the face.

'However, another matter perturbs me far more. The seat of war in the Levant is no longer Egypt but Syria. The only way in which Bonaparte can reach Constantinople is by a march along the coast and our only chance of preventing him from doing so is by giving our greatest possible support to the Turks in the coastal fortresses he will have to attack. The blockade of the Egyptian coast could easily be maintained by two frigates and some smaller craft. It had, therefore, been my intention to order Captain Hood to join me here with his line-of-battle ships. This is where they should be, and they would have proved invaluable. But, alas, I have been deprived of the right to make proper use of them.'

Roger took a good pull at his glass of claret and replied, 'Sir Horatio's treatment of me rankles somewhat; but I share the universal admiration of his genius as a sailor. Therefore I feel that I can say without prejudice that I judge you to be right. Pray tell me now of the present situation.'

'Bonaparte has twice smashed the Turks—at El Arish and at Jaffa. He is now advancing along the coast opposite us and

obviously intends to invest St. Jean d'Acre. As you will know, it
is a mighty walled city. Its fortifications were built by the
Crusaders who held it for many years against the Saracen. At
present, Djezzar Pasha commands there. He is a most vile man
and capable of any barbarity; but he has an abundance of courage
and determination. If he can hold it all will be well. If he fails
all will be lost, for it is the key to Syria.'

'How do you regard his chances?'

The Commodore shrugged. 'I would say fifty-fifty. I've no
reliable information about the size of Bonaparte's Army, but it
cannot be very large. Moreover he is so ill-found for provisions
that he had to commit the enormity of massacring two thousand
prisoners taken at Jaffa, because he could neither feed them nor
spare the troops to march them back to Egypt and dared not
leave them in his rear.'

'Yes. I heard about that.'

'Another factor is that plague has broken out in his Army. If
it becomes an epidemic that may relieve us of our anxieties. But
should it not, the French will remain extremely formidable. On
the other hand, the Turks are mustering two Armies—one in
Rhodes and the other in Damascus—both designed for the relief
of Acre when it is invested. The question is whether either will
arrive in time to relieve the fortress.'

'Should they fail to do so, Bonaparte would still have to fight
them afterwards.'

'That is true, but the odds would then be in his favour. I am
informed that he has sent emissaries to the Christian Druses and
other peoples who are restless under the Turkish yoke. At the
moment they are sitting on the fence, waiting to see if he can
succeed in taking Acre. If he does, they will rise and join him.
That could mean his gaining the adherence of no fewer than
eighty thousand auxiliaries. With such a force at his disposal it
would prove the end of the Sultan's Empire. You will see now
how everything depends on our holding Acre.'

'I do, indeed. How far do you think you can assist in that?'

'From off-shore the guns of my little Squadron should seriously
interfere with the attacks of the French, but the crux of the
matter will lie in Djezzar Pasha's ability to defend the walls of
the city. Since you know of my escape from the Temple, you
may have heard that it was made possible by a good friend of
mine: Colonel Phélippeaux. He was a Colonel of Engineers in

the old Royal Army of France, and is a great expert on fortifications. He accompanied me to the Levant and, before I sailed from Alexandria early in the month, I sent him and Captain Miller ahead of me in *Theseus*. He is now in Acre inspecting the defences and, if his recommendations are accepted, I have hopes that by now they are being greatly strengthened.'

As the meal proceeded, Roger described to his host the collapse of the Neapolitan invasion of the Roman States, the evacuation of the Royal Family and the horror which had subsequently descended on Naples. They then talked of the Russo-Swedish war and the French Revolution. Later Sir Sidney gave Roger an account of his capture at Le Havre.

He said there was no foundation in the story that he had attempted to blow up the docks. He had been given command of the frigate *Diamond* and a flotilla of small craft, with orders to clear the Channel of French privateers that were then seriously interfering with British commerce. In the course of a year he had captured or destroyed a great number of them; but one, owing to her exceptional speed, continued to elude him. Learning that she was in Le Havre, he had determined to cut her out. Having no Lieutenant available upon whom he could rely, he had taken in the boats himself. The lugger was taken by surprise and captured almost without resistance. However, when Sir Sidney went on board and the lugger was got out into the river, she was caught by a flood-tide and carried upstream. They hoisted sail but the wind had fallen; so at daybreak she was still above the town and becalmed. The French then attacked her from both the water and the land with all the forces the big port could muster; so against such overwhelming odds Sir Sidney and his men had been compelled to surrender.

When they were halfway through a decanter of rich Malaga wine Roger said, 'You will appreciate that, as I owe allegiance only to Mr. Pitt, I can refuse to accept your orders. But placed as I am I feel it would be unpatriotic to deny you such help as you may in reason ask from me. On this I would be glad to hear you views.'

The Commodore remained thoughtful for a moment, then he replied, 'The thing that would be of most value to us would be an accurate appreciation of Bonaparte's forces and his supplies. Upon such information we could settle the best tactics to use in the defence of Acre. If he has strength and staying power it would, I think, pay Djezzar Pasha best to make a number of determined sorties and so prevent the French from creating a strong, entrenched position and from tunnelling beneath the walls. But if the previous engagements of the French, and now the plague, have seriously weakened them, Djezzar would do better to take no risk of his best troops being cut up outside the city, but sit tight and wait until starvation and disease cause the French Army to fall to pieces.'

'That is sound reasoning,' Roger agreed. 'Now I must be frank. I have no intention of risking death going backwards and forwards in the desert, or of spending several months at Bonaparte's headquarters endeavouring to get periodical reports back to you of how matters are going there. If in a single mission I can secure for you the information you require, will you agree to send me back to England at the first opportunity? '

'Yes,' replied the Commodore, without hesitation. 'That is a fair offer and I willingly agree to your conditions.'

'Good,' Roger nodded. 'The next question is how am I to make connection with the French? Although the Turks are our allies, you cannot simply put me ashore. It is certain that I should fall in with a band of marauding Arabs who would promptly murder me.'

'We could disguise you as an Arab,' Sir Sidney suggested.

'Thank you, no,' replied Roger with a quick shake of his head. 'Your Arabic may have been good enough for you to pass as an Arab in Morocco, but mine is not good enough for me to pass as one in Palestine. And, as these people cannot read any *laissez-passer* with which you might furnish me, it would be useless.'

'It is a pretty problem,' the Commodore admitted.

After a moment's thought Roger said, 'There is one way in which it might be done: that is by an exchange of prisoners. To the French I am known as Colonel Breuc. If the French have a British prisoner of equivalent rank you could send a flag of truce and, perhaps, arrange an exchange. You would get something for nothing and without being subject to any danger I should be taken straight to Bonaparte's headquarters.'

'That is certainly an idea. Unfortunately, though, as it happens, the French have taken none of my people except a few seamen from boats sent in with reconnaissance parties. And it would look far too fishy should I propose an offer of a Colonel on the General-in-Chief's Staff in exchange for those poor fellows.'

'I fear it would,' Roger agreed. 'We are, then, at a dead end, and must continue so until we can devise some plan by which I can reappear at Bonaparte's headquarters as an escaped prisoner without having first to be landed and make my way alone across country infested with murderous tribesmen.'

During the week that followed, neither of them could think of any way in which this could be accomplished. Roger took all his meals with Sir Sidney, who was his senior by only three years, and they had much in common. As they reminisced over events in which, although then unknown to one another, both had played a part, their mutual liking grew. Before long, too, Roger realized why it was that Sir Sidney was unpopular with his naval colleagues. He was by nature haughty and extremely intolerant of those typical naval Captains who were expert seamen but almost entirely ignorant of matters outside their profession. He spoke several languages fluently, was widely read, had an intimate knowledge of events which had led to the present international relationships and possessed a swift, inventive mind. It also emerged that he took good care of his men and that they reciprocated with respect and affection.

On the 15th they dropped anchor opposite the Crusaders' great fortress city of Acre. It lay on a rocky promontory, rectangular in shape and joined to the mainland by a wide area of flat desert and marsh. Thus, as Sir Sidney pointed out to Roger, ships anchored to north and south of the city would be in an excellent position to assist the defence by enfilading assaulting columns. They went ashore and, accompanied by Colonel Phélippeaux, carried out an inspection of the defences.

Roger was amazed at their strength and depth. The four-mile-long wall encircling the town was in most places a hundred feet high and so broad that three coaches could have been driven abreast round the top. Every few hundred feet great bastions jutted out, enabling cross-fire to be poured down on attackers. The succession of culverts, moraines and fosses seemed unending and it appeared impossible that the city could be taken by assault.

But Phélippeaux pointed out that in many places the walls were crumbling and that several of the towers had become unsafe, so would come down easily under bombardment; that some of the moats had become choked, having been used for generations as refuse dumps and that fields of fire had been rendered useless because groups of shanties had been erected outside the walls, masking the lines of sight. He was particularly concerned about the north-eastern corner of the city, which was the furthest from the shore and largely an area of ruins. An enormous tower stood there but, if once seized, it would be very difficult to recapture, and possession of it would give the enemy dominance over the whole of that quarter.

However, he reported that Djezzar was doing his utmost to strengthen the defences and, as evidence of this, they saw many gangs of Arab men, women and children—hundreds strong—toiling at clearing twenty-foot-deep ditches and hacking down and burning scores of miserable huts.

Two days later a sloop came alongside *Tigre,* with the news that a French flotilla, composed of small craft, had passed Jaffa and, keeping close inshore, was coming up the coast. The Commodore at once ordered sail to be set and the Squadron headed south to meet it. Sir Sidney's luck was in. They surprised the flotilla that night as it rounded the promontory at the southern end of the long bay. There followed a sharp encounter and the French endeavoured to beach their ships, upon which every boat possessed by the British was sent in and a skirmish ensued on shore that ended in the capture by the British of every ship in the flotilla.

It proved to be a prize of incalculable value as it consisted of seven gunboats mounting thirty-four cannon, which could be used in defence of Acre, and the whole of Bonaparte's siege artillery, amounting to nearly forty heavy guns and a great quantity of ammunition. It would have required a labour force thousands strong to drag these heavy cannon all the way from Egypt by the camel-track that linked the coast towns; so Bonaparte had had no alternative but to send them up by water. Later it transpired that, on finding Sir Sidney Smith's Squadron in the Bay of Acre, he had sent a message back to Jaffa, ordering the flotilla to remain there; but by the time the message arrived the flotilla had already set sail.

It was a body blow to the French, for not only did the loss of their siege train deprive them of the swiftest means of reducing Acre but, as the material had been captured intact, it could now be used against them. Phélippeaux was overjoyed and at once set about landing the cannon at the Mole so that they could be installed, as he directed, to strengthen the weakest places in he fortress's defences, and Sir Sidney sent ashore to man them all the gunners he could spare.

Roger's future was also decided by this action. One of the boat parties had rashly chased the French too far from the shore, then found itself surrounded by superior numbers and forced to surrender. The party consisted of a Lieutenant, a Midshipman, a Petty Officer and seven seamen, and Sir Sidney thought it possible that the ten sailors might be released in exchange for one French Colonel. A flag of truce was sent ashore at the southern point of the long bay, on which lay the little port of Haifa, near which the flotilla had been captured. Two hours later the Lieutenant who had been sent ashore returned to report that a French officer there had agreed to the exchange.

During Roger's week in *Tigre* he had formed such a firm friendship with the adventurous Sir Sidney that he had, on several occasions, been tempted to tell him his real name and the whole truth about himself. But his natural caution caused him to refrain because, even under the seal of secrecy, the fewer people who knew that Roger Brook and Robert MacElfic were the same person, the better. But he now had to become Colonel Breuc again, and how he should account to Bonaparte for the five months he had spent as Robert MacElfic had given him considerable thought.

He decided finally to say that, according to plan, he had gone aboard a Greek ship in Alexandria, had posed as an Englishman and had passed safely through the British blockade. But a fortnight later the ship had been captured by Corsairs and taken to Tripoli where, for two and a half months, he had had a hideous time as a slave loading cargo in the harbour. He had then managed to escape by concealing himself in the hold of a merchant ship and, when she was well out at sea, he had given himself up as a stowaway. To his delight, he found that the merchantman was a French blockade-runner and bound for Marseilles; so he had no hesitation in declaring himself to be Colonel Breuc and her Captain had treated him with the greatest politeness. On board he also met the owner of the ship's cargo, a Monsieur Drapeau, whom it happened that he had known well in Paris some years earlier; so there could be no question of his identity. But when the ship was sneaking by night through the narrows south of Malta his luck turned. She ran straight into

Sir Sidney Smith's Squadron on its way to Egypt, and was captured. As he was known to Drapeau, it had been out of the question to pretend that he had lied to the Captain about being Colonel Breuc and that he was in fact an Englishman; so, since Sir Sidney was not calling at any port under British control, he had been carried on to Syria as a prisoner.

At that time ships were being captured almost daily throughout the Mediterranean, either by Barbary pirates or the ships of the warring nations; so there was nothing in the least improbable in such a story, which provided a complete explanation of his never having reached France.

By six o'clock he had first cut then shaved off the fine, brown, curly beard that he had grown as MacElfic, and was ready to go ashore. Compared with other missions he had undertaken, he did not expect this last hazard in the Near East to prove particularly difficult or dangerous. Now that the French Army was arriving outside Acre there was no longer anything to be feared from marauding Arabs and Sir Sidney's gunboats would be constantly patrolling within cannon shot of the coast. He would be escorted at once to Bonaparte's headquarters and a few days there should be sufficient to inform himself of the size and resources of the Army. The odds were that the headquarters would be no more than a few miles from the coast; so he should be able to slip away from them one night and, as a Colonel, no French picket would interfere with his making his way to the shore. Only then might he meet with difficulties. However, there were still plenty of native-owned fishing boats coming and going in the long bay and before dawn he should be able to find one whose master could be bribed to take him off to the nearest British ship.

Sir Sidney wished him the best of luck and a speedy return. Having taken a cordial farewell of the gallant Commodore, Roger went over the side into a waiting boat. Half an hour later he landed, with the Lieutenant who had carried the flag of truce, at a previously agreed point about halfway along the Gulf, some six miles south of Acre.

A small body of French troops, headed by an officer, was waiting there and with them were the British sailors who had been taken prisoner the previous night. The formalities were soon concluded. The sailors, hilarious with joy that their captivity should have been of such short duration, clambered into the boat and it pushed off. Meanwhile the French officer had saluted Roger and introduced himself as Captain Elbée of the Camel Corps.

Roger remarked on the smart, although now slightly faded, sky-blue uniform of these French troops as it was new to him. After congratulating him on having regained his freedom, the Captain explained, ' We are a new regiment, created by the General-in-Chief last autumn. My men sit back to back, two to each dromedary; but, even so, we can travel at a considerable speed and can range the desert for several days without having to provide water for our animals. The regiment was formed to suppress the many roving bands of these accursed Arabs, and has been most successful. Very soon we became an élite Corps and now it is regarded as an honour to be transferred to us.'

' Then I congratulate you,' Roger replied. ' But, since you have such a fine turn of speed, I wonder that you are not being made use of in the advance guard.'

' We are the advance guard,' the Captain replied. ' At least, as far as the coast is concerned. The bulk of the Army has now spread out and is enveloping the city. It was, I believe, expected that other advance units would reach the coast north of Acre today. If so, the siege will begin tomorrow. My troop will not now be moving on until I receive further orders.'

' Do you know the whereabouts of the General-in-Chief's present headquarters? ' Roger enquired. ' If you do I should like to proceed there tonight, so that I can report myself without delay.'

The Captain shook his head. ' I regret, *mon Colonel,* but that is not possible. I am told that the General-in-Chief intends to establish himself somewhere on the slopes of Mount Carmel, so that he can overlook the city. But as you can see we are a considerable distance from the Mount. Parties of enemy skirmishers have been coming out of Acre all day and roving the plain. It is certain they will continue to be active at night. If you proceeded on your own, you would run a grave risk of capture and I have not enough men to spare an escort for you.'

While talking, they had crossed the half-mile inland to the spot where, just out of range of the guns of the British ships, Elbée had made his camp. It was in a wide depression between two rolling sand-dunes on the crests of which look-outs were posted. In the flat valley bottom the remainder of the troops were gathered round a fire at which some of them were cooking supper, and beyond it a score of seated dromedaries were picketed in a neat line.

In all there were about thirty men, but no other officer. Elbée told Roger that since leaving Jaffa he had lost six of his men and his Lieutenant in skirmishes, then he apologized for lacking the means to entertain his guest in the way he would have wished. The baggage camels could carry only water, food and a reserve of ammunition; so there were no tents and supper would be only boiled beans, a mouthful of one of the two rabbits that had been snared and cornmush pudding. He added that one of the reasons for which his Colonel had been only too pleased to exchange the ten British sailors for Roger was that they had little enough food for themselves, let alone prisoners.

As darkness fell they ate their meagre meal, a little apart from the troops. While he ate, Roger, who had been unable to produce identity papers, set about removing any suspicion which might lurk in the Captain's mind that he might be a French Royalist whom the British had planted as a spy. He naturally refrained from disclosing why Bonaparte had sent him back to France or that he had posed during part of his voyage as an Englishman; but in other respects he gave the fictitious account that he had thought out of his adventures in the past five months, calling lavishly on his imagination as he described his sufferings while a slave in Tripoli. He then began to enquire after his many friends in the Army, displaying a familiarity with them that no ordinary spy could have shown.

Elbée, now clearly convinced of Roger's *bona fides*, replied to his enquiries as well as he was able, and gave him an account of the Syrian campaign to date. The Army had had a terrible time while crossing the barren territory of Sinai, but the spirit of the men had revived again on seeing the wooded hills and fertile plains of Syria. Before El Arish had been taken there had been a fierce encounter with what remained of Ibrahim Bey's Mamelukes, in which Reynier's Division had suffered heavily, but that of Kléber had come to his rescue and had turned a possible defeat into victory. The taking of Jaffa had been a most bloody business. The dauntless Lannes led the final assault that had broken the resistance of the garrison; then, as the city had refused terms, it was put to the sack. Consumed by thirst and half starving, the troops looted, slew and raped without pause for twenty-four hours.

Roger broke in to say that he had been told about the massacre of the prisoners and had been greatly shocked by it, but Elbée sprang instantly to his General-in-Chief's defence.

'What other course was open to him?' he demanded. 'I am told that he nearly took the heads off the two officers who accepted the surrender of the troops who had broken their parole, because it forced this awful decision on him. For two whole days he wrestled with this problem and twice called a conference of all his Generals to debate it with them. There was not enough food to fill the bellies of our own men, let alone these two thousand prisoners. They could not be sent back by ship to Egypt because of the British, and escorts to march them back overland could not possibly be spared. If they had been released they would have made their way up here to St. Jean d'Acre, and many of them would for the third time have taken French lives. The opinion of the conference of Generals was unanimous. The poor wretches had to be taken out and shot.'

With subtle intent Roger said, 'But, surely, the Army is not so reduced in numbers that a few hundred men could not have been spared to march the captives back to Egypt?'

Elbée shrugged and supplied the desired information. 'I can give you only rough figures, but I cannot be far out if I say that General Desaix has been left with at least ten thousand men to hold Egypt. With the casualties we have suffered in the past eight months that cannot leave many more than twelve thousand of the original expeditionary force, and we have not received a single reinforcement. In any case, only four Divisions entered Syria: those of Kléber, Reynier, Bon and Lannes, plus the cavalry under Murat. All of them are far below strength; and now, to the terror of us all, they are being further reduced by plague.'

'That,' said Roger, 'is by far the worst news you have given me. Has the infection become serious?'

The Captain sighed. 'I am told that a few cases occurred while General Kléber's troops were still in Alexandria, but there was no serious outbreak until his Division reached Jaffa. He then lost some two hundred men in the course of a few days, and it is said to be spreading in an alarming fashion. My own men, thank God, have remained free from infection. But, to be honest, we all now refrain from shaking hands with any man from another unit, for fear that we may contract the pestilence.'

It was now about ten o'clock. Except for the sentries, the troops had wrapped themselves in their cloaks and gone to sleep. Roger and his host decided to do likewise. Having dug holes for their hips in the soft sand, they settled down. As Roger spread his handkerchief on a mound of sand that he had scooped up to make a pillow, he was aglow with satisfaction. Without even going to Bonaparte's headquarters he had learned the basic facts of the situation. The French were approximately twelve thousand strong; he knew the names of the Generals who were commanding the Divisions, and had also learned that the Army was existing on a minimum of rations and that it was now being scourged by the plague.

That information was all Sir Sidney had asked him to supply. With a clear conscience he could give it and require in return that he should be given a passage home. All he had now to do was to set out next day, ostensibly for Bonaparte's headquarters, rid himself somehow of the guide he would be given and, the following night, bribe an Arab fisherman to take him off to a British warship. With this happy prospect in mind, he fell asleep.

Soon after one o'clock in the morning the sound of a single warning shot pierced his dormant brain. He started up, wide awake. Next minute he heard the thunder of horses' hooves. Elbée sprang up beside him and they drew their swords. There was no moon so it was almost dark but, above the ridge, against the night sky, they glimpsed a formidable mass of cavalry charging down the slope.

They had hardly time to draw breath before Djezzar's yelling horsemen were upon them. Roger never knew what happened to Elbée. He was assailed simultaneously by two mounted men, clad in flowing robes and wearing large turbans. He thrust upward with his sword at the one on his right. The point of the sword pierced the man's side and he gave a hideous howl. But at the same instant he had struck at Roger with his scimitar, and the side of the blade caught Roger on the head, knocking him half unconscious. As he staggered back, the man on his left grabbed him by the hair, dragged him off his feet and, exerting terrific strength, hauled him up across his saddle-bow.

His senses whirling, amidst a babel of shots, screams and curses, Roger was carried off into the darkness. After galloping for a mile or more his captor reined in. By then Roger had recovered sufficiently to struggle. Holding him down, the man who had taken him prisoner thrust a cord with a slip knot over his left wrist, then pulled it tight and thrust him off, so that he fell to the ground.

For a few moments he lay there, bruised and panting. A pull on the stout cord jerked him to his knees. The light was just sufficient for him to see that he was among a body of horsemen. To his right he glimpsed another prisoner in a similar situation to his own. A command rang out in Turkish. The body of cavalry began to move forward at a trot. The pull on his wrist yanked him to his feet. Still half dazed, he found himself running, jumping, staggering breathlessly over rough ground, in a desperate endeavour to keep himself from falling and being dragged face downward across it.

Bemused by pain and terror as he was, he was still capable of realizing the awful thing that had happened to him. He could now no longer hope for a swift completion of his mission and a passage home. Instead, he was a captive and being taken to Acre. There the odds were that Djezzar Pasha, with his notorious lust for cruelty, would put him to death in some hideous fashion. At the very best he would become a slave. Only that evening he had amused himself by describing to Captain Elbée the imaginary miseries he had suffered as a slave in Tripoli. He had little thought then that they might actually be inflicted on him before another day had passed.

18

The Siege of Acre

GASPING for breath, his feet hardly touching the ground, Roger
blundered on. His left wrist was already galled to bleeding point
by the cord looped round it, he was blinded by the sand kicked
up by the hooves of the horses and, from the pull his captor had
extered on his hair, his head burned as though vitriol had been
poured upon it. Unaided, he could never have run so far at such
a pace. The cord drew him on, relieving him of any effort to
force his body forward, but the strain of keeping upright was
appalling. How long his ordeal lasted he had no idea, but it
seemed to him that he had been running with bursting lungs for
hours on end before the cord at last slackened. Streaming with
sweat, coated with sand and with agony in every limb, he fell to
the ground and fainted.

When he came to he was again lying face down across his
captor's saddle-bow. After a few minutes the clatter of the horses'
hooves on cobbles told him that they had entered the city. Ten
minutes later they halted, he was thrust from the saddle and came
down in a heap on stone paving. His body was so racked with
pain that he hardly felt the thump on his backside and squirmed
up into a sitting position. His view was partially obscured by a
forest of horses' legs and those of their riders, who were now dis-
mounting; but he could see enough to know that he was in a large
courtyard lit by men holding smoking torches.

His captor bent over him, roughly untied the loop of cord
round his wrist, spat in his face and kicked him. The man then
took the bridle of his horse and joined his companions, who were
leading away their horses. Other dark-faced, turbaned men came
forward. Two of them dragged Roger to his feet and hustled him

across the courtyard to a low doorway. As they did so he saw that he had three companions in misfortune. The four of them were pushed through the door, along a short passage and down a spiral stairway. At the bottom a negro opened a massive wooden door with thick, iron bolts. The light from the torches showed that it gave on to a low, barrel-vaulted dungeon. The prisoners were thrown head first into it, the door clanged to and total darkness descended on them.

The four captives were too utterly exhausted and bemused by pain even to speak to one another. They simply lay where they had been thrown, sobbing and groaning. After what seemed an interminable time, nature took charge and Roger fell into an uneasy dose.

He was aroused by a hoarse voice croaking for water. He had none to give the sufferer and realized that he was terribly parched himself. As he sat up he gave an 'ouch' of pain, for he had used his left hand in raising his body. Gingerly he felt his wrist and feared it had been dislocated. He was a mass of aching bruises and his scalp still pained him; but he decided that apart from his wrist, he had sustained no serious injury.

Out of the darkness came another voice that asked, 'Who are you fellows?'

'I am Colonel Breuc,' Roger replied, and the prisoner who had been moaning for water answered:

'I'm Trooper Auby.'

'And I'm Corporal Gensonné.' There was a short silence, then the Corporal spoke again. 'There was four of us. Come on; speak up, number four.'

Silence fell again, then came the sound of scraping. Sparks appeared, a small flame flared and by its light Roger saw two gnarled hands with a grimy, grey-moustached face above them. It was the Corporal; with a tinder-box he had lit a scrap of paper. Carefully guarding the flame, he moved it till the light fell on the others. The glimpse Roger got of Auby showed the trooper to be little more than a boy. His cheek had been laid open by a slash from a scimitar and the blood had congealed on it. The fourth prisoner lay on his back, quite still. After one look at him, the Corporal said:

''E's got nothing to worry about. 'E's a gonner.'

'Worry', thought Roger, was the appropriate word. As Bonaparte would not even be starting his siege operations until that

L

day or the next, there was no possible hope of rescue. On considering matters he found it surprising that he was still alive, for the Turks normally took no prisoners. He could only suppose that Djezzar had ordered one of his captains to bring in a few so that they could be questioned about the French dispositions. As the word ' questioned ' ran through Roger's mind, it gave him another shudder. Being ' put to the question ' was synonymous with being tortured, and he had no doubt whatever that whether they remained silent, lied to please their enemies or told the truth the Turks would use torture on them. They would then be made slaves or, quite probably, as the Pasha was reported to be a monster of cruelty, put to death in some hideous manner.

The Corporal's spill had soon flickered out and he asked if either of the others had any paper on him. Auby had none, neither had Roger, except for Bonaparte's letters which were still sewn into the hem of his travelling coat; and he had no intention of giving those up, unless he saw a chance of buying his life with them.

In hoarse whispers they continued occasionally to exchange remarks. Young Auby was a conscript and the son of a farmer in the Beuce. He had been about to marry his sweetheart when he was compelled to leave her for the Army. In addition to the wound on his face, he had been shot in the side and was evidently in a very bad way. The Corporal was a Lyonnais who for many years had been a professional soldier. He did not seem to be afraid of death, and only grumbled that it looked as if it had caught up with him just after he had had the ill luck to miss the sack of Jaffa, at which he could have had a last, glorious fling slitting the throats of Turks and raping their women.

They had no idea of the time and were too miserable to feel hungry, but thirst plagued them more and more as the hours crawled by. Now and then they heard a faint scampering that told them that rats had been attracted to the dungeon by their subtle knowledge that there was a corpse in it. The thought that the brutes had begun to eat their dead companion filled Roger with horror.

None of them had been searched; so Roger still had his moneybelt round his waist and he wondered if, with its contents, he might possibly bribe one of his jailers to help him escape, but he thought it highly unlikely. Why should any of them risk death? If he showed his gold to one of them it was all Lombard Street to a China orange that the man would simply knock him down and take it from him.

At last a streak of light showed under the heavy door, the bolts were shot back and it was pulled open In the glare of the torches Roger glimpsed the rats scampering away from the dead trooper's body. A Turk, who was evidently the senior jailer, shouted, 'Up dogs of Christians! Up, I say, that you may be sent to your maker, Iblis.'

Roger drew a sharp breath. He had picked up enough Turkish to know that Iblis was the Devil, and to be sent to him signified that they were about to die. He got to his feet and his companions followed his example. Surrounded by armed guards they were taken up the stone stairway and out into the courtyard.

It was late afternoon and a sunny day. From the immensely strong square tower that reared up on the landward side of the court Roger could tell now that they were in the great citadel of the fortress, as he had several times studied it through a telescope from the deck of *Tigre*.

His glance next fell on a group of half a hundred men grouped beneath the tall *casbah*. A low dais had been erected there and a solitary figure was seated cross-legged on it on a pile of cushions. From the richness of his robes, the rings that sparkled on his fingers, his jewel-hilted scimitar and the great pigeon's-blood ruby that held an aigrette erect in his enormous, flat turban, Roger had no doubt that he was Djezzar Pasha. To either side and behind him were ranged his entourage. Their costume had changed little since the days of the Saracens and in their circular, pointed helmets, from which depended chain-mail ear-pieces, burnished corselets, jewelled girdles and colourful tunics, they presented a splendid spectacle. Near the dais was a small, wizened man, evidently a Councillor, wearing a green turban, showing that he had made the pilgrimage to Mecca. Beside him towered an enormous negro, naked to the waist and carrying a drawn scimitar. He was obviously the official executioner.

But Roger's glance rested only for an instant on this brilliant array of warriors. At the sight of another erection in front of the dais he had gone white to the lips. It consisted of eight small platforms, about three feet in height, arranged in pairs, each pair being a yard apart. Between the pairs stood four stout stakes, the height of a man and sharply pointed at the upper ends. He gulped, gave a shudder and instantly began to sweat with terror. It was clear to him now that the fiendish Pasha had told his cavalry to bring in prisoners not so that he might extract information from them, but simply to have them killed in his presence for his amusement.

That row of stakes could mean only one thing. A favourite method with the Turks of putting criminals to death was to impale them, and that was the ghastly end which Djezzar clearly meant to inflict on Roger and his companions.

Corporal Gensonné and Trooper Auby, being ignorant of Turkish customs, had evidently not realized the awful purpose that the stakes were to serve. The Corporal was marching forward between his guards, unaided and with set but courageous mien. The Trooper's wound had opened and blood from his right side was seeping down his pale-blue breeches. With the help of two guards, he was limping forward. His face showed fright but no special terror. Roger had halted in his tracks, but was pushed on by the men on either side of him.

As he advanced, he was visualizing the ghastly scene which must soon be enacted. Each pair of guards would mount the low platforms, dragging their prisoner up with them. They would lift him breast-high, force his legs apart, bringing the point of the stake in contact with his anus. Then, each seizing a leg, they would jump down from their platforms, so that their weight would drive the stake up into their victim's body. If they did their work well the point of the stake would come out of the prisoner's mouth or the top of his head. If they bungled it it would emerge through his chest or the side of his neck. But for him that would be a matter of no importance for, in any case, as the stake pierced his vitals he would suffer unimaginable agony.

The prisoners were brought to within a few yards of Djezzar. Roger found himself staring into the cruel, hook-nosed face with its handsome, curly beard and fine, upturned moustaches. Suddenly, in a hoarse voice, he began to plead for himself and his companions. One of his guards struck him in the mouth, reducing him to silence.

The Pasha gave a curt order that the executions should begin and pointed to young Auby. His guards flung him to the ground and ripped off his breeches. Either from terror or because he had lost so much blood from his wound, he fainted. The two muscular

Turks lugged him up between them and forced his limp body on to the stake. Suddenly he came to, his eyes starting from his head, and he gave an awful groan. But it was all over in a moment. The point of the stake came out from his neck and his head flopped forward.

As the deed was done, Roger heard a sudden chatter of excited female voices. Looking round, he saw that about twenty feet up from the courtyard, in a wall at right-angles to the line of stakes, there was a row of open arches. They were filled by about twenty veiled women, who had evidently been summoned to see the fun. A few of them had their eyes averted, or covered with a hand, to shut out the atrocious sight of Auby's sagging body. But the majority were staring down eagerly at it and some were crying in shrill voices:

'Praise be to Allah and blessed be His Prophet! Death to the Infidels! Death to the Unbelievers!'

But Roger's glance rested on them only for a moment. At the sight of Auby's death, Corporal Gensonné realized what was in store for him. Giving a furious curse he turned on the guard who stood on his right and with one blow knocked him down. The other guard grabbed him by the shoulders. But Gensonné wriggled free and kicked him in the groin. Swerving away, he dodged a third man who had come at him and ran towards the great gate, which stood wide open.

For a moment Roger was seized by an impulse to follow his example. But there had been half a dozen guards lounging by the gate. They were now running in a group to intercept the Corporal and the head jailer with three of his men had dashed in pursuit of him. Against such odds no attempt to escape could possibly succeed.

Djezzar was roaring with laughter at the discomfiture of the two guards who had been standing on either side of Gensonné. But the Corporal's bravery did not incline the sadistic Pasha to clemency. With an amused smile he waited as the ten Turks closed round the solitary Frenchman, seized him by the arms and dragged him, blaspheming wildly, back to the line of stakes. While four of them held him, two others wrenched the breeches from his kicking legs, then they carried him between them to the stake next to that upon which Auby's body hung impaled. Roger closed his eyes to shut out the horror of what followed. The Corporal screamed and screamed and screamed, then suddenly fell silent.

Again there came from the women's balcony treble cries of:
'Death to the Christian dogs! To Iblis with the Unbelievers!'

Roger knew then that his turn had come. Within the next few minutes life for him would be over. Never more would he enjoy the passionate embrace of his beautiful Georgina, never again see the green fields of England. Starting forward, he shouted to the Pasha in the best Turkish he could muster, and with all the strength of his lungs:

'Excellency! If you have me killed Allah will call you to account for my death. I have had no trial, but could prove my innocence. I am no enemy but a friend. I have papers to prove it. Sir Sidney Smith will vouch for me. I am not a Frenchman but English and your ally.'

One of the guards again silenced him by striking him on the mouth. Suddenly one of the women up in the balcony cried, 'He lies. He is a French Colonel. I knew him in Cairo.'

Instantly Roger recognized the voice. It was Zanthé's. Looking up he saw her leaning right out over the balcony. The tawny eyes above her yashmak marked her out from the other dark-eyed women. Djezzar also looked up and called back:

'Then, moon of my delight, we'll make him wriggle on a stick.'

'No, Pasha, no!' she cried. 'Such a death is too swift for him. In Cairo he insulted me. I pray you to give him to me so that I may see him die by inches. Give him to me for a plaything so that I may be avenged on him.'

Giving a bellow of laughter, the bearded Pasha waved a hand to her and shouted, 'Beautiful one, when your red lips speak, to hear is to obey. He is yours, to do with as you will.'

'May Allah reward you, mighty Pasha,' she called down. 'I'll have him castrated, then he shall live on offal served in our chamber-pots.'

The mail-clad men surrounding Djezzar roared their applause and the women up in the balcony with Zanthé broke into peals of shrill laughter.

At a sign from the Pasha, two of the guards took Roger by the elbows, hurried him away across the courtyard, down the spiral stairs, thrust him back into the dungeon and again shut him up there in the pitch darkness.

Sinking down on the floor, he propped his back against the slimy wall. His thoughts were so chaotic that for a few minutes he could hardly grasp that, temporarily at least, his life was safe.

By a miracle he had escaped the excruciating agony of having a four-inch stake rammed through his intestines and dying with its point lodged in his gullet.

Zanthé's unexpected appearance at the critical moment had at first amazed him. But after a few moments' thought he realized that it was not particularly surprising. When the Sultan had declared war on France the previous autumn, the Turkish officials in Cairo would have been secretly apprised of it long before Bona- parte learned that the Porte had openly become his enemy. Naturally, on one excuse or other, the highly placed Turks in Egypt would have slipped away to Syria, taking their women with them. As Acre was the capital of Syria it was logical that Zanthé, and whoever was now her protector, should have taken refuge there.

As Roger's mind cleared he began fearfully to speculate on what was in store for him. He had been saved from an agonizing death, but only by a woman who nursed a bitter hatred for him. She had shouted down that she intended to have him castrated. At the thought the saliva ran hot in his mouth and his flesh crept. swallowing hard, he wondered if he would not have been more fortunate had he suffered those few minutes of searing pain and now was dead.

In a swift series of pictures his mind ran back over the key episodes in his association with Zanthé. He had taken her by force, enjoyed her, then found that she had spoken the truth when she had declared herself to be a virgin. Yet he had been for several weeks afterwards under the illusion that, although she had at first fought him off, the pleasure she had later felt during his embrace, wordlessly confessed beyond dispute by her passionate response, had been a positive indication that next time she would give herself willingly to him.

But when he had carried her off from the Viceroy's palace he had swiftly shattered that optimistic belief. With renewed distress, and now with fear, he recalled how she had declared that should he again attempt her she would resist him to the utmost. He remembered also the intense resentment she had expressed at his having ravished her on that first occasion.

And now she had him at her mercy. She could not have made plainer her reason for asking of Djezzar his life. Clearly, she intended to revenge herself on him by depriving him of his man- hood and, not content with that, meant to extract payment from him, by hours of degradation and torment, for every moment of pleasure he had had with her.

He did not have very long to wait before his punishment began. After he had spent about an hour in miserable contemplation of his fate the jailers came for him again. They marched him up to the courtyard, across it and through a door under the balcony from which the women had watched the impaling of Auby and Gensonné, then up a flight of stairs and through several passages to a door on which the Chief Jailer knocked loudly with the hilt of his dagger. After a few moments an iron grille was lifted and a pair of heavily lidded eyes peered at them. The door was then opened by a hugely fat negro with several chins, whom Roger at once placed as a eunuch. At a piping call from him, two other eunuchs appeared, took the prisoner over from the jailers and hustled him inside.

The vestibule through which they took him was lit by hanging lanterns made from silver filigree work, encrusted with coloured glass. By the soft light they gave he saw that the walls were hung with rich silk Persian rugs of beautiful design and that the place was furnished with chests of rare wood inlaid with ivory. No sound penetrated to this luxurious apartment and the delicious scent of jasmine hung on the still air.

Roger was taken through a hanging curtain of beads, down a corridor, through another room—an aviary, where dozens of cages held twittering birds of every rainbow hue—then into a loftier chamber with on one side slim, marble pillars supporting arches of lace-like carved stone. The arches gave on to a long balcony that had a lovely view over the bay, in which the ships of Sir Sidney Smith's Squadron were lying at anchor.

But Roger knew that they were much too far off for anyone in them to hear a cry for help, however loud his shouts, and after one glance to seaward his gaze became riveted on Zanthé. She was seated at the far end of the room, cross-legged on a low divan heaped with cushions. Squatting on the floor near her were two other women and behind the divan stood a fat, elderly negress. All the women were wearing yashmaks, but the silk of Zanthé's was so diaphanous that, as Roger advanced, he could see her lower features clearly through it.

Agitated as he was, he still found her beauty breath-taking. Her curling hair, with its rich bronze lights, serene forehead, dark, tapering eyebrows, magnificent tawny eyes and red, full-lipped, cupid's-bow mouth were all as he remembered them and as he had so often visualized them when daydreaming about her. When he arrived at about ten feet from her divan he was about to bow to her but was not given the chance.

Two of the powerful eunuchs seized him by the arms, forced him to his knees, then pushed his head forward towards the floor, while the third shouted in the thin, high voice of a castrato:

'Down, Christian dog! Down! Lick the floor in obeisance to Her Exalted Highness, daughter of the Sultan Abd-ul-Hamid, Descendant of the Prophet, Shadow of Allah upon Earth, Padishah and . . .'

He was still declaiming shrilly when one of the other eunuchs struck Roger a sharp blow on the back of the head. His face hit the marble floor with such force that his lips were bruised and his nose began to bleed. Jerking up his head he stared at Zanthé and exclaimed in French:

'Can that which was said in jest really be true? That . . . that you are a daughter of the Sultan?'

Her face remained impassive, but she gave a slight shrug and replied in the same language, 'I am the only daughter of the late Sultan. But do you take me for such a fool as to have revealed it to you while I was in Cairo? Had I done so when we first met you would have demanded a King's ransom for me and, on the second occasion, your General would have kept me as a valuable hostage.'

'But . . . but,' Roger stammered, 'how can you be? You . . . you said that you were French.'

'I told you that my mother is French, and that is true.'

The enormity of his crime now came home to Roger. To lay hands on a woman of royal blood in any country was *lèse-majesté*; and in Turkey, where all women of good class were so jealously guarded, to have forcibly deflowered a Princess must merit the most ghastly tortures that the Eastern mind was capable of conceiving.

'Had I but known——' he began.

'That which is done is done,' she said sharply, 'and had I been but a merchant's daughter I would have felt no less the disgrace you inflicted on me.' Then she gave an order in Turkish to her Chief Eunuch, the meaning of which Roger did not grasp.

The eunuch clapped his plump hands and two more eunuchs, who had evidently been waiting in an adjoining chamber, came waddling in. One of them carried a large bowl filled with water, the other brought soap and towels and, under one arm, two long bamboo poles. The eunuchs on either side of Roger continued to hold him down on his knees while the basin was set in front of him. The blood from his nose was running down over his lips and dripping from his chin, so he thought he was about to be allowed to wash it from his face. He was swiftly disillusioned.

One of the newcomers splashed water on his head while the other rubbed soap on it, until his hair was in a thick lather. The Chief Eunuch then produced a razor. Suddenly realizing that they intended to shave his head, he began to shout and struggle. In spite of their rolls of surplus fat, the men who held him were very strong; so in his weakened state he could not have got away from them, and he did not try for long. The Chief Eunuch gave the top of his right ear a sharp nick with the razor. Fearing that if he resisted further his ear might be cut off, Roger let himself go limp and submitted to having his head shaved.

It was over twenty hours since he had had anything to drink, but the craving he had felt during the early part of the day had later receded to the back of his mind under the compulsion of far stronger emotions. Now the sight of the bowl of water caused his thirst to return with such force that he even licked in with his parched tongue some of the soapy water that ran down from his head to the corners of his mouth. Unpleasant as it tasted, as soon as the last locks of his hair had been thrown aside he wrenched himself forward, plunged his face into the basin and lapped up several gulps of the water remaining in it.

When the eunuchs had dried Roger's head with a towel and stood back from him, Zanthé surveyed their handiwork with a smile, her two women burst out laughing and the negress gave vent to a strange cackling sound. At a word from Zanthé the old woman brought a mirror and held it up in front of Roger, so that he could see himself. The sight of his head, as bald as an egg, came as a horrid shock and his bronzed face surmounted by the pinkish scalp from which the hair had been shorn gave him the appearance of a clown. As he was inclined to be vain of his normal good looks he could have wept with anger. But far worse was to follow.

Pushing him over on his back, two of the eunuchs held him down while two others pulled off his boots and stockings. They then lashed his bare feet securely to the bamboo poles and lifted them waist-high, so that his body, shoulders, arms and legs still lay sprawled upon the ground. When the poles had been brought in, he had wondered to what use they were to be put. Now a memory flashed into his mind of someone once telling him of the Turkish torture known as the bastinado. It consisted of whipping the sensitive soles of the feet with a thin, springy rod.

Next moment he was experiencing that form of torture. The Chief Eunuch produced a rod and he brought it sharply down in Roger's upturned left foot. He let out a yell. The rod swished down on his right foot. He yelled again and began to beg for mercy, but his pleas were ignored. Swish, swish, swish, the cuts came down with ruthless regularity, while he squirmed and twisted, shouting, screaming and vainly beating his hands on the floor. By the time Zanthé called a halt to his flagellation, the soles of his feet were raw, bleeding and giving him as much pain as though they had been held in front of a red-hot fire.

When the cords that tied his ankles to the poles had been untied, he was near fainting and lay, a sobbing wreck of a man, before the divan on which sat the beautiful girl whom he had robbed of her virginity. But she had not done with him yet. At an abrupt word from her the eunuchs began to strip him.

Pulling off the crumpled and dirty travelling coat that he had worn since soon after his arrival in Naples, and throwing it aside, they quickly divested him of his other garments. In his present state he was indifferent to the shame of being exposed naked, but when his money-belt was taken from him he rallied himself sufficiently to call out to Zanthé, 'In that you'll find a blue diamond that I procured as a gift for you while away in Alexandria.'

The belt was handed to her and after going through several of its pockets she fished out the slender chain from which depended the jewel that Sarodopulous had given him. His fleeting thought that the gift might serve to appease her was swiftly dashed. After a casual glance at it she threw it down on the divan beside her and said contemptuously:

'I have a score of stones, each worth not less than fifty times the value of this little bauble. But it will serve as a gift for one of my tire-women who is about to marry.' Then she looked at the Chief Eunuch and added, 'Go to it now. Let us get finished with this business.'

Again water, soap and towels were brought. Roger was thrown

on his back and one of the eunuchs sat on his chest so that he could not see what was being done to him; but he felt his private parts being lathered, then shaved, and he dared not move from fear of receiving a severe cut.

The weight of the eunuch on his chest drove the breath from his lungs, the soles of his bleeding feet felt as though they were being held before a fire, his injured wrist was aching dully. Yet his mind was suffering greater torture than his body as he visualized the awful thing that was about to happen to him.

He felt the rough towel against his flesh again, then a loop of string was put over his testicles and drawn tight. His eyes starting from his head he yelled to Zanthé to have mercy on him.

Her cold and imperative voice cut through his shouts. 'Enough! Be silent! This is only preparation. It will be a week yet before we make a neuter of you.'

The eunuch got up off him and two others hauled him to his feet. They pained him so much that he could not stand on them. Between them the eunuchs got his shirt over his head and threw his travelling coat round his shoulders, then half-dragged and half-carried him out through a side door, up two flights of stairs and into a sparsely furnished attic. It had a narrow, open, arrow-slit window and he was just sufficiently conscious to realize that night had fallen. The eunuchs threw him on a narrow divan and left him, locking the door behind them.

For a time he lay where they had thrown him, drenched in sweat and half comatose, his head throbbing as though about to burst. Gradually his greater torments took first place in his consciousness. His feet caused him such pain that had he had a hatchet he would have been tempted to hack them off; his testicles, too, throbbed violently. With an effort, he sat up and endeavoured to untie the string which bit into the flesh at their base; but it was thin and waxed, so he found it impossible to unpick the knot.

Knowing little about castration, he had always supposed that the operation was performed with a knife; but he now thought that that could only be in the case of young boys, such as those the Pope annually ordered to be castrated so that they could continue to sing in the choir of the Vatican. From what Zanthé had said it seemed probable that the Turkish method with fully grown men was to restrict the flow of blood, tightening the string a little each day until the testicles became partially atrophied, and then could be cut off without the risk that the victim would die from loss of blood.

For what seemed an age he lay there, slowly turning his tortured body from side to side and groaning as the tears seeped out of the corners of his eyes. Then the door opened. Raising his head a little he recognized the old negress. In one hand she held an oil-lamp and in the other a large basket. Setting them down, she pulled open his coat and had a good look at him. Producing a small pair of clippers she cut the string confining his testicles, bringing him swift relief in that quarter. From her basket she then took a pot of salve, with which she anointed the soles of his feet and his lacerated wrist. Having bandaged them, she went to her basket again, took from it a bowl of warm, highly spiced soup and lifted his head while he gratefully drank it down. As she let his head fall back he muttered his thanks but she made no reply and, having collected her basket, left the room.

With his pains considerably lessened, he lay still for some moments and soon became drowsy. The sensation told him that the soup must have contained opium or some other Eastern drug and before he could consider the matter further he fell asleep.

When he woke it was past midday. He felt terribly stiff and his feet still pained him badly; but on a small chest beneath the window he saw that food and drink had been left for him, and he now felt hungry. He swung his legs off the divan and gingerly tried his weight on them. He could not have walked any distance but, advancing on tiptoe, he reached the chest and sat down on a stool within reach of it.

The food consisted of some pieces of cold meat on a skewer, a dish of sweet cakes and fruit. A jug contained a mixture of orange and lemon juice that went down like nectar. As he ate he peered out of the arrow-slit window. Only a small section of the bay was visible through it and the wall it pierced was as thick as his arm was long; so he had to give up any idea of trying to attract the attention of one of the ships in the bay. When he had finished his meal he made his way unsteadily back to the divan and lay down, to be racked again by unnerving thoughts.

From the treatment he was now receiving he could only suppose that Zanthé, with a typically Eastern refinement of cruelty, was fattening him for the kill or at least enabling him to recruit his strength so that he might the better support further torment. If, too, his new theory about methods of castration was right, the string had been removed from his testicles only temporarily. It now seemed probable that to apply it only for a few hours each day would, in due course, have sufficient effect to make the final operation possible without danger. Grimly, he forced himself to accept that he must soon expect a visit from the eunuchs; but the afternoon wore on into evening, and they did not come.

As twilight deepened he fell into a doze, but started wide awake filled with apprehension when, an hour or two later, he heard footsteps outside the door. To his relief it proved to be the old negress. In her basket she had brought him up another meal. Setting it on the chest, she examined his feet and wrist, put more of the healing ointment on them and rebandaged them. Noticing that the chamber-pot which stood in a corner had not been emptied, she picked it up and deftly pitched its contents out through the arrow-slit window.

This time he was able to thank her more coherently for her ministrations, but she again remained silent. When he asked her name she grinned at him, opened her mouth wide and held up the lamp so that he could see into it. To his horror she had no tongue. It had evidently been torn out at the roots, to make her a mute and ensure that she did not disclose any secrets she might learn while in the seraglio.

Roger spent a better night and the day that followed differed from its predecessor only in that he was awake when the negress brought him his morning meal. With it she brought a basin of water for him to wash. From then on for a fortnight his days and nights kept the same pattern. His many bruises disappeared, the soles of his feet healed and his wrenched wrist returned to normal. He had nothing to read and no means whatever of employing himself; so he could spend his waking hours only in an endless series of speculations.

Having considered the possibilities of an attempt to escape, he had soon concluded that it would prove hopeless. The window was so narrow that he doubted if he would have been able to force his body through it and, even if he could, he could not have made from the material available in the room a rope anywhere near long enough to reach the ground. As his money-belt had been taken from him he could not bribe the old negress to help him, even if she had proved bribable. After the way in which she had tended him he could have brought himself to stun

her only if his life had depended on it and, even if he had ruthlessly overcome her, his chances of escaping from the citadel and
out of the city would have been infinitesimal.

His only means of judging the progress of the siege were from
the sounds that reached him. On the fourth day of his confinement he heard gunfire and as it did not, as far as he could tell,
come from the ships in the bay, he judged that Bonaparte had
begun to bombard the city with such light field artillery as he
had been able to bring overland with him. Next day he caught a
rumbling sound, as though a small earthquake were taking place.
It lasted for two or three minutes, and he guessed that one of
the great towers must have collapsed. That would have meant
a breach in the walls, enabling the French infantry to launch an
assault. The thought raised his spirits considerably for, much as
he would have wished the Anglo-Turkish force to succeed in
holding Acre, his life or, hardly less precious, his virility was at
stake and his only hope of saving one or the other lay in the
French capturing the city and rescuing him.

During the week that followed it was obvious that they were
doing their utmost to capture Acre, for Sir Sidney's Squadron
and, close inshore, the gunboats he had captured were almost
constantly in action. Then, towards the end of the month, the
firing died down, from which Roger judged that the assaults had
all been repelled by Phélippeaux's cannon on the walls and the
enfilading fire from the ships. So Bonaparte had failed in his
attempt to take the city by storm and had been reduced to
approaching the walls by a system of trenches, from which mines
could be laid beneath the fortifications.

Such an operation would take weeks, so Roger's hopes for
himself sank again. By then he had recovered physically, but at
times was harassed by black periods of depression and fear. He
could only suppose that, as no further steps had been taken
towards his castration, Zanthé was playing a cat-and-mouse game.
He dare not hope that she had either forgotten or pardoned him
and, if his reprieve could be explained by her having fallen ill,
that could only mean a postponement of his martyrdom.

It was on April 3rd, about midnight, that he was roused from a
deep sleep. He had not heard the door being unlocked and
opened his eyes to find a figure bending over him. The starlight
coming through the arrow-slit was just sufficient for him to make
out that his visitor was clad in flowing robes, but he could not

tell if they were worn by a man or a woman. His heart began to hammer wildly, for his first waking thought was that Zanthé had sent one of her people either to murder him or fetch him to be further tortured in front of her.

Suddenly the figure flung a pair of arms across his chest and fell in a kneeling posture beside his divan. There came a loud sob, then a heart-rending cry.

'Oh, monsieur! Can you ever forgive me for what I have done to you?'

'Zanthé!' he exclaimed and, struggling up, instinctively put his arms about her bowed shoulders.

'There was no other way,' she sobbed, 'no other way. Having saved you from Djezzar, what else could I do? Had I not had you treated as I did, the eunuchs would have betrayed me and you would have been taken away to your death. I could justify keeping you here only because I said that you had insulted me and I wished to be revenged on you. Oh, my poor love! How you must have suffered! And I, forced to order all that was done to you, then be a witness to it.'

For a moment this extraordinary revelation, that she had saved him from impalement not out of hate but out of love, left Roger tongue-tied. That she had then been compelled to carry through the role she had adopted needed no further explaining. Finding his voice, he murmured:

'Think no more of it. Cease your tears, I beg. I owe my life to you and you love me. That is all that matters.' Then with one hand he started to stroke her hair and added, 'But . . . but when did you find that you loved me?'

Her sobs ceased and she began to speak in a breathless voice. 'Love begets love. That first night, I could not help but be drawn to you. Your looks, those fine shoulders and slim hips. They would attract any woman with warm blood in her veins. That . . . that was why, in the end, I gave myself so fully. How could I not? But that is not love. I counted you no better than any other soldier who had not lain with a woman for months, and would have taken any little slave-girl just as fiercely. And you, an uncircumcised Christian, had robbed me, a Princess of the Imperial Line, of my virginity! I saw it as my people would —a crime unthinkable. My passion spent, I hated you for it and determined to escape. As you must know, while you were away in Alexandria the merchant ben-Jussif, who owned the house, and his sons rescued me. I sought asylum with the Viceroy's ladies. Then, during the October rebellion, you broke into the seraglio. By then I thought you would at least have found out that I was the widow of the Commander of the Cairo garrison and a woman of high rank. But you claimed me as your slave. Can you wonder at my resentment?'

'I cannot now,' Roger said gently. 'But what then?'

She stifled a sob and went on, 'Being carried off by you again re-aroused my passions. I could not stop thinking of that night in ben-Jussif's house. I wanted you to take me again, to possess me utterly. But I would not show it. I am by nature proud. The very thought that I should wish to give myself to a man who wanted me as nothing more than a concubine degraded me in my own eyes. After what had passed between us I would have died of humiliation had I been weak enough to give you the least sign of encouragement. But there came the morning of your return. You were placed under arrest by that Colonel Duroc. Before you left the house you said to me that, whatever your punishment, you would do the same again for an hour in my company. I knew then that it could not be only as a plaything that you thought of me. It came as a revelation that you must really love me. I felt a dizziness, and my heart melted within me.'

'Had I but known, nothing would have induced me to leave Egypt.'

Zanthé raised her head and said in surprise, 'I did not know you had. Have you been far?'

He nodded. 'Yes. General Bonaparte sent me on a mission. It necessitated a long voyage. It was soon after landing, on the night of my return, that Djezzar's men captured me.'

Again she lowered her head and began to sob. 'And then . . . and then I saw you there in the courtyard. You were in different clothes, you hair disordered and in a terrible state. I did not recognize you until you spoke. Oh, Allah be praised that you cried out to Djezzar when you did. Had you not, you would have been impaled before my very eyes. My heart came up into my mouth. I nearly fainted . . .'

'But, brave girl that you are, you didn't. You kept your head and saved me.'

'I know; but at what a price.'

'I pray you, forget that. It is all over now. At least . . .' Roger added, with sudden uneasiness, 'I hope so.'

'Yes; yes. You have nothing more to fear. That is, provided it is not discovered that you have not been made a eunuch.'

'Am I then supposed to have been?'

'Of course; otherwise I could not have kept you in my private apartments. The horrid business is supposed to have taken a week. By then that string they tied about you would have done its work, had not my faithful Gezubb come up here and cut it off. A further week would be needed for your recovery; so it is expected that tomorrow you will come down and take up the duties I shall give you.' Again her tears began to flow as she added, 'It is I who should be your slave, not you mine. And to begin with, I shall have to treat you harshly. For that I implore you not to hate me. I . . .'

Putting his hand gently over her mouth he checked her lamentations and said, 'Hush! I could never hate you. Use me as you will. Allot me the meanest tasks. The worse you treat me, the less likely it is that anyone will suspect the truth. A smile from your lovely eyes when no one is looking is all the compensation I ask.'

Her tears had ceased and suddenly she gave a low laugh. 'I can come to you secretly at night, like this, and only old Gezubb will know of it. Then you can ask of me smiles, kisses, caresses and every pleasure imaginable. Tell me, my beloved one, are you now well again and all your poor wounds fully healed?'

He laughed in reply. 'I have never felt better, as I will show you if you wish.'

'If I wish!' she echoed. 'How can you know the restraint I have put upon myself this past fortnight? For me to have come to you while you were still in pain could only have proved a terrible frustration for us both. At least for both had I found you willing to forgive me. My most awful fear was that you might not, and had you cast me aside I think I would have killed myself. But in more sanguine moments I imagined myself again lying in your arms. Night after night my heart has beat near to bursting-point at the thought of it. Allah alone knows the strength of my passion for you; and now . . . now that I can feel your hands upon me I have become a furnace of desire.'

Next moment their mouths met in a long, fierce kiss. Breathless, they drew apart and she stood up. With a swift movement she threw off her robe. Beneath it she had on only a voluminous pair of almost transparent Turkish trousers. Undoing her girdle she slid them down, stepped out of them and kicked off her sandals. While they had been talking the moon had risen and a beam of moonlight coming through the arrow-slit silvered her magnificent body as she stood beside him, naked. The light flickered in tiny blue sparks in the valley between her breasts and Roger exclaimed:

'Why, you are wearing the little diamond I procured for you.'

'Of course,' she laughed. 'It is my most treasured possession and I shall always wear it.'

He threw back the coverlet of the divan and pulled his shirt off over his head. As he did so she moved round to the foot of the divan, fell to her knees, took both his feet in her hands and began to kiss them.

Striving to pull them away, he cried, 'No, no, beloved, you must not do that. Come here this instant and let me take you in my arms.'

'Nay,' her low laugh came again. 'This is my rightful place. Did you not know that, when the Sultan sends for one of his women, they greet him by kissing his feet then, humbly conscious of the honour he does them, steal gently up upon him until they can kiss his chest? And you are my Sultan.'

'I am also your slave,' he laughed back. 'Enough of that.' Then, sitting up, he stretched out his hands and drew her swiftly to him.

Later, lying side by side and still embraced, they talked in whispers. As he had supposed, her husband, like many Turks, had cared only for young boys. He had married her solely for the prestige that an alliance with the Imperial House would bring him and had had two other wives, but never slept with either of them. Instead he made his wives flog the boys with rods and birches and it was the performance of this cruel task that had made her hate him.

She had made up the story of her flight from Cairo. The truth was that, after the news of her husband's death had arrived, the guard of Janissaries left at the palace had deserted. Fearing that the palace would be attacked by the mob, she had decided to seek safety with the Viceroy and had urged the other two wives to accompany her. But they had been too frightened to face the streets without a proper guard. So she had set off on her own, accompanied only by her maid and one faithful manservant; on their way they had had the misfortune to be seized by the Sergeant.

She then told Roger that her mother had been a Mademoiselle Aimée Dubucq de Rivery, born in Martinique. In 1780 she had been sent to finish her education in France with the Dames de la Visitation in their Conent at Nantes. After some years there she was on her way home when the ship in which she was travelling nearly sank in a violent storm. The passengers were rescued by a Spanish trader which took them round into the Mediterranean. There the Spanish ship had been captured by Corsairs and everyone in her taken as prisoners to Algiers. When the Bey— Baba Mohammed ben Osman—had heard that among the prisoners there was a beautiful, golden-haired, blue-eyed French girl of noble birth, he had sent for her and at once decided that he would win high favour by sending her as an offering to his overlord, the Sultan.

On hearing this, Roger exclaimed, 'But this is amazing! I know your mother's story. She is a cousin of the Vicomtesse de Beauharnis, who is now Madame Bonaparte, and who was also born in Martinique. She is a friend of mine and told me once how, while still in her teens, she, your mother and a third young girl all went to an Irish sybil to have their fortunes told. It was predicted that both Madame Bonaparte and your mother would become the wives of great Sovereigns and that their children would become Kings and Queens.'

'In my mother's case,' Zanthé replied, 'the first part of the prediction came true. In the Sultan's harem there are always several hundred odalisques, each one picked for her looks; yet my mother was so lovely that they named her *Naksh*, which means "the beautiful one", and my father made her his favourite Kadine.'

'Since you must take after her, I don't wonder. She must also be a woman of great character to have survived the jealousy and intrigues of so many rivals.'

'She is; but she had the help of two powerful allies: *Son Altesse Noire,* a most intelligent Nubian who is Chief of the Black Eunuchs, and the Circassian Kadine, the widow of my father's predecessor Mustapha III. It is her son, my cousin Selim, who is the present Sultan and, as his mother, she wields great power. She is known as the Sultan Valideh—the head of all the veiled women of Islam. These two put my mother forward as a good influence to help sweep away many barbarous old customs and open the way for Turkey to receive the new scientific knowledge from the West. They hoped, too, that she might gain France's support for Turkey against our hereditary enemies, the Russians. It is owing to her that we now have many French officers in the Turkish Army.'

'What of the latter part of the prophecy?' Roger asked. 'Have you a brother who is likely to succeed the present Sultan?'

'I have one brother, Mahmoud, but he is not the heir apparent. The Sultanate passes not from father to son, but to the eldest male member of the Osmali family. Mustapha, my father's eldest son by a Turkish Kadine, is the next in line. Only should he die will my brother ever come to the throne.'[1]

'I wonder,' Roger mused, 'if the prophecy will come true for Madame Bonaparte. In Paris, a few years ago, when the General was almost unknown, another sybil named La Normande made a very similar prediction about her future. I think, though, that the General has a long way to go yet before he can make himself a King. Tell me, now, how is the siege going?'

'There was most furious fighting up to a few days ago,' Zanthé replied. 'But the garrison is holding its own; largely, I believe, owing to the help given by the English. It is said that the Admiral Sir Smith often comes ashore and says how the fighting should be conducted. He has, too, several able Lieutenants. There is a Colonel Phélippeaux who has mounted many cannon on our walls and a Captain Miller who commands the British gun teams that have been sent into the city to help in its defence. Even so, the French are making progress in the north-east quarter. I expect you heard that terrible rumbling a few days after you were put in this room. That was a part of the great tower tumbling down in ruins after the French exploded a mine under it, and since then they have held a small section of the outer wall.'

For a few moments they fell silent, then instinctively they began to kiss and made love again. When their passion was temporarily spent Roger remarked:

'From the way in which Djezzar addressed you as "my beautiful one" when he granted your request to spare my life, I imagined that, as you had become a widow, he had taken you as one of his wives.'

She shook her head. 'That he has lustful thoughts about me is

---

[1] Historical note:

Aimée Dubucq de Rivery's son, known as 'The Reformer', became the Sultan Mahmoud II and reigned from 1808 to 1839.

true. His eyes devour me whenever he sees me, even at a distance. He sent his Chief Eunuch to me shortly after I arrived here, offering to divorce one of his wives and take me in her place. He is a most horrible man, so naturally I declined his offer.'

'Have you no fear that he may attempt to take you against your will?' Roger asked anxiously.

She kissed him. 'You need have no fear of that, dear love. As I am the daughter of a Sultan he had to provide me with my own suite of apartments, and custom forbids him to enter them. Before the war it would have been a different matter. Then he was virtually an independent ruler and all Syria bowed the knee to him. Married or single, I would not have risked a visit to his city of Acre. But now he is dependent on the Turkish forces and the goodwill of the Porte to maintain himself against the French. It is the right of my cousin, the present Sultan, to give me again in marriage to whom he will, and he certainly would not give me to a Pasha who in the past has flouted his authority. For Djezzar to force me into marriage without my cousin's consent, or molest me, would mean risking his whole future. Being an ambitious man, you may be sure he will not do that.'

With her head on Roger's chest they dozed for a while, then she roused and began gently to caress him. For a few minutes he pretended to be asleep then, with a laugh of delight, crushed her to him. For a third time their mutual passion carried them to Paradise. Then with long, happy sighs, they lay still.

Soon afterwards the first flush of dawn showed through the arrow-slit window. With great reluctance Zanthé sat up and said that she must leave him, but before doing so she gave him most careful instructions to guide his behaviour during the coming day. After another score of lingering kisses and endearments they tore themselves apart.

A few hours later the old negress, Gezubb, roused him from a heavy sleep. With her she brought the garments and sandals of a eunuch. Having washed himself and put on the clothes, he accompanied her downstairs. Zanthé had told him that no one in the seraglio understood French and that he should pretend that he knew no Turkish or Arabic. He could not then be called on to answer awkward questions and, when he did have to appear to have picked up a few words of Turkish, he must try, as far as possible, to imitate the high, piping voices of the eunuchs.

The enormously fat Chief Eunuch was a lazy, normally good-tempered man. He showed no hostility to Roger and, by signs, set him to clear out the bird cages in the aviary. It was not a particularly unpleasant task and occupied him for most of the morning. But when he had finished, two other eunuchs cornered him, and, with cries of 'Christian dog', set about him with their heavy, leather belts.

He knew that if he seriously injured either of them it would be certain to cause trouble and put Zanthé in a difficult situation; so he defended himself as best he could without striking out. Grimly he put up with quite a beating but, before it was over, by good luck, Zanthé came into the room.

Immediately they caught sight of her they stopped, but with her tawny eyes blazing she walked purposefully towards them. Seizing each of them by an ear, she smashed their faces one against the other with all her strength and, from his night's experience, Roger knew that her splendid limbs were as strong as those of many a man. As she continued to bash their heads together they set up a shrill yelling, which brought all the others running into the room.

Letting her victims go, Zanthé pointed at Roger then cried to the assembled group in tones of fury, 'The Roumi is not for you. He is here as my slave and plaything. Should any of you dare to lay a finger on him I'll have you bastinadoed.' Then, turning on Roger, she slapped him twice hard across the face.

That evening, as a further demonstration of her apparent feelings towards him, she made him turn somersaults in front of her divan. Each time his legs were in the air she jabbed a bamboo pole into his side, causing him to fall in a flurry of arms and legs on to the hard floor.

When she came to his room again at midnight she implored his pardon; but he assured her that none of his falls had hurt, and that such treatment was just what was needed to convince the eunuchs that tormenting him and making him a laughing stock for her women gave her pleasure.

Again they spent the greater part of the night giving free rein to their passionate delight in one another, or lying embraced in a blissful doze. Before she left him they devised other ways in which, without causing him any serious pain, she could appear to chastise and humiliate him.

For more than a month matters continued in much the same way, except that during the daytime Zanthé gradually relaxed her severity towards him. The unspoken excuse provided by her to the eunuchs for so doing was that no one else in the seraglio understood French, whereas Roger could read the books in that language which she had brought from Cairo in her baggage. In the morning he continued to clean out the cages in the aviary and later in the day spent hours reading aloud to her.

Night after night, after they had revelled together, she gave him such news of the siege as reached her. During April the French succeeded in bringing their trenches right up to the walls and exploding a number of mines under them. However, in the middle of that month their efforts against the city had been greatly reduced, owing to the approach of relieving forces. A body of troops, said to be commanded by General Junot, had been detached and had inflicted a heavy defeat on a Turkish force near Nazareth. Then, a week later, Bonaparte was reported to have left his headquarters and to have gained a victory over the larger part of the Army of the Pasha of Damascus.

After that the French attacks had been resumed in full force and they had been greatly strengthened by the success of some ships from Alexandria in landing six heavy siege cannon near the foot of Mount Carmel. On the 25th two more towers had been brought down and most desperate fighting had followed. But the Mamelukes, Janissaries and British marines were holding, with desperate valour, the breaches that had been made in the crumbling walls.

Each day the sounds of the fighting grew nearer and, on May 1st, Djezzar's great fortress palace was attacked. Through the thunder of cannon and the rattle of musketry, the battle-cries and screams of the wounded could be clearly heard. The French broke into the palace garden, but were driven out by Djezzar's renowned Albanian guards. On the two succeeding days there was a lull, but on the 4th another tower was blown up by a mine and the French launched a most determined assault through this new breach they had made in the defences. There was fighting in the streets which went on for three days; but Sir Sidney Smith landed his sailors, armed with pikes and cutlasses. The British tars turned the tide of battle and, once again, the French were driven back.

On the 7th great news came in for the defenders. The other Army that had been formed for the relief of Acre was coming by sea from Rhodes and the Fleet carrying it had been sighted.

There was tremendous excitement in the city, and by afternoon the Turkish Fleet could be seen on the horizon. But it was watched with almost unbearable suspense, because a complete calm had fallen and the boats that had been sent out to tow it in could draw it towards the harbour at no more than a mile or so an hour.

At midnight on the 8th Zanthé came to Roger's room as usual; but instead of giving him her normal, loving greeting she flung herself, weeping, on his breast, her eyes distended by tears.

'What is it, my love?' he cried, clutching her to him and turning her lovely tear-stained face up to his. 'What has happened! Have we been discovered?'

'No,' she sobbed, 'no, but Fate has dealt us a most terrible blow. An oared galley from the Turkish Fleet made harbour this evening. The Commander brought a despatch for Djezzar. It seems that he wrote to Constantinople, asking a reward for having defended Acre so valiantly. My cousin has sent a *firman* granting his request. It . . . it was that he should have me for a wife. And he will brook no delay. I am to marry him tomorrow.'

19

A Bolt from the Blue

IT was seven weeks since Roger had been captured, and for the greater part of that time he had been Zanthé's lover. The other inmates of the seraglio had become used to him and, since he had become her reader, accepted that she should no longer treat him harshly; so his days passed pleasantly. His period of convalescense and the lazy life he had since led provided the best possible conditions for him to meet Zanthé's desire for him with a continued passion as great as her own. Also, since she found a thousand questions to ask him about France and other countries in which he had travelled and he never tired of hearing her talk of the strange life led in the great seraglio at Constantinople, the hours of the nights they spent together never seemed long enough.

Even had he been given a chance to escape, he would have thought twice before taking it. Any information with which he could have furnished Sir Sidney Smith would have been hopelessly out-of-date, so there was no duty that his conscience urged him to perform. As long as the fact that he had not been castrated remained undiscovered he was safe, and he was quite content to wait upon events.

Up till now Bonaparte had not suffered a single defeat in Italy, Egypt or Syria, so it seemed most unlikely that he would fail to take Acre. The reinforcements brought by the Turkish Fleet might enable the city to hold out longer; but the French had breached the walls in many places and, it was said, so widely in one part that an assault of fifty men abreast could pass through the gap. In view of this Roger still believed that any day might see them victorious and the only anxiety he felt was about what might happen on the day of their victory.

If Djezzar's palace were stormed, Zanthé and he might become involved in some wild *mêlée* in which one or both of them might be killed or injured. It was certain, too, that the city would be given over to the sack and, if they were caught with the other women and the eunuchs, it might prove difficult for him, with his appearance as a eunuch, to protect Zanthé from the brutal and licentious soldiery. But his quickness of mind had always served him well at times of crisis. He was optimistic, therefore, about their surviving those few hours of danger and succeeding in convincing the attackers that he was a French officer who had been captured. Once they accepted him as Colonel Breuc, Zanthé would be safe from molestation and, as soon as the fury of the sack had died down, he intended to take her to Bonaparte's headquarters.

He would have greatly preferred to take her to Sir Sidney Smith; but his only means of protecting her during those dangerous hours would be by declaring himself a Frenchman and, once the city was in the hands of the French, it would be next to impossible to get her away to a British ship. It was owing to this assessment of the probable course events would take that, much as he loved her, he had decided against confiding to her the truth about himself. Since there seemed no escape from again taking up the role of one of Bonaparte's aides-de-camp it was better not to burden her with the knowledge that he would be a spy in the camp of his enemies, at least until he saw a good prospect of getting her safely away from the French Army. Where he would take her when he did get that chance he had not yet even considered. It must depend on unforeseeable circumstances which would arise in the future. In the meantime his mind had been almost entirely obsessed with her beauty and charm, and he was content to remain a prisoner for the sake of the hundred delights she so willingly afforded him.

But now the jealous gods had launched a thunderbolt which threatened to put a swift and permanent end to their happiness. Not only was his beautiful Zanthé to be torn from him; she was to be forced to give herself to, of all people, Djezzar Pasha, that monster whose name throughout the whole Middle East was synonymous with cruelty. The thought made Roger's heart contract. A sudden nausea rose in him. Nearly sick with rage and apprehension, he cried aghast:

'It cannot be true! The very idea fills me with horror. Are you quite certain that this is not a trick?'

'Dear love, I am certain,' she moaned. 'The Chief Eunuch of Djezzar's own seraglio brought . . . brought the *firman* from the Sultan for me to see, and . . . and with it many rich presents of silks and jewels.'

'Can you not flatly refuse to marry him?'

'How can I? Any female of the Imperial Family is the Sultan's, to dispose of, and it is unthinkable that I, the daughter of a Sultan should set an example of defiance. As soon as Selim learned what I had done he would be forced to make an example of me. He would send an order for me to be strangled by the bowstring.'

'To refuse would at least gain us time,' Roger argued. 'It would take weeks for the news to reach Constantinople and an order for your execution to be conveyed to Acre. Meanwhile——'

'No, no!' she cut him short. 'It would gain us nothing. Djezzar has long desired me and he is not the man to wait on ceremony. Now that he has my cousin's consent he will take no refusal. He will have the Imam pronounce the words over us whether I will or no. Then if I resist he will whip me until I consent to perform all the bestial acts that the women of his seraglio have told me he demands of them.'

'Then we must escape tonight.'

'Oh, if only we could,' she sobbed. 'But it is not possible.'

'It is,' Roger insisted. 'It must be. It would have been far easier to contrive had we had even a few days' warning. But we must do without. We'll manage somehow.'

'I know you to be brave, but bravery is not enough she protested tearfully. 'They would catch us both and inflict some ghastly death upon you. It is my fate that I must suffer, but I'll not allow you to give your life to no purpose. You must remain here, continuing to pose as a eunuch. There is at least a chance that the French will take the city and you will be rescued before your imposture is discovered.'

'Oh, my sweet, courageous Zanthé!' He turned her face up to his and kissed her tear-stained cheeks. 'What sort of man do you take me for to think that I would give you up to that brutal sadist while skulking here in safety? It would, I admit, be next to impossible for me to escape alone. For you to do so alone would be equally difficult. But together I have good hopes that we may.

You know the palace. You can judge at which exit we are likely
to be faced with the fewest obstacles and guide me to it. I have
the strength you lack to break down all but the strongest barriers.
Provide me with a good weapon and, should our escape be
opposed, I'll hack my way through half a dozen guards to carry
you to safety.'

She closed her eyes and clung more fiercely to him. 'My splendid love! My paladin! I know you would. I am blessed beyond
all women that so fine a man should be willing to die for me.
But we cannot escape! We cannot! There is a eunuch on duty
day and night at the only entrance to these apartments. You
could not kill him before he gave the alarm. Within a few
moments the others would be upon you. Did you overcome them,
that would still be only the beginning. Outside the door there is a
sentry. Hearing the noise within he would summon the guard.
Those Albanians are as brave as yourself and armed to the
teeth. You could not possibly succeed in cutting a way for us
through them. I should see you killed before my eyes. No, no! I
would rather let Djezzar inflict what he will upon me.'

'I'll not have it,' Roger said firmly, 'and by the door is not
the only way out. There is the balcony overlooking the harbour.'

'But it is thirty feet from the ground.'

'No matter. We will make a rope from the coverlets of divans.
I will lower you by it and follow after. Quick now. We have no
time to lose. You can rely on old Gezubb, can you not? Go now
and get her to help you. I'll come down and join you the moment
I have dressed.'

Zanthé hesitated. 'Do you . . . do you really think . . . ?'

'I do indeed.' He gave her a quick kiss. 'Go now, I beg you.
Find me a weapon, then start making a rope. It should be thick
and the knots secure, otherwise it may part and one of us may
break our neck.'

With sudden resolution she took her arms from around him
and turned to the door. 'So be it, then. In the worst event we can
but die together. I pray Allah to protect us.'

As soon as she had left him, Roger dressed. Over his eunuch's
robes he put on his worn travelling coat and, kicking aside the
sandals he had worn during his captivity, drew on his top boots.
Tiptoeing from his room and down the stairs he entered Zanthé's
apartments. Here and there a light had been left burning in one
of the hanging lanterns and, knowing the rooms so well, he had

no difficulty in finding his way to the main apartment. At the far end, to the right, there was a curtained archway that he knew led to Zanthé's sleeping chamber. He had never been in it but now, thrusting aside the curtain, he walked through to her.

The scent of jasmine hung heavily about it and it was furnished with the utmost luxury. But he hardly noticed that. To his relief he saw that Zanthé had already put on black robes similar to those in which he had first seen her and that she and her faithful negress were sitting side by side on the divan, making a rope from a hurriedly assembled assortment of silk materials.

As he entered the room Zanthé stood up. She handed him a scimitar, a curved dagger and the money-belt that had been taken from him. He buckled on the belt and examined the weapons, to find that both were razor-sharp. Then he said, ' We must keep our hands free, so can carry nothing with us. But take your jewels. Find a small bag to put them in, then tie it round your neck by a thick ribbon so that the bag is tight up under your left armpit.'

While Zanthé did as he bade her and drew on a pair of soft leather boots, Gezubb finished the rope to his satisfaction. Together they carried it out on to the balcony. For several minutes he peered over in the semi-darkness until he felt certain that the coast was clear, then he lashed one end of the rope securely to a pillar and put the other end in a loop round Zanthé's body below her arms. Gezubb, her eyes streaming with tears, knelt down and kissed her mistress's feet, while Roger kissed Zanthé on the mouth and told her that she had nothing to fear. Then she threw her legs over the balustrade of the balcony. Roger and Gezubb took the strain on the knotted rope and lowered her to the ground. The rope slackened and she called up to them in a low voice that all was well. Giving the weeping negress a friendly pat on the shoulder, Roger grasped the rope firmly and went down it hand over hand.

When he reached Zanthé, he peered anxiously into the shadows on either side, while old Gezubb pulled up the rope behind them so that it should not be discovered. The moon was up, but low in the sky; so he could not see far by its light. But this side of the great fortress palace had remained secure from attack and every available man was now needed to guard the garden side; so Roger was hoping that even if sentries normally patrolled the seafront they would now have been withdrawn.

The day's battle had long since died down. Occasionally there came a solitary shot or a short burst of musketry as a sentry on one side or the other imagined that he saw enemies approaching out of the darkness. After a few moments Roger took Zanthé's arm and said:

'Come, beloved, we must now to try to find a boat.'

'A boat!' she echoed in surprise. 'Surely it would be rash to leave the harbour and try to make our way along the coast. We might be captured by the British.'

Now that an escape from Djezzar's palace had been forced upon Roger, the fact that the French had not yet taken Acre had, during the past hour, caused him to change his plans completely. As matters stood it would be difficult and dangerous to attempt to reach the French, whereas it should prove comparatively easy to get taken aboard a British ship. Drawing her forward, he said:

'That is just what I intend. We must place ourselves under the protection of Sir Sidney Smith as soon as possible.'

'But,' she objected, 'as a Frenchman they will make you a prisoner-of-war.'

There was no time to start explaining to her the complicated ramifications of the life he had long been leading; so he replied quickly, 'No matter. The English are chivalrous people. They will do me no harm, and placing ourselves in their hands is by far the simplest way of saving you from Djezzar.'

'No, no! You are mistaken,' she cried, pulling back. 'The English are Djezzar's allies. When he learns that I have fled he will be berserk with rage and have a search made for me everywhere. It would be impossible to conceal the fact that I have taken refuge on a British ship. The news that a Turkish lady had been brought aboard by a French Colonel would swiftly spread. Djezzar would demand my return and the English Admiral would have to hand me over.'

'Dearest, he would not,' Roger replied. 'Sir Sidney Smith is a most chivalrous man. When he hears that a blackguard like Djezzar means to force you to marry him you may be sure he will give you his protection.'

'You are wrong,' she argued breathlessly. 'In time of war great Captains cannot afford to allow their actions to be governed by sentiment. Recall what happened in Cairo. The French then regarded the Turks as their allies. To appease the Viceroy, General Bonaparte returned me to him and dismissed you,

although you were one of his favourite officers. In this case you
would not have even that much in your favour. You'd be no
more than an enemy officer who had given himself up. How
could the Admiral refuse to send back to Djezzar a woman whom
he has the Sultan's permission to marry?'

This was a possibility that had not occurred to Roger during
the brief time since he had made his change of plan. The influence
he could exert on Sir Sidney was very much greater than Zanthé
knew. Even so, would it be sufficient to protect her? The British
Commander must place the interests of his country before all
else and, in this case, they were that, in order to inflict as much
damage as possible on the French, Acre must be held for as
long as human endeavours could hold it. A bitter quarrel with
Djezzar might have disastrous results. The Pasha had a reputation not only for cruelty but also for treachery. Rather than
sacrifice more men in desperate assaults, Bonaparte might be
willing to negotiate with him and give him generous terms to
surrender the city. Sir Sidney could not be expected to risk that
for the sake of a woman.

As these thoughts were running through Roger's mind, Zanthé
clung to his arm and implored him, ' Please! Please, my love, let
us go to the French. Only with them will I be safe from Djezzar.
If you take me to the English our escape will be in vain. You
will have sacrificed yourself for me by becoming their prisoner
and within two days at most I shall be in Djezzar's seraglio and
at his mercy.'

' You are right, my sweet,' Roger admitted reluctantly, ' but it
means exposing ourselves to much greater danger. We needs
must pass through the battle zone before we can consider
ourselves safe, and risk being shot at by the sentries on both
sides.'

' I am not frightened. You are so brave that I know you will
get me through.'

Roger knew only too well that this was no question of bravery.
He could only exercise the utmost caution and hope for luck.
But now that he was again in danger his mind had become
extraordinarily alert, and he knew that he could rely on those
faculties of wariness, keen sight, swift decision and violent action
which in the past had served him so well.

Placing her on his left so that his sword-arm was free, he
said, ' We must walk forward at a natural pace. If you see

anyone ahead of us just press my arm but do not speak. If anyone challenges us say that you are a midwife and that I am escorting you to a birth. Should we be attacked do not run away unless I tell you to.'

Heading towards the northern side of the city, they advanced for some two hundred yards alongside the wall of the palace until the wharf on their other side ended. In the narrow street beyond it two men stood talking, but they took no notice of Roger and Zanthé as they passed. A hundred yards further on they came upon the first rubble they had encountered. It was the remains of a house that had collapsed when a cannon ball had carried away one of the main beams. Scrambling over it, they entered a small square. Half a hundred soldiers of the garrison were lying or squatting there. Most of them were utterly exhausted after the day's fighting. It was necessary to pick a way among them, but only one or two wakeful ones muttered at them as they did so. On the far side of the square they entered another street, almost choked with rubble which in some places was fifteen feet high.

In a whisper Zanthé suggested trying another route, but Roger whispered back, ' No, where the way is fairly clear it is certain there will be squads of soldiers posted ready to resist a surprise night attack. No surprise could be achieved through a blocked street like this; so we are much less likely to run into an officer who'll demand to know where we're going, and there won't be any women about to give birth out here.'

Laboriously they climbed the mountain of fallen brick and charred woodwork, then stumbled across its uneven surface for some three hundred yards. Now and then they slipped or tripped and twice ran into rotting bodies. The stench was terrible and the rats, which had multiplied enormously during the siege, peered at them boldly with little, fiery eyes. Roger helped Zanthé as best he could but, as they could see only vaguely where they were putting their feet, both of them fell down several times. At length they scrambled down into an open space with trees in it. It must once have been a garden. There, with bruised knees and scratched hands, they sat down for some minutes to get back their breath.

When they went on again they moved cautiously from tree to tree, pausing in the deeper shadow cast by each to listen and peer forward. From near the far edge of the trees they could see

M

against the night sky a huge ruin and, to the left of it, a row of broken arches. Zanthé whispered, 'That must be all that is left of the great north-east tower; beyond it is the Roman aqueduct.'

A moment later they caught the sound of footseps, so quickly crouched down behind a nearby bush. I proved to be a squad of troops emerging from one of the unblocked entrances to the city. Their boots kicking against fallen stones and bricks, they marched across to the right of the ruined tower. When they had passed, Roger and Zanthé set off towards the aqueduct. To reach it they had to cross another patch of rubble; but it was lighter there than it had been between the remains of houses in the wrecked street, so they got through it more easily. Beyond it rose the aqueduct.

Cautiously approaching the nearest arch, Roger looked through it. At the far end, leaning against the wall, barely a dozen feet away, stood a figure. It was a sentry, but he was keeping watch for anyone approaching the city and his back was turned. With Zanthé behind him Roger tiptoed forward. The thought of killing a man taken unawares had always been repugnant to him, so he reversed his scimitar. At that moment the sentry sensed that there was someone behind him and half turned. Before he could do more Roger struck him hard on the head with the thick, back edge of the curved blade.

The man fell to his knees, but the thickness of his turban had saved him from being knocked senseless. He opened his mouth and there issued from it the beginnings of a shout. Springing past Roger with the swiftness of a panther, Zanthé buried a dagger in the man's neck, reducing his shout to a horrible gurgle.

It shook Roger to see a lovely girl of seventeen kill a man so ruthlessly, but he knew that standards were different in the East and life was held cheap. Moreover he realized that she had probably saved them from capture, so he commended her warmly for her swiftness and courage.

A hundred yards beyond the aqueduct lay the great wall, but that sector of it had been battered to pieces by Bonaparte's artillery. It was now no more than a long, high mound, composed of the earth in its interior and chunks of brickwork that had been its casing. Again they climbed until they were fifty feet above ground-level. As they neared the top of the ridge Roger went down on his hands and knees and whispered to Zanthé to be extra cautious, as he expected there would be an outer line of sentries posted here. In that he proved mistaken and they soon learned the reason.

Having reached the crest they lay side by side for some minutes, looking about them and listening intently, then Roger said, 'I think the coast is clear, so we'll go forward.' Not realizing that she would be exposing herself against the skyline, Zanthé incautiously stood up. Next minute a series of flashes stabbed the darkness, both in front of and behind them, and the stillness was shattred by the reports of half a dozen muskets. In an instant Roger pulled her down and the bullets whizzed and spattered harmlessly to either side of them, but it was a nasty moment.

Being shot at both from front and rear had made it obvious that they were now in no man's land. Roger drew Zanthé back a few yards down the city side of the slope, then they crawled along until they had put some distance between themselves and the place where she had been fired at. Still on their stomachs they wriggled over the ridge and down the far side. As they advanced, the stench of dead bodies increased to nausea-point, and near the bottom of the slope they suddenly slid into a deep ditch that was half full of corpses.

Giving a shudder, Zanthé gulped, 'Allah defend us; this is horrible! Help me out of here, dear one, or I'll be sick.'

Quickly, Roger gave her a hand to scramble up over the far side of the ditch. As he did so, he whispered, 'Crawl twenty yards, then wait for me. This is just what I was hoping to come upon. I may be quite a time, but don't worry.' Then he let himself slide back on to the pile of dead bodies.

The light was only just sufficient for him to make them out individually. They had evidently been killed in a recent assault, as none of them was in a state of actual decay. There were about thirty of them, mostly French, with a few turbaned Muslims among them. Mainly by feel, he formed an idea of their size and it did not take him long to find a body of roughly his own build; but it was no easy matter to get the dead man's uniform from his stiff corpse. To do so, Roger had to use his dagger and cut the cloth in several places. However, he felt that by now Bonaparte's troops had been reduced to such a ragged state that the hacked condition of the uniform would not cause comment. Taking off his own worn travelling coat, he struggled into the tail-coat and breeches of the soldier. He then cut off that part of the hem of the travelling coat in which Bonaparte's despatches had for many months lain rolled up and put the piece of cloth containing them in his pocket.

It was a more difficult matter to find a uniform suitable for Zanthé. Holding his nose now and then to prevent himself from vomiting, he continued to search until he came upon a shortish man who, although much broader than Zanthé, looked about her height. Having got the uniform off this second man, he hunted round till he found two muskets, two bandoliers and a grenadier's shako.

This repulsive labour took him the best part of an hour, but he found Zanthé waiting in patient confidence that he would rejoin her as soon as he could. Loath as she was to exchange her silken robe for the bloodstained uniform, she made no protest about so doing. He put one of the bandoliers over her shoulders and concealed her long hair by tucking it up under the shako, but he kept both muskets to carry himself.

Giving her a kiss, he told her that he now felt their chances of getting into the French lines without being fired upon were much better and, standing up, they walked forward. As they advanced, Roger began to curse loudly in French, using phrases which would give the impression to anyone who heard him that he had lost his way in the darkness.

When they had covered a few hundred yards a voice to their right and a little to their rear suddenly shouted, ' Who are you? And where the hell d'you think you're going? '

Halting, Roger gave one of the muskets to Zanthé and shouted back, ' We're lost. Can you tell us the way to Company Headquarters? '

A tall figure, wearing the same type of shako as Zanthé's, emerged out of the darkness. With the rasping scorn of a typical Sergeant-of-the-line, he bellowed at them, ' Company Headquarters, indeed! Why not ask the way to the " Little Corporal's " headquarters and tell me he's invited you to breakfast? ' Jerking a thumb over his shoulder, he added, ' 'Cos I'm new to the Company, don't think you can put it over on me. Get back to the rest and give a hand with them sandbags, or I'll have the hide off the two of you.'

In the face of this threat Roger swiftly decided that, should he declare himself to be one of Bonaparte's aides-de-camp, he would not be believed and would land himself in a packet of trouble. Adopting the only alternative he set off, with Zanthé beside him, in the direction of the Sergeant had indicated, hoping that they would soon be rid of him. But he turned and followed them until they came upon a platoon of troops, some of whom were filling sandbags and others carrying off the filled sacks through the semi-darkness.

Stacking their muskets with others, they picked up two spades, intending to fill some of the sacks; but the men who had this easier job cursed them and pushed them aside, so they were forced to join the chain of sack carriers. The stronger men were carrying a sack apiece, but a number had been so weakened by lack of nourishing rations that they could manage only a sack between two. This enabled Roger and Zanthé to work together but, even so, it was fortunate that she was a strong-limbed girl, as she had to support one end of the sack and each one seemed to weigh half a ton.

The task of the working party was to build, while darkness lasted, a series of small redoubts for the protection of gun teams, so that the artillery men could bring up their field-pieces closer to the city. But they were never completed. After Roger and Zanthé had been wearily carrying sandbags for over two hours, without any chance having arisen for them to get away undetected, several shots suddenly rang out. They were followed by shouting and a bugle call.

Dropping their burdens, the men ran back to the place where they had stacked their muskets, grabbed them, ran on another twenty yards and jumped down into a trench. Roger and Zanthé lost no time in following them. The shouting increased, there came the noise of hundreds of feet running down the outer slope of what had been the great wall and Roger guessed at once that this must be one of the sorties that the garrison had frequently made during the siege to prevent the French getting a firm hold on any of the breaches they had made in the walls.

Pushing Zanthé behind him, Roger took a firm grip of his musket. The thundering feet came nearer, the shouting of war-cries became deafening. The men on either side of Roger were up on the fire-step of the trench with their muskets levelled. Someone gave the order to fire. Seconds later there came the crash of the volley. It was succeeded by yells and screams, but the attackers still came on. A Muslim of no great size, but with huge, black moustaches and fiery eyes, suddenly appeared above the trench, then leapt down on Roger.

It was his last leap. Roger had never practised bayonet fighting; but he knew that if he failed to kill this kind of fanatic outright he was liable, however seriously wounded his enemy, to be killed himself. With the barrel of his musket he parried the Muslim's spear-thrust, then jabbed the bayonet in below the man's ribs. The Muslim's own weight forced the point up into his heart. He made another feeble stab with his spear, then his eyes rolled up and he was dead.

A second Muslim sprang over Roger's head across the trench, another and yet another followed. In the immediate vicinity, apart from hand-to-hand encounters that were going on to either side some way along the trench, there came a brief lull. But bugles were blaring in all directions and a battery of guns opened somewhere in the rear.

There came the sound of running feet again, this time from the opposite direction. The French infantry, in the reserve trenches had held the attack and were now driving the enemy back. A wounded Muslim tumbled into the trench behind Zanthé. Squirming round, he made a slash at her ankles with his scimitar. Just in time, Roger took the swipe on his bayonet, then jabbed it with all his force into the man's gullet. As he put his foot on the Muslim's chest to wrench the bayonet free from his contracted neck muscles, three or more other Muslims leapt the trench in flight back to the city. Hard on their heels came the French.

The Sergeant, twenty yards away to Roger's left, was yelling: 'Up you go, lads! Get after the swine! No quarter! Give it 'em in the kidneys as they run. Come on now!' He was already out on the parapet and the men on either side were scrambling up over it.

Swiftly, Roger took advantage of the fact that the light was not sufficient for his actions to be seen from any distance. Falling on his knees, he pulled Zanthé down and said, 'Lie on your stomach with an arm twisted behind you. We must sham dead, or the Sergeant will force us to take part in the fighting.'

As she obeyed him, he thrust a hand on to the wound of the nearest dead Muslim, smeared blood from it over his own face and threw himself on his back across Zanthé's legs. He had acted none too soon. The Sergeant was striding along the parapet of the trench, routing out laggards with a spate of curses. But after one glance at Roger's bloody face and the tangle of bodies about him he passed on.

Having given him time to get well away, Roger got to his feet, jumped up on the fire-step and peered about him. It was getting a little lighter, the stars were paling in the east and dawn could not be far off, but he still could not see very far because the smoke from the muskets now helped to limit the field of vision. As far as he could make out, the Muslims had rallied on the crest of what remained of the wall and a fierce conflict was taking place there.

So far, during the long night, he had been buoyed up by the need for being constantly on the alert and the knowledge that, one after the other, he was surmounting the perils that beset him. But now he was suddenly seized with fears and forebodings. They had escaped from Djezzar's palace, come through the city unchallenged, overcome the one sentry who had endangered their flight, secured uniforms which would protect them from being shot on sight by the French and succeeded in reaching the French lines. But now fortune seemed to have deserted them. They had become caught up in the midst of a battle and he could see no way of getting them out of it.

20

The Unholy Land

ROGER was in a terrible quandary. Now that a battle had begun
it seemed certain that both sides would throw in reinforcements
and the struggle in that sector would continue for many hours.
If he and Zanthé continued to sham dead and within a short
time the Muslims re-took the trench they would, as was their
custom, slaughter any wounded and mutilate any dead they
found there. If the Muslims were held at bay French stretcher-
bearers would make their appearance. Having collected the
wounded they would, as they invariably did, search the dead for
any items of value they might have on them. When they found
him and Zanthé apparently unconscious, but still alive, they
would revive them and force them to go forward to join in the
fighting. Worse, should an officer be present he would arrest
them and give them short shrift as cowardly malingerers. Even
should they escape such calamitous attentions they could not possibly remain there shamming dead all day. Heat, thirst, the stench
and the myriads of flies that would be attracted by the wounds of
the dead would force them into making a move in one direction
or the other. But which?

If they went forward they could not escape becoming involved
in the fighting. Against the fanatical Muslims Roger knew he
would have all his work cut out to defend himself. It would be
almost impossible to protect Zanthé at the same time, and the
thought of her being cut down or having a pike thrust through
her body was unbearable. Yet if they made for the rear that
held the worst risk of all. They could not possibly get far without
meeting other troops. As they were unwounded it would at once
be assumed that they had turned tail and run. In Bonaparte's

Army there was only one penalty for deserting one's comrades when in action: it was to be shot out of hand without even the formality of a drumhead court martial.

As Roger wrestled with this problem, a tall soldier came lurching out of the murk towards the trench. Staggering from side to side, he reached its parapet some ten yards to Roger's right, tripped on it and fell headlong into the trench. Roger had seen that the man was carrying something that projected a good two feet above his head. Wondering what it could be, he scrambled along to find out. As he came nearer and realized what the object was, he gave a cry of delight. The man was a giant Sergeant of Grenadiers, and he was clutching to his chest a captured Turkish standard.

The Sergeant lay twisted sideways. From his mouth a stream of blood gushed, then he was quite still. Obviously he had received a mortal internal wound and his fall into the trench had finished him. Stooping, Roger took the standard from the clutching fingers. The lower few feet of the pole had been broken off, but the standard itself was intact. It was not a flag, but a flat, diamond-shaped sheet of silver cut out to form an intricate design of Arabic letters. It was surmounted by a crescent lying on its back, from which hung a fine horse-tail.

Carrying it back to Zanthé, he exclaimed, ' My sweet, your prayers to Allah for our safety have been answered. See, he has sent us this. It will prove our safe-conduct to the rear of the French lines. We have only to tell everyone we meet that we have been ordered to take it to Bonaparte.'

Without losing a moment they climbed out over the back of the trench and set off. But they were not yet out of danger. The guns of the city were replying to the French artillery and were trained on reinforcements that were hurrying forward. They had covered only fifty yards when a cannon ball bounded past within two feet of Zanthé. There was little cover but, zigzagging from side to side, they ran on, taking such advantage of the ground as they could.

Dawn had now come. Ahead of them they saw a company of infantry coming towards them at the double. Roger raised the captured standard high above his head and cried, '*Vive la France! Vive Bonaparte!*' The nearest officer grinned and waved his sword in reply. The men broke into cheers as they streamed past them.

Another five minutes and they were out of range of the guns. Pulling up, they sat down on some rocks to regain their breath. Laughing, they hugged one another, then Roger said :

' I have as yet had little chance to think of your situation while with the French Army, but I count it unlikely that there will be other women at headquarters. For your protection it seems best that I should give out that you are my fiancée.'

Lifting his hand, she kissed it then gave him her most ravishing smile. ' The will of Allah has made you my dear lord, and I am happy that you should wish everyone to know it.'

Soon afterwards they set off at a walk and, although the strain of the past night was now telling heavily on them, they met with no difficulties. Everywhere they were greeted with cheers and, after many enquiries, learned the whereabouts of the General-in-Chief's headquarters. He had come up from Mount Carmel to direct the battle and had taken up his position on a slight rise about three miles from the city.

As they trudged up the slope, they saw that a marquee had been set up for him and that he was standing in front of it with his telescope to his eye, surrounded by his Staff, several of whom were mounted ready to gallop off with his orders to the different Divisions and Brigades. Not thinking it fitting to approach him while he was making his decisions, Roger halted some thirty yards from the edge of the group, then he and Zanthé turned to look back across the plain at the city from which they had escaped.

The whole field of battle lay spread before them. Full daylight had come and the sun glinted on the domes and minarets of the great fortress city. Parts of it were wreathed in smoke which was stabbed every moment by the flash of cannon. The still-standing towers stood out sharply against the blue sky and the whole was framed by the background of the bay, where lay the British frigates and gunboats. They too were partially obscured by smoke and rows of little white puffs kept on bursting from them as they fired broadside after broadside at the attackers. In three places where breaches had been made in the walls solid columns of infantry were carrying out assaults. Dotted about the plain were batteries of guns and dozens of other regiments, awaiting orders to enter the battle. The French Army numbered close on ten thousand men and was supported by several thousand auxiliaries: Copts, Druses, Armenians and other Christian warriors whom Bonaparte had enlisted in his war against the Turks. Even at that distance the roar of the guns and the constant discharge of thousands of firearms came to them like the rolling of thunder. To witness such a vast assembly—white, brown and black—which, including the garrison and the British ships' crews, amounted to some fifty thousand men engaged in conflict, was an unforgettable spectacle.

Roger's gaze was still roving over the amazing panorama when Zanthé touched his arm. An officer was calling to them and Bonaparte was beckoning. Side by side, they walked quickly forward. When they arrived within ten feet of him Roger stood stiffly to attention and lowered the standard until its crescent top touched the ground.

'*Mon brave,* I thank you,' Bonaparte said loudly. 'Where did you capture this standard and when?'

'Near the north-east tower, *mon Général,* shortly before dawn this morning,' replied Roger promptly.

Bonaparte gave him a closer look and said, 'I know your face. Where have I spoken with you before?'

Roger gave a sudden laugh. '*Mon Général,* you should know it. I am your Colonel Breuc.'

The Corsican's big, dark eyes widened and he exclaimed, 'Breuc! By all that's wonderful! Where in thunder have you sprung from?'

'For the past seven weeks I have been a prisoner in Acre; but last night, with the aid of my companion, I succeeded in escaping.'

'Bonaparte's glance turned to Zanthé's dirt-smeared face above the far-too-large uniform coat, the shoulders of which sagged halfway to her elbows, and he frowned. 'If you were issued with that garment I'll crime your Quartermaster-Sergeant. No soldier could be expected to fight his best in so cumbersome a uniform.'

'We took our uniforms off the dead,' Roger answered for her, 'and my companion is not a soldier of your Army. You will recall the reason for your sending me away from Cairo. Allow me to present the lady in the case—the widow of the Commander of the Turkish garrison.

'Breuc, your audacity astounds me! To have captured both her and a Turkish standard you must be the Devil in person. But does this mean that instead of obeying my instructions you followed her to Acre?'

'No, *mon Général*, far from it. But, alas, I never reached France. I was taken first by Barbary Corsairs, escaped, was recaptured by the English and brought to Acre as a prisoner by Sir Sidney Smith. I am, though, happy to report that I succeeded in preventing that with which you entrusted me from falling into the hands of the enemy.'

'God be praised for that!'

'I was about to add,' Roger went on, 'that this lady is not my captive. She left Acre of her free will, and has done me the honour to promise to become my wife.'

Turning back to Zanthé, Bonaparte smiled. 'Then I congratulate you. For your husband you will have one of the bravest and most resourceful officers in my Army. What is your name, madame?'

She went down on one knee. 'May it please you, *Monsieur le Général*, I am called Zanthé. Although I am a stranger to you, it is possible that you have heard of my mother. She was a Mademoiselle Dubucq de Rivery. She later became the Sultana of *Son Majesté Impérial le Sultan Abd-ul-Hamid*.'

Again Bonaparte's eyes opened wide. He had not yet become used to Princesses kneeling to him. Stepping swiftly forward, he took both her hands and raised her to her feet exclaiming, 'I have indeed heard of Your Highness's mother! When young, in Martinique, Her Majesty and my wife were cousins and close friends.' Then, with his invariable courtesy towards women, he added, 'I am honoured to have Your Highness as a guest in my camp. We are but rough soldiers, and at the moment very badly found. But you shall lack for nothing with which it is possible for us to provide you.' Turning back to Roger, he said with a smile:

'A moment ago I erred. It is not *Madame* I should have congratulated but you, *mon brave Breuc*. And to have you back rejoices me. You are, of course, reinstated as one of my aides-de-camp and in my next Order to the Army I shall make mention of your return with this standard. It is the seventeenth that we have captured from the Turks.'

As Roger thanked him, he spoke to his step-son, who was standing just behind him, then lifted his telescope to make another survey of the battle.

Young Eugène de Beauharnais bowed to Zanthé, shook Roger warmly by the hand and led them round the side of the marquee. On the slope behind it thirty or forty tents had been erected. Showing Zanthé into one, he said he would send a servant with water for her to wash and a light meal, and suggested that she should then get some sleep while he sent to Main Headquarters for some more suitable clothes for her. Roger he took to a larger tent, shared by the aides-de-camp, and told a servant to look after him.

With water from a canvas bucket, Roger washed the blood from his face and hands then ate a little fruit, washed it down with two glasses of wine, stripped off his outer clothes and lay down on the camp cot. Although it was barely twelve hours since Zanthé had come weeping to his room with the news that Djezzar meant to force her to marry him, that now seemed days away and he was desperately tired. Her plight had prevented him taking her aboard a British ship and so securing his longed-for passage home. But he knew that they had both been incredibly lucky to have come through the night unscathed, and Bonaparte's reception of them could not have been kinder.

His thoughts turned to the future and he recalled the heartiness of Bonaparte's congratulations on his having become affianced to an Imperial Princess. When suggesting that he should present her as his fiancée he had intended no more than the adoption of a measure which would ensure that no other man attempted to force his attentions on her; but her reply had implied that she had expected nothing less of him. He realized that, now she had cut herself off entirely from her own people, he was responsible for her. Previously the idea of marrying her had never entered his head, but now he had to consider doing so. And why should he not? She was utterly devoted to him, intelligent, charming, passionate and one of the most beautiful girls he had ever seen. Still musing over this thought, he fell asleep.

It was evening when he awoke, and shortly afterwards Eugène entered the tent. He brought with him the uniform of an officer of Chasseurs, who had been about Roger's build and had died of wounds a few hours earlier, and one of the scarfs, that distinguished aides-de-camp, for Roger to wear round his arm. He said that the man he had sent to Main Headquarters had rummaged through several chests there which contained loot from Jaffa and had found in them a number of rich, silk garments, jewelled girdles and sandals. These he had sent to Her Highness's tent; he had also raked up some spare shirts, a razor and other kit for Roger. Roger thanked him and asked the result of the day's battle.

Eugène shook his head and replied, 'Since dawn there has been most desperate fighting and rumour has it that we have lost several of our best men. But the fighting continues and for the first time our troops have managed to force their way into the streets of Acre. My step-father is throwing everything in. His hope is to overcome all resistance before the reinforcements brought by the Turkish Fleet can be landed. But whether he will succeed in that still lies in the lap of the gods. You are to sup with him and he will probably give his views then on our prospects.'

When Roger had put on the uniform of the dead officer of Chasseurs he went along to Zanthé's tent. He found her again dressed as a woman and the silk garments that had been brought to her did not, owing to their flowing nature, appear unsuitable. There was a young Arab woman with her, who had been brought from a nearby village to be her servant. When he had kissed her she asked him if he could come to her that night, but he shook his head:

'Alas no, my dearest. For the time being we must be most circumspect. Bonaparte has displayed a high regard for you. I could not spend the nights here undetected and discovery would lead to a scandal that would destroy your prestige in his eyes. We dare not risk that. I will seek your sweet company whenever possible, but until conditions are more favourable we must restrain as best we may our impatience to enjoy love's revels.'

After spending some time with her, talking over the excitements of the past night, he went to the marquee. There he was surrounded by a dozen of his old friends, all of whom slapped him on the back, congratulated him on his escape and wanted to hear what had happened to him. However, after the friendly welcome he soon realized that the general atmosphere was one of gloom and learned the reason. Generals Rambout and Langier had both been killed that day, Lannes had been so terribly wounded that his life was despaired of and Duroc had just been carried in with a wound in the thigh.

At supper Bonaparte placed Roger on his right and asked him for an account of his doings. Roger gave a fictitious description of his capture by Corsairs, his weeks of slavery in Tripoli, as a prisoner in a British ship and, more recently, in Acre. Contrary to custom, Bonaparte listened without interrupting and made only one comment, 'I see you have had your hair cut.'

During the past seven weeks Roger's hair had grown a good

inch. It now stood up stiffly all over his head and, where before his previous ordeals had caused it to become prematurely grey only at the temples, the new hair was mainly white as a result of the terror he had experienced during his first day and night in Djezzar's palace. But he did not mind that, as older men still used powder on their hair in England. With a laugh, he replied:

'It was cut for me, but I do not resent that: it is much more sanitary.'

'You are right,' Bonaparte nodded, then added with a frown, 'You have no doubt been told that there is a serious outbreak of plague inflicting the Army?'

'I had, *mon Général*, and was greatly distressed to hear it.'

'It has already robbed me of six hundred men,' Bonaparte went on gloomily, 'and as we have no hope of receiving reinforcements I can ill afford them.'

After the meal Bonaparte said nothing of the battle. Obviously much upset by the day's losses, and particularly about Lannes and Duroc having been wounded, he said that he was going to bed. But before leaving the mess for his sleeping quarters he drew Roger aside and asked in a low voice:

'My letters. What did you do with them?'

Producing the part of the hem of his travelling coat that he had cut off, Roger replied, 'They are still stitched up in this, *mon Général*. I was loath to destroy them as long as there was any hope of my getting through to France, but the Fates were against me.'

Bonaparte nodded and pulled his ear. 'You have nothing with which to reproach yourself. No man could have done more. See Bourrienne in the morning, give him such intelligence as you can and he will inform you of our situation.'

Next morning, after a visit to Zanthé, Roger repaired to a tent that had been set apart as an office for Bourrienne. On the previous evening he had thought that the *Chef de Cabinet* looked far from well, and his friend told him something of the trials that had seriously undermined the health of the Army during the past three months.

The march from Suez across the desert of Sinai had been as bad as the original advance from Alexandria. The sufferings from thirst of everyone had been terrible and conditions had been little better while coming up the coast. The weary infantry had often openly cursed their own senior officers because, being mounted, the demands on the latter's endurance were not so great. Yet in spite of great reluctance to embark on the campaign, and terrible privations during it, the fighting spirit of the Army had remained unimpaired.

Apart from their capture of El Arish and Jaffa, and exposure to death or wounds for seven weeks under the walls of Acre, that spirit had been most gloriously displayed in a brief campaign against Abdullah, Pasha of Damascus. Early in April they had learned that the Pasha was assembling an Army, estimated at thirty thousand strong, for the relief of Acre. Bonaparte, with his usual aptitude for taking time by the forelock, at once despatched a force to attack he Turkish Army before it was fully organized. Junot led a reconnaissance in force with five hundred men, and Kléber's Division followed. On the road to Nazareth, Junot was surrounded by several thousand Nablousian warriors, but drove them off with terrible losses and captured five standards.

The Pasha's main Army had, in the meantime, crossed the Jordan and when Kléber, with his three thousand men, reached the base of Mount Tabor, he found himself opposed to at least eight times his own number. The French fought in square until on every side it had a breast-high rampart of dead horses, camels, Mamelukes, Syrians, Turks and Arnauts. After six hours of heroic resistance Bonaparte—from a feeling that Kléber might get into difficulties—arrived unexpectedly on the scene with Bon's Division. Forming it into two squares behind that of Kléber he surprised and enveloped the enemy, bringing utter destruction on the Pasha's Army and capturing his camp, four hundred camels and a great quantity of booty.

But gallant General Bon was dead and so was their beloved Chief Engineer, the one-legged General Caffarelli. On the 9th April he had been inspecting a trench and the men there had warned him that to show any part of himself was to risk being shot by an Albanian sniper. He had been careless and received a bullet in the elbow. His arm had been amputated but he had failed to recover. Bourrienne wept as he related to Roger how, eighteen days later, their gifted friend had died in his arms.

Bourrienne estimated that they had lost three thousand French troops from death in action, serious wounds, capture and death from plague; so the backbone of the Army of Syria had been reduced by nearly a third of its original strength. But if Acre could be captured they would not have suffered in vain. Bonaparte had already planned his march on Damascus and Aleppo and his prospects would be brighter than they had ever been.

The Turkish rule was so oppressive that many Chieftains in Palestine, Mesopotamia and Asia Minor were in secret negotiations with French agents and had expressed their readiness, when Bonaparte could march on Constantinople, to throw off the Turkish yoke and join him. There were also the Christian subjects of the Sultan, all of whom were ready to welcome the French. The warriors of these peoples totalled near a hundred thousand men. At present they were sitting on the fence. But once Acre had fallen Bonaparte would have a vast army at his disposal and, with his organizing genius, there could be little doubt that Constantinople and the whole of the Turkish Empire would fall like a ripe plum into his hands.

'He has never failed in anything he has yet attempted,' Roger remarked; 'so I cannot believe he will in this, unless it be through something beyond his control, such as the spreading of the plague.'

Bourrienne nodded. 'It is from that we have most to fear. But apart from it the odds against us are damnably heavy. By now we must have killed many thousands of Djezzar's men and we have taken many prisoners. Yesterday alone eight hundred of them were brought in. But the garrison is still as numerous as a swarm of ants, and I am told that the reinforcements, which by now must be landing from the Turkish Fleet, number twelve thousand. A matter, too, that causes me great anxiety is that we are running short of gunpowder. It is bad enough that, for weeks past, we have had to rely on the British to supply us with cannon balls; but there is now way in which we can secure powder from them.'

'How mean you,' Roger asked, 'that they supply us with cannon balls?'

'We ran out long ago,' Bourrienne replied, with a sad smile, 'but they appear to have unlimited supplies. They will even fire on our men when a few of them go down to the seashore to bathe. Our little man was prompt as ever to think of a way to remedy our shortage. He offered the troops ten sous for every ball they could bring in. So there is now a nightly hunt for British shot and next day we fire it back at Acre.'

After a moment Bourrienne went on, 'We would have been in Acre, as we were in Jaffa, within a week, had it not been for those accursed English. They have good grounds for having adopted the bulldog as their symbol. The six hundred gunners whom, as we have learned from prisoners, they sent ashore to strengthen the defences have proved the rock upon which our assaults have been shattered. Their Commander is said to be no more than a Commodore, but he deserves to be a High Admiral. He is as courageous as their other seadogs, but far superior to them in brain. By using his intelligence he has caused us endless trouble. Aboard one of his ships he has a printing press, and he has used to run off thousands of leaflets. Some of them are distributed through Arab agents bought with British gold among our own troops. They are to the effect that Bonaparte is giving their lives not for France but only to advance his own ambitions. Others, distributed among the Christians of the Lebanon, contain a version of the proclamation issued by our General within a few hours of his first entering Alexandria. You will recall that he said in it that he regarded the Mohammedan religion as more sensible than the Christian.'

Roger grinned. 'So it has become a boomerang, eh? Has this propaganda had any serious effect?'

'Naturally. It has disturbed the minds of the troops and has had a most adverse effect on the Christian tribes, on whom we have been counting as our future allies. Our little man was so enraged by it that he issued an order stating that Sir Smith is mad, and that anyone found in possession of pamphlets issued by him would be liable to severe punishment. At that, though you'd scarce credit it, Sir Smith sent a flag of truce ashore challenging the General-in-Chief to a duel.'

'What reply was sent to him?' Roger asked with amused interest.

Bourrienne shrugged. 'The English are mad. Everyone knows it. No man of any other nation would have even thought of such a thing. Bonaparte naturally replied that he had many other matters to engage his attention. But, with a touch of humour, he added that if, at any time, Sir Smith could produce Marlborough to fight him, that would be a different matter.'

They then talked of the European situation, as far as they knew it. Roger could give only such information as he would have picked up as a prisoner when captured off Malta by Sir Sidney Smith in March. He gave a sketchy account of the Neapolitan war, adding that he understood that the French had finally subdued

Naples early in February and that England, Russia and Turkey had formed another Coalition against France.

Bourrienne's information, from neutrals and blockade-runners, was little better, but he could add that Austria had joined the Coalition and had declared war on France on March 12th. Rumour had it that the French were now having great difficulty in keeping control of the population in the recently created Republican States in Italy. No despatch from the Directors had reached Bonaparte since March. In this last despatch, they had given him the choice of striking at either Constantinople or India; but, as it had left Paris as far back as November, such news as it contained was already stale.

This exchange of views over, Roger went out into the brilliant May sunshine. The assaults on Acre were being continued with unflagging vigour and the General-in-Chief had gone up to the front to supervise them personally; so Roger was free to visit Zanthé. He found her outside her tent. A small table had been procured for her and she was sitting at it playing against herself the oldest paper game in the world, a form of noughts and crosses.

Not far from her two Mamelukes stood, leaning on their weapons. When Roger asked what they were doing, she replied, 'General Bonaparte has detached six of them from his regiment of Mamelukes to act as a guard of honour for me. I am greatly touched by this attention; but, alas, it is going to make it still more difficult for you to come to me at night without your visits becoming common knowledge.'

'I fear it is,' he agreed. 'We must do our best to remain patient.' As he had received no orders, he enjoyed a picnic lunch with her and remained talking to her for most of the day. Then, as the shadows lengthened, he went to the big marquee.

It was May 10th. For thirty-six hours the all-out assault had now been raging. The troops who had penetrated to the streets of Acre the previous afternoon had been halted and cut off. Two hundred of them had taken refuge in a mosque and held it all through the night. Sir Sidney Smith, who had come ashore to take personal charge of the city's defence, had generously saved this little party from massacre by forcing the Turks to allow it to withdraw; but that had put an end to the French penetration of the city. The Turkish troops who had been brought by sea were now taking up positions to defend the breaches made in the walls, and the French had suffered so severely that Bonaparte had decided to put a stop to the assaults.

In the French camp there were now twelve hundred wounded, but the British Squadron, which had become an integral part of the city defences, dared not leave its moorings; so the coastal waters from a few miles south of Acre were no longer under its control, and many of the French wounded were carried down in litters to the little port of Haifa, from which they were being sent by ship to Egypt. The indomitable Lannes still miraculously clung to life. He had already been severely wounded in the assault on Jaffa and on the previous day, when twice wounded, his Grenadiers had had to drag him out of the battle by his feet. The doctors said of him that his bones must be made of rubber, as it seemed that when hit by musket balls they bent but rarely broke. Bonaparte ordered a special litter to be made for him which sixteen Turkish prisoners were to carry in teams of eight.

Between the 11th and 18th of May the siege continued, but with less intensity; so Roger was not called on to run much risk in delivering orders from the General-in-Chief to officers commanding units down in the plain. Zanthé slept through the hottest hours of the day and spent the rest of the time sitting outside her tent. Some French books had been found for her to read and in the evenings a little Court, composed of Roger and friends whom he had introduced to her, surrounded her. All of them, having been deprived for so long of female society, found delight in her company.

It was on the evening of the 18th that Bonaparte sent for Roger and said, 'Breuc, have a comfortable litter made for Her Highness, and take as many prisoners to carry it as you wish. Tomorrow she is to set off to Egypt and, as I shall not require you on our march, you have my leave to accompany her.'

'On our march! . . .' Roger exclaimed. 'Can you mean . . . ?'

The Corsican nodded. 'Yes. You will speak of this to no one. So far, I have told only Bourrienne and a few members of my personal Staff who will have to make the necessary preparations. If it got about that I mean to retreat, the whole garrison of Acre might sally forth and overwhelm our rearguard. But on the night of the 20th I intend to break off the siege.'

'It was a terrible decision to have to take,' Roger murmured.

'I had no alternative. Scattered about Egypt we now have only some ten thousand troops, and a despatch from Menou informs me that trouble is brewing there. In high summer, too, conditions will be favourable for an invasion and I cannot doubt that the Turks will despatch a great Army by sea for an attempt to re-conquer the country. If I do not return there all my labours to make it a prosperous French colony will have been in vain and, with the loss of the ports, we would lose our one hope of receiving reinforcements.'

'You think then that there is still a chance that the Directory may send them?'

'One can but hope. The Brest Fleet under Admiral Bruix is still intact. With that of the Spaniards it could form a formidable armament and stand a good chance of bringing troops round to us through the Mediterranean. For months now I have been sending despatch after despatch, urging this course upon the Directors. It may be that they are so eaten up with jealousy of me that, rather than aid me to further triumphs, they would sooner see a French Army founder here. But it may be that I am unjust and that all my despatches have been captured by the accursed English.'

'They have proved a most ugly thorn in our side here,' Roger commented.

'You are right there. Had it not been for them, I should have been in Acre weeks ago and by now halfway to Constantinople. Do you know that the Sheiks have already offered me the keys of Damascus? Could we but advance the whole of Syria and the Lebanon would rise to aid us. But it is not to be. One man has robbed me of my greatest ambition. Nelson did no more than cut us off in Egypt, and there I proved that we could be self-supporting. But this Sir Smith has dealt me a vital blow. To my mind, he far surpasses any other English Commander. He has shown not only the greatest tenacity but the highest intelligence in handling his very limited forces, and in addition he has throughout maintained a most chivalrous attitude towards our wounded and our prisoners. Whatever his future may be he must now go down in history as the man who changed the fate of the whole Eastern world.'

As Roger left the tent with Bonaparte's generous tribute ringing in his ears he could not help recalling the contempt with which the British in Palermo had spoken of Sir Sidney Smith, dubbing him 'The Swedish Knight' and 'The Great Plenip'. He wondered if Nelson was still there, bewitched by Emma and dancing attendance on the despicable King and Queen of the Two Sicilies. But of one thing there could be no question. Sir Sidney had inflicted on Bonaparte his first defeat. Time was to show that on land no other British Commander, with the exception of Wellington, would ever defeat him.

On the following day Roger and Zanthé set off southward. He rode beside her litter, they were escorted by her Mameluke guard who kept in order the prisoners who acted as bearers and the rear was brought up by two camels carrying Zanthé's Arab woman servant and the baggage. That afternoon they crossed the river Kishon and in the evening made camp on the far slope of Mount Carmel. No longer fearing that his actions would be reported to Bonaparte to the detriment of Zanthé's reputation, Roger and his beautiful mistress spent a night of delight together.

During the next three days they followed the coast along the edge of the plain of Sharon, reaching Jaffa on the evening of the 22nd. Roger would have liked to press on, but the bearers were by then in very poor shape. As prisoners, their rations for the past ten days had been barely sufficient to keep life in their bodies. Most of them were suffering from dysentery and three, from complete exhaustion, had already had to be left at the wayside with a flask of water to fend for themselves. Soon after leaving Jaffa they would be entering the hundred miles of almost uninhabited coast with its long stretches of desert, where the going would be hard and water scarce; so before proceeding on this worst part of the journey Roger decided to give his people two days' rest.

While on the march there had always been other little caravans, mostly carrying wounded, within sight and, on the first day they spent in a little camp they made among some palm trees outside the town, the number of these increased considerably. On the second day the advance guard of the retreating Army arrived, and with it Bonaparte.

Food of all kinds had already reached famine prices; but Roger went into the town hoping still to be able to buy with gold some boxes of figs, dates or other preserved foods that would not be affected by the heat. In the *muski* he ran into Eugène de Beauharnais, bent on the same errand. That normally cheerful young man was looking exceptionally glum, and Roger soon learned the reason.

There had been only a few sailing boats in which to send off sick and wounded from Haifa, but here there were many more and, with his indefatigable energy, Bonaparte was arranging for his hundreds of casualties to be shipped to Egypt. But it was not that which so perturbed Eugène. His step-father had visited the hospitals, urging everyone there who was capable of standing to get up and go aboard one of the ships in the harbour, rather than remain to be captured by the Turks. He had then gone into the plague ward and had spoken to the poor wretches there. It was a noble gesture but Eugène condemned its rashness, declaring that should his beloved step-father fall a victim to the plague the retreating Army would founder and be lost without his leadership.

Roger agreed with him. Then, during the few minutes that they continued to talk, Eugène urged Roger to set off from Jaffa with as little delay as possible. He said that, as soon as the retreat began, the Nablousian tribesmen had come down from the mountains in hordes, to harass the columns and cut off stragglers. The General-in-Chief had decreed a policy of scorching the earth. Every village and all crops were being burnt, and the wells stopped up, so that the Army would leave a great area of desolation behind it. But it was feared that it would not entirely stop these fierce irregulars and the pursuing Turkish cavalry.

Eugène's warning determined Roger to make a start that evening, but when he got back to his small camp he was met by terrible news. One of the Turkish prisoners had been vomoting and the others declared there could be no doubt that he had caught the plague. He had been carried some distance apart and a friend of his had volunteered to stay behind and do what could be done for him.

But that was not the end of the matter. Zanthé, having been brought up in Constantinople, which was rarely free from cases of plague, knew a certain amount about the disease. She assured Roger that the pestilence was not catching through the breath nor, if care were exercised, through touch, but was conveyed by fleas that lived on animals.

Roger was aware that the Arabs had inherited the knowledge of the ancient civilizations and that, in many respects, their medicine was still in advance of European doctoring. He accepted without question what Zanthé said and, when she insisted that one of their camels must be the carrier and that both of them should be killed, he felt that not to follow her advice would be flying in the face of Providence.

He had the camels taken away and slaughtered; but only with great reluctance, for he was now faced with the problem of how they were to proceed. Zanthé's woman could walk with the men; but they would need the tent to shelter them from the blazing sun during the middle of the day, and the spare litter-bearers, after their spells of carrying Zanthé, would collapse if they then had to take up burdens of food and water which, to start with must be sufficient for several days' journey.

He still had enough money on him to buy a score of camels at their normal price, but in the present circumstances he doubted if it would buy a couple. He proved right. Going into the town again, he spent the whole evening endeavouring to buy animals; but he could find no sellers until at last he came upon a peasant whom he persuaded to part with his donkey for five gold pieces.

It was by then too late to start that night; so they set off very early next morning. Even so, they now found themselves in the midst of the Army. Only a few of the regiments had been halted in Jaffa, to assist the engineers in destroying its defences. The main body had been ordered to reach Egypt with as little delay as possible, and was taking advantage of the cool of the night for the greater part of the marches.

The condition of both officers and men was pitiful. Their uniforms were faded, torn and blood-stained, and every third man had a bandage round his head or face or his arm in a sling. The horses of those who were mounted were skin and bone, as were also those which drew guns or light vehicles. The bands no longer had the strength to play. The only words uttered were curses and in quarrels over water. There were still many seriously wounded among them, either being carried in hammocks and reclining on the water and ration carts. Attempt was no longer made to march in formation. They trudged blindly on in ragged little groups, in couples and singles. All discipline had ceased to exist.

It was now less than a month until the longest day in the year. The sun rose each morning soon after five o'clock. By nine it was blazing down from a brassy sky; by midday the barren land became as hot as the inside of a furnace. During the hours of intolerable heat the troops threw themselves down on the burning sands and lay as though dead until well into the afternoon. They suffered most terribly from sunburn and frequently some poor wretch would go off his head with sunstroke.

On the fourth day out from Acre an order was passed down from the General-in-Chief that the wounded must be everybody's first consideration. All mounted men, officers included and of whatever rank, were to give up their horses to the sick or injured. For two days past Roger had not been feeling very well, so he was most loath to give up his mount; but since he had to do so he felt that Zanthé was *his* first consideration. They had lost three more bearers, which had reduced their number to nine, and it was a pitiful sight to see six of them at a time staggering along with the litter. Should many more of them collapse the litter would have to be abandoned, and he then intended to mount Zanthé on his horse. Although she was not wounded he knew that no Frenchman would cavil at her riding it. So to keep the animal with them he made her mount it there and then, which also relieved the wretched bearers and gave them a better chance of surviving as they then had only to carry the baggage in the litter.

Zanthé's hard Mameluke guard were bearing up well and, although Roger had to walk himself, he felt decidedly better. Next day, however, he developed a splitting headache. By midday he knew that he was running a high temperature and he assumed that his wretched state could be put down to a touch of sunstroke; but he was puzzled by a stiffness that seemed to be affecting his limbs and the strong light began to hurt his eyes.

When these disorders came quite suddenly upon him he was lying beside Zanthé in the shade of the tent. Seeing his distress she anxiously questioned him, then, undoing his tunic, slid her hands up to his armpits. Under the left one her fingers felt a lump. Her great tawny eyes distended with terror, but she did not cry out. With a sob in her voice, she said:

' My love! My love! It is useless to conceal it from you. Four to six days is the usual period for the horror to reveal itself after one has been infected. Oh, that accursed camel! A flea from it has given you the plague.'

21
Plague and the Great
Temptation

HAD it not been for Zanthé there is little doubt that at the age of thirty-one Roger would have died in Palestine. During that terrible retreat the French Army went to pieces. The men fought among themselves for water. In many cases wounded officers who were being carried in litters were abandoned at night by the bearers, who stole the supply of water that had been allotted to the officers, and their valuables. Anyone showing symptoms of the plague was driven away by his comrades and left to die alone or be butchered by the Arabs. As the French retreated, setting fire to every village, farm and field of crops that they left behind them, the numbers of desperate, homeless Arabs seeking vengeance constantly increased. Like the carrion crows that hung in clouds on the rear and flanks of the Army, bands of these Arabs pressed on it night and day, forcing it to keep to the shore and falling upon any small parties rash enough to seek shelter or water by leaving the main, straggling line of march.

The course of Roger's affliction was no exception to the rule. First the rather seedy feeling for a day or so, recovery to normal spirits for about forty-eight hours then, almost without warning, the onset of stiffness, blinding headaches, nausea and rise in temperature. He was overcome so swiftly that he would not have been capable even of sending the Mamelukes among the retreating Army to try to find a doctor or a senior officer who would at least have ensured that he would not be abandoned by the road-side, and but for Zanthé that would have been his fate.

Neither could a European woman have saved him, however great her courage and devotion, for the Mamelukes and Turks would certainly have made off with the water and left her to die with him. As it was, when she told them that the *Effendi* was smitten with the pestilence they accepted the situation with the fatalism of Orientals and, through a mixture of devotion and fear, continued to accept her orders. The devotion of the Mamelukes was partly inspired by Bonaparte's having entrusted her safety to them; since, as a great leader of fighting men, he had inspired an almost religious respect in them, and partly because she was a beautiful woman. The element of fear, which equally affected the Turkish prisoners, was due to the fact that, as the daughter of a Sultan, she had in her veins the Blood of the Prophet; so to abandon her would have meant certain hell-fire in the Hereafter.

She explained to them that plague was neither infectious nor contagious, unless pus from a plague boil came in contact with a scratch or open wound. She then had Roger lifted into the litter and carried down to the seashore. There, while with glassy, staring eyes he twisted and moaned, she got his clothes off and had the men in turns support his head as he lay in the creamy surf. By this means she reduced the heat of his fevered body until the sun went down. She made them strip, too, search all their garments minutely, in case they were harbouring a flea, wash them in the sea and bathe themselves.

All night and for most of the two days that followed Roger was delirious. For a part of the time he raved in English but, as he had spoken and thought in French for a long time past, broken sentences in that tongue came equally often from his cracked lips and at times he shouted in Turkish. His eyes were red and inflamed, his tongue swollen and covered with white fur. From time to time he vomited and, although Zanthé kept him for hours each day immersed in the surf, he broke out in profuse sweats when taken from it. On the third day he was prostrate with exhaustion, but Zanthé still had hopes for him because he was constipated and that, in a case of plague, she knew to be a good sign.

In addition to her intense anxiety about Roger she had another. The shattered Army was, all this time, trudging past them on the track a hundred yards away. Bonaparte's policy of scorching the earth might delay the pursuit by regular Turkish cavalry, but the merciless Arabs would, she knew, be close on the heels of the French rearguard and, even should they spare her, she felt sure they would murder Roger. In consequence, on the morning of May 30th she decided that they must abandon the little camp they had made by the seashore and move on.

But when she examined Roger soon after dawn she found that the bubo under his arm was so swollen that it was ready to burst. As he was conscious she had two of the Mamelukes hold him down, then lanced the great swelling with her sharp dagger, squeezed out the pus and washed out the cavity with seawater. He was then put in the litter and they took the road again.

After the operation he sank into a coma and all day Zanthé feared that any moment he might die from weakness, but when they made camp that evening he was conscious and able to mutter a few words. Again they bathed him in the sea and for the first time in four nights he slept. Next day he was a little easier and, provided his heart held out, it began to look as if he would pull through.

The halt of two days had been a welcome respite for the prisoners and the seabathing had helped to recruit their strength, so they were now making better progress. But, by then, their store of water was running low. The seawater thereabouts had an exceptionally high degree of salt and, if allowed to dry on Roger after his immersions, it tended to clog his pores and prevent him from perspiring. As he could not be rubbed down hard Zanthé had to sponge off the salt with a moistened cloth, and this had eaten into their limited supplies of water. By June 3rd their need had become desperate so, at sundown that evening, she sent four of the Mamelukes out with orders to get water, even if they had to kill for it.

Some hours later they returned in triumph with several gallons of water, and they had not had to rob others in order to obtain the precious liquid. In certain places along the coast, near the southern end of the Syrian desert, there are small sand-dunes, composed of such fine sand that the heavy rains in winter are absorbed by them as though they were giant sponges. Later, when the dry weather comes, their crust hardens; but it can be pierced with a stick and, even after many months, water will trickle out. The Mamelukes had recognized some dunes as this type of natural reservoir and laboriously, but joyfully, filled from them the empty waterskins they carried.

After a further four days' march they reached the Roman

ruins of Pelusium. At the nearby village on the shore Zanthé succeeded in hiring a native dhow, so that they could make the remainder of the journey by sea. For much of the time Roger had been sunk in a lethargy, and still had hardly the strength to raise his arm. But he had recovered sufficiently to know what was going on round him and, when Zanthé told him about the boat, he asked her to release the Turkish prisoners and make for Alexandria.

They called at Damietta, where Zanthé went ashore with two of the Mamelukes to buy more palatable provisions, fruit and various other things. On her return Roger dictated to her a letter to Bonaparte, which they later sent ashore to the garrison Commander, General Menou, for forwarding. In this letter Roger reported his misfortune and narrow escape from death, then said that he proposed to convalesce in Alexandria at the villa of his friend the Greek banker, Sarodopoulous.

On June 14th they reached Alexandria. It was now two and a half weeks since Roger had been smitten with the pestilence and the past week spent at sea had done him a lot of good; but, even so, he was still so weak that he could not walk without assistance and had to be carried in a litter by the Mamelukes out to Sarodopoulous's villa.

He had lost so much flesh that his face was gaunt and his clothes hung loose about him. For a moment Madame Sarodopulous failed to recognize him; then, greatly shocked by his appearance, she gave him a most friendly welcome which was fully endorsed by her brother-in-law and son when, that evening, they returned from their counting house in the city. Roger had already been put to bed and it was Zanthé who, while dining with the family, gave them a full account of the grim time he had been through since he had been taken prisoner three months earlier at Acre.

Next day Roger signed a chit empowering the banker to draw for him his arrears of pay from the French Paymaster in Alexandria and asked the Greek to have the blades of six fine scimitars engraved. Each was to be inscribed with the name of the Mameluke concerned and the words: ' Member of the guard that conveyed Her Highness Princess Zanthé safely from Acre to Alexandria during the great retreat in the year of the Hegira 1177. For courage and fidelity, from Colonel Breuc, aide-de-camp to General-in-Chief Bonaparte.'

When the scimitars were ready Roger asked Zanthé to present them. Then, giving each of the Mamelukes a handsome present of money, he thanked them for all they had done and ordered them to proceed to Cairo and rejoin their regiment. Overwhelmed by such kindness, these simple but magnificent fighting men kissed Zanthé's feet and, with tears in their eyes, took leave of Roger.

Roger had been helped down to the terrace for this little ceremony and it became his routine to spend most of his time there dozing, talking or walking up and down leaning on Zanthé's arm, for gradually more lengthy periods. The Sarodopulouses could not do enough for them. Nowhere could Roger have been provided with more nourishing fare to restore his vitality. Breasts of quail, chicken livers *à la brochette*, curried lobster, gazelle meat stewed in wine, soups made from pressed wild duck and the finest fruits succeeded one another to tempt his appetite. The Sarodopulouses displayed the greatest admiration for Zanthé's courage in having nursed Roger through the pestilence and, without servility, showed how honoured they felt at having as their guest a Princess of the Imperial House. Madame Sarodopulous insisted on replenishing Zanthé's wardrobe with many beautiful garments and her son Achilles made himself her slave, endeavouring to anticipate her every wish and thinking up all sorts of pastimes to amuse her.

Even Zanthé's efforts to save Roger's life might have proved unavailing had it not been for his splendid constitution. For many years he had frequently ridden long distances at the utmost speed possible. Whenever he had had no serious matter to attend to, he had always spent an hour or more a day in a fencing school and, when shooting game, had been capable of walking many miles without feeling fatigue. In consequence, his health had been excellent and his muscles as strong as whipcord. Now, his splendid physical condition before he caught the pestilence stood him in good stead. With every comfort, the most nourishing food and no worries, he began to put on flesh and feel like his old self again.

For the first few days Roger remained too lethargic to think of much besides his miraculous preservation, Zanthé's love and her devotion to him, the kindness of the Sarodopulouses and the joy of having his recovery aided by security, quiet and lazing in the shade of the terrace watching little green lizards darting from place to place along the sunlit balustrade. But, as his mental faculties returned to him, he began again to enjoy speculating with his host on the course of the war.

As usual, Sarodopulous's agents had kept him well informed; so he was able to tell Roger of the major events that had taken place in Europe up till about eight weeks earlier.

Austria had dragged her feet in the matter of actually committing her Armies to the new war of the Second Coalition. Although already negotiating an offensive alliance with Russia, Turkey and Britain in the winter, she had allowed both Piedmont and Naples to be overrun by the French without lifting a finger, and in the early spring had still shown great reluctance to take positive action. At length it had been forced upon her through the entry of a Russian Army into Austria, under the late Catherine the Great's famous Commander, General Suvóroff. The French had demanded that, within eight days, the Russians should withdraw from Austrian territory; the Emperor had ignored the demand and it had then been tacitly accepted by the two countries that a state of war existed between them.

The Directory, made over-confident by the long series of victories won by Bonaparte in Italy, had, regardless of numbers, instructed its principal Commanders—the Republican veteran Jourdan on the borders of Austria, and Masséna in Switzerland —to assume the offensive at once.

Apparently the strategy of the French had been based on the idea that, if they could secure the bastion of the Alps, they would at any time be able to emerge from it and dictate the situation in the neighbouring plains; so they had given little attention to the upper reaches of the Danube or the Rhine. On March 1st Jourdan crossed the latter and on the 6th Masséna moved into the Grissons to expel the bands of anti-French Swiss there, who were eagerly awaiting Austrian support.

Jourdan, meanwhile, advanced into the Black Forest between the source of the Danube and Lake Constance; so the war seemed to have opened well for the French. But, during the uneasy peace, the Austrian Emperor had been extremely active in reorganizing his Army, calling up and training reserves and making every sort of preparation against another outbreak of war. In consequence, he had been able to put into the field two hundred and twenty-five thousand well-equipped troops, which far outnumbered those with which the French could oppose him.

The first fruits of this numerical superiority were seen on

March 21st, in the first collision of the Armies. Jourdan's thirty-six thousand French clashed head-on with some seventy-eight thousand Austrians under the Emperor's most capable General, the Archduke Charles. The French fought courageously, but were forced to give way and retire on the village of Stockach.

The village was of considerable strategic importance, because the roads from Switzerland and Swabia met there. Rallying his forces there on the 25th, Jourdan decided to advance and give battle. The Archduke also advanced troops in that direction, intending only to make a reconnaissance in force. Confused fighting resulted, which later developed into a most desperate conflict involving both armies fully. Although Jourdan had Lefebvre and St. Cyr among his Divisional Commanders, the French were heavily defeated and a large part of their Army fled in terrible confusion across the plain of Liptingen.

Jourdan retired with the remnants of his force into the Black Forest, while Masséna's offensive had been checked and he was being hard pressed in Switzerland by another Austrian Army. At the same time the Allies launched a third powerful Army, consisting of thirty-six thousand Austrians and Suvóroff's eighteen thousand Russians, into northern Italy. They were opposed there by General Schérer, who had one hundred and two thousand men under him. But the French were widely scattered and Schérer, one of the old-type Republican Generals, was incapable of co-ordinating his forces effectively. The French were driven back over river after river until they were behind the Adda, and there Schérer was relieved of his Command by Moreau.

Yet even that hero of many victories could not hold the enemy. Suvóroff's Russians, fighting like tigers, forced the bridge at Cassano and on April 27th captured General Sérurier with three thousand men. The French had already had to leave the great fortress of Mantua to be besieged and now the Allies entered Milan.

In southern Italy also the French had suffered a severe blow. Called on for help, General Macdonald left strong garrisons in the three great castles at Naples then marched north with thirty-six thousand men. The withdrawal of his Army at once resulted in a peasant rising, led by a militant Cardinal named Ruffo, and in April there ensued the massacre of the Neapolitans who had collaborated with the French. To complete this tale of woe for the Republic, although their garrison on Malta continued to hold out, Corfu was captured from them by a combined Russo-Turkish Fleet towards the end of April.

Another matter about which Sarodopulous told Roger was the ending of the Conference of Rastatt, and how the manner of it had excited indignation in every Court in Europe. Ever since the late autumn of '97 the French plenipotentiaries had remained at Rastatt, negotiating with Austria and a horde of German and Italian petty Sovereigns, on the final clauses to be inserted in the Treaty of Campo Formio. By that treaty, the Austrians conceded to the French the Germanic territories up to the left bank of the Rhine and recognized the Cisapline Republic, which embraced the greater part of northern Italy. The object of the Conference had been to compensate such Princes as had been dispossessed of their territories by giving them others.

The plenipotentiaries chosen by the Directory had been the most vulgar, brutal type of die-hard revolutionaries. Making capital out of Bonaparte's recently concluded Italian campaign, they had behaved with the utmost arrogance and had acted throughout like bullies rather than diplomats. On several occasions the Austrian plenipotentiaries had withdrawn in disgust, but the French had kept the Conference going with the Princes and Grand Dukes on the excuse that their future status could not be left unsettled. After sitting for a year the Conference became a complete farce, for by then a French Army was besieging the fortress of Ehrenbreitstein on the Rhine and, when it surrendered, the Emperor decided that no possible good come of continuing the negotiations.

But the French plenipotentiaries refused to depart. Even when Austria and France became openly at war, and after the Archduke Charles's victory at Stockach, they still remained there, chaffering with the Princes and seeking to undermine the Empire by tempting them with offers of territories which were to be taken from the Church lands ruled by the German Prince-Bishops.

At last, on April 8th, the Emperor formally decreed the Conference at an end and annulled all its acts. The Germans withdrew but the French protested violently and stayed on until a military force was sent to turn them out. On the evening of April 28th they left with their families, in three coaches. Just outside the town they were set upon by a regiment of Szekler Hussars and dragged from their coaches. Two of the plenipotentiaries

N

were murdered in the presence of their horrified wives and the
third escaped only because he was left for dead after a terrible
beating. That the men themselves had been brutal ex-terrorists
was beside the point, and on all sides Austria was condemned
for this shocking breach of the immunity always accorded to
diplomatic representatives.

By the end of June, Roger was still very much an invalid
physically, but sufficiently alert mentally to give some thought to
his future and that of Zanthé's. Since their brief conversation on
the morning after they had escaped from Acre, neither of
them had mentioned marriage; but he had introduced her to
the Sarodopulouses as his fiancée and he felt sure that she
expected him to make her his wife as soon as he was fully
recovered.

His recollections of her as a mistress were such that, although
his health debarred him, for the time being, from resuming his
role of her lover, he had begun to long for the time when they
could again share a divan. Even so, being no callow youth and
having been the lover of a number of beautiful women, he could
not help wondering for how long the passionate attraction
between them would last. Through the years Georgina had never
failed to rouse him, but hers was a case apart. Moreover he
knew there to be a great deal in her contention that their continued physical desire for one another was largely due to the
fact that they had never lived together for more than a few
months at a time, and even then at long intervals.

In Zanthé's case, although he reproached himself for thinking
of it, there was a special reason why her attraction for him
should decline more swiftly than would that of other beautiful
women he had known. When he had met her ten months ago she
had been seventeen but by European standards looked to be in
her early twenties. She was now eighteen, but in England would
not have been put down at less than twenty-five. The cause was
her half-Eastern blood and her wholly Eastern upbringing.
Eastern women aged much more swiftly than Europeans and
Zanthé also had the normal Eastern woman's love of rich foods
and sweetmeats. With a true fatalist's disregard for her figure, she
ate Rahat Lacoum, sugared nuts and preserved fruits by the
pound. It would have been as agonizing for her to deprive herself of them as it would have been for a Frenchman to deny
himself wine; so the odds were that by the time she was thirty she

would, like most upperclass women of that age in the East, be able
only to waddle.

There was also the factor that, unless Georgina would change
her mind and have him, Roger had not wanted to marry again; at
least, not for another few years and then only should he find
someone to whom he was greatly attracted and who would also
make a suitable step-mother for his little daughter Susan. And
how could Zanthé, with the best will in the world, be expected
to bring up a young English girl fittingly and launch her in
Society?

On the other hand, physical attractions apart, Zanthé was of a
most lovable disposition, had been well educated by her French
mother and was quick to learn. With such qualities, Roger had
no doubt that she would take Susan to her heart, prove as good-
tempered a wife as any man could wish for and perhaps, after a
while, acquire the manners and attitude of mind of an English
lady of quality.

In any case, the more he thought about it the more convinced
he became that honour demanded that he take a gamble on the
future. Zanthé had twice saved his life and now, having severed
herself from her own people, all she had in the world were some
valuable jewels and himself. Sarodopulous had examined her
jewels and had declared that, if sold, they would provide her with
a handsome dowry; so, had Roger decided against marrying her,
she could have found another husband. But he believed that it
would break her heart to have to do so, and after all she had
been to him he could not bring himself to do that.

As a result of these deliberations, he broached the subject to
her, one afternoon during the first week in July, on the score that,
as in another month or six weeks he hoped to be fully restored to
health, they ought to begin making plans. Just as he expected,
she at once raised the question of religion. He had no intention
of becoming a Mohammedan and had thought it probable that,
as they would in due course be going to make their home in
Europe, she would consent to becoming a Christian.

He was not disappointed in that but, to his surprise and dismay, he met with most determined opposition when, evading the
awkward implications of saying he was Church of England, he
declared himself to be a Protestant. Zanthé's mother had been
brought up as a Roman Catholic, so she respected that faith and
was perfectly willing to subscribe to it in order to marry him.

But she had been taught that Protestants of all denominations were as evil as Jews and was greatly shocked to learn that Roger was what Christians of her mother's faith termed a 'heretic'.

During the next few days they had several sessions in which they argued the matter passionately. Zanthé suggested that both of them should become Catholics, but Roger would not hear of it. He was far from being a religious man but, like most Englishmen of his day, had been brought up to regard the Pope as anti-Christ and all his works as of the Devil. Such beliefs, when inculcated young, die hard, and he was fully convinced that he would lose his hope of salvation should he become a Catholic as she was that she would lose hers should she become a Protestant.

The resistance she displayed might have caused another man to have seized on it as an excuse to refuse to pursue matters further, but in Roger it only aroused a determination to make her his wife. He suggested that they should be content with a civil marriage, which was now the normal form of ceremony in Republican France. But Zanthé would not hear of it. She protested that, unless their marriage were blessed either by a Mulim imam or a Catholic priest, it would be no marriage in the sight of Heaven. Then, in tears, she declared that, if Roger were not prepared to sacrifice his scruples to make her his wife, she loved him so dearly that she would accept the terrible humiliation of accompanying him back to France as his concubine.

This impasse continued for some days until on July 11th Roger was given other things to think about. On that day Sir Sidney Smith's Squadron appeared off Alexandria, convoying an armada of transports carrying a considerable Turkish Army. For the past week Roger had been going for short rides, accompanied by a groom. In view of this emergency he felt that, to maintain his status as an aide-de-camp to the General-in-Chief, he must, although still far from strong, offer his services.

Ignoring the protests of Zanthé and the Sarodopulouses, he rode into Alexandria and reported to Marmont, who was now in command there. The young General was a gunner. He was one of Bonaparte's oldest friends and had served with him at the siege of Toulon, where Roger had also met him. Their greeting was cordial but, after one look at Roger, Marmont declared him unfit for active service. However, he said that he would welcome his help in his bureau; so Roger was given a desk and set about dealing with urgent administrative matters.

Couriers had been sent post-haste to Bonaparte at Ghizeh. They reached him on the 15th and he at once set out for Rhmaniyeh. From there, he ordered a concentration of troops headed by Kléber's Division, then at Rosetta. By the 21st he had at his disposal an Army nearly as large as that of the Turks, which was reported to number ten thousand men. Meanwhile the Turks had landed on the peninsular of Aboukir, massacred the garrison of the small fort there and dug themselves in behind a double line of entrenchments.

On July 25th Bonaparte attacked. Lannes, amazingly recovered from his wounds, and d'Estang outflanked the village which formed the strongpoint centre of the first line of Turkish defences, then Murat followed with his cavalry and drove a great number of the Turks into the sea.

During the terrible heat of midday Bonaparte gave his troops two hours' rest. He then sent them in against the Turks' second line, which had a strong redoubt in its centre. Again the French charged with tremendous élan but this time the attack failed, largely owing to the supporting fire of the Turkish gunboats that had been brought close inshore. The Turks, confident of victory, surged out of their entrenchments, but delayed to butcher the wounded French and mutilate the dead. Seeing them to be scattered while engaged in this barbarous business, Bonaparte ordered another attack. Catching the Turks at a disadvantage, the French reached and seized the second line of trenches. Murat, with his cavalry and camelry, again drove the fleeing Turks into the surf and hundreds of them were either sabred or pursued into deep water until they drowned. Heavy cannon were then brought up to bombard the small fortress into which the surviving Turks had crammed themselves. It became a massacre. After two days, two thousand of the Turks surrendered—all that was left of an Army of ten thousand.

Roger saw nothing of this, but received gruesome accounts of it while working at Alexandria in Marmont's office. The emergency over, he returned to Sarodopulous's villa, a little tired from his exertions but otherwise in good heart, to continue his convalescence.

It was on the day after his return that he had a most unnerving experience. While sitting on the privy, he felt something furry tickling his left buttock. Leaping up, he found it to be a large scorpion. At his sudden action the poisonous beast fell off on to the floor. Next moment he had crushed it with his boot; but he stood there for a few moments, white and shaking. Had it stung him he might have died in agony. Shortly afterwards, on returning to the villa, he told Zanthé of his lucky escape and added:

'This is the most accursed country. I managed to escape from it once. When next a chance comes for me to do so I'll take it, and never, never will I return. Not even wild horses shall drag me back to it again.'

Three days later it so happened that he was given a chance to leave Egypt. The fortnight he had spent working in Marmont's office had proved no undue strain upon him. On the contrary, he was inclined to think that, before it, he had allowed Zanthé and the Sarodopulouses to pamper him too much; for on his return to the villa he felt considerably fitter. In the early mornings, before the sun got too hot, he was going out riding on his own and ever further afield.

On the morning of July 30th, having ridden some five miles along the coast to the west, he trotted to the top of a big sand-dune and saw below, in the little bay, a group of men. A British sloop-of-war was lying about half a mile off-shore and the men had obviously landed from her. At a glance he saw what they were about.

The coast of Egypt was far too long for the French, with their limited number of troops, to patrol the whole of it regularly; so at times the blockading ships landed parties on deserted stretches of coast to collect springwater. Such sources were too small for the larger ships to pick up the hundreds of gallons they required, so from time to time they had to water at Crete or Cyprus; but even half a barrel of fresh springwater was a great luxury so now and then, in order to obtain it, blockading vessels took the risk of their parties being surprised by the French.

Down in the bay a semi-circle of half a dozen sailors with muskets kept guard some distance from a cluster of rocks above the tide-line. Among the rocks, under the supervision of an officer, others were filling three small casks from the spring with pannikins while, a hundred yards away, a boat was being kept in readiness to take them off.

As Roger brought his mount to a halt on the top of the dune, the sailors spotted him, gave the alarm and raised their muskets. Before they could draw a bead on him he swung his horse round, put spurs to it and, crouching low in the saddle, cantered off back down the slope. But as soon as he was well under cover of the crest he pulled up.

Wild thoughts were racing through his mind. He was alone; so if he appeared again, waving his white handkerchief, the men would not fire upon him. He had only to ride down to them and give himself up to be taken aboard the British sloop. Within a few days he could get himself transferred to *Tigre* and be again with Sir Sidney Smith. After all he had been through he had no doubt at all that the Commodore would take the first opportunity to send him home.

It was seventeen months since he had left England. During that time he had twice secured important despatches from Bonaparte, and had also sent back from Naples a very full report on the resources of the French Army in Egypt. Meanwhile, he had suffered grievously and several times had narrowly escaped losing his life. No one, with the possible exception of the fanatically patriotic Nelson, could possibly contend that he was not now entitled to give up the desperately dangerous double life that he had been leading for so long.

If he did not take this chance, in a few weeks he must return to duty in Cairo. And what then? On re-entering Egypt Bonaparte had issued a proclamation containing more flagrant lies than even he had ever before given out. He claimed that he had totally destroyed Acre and that this had been his only object in invading Syria. He declared his total casualties to number a mere five hundred, when everyone in the Army knew that they ran into thousands. With superb effrontery he had organized a triumphant entry into Cairo, with the captured Turkish standards being carried before him, and claimed to have returned from a campaign of victories equalling those he had achieved in Italy.

This unscrupulous propaganda had deceived the greater part of the Egyptian people and had even, to some extent, been swallowed by the French regiments which had not taken part in the Syrian campaign. But Roger knew the truth.

During its thirteen months in Egypt the French Army had been reduced, by casualties and pestilence, to little more than half its original number. It had not received a single reinforcement from home and, as long as the British blockade continued could not hope to do so. Even with the regiments of Mamelukes and other natives who had been enlisted, it was now barely strong enough to hold Egypt, let alone undertake other campaigns further afield. All prospect of raising the Arab races against their overlord, the Sultan, had vanished with the failure to take Acre. Gone, too, was the dream of capturing the Red Sea ports and from them invading India as a prelude to creating a great Empire in the East. Now the French were like a garrison in a besieged city that had no hope of relief, and in which the population was hostile. From attacks on their convoys by Bedouin, knifings by night in the streets, accident and disease, they must gradually be weakened to a point at which the Egyptians felt strong enough to rise and massacre them.

As Roger thought of those months ahead during which, if he remained in Egypt, he must continue to suffer from the sweltering heat, myriads of flies, possibility of being killed by an Arab or stung by a poisonous reptile, and living all his time among companions growing daily more desperate with fear about their future, he had never before so greatly longed to be back in the green fields of England.

Only the thought of Zanthé deterred him from galloping back over the crest, pulling out his white handkerchief and waving it aloft for the little party of seamen who meant home and safety to him. She had given him intense pleasure. She loved and needed him. She had twice saved his life and had nursed him back to health. Could he possibly desert her? Still worse, could he simply disappear without a word, leaving her to months of misery, wondering whether he were dead or alive and what had happened to him? She was very beautiful and he would soon be strong enough to become again her lover in the fullest sense. But there were other women as beautiful, even if in a different way, and as passionate in England. In a few years she would look middle-aged and have become fat and unwieldy. Why should he sacrifice every other thing for which he craved to saddle himself with a half-Asiatic girl whom he would have to take with him as his wife wherever they went, whether they actually married or not?

For a few agonizing minutes he wrestled with the most terrible temptation that had ever beset him. Then he knew that he could not give in to it. The shame of having left her, after all she had been to him, would haunt him all his days. He must remain in Egypt and share the lot of Bonaparte's ill-fated Army. Sadly, he kneed his horse into a walk and rode back to Alexandria.

Having resolved not to abandon Zanthé, he committed himself to her still further that evening. It chanced that the Patriarch of Alexandria called at the villa to solicit a large sum from Sarodopulous for a charity. He was a big, jolly man with a fine, curly black beard and, while they were all consuming coffee and cakes, the talk turned to different faiths.

When Roger was in St. Petersburg he found that, under Catherine the Great, Russia was then the most tolerant country in the world with regard to religious matters. Priests of all denominations were encouraged by the Empress to establish churches there, and every year the Metropolitan gave a reception to which he invited Catholics, Lutherans and Calvinists as well as brethren of his own Church. Three kinds of wine were served at these receptions, and it was his custom to welcome his guests with the words: 'Gentlemen, these wines are different; but all of them are good, and so are the different faiths which we follow.'

Recalling that, Roger was not at all surprised to find that the Patriarch showed a most tolerant respect for other Christian faiths; but he stoutly maintained that, owing to its unbroken descent from the first teachings in the Holy Land, the Eastern Orthodox Church adhered more closely to the true principles of Christianity than any other religion.

Zanthé showed great interest and questioned him closely. Roger, too, was intrigued and it occurred to him that, while nothing would have induced him to become a Roman Catholic, the undemanding tolerance of the Orthodox Church would make a ceremony performed by one of its priests quite a different matter. In consequence, when the Patriarch had gone he took Zanthé aside and asked her how she felt about it.

To his delight he found that, while her abhorrence of Protestants still equalled his of Popery, she had always regarded the Orthodox Christians with respect. She could hardly contain her joy at his having proposed a way in which he could make her his wife in the sight of God, without either of them having to commit an act that they would have detested.

When they told the Sarodopulouses of their intention, the banker and his family showed the greatest happiness and Madame Sarodopulous began to describe to them the charming marriage ceremony of the Orthodox Church, at which they would both wear crowns and carry candles. But her brother-in-law warned them that their marriage could not take place for at least a month. They would first have to receive instruction in the Orthodox faith and learn by heart its catechism and numerous prayers and responses.

On hearing this the tall, dark, handsome Achilles, who, ever since they had arrived at the villa, had made himself Zanthé's willing slave, at once offered to act as their tutor. It was agreed that he should coach them daily in the Orthodox prayer book and that it should be arranged for them to visit the friendly Patriarch twice a week to be prepared for reception into his Church.

Later that evening Roger again drew Zanthé aside and said to her with a smile, ' My beautiful. For having arranged matters like this I feel that I may ask a reward from you.'

' Count it already given,' she smiled back. ' What is it that you wish? '

' That you should let me come to your room tonight,' he whispered.

She hesitated a moment. ' Dear love, you cannot believe how terribly I have desired you during these two months since you were stricken. But, as long as we remain guests here, we are not free to do as we will. Should we be discovered, what Madame Sarodopulous think of us? For having abused her hospitality in such a way I would die of shame.'

' Oh, come! ' Roger protested. ' Your room is but a few yards from mine, and I will use the utmost discretion. I'll not come to you until everyone has retired for above an hour and should be sound asleep, and I'll leave you well before the servants are awake. For the past fortnight or more I have thought of little but making love to you again. And you have already said that you would grant my wish.'

' But . . . but,' she murmured, ' will it not harm you? Nothing must interfere with your complete recovery. And if . . . if it is for your good, I . . . I can still wait.'

' On the score of my fitness have no fears, my sweet,' he smiled. ' I have reached a point at which to be denied your caresses would harm me more.'

Her big, tawny eyes had become moist and she was trembling as she replied, ' I would have to be made of iron to resist your pleading. But I'll allow you to stay with me no more than half an hour. On that, for your health's sake, I insist.'

So that night Roger again entered Paradise in the arms of his beautiful fiancée.

During the three weeks that followed they visited the Patriarch regularly and learned from the red lips of the dark, flashing-eyed Achilles to recite the Greek Church credo and other religious pieces from the Orthodox prayer book. Meanwhile, Zanthé put great restraint upon herself and refused to allow Roger to come to her room more than two nights a week. But on those nights they gave themselves up to their mutual passion with as much ardour as they had while in Acre.

It was on August 16th that a blockade-runner brought Sarodopulous further news of events in Europe. Throughout May and June matters had gone from bad to worse with the French. Towards the end of the former month the Allies, with the help the the Piedmontese Royalists, had regained possession of Turin. Moreau had only with great difficulty cut his way through the passes of the Alps to seek safety in Genoa.

Macdonald, arriving in the north with the French Army that had occupied the Kingdom of Naples, had, in mid-June, defeated the Austrians at Modena; but Suvóroff, by a rapid concentration and forced march, had thrown his Russians on Macdonald's force before Moreau could come to his aid. Three days of desperate fighting had ensued, at the end of which the terrible Muscovites had proved the masters of the French. Macdonald's troops had broken and, in small parties, staggered back across the Apennines, to reach Genoa in a state of utter exhaustion. Suvóroff, for these brilliant victories in the Allied cause, had been given the title of Prince *Italiski*.

These disasters to the French had led to the fall of the puppet States they had created: the Cisapline, Roman and Parthenopean Republics. On all sides priests, Royalists, bourgeoisie and fanatical peasants were exacting vengeance for the repression, brutality and robbery to which they had been subjected by the bringers of 'Liberty'. Mob leaders, gentle intellectuals with Liberal views and all who had collaborated with the French from either the worst or best motives were, through the length and breadth of the peninsula, impartially dragged from their homes by the hundred and shot, hanged, slashed to death or burnt in public.

It was in the south that this ferocious vengeance reached its peak. In Naples the three castles, garrisoned by French troops and so-called 'patriots', continued to hold out; but by mid-

June Cardinal Ruffo's irregulars had entered the city, butchered every Republican they could find and laid siege to the castles.

Ruffo, wishing to pacify the kingdom, offered these garrisons the honours of war and a safe-conduct to France if they would capitulate. The Republicans agreed to these generous terms and Captain Foote, then the senior officer with the British Squadron lying off Naples, also signed the terms of capitulation.

But on June 24th Nelson arrived, invested with unlimited powers by King Ferdinand who was still in Palermo. The British Admiral promptly asserted that Cardinal Ruffo and Captain Foote had exceeded their authority in granting terms to the enemy garrisons. He declared the capitulation agreement null and void and, with a vindictiveness difficult to understand in so gentle a man, but evidently largely inspired by Emma Hamilton as the mouthpiece of the Queen, had the Republican leaders who had surrendered executed and the Neapolitan Admiral Caracciolo hanged from his own yardarm.

Secretly, as an Englishman, Roger rejoiced to hear these tidings. Although he had the warmest personal feelings for many friends he had made among the French, he had never wavered in his conviction that the hyrda-headed monster that had been produced by the Revolution could bring only evil to the peoples whom it first fascinated and then enslaved. It was excellent news that the Italians were, with the help of the Austrians and Russians, again achieving their freedom and from a worse tyranny than any they had known before. He hoped that it heralded the downfall of the collection of atheists, murderers and thieves who had for so long controlled the destinies of France.

But policy demanded that he should allow the Sarodopulouses to continue to believe that he was a French Colonel, and he had felt that it would be time enough to disclose to Zanthé the truth about himself when, and if, he could succeed in getting her out of Egypt. So, at this latest news from Europe, he had to pull a long face and pretend grave concern.

Roger and Zanthé had fixed the date of their marriage as August 29th. On the evening of August 22nd, just as the sun was about to set, a Lieutenant of Bonaparte's favourite regiment, the Guides, rode up to the villa on a lathered horse, bringing a despatch. Tearing it open, Roger saw it was in Bourrienne's writing and was an order signed by the General-in-Chief. It read:

I require you to report to me immediately. You will accompany the bearer of this with a minimum of delay.

Roger was greatly puzzled, but felt that he could not possibly ignore the summons. Thinking it unlikely that he would be away for long, he told Zanthé that he would send her a message as soon as he possibly could and, in any case, would get permission to return for their wedding day. While he was taking leave of her and the Sarodopulouses, a horse was being saddled for him. Ten minutes later he rode away with the Lieutenant of Guides.

When Roger asked the Lieutenant where they were making for the latter replied, ' I regret, *mon Colonel,* that I am under orders not to reveal the whereabouts of the General-in-Chief; but we have no great distance to go. We must, though, make all speed, because I lost my way when coming to find you and so was more than an hour behind time in delivering my despatch.'

The Lieutenant had turned west and, alternately trotting and cantering, they rode along the coast until they reached the little bay in which Roger had come upon the British landing party collecting springwater. Darkness had fallen, but a solitary boat lay there in which were men with lanterns. Their light showed thirty or forty saddled but riderless horses wandering loose about the beach. As soon as Roger reached the shore, a naval officer in the boat shouted to him to be quick and come aboard.

More puzzled than ever he dismounted, abandoned his horse and, followed by the Lieutenant, scrambled over the gunwale. The boat pushed off at once and, after fifteen minutes' rowing, came alongside a ship that Roger judged to be a frigate. The crew were in the act of setting sail.

He found a group of men on the quarter-deck which was lit by flambeaux. In its centre stood Bonaparte. With him were Berthier, Murat, Lannes, Marmont, Bessières, Andréossi, Monge, Berthollet, Bourrienne, Duroc, de Beauharnais, and the other members of his personal Staff. Marching up to him, Roger saluted and said:

' *Mon Général.* You sent for me.'

Bonaparte nodded. ' You are late, and lucky to be taken off in time.'

' Your pardon, but in time for what? ' Roger asked.

' Why, to accompany me back to France, of course,' snapped the pale-faced little Corsican. ' Where else should I be going in a frigate? '

Roger stared at him aghast. The boat in which he had been brought aboard was being hauled in. The frigate's sails were filled with wind and she was already moving through the water. It was now too late to ask to be set ashore. Bleakly, he realized that his marriage to Zanthé would now never take place. Three weeks earlier he had overcome the temptation to desert her. Now Fate had decreed that without having any say in the matter he should do so. But he was not going home.

22

Back into the Secret Battle

THERE was tremendous jubilation aboard the frigate. It was fifteen months since Bonaparte's expedition had sailed from Toulon and those who accompanied him had said good-bye to their wives and sweethearts. During thirteen of those months they had lived in an utterly alien land, where white women were as rare as white blackbirds, where wine was almost unobtainable and where the food was unappetizing and monotonous. As soldiers it was their trade to face danger but there had been added to it terrible marches under a blistering sun, days of torture from thirst, fear of the plague and a never-ending irritation from swarms of flies. Now, the seemingly impossible had happened. The nightmare that was Egypt was being left behind. The frigate was actually under sail. They were on their way back to France, which meant everything in life they held dear. Roger could not wonder that joy was depicted on every face.

He soon learned the reason for his inclusion and why it had been so belated. When those selected by Bonaparte to accompany him were already on board, Marmont happened to mention to Eugène de Beauharnis the help that Roger had given him in his office at Alexandria during the emergency caused by the Turkish landing. Eugène spoke to his step-father and the General-in-Chief at once agreed that ' le brave Breuc ' must not be left behind if there was still time to fetch him. As Roger thanked the chubby-faced youngster he felt that never had so handsome a return been made for a pair of pistols as for those he had given Eugène when only a boy of fifteen.

From Eugène he learned that there were two frigates, *Muriou* and *Carrère*, under the command of Vice-Admiral Gantheaume.

They had been sheltering in the harbour of Alexandria and, at
Bonaparte's orders, had been secretly prepared for sea. But
Bonaparte's departure had been made possible only because Sir
Sidney Smith had had to withdraw his Squadron to Cyprus for
repairs, thus raising the blockade temporarily and leaving the
coast clear.

Bonaparte had packed nearly five hundred passengers into the
two frigates. They consisted of the pick of his officers, a number
of the most gifted savants, a big bodyguard of his Guides and
many personal servants. As Roger heard this he realized that
had he been left behind the fate he had dreaded would have
been more likely than ever to overtake him. Bonaparte had not
only abandoned his Army, but had weakened it immeasurably by
taking with him the greater part of its brains and guts.

Of the best Generals, only Kléber, Desaix and Junot had been
left behind, and the two latter only because they were too distant
to recall in time. Desaix was in command of the forces in Upper
Egypt and Junot, with his Division, was on the Syrian border.
Kléber had been nominated General-in-Chief. He was a fine
fighting man, but had little talent for administration; and it was
that, above all, which was needed at headquarters if the Army
was to be kept from becoming mutinous from despair and
shattered morale.

But at the moment those who had escaped were not thinking
of the fate to which they had left their comrades. The wind was
light but steady, the sea calm and the frigate carried a good stock
of wine. For hours they laughed, drank and sang gay choruses.
Roger joined in. It would have been contrary to his nature not
to do so; but, later, when he lay in a narrow cabin, cheek-by-
jowl with the other aides-de-camp, it was a long time before he
could get to sleep from picturing Zanthé's distress when she
learned that he had left her.

Next day he had a talk with his old friend Bourrienne, and
learned what had led to their master talking his momentous
decision. At the recent battle of Aboukir the Turks had taken a
number of captives. Sir Sidney Smith had intervened to prevent
their being murdered, then arranged with Bonaparte an exchange
of prisoners. The Commodore had also sent ashore a number of
French wounded whom he had rescued from Jaffa. To show
appreciation of the Englishman's chivalrous behaviour, Bonaparte had sent some presents to him. Sir Sidney had returned the

compilment, and among his gifts had been a bundle of news-sheets covering events in Europe up to June 10th.

It was ten months since any official news had been received from France. By way of Algiers and Tripoli, or Greece and Crete, carried by blockade-runners, rumours had trickled through to the effect that Austria was again at war with France and that all was not well in Italy. But it was not until the night of August 2nd-3rd, during which Bonaparte had sat up until the small hours in Alexandria reading these news-sheets, that he had realized the seriousness of the situation. The following morning he had exclaimed to Bourrienne:

'My presentiments have come true; The fools have lost Italy! All the fruits of our victories are gone. I must leave Egypt in order to save France.'

Having taken his decision, he acted with speed and secrecy. He told only Berthier and Gantheaume; ordering the latter to pre-pare the two frigates and two small supply ships with enough food for a two-month voyage. On August 5th he left Alexandria, on the 10th he arrived in Cairo. There, he gave out that he intended to carry out an inspection of Desaix's force in Upper Egypt. A few days later he announced a change of plan: he was going to make a tour of the Delta. Meanwhile Bourrienne had collected all the people Bonaparte intended to take with him, but it was not until they reached Alexandria on the 22nd that any of them were told that they were going home to France.

Kléber had been at Damietta and Bonaparte had written, asking him to meet him for a conference at Rosetta. But with the duplicity that was typical of his methods the Corsican had never intended to keep the appointment. To escape protests and reproaches, he had simply sent a letter to await Kléber's arrival. It appointed him General-in-Chief, with powers to surrender to the British, but only if the ravages of the plague became so bad that the Army became incapable of resistance. The unfortunate Kléber had been left to find out for himself that the Army was ten million francs in debt and that Bonaparte had taken with him every sou of ready money.

When Roger asked Bourrienne for the news that had been gleaned from the papers sent by Sir Sidney Smith, the *Chef de Cabinet* told him of the serious reverses the French had met with in the neighbourhood of the Rhine and from north to south in Italy. Roger had already learned most of this from Sarodopulous, but there was later news about Switzerland. Matters were going badly for the French there also. Masséna had been compelled to relinquish the Grissons; then, on May 24th, two Austrian armies, joining forces, had brought such a weight of numbers against him that he had been driven back to the line of the river Limmat and Zürich.

Bourrienne, with intense indignation, gave an account of the murder of the French envoys at Rastatt and went on to speak of affairs in Paris. In mid-May the retirement by ballot of one of the Directors had become due and this time the lot had fallen on Jean-François Rewbell. The handsome, corrupt, licentious aristocrat Barras had been the most prominent figure in the Directory, right from its formation; but it was the coarse, ruthless, dyed-in-the-wool revolutionary Rewbell who had managed it and, time after time, frustrated the attempts of the Moderate majority in the Legislative Assembly to restore some degree of true liberty to the French people.

Rewbell had been replaced by the Abbé Sieyès, one of the strangest figures of the Revolution. He had become prominent in its earliest days and had remained so ever since. When asked, in after years, what he had done in the Revolution he replied, 'I survived.' For anyone who had been one of the original leaders that was no small feat. A few others, such as Talleyrand, had done so, but only by going into exile during the worst years of the Terror. Sieyès, the most subtle of intriguers, had, by changing his coat a dozen times, not only kept his head on his shoulders but occupied some post of importance in every successive Government.

He was not a bloodthirsty man but had an intense hatred of the aristocracy and was incredibly vain of his intellectual powers. Above all he fancied himself as a drafter of Constitutions, although many of his ideas on the subject were impracticable. On the fall of Robespierre he had been among the first chosen by the rump Convention to be one of the new governing body of five—the Directory. But as his proposals for a new Constitution had been rejected he had, in a huff, refused office.

This change in the personnel of the Directory was of far greater importance than any which had preceded it, and later in the day Roger pondered over its possible results. As Sieyès was a renegade and an atheist, his appointment would not lead to greater religious toleration and, as a revolutionary, he would, no doubt, support the Directory in their policy of continuing to repress individual liberty. But he was far too careful of his own skin to act as Rewbell would have done in a crisis and back his opinions with ruthless force. In consequence, this change in the Directory must greatly weaken it; and for a long time past it had been hated and despised by both the great mass of the people and the Liberal majority which sat, powerless under its rule, in the Legislative Assembly. Therefore, it now needed only a strong man to play Cromwell in order to put an end to the Directory.

Roger had no doubt that Bonaparte must be well aware of this. Overtures to lead a *coup d'état* to overthrow the Directory had been made to him in the spring of '98 and Talleyrand had told Roger that the little Corsican had refrained only because, being an extremely astute politician, he had decided that the time was not yet ripe. Instead he had gone off to Egypt, with the possibility of carving for himself an Empire in the East while time worked for him in France. He had failed in the first, but time had marched on just the same and now the plum looked ripe for the picking.

As Roger thought of this he realized that a sudden change had taken place in his own mentality. He had gone to Egypt only because Talleyrand had virtually forced him to. While there he had twice furnished Nelson with valuable information about Bonaparte's intentions. But that had given him no great satisfaction. It was not to secure information about the situation of an Army operating three thousand miles from England that Mr. Pitt had sent him to Paris. The work in which he had specialized for so long and in which he had been so successful was using his wide acquaintance with enemies in high places to assess the future policy of their Governments. To be back in Paris again and, perhaps, be able, to some degree, to influence events in favour of his country was a very different matter from remaining virtually useless and cut off from all the amenities of life in Egypt.

One thing seemed certain: Bonaparte's return to Paris would lead to a crisis of some kind, and the more Roger speculated on its possibly far-reaching results the more eager he became for the voyage to be over.

For some days, and particularly at nights, he was haunted by thoughts of Zanthé. When the news reached her that Bonaparte had decamped, taking his finest Generals and his personal Staff with him, she would realize that Roger was with them and on his way back to France; but she could not be expected to guess that he had not had the option of refusing to leave her, or even the opportunity to send her a message. She could only suppose that, having been given the chance, he had callously deserted her. That worried him even more than having lost her; although at times such was his feeling for her that he almost wished he had been left behind to marry her as they had planned.

It was on the third day out that, up on the quarter-deck, Bonaparte suddenly asked him, 'What happened to your Princess?'

Roger told him; but the Corsican only gave a grunt, then said, 'I, too, have had to deprive myself of much happiness by leaving behind in Cairo my little *Bellilotte*. She implored me to take her with me, but I refused. We have to face the fact that we may be captured by the English. Most of the English sailors have been without women for many months and I could not bear to think what might happen to her if she fell into their hands.'

Roger was so shocked by this slur on British chivalry that only long habit prevented him from making his leanings suspect by entering on an angry defence of his countrymen. That he would have been amply justified was proved some months later, when the Corsican's violet-eyed mistress endeavoured to follow him to France in a blockade-runner. The ship was captured by the English. They delighted in her company, entertained her royally and went out of their way to set her safely ashore in France.

While Roger was inwardly seething, Bonaparte, being in one of his confidential moods, went on, 'I should have liked to have had a child by her; but the little stupid seemed incapable of producing one. She vowed that it was not her fault, and implied that because I have never yet begotten one it must be mine. Yet I'm as virile as other men, so I'll not accept it that I'm incapable of becoming a father.'

Raising a smile with difficulty, Roger replied, 'You are not yet thirty, so have ample time. It may be that one's mental state when making love has an effect on such matters. You are constantly beset by so many urgent problems that it would surprise me if you ever gave your whole thoughts to a woman even for a few moments.'

Bonaparte gave him a swift glance. 'That is an interesting thought. Perhaps you are right. At least it gives me some comfort. But there are more important things in life than women. One's country must come first, and you shall see what I will do in Paris. As I've often said I would, I'll put an end to these fops and puppies who are bringing about our ruin.'

This conversation did not console Roger for the loss of Zanthé; but it did help a little to take his thoughts from her, for Bonaparte had confirmed his belief that exciting imes lay ahead when they reached the French capital and the various ways in which events might develop gave him much on which to ponder.

However, it was to be many weeks before they reached Paris. After their propitious start the weather became unfavourable. As in the case of the outward journey, Bonaparte allowed their Admiral no say about the course he should take, preferring to trust in his own star rather than let anyone else decide how they should endeavour to evade Nelson's ships.

He ordered Gantheaume to hug the coasts of Tripoli and Tunisia until they came opposite the ruins of ancient Carthage, then head north for Sardinia. His plan was sound, for if they had encountered British warships in the open sea they must either have surrendered or been sunk; whereas, should they be intercepted near the coast, it was his intention to have the frigates run ashore then, accompanied by some eight to nine hundred fighting men, make his way to an African port, from which he might hope to get another ship and again attempt to reach France. But for twenty-one days without intermission the winds were adverse. Laboriously the frigates tacked from side to side, making a few miles each night, only to be blown back towards Alexandria next day.

The gaiety on board soon subsided. For three whole weeks the voyagers suffered the most agonizing frustration and apprehension. Each morning it seemed impossible that dusk should again fall without Sir Sidney Smith's squadron having come upon them. The sighting of even the smallest sail on the horizon made Bonaparte's pale face still paler, from fear that he was about to be captured; for he knew that there could be no escape and that resistance would be futile.

His companions did everything they could to distract him, almost forcing him to play cards and letting him cheat as much as he liked at vingt-et-un; for he could not bear to lose at any game, although he always gave away his winnings.

At last, in mid-September, the wind changed and for long, monotonous days they sailed west along the coast of Africa until they rounded Cape Bon. Soon afterwards they entered on the worst hazard of their journey—the hundred-and-fifty-mile run from the neighbourhood of Bizerta across to the southern tip of Sardinia—for the narrows there were always patrolled by British ships. Fortune favoured them and fair winds continued to carry them up the west side of the big island. But when they had passed it a great storm blew up, driving them with it into the Gulf of Ajaccio, and, failing to beat their way out, the frigates were forced to put into the port.

Far from being pleased at this opportunity to revisit his birth-place and see his relations, Bonaparte was furious at the delay. Moreover, he had long since lost all interest in Corsica and pre-sented a surly face to the innumerable people anxious to claim kinship with him and the scores of mothers who presented their offspring to him vowing that, although the great man's memory might have failed him about such trivialities, he was the god-father of their children.

In Ajaccio they learned that further disasters had befallen the French in northern Italy. On July 22nd the citadel of Alessandria had surrendered and, eight days later, the great fortress of Mantua had fallen. The successful end to these sieges had released many thousands of Austrian troops. In addition, Suvóroff had received reinforcements which brought the strength of the Russians up to twenty-seven thousand men.

Joubert, a young General of great promise, had been sent to Genoa to supersede the veteran Moreau. Ambitious to win laurels for himself but unaware that Mantua had fallen, and hoping to save it, Joubert had left the shelter of Genoa and advanced to Novi where he had seized the heights above the town. There he was attacked by an Austrian Army, under General Kray, and Suvóroff's Russians. Early in the day the young Joubert's promis-ing career was cut short during an encounter with skirmishers. In spite of having lost their General, the French fought valiantly but were surrounded. In the final phase of the battle they had to retreat down a valley choked with their own baggage wagons. Hungarian troops had moved round to the heights commanding it and poured down a relentless fire upon them. The valley became a shambles. Only a remnant of the French got away and at Novi they had lost twelve thousand men.

Meanwhile, terrible things were happening in the south. Nelson had refused to recognize the capitulation of the garrisons of the castle at Naples that had been agreed with Cardinal Ruffo, so these unfortunates became the victims of a White Terror. Instead of being given a safe-conduct to France, as they had been promised, many hundreds of them were executed. King Ferdinand had arrived from Palermo and made his headquarters in Nelson's flagship. Bewitched out of all sense of reason by his Neapolitan friends, Nelson allowed himself to be made their sword of vengeance. Even one hundred and twenty of the noble *Eletti,* who had endeavoured to maintain order in the city after the departure of the Sovereigns, were summarily put to death. As chief executioner in this blood bath, Nelson was created Duke of Bronte by His Sicilian Majesty. But when he later returned to England his own Sovereign, King George III, received him with chilling coldness.

On October 7th the two frigates left Ajaccio on their last desperate run for the French coast. Another thing Bonaparte had learned in Ajaccio was that, as far back as the preceding April, Admiral Bruix had brought his Atlantic Fleet round into the Mediterranean. But instead of employing it to convoy reinforcements to Egypt, as Bonaparte had so consistently implored the Directory to do, they had retained it to protect the south coast of France.

Even so, the Corsican was still haunted by the fear that he might yet be captured; so while in Ajaccio he had had a cutter built. It was to be towed behind *Murion,* with twelve stout rowers in it, so that should the frigate be intercepted by the British, he could at once jump into it and still have a chance of landing in France.

From having to take to it he had the narrowest of escapes. The weather proved fair, but on their second evening out they sighted a British Squadron of fourteen sail. The Squadron recognized the two frigates as Venetian-built and, knowing that the Venetian Fleet had been stolen by the French, at once altered course and came in pursuit. Darkness fell, but they were still in danger of capture. All night, as they heard the reports of the signal guns of the British ships, they sweated in panic. It seemed inevitable that when morning came they would again be sighted, then run down. Their voyage had lasted nearly seven weeks and the thought of being taken prisoner on the very last day drove them frantic with despair. Gantheaume lost his head and urged an attempt to get back to Ajaccio; but Bonaparte, practically alone among them kept calm. He ordered every sail to be spread and, instead of trying to reach Toulon, decided that a course should be set to the north-west. By morning it brought them to St. Raphael, the harbour village that served the ancient town of Fréjus.

Intense as was their relief at their safe arrival, there was another matter that had caused Bonaparte grave concern. Having come from the Near East, where plague was endemic, they were subject to three weeks' quarantine. But a sailing boat came out and hailed them. As soon as it was known that Bonaparte was on board, scores of craft, crammed with people, put out from the little harbour. Shouting, cheering, they forced their way on board, determined to give the conqueror of Italy an unforgettable welcome back to France. Crowding round the slim, pale-faced figure on the quarter-deck, they fought to wring him by the hand or even kiss the hem of his coat. Owing to this the quarantine was rendered pointless. If the frigates had brought plague with them, the populace of Fréjus had been exposed to infection. So by mid-morning it was decided that Bonaparte and his entourage should go ashore.

The latest news to be had in this remote little town was still of French disasters. Of all Italy, France now held only Genoa and the narrow lands of the Ligurian Republic of which it was the capital. The Army of the Archduke Charles was besieging Phillipsburg and Mainz. Suvóroff's Russians had crossed the Alps and entered Switzerland, where another Russian Army, under General Korsakoff, reported to be thirty thousand strong, had joined him for an attempt to crush Masséna. Lastly, the French were being attacked on yet another front. On August 27th a British Army commanded by the Duke of York landed at the Helder and, assisted by Dutch Royalists, had seized the Fleet moored at the Texel. Then, a fortnight later, the British had been joined by a Russian contingent of seventeen thousand men, brought round by sea from the Baltic by General Hermann.

With such enormous forces arrayed against her it was clear that France's situation was now desperate and that before winter set in she might be invaded. Bad as was the news, all Bonaparte's companions knew that it favoured the prospects of their master. His reception at Fréjus could not have been more enthusiastic, but Fréjus was only one small town. Paris and the greater part of France might give him anything but a warm welcome. He had left his Army to rot in the sands of Egypt and families all over the country had husbands, brothers, sons and lovers among those he had abandoned there. When sending him out, the Directory had given him a somewhat ambiguous permission to return in certain circumstances; but he would have to account for his act to the Minister of War, and that Minister was his enemy Bernadotte. There was, too, the awful possibility that he had brought plague to France. He would, therefore, stand or fall by the country's need of him. Only a great public outcry, that he was the one man who could save France, could safeguard him from his enemies.

Roger's little château lay only a few miles away in the direction of St. Maxime, so he naturally offered it for his master's accommodation. But Bonaparte was anxious not to lose a moment in getting to Paris and, as soon as coaches and horses could be collected, he set off with his Generals and personal Staff.

The journey took seven days and proved a triumphal progress. The news of Bonaparte's return had spread like wildfire. People came from miles round to stand along the roadside and cheer him; the streets of the towns and cities through which they passed were choked with crowds hailing him as their deliverer, and from every balcony the women threw down autumn flowers on the little cavalcade. After the first day it was already clear that not one in ten thousand in those seething crowds was giving a thought to Egypt. To them the little, pale-faced General was the heroic conqueror of Italy and the one man who might hold France's enemies at bay.

On October 16th they arrived in Paris. Bonaparte drove straight to his house in the Rue de la Victoire, Roger to his old quarters at La Belle Étoile. The good Norman couple were, as ever, delighted to see him and asked him to dine with them. Over the meal Maître Blanchard gave him the latest news, which confirmed rumours he had heard while on the road, that things had taken a turn for the better.

General Brune's Army in Holland had, on September 19th, inflicted a severe defeat on the Anglo-Russian expeditionary force, so that it was now on the defensive. Better still, from the main theatre of war came the news of a great triumph in Switzerland. One of Masséna's lieutenants, General Lecourbe, with troops used to mountain warfare, had taken heavy toll of Suvóroff's Army as it had forced its way through the defiles of the Alps. Korsakoff, meanwhile, had stormed Zürich. Using the divisions of Mortier and Soult to bar his further advance, Masséna despatched Oudinot's corps of fifteen thousand men to encircle the Russian rear. Korsakoff had then found himself caught in the city with his back to the lake and the river Limmat. A terrific battle had raged for two days until, on September 25th, Korsakofl had formed his infantry into a solid mass and cut his way out through Oudinot's corps. But eight thousand Russian prisoners, a hundred cannon and the whole of Korsakoff's treasure and supplies had been taken. The bastion of Switzerland remained in the hands of France and Masséna had earned himself a place among the greatest of her Generals.

For the time being at least France was no longer in danger and Roger wondered how seriously that might detract from the popularity that Bonaparte had enjoyed during the past week with the fickle masses. His thoughts were, however, abruptly diverted by a serving man coming in to say that M. de Beauharnais was outside and asking to see him urgently.

Apologizing to his host and hostess, Roger left the parlour and went out to find Eugène in a state of great agitation and distress. Taking his young friend by the arm Roger led him into a small room nearby that was empty, sat him down and asked him what was the matter.

Manfully choking back his sobs, Eugéne poured out his story. His step-father had thrown his mother out of the house and intended to divorce her.

The former statement was not strictly accurate, but as near the truth as made no difference. Eugène had learned from the servants that, on the previous day, his mother had dined with Louis Jérome Gohier, who in June had been made a member of the Directory. As, by rota, he was that month its President, a despatch announcing that Bonaparte had landed in France was brought to him. It arrived in the middle of the meal and he informed Josephine of its contents. She had at once gone home, packed her prettiest clothes, ordered her fastest horses and set out to meet her husband. But she had guessed wrongly the road by which he would come, so had missed him.

When Bonaparte arrived in the Rue de la Victoire, instead of finding his wife he was met by his mother. Soon afterwards they were joined by the rest of the Bonaparte clan. One after the other, and at several of them together, they poured into his ears the tale of Josephine's infamies. She had always been hopeless about money and during his absence had piled up a mountain of debt. Before leaving for Egypt, he had said that he would like to have a small house in the country; so Josephine had bought, for four hundred thousand francs, the Château of Malmaison and had furnished it as though it were a palace. But, infinitely worse, they accused her of having hopped into bed with practically every man who had asked her. They then nailed her infidelity beyond question by stating that his servants would confirm that, for weeks at a stretch, she had lived openly and at Malmaison with M. Hippolyte Charles.

Roger knew all about M. Hippolyte Charles. He was just the sort of handsome, amusing blackguard that women adored, and an old flame of Josephine's. When, in the first year of their marriage, she had at last given way to Bonaparte's passionate appeals to join him in Italy, two of the officers who had escorted her had been Junot and Charles. The former had earned her displeasure by making love during the journey to her pretty maid-companion, Louise Compoint, and Roger was inclined to wonder now if it had not been, at least in part, a desire to pay her out that had prompted Junot to show Bonaparte in Egypt the letter reporting her infidelity.

However that might be, dashing Lieutenant Charles had been the life and soul of the party; so much so that soon after its arrival in Italy Bonaparte had found a pretext for forcing him to resign his commission.

That had not worried Hippolyte in the least. He was already performing profitable services for Army contractors, so he became one himself and was said to have since made a fortune.

Eugène maintained that his mother had been indiscreet in seeking distraction during her husband's long absence, but certainly no more. Roger did not contradict him but, knowing Josephine's congenital inability to say 'No' to any request and the warmth of her Creole temperament, he had no doubt at all that out at Malmaison she had given Hippolyte the fullest proofs of her affection. She must, of course, have been scared almost out of her wits by the news of Bonaparte's unexpected return and by the thought that his family were certain to tell him about the sort of life she had been leading. Her only hope had been to reach him before they did and do her utmost to re-arouse his old desire for her; but she had missed him and they had got hold of him first.

When Bonaparte, foaming at the mouth with grief and rage at his worst suspicions having been so fully confirmed, had at last got rid of his puritanical mother, his grave-faced brothers and his screaming sisters, he had gone upstairs, rammed all Josephine's belongings into several trunks, had them carried down into the hall for her to collect, then locked himself in his bedroom and refused to see anyone.

When Eugène had finished his woeful tale Roger considered the situation, both from the personal angle and as it might affect his duty as a secret agent of Mr. Pitt. He had had a considerable hand in the intrigue that had led to Bonaparte marrying Josephine. In fact, but for a great service he had rendered her, the marriage would probably never have taken place. She had more than repaid that by unfailing kindness to him and by saving his life in Venice. These ties constituted a bond between them that would prove invaluable should Bonaparte's star continue in the ascendant and he succeed in his ambition to secure a dominant voice in the future direction of affairs in France. On the other hand, if he rid himself of Josephine he would soon, his temperament being what it was, find himself another woman to fill her place. To establish the same sort of relations with a newcomer would at best mean an immense amount of work, or might even prove impossible. It took Roger less than a minute to decide that friendship and duty marched hand in hand. Clearly he must help in any way he could to prevent Bonaparte from divorcing Josephine; so he said to Eugène:

'I think your mother's future lies not in her hands but in yours. As things are at the moment it is certain that, whether she be guilty or not, your step-father will not listen to her. His family must have poisoned his mind against her to such an extent that nothing she can say will move him. But his weak point is children. He would, I know, greatly like to have one of his own, but so far his attempts in that have been unavailing. Meanwhile, you and your sister partly fill his craving to be a father. He is devoted to you both. My advice, for what it is worth, is that you should return and not only plead your mother's cause but say that, if he abandons her, you and your sister will be driven to despair, because where she goes duty requires you to follow. But you both love him so dearly that to have to leave him would break your hearts.'

Eugène thanked him for his counsel and left the inn. As Roger watched him go, he was far from sanguine about Josephine's chances. He felt that, had *La Bellilotte* accompanied Bonaparte back to Paris, there would have been no hope at all for Josephine; but after his two-month journey the passionate little Corsican must be in a susceptible state with regard to women, so it was just on the cards that, if only Eugène could persuade him to see Josephine, she might arouse his old passion for her and win him back.

Early next morning Eugène came to La Belle Étoile again. He was tired but beaming, and told Roger about the terrible time he had been through. During his absence the previous evening his mother had got back to Paris, found her trunks in the hall and, overwhelmed with despair, gone to pour out her woe to Madame de Château-Renault. Her friend had insisted that she make a fight for it and sent her back. Eugène had found her kneeling outside Bonaparte's door, pleading with him, but he had maintained a stony silence. With his fifteen-year-old sister, Hortense, Eugène took his mother's place. Alternately they implored their step-father to have mercy on their mother and themselves, while Josephine lay at the bottom of the stairs weeping hysterically. At last, the children had persuaded Bonaparte to see his wife. Josephine had staggered up on to the landing. The door had opened. The faces of both were streaming with tears. Without a word, they had fallen into one another's arms.

Pleased and relieved at the outcome of this domestic crisis, Roger sallied forth to savour the autumn air of Paris and order some new uniforms. Later in the day he heard that during the morning Bonaparte had made an official call on the Directors. It was reported in the cafés that they had received him coldly and rumoured that Bernadotte had urged that, for having deserted his Army, he should be arrested. But the *Moniteur* carried heavy headlines announcing his arrival in Paris, and giving an account he had sent them of what he termed his ' greatest victory '.

With splendid effrontery de declared that at Aboukir he had driven thirty thousand Turks into the sea, thus permanently destroying the power of the Sultan to make any further attempt to regain Egypt. He stated that, but for this achievement, he would never have left his beloved Army; but it was in good health and splendid spirits so, with Egypt secure, he had felt it his duty to return and place his sword at the disposal of the Government against the enemies of France nearer home.

It was the first news to be given out in France about the battle of Aboukir, and Paris was thrilled by it. For so many years the Parisians had been fed on accounts of victories in Europe, or defeats that had been more or less covered up as brilliant strategic withdrawals, that such news meant little to them. But the picture conveyed of a few thousand Frenchmen, far from home, triumphing over ten times their number of ferocious barbarians was something new about which to cheer in earnest. Brue's able generalship in Holland and the fact that Masséna had in Switzerland saved France from invasion by a Russian horde were, in a moment, forgotten. Bonaparte was once more the hero of the hour, the idol of the populace.

Roger felt that he had good reason to be pleased with things. The master to whom he had attached himself might be a liar and an opportunist, but he was in most ways a far finer man than the corrupt and inefficient politicians to whom he was secretly opposed; and he was more than holding his own against them. Josephine, meanwhile, had been reinstated. She was once more being hailed by the people as 'Our Lady of Victories' and Roger knew he could count on her friendship.

His own position left nothing to be desired. He had now been a member of the great man's Staff for well over two years and had become one of his intimates. That he did not fully deserve his companions' belief in his bravery he was well aware, as several of his exploits had been faked. But everyone believed that he had escaped from the British after the battle of the Nile, escaped from slavery in Tripoli, escaped again from Djezzar during the siege of Acre and brought with him a Turkish standard. That he had actually come through several desperate situations by his own courage and resource was beside the point. He had been cited in an Order of the Day by Bonaparte, after personally defending him near Venice, and had been presented with a sword of honour. He had again been cited in an Order of the Day, after rejoining Bonaparte outside Acre, and was now known in the Army as '*le brave Brecu*'. Conning over his record to himself, he felt that even the astute Talleyrand must now be convinced that at heart he was truly French. It had needed only that to make his position unassailable.

That evening he decided to call upon his charming and brilliant friend. Before doing so he returned to La Belle Étoile to freshen himself up and have the patched and faded uniform he still wore smartened up as far as that was possible. As he entered the inn a potman gave him a letter. Opening it he saw that it was headed, ' Ministry of Police '. It read:

The Minister presents his compliments to Colonel Breuc and desires him to call upon him at his earliest convenience.

It was signed *Joseph Fouché.*

Roger went as white as the paper on which the letter was written. It seemed incredible, yet it must be true. Somehow, during his absence from France, the subtle, scheming, ex-terrorist had succeeded in climbing from obscurity back to power. Fouché was Roger's most deadly enemy, the one man who had it in his power to ruin him utterly. And he was now Minister of Police.

23

Out of the Past

ROGER had absorbed the contents of the communication at a single glance. Its very brevity precluded any possibility of mistake and it was a summons that he dared not ignore. Abruptly he told the potman to bring him a pint of Anjou wine. Then he sat down to think.

He had last seen Fouché in March, '96. Unlike a number of other prominent terrorists who had saved their own necks by conspiring to bring about Robespierre's downfall in the summer of '94, Fouché's record had been so black that he had been hounded out of the Convention. All his skill at intrigue had failed to save him from the malice of his enemies, and for close on two years he had lived in obscurity and poverty. In the spring of '96 he had striven to secure for himself, by a pretty piece of blackmail, at least a minor post in one of the Ministries; but Roger had outwitted him. Still worse, for him, as his activities had menaced Barras's plans the all-powerful Director had issued an order of banishment, forbidding him to reside within sixty miles of Paris.

How, Roger wondered, with Barras still the most prominent man in the Directory, had Fouché not only secured permission to return to Paris but become Minister of Police, the most powerful official in the capital? Before opening Fouche's letter he had felt so fully assured of his own security. Now, as he slowly drank his wine, he endeavoured to assess how seriously it might be threatened by this extraordinary change in the fortunes of his old enemy.

Had Fouché emerged again as a private individual or even in

some minor post, Roger would have had little to fear. Apart from occurrences during his first year in France, of which only Talley-rand and Fouché knew, his record was unassailable. With his many friends in high places, Barras and Bonaparte among them, he could have laughed to scorn an accusation by any ordinary ex-terrorist; but if the Minister of Police personally vouched for it that he knew Colonel Breuc to be an Englishman and a secret agent, that would be a very different matter.

In France, for the past eight years, all protection of the liberty of the individual had ceased to exist. There was no such law as Habeas Corpus, or any Court before which an accused person might demand to be heard. The country had been ruled by a succession of tyrants who maintained themselves by giving full powers to their secret police to suppress all opposition. Many thousands of people had been arrested merely on suspicion and had been imprisoned indefinitely or shipped off to die in the fever-ridden penal settlements at Cayenne. So Roger now had to face the appalling thought that Fouché could arrest him and, unless he could very speedily get help, order his immediate transportation. Roger had no doubt that Bonaparte would inter-vene on his behalf. But the Corsican must be immersed as never before in his secret struggle with the Directory; and he might not even hear of Roger's arrest until the latter was a prisoner in the hold of a ship well out in the Atlantic.

Before many minutes had passed, he decided that his one hope of protecting himself lay in informing his friends of his danger so that, should he fail to return from his interview with Fouché, they would at once take steps to do what they could for him. Yet he also saw that for him to run round Paris telling all and sundry that he feared he was about to be arrested as an English spy was out of the question. The old adage, ' *qui s'excuse, s'accuse* ', flashed into his mind. As yet he had not even been accused, so what possible grounds could he give for fearing that he would be?

It was then he recalled that, at the moment he had received the bombshell, he had been about to freshen himself up before going to call on Talleyrand. He finished his wine at a draught, then went up to his room. Talleyrand was the one man who knew as much about him as did Fouché, so he could at least consult him without throwing suspicion on himself. It was most unfortunate that the ex-Bishop was no longer Foreign Minister; but though he now

O

lacked the power to protect a friend he could still be counted on for good advice.

Fifteen minutes later Roger left La Belle Étoile in a sedan chair for the Rue Taitbout, where he learned that Talleyrand had moved on leaving the official residence of the Foreign Minister in the Rue de Bac. Darkness had come and rain with it, converting the surface of the streets into inch-deep mud. As his chairmen sloshed through it Roger thought how terribly the state of Paris had deteriorated since he had first known it.

Then, though the streets were narrow, they had been reasonably clean and there were scores of fine mansions in which hundreds of wax candles burned every night. Now, the streets were pot-holed and half choked with refuse. Hardly a glimmer of light was to be seen. The mansions had leaking roofs and broken windows; most of them had become rat-infested tenements, while many of the formerly splendid churches had been turned into shoddy dance halls or gaming dens. The Armies of France had sent back thousands of millions of francs, extorted from conquered countries, yet the Governments had been so corrupt and inefficient that money was never forthcoming to stop the capital from falling into an ever-worse state of rack and ruin.

Talleyrand's house had a courtyard flanked by two pavilions. It was one of the few that, owing to his genius for acquiring money and a good taste that no money could buy, was kept up with the same elegance that had graced those of the old nobility. After Roger's many months spent in the cramped quarters of ships going to and fro across the Mediterranean, and in the insalubrious East, the very sight and warmth of the handsomely furnished hall cheered him a little; but to his annoyance he learned that the master was out, making a round of the salons.

When he said he would await M. de Talleyrand's return, the footman fetched the Majordomo. This portly factotum recognized Roger and said he feared his master might not return home for several hours. But Roger said it was imperative that he should see M. de Talleyrand that night; so the Majordomo showed him into an ante-room, had the footman bring him wine and biscuits, then left him.

For a while he continued to muse over the alarming turn his fortunes had so suddenly taken; but after a time it struck him that no good could come from his spending half the night brooding, so he had better find some other way to employ his mind.

The ante-room contained two bookcases and a large, mahogany rack containing news-sheets. On glancing at these he found that they were the files of the *Moniteur* for several months past; so he spread out some of the sheets on the table and began to look through them.

He already knew that in the previous June there had been a further change in the Directory and another bloodless revolution, termed the *coup d'état* of Prairial. Now he was able to follow its course through the official reports of speeches in the Five Hundred and, from his knowledge of the principal participants, more or less read between the lines what had taken place.

It was clear to him that, when Rewbell had retired from the Directory in May, the Abbé Sieyès—then the Ambassador of France in Berlin—had been elected in his place, not because the remaining Directors wanted him but because the Assembly had forced him upon them.

That they had done so was further evidence of the country's desperate desire for an end of corruption and inefficiency. Sieyès at least had a reputation for honesty and, although he was cunning enough to make few public pronouncements, he was credited with profound wisdom. The Directory had failed so dismally as a form of government that it was felt on all sides that a change in the Constitution was long overdue. Who could produce one with more likelihood of converting the muck-heap inherited from the Revolution into a modern Utopia than this dry-as-dust little Abbé who, for years, had posed as another Solon? Moreover while on the one had he had never been an active terrorist, so would curb the Jacobins, on the other he was a veteran anti-Royalist and had voted for the King's death, so could be trusted to preserve the principles of the Revolution.

But by the time Sieyès had arrived from Berlin new elections had taken place, greatly strengthening the Jacobin Party in the Five Hundred. They had violently denounced the Directory and forced through a law restoring freedom to the Press. This had led to scores of articles and pamphlets appearing, attacking the Directory and especially the opposition to reform displayed by Larevellière, Merlin and Treilhard. Sieyès had obviously seen the necessity for getting rid of them, and Barras, playing as ever for his own hand, must have aided him.

As a first step, although Treilhard had served on the Directory for a year, an illegality disqualifying him from holding office was suddenly discovered, and Gohier, a staunch Republican who had formerly been a Minister of Justice, was elected in his place. Then, on the 30th of Prairial, they had put on the time-worn act of sending a message to the two Chambers, declaring the country 'to be in danger'. Uproar had followed and that evening, to prevent bloodshed. Larevellière and Merlin had agreed to resign. To succeed them the Councils had elected Roger Ducos—who, like Sieyès, never committed himself to anything for which he might later be called to account—and General Moulins, a morose and incompetent man who had been put up because he was too stupid to prove a menace to anyone.

If the object of all these intrigues, vitriolic articles and night-long hurling of insults in the Two Chambers had been to introduce a more moderate form of government, then it had failed dismally. The Jacobins, not so much through numbers as by threats of violence, now dominated the Five Hundred, and both the *Anciens* and the Directory appeared incapable of controlling them.

They had resurrected the Jacobin Club. Over one hundred and fifty Deputies joined it and its sessions were held in the *Manège*, where Danton had thundered, Robespierre had advocated merciless decrees and the King's death had been voted. They had formed a Committee of Eleven which was laying claim to the powers of the old Committee of Public Safety. All this had the full approval of the two fanatically Republican Directors—Gohier and Moulins—and three Generals of the first rank—Bernadotte, Jourdain and Augereau—belonged to their party.

Their attitude was typified by the Law of Hostages, which they had succeeded in pushing through in July. Hoche, by securing a degree of toleration for the Catholics in La Vendée, had at last succeeded in pacifying Brittany; but the Government had not kept its side of the bargain, so fresh disturbances had broken out there. To suppress them it had been decreed that, in the twelve rebellious Departments, the Republican authorities should choose hostages from among the relations of *émigrés* and *ci-devant* nobles. These innocent people were to be imprisoned forthwith. Then, for every Republican killed by the partisans, four hostages were to have their entire property seized and to be transported to Cayenne.

The Jacobins were hated by the vast majority of the people, but they were also feared; for their ruthless minority included among its members not only Directors, Generals and many

Deputies, but a great number of officials in the administration and the police. It was reported that at the Café Godeau, near the Tuileries, the revolutionaries who assembled there had vowed that they would slaughter ten thousand victims to the shade of Robespierre, and that they drank nightly to a return to the days of '93 when they would again see the guillotine at work in the Place du Carrousel.

As Roger absorbed this he no longer had cause to wonder how it was that a man with Joseph Fouchés record had succeeded in getting himself made Minister of Police.

It was past midnight when Talleyrand appeared. Despising cloth for evening wear as plebeian, he was dressed in wine-coloured satin and, indifferent to the jibes of the Jacobins, still wore his hair powdered. Raising his quizzing-glass on its broad black ribbon, he eyed Roger through it from the doorway, bowed and said with a smile:

'My poor friend, I am told you have been waiting here for hours. If only I had known——'

'But you did not,' Roger said quickly, 'and it is I who should apologize for bothering you at such an hour. I trust, though, that you will give me a few minutes, as the matter is urgent.'

'Why, certainly. But what do I see?' The statesman's glance fell on the table. 'Cold Claret and a few biscuits. My people have neglected you shamefully. This is no fit fare for that gallant soldier "*le brave Breuc*".'

Roger flushed slightly. 'I've done little to earn such an appellation and wonder that anyone should have told you of it.'

'One hears things, you know; one hears things.' Talleyrand turned to the footman behind him. 'Henri, have the centres of some *brioches* removed and the shells stuffed with foie-gras; and fetch a bottle of champagne from the ice locker.' Turning back to Roger, he added:

'Champagne is the only possible drink after midnight. Tell me now; in what way can I be of service to you?'

'It seems,' Roger replied, 'that you have heard something of the way in which I have risked my life several times during the past seventeen months. May I ask whether you are now fully convinced about what I told you when last we met—that, since joining General Bonaparte's Staff, I have regarded myself as a Frenchman?'

'Why, yes. That is, dear friend, as fully convinced as my unhappily low assessment of human nature ever allows me to be about anything. But at least I know you to be no fool. Having laid the foundations of such a promising career for yourself in France, I cannot think you would be so stupid as to risk throwing it away by aiding France's enemies.'

'I am relieved to hear it; for one person remains who, like yourself, knows that I am Admiral Brook's son. And I have reason to fear that he intends to ruin me.'

'Who is this tiresome individual?'

'Joseph Fouché.'

Talleyrand raised his eyebrows. 'Indeed! That is most unfortunate. Fouché is the most dangerous blackguard unhung, and if you have made an enemy of him in the past your case is serious.'

'Alas, I have; and this evening I received a letter from him requiring me to report to him at his Ministry. Should he arrest me, I was hoping that I might count on your protection.'

Before replying, Talleyrand took out his snuff-box, tapped the lid, took a pinch and dusted the specks from his satin coat with a flick of his lace handkerchief. Then he said gravely, 'I would give it you willingly, had I the means; but I am at the moment no more than a private citizen.'

Roger nodded. 'I knew that you were no longer Foreign Minister. A rumour reached us in Egypt that you had been deprived of your post owing to a difference of opinion with some Americans, and I was most distressed to hear it.'

'Oh, that!' Talleyrand gave his low, rich laugh. 'My compliments on the delicacy of the way in which you put it. Our "difference of opinion" was that those boors refused to subscribe to accepted European custom and pay me a miserable hundred thousand francs before I would enter into negotiations with them about some of their ships we were holding. But I was not deprived of my post. I resigned, and that although no pressure was brought on me to do so.'

'You surprise me.' Roger raised his eyebrows. 'May one ask what led you to give up such an interesting and er . . . lucrative post?'

'You may. I had made enough out of it to live respectably for some time to come and, although I should resent anyone else terming me a rat, you will know the old proverb about rats leaving the sinking ship. The Directory is doomed and I have an aversion to being drowned. Moreover, the *canaille* had become so vociferous about me that I felt it politic to retire into private life for a while. When the Legislature again gave freedom to the Press I became the target for every kind of abuse. They even had the impudence to write most scurrilously about my private life and, still worse, to question my foreign policy. As you are aware, I have always maintained that the only hope for lasting peace and prosperity in Europe lies in a rapprochement between France and Britain. They dubbed me an *émigré* Anglophile and asserted that my aim was to wreck the Revolution. As though it could be wrecked further than it already had been by those foul-mouthed, bloodthirsty Jacobins.'

At that moment the footman arrived with the champagne and *brioches*. Standing up, Talleyrand limped over to the table and poured the wine himself. As he handed a glass to Roger he went on, ' So, by resigning when I did, I both diverted the attentions of the mud-slingers from myself and gracefully bowed my way out of this Government that is now execrated by everybody. But, of course, I took steps to continue doing what little I could to prevent the Directory from further poisoning our foreign relations. I persuaded them to appoint my old friend, Reinhard, in my place. He is a most admirable man nad accepts my guidance without question. He realizes, too, that he is no more than a stop-gap and will take no umbrage at my replacing him as soon as we can get rid of these dolts now occupying the Luxembourg.'

' You are convinced, then, that the Government will fall? ' Roger asked, before taking a large bite out of one of the delicious *brioches*.

' As certain as one can be of anything. But I have digressed too long. When do you propose to pay your call on Fouché? '

' Tomorrow; or rather, this morning. It would certainly not improve my case to wait until he has me fetched. All I can do is put a bold face on matters, endeavour to convince him, as I have you, that I have served France well in these past two years and intend to continue to do so; and trust that, powerful though he has become, he will think twice about having me arrested as a secret agent. After all, it is only his word against mine that I was not born a Frenchman, and should he arbitrarily spirit me away I am sure you will be good enough to set on foot enquiries as to what has become of me.'

' On that you may rely. Go to him early. Tell him you have an appointment with me here at midday. That may give him pause. Should you not be here by twelve o'clock I will go straight to Bonaparte. I had a long interview with him this morning and during it enquired after you. He holds you in high regard and, as you are one of his aides-de-camp, he is entitled to demand an explanation as to why you are being held. Even so, I shall be much relieved if you are able to keep our appointment. As Minister of Police, Fouché has almost unlimited powers and is answerable to no one other than the Directory. If he does detain you it may prove far from easy to get you out of his clutches.'

' It is that I fear. And I am most grateful to you for what you propose to do. When last I saw him, he had just received an order of banishment signed by Barras. To find him back here in Paris and wielding such power came as a great shock to me. How in the world has such a villain succeeded in making his way back into public life? '

Talleyrand smiled. ' Dear friend, you have answered yourself. Because he is a villain. Birds of a feather, you know. This past year or more, the Directory has had the greatest difficulty in surviving. It has succeeded only by the use of bribery, blackmail and treachery. It is by no means easy to find officials willing to employ such methods who are, at the same time, capable administrators. And no one could question Fouché's ability. When he bobbed up again, they decided to let bygones be bygones and reap the benefit of his special talent for villainy.'

' It still amazes me that they should have put into his hands the immense powers enjoyed by a Minister of Police.'

' They did not do so to begin with. If you wish, I could give you particulars of his rogue's progress.'

Roger replied that he would very much like to hear them; so his host took his malacca cane and, with his graceful limp, left the room. Some minutes later he returned carrying a folder. As he sat down again and opened it he said, ' While I was at the Foreign Ministry I naturally had my own intelligence service. When I was about to leave, it occurred to me that if I brought some of these dossiers with me they might later prove useful.'

Flicking over the contents of the folder, he went on, ' There are pages and pages about Fouchés activities during the Terror, but no doubt you are already informed thereon. Ah, here we are! " Banished from Paris by order of Director Barras. Settled in Montmorency Valley. Near destitute. Started pig-farming on a capital said to be less than one hundred louis." ' Talleyrand sniffed. ' What a revolting occupation to choose. But I suppose there is money in it.'

' He had a pig farm on the outskirts of Paris before he was banished,' Roger volunteered. ' I gathered, though, that he was making very little out of it because someone else had put up the capital. But, I pray you, continue.'

' " Early in '97 returned to Paris, started a small company for delivering food to troops in north-west France. Got rid of partners and began to do well on his own. Helped to secure the acquittal of the financier Hinguerlot from charges preferred against him before the Tribunal of Melun. This led to establishing valuable connections with the other Parisian bankers. Undertook the organization of profitable smuggling operations on the Dutch frontier. Made overtures to the self-styled King Louis XVIII, then at Mitau. Offered information and assistance to bring about a Restoration." '

' Can that really be true? ' Roger asked. ' I would not have thought even Fouché capable of such a volte-face. Besides, he is a regicide and must have been crazy to imagine that the King would take into his service one of his brother's murderers.'

Talleyrand shrugged and took a drink of wine. ' Stranger things have happened, and only Sieyès is more adept than Fouché at turning his coat. This, of course, occurred in the summer of '97, when there came the great reaction to the Right led by the *Clichiens*. To uninformed people, as Fouché then was, it must have looked quite likely that Pichegru and his friends would succeed in restoring the Monarchy. No doubt our wily friend thought that by a stitch in time he might at least earn a pardon. But you are right. The Royalists would have nothing to do with him.'

Again scanning the dossier, Talleyrand went on, ' " His reaction to this rebuff was to throw himself heart and soul into the movement of the Left, which culminated in the coup of *Fructidor* by which General Augereau swept away the Royalist elements in the Legislature. It was Fouché's activities at this time that earned him the approbation of the Directory and led to his Order of Banishment being rescinded. In September, '98, he was sent as Ambassador to the Cisalpine Republic. While there, he saw the folly of seeking to dictate to the Italians rather than win them as willing allies and, in this, he had the support of General Joubert. The

Directory did not approve this policy and he was recalled." '

Breaking off for a moment, Talleyrand remarked, 'It was I who urged that policy upon him. Because the Directory counter-manded it France has since paid the penalty. Had we not oppressed the Italians they might have sided with us against Suvóroff's Russians. But no matter. " On his return he was sent as Ambassador to the Batavian Republic. Its Government, owing to French oppression, was toying with the idea of coming to terms with the Orange Party, which was under the influence of England. By skilful diplomacy he prevented that. This resulted in the Dutch Army under General Daendles siding with France when the Anglo-Russian force landed in Holland a month later. In July he was recalled and made Minister of Police. On August 13th, he closed the Jacobin Club.'

'What!' exclaimed Roger. 'Is it possible? Next you'll be telling me that he has gone to Mass in Notre Dame.'

'Os, he will, sooner or later,' Talleyrand replied. It is no longer the fashion to feed donkeys on the Host and tie Bibles to their tails, as he did when representing the Committee of Public Safety in Lyons. It is simply that, now he has become a Minister, he wants to remain one. He is, therefore, prepared to use repressive measures against either side, if it looks like making trouble. He has courage, you know, as well as brains.'

They talked for a while longer and finished the champagne. Then, as Talleyrand accompanied Roger out into the hall, he said:

'You and I have always held the same views about what is best for Europe and events in the next few weeks may decide the future of Europe for many years to come. You are both Bonaparte's friend and mine. Since we both trust you, I had hoped that you would act as a contact between us at times when it would be wiser for neither of us to call upon the other. That apart, such an evil chance having beset you distresses me greatly. I would give much to be able to protect you from Fouché. As that is beyond my power, I can only wish you well and promise that, should your worst fears be realized, I will do my utmost to have you brought to trial and see that you get a fair hearing.'

This was cold comfort, for Roger knew that should he be brought to trial he would, for ever afterwards, remain suspect, even if he were acquitted, so he would be finished as a secret agent. But at least Talleyrand would provide a life-line which would prevent his being spirited away and dealt with summarily before his friends had had time to start wondering what had become of him.

He found his two chairmen curled up asleep beside a brazier under the *porte-cocheur*. As he roused them, Talleyrand came down the steps from the house and said, 'I see that, not realizing that your return would be at such a late hour, you brought no link-man. I will send my night-watchman to light you on your way. He can lock the courtyard gate behind him.'

'I thank you for the thought,' Roger replied, 'but this is a public chair. I am sure the bearers must know Paris well and will have no difficulty in finding their way back to my inn.'

'It is not a question of finding the way. You must have light, to shine upon your sword or a pistol held so that it can be seen through the window of the chair; otherwise you will be attacked.'

'Attacked! By whom? Why should I be?'

Talleyrand gave a cynical laugh. 'My friend, you are a stranger in Paris. Otherwise you would know that our Government is much too occupied with other matters to prevent a thousand footpads roaming the streets every night. Why, the banker who finances the gaming rooms at the Palais Royal has to hire a troop of cavalry to escort his cashier's barouche to the bank with each day's takings. Did he not, he would soon find it hard to get cashiers, for, night after night, their throats would be cut.'

Roger made no further protest about accepting the services of the watchman. He reached home without incident, a little afer two o'clock in the morning. In spite of his anxiety, he dropped off to sleep almost as soon as his head touched the pillow.

By half past nine next morning he was at the Ministry of Police. On his producing Fouché's letter a bearded official, wearing a seedy overcoat, wrote his name in a book then took him to a bare, chilly waiting room. His nerves taut with apprehension about the coming interview, he paced to and fro between the window and the door. Ten minutes passed, fifteen, but nobody came for him; so he sat down on a wooden bench. The only printed matter in the room was police notices on the walls. Inevitably, his mind drifted to Joseph Fouché and what he knew of that strange, devious-minded man.

Fouché had been born in Nantes, of middle-class parents. The family were merchants and shipowners and owned a plantation in the West Indies, but Joseph was put into the Church. He never actually took Orders, but for ten years wore the tonsure as a lay brother of the Oratorian Fathers and taught in their seminaries. From his teens, he had taken an interest in police work and one of his hobbies was playing the amateur detective. The other was science, with special interest in balloon ascents such as those of the Montgolfier brothers, which were then arousing great interest.

In '89, still as an Oratorian schoolteacher, he was living in Arras. There he became friendly with Robespierre and his family. So close was the friendship that he had contemplated marrying Robespierre's sister Charlotte and, when Robespierre had been elected as a Deputy to the Third Estate, it was Fouché who had lent the impecunious lawyer the money to go to Paris.

Imbued with the revolutionary ideas of the Arras circle of which Carnot, then stationed there as an Officer of Engineers, had also been a member, he had returned to Nantes, left the Oratorians and became a professional agitator. In September, '92, he had been elected as a Deputy for Loire Inférure. In the same month he had married a Mademoiselle Coignaud, the daughter of a local official. She had red hair and eyebrows, a pale, pimply face and was terribly ugly. Yet Fouché adored her. His love for her and the children he had by her was the one constant and decent emotion he displayed in his whole life.

In Paris, as a member of the Convention, he had soon made his mark. In '93, the Committee of Public Safety had sent him as *Représentant en Mission* to Nevers. With unlimited powers, he had given free rein to a fanatical atheism, sacked all the churches, sent all their sacred vessels to Paris to be melted down and made the Archbishop wear the Red Cap of Liberty. Transferred to Moulins, he had carried out similar desecrations. But it was in Lyons that he had made his name for ever infamous.

In the autumn of '93 a Liberal reaction had taken place in Lyons, which resulted in a noted revolutionary named Chalier being executed. Robespierre had sent Collot d'Herbois and Fouché to purge the city. With merciless frenzy they had attacked the bourgeoisie, throwing hundreds of them into prison, looting their homes from garret to cellar and even stripping them of their clothes. Their final enormity had been to enjoy, from a dais they had erected in a field, a spectacle of mass murder. Scores of prisoners lashed together in couples had been lined up in front of two trenches, then mown down by grape-shot fired from cannon at close quarters. Those who survived the blasts were then hacked to pieces by the troops, on the orders of Collot and Fouché.

But in the summer of '94, Robespierre's egomania began to be dreaded even by his closest collaborators. The slightest deviation from his principles by one of his followers could lead to that rash individual's head landing in the basket of the guillotine within twenty-four hours. As the only hope of saving themselves, Fouché, Tallien, Freron and other terrorists had conspired with some of the Moderate leaders and it was Robespierre who had gone to the guillotine. By timely turning of his coat Fouché had saved his life, but had bought it at the price of his career. Having made use of him, the Thermidorians had thrown him aside and for four years he had been compelled to eat in poverty the bitter bread of frustrated ambition.

Such was the man upon whose pleasure Roger waited.

And wait he did. Half an hour went by, an hour, two hours, yet still no one came for him. At half past eleven he went out to the bearded official and sent a message up that M. de Talleyrand was expecting him at twelve; so he could not remain there much longer. A reply came down that the Minister regretted the delay. Would he be good enough to return at six o'clock?

Having said that he would, he left the building. His interminable wait had frayed his nerves almost to breaking-point and now he had another six hours to get through somehow before he would know Fouché's intentions towards him. Hailing a hackney-coach, he had himself driven to the Rue Taitbout. Talleyrand received him with his usual affability, listened sympathetically to his angry account of the way in which he had been treated, then said:

'To keep you on tenterhooks like this is typical of Fouché's methods. He hopes to undermine your confidence in yourself. You must not let him. It is obvious that this wretched business has already had a serious effect on you. If you brood on it all the afternoon that may prove disastrous. I shall prescribe for you. First, a good gallop. I will order a horse to be saddled. Ride him out to Vincennes and ride hard. If you kill the animal, no matter. On your return, go to a fencing school. Spend two hours there and fight at least six bouts. Then dinner. Eat fish, not meat, for that is heavy and would dull your brain. With dinner a pint of champagne, but no other alcohol either before or after. Tonight I am holding a reception. I shall hope that you will be free to attend it. But, should you not, Bonaparte will be here and I will tell him of my fears for you.'

With a thin smile, Roger thanked him for his counsel and promised to follow it. The fresh air and violent exercise did him a world of good. Soon after five o'clock he sat down at La Belle Étoile to a large Sole Colbert, and took with it his 'medicine as directed'. At six o'clock he was back at the Ministry of Police, still extremely anxious but now able to make himself look as though he had nothing to worry about.

This time he was taken straight upstairs to the Minister's room, a large apartment the walls of which were entirely hidden by row upon row of filing cabinets. Fouché was sitting at a big desk with his back to a tall window, but it was now dark and lamps had been lit which shed their light only on his desk and on any visitor seated opposite him.

He was now forty and, in appearance, quite exceptionally un-attractive. Although strong, his tall body was so lean and angular that it gave the impression that he was suffering from some wasting disease. His face was thin and bony, with the complexion of a corpse. From the point of his large, sharp nose there frequently hung a drop, as all his life he suffered from a perpetual cold. His red hair was sparse and brushed over his scalp in rats' tails. His lips were thin and his heavily lidded eyes greenish. They had a fish-like appearance, but few people had ever looked right into them because, when talking to anyone, he always kept his glance averted. Nobody who did not know him would have thought it possible that he was capable of working twenty hours a day, as he often did for long periods; for he seemed to be so drained of all vitality that within the week he would be measured for his coffin.

Without looking at Roger he stood up, made a slight bow, waved his bony hand towards the chair opposite his desk and said, 'So we old acquaintances meet again.'

'A classic phrase,' smiled Roger, sitting down. 'And I am happy to think that we are both better situated than when last we met.'

'I must congratulate you on having become a Colonel in the French Army.'

'And I you in having become Minister of Police.'

Fouché studied the fingernails of his right hand. 'You may also do so on another count. You will recall that when last we parted I was penniless and about to go into banishment. I have since succeeded in making for myself a . . . well, let us call it a modest fortune.'

'I am glad to hear it.'

'You will also recall that, on the occasion to which I refer, you gave me a hundred louis.'

'That is so,' Roger murmured, greatly surprised at the turn the conversation had taken. He thought it hardly possible that Fouché could have raised the matter with the intention of showing gratitude, but added:

'Instead of exile in penury, you had been counting on Barras giving you some minor appointment which would have supported you. You were, I remember, greatly distressed by the thought of the hardship your wife would have to endure. That was my reason for giving you a sum to go on with.'

'I know it. At the time I believed that you had thrown it to me as a sop because you had cheated me. But later I learned that, although you had got the better of me by your wits, it was through no fault of yours that Barras treated me so abominably. I am now able to repay your generous gesture.'

As he spoke, Fouché produced from a drawer in his desk a little sack. It clinked as he pushed it across to Roger, and he added, 'There are a hundred louis. The hundred you lent me proved the basis of my fortune.'

Scarcely able to believe his eyes and ears, Roger leaned forward, took up the sack, and said with a smile, 'Many thanks, *Monsieur le Ministre*. You enable me to hope that, in future, relations between us may be more cordial.'

Fouché gave a loud sniff then, with a swift, covert glance from beneath his heavy eyelids, replied, 'I have only one regret. It is that I could not put guineas into the bag instead of louis. The coin of your own country might have proved more useful to you, Mr. Brook; er . . . that is, if my police had allowed you to get out of Paris with it.'

24

The Great Conspiracy

ROGER'S smile froze on his lips. In spite of his amazement at finding Fouché's attitude to him so different from the hostility he had expected, he had for a few moments allowed himself to be deceived into thinking that his old enemy had sent for him only to repay a debt. But nothing of the kind. He had simply been playing the sort of cat-and-mouse game in which he delighted. Again there arose in Roger's mind those awful visions of years spent forgotten in a dark dungeon in some remote fortress, or dying of yellow fever at Cayenne. With a supreme effort he succeeded in preventing his face from showing any marked reaction, and asked quietly:

'Why should you suppose that I wish to leave Paris?'

'Does not every man wish at times to return to his own country?'

'France is my country.'

'Oh, come!' Fouché's thin-lipped mouth twitched in a faint smile. 'Others appear to believe that, but you cannot expect me to accept such a barefaced lie. Need I remind you that, when first I came upon you as a boy in Rennes, you admitted to me that you were the son of Admiral Brook and had run away from home?'

'In for a penny, in for a pound,' thought Roger, so he snapped back, 'I need no reminding of how you murdered poor old Doctor Fénelon and stole our money.'

Fouché gave a slight shrug. 'It was not murder. My pistol went off by accident. And I needed the money. But, your admission apart, four years later I followed you to England in the hope of earning the reward offered for the documents you stole from the

Marquis de Rochambeau. I came upon you at your home, Grove Place, at Lymington. You cannot deny that.'

'I do not seek to do so; nor deny that I am Admiral Brook's son.'

'Then you admit that you are an English spy?'

'I certainly do not. The Marquis's papers came into my hands by chance. Young as I was I realized that, if I could get them to London, it might prevent a war between England and France. I proved right in that. It was your misfortune that, after you regained the papers, I got them back. But at that time we were private individuals. Neither you nor I were then agents employed by our Governments.'

'That is true; also that you got the better of me. It was the first time, but not the last. I will admit that you are a most redoubtable opponent. The way in which you made off with the Dauphin was masterly. Yet had I left Paris but half an hour earlier I would have caught you and had you guillotined for it.'

In spite of the peril he was now in, Roger felt on the top of his mettle and replied with a laugh, 'For that again, you cannot accuse me of espionage. I acted as I did on account of a personal promise that I had made to Queen Marie Antoinette, not as the agent of a foreign Power.'

That was only a half-truth, but Fouché could not contest it. He was doodling on a piece of paper and, without looking up, said, 'Later, you deceived me into believing that you still had the boy, then told me he was dead. What was the truth of the matter?'

For a moment Roger hesitated, then he replied, 'You will recall that, as I pushed off with him in the boat, you and your men fired upon us. He was hit by a ball and died that night.' That was not the truth, but was near enough, for the boy was dead before Roger landed on the far shore of Lake Geneva. After a moment he went on:

'Neither can you accuse me of espionage in the matter of Madame Bonaparte's diary. I retrieved it from you only because Barras wished her to marry his protégé, the young General. She would have refused to do so had we not suppressed the evidence that her first marriage to de Beauharnais was bigamous, owing to her having already married William de Kay while still in her teens.'

'Yes, yes; but all this does not make you a Frenchman.'

'Not legally, I agree. Yet for many years past I have lived in

France and thought of myself as a Frenchman. You are well aware of the part I played during the Revolution. Admittedly, it is known to you that at heart I was a Royalist. But what of it? Thousands of Royalists have since become good Republicans, and thousands of Republicans would tomorrow, if they thought a Restoration likely, become Royalists.'

'That is true. But the fact remains that you, an Englishman, now pose as a Frenchman born in Strasbourg, and that you have succeeded in getting yourself appointed as one of General Bonaparte's aides-de-camp. In such a position you must become privy to many State secrets.'

'Certainly, and why should I not?' Roger asked boldly. 'My relatives in England long since cast me off, owing to my Liberal opinions. I am making a career for myself in France, and a fine one. To betray the country of my adoption for the sake of the country of my birth would be to cut off my nose to spite my face. Surely you see that?'

For a full minute Fouché continued to doodle, then he said, 'You once did me a kindness but, on balance, I have no cause to love you; and in the past you have given me ample proof that you are a very dangerous man. I can see no reason why I should allow you to continue to perpetrate upon General Bonaparte and others the fraud that you were born a Frenchman. Since I have personal knowledge of your origin, any form of trial would be redundant and, as Minister of Police, I am in a position to have you swiftly eliminated. To do so seems to me only a sensible precaution against the possibility that you are lying to me.'

Realizing that the crisis of the interview was at hand, Roger said firmly, 'I agree that you have the power to give orders that I should be carted off to some hideous fate, before my friends could even demand that I be formally accused and tried. But what of afterwards? Let us consider two possibilities.

'First, we will assume that I am at heart loyal to France. You would then have deprived your country of a useful servant. There would be only your word for it that I was a traitor. No one would believe you. It would be thought that you had abused your position to exact a private vengeance. Bonaparte, Talleyrand and a dozen other of my friends would never forgive you. And the Army, which now terms me "*le brave Breuc*", would execrate your name.

'Secondly, we will assume that I am a spy. You might employ

false witnesses, but you could produce no convincing proof that I am Admiral Brook's son. Again you would be disbelieved, and attract to yourself the same enmity and opprobrium. But more. Were I an agent of Mr. Pitt, can you really believe that I should come here like a lamb to the slaughter? Certainly not. I should be hand in glove with the Royalist agents. I should have learned from them that, in the summer of '97, a certain Citizen Joseph Fouché offered his aid in an attempt to place Louis XVIII on the throne of France. I should——'

'There is not one word of truth in that,' Fouché broke in quickly.

'Of course not,' Roger agreed smoothly, 'nor is there in your fanciful idea that I am an English agent. Yet if I were, you may be certain that, before placing myself in your hands, I would have arranged with my friends that, if you dealt with me as a spy, they should at once put it about all over Paris that, when the Government of France ceased to give you employment, you had offered to betray the Revolution. To that one should add that, just as you might employ false witnesses against me, so the Royalist agents would produce letters, er . . . faked of course, that people might accept as proof, that you had been in communication with the Court at Mitau.'

It was Roger's only card, a bluff based on the information Talleyrand had given him. There might be no incriminating letters in existence, for Fouché was so cautious in all his dealings that he had probably communicated with Mitau only through a third party and had never put pen to paper. But such letters could be forged and it was a certainly that the Royalists in Mitau would willingly have co-operated in attempting to ruin an ex-terrorist of Fouché's standing.

As the cadaverous Minister continued to stare silently at his desk, Roger went on in a conciliatory tone, ' But all this is beside the point. No one could ever seriously accuse you of scheming to betray the Republic that you played so large a part in establishing, any more than anyone other than yourself could seriously accuse me of being one of Mr. Pitt's agents. And that is the crux of the matter. That I was born an Englishman, to you I readily admit; but that I am a spy, I deny. Therefore, should you use your power arbitrarily to terminate my career, you will be doing a deliberate disservice to your country for the purpose of satisfying your private malice.'

' No, no! ' Fouché shook his head. ' I am not a malicious man. I have never willingly made an enemy in my life. My only enemies are those who are jealous of me.'

' Then why make one of General Bonaparte, as you certainly will if you make away with a man whose services he regards as valuable? '

Fouché sniffed, then repeated, ' General Bonaparte. I gather that you are on intimate terms with him? '

' That I can certainly claim to be, and something more than an ordinary military aide-de-camp. In the winter of '98, I went to England on a secret mission for him and brought him back accurate information about the defences on the south coast there. How can you reconcile that with your idea that I am here as a spy for England? '

' I would like to have your opinion of Bonaparte.'

' It is that he is the most remarkable man alive. As a soldier, he is head and shoulders above any other General. But not only that. He is a great administrator. His head is stuffed with more general knowledge than those of any other ten men you could name, yet his mind is so lucid that he never confuses issues. He has immense courage and the ability to make decisions on the instant.'

' You confirm all that I have heard from other sources. Do you think that he intends to stage a *coup d'etat*? '

' If I knew, I certainly should not tell you. But I will offer you a piece of advice. Everyone knows that the Directory is on its last legs. Whatever may emerge from its downfall, you can be certain that Bonaparte is too strong a man to allow himself to be trampled underfoot and, if he does seek power, he will have many friends to aid him. Yet, at this time, when the future is still in doubt, he cannot have too many friends. You would be wise to become one of them.'

Fouché's fish-like eyes suddenly flickered over Roger's face. Looking away again, he said, ' Advice from a man like yourself is worthy of very serious consideration. In my view, though, it will be all or nothing. The Jacobins are again very powerful, and he is not a politician. If, before he is ready to strike, they accuse him in the Five Hundred of conspiring to become a Dictator, nothing can save him. He will be declared an Outlaw, then no one will dare raise a voice in his defence. On the other hand, if he does intend to bring about a *coup d'état* and is successful, he'll brook no rivals in the new Government. He will seize supreme power for himself.'

'And, as a result,' Roger added, 'every plum on the tree will go to those who have aided him. In my position, devoted to him as I am, I stand to make my fortune. Can you any longer suppose that I should throw such a chance away because I happen to have been born in England?'

A bleak smile again twitched Fouché's thin lips as he replied, 'I have never taken you for a sentimentalist. But, er . . . with regard to your advice. When Bonaparte was last in Paris, I was busying myself with a commercial venture in northern France; so I have never met him. I should find it interesting to do so, in order that I can form my own opinion of the man.'

Roger's heart suddenly began to hammer in his chest. Each beat was as if it cried aloud, 'I've won! I've won! I've won!' With a little bow, he said, 'I should be very happy to arrange a meeting.'

'That would be to add to my indebtedness to you,' Fouché's shifty glance again met Roger's for an instant. 'However, when suggesting it to him, please do not give the impression that I intend to commit myself to anything.'

'Assuredly not. But, in the event of your impression proving favourable and certain movements being set on foot, you would, no doubt, wish to keep in touch with him. It might be ill-advised to do so openly with any frequency. If you felt that, and were also averse to putting anything on paper . . .'

'*Mon cher Colonel,* I take your thought. And I am sure that I can count on your discretion as a verbal courier between us. After all, although you and I differed in our political opinions we worked together for the overthrow of Robespierre, did we not? In this case it seems unlikely that even our political opinions would differ.'

'*Monsieur le Ministre,* I am delighted that you should think that, but not at all surprised. France is in a wretched state and has been so for far too long. All sensible men now seem to agree that what the country needs is a strong man, capable of bringing order out of chaos. General Bonaparte is such a man, and one can think of no other.'

Having given a nod of agreement, Fouché swiftly hedged. 'You will, of course, appreciate that in my position I could not take a personal part in any movement. Such action as is taken would be entirely his affair. I should remain merely an observer.'

'Naturally,' Roger agreed gravely. 'And, after all, we are talking of something that may never take place. Let us leave it that you are to meet the General. Should you then feel about him as do others who know him well, and should he contemplate anything, you might, perhaps, be willing to view the project with benevolent neutrality?'

'Benevolent neutrality. That is an apt phrase; most apt. I see that we understand one another very well.' Coming slowly to his feet, Fouché added, 'And now, *mon cher Colonel,* it remains only for me to thank you for having called upon me.'

Roger rose and took the moist, bony hand offered him. '*Monsieur le Ministre,* it has been a great pleasure to me to renew our acquaintance in such circumstances. In future you may rely upon me to have your interests at heart.'

'You are most kind. Life could be so much simpler if one had only to deal with friends. For my part, should you have any little personal troubles at any time please remember that the Ministry of Police can usually find ways to smooth them out, and that it is at your service.'

Five minutes later Roger was out in the street. His relief at emerging from the Ministry was submerged in elation. He could hardly believe that he was not dreaming. Fouché might still have suspicions about him, but, if so, they could be only lingering ones which he was prepared to ignore unless given fresh cause to believe that Colonel Breuc was betraying France. In his tussle with Talleyrand Roger had been worsted and, to convince him of his *bona fides,* had been compelled to spend seventeen arduous months in the Near East and Mediterranean. But in this far more dangerous battle of wits with Fouché it was he who had come off best, for not only had he retained his freedom but, to his amazement, had also placed himself in a situation that could prove enormously to his advantage.

When he arrived at Talleyrand's reception he found, receiving with him, a woman of quite exceptional beauty. She was past her first youth but had a lovely figure, a marvellous complexion, big blue eyes, masses of golden hair and a slightly *retroussé* nose, not unlike that of Talleyrand. Roger bowed over her hand, gave Talleyrand a smiling nod to indicate that he had successfully survived his interview with Fouché, then moved away into the crowd.

At the buffet, he found himself next to an old acquaintance: a handsome gentleman known as *le beau* Montrond '. He was a wit, a dandy, a gambler, a formidable duellist and a great personal friend of Talleyrand's. He had attached himself to the statesman and rendered him many useful services. It was said of him that on one occasion Talleyrand had remarked to a third party in de Montrond's presence, ' You know, I like de Montrond because he is not overburdened with scruples.' Upon which de Montrond put in, ' And I like de Talleyrand because he has no scruples at all.'

To de Montrond Roger said, ' Tell me, who is that beautiful woman who is acting as hostess for our host? '

De Montrond looked at him in surprise. ' Do you not know? But, of course, you have been long abroad. She is a Madame Grand and is known as " The Indian " because, although the daughter of a Frenchman, she was born in Pondicherry. From her teens she has been a most notorious whore; but no one can deny her beauty and our dear Charles-Maurice has made her, for all practical purposes, his wife.'

Roger needed to ask no more for, although he had never met Catherine Grand when he was in Calcutta, her name had still been a legend in Society there. At the age of fifteen she had married an official of the India Company named Grand. Her dazzling beauty had soon attracted the interest of Sir Philip Francis, a member of the Supreme Council of Bengal: the man who, with vitriolic venom, had, as a friend of Charles James Fox and in the Whig interests, consistently thwarted the work of India's greatest Governor, Warren Hastings. One night, Grand's Indian servants had found a ladder made of sections of bamboo swinging from Mrs. Grand's window. Believing that burglars had used it to gain entry the servants had roused the house. Sir Philip had then been found in the bed of its luscious sixteen-year-old mistress.

Mr. Grand had promptly returned the young lady to her parents and sued Sir Philip for heavy damages. Although the case had gone against him, Sir Philip had performed the extraordinary feat of persuading his wife that his interest in his enchanting little mistress was no more than paternal; so she had lived for a year in their house. Then, having tired of her elderly lover, she had run away with a younger one to Paris.

From that point, de Montrond gave Roger her biography up-to-date. In the years preceding the Revolution she had passed

through the hands of a long succession of aristocrats. During the
Terror she had taken refuge in England. On her return to Paris
the police had believed that she had been sent over by the English
as a spy. In the hope of clearing herself she had requested an
interview with the Foreign Minister. Talleyrand had consented
to see her. They had talked through the afternoon and evening
and, presumably, for some part of the night. In fact, she had
never again left the Foreign Ministry until she moved with
Talleyrand to the Rue Taitbout. Unblushingly he had installed
her overnight in the Ministry of Foreign Affairs as his mistress,
and from then on she had acted as his official hostess.

'But,' Roger protested, 'in Calcutta people said of her that she
was the most stupid woman alive; that her brain is no bigger
than a pea and that her whole conversation is sprinkled with
absurdities. If that is so, how can a man of Talleyrand's brilliant
intellect possibly have put up with her for so long?'

De Montrond laughed. 'You are right. She is the veriest fool,
but when questioned about it he replies lightly that " she has the
wit of a rose ". Quite seriously, though, he once said to me, " My
dear fellow, you need to have been the lover of so intelligent a
woman as Madame de Staël to appreciate the joy of having in
your bed anyone so silly as Catherine ".'

The sally made Roger laugh, but the thought of Talleyrand's
having been bewitched by a beautiful face and body reminded
him of how he had himself been bewitched in Cairo by Zanthé.
It was now just a year since the October rebellion there, and he
had then known nothing of her mental qualities; yet he had
risked his whole future with Bonaparte to break into the Viceroy's
palace and abduct her.

He still thought of her now and then, sometimes with longing,
sometimes with guilt. He considered it probable that, in spite of
the blockade, Ouvrard, or some other Parisian banker who had
dealings with Sarodopulous, would be able to get a letter from
him through to Egypt for her. Yet, anxious as he was to let her
know that he had not wilfully deserted her, he could hardly, in
the same letter, tell her that he regarded himself as no longer
engaged to her.

On the contrary, his conscience told him that he ought to ask
her to endeavour to join him in France. Such journeys always
had their hazards; but Sarodopulous could arrange a passage for
her in a neutral ship, provide her with a suitable escort and furnish

her with introductions to bankers of his acquaintance in all the principal ports at which she might have to change ship or be carried to by misadventure, so the chances of her arriving safely in France in two or three months' time were decidedly favourable.

Yet Bonaparte's having arbitrarily freed him from his entanglement seemed to Roger, in his more sober moments, an act of Providence. Much as he delighted in Zanthé, he knew in his heart of hearts that the main basis for their attraction for one another had been an overwhelming physical desire; and the thought that in a few years' time he would have for his wife a large Eastern lady who had run to seed continued to plague him.

There was also the point that, once the current crisis had resolved itself, it was his duty to return to England at the earliest possible moment in order to inform Mr. Pitt about changes of policy that the new Government in France was likely to make. And once home, the very last thing he wanted to do was to leave England again. But he could not ask Zanthé to join him there, because he dared not put on paper his reasons for wishing her to do so. So if he sent for her at all he would have to return to France to meet her.

Lastly, there was the tricky problem of his dual nationality. She still believed him to be a Frenchman. As nothing would have induced him to spend the rest of his life in France, he would have to tell her the truth about himself. Since she was half French, he had no means of judging how she would take that and, if she did agree to go to England with him, how was he going to get her there? It was one thing for a man like himself to make a clandestine crossing of the Channel in wartime, but quite another to take a woman with him.

All these considerations were inducements to continue to let matters slide; and the long voyage from Egypt, coupled with the excitement of once again being up to the neck in his old work, were inclining him, more and more, to think of her only as one of his loves of the past.

Before he left the reception Talleyrand drew him aside, but only for a few words. Roger confirmed that he now had nothing to fear from Fouché and Talleyrand asked him to breakfast with him two days hence.

Next morning Roger went to the Rue de la Victoire, where he found Bonaparte in a most evil temper. With him were several of the officers who had accompanied him back from Egypt, and all of them had long faces. The reason soon transpired. They had made all speed to Paris, leaving their baggage to follow in wagons. The news had just come through that the whole of it had been captured by brigands. As Roger had left Egypt with only the clothes he stood up in, he could afford to laugh, although he was much too tactful to do so. But the others had all brought rich cashmeres, silks and Eastern perfumes for their women, and jewelled scimitars, armour, saddlery, etc. of considerable value as souvenirs for themselves. With good reason they were cursing the Government that had allowed the country to fall into such a state of open lawlessness.

As Bonaparte's glance fell on Roger he snapped at him, 'Where the devil were you yesterday? You know full well that it was your duty to attend upon me.'

Actually Roger had been far too anxious about what Fouché might do to him to think of anything else, but now he was able to reply with a smile, ' *Mon Général*, I was, as ever, being active in your service.'

'What the hell d'you mean by that?'

'Grant me but a moment in your cabinet, and I will inform you.'

Bonaparte's insatiable craving for information of all kinds could always be counted on. With a jerk of his head, he led the way out of the drawing room and across the passage to the room where he and Bourrienne worked. Closing the door, he asked sharply, 'Well? What is all this mystery?'

Roger lowered his voice. 'I think I can say that I have put the Minister of Police in your pocket.'

'What! Fouché?' the Corsican exclaimed. 'A most dangerous man.'

'Dangerous to his enemies, but a most powerful friend. No one is in a stronger position to assist you when you launch your *coup d'état*.'

'Who said that I intend to launch a *coup d'état*? I am a loyal servant of the Government.'

'Of course,' Roger shrugged, 'for as long as it suits you. But in Egypt and during our voyage home you said time and again that, when you got here, you would throw all these fops and puppies into the Seine.'

'Perhaps, but I was not speaking literally. I meant only that the Government needed reconstructing. They have offered me the

Command of any Army I choose; so I might go back to Italy.'

'It is an idea,' Roger agreed. 'And, like Fouché, I might take up pig-farming. I don't think either of us will; but if you feel that I am no longer capable of acting in your best interests, I shall have to consider some other——'

'No, no!' Bonaparte interrupted swiftly. 'I have every confidence in you. So has Talleyrand. We agreed that if . . . but that is another matter. Tell me about this conversation you had with Fouché.'

'We were discussing the appalling state into which France has fallen and agreed that a change of Government is the only remedy. Your name is on every tongue, so naturally it came up. I said that if you had any plans I knew nothing of them, but was convinced that you were the only man in France strong enough to prevent the country from falling into a state of open anarchy. He was inclined to agree and would like to meet you. If you mean to return to Italy it would be a waste of time, but if you . . . well, you have only to promise him that he shall keep his Ministry and he will observe a benevolent neutrality. I need hardly remark that many a crown has been won or lost owing to the attitude of a Minister of Police.'

'Crowns! No, no! I am a loyal Republican. But you have done well, Breuc, you have done well. Even so, I do not feel that it would be wise for me to meet Fouché yet. So many things are still uncertain, and the stronger the hand I can show him when we do meet the better. Keep him in play for a few days. Tell him I look forward to making his acquaintance but have been asked by the Directors to advise on the reorganization of the Armies, and that for the time being I must give that matter my whole attention.'

Next day, the 21st, Roger breakfasted with Talleyrand. When he had told him how he had spiked Fouché's guns by referring to his overtures to Mitau and what had followed from it, the statesman was both amused and delighted. He said:

'As a soldier, *mon vieux*, you are entirely wasted. No diplomat could have achieved a finer coup than bringing Fouché over to us. He is the exceptional leopard who is really capable of changing his spots. The thought of his past crimes makes one shudder but I am convinced that, like the convert to Rome, now that he has achieved respectability he is likely to become more of an anti-Jacobin than any of us. His closing of their club was the first evidence of it. I was hoping to win his support for Bonaparte and you have paved the way for that most admirably. As far as the little General is concerned, I regret to say I have found him far from certain of himself; but one cannot blame him for being cautious, and perhaps it is as well that he should have declined a meeting with Fouché for the moment.'

Dabbing rich Brittany butter on a *croissant*, Talleyrand went on, ' I asked you here this morning because, if you are to be of maximum value to us, you must be informed of what has so far gone on behind the scenes. As you know, greatly against the will of the Directors, Sieyès was elected to fill Rewbell's place last May. Although it is not generally known, that was my doing. I secretly buttonholed every Deputy who I believed wished for an end to the devilish uncertainties that beset us, and urged upon them that Sieyès was the only man capable of directing a stable Government.'

' Why Sieyès? ' Roger asked. ' He is timid, and clever only at saving his own skin. He would run a mile rather than take any decisive action. It surprises me that you should choose such a weak tool for your business.'

Talleyrand smiled. ' Dear friend, you have yet quite a lot to learn. The majority of successful revolutions are made not from without, but from within. However impracticable Sieyès's ideas may be, he has persuaded nearly everybody that he has long had a Utopian Constitution in his pocket. Being eaten up with vanity as he is, it was a certainty that, as soon as he was given power, he would not be able to resist the itch to foist his unwieldy child upon the nation. What is more, believing him to be a wizard, the public would support him in any steps he took to do so.

' The first step was to hack away the dead wood in the Directory. By the bloodless *coup d'état* of *Prairial* we got rid of three of them; but unfortunately things did not go quite as well as we had hoped. The Deputies landed us with Gohier, Moulins and Roger Ducos. The first two may give us some trouble; but the situation was at least improved by the inclusion of Ducos, because he is another trimmer and will follow Sieyès's lead in everything.

' By then, Sieyès was burning to give birth to his ponderous brain-child, but he at least has sufficient sense to realize that for that business he needs a capable midwife. To quote his own words,

" What the nation needs is a brain and a sword." He, of course, was to be the brain; but who the sword?

' His first thought was of young Joubert. A good soldier and a sensible man; but he had never directed a victorious campaign, so it was doubtful if the Army could be counted on to support him. It was in the hope that he would win for himself suitable laurels that we sent him to supersede Moreau in Italy. But, as you know, he met only with defeat and was killed at Novi.

' Sieyès's next choice was Moreau. His brow was already heavy with laurels won on the Rhine and elsewhere. His popularity as a General is beyond question; but he is no politician. He proved as timid about taking any action that might lead to his being outlawed as Sieyès is himself. When the news arrived of Bonaparte's having landed at Fréjus, Moreau was with Sieyès and he exclaimed with relief, " Here is your man! " '

Roger nodded and asked, ' How are they getting on together? '

Talleyrand threw up his hands and raised his eyes to heaven. ' Getting on! They have not yet even met. Between them they are driving me to distraction. The two of them are behaving like two old dowagers whose arms have the same number of quarterings. Each considers it to be beneath his dignity to be the first to call upon the other.'

' I no longer wonder, then, that I found our little man in such a state of uncertainty when I spoke to him about Fouché. He even talked about going off to take command of the Army in Italy; although I feel sure he does not mean to.'

' No, he will not do that. At the moment he is angling to have himself made a Director.'

' Since he is only thirty, and the lowest age at which one can qualify is forty, he would first have to get passed an amendment to the Constitution.'

' Exactly, and his chances of doing that are negligible. The Jacobins would oppose it tooth and nail; and so would Gohier and Moulins. They would never agree to have him as one of them.'

' Then it seems things have come to a stalemate.'

' Yes. Four precious days have already been lost, and his refusal to meet either Sieyès or Fouché is deplorable. Somehow I must bring him and Sieyès together. In the meantime, I pray you do your utmost to nurse Fouché and prevent him from getting the idea that he has been cold-shouldered.'

'I wrote to him yesterday and took a gamble on saying that " our friend was eager to meet him ", etc., then asked on what days next week he would be free to take breakfast in some place where the meeting was unlikely to be observed and reported.'

'Good! Good! Somehow we will get Bonaparte there, even if we have to drag him by the coat-tails.'

'Ah, but where? I can think of only one suitable place, if it is available. Have you still your little house out at Passy? '

Talleyrand smiled, 'Why, yes. The Velots still look after it for me and occasionally I use it as a rendezvous to ascertain the colour of some pretty creature's garters. It is an admirable choice. You have only to let me know the day and I will arrange matters. Within recent months, Fouché and I have become upon quite tolerable terms and he will be more inclined to come in with us when he realizes that I am giving Bonaparte my support. As host, I can serve as the oil between the wheels; but, later, you and I must leave them alone together.'

'So be it then. I only pray that our little man will not bring about his own ruin by too lengthy a hesitation. Fouché feared that, if he failed to act promptly, he might be denounced in the Assembly as a conspirator, and that would prove the end of him.'

'That is my own fear, but I have taken a precaution against it. Today, unless matters go very wrong, as an honour to the General his brother Lucien is to be elected President for the month of the Five Hundred. He is a most revolting young firebrand, but he has a good head on his shoulders and is devoted to his brother. For his term as President we can count on him to quash any measure likely to thwart the ambitions of our formidable nursling.'

When they had finished breakfast, Talleyrand gave Roger a lift to his tailor's then drove on to Bonaparte's. After trying on his new uniforms, Roger followed him there. By then Talleyrand had left, but there were half a dozen officers in the drawing room, gathered round the General, among them Admiral Bruix who, since Breuy's death, had been the senior Commander in the French Navy. Having talked for a while with some of those present, Roger slipped away to the little cabinet where, as he expected, he found Bourrienne at work.

He confided to his old friend the situation regarding Fouché and asked his help, but the *Chef de Cabinet* shook his head. 'I do not feel that it is for me to attempt to influence our master in these matters. Talleyrand has been at him this morning urging him to call on Sieyès, and he has made a half-promise to do so; but I doubt if any good will come of it. The temperaments of the two men are so utterly at variance. If he does ally himself with one of the Directors it is much more likely to be his old patron, Barras. Although he despises him they have much more in common.'

'Including Josephine,' remarked Roger with a smile.

Bourrienne gave him a reproving look. '*Mon vieux,* you should not say such things. What is past is past.'

'But is it? Rumour says that, before our return, she was from time to time still being kind to him for old acquaintance's sake; although Gohier appears to have been her latest interest.'

'You would be more correct in saying that Gohier is in love with her and that, by encouraging him without going too far, she is preventing him from joining her husband's enemies.'

'Bless you, Bourrienne, for a dear, kindly fellow,' Roger laughed. 'All I pray is that she will be discreet. Our little man is in no mood to stand for further infidelities, and she is so good-hearted a creature it would be a tragedy if some scheming harridan were put in her place.'

The next morning Roger witnessed a fine flare-up in the Bona-partes' drawing room. The General had been prevailed upon by Talleyrand and had sent an aide-de-camp to Sieyès to say that he proposed to call on him the following morning. Evidently the inordinately vain Sieyès considered himself insulted because Bonaparte had already been a week in Paris without troubling to present himself officially to him as one of the heads of the Government; so he had sent back a message saying that the hour proposed would be inconvenient.

Thereupon, Bonaparte flew into one of his passions. He declared that the aide-de-camp had acted without orders and had not been sent by him. Then he raved to those around him that he paid calls on nobody. He was the glory of the nation and if people wished to see him they must call on him.

Much perturbed, Roger slipped away, signalled a coach and drove hell-for-leather to the Rue Taitbout. On hearing Roger's news, Talleyrand was equally furious but controlled his temper better. Roger had retained the coach and they drove back to the Rue de la Victoire together. By then, Bonaparte had calmed down a little and let Talleyrand lead him out into the small garden. They remained there, wrangling heatedly, for half an hour. Later, when Talleyrand left the house, Roger accompanied him. When they were out in the street, the statesman exclaimed:

'God preserve me from such conceited fools. The two of them have come within an ace of wrecking all my labours to give France a stable Government and peace. But I stood no nonsense. I told him that he was behaving like a petulant schoolboy and understood no more about politics than a kitchenmaid. Apparently, he has been toying with the idea of allying himself with Barras. To do so would be suicidal. Barras is now a washed-out rag and hated by one and all for his corruption and incompetence; whereas Sieyès is the new broom at the Directory and people expect great things of him. In the end, I got my way. He has given me his firm promise to call on Sieyès tomorrow. At the same time, I took the opportunity to force his hand about Fouché.'

'You did! Thank God for that. I have been on tenterhooks lest he should refuse a meeting.'

'You need worry no more. It was Sieyès who got Fouché made Minister of Police; so I pointed out to our man that the two run in double harness and to become on terms with one but not the other would be invidious. I pray you now, lose no time in fixing a day for them to breakfast with us out at Passy.'

Roger went straight to the Ministry of Police, saw Fouché, told him that Bonaparte was now eager to meet him, and provisionally arranged for the meeting to be on the 25th. That afternoon he again saw Bonaparte who agreed to the date.

Next day, the 23rd, Bonaparte paid his call on Sieyès, but the meeting was far from a success. The ex-Abbé was frightened by the General's forthright manner and obvious determination, in the event of a successful coup, to have a big say in the Government. The General scarcely veiled his contempt for the ex-Abbé's timidity and Utopian ideas. Nevertheless the ice had been broken and, on the 24th, Sieyès accompanied by Roger Ducos, returned Bonaparte's call.

On the morning of the 25th, Talleyrand and Roger drove out to the former's charming little house in the garden suburb of Passy. Old Antoine Velot and his wife Marie, who for many years had lived there as butler and cook, were overjoyed to see Roger again. He had supported them all through Talleyrand's exile and they had looked after him while he had lived in hiding there during some of the darkest weeks of the Terror. The house brought back to him many memories of those desperate days, but also fond ones of his dead wife, Amanda, who had lived there with him for a while, and of the shock he had received on going out there unexpectedly one night to find his beautiful mistress, Athenaïs de Rochambeau, occupying his wife's bed.

Bonaparte and Fouché arrived within a few minutes of one another and, to Talleyrand's great relief, got on well together. In spite of the frank manner of the one and the shiftiness of the other, they were both practical men who knew what they wanted and their ideas of what should be done had much in common. By the time they were halfway through breakfast both had stated their views with a degree of frankness that made it unnecessary for Talleyrand and Roger to leave them alone together afterwards; so Roger heard the whole of their conversation.

Fouché agreed with Talleyrand that the revolution must be brought about from within, so with apparent legality. It was, therefore, essential that Sieyès should be entirely won over. Fouché then promised to work on Sieyès with the object of making the latter's relations with Bonaparte more cordial, while Bonaparte agreed at all events to pretend to accept Sieyès's proposals for a new Constitution and to flatter his vanity at their future meetings.

Before they parted, the Minister of Police displayed his usual caution. Snuffling, he said it would be ill-advised for him to give anyone, apart from Sieyès, the impression that he thought highly of Bonaparte in any other way than as a soldier; so it would be wise for them not to meet, except by chance and socially and, since Roger was one of the General's aides-de-camp, it might arouse unwelcome comment if he were to act frequently as a go-between. Therefore for that purpose he proposed to employ, alternately with Roger, Commissioner Réal, the Chief-of-Police of the Paris District, for whose trustworthiness he could vouch. He would also give Réal a special assignment to have the Jacobin members of the Five Hundred kept under observation, with the object of obtaining advance information of any plot against Bonaparte in which they might engage.

When Bonaparte and Fouché had left in their respective coaches, Talleyrand and Roger settled down to enjoy another glass of *Grande Echézaux*. The statesman savoured a mouthful of the fine wine, then smiled across the table and said:

'My dear friend, we may congratulate ourselves. At last

P

something definite has been achieved. Bonaparte has promised to butter up that idiotically vain creature, Sieyès. Fouché foresees security for himself in a triumph for Bonaparte so, although unheard and unseen, will prove our most powerful ally. At last these diverse elements are about to coalesce for a single purpose. This morning, the Corsican has committed himself. The Jacobins are powerful and ruthless. They will do their utmost to destroy him and, if the ex-*sans-culottes* in the garrison of Paris side with them, it may prove the end of people like us. But the battle is now joined. There can be no turning back.'

25

The Fateful Days of *Brumaire*

DURING the few days that followed this highly satisfactory meeting there were endless comings and goings. Only a handful of people were let into the secret that Bonaparte was now committed to play the principal role in a *coup d'état*, but everyone knew that an upheaval was imminent, and the little house in the Rue de la Victoire was crowded from morning to night with officers who wanted to express their loyalty to him, and others who went there hoping to find out which way the wind was blowing. Those who were in the plot—Berthier, Bruix and Murat among the senior officers then in Paris, and Talleyrand, Röederer and the Minister of Justice Cambacérès among the politicians—worked desperately hard to win him the support, 'should he be called upon', of doubtful elements.

In this respect Josephine also performed prodigies. In spite of the fact that, after her release from prison at the ending of the Terror, she had become little better than a highly paid *demi-mondaine*, she had attained a high place in the new Society. Undoubtedly the fact that she was an aristocrat by birth and the widow of a Vicomte had been part of her attraction for Bonaparte, and he felt that by marrying her he had improved his social status. Since then she had enjoyed the added lustre of his name and, for the past three years, had been hailed everywhere as ' Our Lady of Victories '. Moreover she was an excellent hostess, possessed great tact and charm and had the ability to make people feel that she wanted to talk only to them. In consequence, her influence over both men and women, although not obvious like that of Madame de Staël's, was considerable, and she proved invaluable in placating people whom her husband's abrupt manner offended.

In her drawing room and the salons of Madame de Staël and Madame Recamier, which Roger again frequented, the talk was largely of the war and, from various conversations, he learned the reason that lay behind the marked improvement that had taken place in the past six weeks in the situation of the French Armies.

After the Austro-Russian victory at Novi in August the two Emperors had quarrelled. Francis of Austria had maintained that, although Suvóroff commanded a Russian Army, he came under the Austrian High Command. This had given umbrage to Paul of Russia, and fuel had been added to the fire by the Allies' capture of Turin. King Charles Emmanuel, having been driven from his capital in December, '98, had taken refuge in his island of Sardinia. Paul instructed Suvóroff to invite him to return, and Britain fully supported Paul's action, but Francis refused to permit it. He maintained that Charles Emmanuel, who had earlier signed a treaty with the French, had thereby become an enemy; although the fact of the matter was that Francis wanted most of northern Italy for Austria and meant to claim Piedmont as part of his indemnity.

It was this legitimate claim by the House of Savoy to the Piedmontese territories that was later to bedevil the relations of all Europe. The immediate upshot of the quarrel had been the withdrawal of Suvóroff's Army from Austrian control and an order from Paul that it should march through the Alps to Switzerland, there to join that of Korsakoff.

This could have proved an excellent move for the Coalition, because the two Russian Armies, together with that of the Archduke Charles, could, by sheer weight of numbers, have overwhelmed Masséna and invaded France. But, with short-sighted selfishness, Francis had withdrawn the Austrian Army from Switzerland and ordered the Archduke to lay siege with it to cities on the Rhine occupied by the French.

His reason for doing so was a jealous fear of Prussia. By sending an Anglo-Russian expeditionary force to Holland, the Allies had hoped to draw Prussia into the Coalition against France, the natural enemy of all Monarchies. But, with cynical disregard for the great stakes at issue, Prussia had held aloof, preferring to keep her forces intact for possible operations on the

Rhine which would attract into her orbit many of the petty German Princes at the expense of Austria, and thus lead to her becoming a Power of the first rank.

The result had been that the withdrawal of the Archduke from Switzerland had cancelled out the arrival of the Russians. Masséna, faced with no greater numbers than before, had been able to achieve his great victory over the latter. Meanwhile in Holland, two days after Bonaparte's arrival in Paris, the Anglo-Russian force, incompetently led by the Duke of York and unsupported by the Prussians, had been compelled to sign a capitulation at Alkmar on terms that compelled its return home with its tail between its legs.

At last, on October 29th, Bonaparte, by unstinted flattery of Sieyès, gained his goodwill and entered into a firm partnership with him. Their plan was that they should get rid of Barras, Gohier and Moulins, launch the ex-Abbé's famous Constitution which, on the Roman model, would have Consuls for its senior officials, and nominate a President.

But, at times of crisis, Barras had so often suddenly re-emerged from his life of debauchery as the strong man that Sieyès was frightened of him; so the wily Talleyrand suggested that Barras be made privy to the plot and led to believe that he would retain his position more or less unchanged. This was agreed and Sieyès succeeded in winning Barras over to their plans.

However, other considerations continued to cause the launching of the coup to hang fire. All the conspirators were aware that any tampering with the principles of the Revolution, as laid down in the existing Constitution, would arouse the fiercest opposition of the Jacobins, and among them were four senior Generals: Lefebvre who commanded the Paris garrison, the veterans Moreau and Jourdan and the fiery Bernadotte. Should any of these call on the troops to defend the 'liberties won in the Revolution', the conspirators might find themselves under arrest before they had time to rally their forces.

It was thought that Lefebvre might be won over at the last minute. Moreau, so brave in battle but so hesitant in politics, was unlikely to take the lead against Bonaparte. But Jourdan well might, and the worst danger of all was Bernadotte. He had been replaced in the previous month as Minister of War by Dubois-Grancé, a sound Republican but a Moderate, who had played a leading part in bringing about Robespierre's fall. As he was an anti-Jacobin it was thought that he would at least remain neutral. But Bernadotte was still a danger with whom to be reckoned.

He had a strain of Moorish blood, which accounted for his dark complexion, crop of coal-black curls and hot-blooded temper. He was firmly Republican in principles and he and Bonaparte disliked one another intensely; so there were very good reasons to fear that he might attempt to wreck the coup. Twice, during these anxious days of late October and early November, he put in an appearance at the Rue de la Victoire. Twice he and Bonaparte would probably have come to blows had not Josephine poured oil on the troubled waters; but there seemed little chance of winning him over.

Early in November Talleyrand began to prepare propaganda to be issued to the public once the coup was under way. In this Röederer, one of the elder statesmen of the Revolution, proved invaluable, as he was a most skilful and lucid writer. Together, in the Rue Taitbout, they prepared posters and leaflets which Röederer's son, by joining a firm of printers as an apprentice managed to get printed at night. The banker Collot put up two million francs for expenses and Ouvrard, the richest financier in Paris, promised to buy Barras's resignation, should he refuse it when confronted with the demand that he should go.

Meanwhile, Bonaparte shunned publicity as far as possible. When he did go out he always wore civilian clothes, and pretended that now he no longer had an active Command his only interest was in the scientific debates at the Institute. But by this time so many people were involved that it was impossible to keep secret any longer the fact that a conspiracy was afoot.

Fouché then employed a clever stratagem to quieten the Directors at whom the coup was aimed. He gave a party to which he invited both the leading conspirators and those who were expected to oppose the coup. On entering the room Gohier innocently fell into the trap by asking jovially, 'Well, my friend, what is the latest news?'

Blinking his fish-like eyes, then looking away, Fouché replied, 'There is none, except about the conspiracy.'

Bonaparte and his friends were electrified, fearing that Fouché had had the house surrounded by his police and was about to betray and arrest them. But Gohier only laughed and said, 'Splendid, we Directors may sleep easy in our beds as long as we have you as Minister of Police.'

On November 6th, the two Chambers gave a banquet in honour of Bonaparte and Moreau. It was held in the Church of St. Sulpice and a great crowd assembled outside to see the notables arrive. When Bonaparte's coach drew up they shouted ' Peace! Peace! Give us Peace! ', as the people now always did whenever he appeared. But he was in a surly mood and would not even wave his hand to them.

The banquet was anything but a success. Bonaparte had brought his own food and wine from fear of being poisoned. The Republican Jourdan failed to appear, and throughout the meal there was general constraint and embarrassment. Barras, who was seated next to Bonaparte, said that what France needed was a President and suggested a General Hedouville for the post, no doubt because Hedouville was a nonentity who could have been easily manipulated. Bonaparte replied only with a stony stare and Barras fell into an uneasy silence. When Bonaparte's health was drunk he replied in only a few words and drank to the ' Union of all Frenchmen '. Then, pleading fatigue, he quickly slipped away.

Next morning twenty of the chief conspirators met at the house of Lemercier, the President of the *Anciens*, and discussed the measures to be taken. It was decided that, in order to prevent either the mob or the Jacobin Generals from interfering with the proceedings, a State of Emergency should be declared, which would enable the place of assembly of both Chambers to be transferred to St. Cloud, and that Bonaparte should be given command of the Paris garrison for their protection.

That evening Fouché sent an urgent message by Réal that the coup must be delayed no longer or it would be nipped in the bud.

On the 8th, the final arrangements were made. Roger went to see Talleyrand and found him none too happy about their prospects. That genius, who had brought the affair to its present point with such labour and skill, told him:

' *Coups d'état* should be unexpected and swift. This one can be neither. Half Paris now knows what we would be at, and is boiling up to defeat us. If we could be finished by tomorrow night, all might be well; but we cannot. It requires a day to move the Legislature out of Paris, so the blow cannot be struck until the day after tomorrow. In twenty-four hours anything can happen. The delay may prove our ruin. All we can do now is hope for the best.'

The morning of the 9th—18th *Brumaire* by the Revolutionary Calendar—dawned bright and mild. At 7 a.m., the *Anciens* met at the Tuileries. Their President announced that the Republic was in danger from a conspiracy hatched by the Jacobins, and proposed that the two Chambers should transfer to St. Cloud to avoid intimidation by the mob. Notice of this early session had been purposely withheld from sixty doubtful members, so it was voted unanimously that the next meetings of the Two Chambers should be held in the Palace of St. Cloud the following day at noon. A decree was then passed that Bonaparte should assume command of all the troops in the Paris area for the purpose of protecting the Legislature in the continuance of its functions. Bonaparte was then sent for.

At a very early hour that morning, he had summoned all the senior officers in Paris to the Rue de la Victoire. Soon after dawn it was packed with excited warriors. Among the first to arrive was Lefebvre. Shaking the Commander of the garrison by the hand, Bonaparte cried, ' Here is the sword I carried at the battle of the Pyramids. I give it you as a mark of my esteem and confidence.' By that shrewd gesture, his old comrade-in-arms was immediately won over.

Berthier, Lannes, Murat, Macdonald, Bessières, Marmont and Moreau all came trooping in, to offer their services. Jourdan, almost alone, ignored the summons and Bernadotte appeared but remained recalcitrant. He was brought by Brother Joseph, came in civilian clothes and still stubbornly refused to have any part in the business.

By the time Bonaparte received the summons from the *Anciens,* he was able to go to them accompanied by scores of the ablest soldiers he had led to victory. In the garden of the Tuileries hundreds of troops were drawn up. Impassively, they watched his arrival. At the bar of the Assembly, he seemed temporarily to have lost his nerve and, on being charged with its protection, made a short, rambling speech about the sacred principles of the Revolution. The Deputy Garat rose to point out that, on his appointment, he had not sworn fidelity to the Constitution; but the President promptly declared all further proceedings out of order.

Once outside the building, the sight of the massed troops

seemed to restore Bonaparte's confidence. Addressing them in ringing tones he cried, 'Soldiers! What have you done with the France which I left so brilliant? I left you peace, I find war. I left you victories, I find defeats. I left you the millions of Italy, I find laws of spoliation and misery.' His oration was met with a tremendous burst of cheering.

But the decrees of the *Anciens* had to be confirmed by at least three out of the five Directors, and notice of them sent to all. Sieyès and Roger Ducos had already agreed to sign and then resign, and Josephine had invited Gohier to breakfast in the hope that she might persuade him also to do so. But Gohier was suspicious and saw no attraction in a rendezvous so early in the morning, so he sent his wife instead. Josephine put the situation to her; but she could not be persuaded to attempt to bring her husband over into the Bonapartist camp, and as soon as Gohier learned what was afoot he declared his intention of continuing as a Director.

Barras was still unaware that the conspirators intended to turn him out, and Gohier and Moulins, believing him to be with them, assumed that, as the three of them constituted the majority, they could not be deposed; so they took no action. But Talleyrand was taking charge of that end of the affair personally.

Roger had been detailed to act as his assistant, so he had that morning gone direct to his house. Soon afterwards, they were joined by Admiral Bruix, Ouvrard and Röederer. Supervised by Talleyrand, Röederer drew up a document of resignation, full of high-sounding phrases, for Barras to sign. Ouvrard then produced a draft on his bank and, handing it to Talleyrand, said, 'Any objections he may have to resigning should be overridden by this.' Roger, who was standing near, did not see the actual sum for which the draft was made out, but he caught sight of the word 'millions'. Then, to fill in time until they learned what had taken place at the *Anciens*, the five of them went into the dining room and ate a hearty breakfast.

At eleven o'clock a message arrived from Bonaparte that all had gone according to plan, so Talleyrand, Bruix and Roger set off in a coach for the Luxembourg.

There they were faced with a somewhat delicate situation, as all five of the Directors occupied suites of apartments in the Palace and it was important that neither Gohier nor Moulins should see Talleyrand calling on Barras. Otherwise, they might have guessed what was happening, insisted on joining him and stiffened his resistance. It was to guard against this that Talleyrand had asked that Roger should accompany him.

Leaving the other two down in the hall, Roger went up the marble staircase, made a swift reconnaissance, then enquired of the footman on the door of Barras' suite if his master was alone. Learning that he was, Roger ran back and called to Talleyrand and the Admiral to come up. As soon as they had entered Barras's apartment Roger told the footman that, if anyone enquired for his master, he was to say that he could not receive them because he was in his bath.

When Talleyrand, kindly but firmly, told Barras what was required of him, he was surprised and somewhat hurt that, after all he had done for Bonaparte, his protégé should have turned against him; but he offered little resistance. For over five years he had enjoyed almost unlimited power and more wine and beautiful women than most men would be granted in twenty lifetimes. He had acquired an enormous fortune and was tired of wrangling with earnest people and windy gasbags like Sieyés. When he had read the declaration and had seen that it announced his honourable retirement after having rendered great services to his country, he signed it without a murmur.

It was not even necessary to offer him the additional fortune that Talleyrand had brought folded up in his waistcoat pocket. What he said to Ouvrard later about the draft no one will ever know; but there is reason to suppose that the banker never got it back. After all, Talleyrand enjoyed collecting money and none of his friends could complain about the way in which he spent it. Escorted by a hundred dragoons, Barras left Paris that afternoon for one of his estates in the country. Untroubled by wars or any responsibility, he continued to enjoy every luxury during his many years of happy retirement.

The three signatures having been obtained to legalize the decrees of the *Anciens*, the next step was to persuade Gohier and Moulins to resign. But both flatly refused to do so. At the Luxembourg there was a royal rumpus, which ended in Bonaparte's hand being forced. The only certain way of preventing the two diehard revolutionaries from raising the mob against him was to arrest them, but in this Bonaparte showed admirable statecraft. He entrusted Moreau with the task of surrounding the Luxembourg with troops and confining the two Directors to their apartments, thus causing the popular veteran to commit himself fully to the conspiracy.

Meanwhile, at midday, the Five Hundred had assembled for a normal sitting in the Palais Bourbon. Lucien Bonaparte, as President, read out the decrees of the *Anciens*: that the two Chambers should remove to St. Cloud and General Bonaparte be given command of all troops in the Paris area. The majority of the members were taken completely by surprise but, before they had a chance to question the measures or make any protest, Lucien abruptly adjourned the session.

Now came the time of danger that Talleyrand had foreseen. The cat was out of the bag. No further legislation could be passed until the Chambers met at St. Cloud at midday the following day. That gave Bonaparte's enemies nearly twenty-four hours in which to concert measures against him.

In the evening, Bonaparte, Sieyès, Talleyrand and their principal supporters met to decide on the course of action to be taken next day. Their object was to abolish the Directory and appoint Provisional Consuls who would recast the Constitution. But what if the Five Hundred refused to pass such a decree? Lucien vouched for his ability to get the measure through, but Talleyrand said he felt certain that a majority would oppose it. He insisted that the only way to make sure of success was to send Réal to ask Fouché to have the forty most violent Jacobin members arrested in the course of the night. But Bonaparte would not hear of it. He declared that such methods were those of the tyranny that had brought France to ruin, that he would lead a Government only if given a mandate to do so by the elected representatives of the People, and that such an act would be in flagrant contradiction to his principles—to restore true liberty and toleration. In consequence, the meeting broke up with nothing settled and the morrow left precariously on the knees of the gods.

At the same hour, in another part of Paris, Bernadotte had assembled the leading Jacobins and they were feverishly debating measures to wreck the *coup d'état*. As a first step, it was agreed that the Five Hundred should pass a decree making Bernadotte joint Commander with Bonaparte of the Paris garrison. He would then be able to veto any move by Bonaparte to use troops, while the Deputies of the Left concerted plans to bring about his ruin.

Next morning there was a very clear indication that the responsible elements of the population favoured and hoped for the overthrow of the Directory, for the Three Per Cents went up several points. But that gave no practical support to the conspirators, as for the past eight years the moneyed classes had been at the mercy of the demagogues. It was, too, more than offset by the news that Santerre, the veteran leader of the *sans-culottes*, was stirring up the mob in the Faubourg St. Antoine.

As the Palace of St. Cloud was not equipped for a meeting of the Legislature, time had had to be allowed for an army of carpenters to fit up benches in its two largest apartments. It was for this reason that the time for opening the proceedings could not be earlier than noon. But many of the Deputies, anxious to learn the latest rumours, arrived at eight o'clock. By midday, the Chambers were still not ready, so the opening had to be postponed until one o'clock.

That gave five hours for the Deputies to form groups outside and discuss the situation. Excitedly they said to one another, 'What is this plot that has been used as a pretext to get us out of Paris?' 'Why were the "patriot" members of the *Anciens* not summoned to its meeting yesterday?' 'What are all these hundreds of troops doing bivouacked in the park? It can only be to coerce us. Bonaparte is a traitor. He intends to betray the Revolution and make himself Dictator.'

As time went on tempers rose, indignation increased and many of even the Moderate Deputies declared their determination to resist any attempt to alter the Constitution. At last, at one o'clock, when the Orangerie was ready to receive the Five Hundred, the Deputies streamed into it, angry, intense and, almost to a man, hostile to Bonaparte.

The clamour was such that Lucien had difficulty in getting a hearing. He called on Gaudin, one of the conspirators, who proposed that a Committee be formed to report on the state of the Republic and that the assembly should adjourn until the report was presented. The proposal was aimed at getting rid of the Five Hundred while giving the *Anciens* time to retrieve the situation. But it did not work. The Deputies saw through it and shouted it down with cries of execration. 'The Constitution or death!' they yelled. 'No Dictatorship! Bayonets do not frighten us! We are free men! Down with the Dictators!'

When the pandemonium had died down, Grandmaison proposed that the members should individually renew their oath to the Constitution. The whole Assembly rose to its feet, shouting '*Vive la Républic!*' The motion was carried by acclamation and the next two and a half hours were passed going through this, in the circumstances, futile ceremony.

The *Anciens* had met in the Gallery of Apollo and things were not going well there either. The Deputies who had deliberately been kept away from the previous day's sitting were indignantly demanding an explanation and, when they asked for particulars of the Jacobin plot, no one could give them any. The five Directors had been sent a formal notification of the session. At half past three the news was received that three of them had resigned and the other two were under arrest. The Deputies who were not in the plot then took alarm, and it looked as though the *Anciens,* too, would turn against Bonaparte.

With Sieyès, Ducos and others of his co-conspirators, Bonaparte was in a room on the first floor of the Palace. Every few minutes news was brought to them of what was going on in the two Chambers. Roger was not among the aides-de-camp who kept them informed. He had been allotted the task of acting as liaison with Talleyrand, and neither Talleyrand nor Fouché was in the Palace.

The wily Minister of Police had preferred to remain in Paris so that, if things went wrong, he could disclaim any connection with the conspirators; but, even so, he rendered them a valuable service. At midday he ordered the gates of Paris to be closed, thus preventing any mobs marching out of the city to support the Jacobin Deputies at St. Cloud.

Talleyrand, the arch-conspirator, was also much averse to taking an active part in *coups d'état.* He preferred on such days to stay at home; but the preceding day he had felt that unless he used his persuasive powers personally Barras might have refused to resign and, as the conference that night had left matters in such an uncertain state, he had decided that he dare not remain more than a few minutes' distance from Bonaparte during the all-important sessions at St. Cloud in case the General made a mess of things. He had, therefore, hired a small house near the Palace and had driven out to it that morning accompanied by Röederer, de Montrond and Roger. As the hours passed they became more and more anxious.

So, too, did Bonaparte. Soon after three o'clock Jourdan

arrived on the scene and, far worse, he brought with him that terrible, swashbuckling revolutionary, General Augereau. Rumours then came in that the Five Hundred had sent representatives back to Paris to raise the mobs and sieze the city. On hearing this Bonaparte decided to make a personal bid for the support of the *Anciens*.

Accompanied by Berthier and Bourrienne he entered the Chamber of Apollo and asked permission to address the Assembly. It was granted but, when he started to speak, it was obvious to everyone that he had lost his nerve.

This was the second important occasion in his career when he had done so. The first had been in Italy, before the battle of Castiglione. On the previous day the castle and village had been in the hands of the French. After only a weak defence, General Valette had allowed the Austrians to push him out of them. As the castle dominated the situation and Bonaparte's Army was already partially surrounded he had been absolutely furious and, on the spot, reduced Valette to the ranks. But that did not improve the situation.

At a morning Council of War Augereau and the other Generals urged that the only possible course was to retake the castle by assault and cut their way out. Bonaparte, faced with this unexpected hitch in his carefully laid plans, temporarily lost his resolution. Fearful of having his unbroken chain of victories brought to an end by a shattering defeat, he refused to give any orders at all. Exclaiming 'I wash my hands of it! I am going away!', to the utter amazement of the others he walked out of the tent. Augereau had shouted after him, 'Who, then, is to take command?' 'You,' Bonaparte shouted back. Augereau had then led his Division in a furious charge up the hill and driven the Austrians out of the castle. Only after it had been taken did Bonaparte actively resume his Command. It was on account of this that, later in his career, whenever anyone complained to him of Augereau's outrageous behaviour, he always excused him by saying, 'Ah, but remember what he did for us at Castiglione.'

Now, again, Bonaparte went all to pieces. He spoke hesitantly, in confused, broken sentences, muttering vaguely that he did not intend to play the part of a Cromwell; that the Jacobins had made a plot; that the Constitution had often been violated before. Horrified at the lack of firmness he was suddenly displaying, when he stammered to a stop not knowing what to say next, Berthier and Bourrienne took him by the arms and hurried him out of the Chamber.

Whitefaced, de Montrond came hurrying over to Talleyrand to tell him what had happened. Clearly disaster was imminent. Talleyrand turned to Roger.

'Go to him, Breuc. He has faith in you. Tell him from me that he must now throw aside all legal scruples. He must use his troops or he is lost.'

Roger set off at a run across the park. By the time he reached the Palace, Bonaparte, his mind still hopelessly confused, had apparently had the idea that he might be better received by the Five Hundred. With four Grenadiers as an escort, he entered the Orangerie. His appearance was met with howls of rage. The Deputies began to fight among themselves, while the greater part of them yelled, 'Down with the Dictator! Down with Cromwell!' A huge Deputy, named Destrem, hurled himself on Bonaparte and struck him several times. His Grenadiers dragged him, bruised and bleeding, from the Chamber. As they did so the terrible cry went up, '*Hors la loi!* Outlaw him! Outlaw him! Death to the traitor!'

As Roger entered the hall he heard those cries which threatened an end not only to the attempt to give France a new Government, but to Bonaparte's life. At the top of the long staircase he saw the General stumbling along between the Grenadiers as they helped him back to the room in which Sieyès and the others waited.

At the foot of the stairs Roger halted. Never in his life had he been faced with alternatives which could have such momentous results as at that moment. By prompt action, the situation might still be saved. But if he refrained from delivering Talleyrand's message Bonaparte was finished. Mr. Pitt believed Bonaparte to be the most dangerous potential leader of Britain's enemies, and close on two years before he had sent Roger to France with definite instructions to do everything he could to wreck the career of the young General. Those were Roger's orders. Chance had put it into his power to carry them out, finally and completely. Dare he ignore them?

Now was the vital moment of decision.

26

The Revolution is Over

As Roger stood there at the foot of the stairs he could feel the pulse throbbing in his temple. There was no time to lose; not a moment. Shouts and screams were still coming from the Orangerie. In there the gangling-limbed Lucien, short-sighted, bespectacled, thin-voiced, was displaying magnificent calmness and courage. A motion was brought that his brother should be outlawed, but he refused to put it to the Assembly. Then, seeing that his hand was about to be forced, he gained some minutes by resigning the Presidency to Chazel. Pandemonium again broke out. Fifty members all wanted to put motions and they fought like tigers to get up on the rostrum, each one who succeeded being dragged off again before he could make himself heard.

Roger's brain was whirling madly. Few men now knew Bonaparte better than he did. The Corsican was by nature a brigand, a thief on the grand scale, an athiest, a born liar, unscrupulous, ruthless and boundlessly ambitious. He was the absolute antithesis of the honour, integrity and high moral standards for which Britain's Prime Minister stood. It could not be wondered at that Mr. Pitt feared to see such a man given power, and had ordered Roger to do all he could to check his advancement.

Instead Roger had performed many useful services for Bonaparte and, for the past month, had done his utmost to aid him in a conspiracy which might, sooner or later, lead to his wielding supreme power. Chance had given Roger the opportunity to bring in Fouché, but that was incidental. Fouché took his own decisions and, his views being as they were, Talleyrand would later have been certain to secure his co-operation. In any case, Roger had been only swimming with the tide. Had he endeavoured to thwart the conspiracy, Fouché would soon have learned of his activities through one of Réal's thousand spies and would have pounced. So Roger would have found himself in prison or, worse, been in his grave. But now, simply by refraining from going upstairs, he could undo all that Talleyrand had striven for with such ardour, patience and skill.

There lay the rub. If he betrayed Bonaparte he would also be betraying Talleyrand, and he had unshakable faith in Talleyrand. He knew that Mr. Pitt disliked and despised Talleyrand even more than he did Bonaparte. But in that Roger had always felt that the shy, cold, passionless Prime Minister erred greatly in confusing morals with interests. Both Bonaparte and Talleyrand stood condemned on their personal records: the one for trickery and theft, the other for corruption and licentiousness. But Bonaparte had a genius for bringing order out of disorder; he had started as a revolutionary, but he had matured into a man of sound Liberal views who at least showed respect for religion and wished to see real liberty and justice restored to his countrymen; while Talleyrand was the man of great vision. All his life he had maintained that only when Britain and France reached an understanding could permanent peace and prosperjty come to Europe. He was the man of Peace. With Bonaparte in power, his influence would be enormous. And everywhere that Bonaparte now went, the people in the streets called to him, 'Peace! Give us Peace.' If he won this desperate gamble, how could he ignore both Talleyrand and the Will of the People?

Sweat had broken out on Roger's forehead. He was now facing 'The Great Risk' that he had always dreaded might some day be forced upon him. If he once again went against Mr. Pitt's judgment, Bonaparte, as Commander of all France's Armies, might decide to carve out for himself in Europe the Empire that he had failed to carve out in the East. If that happened, it would mean the shedding of tears by a million women and the shedding of blood by a million men. The burden of such a decision was almost too great for any one man's shoulders. But Roger took it. He put one foot on the lowest stair. Then he began to run.

As he burst into the room where Bonaparte had spent most of the day he saw that he was slumped in a chair, his features haggard, his hair in disorder, mopping the blood from a cut on his face. Next moment Roger had seized him by the arm, pulled him to his feet and was shouting:

'Quick! You have not a moment to lose! In the Five Hundred they are murdering your brother and are about to outlaw you! Do you understand? To outlaw you! Order the troops to clear the Orangerie. Talleyrand sent me. It is your only chance. It is now their lives or yours. Fail to act and tomorrow they will send you in an iron cage to Cayenne.'

Bonaparte shook Roger off. But, as though he had received an electric shock, his old vitality returned to him. His dark eyes flashed, he strode to the window and out on to the balcony. Drawing his sword he cried in his harsh Italian accent to the troops lined up below:

'Soldiers I will stand for no more. I have observed the laws, but the Five Hundred is filled with traitors. I went among them to plead for an end to the measures that have brought France to ruin. They insulted and reviled me. They attacked me with daggers. They are about to murder my brother. The peace must be kept. I order you to go in and rescue him.'

His mind had cleared and had seized upon a feature in the situation by which he might later whitewash himself. He had not ordered the troops to put an end arbitrarily to the session, but simply to rescue his brother.

Murat took off his feathered hat, waved it and ordered the troops to fix bayonets. A great cheer went up. With Murat at their head, holding high his sabre, they charged into the Orangerie.

Roger, utterly spent by the mental ordeal he had been through, sank down in the chair from which he had pulled Bonaparte. Later he heard about the final scene in the drama. When Murat burst into the Orangerie, Lucien had again got possession of the rostrum but was spreadeagled and clinging to it. At the sight of the bayonets and busbies the Deputies had scattered. In terror of their lives, most of them jumped out of the windows. Some made their way back to Paris; others, fearing arrest and execution, spent the night wandering miserably about the park and forest.

In spite of the rough handling he had received Lucien, when escorted outside, mounted a horse, grabbed a sword and, pointing it at the General, who had come down to meet him, cried, 'Should my brother ever attempt anything against our liberties, I will plunge this into his heart.' This theatrical gesture brought cheers from even the soldiers of the Legislative Guard, who had previously shown some doubt about where their duty lay.

Proceeding to the *Anciens* Lucien reported to them, with tears streaming down his cheeks, how Deputies of the Five Hundred had drawn their daggers on his brother, how, mercifully, he had been spared, and then how, fearful of being called to account for their act, the Deputies had disappeared of their own accord.

Having expressed their horror at the attack, the *Anciens* passed a decree appointing Bonaparte, Sieyès and Ducos Provisional Consuls, formed an interim Legislative Committee from among themselves and adjourned the Councils until February 20th.

But the decrees of the *Anciens* still required ratification by the Five Hundred to make them fully legal. By then the majority of its members were lost in the damp mists of the November night: hungry, scared out of their wits and tearing their red robes as they hunted for hiding places among thickets of thorn bushes. But a handful of Bonaparte's supporters had known flight to be unnecessary, so were still hanging about. The indefatigable Lucien gathered together some twenty-five of them. Then, by the dim light of three candles, they ratified the decrees and also decreed the expulsion of the sixty Jacobin members. At one o'clock in the morning the three Provisional Consuls took the oath before both Chambers and formally assumed office.

The day was Bonaparte's, but only owing to the courage and tenacity displayed by his brother Lucien.

Meanwhile Talleyrand, accompanied by Röederer, de Montrond and Roger, had driven the few miles to Melun. He had had the foresight to arrange with a Madame Simons, a charming ex-actress who had married well and was an ex-mistress of his, to provide them with dinner at her pretty little house there. It had been a long and trying day. While others still argued about formalities in the chilly corridors at St. Cloud or wandered disconsolate in the woods, the arch-conspirators warm and cosy in the soft candlelight, with fine wine, well-chosen dishes and a pretty woman for hostess, proceeded to enjoy themselves.

·   ·   ·

The coup of the 18th *Brumaire* had infinitely more far-reaching results than any of the conspirators intended. Their aim had been to overthrow the Directory and make certain adjustments to the existing Legislature. Not only did it result in the abolition of the Directory but of the two Chambers as well. That fact was not immediately understood but, even had it been, all the best elements of the French nation would have approved. They were utterly weary of being ruled by Assemblies composed mainly of soapbox orators and cunning lawyers, with temperaments that ranged from those of incompetent idealists to tyrannical murderers. They wanted a strong and stable Government, led by a practical man; and now they had it. Even had they known that for the next fifteen years the 'Will of the People', to establish which the Revolution had been brought about, was to be ignored by a dictator, it is probable that the bulk of the nation would still have been prepared to accept that as the price for the restoration of a reasonable degree of freedom and religious toleration, the protection of private property, justice in the Courts and a stable financial situation.

Owing to the coup having been spaced over forty-eight hours it had been within an ace of failure, but once accomplished it was accounted a triumph. No blood had been spilt and all the actions taken had at least a semblance of legality. By the adjournement of the Chambers until February 20th, which was followed by the arrest of fifty-seven prominent Jacobin Deputies, all opposition had been crushed and the rejoicing throughout Paris was almost universal.

On the day following the coup the three Provisional Consuls occupied the apartments at the Luxembourg vacated by the Directors. For the time being they enjoyed equal powers: but it was soon agreed that Bonaparte should handle all administrative matters, with the assistance of two Committees each of twenty-five members elected from the two Chambers, while Sieyès drafted the new Constitution. Fouché was, of course, retained as Minister of Police. Berthier took over the War Office and Gaudin, a Deputy who had spent most of his life in the Treasury and was a highly competent man, was made Minister of Finance. For the time being, Talleyrand remained in the background but was in constant touch with Bonaparte.

During the remainder of November and the first three weeks of December, Bonaparte and Sieyès met daily to discuss the many articles in the proposed Constitution. Fundamentally their ideas on the subject had little in common; but the General was clever enough to continue to flatter the ex-Abbé, and so succeeded in getting included the clauses he considered essential. The most important of these was that, instead of appointing a Grand Elector as the Head of State, as Sieyès's wished, one of the three Consuls should act in that capacity with very extensive powers, while the other two would be little more than his advisers.

Meanwhile, they added considerably to their popularity by annulling the terrible Law of Hostages; sending General Hedouville, who had assisted Hoche to pacify the Vendée, back there to pacify it again; authorizing the return to France of every proscribed person who had been condemned to transportation without trial, and repealing laws which imposed crippling burdens of taxation.

Throughout these weeks Roger continued his duties as one of Bonaparte's aides-de-camp with as much patience as he could muster. For better or for worse, he had made his contribution to the present state of things; but as yet there was no point in his slipping off to London and confessing to Mr. Pitt that he had flagrantly disobeyed his orders. The fact that the Directory had been overthrown would have reached the Prime Minister within a few day of its happening. What he would want to know was what changes in French foreign policy, if any, were likely to result from it, and whether the new Constitution was likely to restore France to stability. Roger could make no assessment of that until it was known who was to wield almost dictorial powers by being appointed First Consul, and that still hung in the balance.

It was not until December 22nd that the notables assembled in the Luxembourg to vote on this momentous issue. Puffed up with vanity, Sieyès had all along visualized himself in the role of First Consul, and it was that which had caused him to agree that the other two should have no power of veto and be virtual nonentities.

Feeling quite sure of himself Sieyès opened the meeting with an address in which he dwelt on the evils of military Dictatorships and how dangerous it would be to appoint a soldier as First Consul. But Bonaparte had devised a clever trick to outwit him. Before the meeting the wily Corsican had told his supporters not to form a group, but to scatter themselves about the hall. Then, when he took Sieyès's hand, they were to give a loud cry of 'Bonaparte!'

As Sieyès brought his address to an end, Bonaparte stepped up to him with a smile and said, 'Let us have no difference of opinion, my friend. I vote for you. For whom do you vote? '

Sieyès, thinking that Bonaparte's vote put his own election beyond all question, replied, out of politeness, ' I vote for you.'

Bonaparte put out his hand, Sieyès took it. Instantly, from all parts of the hall, there were loud cries of ' Bonaparte! Bonaparte! ' The General's scattered supporters infected their neighbours and in another minute everyone was crying *'Vive Bonaparte!'* Thus the wretched Seiyès was discomfited and the Corsican elected First Consul by acclamation.

Sieyès, almost speechless and half out of his mind with rage, refused the honourable post of Second Consul: so the Committees elected Cambacérès in this capacity and Lebrun as Third Consul. On the following day Bonaparte, whose word had now become, for all practical purposes, law, sent Reinhard as Ambassador to the Helvetic Republic and handed the portfolio of Foreign Minister back to Talleyrand.

Had Seiyès become First Consul, Bonaparte might well have decided, rather than remain as little more than a cipher in Paris, to take supreme command in the war against Austria. Sieyès would gladly have got rid of him at that price. Then the Jacobins would have striven again to impose their rule of Terror and the Royalists plotted again to bring about a Restoration. Once more the future would have been in the melting pot; but with Bonaparte as Head of State, firmly supported by Talleyrand and Fouchè, Roger could go back to England and report that the Revolution was over.

Now that the situation had clarified, his longing to get home became almost unbearable, and he saw no reason why he should not set out almost immediately. He had only to tell Bonaparte that the winter weather was again affecting his, mythically, weak chest to be given leave to go to his little château in the south of France. He could then set out in that direction, make a detour that would bring him to one of the Normandy ports and pay a smuggler well to run him across the Channel. As it was already the 23rd he could not get home for Christmas, but he should be able to do so well before the New Year.

That night he went to the Luxembourg, intending to ask his master for leave. There was a crowd of people there, but Bonaparte was busy in his cabinet with Bourrienne. After a while Josephine caught sight of Roger and beckoned him over. As he made a smiling bow to her, she said:

'*Cher ami.* Have you heard the wonderful news? The General and I are to move to the Tuileries. After living in our little house for so long, I'll feel like a pea in a box. But just think of the splendour of it, and the parties I'll be able to give there.'

Roger bowed again. 'Our Lady of Victories will shine there more brightly than ever did any Queen of France.'

Her big eyes sparkled and she tapped him with her fan. '*Cher, cher Colonel.* You have always stood out among our soldiers as a courtier, and there will be the warmest welcome for you always, at any time, at the Palace. Our first great reception is to be on Christmas Day and, of course, we shall count on you.'

Christmas had long since been abolished by the revolutionaries. Not only did it hold no place in the calendar as a Revolutionary Festival, but for years past no one had dared to treat it as other than an ordinary working day. Much surprised, Roger raised an eyebrow a fraction.

Josephine laughed, flicked open her fan and behind it whispered to him, 'The choice is deliberate. The preparations for us to occupy the Palace are being hurried forward on that account. The General wishes to show the people that he is without prejudices and will permit religious persecution no longer.'

'*Madame,* that is excellent news,' Roger said quickly, 'and a truly wise measure. No ruler, however strong, can have too much support and, by granting religious toleration, our General will win the love of countless thousands of, yes . . . why should we not say it . . . his subjects—and yours.'

'No, no,' she chided him. 'You must not say such things. He insists that he is no more than an ordinary citizen charged with the duty of giving expression to the wishes of his fellows. But I had almost forgotten. There is special reason why you must not fail to be in attendance at the Tuileries on Christmas night. There is someone who by then will be in Paris and whom I shall invite: someone who is eagerly seeking news of you. I received the letter only yesterday from M. Ouvrard, who corresponds with a Greek banker named Sarodopulous. This lady is the daughter of one of my girlhood friends, who in the most romantic way has become the favourite wife of the Great Turk.'

.   .   .   .   .   .

For a moment, Roger was struck dumb. It could not possibly be anyone other than Zanthé to whom Josephine referred. Clearly Sarodopulous had made arrangements for her to travel to France, and she had arrived safely. Her only possible reason for undertaking the hazardous journey must be to rejoin and marry him. At the thought Roger felt panic rising in him. Only long practice at concealing his emotions enabled him to prevent Josephine from realizing the shock he had received.

She was going gaily on with an account of Aimée Dubucq de Rivery's capture by Corsairs and how, by her entrancing beauty, she had captivated the Sultan. Roger listened with a fixed grin, hardly taking in a word she said. As soon as he decently could he turned the conversation, drew two other visitors into it, then bowed himself away and left the apartment.

Back at La Belle Étoile he went up to his room, flung himself into an elbow chair and gave himself furiously to think. He could still return to the Luxembourg in the morning and ask Bonaparte for leave; but now it was most unlikely that the General would grant it until after Christmas Day. At his first reception as First Consul he would naturally wish to have all his paladins around him, ' *le brave Breuc* ' among them.

It occurred to Roger that he could cut loose. If he did not put in an appearance next day no one would start a hue-an-cry after him. By taking horse that night he could reach the coast before anyone even started enquiring about him. But he was very loath to do that.

While in Egypt he would have given anything to free himself from the double life he was leading, but since his return to Paris the excitement of being in the vortex of the political cyclone had again got hold of him. He had with pain and grief overcome the two great threats to his career as a secret agent. Talleyrand was now convinced of his loyalty and Fouché had forgone the chance to question his past, in return for a collaboration which would now make it impossible for him to do so and be believed. Added to which Roger enjoyed the friendship and confidence of the new master of France.

If Georgina were still free and willing to become his wife, he would have been happy to leave Mr. Pitt's service and settle down with her. But it was close on two years since he had seen her and, even if she were still free, he doubted if he could persuade her to marry him. Failing that, what did the future hold? A few happy, carefree months in England then, as he so well knew, the itch to be at the centre of great events would get him again. To set off without explanation would be to become a deserter, and to throw away the extraordinary position he had achieved might later cause him the most bitter regrets.

There was then the personal problem. As Zanthé had risked shipwreck and capture to follow him to France, how could he possibly requite such love and courage by ignoring his obligation to her; still worse, leave her stranded in Paris? As he thought of her, his heart began to glow again with memories of her beauty, the intensity of her passion and the wonderful nights they had spent together.

It was still his inescapable duty to return to England and report to Mr. Pitt as soon as possible. That he must do. But at least he must remain in Paris over Christmas to welcome Zanthé. Then, on some pretext of duty, he would slip away and secretly cross the Channel. Yet not for the long, carefree months to which he had so greatly looked forward. Every decent instinct he had cried aloud that he must get back to France as soon as he could and take Zanthé for his wife.

In this frame of mind, wearing a new and brilliant uniform, he went to the Tuileries on the evening of Christmas Day. It was the first of scores of receptions that Bonaparte and Josephine were to hold there. In due course Kings, Princes, Grand Dukes and Eastern Potentates would be ceremoniously announced and bow before them, but this was just a large, jolly party drawn from every strata of society.

There were a handful of aristocrats who, like Talleyrand, had survived the Revolution and a number of the Members of the Institute who came from well-to-do families; but the majority of the guests had once been poor and were still ill-educated. There were the soldiers, clinking about in their spurred top-boots, as yet innocent of sonorous titles and glittering Orders. They used the language of the camp. Lannes and Augereau were incapable of opening their mouths without using some obscene expression and most of the others were little better. With them they brought their wives, nearly all looking awkward in their hastily assembled finery. They had no idea how to adjust feathers in their hair or make a curtsey in response to the bow of a gentleman. Many of them were ex-prostitutes who talked the argot of the gutter and Lefebvre's wife had, when Bonaparte was a seedy young Lieutenant, been his washerwoman. The remainder of the guests were mostly sharp-featured or florid-faced politicians in ill-fitting cloth suits and their women were no worse, but no better, than those of the soldiers.

Among this motley throng Roger took his place in a queue that was moving slowly up the grand staircase. At the top Josephine and Bonaparte were receiving. Grouped on either side of them were already a score of attendant men and women. Having made his bow Roger, as an aide-de-camp, was about to take his place among them; but Josephine turned her head and signed to one of the women near her to come forward. She was Zanthé, but dressed in European clothes, which accounted for Roger's not at once catching sight of her.

His heart throbbing, he smiled a greeting. To their right, in the great salon, the band had just struck up for the first dance. To cover his confusion Roger bowed to Josephine again, then gave Zanthé his arm and led her into the ballroom. For a few moments they were both tongue-tied, then he said:

'How wonderful it is to see you again.'

'I am glad you feel that,' she murmured. 'I was somewhat doubtful if you would be.'

'That is not surprising, seeing the way I left you.'

'I learned that you had sailed with General Bonaparte, but I took it hard that you lacked the courage to say goodbye to me or even leave a message.'

'When I rode away that night I had no knowledge of the General's intentions, and it had occurred to him to take me with him only at the last moment. When I got aboard the anchor was already weighed.'

At that moment, Murat called to Roger, 'Come, Breuc! You and the lovely lady you have with you are just what we need to make up a set.'

Roger could hardly refuse, so he led Zanthé out and they took their corner for a minuet. The dance that ensued had little resemblance to those trodden by Marie Antoinette, her ladies and their gallants in the royal palaces of France. Zanthé was not alone in never having before danced such a measure. Fewer than half the dancers knew the figures, but they gaily clumped round, twirled the women about and—shades of Versailles—two of the men committed the impropriety of embracing and kissing their partners when they met at corners.

Almost unconscious of the barn-dance behaviour that was going on round him, Roger bowed and twirled with the others. At the first sight of Zanthé he had been chilled by the realization that the European clohes she was wearing robbed her of much of her glamour; but her face and figure were as lovely as he remembered them and within a few minutes he was again under her spell.

When the dance was over he led her into one of the long, broad corridors that were furnished with settees for sitting out. As soon as they had settled themselves he decided that this was no case for half-measures. Since he was to marry her, she must not be allowed even to suspect that he had ever had second thoughts about doing so. Taking her hand, he said:

' As I was telling you, Bonaparte gave me no chance to decline to go with him. Otherwise I would have done so and returned to you so that we could be married.'

Her big eyes opened wide in surprise and she stammered, ' But . . . but you said yourself that if you ever got another chance to leave Egypt you would take it, and that nothing would ever induce you to come back.'

' No, surely! ' he protested. ' I have no memory of ever having said anything like that.'

' You did. It was on the occasion when you were nearly stung by a scorpion.'

' Why, yes. I do remember now. But when I spoke of a chance to leave Egypt, I meant one that would have enabled me to take you with me. As things were, my voyage back occupied near two months, and for the past six weeks everything here has been in a state of great uncertainty. Now that Paris has settled down I intended to write to M. Sarodopulous and ask him to arrange for you to travel, with as much safety as he could devise, to France.'

' What! ' she exclaimed, her lip trembling. ' You meant to send for me? '

' Of course. But, brave girl that you are, you took it on your-self to make the voyage. So you have rejoined me three months or more before I could have hoped you would. All we have to do now is find a priest of the Orthodox Church to marry us.'

Zanthé swayed towards him. For a moment he thought that she was about to faint, but she recovered herself and gasped, 'Marry! But I am already married.'

'What say you!' Roger exclaimed. 'To . . . to whom?'

'Achilles . . . Achilles Sarodopulous,' she stammered. 'Did not Madame Bonaparte tell you?'

He shook his head. Still too astonished to be certain if he was pleased or sorry, he muttered, 'Then you did not come to Paris on my account?'

'No. The relations which were opened by you between M. Sarodopulous and the French Army have proved so profitable that Achilles has been sent here to open a branch of the Sarodopulous bank.'

Roger's work often made it necessary for him to lie, but he was no hypocrite. Realizing now how much having regained his freedom meant to him, he could not bring himself to reproach her; but it would have been unkind to her not to appear distressed, so he asked in a low voice, 'How did this come about?'

For a moment she was silent, then she said, 'From the way in which Achilles was always so eager to please me you surely must have realized that he had fallen in love with me. But he attempted nothing dishonourable against you. When . . . when you had gone, neither of us thought you would ever come back and he did his best to console me. He is a fine man, kind, generous and of the East—so in some ways better suited as a husband for me than you would have been.'

'I understand,' said Roger gently, 'and, if the fault for our separation lies with anyone, it is with me rather than with you.'

'It was the Will of Allah—blessed be the name of His Prophet. But . . . but there was another reason. I mean why I decided to accept Achilles soon after you had gone, instead of waiting in case some message came from you.'

Roger gave her a quick look of enquiry.

She nodded. 'Yes, I am enceinte. While we were in Acre old Gezubb, who was wise in such things, looked after me. But during that last fortnight at the Sarodopulouses' . . . it was then. Your son . . . I know it will be a son . . . will be born in May.'

'Does Achilles . . .?' Roger hesitated.

'No. I hate deceit, but he adores me and has made me truly

fond of him. It is much kinder to him that he should believe himself the father and that it is a seven-month child.'

All that had to be said between them had been said. Roger was quick to realize that for them to prolong their talk now must lead to embarrassment for both of them. If they remained there discussing the affair further he could not, in decency, do less than pretend acute distress at having lost her. Then if she loved him still, as he believed she did, she might break down and avow it. Inwardly wincing at his own words, he said:

' I must try to accept my misfortune with courage. Let us find Achilles, so that I can congratulate him.'

Ten minutes later they came upon the handsome young Greek in the card-room. The game he was about to join had not yet started. On seeing Roger approach he gave him an uneasy smile; but Roger, lightly touching Zanthé's hand, which rested on his left arm, said:

' Since it was fated that this pearl among women was not to become my wife, I could wish for her no better husband than yourself.' They then cordially shook hands and talked for a few minutes about the future. The Sarodopulouses were to take a house in Paris and live there permanently. Roger said that he would shortly be leaving for the south of France, but on his return in the spring would look forward to calling on them. As the game was by then about to start Roger asked Zanthé if she would like to dance again, but she tactfully replied:

' No, I thank you. Achilles says that I always bring him luck, so I will remain here and watch him play.'

Roger took a last look into the magnificent tawny eyes of the woman who had twice saved his life and said she was going to bear him a son. Tears sprang involuntarily to his own. He made her a deep bow, then quickly turned away.

. . . . .

Half an hour later he came upon Talleyrand. Limping gracefully along on his malacca cane, the statesman looked like a peacock that had by mistake got into a hen-yard. From his powdered hair to the diamond buckles on his shoes, not an item of his apparel would have been different had time moved back ten years and this been a gala night at the Court of Queen Marie Antoinette.

Roger had not seen him since, two days before, Bonaparte had reappointed him Foreign Minister. As they bowed to one another Roger congratulated him with the greatest heartiness.

Talleyrand took snuff, smiled and said, 'Thank you, dear friend. But with the good Reinhard sitting in the chair, I have never really ceased to be Foreign Minister. Unfortunately, those miserable little people at the Luxembourg were too stupid to take the advice I sent them through him; but now things will be better.'

Pausing, he surveyed the crowd through his quizzing-glass, sniffed at his perfumed lace handkerchief and went on, 'Are they not terrible? Many of them smell! What sacrifices people like you and me make for France by hob-nobbing with them. Take me away from them, Breuc. Take me away.'

Roger laughed. 'But where? We are expected to remain here for at least another three hours.'

'Yes, yes. We will not leave the building, but will go to the west wing. Our little man has provided a room for me there. The idea is that I should occupy it at especially busy times, and thus produce my rabbits for him more swiftly than if I had to go back and forth to my Ministry.'

As they strolled slowly down one of the long corridors, he continued, 'No doubt he thinks that I shall labour there day and night. In that he is much mistaken. I am no Bourrienne. How I pity that good fellow. He cannot have had time for a decent meal or a pretty woman in months. I have never liked work; and to do too much of it is folly, because it exhausts one. Do you know, I never draft despatches myself. I tell others what I want said and, at most, scribble a few notes for them. The most important maxim to observe, if one wishes for a happy life, is " Never do anything yourself that you can get someone else to do for you." '

By this time they had reached the end of the corridor. There, they entered a lofty room that looked out on the Tuileries garden. Taking a key from the fob pocket of his satin breeches Talleyrand unlocked a cabinet, took a paper from one of the pigeonholes and handing it to Roger, said:

'The first fruits of my new Ministry, dear friend. I should be glad to have your opinion upon it.'

Roger spread out the paper; translated, it read:

PARIS, le 5 Nivôse, an VIII

FRENCH REPUBLIC

SOVEREIGNTY OF THE PEOPLE—
LIBERTY—EQUALITY

Bonaparte, First Consul of the Republic, to His Majesty the King of Great Britain and Ireland

Called by the wishes of the French nation to occupy the First Magistracy of the Republic, I have thought proper, in commencing the discharge of the duties of this office, to communicate the event directly to Your Majesty.

Must the war which for eight years has ravaged the four quarters of the world be eternal? Is there no room for accommodation? How can the two most enlightened nations in Europe, stronger and more powerful than is necessary for their safety and independence, sacrifice commercial advantages, internal prosperity and domestic happiness to vain ideas of grandeur? Whence is it that they do not feel peace to be the first of wants as well as the first of glories?

These sentiments cannot be new to the heart of Your Majesty, who rules over a free nation with no other view than to render it happy.

Your Majesty will see in this overture only my sincere desire to contribute effectually, for the second time, to a general pacification by a prompt step taken in confidence and free from those forms which, however necessary to disguise the apprehensions of feeble States, only discover in those that are powerful a mutual wish to deceive.

France and England may, by the abuse of their strength, long defer the period of its utter exhaustion, unhappily for all nations. But I will venture to say that the fate of all the civilized nations is concerned in the termination of a war the flames of which are raging throughout the whole world.

I have the honour to be, etc.,

(Signed) Bonaparte.

Tears had sprung to Roger's eyes three-quarters of an hour earlier when he had left Zanthé in the card-room. As he finished reading the document they again welled up, then flowed over.

'But this is Peace!' he cried. 'Peace! Blessed Peace!'

Talleyrand for once betrayed emotion. He put both arms about Roger's shoulders and embraced him as he said, with a catch in his deep voice, 'Yes; the Peace for which we have striven for so long. At last we triumph.'

'I . . . I have done nothing,' Roger murmured.

'Nay, you have done much. I know you for an Englishman by birth, but you have ever put your trust in me and aided me whenever possible. Besides, was it not you who pushed Bonaparte out on to the balcony at St. Cloud? But for that neither he nor we would be here tonight. Tomorrow morning come to my Ministry. I will then give you this, and all the papers necessary for your journey to London.'

'To London!' Roger exclaimed.

'Why, yes,' Talleyrand smiled. 'Who could be more suitable than yourself to carry this message of goodwill to England? When I suggested it to our little man, he at once agreed. You will travel in a frigate flying a flag of truce, as our Envoy Extraordinary to the Court of St. James.'

Roger could hardly believe that he was not dreaming. He had taken the Great Risk and had again proved right in doing so. But that he was to be the bearer of this wonderful news was a triumph beyond anything for which he had ever hoped.

He stammered his thanks and they continued talking for a further ten minutes, then Talleyrand said he thought the time had come when they ought to show themselves again.

As they were about to re-enter the ballroom they approached a tall, handsome, fair-haired man, standing alone near the wall. In a low voice Talleyrand said to Roger, 'That is the Baron von Haugwitz, the new Prussian Ambassador. He has just been transferred from London and presented his credentials only this morning. From a talk with him you might gather useful information of recent developments in the English capital.'

Talleyrand made the introduction, bowed and moved away. Roger opened the conversation by saying that he knew London well and hoped that while His Excellency had been *en poste* there he had found life pleasant.

The Baron, who found himself very much a fish out of water in this strange new French society, was delighted to talk about the three years he had spent in England. For a while they talked of the Government and British foreign policy, then of Vauxhall Gardens, Cremorne and the social whirl of London. Roger then asked a question that he had had in mind for several minutes.

'Did Your Excellency perchance make the acquaintance of the Countess of St. Ermins?'

'Why, yes,' replied the Baron. 'A most lovely lady and one with an enchanting wit. She moves much in political and diplomatic circles, and at her house in Berkeley Square I met many interesting people.'

Roger gave an inaudible sigh of relief. Georgina had not then remarried, otherwise the Baron either would not have known her by her old title, or would have told him of her marriage.

But the Prussian's face became grave as he went on, 'Alas, when I left London, all Lady St. Ermins's friends were greatly concerned for her. She has two children. They caught scarlet fever and she contracted it from them. In children, the disease is not as a rule dangerous. But in an adult it can be fatal. It was feared that Her Ladyship might die of it.'

.   .   .   .   .   .

The following afternoon Roger was driving towards Calais with all the speed that six good horses could give a well-sprung coach. With him were a middle-aged Foreign Office official named Broussalt, whom Talleyrand had nominated to advise Roger on protocol, a secretary and a valet, also provided by Talleyrand.

As the coach bounded along the rutty roads, Roger could think of only one thing. Beautiful Zanthé had gone from his mind like yesterday's ten thousand years. Even the fact that he carried Peace in his pocket and had achieved the greatest triumph of his career meant nothing to him now. His beloved Georgina, the one woman in the world who really mattered to him, had been stricken by a fell disease and lay in danger of her life. She might even by now be dead.

At that terrible thought he groaned aloud. Broussalt anxiously enquired what ailed him. He brusquely replied that it was the bumping of the coach but, when the others pleaded with him to order the postilion to reduce the pace, he would not hear of it.

By using his powers unscrupulously to deprive other travellers of their relays, by threatening laggard Postmasters with the loss of their positions, by bribes, curses and twice using across men's

Q

shoulders the riding switch he carried, he kept the coach hurtling through the night, so that his companions, now hungry because he refused to stop for meals, thought that they had been saddled with a madman.

He performed the seemingly impossible at that time, and reached Calais in twenty hours. Driving straight to the Port Authority, he presented his credentials and demanded the immediate use of the fastest vessel in the harbour. In vain Broussalt remonstrated with him that it was beneath the dignity of an Envoy Extraordinary to sail in anything less han a twenty-gun frigate. Neither of the frigates in Calais Roads could be made ready to sail before night; but a Revenue cutter was about to drop down to Boulogne, so he commandeered it and went aboard.

Since Britain and France were at war, the French Embassy in London was closed and empty. Therefore, the proper procedure would have been for the vessel carrying him to sail up the Thames and anchor in the Pool below the Tower, so that she could be used as a temporary Embassy. But Roger knew well that, if the wind were unfavourable, a day or more could be lost while tacking up the twisting bends of the river; so he ordered the Captain of the cutter to land him at Dover.

Fortunately the weather was mild, so the crossing was smooth and took less than three hours. Five miles out from the English coast they were challenged by a frigate; but they ran up the white flag with the Tricolour, and the frigate escorted them into Dover harbour.

There, Roger told Broussalt that it was his intention to go to London by road. He then ordered him to remain in the cutter and arrange for it to be escorted round to the Pool, where it was to await his pleasure.

The unhappy official threw his hands in the air and turned up his eyes to heaven. It was, he declared, unheard of for an Envoy Extraordinary to arrive unaccompanied at a foreign capital. The loss of prestige! What would the English think of them? He might have argued with a stone statue for all the satisfaction he got. Roger told him that the the First Consul did not have a red carpet put down before giving battle and that he, Roger, needed no frills to aid him in conducting the mission upon which he had been sent.

By the time he landed it was five o'clock and already dark. He was received by a group of officers, all extremely curious to know his business. Now he had to be careful and remember that he was supposed to be a Frenchman; so he told them in broken English that he carried letters for the Foreign Secretary and wished to be conveyed to London with all possible speed.

But at Dover he was subjected to infuriating delays. First he had to explain his business to an Admiral, then he was taken up to the castle and kept waiting there for over an hour before being interviewed by an elderly General. After asking a score of questions, the majority of which were quite irrelevant, the General said he thought it would be best if Roger remained at Dover until London had been notified of his arrival and instructions received about him.'

At that Roger had great difficulty in keeping his temper. But, with a heavy accent, he said icily, ' You appear to mistake me, *Monsieur le Général*, for a prisoner-of-war. I am nothing of the kind. I am a diplomatic representative and, unless you treat me as such, I shall make complaint of you to your Duke of York.'

Having no desire to risk the displeasure of his Commander-in-Chief, the General grumpily agreed to send Roger to London that night. He was given a good meal, then set off in a coach. A Captain Denistoun rode with him and he was accompanied by a mounted escort.

The roads in England were infinitely better than those in France so, although they travelled fairly fast, the going was not too rough to prevent Roger from dozing for a good part of the way. They reached London very early in the morning. Rousing as the coach rumbled along the Old Kent Road, Roger asked Denistoun whether he was taking him direct to the Foreign Office.

' No,' replied he Captain. ' As yet nobody there will have risen. My orders are to leave you in charge of the Officer of the Guard at the Horse Guards, then report your arrival to Lord Grenville as soon as he is available.'

That was more or less what Roger had expected. He then told Denistoun that before the war he had lived for some time in London and that he had heard just before leaving Paris that a great friend of his, the Countess of St. Ermins, was dangerously ill; so he was anxious to enquire about her.

The Captain agreed that they should call at the St. Ermins mansion in Berkeley Square. When they reached it the blinds were down. Roger, dreading the worst, was almost incoherent with distress; but Denistoun, fearing some trick by this 'frog-eater' of whom he had been given charge, would not let him leave the coach. Instead he got out, knocked up the house and himself made enquiries from a sleepy footman.

He returned to say that Lady St. Ermins was at Stillwaters, her country home in Surrey. The servants in Berkeley Square had had no news of her for the past two days; but they were greatly worried, as it was feared that she would not recover from her illness.

Roger breathed again. At least she had still been alive the previous day, or they would have been sent news of her death. Now he must get to Stillwaters at the earliest possible moment. After some argument, on the plea that his business was of the utmost urgency, he persuaded Denistoun to take him straight to the Foreign Office.

By then it was seven o'clock. The Groom of the Chambers, who happened to be in the hall on their arrival, told them that His Lordship was not yet up, but was taking his morning choco-late in bed. Roger asked for pen, ink, paper and sealing wax, then wrote a brief note, which ran:

My Lord,

> *I pray you, show no recognition on receiving me. I am come to London under escort as Envoy Extraordinary from General Bonaparte. My business is most urgent, so I beg you to receive me without delay.*

Having signed the note with his own name he sealed it, slipped a gold louis into the palm of the Groom of the Chambers and asked him to take it up. Five minutes later he was taken upstairs and shown into the Foreign Secretary's bedroom.

Lord Grenville was by nature a cold man and as little given to showing emotion as his cousin the Prime Minister. But on this occasion he did express surprise and his greeting was warm. Without a moment's delay Roger plunged into his business. Pro-ducing two letters, he said:

'My Lord, I bring great news. General Bonaparte has now been elected First Consul of the French Republic, with virtually dictatorial powers, and he desires Peace. This letter gives expres-sion to his sentiments. The other is from M. de Talleyrand, who is again Foreign Minister, and it sets out the basic terms upon which the French are prepared to negotiate.'

'Overtures for Peace!' Grenville exclaimed, taking the first letter. 'And from the Corsican, of all people! I can scarce believe it.' Breaking the seals of Bonaparte's letter, he opened it and quickly read it through. As he laid it down on the counterpane, he said:

'It has the air of honesty and must receive our most earnest consideration. As soon as I have risen I will take it to the Prime Minister.'

'How soon can Your Lordship expect to hand me a reply?' Roger asked.

Grenville considered for a moment. 'It must be laid before His Majesty, and my colleagues in the Cabinet must be given time to consider the terms that are proposed. Three days should suffice. Today is the 28th, a meeting of the Cabinet could be called for the morning of the 31st, I could let you know the result that afternoon.'

'Until then, my Lord, I pray you to excuse me. Most urgent private affairs claim my attention. I pray you, too, to relieve me of my watchdog, a Captain Denistoun, who waits below, and also to lend me a horse. I must at once ride down into Surrey.'

The Foreign Secretary made a mild protest, as he would have liked Roger to remain with him for some time and give him the latest news from France; but, seeing Roger's extreme agitation, he rang his bell and gave the orders that had been requested of him. A quarter of an hour later Roger was on his way out of London.

The village of Ripley, near which Stillwaters lay, was no more than twenty-five miles distant. Roger was now very tired. It was over forty-eight hours since he had had a chance to do more than doze, and for more than half that time he had been swaying from side to side in fast-driven coaches. Yet his desperate anxiety gave him the energy to fight down fatigue, and he reached Stillwaters soon after ten o'clock.

Throwing the reins of his horse over a stone vase, he ran up the steps and into the hall. A footman, carrying a tray, was crossing it. White-faced, Roger shouted at him:

'Her Ladyship! Is she alive? Is she alive?'

The man nodded. 'Yes, sir; but, alas, very low.'

'Is Colonel Thursby here?'

'Yes, sir. He is up in Her Ladyship's boudoir.'

Roger mounted the stairs three at a time and burst into the

room. Georgina's father looked up with a start. He had been another father to Roger and Georgina was the greatest treasure in the world to both of them. Coming to his feet, the Colonel exclaimed:

'Roger! Dear boy, how glad I am to see you. But you find us in dire distress.'

'How is she?' Roger gasped.

The Colonel shook his head. 'Alas, we now have little hope for her. It was scarlet fever. But you must have heard. She caught it from the children. They, thank God, are now fully recovered. But for an adult the disease is serious; or rather, its after-effects.'

'May I see her?'

'Yes. But she will not recognize you. She is in a coma.'

They went next door, into the big bedroom. Georgina was lying in her great canopied bed, pale as a corpse. Jenny, her faithful maid, her eyes red with weeping, was sitting beside her. Turning down the sheet, Roger took Georgina's wrist and felt her pulse. Looking across at the Colonel, he groaned, 'It hardly beats.'

Tears welled up into the Colonel's tired eyes. 'I know it. I fear she is sinking fast.'

'She is so deathly pale,' Roger murmured. 'Did they purge and bleed her? They must have, for her vitality to be so low.'

'Yes. They did it to reduce the fever. It is the usual practice, as you must know.'

'Then the fools bled her too much,' cried Roger furiously. 'It is lack of blood from which she is dying. Upon what are you feeding her?'

'A little milk is all that she can take.'

With an impatient shake of his head, Roger cried, ''Tis not milk she needs but iron.'

'Iron?' repeated the Colonel, with a puzzled look.'

'Yes. While on my travels I learned that iron is the sovereign remedy for loss of blood. In many aspects of medicine, the peoples of the East are more knowledgeable than ourselves; for among them the learning of the ancient Greeks has not been smothered by Christian taboos and monkish superstition. When I was residing in Alexandria with the Greek banker Sarodopulous, one of his servants attempted to commit suicide by cutting her wrists with a knife. Before she was found and her wounds bound up, she had lost so much blood that she certainly would have died had they not promptly forced her to swallow all the iron she could stomach.'

'But, my dear boy, one can neither eat nor drink iron. How is it possible to administer it to a patient?'

'I'll show you. But let's not waste a moment.' Roger turned to Jenny. 'Quick. Run downstairs. Get me a bottle of Claret and a large pewter mug.'

As Jenny ran from the room, Roger said to the Colonel, 'The Greeks heat an old sword or dagger in the fire until it is red hot, then plunge it into the wine. Among the ignorant, this practice has come to be regarded as magic, owing to the symbolical union of virtue and strength giving the potion life-saving properties; but in fact it is the essence of the iron entering the wine that fortifies the body and makes new blood. To use a weapon is unnecessary. Any piece of iron that has a roughened surface will serve our purpose.'

Crossing the room, Roger seized the poker and thrust it into the heart of the glowing log fire.

A few minutes later Jenny came bustling in with a pint tankard already filled with Claret. Impatiently they waited until the end of the poker was red hot, then Roger took it from the fire and plunged it into the wine. The liquid hissed and bubbled fiercely. When it had settled down, he withdrew the poker and put it back into the fire until it was again red hot. Three times he repeated the process, then with a spoon tasted the mulled wine to test its heat. Satisfied that if each spoonful was first blown upon it would not burn Georgina's mouth, he carried the tankard over to her bedside and, while Jenny held her mistress's head, he carefully fed a dozen spoonsful between her pale lips.

When they had done, Roger said to the Colonel, 'I have come at all speed from Paris and am near the end of my tether. If I do not get to bed soon I'll drop; so I pray you to excuse me. As you have seen, the preparation of the potion presents no difficulty. I'll leave you to give Georgina a further dozen spoonsful of a new brew every hour, then, when I am restored by a few hours' sleep, I will rejoin you.'

Jenny gave him a pale smile. 'Seeing how fatigued you looked on your arrival, sir, when I went downstairs for the wine I told them to get your usual room ready at once. By now there should be a fire lit there and a warming pan in the bed.'

'Bless you for a good, thoughtful girl, Jenny,' Roger smiled back. Then he left them, crossed Georgina's boudoir to the bedroom beyond it, struggled out of his clothes and at last relaxed between the warm sheets.

For the next five hours he lay as though dead himself, then he was roused by Colonel Thursby, who said, 'The doctor is here, Roger, and I have told him about the method by which we are endeavouring to save our dear Georgina. I woke you only because I felt you might wish to discuss her condition with him.'

Rubbing the sleep from his eyes, Roger murmured, 'I see nothing to discuss; but I welcome the opportunity to tell him that if she dies it will be through his excessive application of leeches, and for that I'll kill him.'

'Nay,' the Colonel shook his head. 'Be not too hard upon him, Roger. He is a very decent man and has done only what any other practitioner would have done in a case where it was necessary to bring down a high fever. Moreover, he takes no umbrage, as many others would have done, at you, a layman, having arbitrarily decreed a treatment of your own for his patient. Indeed, he expressed interest in your belief in the efficacy of iron to make blood.'

Slipping on a chamber robe that had been brought to him, Roger accompanied the Colonel into Georgina's bedroom and greeted the doctor with restrained civility. Together they looked down on the still figure in the great bed. Georgina showed no sign of life and no stranger, seeing her now, would have believed that only a few weeks ago her face had been richly coloured and radiant with beauty. There were deep shadows under her closed eyes, her once-pink cheeks had fallen in and their flesh had taken on a transparent hue, her lips had a bluish tinge and, already, she had the appearance of one dead.

In vain Roger searched her features for some slight indication that his remedy had bettered her condition, but, if anything, they seemed more drawn and lifeless than when he had arrived at her bedside that morning. The doctor said in a low voice:

'Mr. Brook, as I have already told Colonel Thursby, I can give you little hope; and there is nothing more that I can do for Her Ladyship. Were she in a better state I would take exception to your most unorthodox conduct in treating her without consulting me. As things are, I can only regret that she shows no signs of responding to your remedy. I fear you must now prepare for the worst; for I doubt her living out the night.'

'I'll not yet despair,' declared Roger hoarsely. 'It may be that the iron needs longer to be absorbed into her system. She is as healthy a woman as any I have ever known. She has sustained no injury and is sound in every other part. 'Tis only blood she needs and iron can give it her. Of that I am convinced.'

The doctor nodded. 'You may be right, sir. I recall a patient of mine who had travelled in the distant East once telling me that the Japanese use iron filings to cure serious cases of anaemia. At the time I doubted such a thing being possible, but . . .'

Roger swung round upon him. 'Iron filings! How did they enable the patient to swallow them? '

'The iron was ground very fine, almost to a powder, then dissolved by stewing with acid fruit and administered to the patient in the form of a purée.'

'We'll give her that too, then. The acid, of course, would act upon the iron. Apple should serve for that.'

Colonel Thursby took Jenny by the arm. 'Off with you, Jenny, to the apple store. Pick out some sound cookers and take them to the kitchen. I'll go to the stables and have our farrier grind down one end of a new horse-shoe.'

It was then decided that every hour Georgina should be given a few spoonsful of the ironized wine and the ironized apple purée alternately and, should it appear that her heart was giving out, a few sips of champagne to reanimate it. The doctor administered to her the first spoonful of the apple purée and swallowing it had the effect of temporarily bringing her out of her coma. For a moment they feared that she was going to sick it up but she kept it down, then relapsed into her previous inertia, except for a low, hesitant breathing.

The two days that followed were filled with hopes and fears. During the first night Roger remained beside Georgina. He did not close his eyes but sat watching the firelight flickering on the ceiling as he listened in the heavy silence to the faint whispering of her breath. It was so light that on three occasions he thought it had stopped and, in a panic, hurriedly forced a few swallows of champagne between her pale lips. But when morning came, they were granted a ray of hope, for they all agreed that there was a very slight colour in her sunken cheeks.

Jenny had also been up for a good part of the night, while Colonel Thursby dozed next door in the boudoir; but in the morning he took over while Roger slept. That evening all three of them were sitting near Georgina's bed when, to their joy, she opened her eyes.

When Roger bent over her, she recognized him, but was not fully conscious. From her whispered words, they gathered that she believed herself to be dead, that Roger had died somewhere abroad before her and, as they had always promised, the first to go should be there to welcome the other.

During the second night, her breathing was easier and she was able to swallow larger doses of the mulled wine and apple purée. On the second day she was obviously stronger and, when awake, hovered in a land halfway between reality and dreams, often murmuring endearments to Roger. But when evening came her temperature rose and she became delirious. Throughout that night, while Georgina tossed and turned and raved, they spent some terribly anxious hours, but at about four o'clock in the morning she again appeared to fall into a coma and, as Roger had to leave that morning, the 31st, for London, Colonel Thursby persuaded him to go to bed.

As soon as he woke, he went in to her again, to find her sleeping; but the doctor, who had arrived on his morning visit, said that all hopes for her recovery now depended entirely on her not having another relapse, for her powers of resistance were still so low that she would die of it from sheer exhaustion.

At ten o'clock she was still asleep and Roger had to tear himself away from her bedside to set out for London. His sleep and a good breakfast had restored his strength to some extent, but the events of the past week had put so great a strain upon him that he was far from being himself; so, still a prey to acute anxiety, he decided that, instead of riding, he would drive up in Colonel Thursby's coach.

When he arrived at the Foreign Office, there was a message for him that he was to go to No. 10 Downing Street at four o'clock. It was cold and miserable and he had two hours to kill. First he went to Amesbury House in Arlington Street, but his old friend ' Droopy Ned ' was not at home. Feeling that he could not face talking to people at his club, instead of going to White's he had a meal in a chop-house. He then spent three-quarters of an hour in Westminster Abbey, praying that Georgina might live.

At four o'clock he was shown up to the Prime Minister's room on the first floor of No. 10. Tall, lean, grey, his face more lined than ever with care, Mr. Pitt was sitting at his desk. Lord Grenville was with him. As Roger entered they both rose and shook him warmly by the hand then, waving him to a chair, the Prime Minister said:

'You have been long away, Mr. Brook, but far from idle as we know. Admiral Nelson wrote twice, commending you most highly for having obtained two of General Bonaparte's despatches for him, and the detailed report of the situation in Egypt that you sent back to me has proved most valuable. But clearly you have been anything but successful in carrying out my wish with regard to Bonaparte. It seems that the cards were stacked against you, and that you might bring about his ruin was too much to expect. At all events he is now firmly in the saddle.'

Roger frowned. 'You surprise me, sir, in harking back to that.'

'Why should I not, seeing that the man has just achieved a position in which he has the power to do this country far greater damage than before?'

'The power, yes; but . . . sir, I do not understand. Your instructions were given to me near two years ago. Since then there have been new developments. The situation has become entirely different. I have never yet deceived you about anything, and I will now admit that I aided General Bonaparte to become First Consul.'

'You . . . you mean to tell me that you deliberately acted contrary to my orders?'

'I did,' replied Roger firmly. 'As an Englishman, watching Britain's interests in a foreign land, I have, in the past, more than once used my own judgement. In this case I did so again. In other matters I have been proved wrong. This time what possible grounds can you advance for bringing my judgment into question? But for General Bonaparte's having become First Consul, with M. de Talleyrand as his Foreign Minister, the letters I delivered to my Lord Grenville three days ago would never have been penned. They offer Peace, sir. Peace after eight years of war! And no other Government in France would ever have made this blessed overture to us.'

Mr. Pitt tapped a paper lying in front of him, then put his fingertips together. 'You refer, Mr. Brook, to this letter. That you should have succeeded in having yourself appointed *Envoyé Extraordinaire* to bring it to London fills me with amazement and admiration. But we have had to bear in mind the man by whom it was written. It is clear to me that you have fallen under his spell. Therefore I attach no blame to you for having become one of his partisans. But we, here in London, judge him by his deeds. He is a proved liar, an atheist, a thief, a blackguard of the meanest order. What faith could His Majesty's Government put in protestations of such a man? I am convinced he has sent this letter only to trick us.'

'Then you are wrong! Wrong, utterly wrong!' Roger burst out. 'I know that he started life as a revolutionary. He may be all you say. But he has other qualities. He is above politics and has only the welfare of France at heart. Apart from a handful of Jacobins, everyone in France longs for peace. General Bonaparte knows that and his most earnest wish is to give it to them. M. de Talleyrand, whom I know well, has ever maintained that no lasting prosperity can come to Britain and France unless they make an accommodation over their differences.'

'Talleyrand,' Grenville cut in. 'That revolting ex-priest, who would sell his own mother for a guinea! His corruption and immortality stink in the nostrils of the whole world.'

'By God, m'Lord, I resent your assessment of him,' Roger cried angrily. 'His morals I'll not seek to defend, but I'd shed my own blood in defence of my opinion that he is the friend of England.'

'Enough, Mr. Brook!' the Prime Minister broke in. 'It is understandable that you should have conceived a personal attachment to these people while so long resident in France. The standards there are very different from our own. But we must view this matter objectively and, sorry as I am to disappoint you, I fear that the answer you must carry back to France will not please the friends that you have made there.'

'What!' Roger exclaimed, aghast. 'Can you possibly mean that you are unwilling to enter into negotiations?'

Grenville had taken a paper from his pocket and he said, 'Here is the answer to Bonaparte's letter which we wish you to carry back.' Then he read:

Lord Grenville in reply to the Minister of Foreign Relations in Paris.
Sir,
   I have read and laid before the King the two letters you have transmitted to me; and His Majesty, seeing no reason to depart

from those forms which have long been established in Europe for transacting business with foreign States, has commanded me to return, in his name, the official answer which I send you herewith enclosed.

Then he added, 'The answer is, of course, that Talleyrand's memorandum of basic requirements is not one upon which we should be prepared to treat.'

'Depart from forms long established!' Roger quoted angrily. 'Sir! My Lord! Can you not realize that we have entered a new age. What matter forms if only we can prevent the war going on and save the lives of a million men? I beg you! I beg you on my knees to reconsider this.'

Mr. Pitt shook his head. 'Nay, Mr. Brook. I realize that your intentions are of the best; but reconsideration is out of the question. His Majesty and the Cabinet are agreed that we might have given the Corsican upstart a chance to prove his sincerity, but for one stipulation. In Talleyrand's memorandum it is stated clearly that France could not agree to King Charles Emmanuel's receiving back his Piedmontese dominions, whereas we have promised to restore him to his throne in Turin.'

'What!' Roger exclaimed, 'and he not even Britain's ally in an effective sense! Can you possibly mean that to restore this petty Italian Prince you would deny Peace to the whole of Europe?'

The Prime Minister drew himself up and said haughtily, 'Mr. Brook, you know well that I have ever desired Peace with my whole heart. But the honour of our country must come before all other consideration, and it is pledged to King Charles Emmanuel.'

'Just as it was pledged to Austria about the restoration of her Belgian lands,' Roger said with an angry sneer. 'Had you been willing three years ago to let the French continue in occupation of them, we could have had Peace then. But, no! And with what result A year later, the Austrians went behind your back and gave them up in exchange for the territories of Venice.'

'Mr. Brook, you forget yourself. . . .'

'I forget nothing,' stormed Roger, getting to his feet. 'As a free Englishman, I'll say my mind to you. Charles Emmanuel still has his island of Sardinia. Let him be content with that rather than that another ocean of British blood should flow to get him back his city of Turin. In your blindness to all that really matters you are rejecting an honest offer. Whatever Bonaparte's past misdeeds, by his sincerity in this he puts you to shame.'

The two statesmen stared at him in awed silence for a moment, then the Prime Minister said, 'Mr. Brook, you look far from well and I judge you to be overwrought. The decision of His Majesty's Government is unalterable and, when you have had a few days in which to recover, in duty bound, as *Envoyé Extraordinaire* of the First Consul, you must carry our answer back to him. In the meantime, we are not unappreciative of the great services you rendered Admiral Nelson, so my Lord Grenville will send to your bank an order for three thousand pounds on the secret funds.'

'I thank you, sir,' retorted Roger sharply, 'but I am not in need of money. Let His Lordship send that sum to Greenwich that it may be used for the relief of our seamen wounded in this war which you have decreed must continue.' Then, white-faced and shaking, he strode from the room.

. . . .

Outside it had commenced to snow. From the Bait and Livery Stable, where he had left Colonel Thursby's coach, Roger picked it up and set out on the drive back to Stillwaters. It was bitterly cold, pitch dark and the horses had already done twenty-five miles; so the pace was slow. He did not arrive until a little before ten o'clock, but when he hurried in good news awaited him.

After her sleep that morning, Georgina had shown a marked improvement. She had become fully conscious and had talked with her father that afternoon, although in the evening she had become fretful and every few moments asked for Roger.

Still shivering, he changed out of his clothes then drank a hot posset that was brought to him. When he went into Georgina he saw that her eyes were open and she smiled at him. Taking her hand he sat down beside her, rejoicing at the much stronger colour now in her cheeks, but he would not let her talk.

After they had sat like that for a long while, he said, 'You must have your mulled wine now. It is already past the time when you should have gone to sleep.'

'My wine,' she whispered. 'Yes. . . . But don't leave me, Roger. Don't leave me. I'd not be alive were it not for you. Lie down here beside me.'

'Oh, my beloved beyond all beloveds,' he whispered back and kissed her gently on the brow.

The old century was ending. From the nearby village the church bells, ushering in the year 1800, came clearly on the winter air. Through the bitter prejudice of British statesmen the terrible war, bringing death and misery to every part of Europe, was destined to continue for another fifteen years. But the French Revolution had ended, so better things might be hoped for France and, perhaps, in time, for Britain too. As the New Year came in, Georgina slept peacefully with her head on Roger's shoulder.

Dennis Wheatley's work has
also been published in

THE UNITED STATES
FRANCE
GERMANY
SWITZERLAND
ITALY
SWEDEN
HOLLAND
SPAIN
HUNGARY
BELGIUM
POLAND
CZECHOSLOVAKIA
DENMARK
FINLAND
PORTUGAL
NORWAY
RUMANIA
BRAZIL

Also in

RUSSIAN
SERBIAN
FLEMISH
ARMENIAN
ARABIC
HINDI
GREEK
TURKISH